I0632505

RAINBOW FANTASIA:
35 Spectrumatic Tales
of Wonder

For Ray Bradbury
Out-of-this-world's most colorful
chronicler of imagi-metaphors.
We love you, Ray.

Forry Ackerman
Anne Hardin

Twice he was seen; and ugly guns flashed at him—guns as different from the simple action ato-guns as life from death. He analyzed them from their effects, the way they smashed down the walls, and made hard metal run like water. Heavy duty electronic guns these, discharging completely disintegrated atoms, a stream of pure electrons that sought union with stable matter in a coruscating fury of senseless desire.

From "Discord in Scarlet" by A. E. van Vogt

RAINBOW FANTASIA:
35 Spectrumatic Tales
of Wonder

Selected by Forrest J Ackerman

Introduction by Anne Hardin

Sense of Wonder Press
JAMES A. ROCK & COMPANY, PUBLISHERS
ROCKVILLE • MARYLAND

Rainbow Fantasia: 35 Spectrumatic Tales of Wonder
All stories selected and with notes by Forrest J Ackerman
Introduction by Anne Hardin (a.k.a "Bo Rayne")

is an imprint of *JAMES A. ROCK & CO., PUBLISHERS*

This compilation Copyright © 2001 by Forrest J Ackerman
Copyright © 2001 by James A. Rock &. Co., Publishers. All applicable copyrights and other rights
reserved worldwide. No part of this publication may be reproduced, in any form
or by any means, for any purpose, without the express, written permission of the publisher.

Address comments and inquiries to:
SENSE OF WONDER PRESS
James A. Rock & Company, Publishers, 113 N. Washington Street, Box 347
Rockville, MD 20850
E-mail:
jrock@rockpublishing.com   lrock@senseofwonderpress.com
Internet URL: www.SenseOfWonderPress.com
Paperbound ISBN: 0-918736-36-6
Printed in the United States of America
First Sense of Wonder Press Edition: August 2001

Cover art for this edition of *Rainbow Fantasia*, Anton Brzezinski: colorization of still
from the silent Soviet scientifilm *AELITA, Queen of Mars (1924)*

Black Absolute by H. L. Gold, *Captain Future*, Fall 1940
Black Harvest of Moraine by Arthur J. Burks, *Weird Tales*, January 1950
Black Butterflies by Elmer Brown Mason, *Popular Publications*, 1916
The Black Curtains by Frederick Stansfiore, *Weird Tales*, March 1925
The Black Stone Statue by Mary Elizabeth Counselman, *Weird Tales*, December 1937
Gray Ghouls by Bassett Morgan, *Weird Tales*, July 1927
Up in Smoke by Tigrina, *copyright* by Tigrina 2001 (July 1946)
The Brown Moccasin by David Baxter, *Weird Tales*, February 1925
The Purple Cincture by H. Thompson Rich, *Weird Tales*, August 1925
The Violet Death by Gustav Meyrink, *Weird Tales*, July 1935
Once in a Blue Moon by Harl Vincent, *Amazing Stories Quarterly*, Winter 1932
The Blue Room by Gordon Philip England, *Weird Tales*, November 1936
The Weird Green Eyes of Sari by Margaret McBride Hoss, *Weird Tales*, March 1925
The Green Monster by Arthur Macom, *Weird Tales*, July 1928
The Man in the Green Coat by Eli Colter, *Weird Tales*, August 1928
The Eighth Green Man by G.G. Pendarves (Gladys Gordon Trenery), *Weird Tales*, March 1928
When the Green Star Waned by Nictzin Dyalhis, *Weird Tales*, April 1925
The Yellow Sign by Robert W. Chambers, from *The King in Yellow*, NY 1895
Yellow Imagicide by Brad Linaweaver, *copyright* © 1999 by Brad Linaweaver
(A previous version of this story appeared as *Imagicide*)
The Golden Whistle by Eli Colter, *Weird Tales*, January 1928
The Golden Chalice by Frank Gruber, *Weird Tales*, July 1940
The Girl in the Golden Atom by Ray Cummings, *Popular Publications*, 1919
The Golden Girl of Munan by Harl Vincent, *Amazing Stories*, June 1928
Executing a Pirouette in Orange by Brad Linaweaver, *copyright* © 1999 by Brad Linaweaver
(A previous version of this story appeared as *Executing a Pirouette for Belphegor*)
The Orange God by Nat Schachner (as Walter Glamis), *Astounding*, October 1933
The Red Plague by P. Schuyler Miller, *Wonder Stories* July 1930
The Red Brain by Donald Wandrei, *Weird Tales*, October 1927
The Red God Laughed by Thorp McClusky, *Weird Tales*, April 1939
Discord in Scarlet by A. E. van Vogt, *Astounding*, December 1939
Lover in Scarlet by Harold Lawlor, *Weird Tales*, January 1949
Scarlet Dream by Catherine L. Moore, Popular Fiction Publishing Company, 1934
The White Lady by Dorothy Quick, *Weird Tales*, January 1942
The White Vampire by Arlton Eadie, *Weird Tales*, September 1928
The White Wizard by Sophie Wenzel Ellis, *Weird Tales*, September 1929
The Rainbow Jade by Gardner F. Fox, *Weird Tales*, September 1949
Résumé of Rays (poem) by Forrest J Ackerman, *copyright* © 1973 by Forrest J Ackerman

CONTENTS

CONTENTS

Illustrations

Special Thanks to Forry Fan David Kurzman for his help
in finding and procuring several elusive texts.

INTRODUCTION
by Anne Hardin

He's Dr. Acula, Karlon Torgosi, Weaver Wright, Spencer Strong, Vespertina (the Transylvanian word for "bat"), Robot Mitchum, undeniably Mr. Sci-Fi, and a host of others, though I must admit my favorite pseudonym is Laurajean Ermayne, who, as the author of a TEASE! article about the 1930 Cecil B. De Mille film *Madam Satan*, "pun-ished" his readers with the caption "Kay Johnson in one Hell of a role, as Madam Satan." From the same film he gave us these words never spoken by Reginald Denny, who was photographed with his arm strategically placed around Johnson's chest in a pre-Hays Code shot, "I don't recognize your face, but your cup size is familiar." Put all these forrynyms together, and you can't help but have one Forrest J (no period) Ackerman, who's such a colorful character it was inevitable that he'd come up with a dramatic spectrumatic selection of sci-fi, fantasy, and horror stories to whet the appetites of JADEd anthology "ackolytes" everywhere. I doubt you'll be familiar with most of these colorful tales, and that's the way Forry "intinted" it. You'll find no "RED Room" or "Horror at RED Hook" or "The RED Peri" or "BLACK Ferris" because these tales by Wells, Lovecraft, Weinbaum, and Bradbury are available elsewhere. As for the original novella version of "The Girl in the GOLDEN Atom" by Ray Cummings and Robert W. Chambers's "The YELLOW Sign," most fans have heard of these legendary titles but never have been able to read them — until now. Forry was raised on the great anthologies of yesteryear edited by Groff Conklin (the king for Forry's tastes), Boucher & McComas, and Bleiler & Dikty. But in a day and age when virtually every theme has been unmercifully exhausted, his remarkable memory as a reader and collector since 1926 allows him to turn back the clock in the Wellsian Time Machine of his mind and rescue works of wonder not available elsewhere. You'll find similar treasures in his other current and forthcoming Sense of Wonder collections: the *Sci-Ants Fiction & Insects Extraordinary* (is this the first ANThology?), the *Sci-Fi WOMANthology*, *Scenes of Wonder: Famous Forry Fotos*, and the projected *MARTIANthology*, co-edited by yours truly. Can a SUPERMANthology anthology be far behind? And who could be better qualified than Forrest Ackerman to produce *Metropolis: 75th Anniversary Edition*, than the man who was a friend of Fritz Lang and has watched that film classic 98 times, at least by this printing.

    The stories in this anthology are taken predominantly from the classic pulp tradition represented by such magazines as *Weird Tales*, that unique repository of

Sci-Fi, horror, and eerie tales with the wonderfully garish and often macabre covers. Stories from *WT* in *Rainbow Fantasia* date from February 1925 ("The BROWN Moccasin" by David Baxter) to January 1950 ("BLACK Harvest of Moraine" by Arthur J. Burks). Other colorful tales first presented in the pulps include such classics as: *Popular Publications* ("BLACK Butterflies" by Elmer Brown Mason), *Captain Future* ("BLACK Absolute" by H. L. Gold), *Amazing Stories* ("The GOLDEN Girl of Munan" by Harl Vincent), and *Astounding Science Fiction* (Nat Schachner's "The ORANGE God"). The stories in *Rainbow Fantasia* span a period of over a hundred years, the oldest being Robert W. Chambers's "The Yellow Sign," from the 1895 story collection, *The King in Yellow* and the most recent two 1999 contributions by Brad Linaweaver.

You'll see the story "When the GREEN Star Waned" by British author Nictzin Dyalhis included here. Dyalhis, who flourished in the pages of *Weird Tales* from 1925 to 1940, had one of the most unpronounceable names of all the *Weird Tales* contributors. It is fortunate that his story had a color of the rainbow in its title, as it is one of the most memorable stories in the magazine's long history. Another distinguished story is Donald Wandrei's "The RED Brain" (*Weird Tales*, October 1927). If you are reading it for the first time here, and you liked the final line of Harry Bates's "Farewell to the Master," it is unlikely you will ever forget its final famous sentence. [By the way, "Farewell to the Master," which was the basis of the film *The Day the Earth Stood Still*, was an Ackerman Agency story.]

Gustav Meyrink was the eccentric Austrian author of *The Golem* (written 1915, translated 1928). This novel is his best-known work, and H. P. Lovecraft praised the book in his *Supernatural Horror in Fiction* (1973), telling of "its haunting shadowy suggestion of marvels and horrors just beyond reach." Meyrink was born in Prague, also home to Franz Kafka. Old Prague, with its ghettos and Gothic architecture, was the perfect setting for the Golem legend. Meyrink's contribution to this anthology is "The VIOLET Death," and it appeared in the July 1935 issue of *Weird Tales*. It's lighter fare than *The Golem*, but typical of Meyrink's fantastic tales. Only you can judge if the specter of Meyrink's Golem haunts you here.

This version of "The Girl in the GOLDEN Atom" is the novella written by Ray Cummings and first published in *All-Story Weekly* in March 1919. It was widely popular as was the 1923 book-length version.

The editor of *All-Story Weekly*, Bob Davis, called Cummings "A Jules Verne returned, and an H. G. Wells going forward." This was one of the first stories that explored the world of the atom, although the concept of a "universe within a universe" was not a new one. Cummings once said that the idea for the story came from seeing an ad showing seemingly endless labels of Quaker Oats, but a more likely source is an 1858 Fitz-James O'Brien story called "The Diamond Lens," which Cummings' tale closely resembles. His characters (the Chemist, the Doctor, the Very Young Man — who follows the Chemist five years later to marry Lylda's sister Aura — follow a similar style popular with late 19th century writers, such as H.G. Wells's in *The Time Machine* and Thomas Love Peacock's *Headlong Hall*. Interestingly enough, Cummings once worked for Thomas Alva Edison.

Book collectors will be interested in the story "The YELLOW Sign" by Robert Chambers. Including the variant edition of "The Mask," Forry has 23 different editions of *The King in Yellow*, the book in which "The YELLOW Sign" first appeared. I counted them!

Forry's story introductions often include shared anecdotes about the authors' lives which provide additional color to this edition, which already closely resembles a Crayola box. As the recipient of the first Hugo Award for Fan Personality of the Year in 1953, his numerous encounters with virtually every writer in the fantasy and sci-fi galaxy are to be expected and his remembrances to be enjoyed. With his 90-year-old mother he met Bassett Morgan. Her "GRAY Ghouls" appeared in *Weird Tales* in July 1927. His mother and Morgan embraced each other and observed, "Well, before long we'll be seeing each other again." He met Eli Colter ("The Man in the GREEN Coat") in Los Angeles toward the end of her life and recollects that the name "Colter came from the gun, a colt." Harl Vincent sent 12-year-old Forry the manuscript of his story "The GOLDEN Girl of Munan." Ackerman later became his literary agent.

Forry never met Dorothy Quick, but while attending the first World Science Fiction Convention in 1939, he came close, talking with her at her front door over the intercom. He once lunched with the noted mystery writer Frank Gruber in his home. He collaborated with Catherine Louise Moore on the fourth most popular sci-fi story of 1935 among Australian fans, "Nyusa, Nymph of Darkness," and ghosted her farewell in "The Faces of Science Fiction" when Alzheimer's had stolen her memory. Her contribution here is "SCARLET Dream" (Weird Tales, May 1934), and features one of her recurring characters, Northwest Smith, and one of her favorite themes, transportation from one dimension to another. This fantastic journey begins, innocuously enough, with Smith's purchase of a colorful shawl from a market vendor on Mars, and it's not long before N.W. has encountered a beautiful woman, people who drink blood, and carnivorous grass. Tigrina, author of "Up in SMOKE" is a long-time Forry-friend and publisher of the world's first Sapphic fanzine, *Vice Versa*. Her story just goes to show where the evils of smoking can lead!

H. L. Gold, the founder and first editor of *Galaxy* magazine, once said to Forry, "Ackerman, you're a basket case of acrimony!" [Or perhaps it was Ackrimony?] Not long afterward, with those harsh words forgotten, Gold asked Forry to be his literary agent. [He is now agent for H. L. Gold, Jr.] Gold's story, "BLACK Absolute," is a chilling story of revenge gone terribly wrong, as are "The PURPLE Cincture" by H. Thompson Rich and "The BLUE Room" by Gordon Philip England.

Certainly one of Forry's most famous clients was *Slan* author, A. E. van Vogt. In 1949, van Vogt sent his best manuscripts to the four leading agents in New York. He then sent Forry some of his throwaway stories to see if he could place them. The outcome is the stuff dreams are made of. The stories, pushed hard by Forry, were quickly accepted for publication, and he added van Vogt's name to an ever-growing list of clients. His "Discord in SCARLET" appears here.

Forry and Anne (Bo Rayne)

We think you'll find stories to cater to any whim — true science fiction with plenty of spaceships and Ak-Blastors, time travel, love stories, specters of demons, heroes and haunts who do their deeds from beyond the grave, stories of great irony, and even a few tales of "nature's own" — snakes, "puppy dog" lizards, orangutans, and butterflies — all with the power to dominate the world they inhabit.

I began this introduction by relating some of Forry Ackerman's favorite pseudonyms. I'll close by revealing the one he gave me when he issued the invitation to join forces for this anthology. All you Forry-philes will not be surprised that in a book called *Rainbow Fantasia*, I was christened "Bo Rayne." My doppelgänger and I are confident you well-RED readers will enjoy every unusual story. After all, they match Forry's heart, which means they're good as "GOLD."

Anne Hardin
August, 2001

RAINBOW FANTASIA:
35 Spectrumatic Tales
of Wonder

BLACK
Absolute

by H. L. Gold

*Absolutely GOLD, from the man who become one of the most influential figures
in Sci-Fi, as founder and first editor of the 1950s magazine success-story:
Galaxy Science Fiction. This deft tale of an "unethical" demonic dentist appeared
in the Fall 1940, Captain Future: Wizard of Science.*

D r. Hudson was trembling with eagerness when he opened the door of his office. Years of habit made him pick up the mail, throw it on his assistant's desk, pull up the shades, and switch on the electric radiator. He was unconscious of those routine activities, just as he scarcely realized he had hung his heavy overcoat in the closet and was rubbing his cold hands.

Walking down the long corridor to his private laboratory at the rear of the five-room office suite, he forced himself to grow calm. He had only thirty minutes to get everything ready for his vengeance!

"Thirty minutes," he whispered impatiently. "It'll seem longer than the fifteen years I've spent hating him. Every second of my life, all those years, I've dreamed of this. I've had to greet him pleasantly, chat with him while I had to look into his mouth, smile when I wanted to torture him in the chair. But in thirty minutes he'll be here, with his jaw swollen and aching—I made sure of that, all right—and begging me to fill that tooth immediately. I certainly will! And that will be my means of vengeance."

Carefully Dr. Hudson pulled down the shades and turned on a single red bulb. It was only twenty watts, so he knew it couldn't be dangerous. But he made certain that no light seeped past the heavy black shades over the closed windows.

He slipped a yellow ring on the middle finger of his right hand. The metal was yellow as gold, but it was an alloy whose formula he would never reveal, except for an enormous price as a weapon of destruction.

"And I'll get my asking price, too!" he muttered vehemently. "As soon as Carter is disposed of, and there's no chance of connecting his death with me, I'll approach the war departments of any country who can afford my price.

1

And I don't care what country it is, as long as the money's sound and there's enough of it."

He left the red-lit laboratory and entered the next room off the corridor. The shades of that room he also pulled down carefully.

Then he went to the door again and stood on the threshold. A single large, compact generator and short-wave machine occupied the room, standing at the distant right-hand corner.

He fixed the position of the machine, closed his eyes tightly, and walked directly to it. When he opened his eyes, his hand was firmly clenching the dial of the automatic switch.

"No chance of a slip," he grinned. "If it doesn't turn off in time, I can find it and turn it off myself."

With a single violent wrench he turned the dial to the last notch. Swiftly he clicked off the light and went back to the blood-red laboratory. He stood trembling in the center of the room, facing the door.

"Four minutes to warm up," he whispered eagerly, glancing at his watch. "Then twenty minutes to prove that I will have my revenge! Exactly twenty minutes—not nineteen or twenty-one. That smug scum has never been late in his life. His appointment is for nine and even the agony I made sure he's suffering won't make him get here earlier or later. And I'll be on time, too!"

Hudson's eyes glittered with anticipation as wispy veils of darkness began to dim his vision. Swirling more rapidly with every second, the veils met, became a ragged shroud through which the red light filtered vaguely.

The rents in the shroud of darkness closed quickly then, and blackness clothed him in an utterly opaque robe.

He whispered experimentally. No sound reached his ears. He shouted with all the power of his deep lungs, yet heard nothing. The completeness of the dark that surrounded him terrorized him although he was its creator.

He had to fight to stay calm.

"Absolute black!" he thought triumphantly. "It works—it works! I've done what every other scientist has failed to do. They called it a theoretical postulate, like the ether and minus-one, but I've made it exist. Blackness that absorbs all radiation and most energy forms, yet radiates and refracts nothing at all! God, it's horrible— to see absolutely nothing but more complete blackness than even the blind suffer, to hear less than the deaf hear! It's like being buried alive in a perfectly sound-proofed grave."

He turned in the blackness and walked to the red bulb. When his exploring fingers found the switch, he clicked it off. His pall of absolute blackness absorbed so thoroughly every bit of radiation that even the dim red light might be dangerous. He had begun to feel warm, and the bulb's twenty watts could have been responsible.

"It's ghastly!" he thought, but enjoying his sense of horror. "I thought I could imagine what complete absence of light and sound would be like. Nobody can, without experiencing it. He'll go mad. Even I would go insane after a few hours of this! He'll tremble in his cloud of absolute blackness until panic drives him out into the sunlight. The blackness will absorb the radiation—and he'll be *cooked!* Then I'll have my vengeance, and the fool won't know I did it, nor why. . . .

"For fifteen years he's been in my way. He married the woman I didn't even have the courage to take out. Without him to defeat me constantly, I could have been top student and athlete at college.

"He took me in as partner when he started his company. But it wasn't making money, and I sold out. It wasn't making money! He must have been turning down orders deliberately—a company certainly doesn't become the biggest in its field two years after it's almost bankrupt!

"I'll make him pay for all that. I've had to struggle along with just my dental practice, while he has a beautiful wife, a town home and two country estates, a hunting lodge, yacht, and six cars. . . . He'll pay for his treachery! I'll put a filling in his aching tooth—but it'll be of the same alloy as my ring—which acts as antenna for my absolute black machine!"

Hudson gritted his teeth as he peered into the wall of utter darkness. Was he beginning to see? He had been keeping count of the minutes, and he knew he could not be more than a few seconds off. The twenty minutes were almost over. He would have just enough time to walk down the corridor, as the blackness was fading, and greet Carter.

He took seven steps, felt the threshold of the laboratory under his left foot, and with the next step he knew he was in the corridor. Slowly he walked toward the office, carefully counting each step. There would be eighteen, and he would be inside the office at precisely nine, just as Carter would be coming in. By then the absolute black robe would be a ragged shroud, and again veils of darkness vanishing into the welcome light. He felt for the threshold of the office, crossed it. The automatic switch, of course, could not really fail. It was the best and most expensive on the market, and it was guaranteed. . . .

For the first time in his life, Carter had been two minutes early for an appointment. He had timed it almost as exactly as he timed everything else, but the pain of his swollen jaw had made him hurry the last three blocks.

Nursing his agonizing tooth, he entered Hudson's office. He looked around anxiously for something that would relieve it until the dentist would appear. The moment he saw the huge diathermy machine, he anticipated relief.

Hudson had often used the machine on him, and he had seen its operation closely enough to know how it worked.

He connected the machine to the rubber-covered metal pad, sat down on the cathode chair, and held the anode plate to his aching jaw.

Reaching over, he switched it on, heard the generator hum rise to a whine, felt the wonderful heat against his cheek.

When he looked up a moment later, he sprang to his feet in astonishment. The most intense black he had ever seen was swirling in the doorway, fading quickly as he watched it.

A white, pain-contorted face gaped out at him. It turned a boiled-red before his eyes, then huge blisters formed and exploded on it, all in the few seconds before it went black and started to shred.

Carter sprang forward, was too late to catch it as it fell. He started to kneel beside the motionless body, but it was charred beyond the endurance of his stomach.

"Hudson!" he moaned. "My best friend—burned to death!"

Dr. Hudson's estimate of the time lapse had been four seconds short. His pall of absolute black, attracted by the ring-antenna, had absorbed the intense radiation of the electric heater and the diathermy machine. His vengeance was complete, for no longer must he endure his enemy's existence. . . .

The BLACK
Harvest of Moraine

by Arthur J. Burks

Prolific writer and career military man, Burks (1898-1974) published in many fields throughout the 30s, 40s and 50s. L. Ron Hubbard said, "Burks' name on a magazine cover would send the circulation rate skyrocketing." This uncanny tale of "alien smut" (which appeared in the January 1950 issue of Weird Tales) shows why!

THE HATED DRAW

I had been afraid of that particular field since I could remember. It was atop a mounded promontory where two whispering draws met. It looked like a monstrous brazen bosom spangled with pebbles of many colors, all of them round and smooth with age. My uncle's farmhouse sat in the side of the draw, perhaps seventy feet below the surface of the field, but sufficiently above the draw's floor to escape sudden inundation. I hated the draw, called Toler Draw, and the nameless other draws that came into it from the east, but both fascinated me so that when I visited my uncle I could not be satisfied without venturing onto the pebbly bosom of the shoulders of the high field and down into the secondary draw.

A "draw," out West, is a deep ravine or gully.

I was fifteen years old when my fear of the field between the two draws came to a head because I could see my ancient fear in the faces of the other harvest hands. I watched Charles Norman, my uncle, who acted as separator tender of the combined harvester. He stood atop the combined harvester and stared moodily out across the half section of wheat we were about to harvest, *if* he gave the word. On the lefthand side of the separator, on his little platform, the sack sewer, a Norwegian, sat on his little box under the twin spouts and watched Charles Norman. He had tried his best to talk Charles out of harvesting this half section. Apparently he had failed, but he had done his best.

Lonnie Keel, fourteen, tended the header. He had affixed a seat to the railing above the open maw of the cylinders at the inner end of the header; he sat on it now, hands engaged in the spokes of the wheel, watching me. I could see he was afraid, too, but excited as only an ambitious youngster can get.

5

I had tended header the two previous harvests, but now I drove the whole shebang, thirty-two head of horses and mules, five teams of six animals each with two leaders. The separator was run by a distillate engine set just behind the teams, at the base of the slanting ladder that led up to the dizzy seat where the driver, myself, Cappy Payne, tried to still the hammering of his heart.

Even yet Charles Norman had not decided for sure. There was danger in the high wheat, nobody knew just how great or varied. Then, the crew was untried, even to the horses and mules. Only the oldest animals had worked ahead of the clamoring engine. I felt it took courage to try to handle the thirty-two animals with only two lines attached to the leaders.

"Well," said Charles Norman, "hang onto the jugheads, we're getting under way!"

I faced the front. Charles Norman, a man of forty or so, climbed down to the distillate engine, cranked it. My horses and mules almost jumped through their collars when the engine broke into raucous song and the hidden machinery of the combined harvester began its roaring. Out of the harvester rose the dust left from last year's last work in the fields, to form a brown cloud about the ponderous machinery.

"Steady, Kate! Hold it, Jerry!" I spoke softly to my leaders, one a sensitive horse mare, the other a steady old mule who had been combined harvester leader since my uncle first owned one of the roaring monsters. I had handled all these animals on other farm equipment, so they knew my voice. I managed to keep them steady.

The blades of the header were tapping at the first of the wheat in the field, folding them back onto the canvas of the conveyor. Even this gentle hammering, for the wooden blades were intended only to keep wheat stalks from bending away under the reaper and being lost behind the machine, emphasized the thing all of us feared: for out of those few heads came the bronze, slicklooking, sooty smut which had turned the old field into a horror.

We all stared at the field as Norman climbed back onto the separator. As far as we could see the heads of wheat which should have gone fifty bushels to the acre, should have been white and firm under the hulls, were a sullen black that threatened to burst from the heads in an ebon inundation.

None of us had ever seen a field so smutted.

"Charlie," John Cavick, the sack sewer had said, "the best thing you can do with that field, for the good of the neighbors if not for yourself, is set it afire! You won't save ten bushels to the acre, and you'll scatter smut from Hades to breakfast!"

"Even ten bushels will keep me out of the red," said Norman. "I've got to take the risk. Of course, if you're afraid to tackle it, maybe I can hire someone else in Waterville."

"I'll do any work anywhere anybody else will," said Cavick, but he kept right after Uncle Charles to the moment I actually started pushing those thirty-two head of animals around the huge field.

There was a weirdness about the field we all recognized. It was surrounded by vast fields of neighbors, and on the north, across the main road, was another half section belonging to Norman, too. No other field in the county suffered smut! How did it happen that this one field alone should be so ridden with it? And why should an aura of *waiting*, of *threat*, of *psychic terror*, hang over this one particular field? I confess my own terrors went back further than those of Cavick, Lonnie, Uncle Charles or anyone else. I kept remembering from childhood, my secret adventures into the two draws, around the mounded bosom of the high field. I remembered badgers drumming into the holes among the sagebrush along the wash at the bottom of the subsidiary draw. I had flushed skulking coyotes, jackrabbits, cottontails, and almost scared myself to death when an occasional sagehen whirred out of hiding in some area of eerie silence. I had heard old tales of strange walkers among the brush, tales told around late supper tables for the sole purpose of scaring kids of the dark.

Charles Norman, atop the separator, hesitated again. I was looking back at him. I held a small rock in my hand. Above the roaring of the engine a man couldn't hear himself think. Charles Norman nodded to me. He had made his final decision. The die was cast.

"Kate! Jerry!" I heaved the rock out ahead of my leaders, careful not to hit either of them. The mules and horses hit their tugs. The huge combined harvester began to move. I had to hold back the animals to keep them from traveling too fast to catch the grain. It was almost as if they, too, feared the field and were running away from it. But for them, as far as I know, it was the motor they feared, and the fact that they could not seem to outrun it.

Almost instantly the harvester and everybody on it, including myself perched out there atop that ladder far in advance of the main body of the machine, including the horses and mules, disappeared into a black-bronze pall, a towering smut cloud that was utterly terrifying. The header, an eighteen-foot "cut," which meant that it cut a swath eighteen feet wide if I held the team so that the header cut its entire width—a driving trick I made up my mind I could manage—laid the smutted wheat back on the drapers, the reapers cut off the stalks, the drapers bore the fallen wheat up the short feed into the body of the machine where the threshing took place. Out of the main body of the machine straw fell into a trap behind the separator, where the header tender, with a long rope attached to his railing, dumped it at intervals in piles behind us. The wheat, separated from the stalks and fanned of chaff, poured into the sacks on Cavick's platform, to be sewn, slid into the carrier beside him, which slanted down to within a few inches of the ground, and tripped when there were six sacks.

Separate from the harvester was the sackbuck, a husky man with a team and a flatbed wagon, who hauled the sacks to central piling areas.

Nobody aboard the harvester saw the sackbuck, Karl Orme, while the harvester moved, because we could not see out of the pall of smut. That cloud, as smut burst from the wheat inside the harvester, belched out of every nook and cranny. Some of the spores burst on hitting the drapers, some when touched by the fanning blades, some burst on the first contact.

The rising smut cloud, which followed us like Nemesis because there was no wind, was worse than any dust storm I had ever witnessed. Looking back and down to the right it was all I could do to see the inner end of the header, to know whether I was cutting too wide a swath and missing some, or using less than I should of the "cut." I could just see. But up ahead, when I tried to see my laboring animals, I could scarcely see Kate and Jerry, my leaders. The horses and mules, even those directly under me, which included the first twelve animals, six abreast, were vague shadowy phantoms in the sooty pall.

I could make out the back of Cavick as he worked like some imp out of hell there on his little platform, fighting the sack-jigger from which poured a stream that would have been wheaten gold if it had not been for the smut. Even with all the fanning, vast amounts of smut went into the wheat sacks. Cavick had turned black and hideous within a few minutes. He had a bright red bandanna about his neck; it became black-bronze in no time. Atop the harvester Lonnie and Uncle Charles were black gnomes in the cloud, and when Uncle Charles walked back to the rear of the separator to study his mazes of wheels, sprockets, belts and pulleys, he mingled so closely with the cloud that I could not see him unless he moved an arm suddenly.

I leaned back and looked up. The sun itself was a blur through the horror. Horror? That's what I said. True or not, there was a terror about smut. Most farmers believed that it could be ignited, that it might at any time explode, if there were enough of it, by spontaneous combustion. No farmer would allow his hands to smoke where there was even the vaguest hint of smut, and every last one of us, before coming to the field, had supposedly ditched his matches at the farmhouse. I could just imagine what it would be like even if the smut did no more than take fire. It expanded outward, that thick cloud, to hold us within its heart and travel along with us around the field, clockwise. A series of swaths had already been cut around the field, some weeks earlier, with a binder. Good hay had been the result, and this was another one of the fear-provoking facts about this particular field. There had been no evidence of smut in the *hay!*

The smut had apparently come full into being between a night and a morning! Horses, mules and farm hands, especially in harvest time, become accustomed to choking dust. I had driven for hours in clouds of ordinary dust as thick as this without much discomfort, though a doctor would have thrown up his hands and uttered all sorts of dire things. I hadn't even coughed. Mules and horses coughed occasionally, but it never seemed to be anything that a good long drink of water at noon and night would not arrange.

Now, though, before I even reached the first corner and started the ponderous swinging of that team—there'd have been fifty-six head if Uncle Charles hadn't "modernized" by attaching the engine to run the separator—everyone on the separator was coughing. Lonnie sounded as if he had whooping cough; deep, rasping, tearing coughs burst from apparently the very bottom of his lungs. Cavick coughed as if he were swearing. Uncle Charles coughed like a consumptive, as if he would spit blood any instant. I coughed as if I were young again, and lost, and sobbing.

But the worst was the coughing of the mules and horses. Men can help themselves. They can stop work. Animals are slaves and must obey their owners and masters. Thirty-two head of mules and horses then, about half of each, struggled grimly through the sooty pall and coughed, deep and drumming, out of their very guts.

I made the first turn. The cloud went with us! It should have gone straight ahead, mind you; why should the *cloud* have turned the corner? I wondered if anybody noticed it but me.

Here were tiny draws in the great field. When we slid down into one I could reach out to right and left and touch the backs of my rearmost animals. When we rose out of the ditch I leaped at the sky like hay on the end of a pitchfork, legs hooked around the jacobstaff to keep from being thrown. These ditches and steep side-hills were why Uncle Charles did not use tractors to pull the harvester in this particular field—mules and horses could manage better.

By the time we reached the second corner of the huge half section, with all its wheat-covered knolls, deep pitches, steep hillsides where the leveler had to be worked like crazy to keep the monster from overturning, I was conscious of something new in the cloud of smut: in some eerie fashion it was *in tune with the chugging of the motor and the drumming of machinery in the guts of the separator, with the low murderous growling of the cylinders especially.* These cylinders now, for the benefit of the mechanically minded, were not the cylinders of the engine; they were the two sets of opposing concave and convex metal "teeth" just behind the short feed from the drapers, through which the wheat passed—the heads to be ripped asunder by the teeth to separate the roughest wheat from the straw. I had known of men to go through those cylinders, come out in fingertip-sized pieces behind the separator.

There was, as I've indicated, an eternal murderous growl about those cylinders when the separator was in gear that made me afraid for the header tender, Lonnie. I'd had that job for two years myself, and always the cylinders had seemed to me to be too close under me for comfort. A bit of dizziness, a fall, and the machine couldn't be thrown out of gear fast enough to keep a man out of the metal teeth.

But why should I fear that now? Because of the sound I *felt* in the sooty cloud— keeping time with the roaring of the cylinders!

The cloud stayed with us as we traveled the far side, slow, ponderous, noisy, every living thing of us coughing his guts out, and started back on the fourth side, which paralleled the subsidiary draw that had always held such terror for me as a child. The side of the draw was steep. I had plowed and seeded it myself, plowing and seeding down as far as I could, to where the streambed was just too steep for anything but a goat—where only sagebrush and rye grass grew. Down there I knew was the perpendicular wash with badger holes in the banks, and big mounds on the streambed. Down there was land that to me, even at fifteen, was terror-land.

You see, I had always, from earliest memories of visits to Uncle Charles's place, been conscious that the entire high field resembled a monstrous grave-mound! It was a feeling I could not escape, of which I could not rid myself. If my feeling had any basis in fact—and I doubted it too much ever to mention it to anyone—*what was buried under it and how far back did it date?*

As we fought our way back to the starting corner, around that gargantuan bosom, or grave mound, I had the strangest feeling that the deep freshet-bed, into which I could not see because of the borders of sagebrush and rye grass, was a-crawl with something. Badgers? Coyotes? Sagehens? Rabbits? What else had I ever seen or heard in the sandy hot wash? Nothing, save in imagination. But in imagination there had been Indian bones, stalking warriors out of elder time—and things man no longer remembered or had heard about, dating back and back and back.

This part of the Big Bend country of the Columbia River was the tag-end of the Great Moraine, almost the exact line on which the Ice Age from the north died, began slowly retreating back to the Arctic.

Why I should remember that in that high field of strangely smutted grain I had no idea, *then.*

Uncle Charles signaled for a halt at the starting spot. The mules and horses, black with sweat all over their bodies, sweat into which the smut was worked like boring maggots, stood and coughed horribly. We all coughed.

The smut cloud did not move on, as it seemed it should. It just stayed there as we stayed, a dome of ebony glistening over and around us. There was a whiteness about the mouths, eyes and nostrils of men and beasts. Our hair and lashes were beaded with smut. Our lungs were afire with it. It tasted bitter as lye on our parched tongues.

I expected Uncle Charles to call it quits, but he was a stubborn man. He signaled for the second round.

II. EBON EXODUS

The same stubbornness, suddenly, was in all of us. We refused to be beaten. How could any of us, simple farm people, have realized *what made us stubborn?* We were just people, descended from pioneer stock, who wouldn't allow a little thing like smut, to which all farmers were occasionally accustomed, to keep us from the harvest. The world was hungry, must be fed, and feeding the world gave us money for luxuries. That was the simple truth of it.

It wouldn't have made any difference, I realize now, if Uncle Charles had given orders to knock off, had decided to let the field rot, for once we had rounded the field we were *committed*. The damage, which we could not even guess at then, was already done.

I'll never know now how we got around that second time. It's a long drag around a half section. At first, if you can make three "rounds" without leaving half the wheat, in half a day, you're doing all right. We made three rounds and that smut cloud never left us. The coughing was hideous. Lonnie especially felt it. He bent double as he coughed. He had had whooping cough that winter, I knew, and his lungs had been weakened by it.

The cloud had expanded and deepened unbelievably. I felt that every spore we had released from the wheat had joined the cloud. I felt that the rhythm I had sensed in the cloud was faster, should have been an audible sound to everybody on the separator, but everybody was too hard at work, too busy coughing, to pay any attention.

We were coming around the shoulder where the two draws merged when the first catastrophe happened—and I was to remember with horror that I had so often thought of this very possibility. *Had I made it happen?*

I heard a scream and whirled on my high perch to see Lonnie Keel fall upon the drapers, bounce, grab for the sides of the feed, ride the canvas into the maw of the machine. He screamed all the way in, until the cylinder teeth got him. His screaming made the mules and horses unmanageable for a full minute, and though Uncle Charles hurried to throw the machinery out of gear, there was no use. Lonnie Keel was doomed from the moment he fell.

And yet, he should have been able to grab the sides of the feed, haul himself out. He had tried, but as I thought of it later it seemed to me that his hands were *snatched* back, the clutching fingers *prevented* from pulling the boy out, saving his life. But of course every farmer knows how to compare hindsight with foresight. I was always one to do a lot of imagining.

The animals wouldn't stop until we made that last corner. Uncle Charles and Cavick were both off the separator, running back behind it. No doubting what they would find—the tiny bloody pieces of Lonnie Keel!

I swung the horses and mules to a halt finally. I fastened the two lines to the whipstock in the rock box, climbed down and killed the distillate-burning engine. Then, sick, coughing, my fear a tangible thing now, I raced back to Uncle Charles and Cavick.

They were bending over something in the stubble.

I bent down, too. I got even sicker. There wasn't enough left of any part of

Lonnie Keel to wad a shotgun! And yet, attached to some of the smallest bits were shreds and patches of his shirt, overalls and shoes!

We three were very close together. "God!" said Uncle Charles. "Go ahead, Cavick, say you told me so! But that don't explain what made the kid fall! There was no reason. I saw him go, and it looked as if he was *pulled* off his seat, *thrown* into the cylinders!"

"I couldn't see," said Cavick, "there's too much machinery between me and the header tender and the smut's too thick anyway!"

We moved back from the combined harvester, the three of us, and noted the pieces of Lonnie Keel, but I think I was the first to notice the real horror of what was just now really starting.

I was staring at a lump of flesh when it seemed to *move*. Then I realized that it wasn't a tiny piece of *Lonnie* that was moving, but something else that was moving *onto* the crimson flesh! It didn't take two shakes to figure out what it was. The smut was alive! It was a tiny glistening army. It crawled onto those pieces of flesh, covered them from sight, *fed upon them!*

Uncle Charles cried out. John Cavick swore savagely. There was nothing we could do for Lonnie, but even so the next move seemed cruel--at *first*. We heard one of the horses scream like a woman in pain. We all three straightened, whirled to look. Several of the horses and mules were down on their bellies in their harness, threshing, coughing—and now several of them followed suit of the first one and screamed. It isn't often, thank God, that a farmer hears a horse scream; usually only when the animal is dying in a fire.

"Get them out!" yelled Uncle Charles. "Get them out of the smut, down to the troughs!"

We didn't forget Lonnie, mind you, nor ourselves. I realized that I was more or less burning up myself, with something more than the heat. A steadily increasing inward pressure was all over my body, and its warmth, too, was increasing.

Uncle Charles didn't ordinarily help with the draft animals, but he did this time. Lonnie usually handled eight head, while Cavick and I took twelve each; but Lonnie wouldn't be doing that kind of work ever again. Uncle Charles had to.

The animals were half crazy but they knew us, knew we were trying to save them, so they stood, fretting a little but not so much, until we had all the tugs unfastened and folded back inside the back-bands.

I mounted Kate. Uncle Charles mounted one of the others, Cavick a third. The rest were apportioned among us, held together by their halter chains. I gave the word to Kate when the rest signaled they were ready.

My twelve head of animals, as if at a signal, broke into a dead run from a standing start. It almost threw me. But behind us the rest came on just as fast, as if invisible whips had suddenly been laid upon the backs of every last one!

My twelve headed for the gate and the main road. I did not try to hold them in.

It would have been no use. I yelled ahead for the chore-man we had left in the barnyard to have the yard gate open. I could see it start swinging inward as we started down the steep rocky grade into the draw. Our galloping had thunder in it, and danger. If one horse or mule even stumbled we would have a murderous pile-up.

I looked back once. Cavick and Uncle Charles were clinging to their riding animals for dear life. I expected somehow to find the smut cloud still with us, but it had halted, rather oddly I thought, partly in and partly outside the field gate. The cloud reached fully a thousand feet into the air and seemed to hover over the entire field.

I thought, as we swung crazily into the gate like chariots taking a dangerous turn, that the smut cloud, on whose sides the sun shone as on the back of a smoothly curried horse, was beginning to sink down upon the field. I saw Karl Orme, the sack-buck, come racing through the gate, standing spread-legged in his flatbed sack wagon, his horses apparently crazy with fear. I saw him fight the lines, turn and face the field from which all of us had just escaped. Yes, even then I used the word, "escaped!" Then Karl Orme did an odd thing, though I didn't see all of it because I had things of my own to do. He jumped from his wagon, lashed his animals into a dead run, and moved slowly back, afoot, to the gate in which the smut cloud seemed to hesitate. It was afterward I remembered that slow, queer return.

Then I lost Karl Orme behind the barn as my animals reached the huge circular galvanized tank in the barnyard, so big that all of Uncle Charles's animals could drink from it at once. I flung myself from Kate's back as Cavick and Uncle Charles swung their animals in against the tank, too.

Uncle Charles yelled at Cavick and me while he himself ran awkwardly toward the blacksmith shop where he kept tools, hoses, odds and ends always needed around a farm.

"Into the tank, both of you!" Uncle Charles yelled. "Get your clothes off! I'll be right back!"

Odd, but I had been wanting to fling myself into the tank. The water in it was about three and a half feet deep. The horses and mules pushed their nostrils clear under. I saw all their eyes bulged. There were lines of white about them.

Aunt Claudia and my two gal cousins came running from the house to ask silly questions just as Uncle Charles came from the shop with a length of hose. He yelled at his wife and daughters:

"Get back away from us! Don't stop for anything, but go on past the house to the next neighbor's. Stay by the telephone there. I'll let you know what to do! *Run!*"

Naturally they thought Uncle Charles was crazy, and I thought so, too, but they turned and fled as their forebears must have fled from charging Indians. Women and girls can run when they're scared.

Uncle Charles flung himself into the tank with Cavick and me.

Cavick and I had both dived in, going clear under, much to the amazement of the horses and mules. Then, standing, we stripped off our clothes, and began to wash our hair, bathe our bodies. Uncle Charles followed suit, but his first thought was of the animals. He affixed one end of the hose to the faucet, turned it on full, and began spraying the horses and mules. The water had plenty of pressure and the stream was strong, but each animal seemed to realize at once that again its best interests were being taken care of.

While he worked on himself Uncle Charles handed the hose to me. I worked on the animals, too. I watched the smut which had covered them vanish into the longer hair under their bellies. I washed that off, too. Karl Orme's team reached the tank, hauling back to stop the wagon as if Orme had still been in it.

I washed them off, too, then John Cavick took a crack at it. Still there were no explanations of anything.

Soon Karl Orme, hatless, his legs pumping like those of a college sprinter, came through the gate, pushed past the animals and flung himself into the trough. Was all this crazy, even a little humorous? Not if you remembered Lonnie Keel and the creeping smut spores which had started devouring his remnants.

Karl Orme stood in the tank, began ripping off his clothes. I noticed that Uncle Charles, standing there in the tank from which now rose the odor of smut, stared up the rounded mound of the drawside at his smutted field. Over the field hung a tremendous black cloud, into which shot tongues of flame. Uncle Charles whirled on Karl Orme.

"What happened, Karl?" he choked. "You were the last out of the field. Did it just take fire?"

"No, Charlie," said Orme grimly, "I took the law into my own hands. Your stubbornness might cost lives. When I saw Lonnie Keel tumble, the rest of what I did was just common sense. I dashed out of the field, freed the horses, turned back and took the greatest chance I ever hope to take. *I threw a match into the cloud!*"

"How dared you do such a thing?" demanded Uncle Charles hoarsely. "You're a hired hand! You've set fire to a half section of wheat. My loss will run into thousands—"

"And how many lives?" said Karl Orme softly. "Listen, Charlie, while I tell you something. I picked up those smutty sacks that John here sewed and dropped. There was smut in all of them. I had piled maybe a hundred in one area, when what do you suppose happened?"

"How would I know?" said Uncle Charles sulkily.

"The sacks began bursting their seams!" said Karl Orme. "They just exploded like over-inflated toy balloons, *and the smut began creeping out, to spread on the ground! I* knew if I didn't take steps your stubbornness would return us all to the field of smut, and no telling what might happen!"

"And now," said Uncle Charles hoarsely, "you've completely released the *things* in the wheat!"

"Things?" said Karl Orme. "What are you talking about? I've burned out that half section, or will have within an hour. The smut won't spread to neighboring fields. The fire—"

"Fire won't do anything to *this*," said Uncle Charles. "It will just complete, a lot faster, the exodus of the—"

What he was going to say I didn't know then, couldn't even guess, for all four of us noticed the same thing at the same time. We had washed from ourselves the smut which had been driving us crazy. We had drunk deeply to wash the stuff out of our gullets. The smut had laid, a thin film, atop the water in the tank. Now we all saw that the stuff had drawn together atop the water, moved slowly to the sides of the tank where it became a thick brown mass. And that mass began crawling up the side of the tank to escape! The horses and mules saw it, snorted, backed away.

We couldn't find a thing to say. We moved to the side of the tank, watching that stuff—and as if it watched us also, and were afraid of being captured, *it gathered speed like some shapeless spider, slid over the rim of the tank, dropped to the ground beyond!* We heard it, and the sound had a kind of jeer in it, strike the ground.

We put our hands on the sides and looked down—just as the smut we had washed off the animals gathered in one place, joined that which had come out of the tank! The mass of smut was dark bronze. It formed a circular smudge, the center of which began to rise perceptibly.

As we stared, our mouths hanging open, the smut-mass doubled in size, doubled again!

"John!" yelled Uncle Charles. "Get a stick of dynamite out of the shed. Cap it, fuse it, bring it here fast!"

It didn't look silly, not now, to see a naked man racing to the blacksmith shop. The mules and horses--as Karl Orme unhitched his two--retreated to a far corner of the barn yard. Orme started for the gate; he, too, was naked. Soon, we hoped, we could get to the house, get into fresh clothes.

John Cavick came running back. He raced to the house to get matches. He had cut the fuse awfully short. The smut-mass was now five feet across, still roughly circular. Then it was ten feet across. Then Cavick was back, and all of us ducked into the water as the stick of dynamite was dropped into the mass.

After the explosion we looked out. The smut-mass was nowhere to be seen. Even then I felt I could hear queer jeering laughter in the very air.

Cavick swore again. Uncle Charles began to pray. I felt like it myself. Not much explanation was needed. Scores of circular smut-masses suddenly sprang into being in the barnyard, and as far in all directions as we could see. That dynamite had blown the mass into tiny bits. But already each bit had grown, expanded, until we could see it.

As each of us noted this, each circular smut-smudge *jumped* in size, its center rose like the crown of a hat, a *peon's* hat, pointed!

"The telephone!" said Uncle Charles, almost moaning. "We've got to have help! And clothes!"

Uncle Charles was an old man as he crawled out of the tank, started a dripping run for the house. As we ran we watched the smut-masses *jumping, spreading, growing,* all around us—and I for one wondered if even we started now, and ran faster and faster, we could ever again escape them.

"Look!" said Karl Orme, as he turned at the door to look back the way we had come. There was now no smoke, no fire, on the high field. There was no smut cloud. But a fringe of bronze extended all along the edge of the field we could see—and as I looked the fringe crept noticeably down the mounded side of the hill where the two draws met!

III. HOPELESS STRUGGLE

By noon of the next day it seemed to me there had never been a time when we hadn't been fighting the smut. We still called it "smut" because that had been the manner of its appearance, but none of us really believed that's what it was—not any more. An agricultural expert from Port Orchard flew in the next morning after Uncle Charles appealed for help by telephone. He put some of the "smut" under his microscope.

"It's not kernel, covered or naked smut," he said. "It's not *tilletia tritici* or *levis*. It's not *Ustilago tritici* or *Urocystis tritici*. In fact, Norman, it's not smut at all! I don't know what it is!"

The horror surrounding the death of Lonnie Keel had long since become a minor thing. Too much else had happened since. In the first place, firing the smut had released every bit of it simultaneously from the wheat by destroying the wheat around it. Fire seemed to have no other effect on the stuff.

Fist, the smut-masses we had washed off ourselves and the horses and mules had widened, spread, grown upward, to meet the brown-black fringe which seemed to be *overflowing* from the high field. That smut, creeping down the bosom of the field like molasses running down outside the neck of a jug was a hellish thing to watch.

Birds, animals, everything in the area, became aware of the creeping horror. Grass on the hillside disappeared, devoured by the stuff. By the next morning, after Uncle Charles had told Aunt Claudia and the cousins to bed down with neighbors, they'd be in the battle line soon enough, hundreds of men and women were helping to fight the smut.

The entire field, which I had seen from an airplane—one of a dozen that constantly circled above the area of spreading spores—was blanketed with the stuff. Moreover, the center of the field was now easily two hundred feet in height. The stuff had moved inexorably out in all directions. Charles Norman's own wheat on the north was being devoured. Some of the men who fought the creeping smut insisted they could hear the stuff *chew,* as if the smut were animal and equipped with a myriad of infinitesimal mandibles. Every kind of fire fighting equipment was on the job that was within reach. Flame-throwers from the nearest army base had been tried. Everything had been hurled into that mess except an atom bomb. It was bent on reaching in all directions, we were all sure, but it would travel slower if we fought it and didn't deliberately spread it.

The smut-mass advanced without the slightest harm into the hottest tongues of flame from the flame throwers which had wrought such havoc among Japs and Germans in World War Two.

Brave men faced the slowly advancing horde with clubs, rifles, wet sacks. They sprayed it with water, with kerosene, gasoline. They fought themselves to a standstill, but the stuff seemed invincible. When the fighters against the growing smutmass thought they had found the answer, the whole mass shuddered, and extended itself in all directions.

Casualties were somewhat high. A dozen men, daring too greatly, had come in contact with the smut and vanished into it, utterly possessed and destroyed by it, as Lonnie Keel had been.

I think every conceivable kind of machine was turned loose on that growing, rising, spreading mass. X-rays, some special secret rays used by the army and navy the exact nature of which I was not informed, were turned on the stuff—and without effect.

The smut-mass did not seem to devour inanimate things—for hours, that second day, we could see the shape of the combined harvester through the growing mass, right where we had left it on the rounded bosom of the hill.

"The smut," said our agricultural expert, and scientists of more kinds than I knew or can remember agreed with him, "is an entity or a vast community of entities. If we don't solve the secret there is no way of telling how far the stuff may go. But where did it come from?"

"It came out of the wheat," my Uncle explained. But when he made it clear, and his neighbors backed him up, that only his field, in all the thousands of acres held by him and his neighbors, had been possessed by the blight, science admitted it had come to a dead end.

"It has to come from somewhere," said Doctor Larsen, the man whom the government entrusted with the secret rays that had been used without effect on our smut-mass. "I can't escape the feeling that in the sudden appearance and spread of this 'smut' there is clear evidence of *intent!*"

Up until I heard that I would not have spoken my thoughts for anything in the world. I'm ordinarily a bit shy. But now I offered my own two cents worth.

"Not only intention," I said, "but scientific implementation of it!"

Larsen whirled on me. "I've been thinking the same thing, kid!" he said. "Just what are you driving at?"

"The field," I said, somewhat breathlessly "lies in the general line of the ancient ice fields which came down, ages ago, from the north. The draws have been dug by ice action and seepage from glaciers. That's what my geology teacher said in high school last term, anyway. If there were intelligent life in the land before the ice came down, what happened to it?"

Tired men, resting for a few minutes from fighting the creeping mass, heard me and snorted.

"Cocky kid!" said someone. "Probably write poetry when he grows up, like his utterly useless old man!"

"Do any of you gentlemen," said Larsen, "have any idea about these secret rays I've been using to fight against your smut?" They shook their heads.

"Then," Larsen continued, "there may be other things ye also wot not of! Go ahead, kid, what's on your mind?"

"I've always felt that the high field was part of some huge grave mound, just because of the shape of it. I've thought since I was little that strange things might be buried in it. Now I wonder what may be a crazy thing—"

"Let us judge what's crazy and what isn't," said Larsen. "Every pathfinder has been crazy in the eyes of his contemporaries. Go on."

"I think there's something under the hill, deep down," I said. "I think it's been there for thousands, maybe millions of years, dormant, resting. Now it has reached out. It is life, whatever life it was that ice destroyed, or forced to flee. The intelligence locked under the hill set a trap for us—the smut! We stepped into it and got caught. It reached up somehow from down under, manifested itself as smut."

"You talk as if this isn't new to you," said Larsen, interrupting. "Why isn't it?" "I've always felt something in the draws, Toler Draw and Norman Draw, the one coming into it from the east," I hurried on. People were close to me now, listening, and I had help from an unexpected quarter.

"I always hated what the kid calls Norman Draw, myself," said Herb Slasser, Uncle Charles's neighbor to the west. "I used to go in there, twenty years ago, before Norman broke the land around it, to get myself a sagehen. *I always felt like running out!* I know there can't be anything in there bigger than badgers or coyotes, yet I finally got so I wouldn't go in there for a sagehen if I was starving!"

"I used to feel," I said, "as if there was someone behind me, who always ducked out of sight when I whirled to look. I always thought I'd run into something hideous around the next turn ahead. I never did, but I always knew why—*it kept just out of sight!*"

"What nonsense!" said the army colonel who commanded the flame throwing equipment and operators. "What can a yokel who has something like second sight tell us that will help combat this stuff?"

A group of people was standing now on the side of the draw opposite where we had left the combine. The draw itself was filled with the smut mass to within a few feet of our level. There was danger, and we all knew it, that it would surge up and out and swallow us all, but the danger was so constant, so commonplace now that we almost ignored it.

"Certainly what he suggests," said Larsen, "can't accomplish less than we have! We've tried now to destroy this creeping stuff with every vibration controlled or operated by man—sound waves, electric currents, X-rays, gamma rays, even cosmic—"

Nobody could think of a destructive implement or technique that hadn't been tried on the smut-mass. As we talked there the sooty, shining, ebony-stir stuff in Toler Draw lurched, came within a few feet of our bodies. We stepped back. I stooped again to look. Tentacles so small, so tenuous as to be almost invisible, were reaching out at us through the interstices of the soil on which we stood! And others were coming upward through the soil. I was right, I had to be right—the source of the danger was somewhere underground, maybe far underground.

Larsen more or less had charge of the sector in which we fought the smut-mass. He put his head together with the heads of the plane crews trying to probe the cloud with radar and sonar, trying to get some picture of just what it might be.

"Can you find out for me," he asked, "whether there are any caverns hereabouts?"

Not until the next day, when three Sprengnether earthquake seismographs graphs were set up at the apices of a triangle several miles on each side, with the high field in the triangle's center, was this question answered. Then they did something they called "seismic prospecting for head waves," carried out under Larsen's supervision—he seemed to know everything about everything—and the seismologists all agreed that there were caverns under the high field, not very far down, either!

No sooner had the word passed than half of Uncle Charles's neighbors said they had always known it. They had walked over the field years before and distinctly heard hollow sounds below! No local yokel was going to get ahead of the oldtimers, even if they had to lie a little.

Even my uncle said there had been times when he had felt hollow vibrations come up through the combined harvester and other heavy machinery. He could also remember times when mules and horses had shied, while working the high field, away from odd underfoot sounds!

But just what did it matter one way or the other? The entire mounded hill was now deeply buried under a sooty, glistening mass several hundred feet deep all over it! There wasn't a chance of any kind of penetrating the hill into a cavern that might be occupied—*by what was such a cavern likely to be occupied?*

When somebody thought to ask that question a dreadful silence settled over everybody, a silence so deep you could hear the little chewing mouths of the smut.

"Find a way or not," some farmer put it in words, "you wouldn't get me even *trying* to get into it for all the gold in the world!"

"There must be some kind of material," I averred, not feeling as smart and cocky as I must have sounded to the others, "in which men can move into and down under the smut-mass. It apparently doesn't eat metal, plastic, things like that."

"But if there happens to be joints, anywhere at all, through which the stuff can reach your body," said Larsen, "you're just the more firmly trapped in something. You have some idea like a diving suit of steel, or plastic, or something, maybe?"

"Yes, sir, and I'll help get into those caverns if somebody will go along, with lights, weapons, and whatever scientists think we need!" I wished I hadn't said that, even before I started, but a kid sometimes gets too big for his britches and keeps right on getting too big when he knows he is.

Larsen started working by telephone on the Navy at Bremerton. Yes, they could furnish water-tight suits, but would they be smut-tight? And how, if the suits worked, would we penetrate the scores of feet of soil, shale, clay and solid rock which intervened between the covering smut and the caverns in which, I think everybody now believed the smut originated, or from which it was directed?

We did some gambling on a wild theory: those entities down under had sought sanctuary from the Ice Age. Therefore they were averse to ice. We could establish a bridgehead on the surface of the ground from which we could operate, if we could freeze the area and keep back the smut at the right spot. That's a little obscure, but for the time being there's no help for it. And I've said it was a wild gamble on a wilder theory—every bit of which might be utterly wrong. We had tried dropping dry ice on the smut-mass and it had had no more effect than fire, rays, explosions, or anything else we had tried.

The three seismologists gave me a thrill, believe me, when I heard them say that the cavern was nearest the surface at a spot deep in the Norman Draw! They made a map for us, covered with what they called "microseisms" which meant nothing at all to me, but Larsen could read without trouble. I was perfectly sure, at this point, that I must have sensed the presence of that cavern when I first sneaked into Norman Draw when I was about six years old.

We were about twenty in number when we finally dared the smut-mass in our air conditioned diving suits. I was allowed to go along because I knew Norman Draw, badger-hole by badger-hole, better even than Uncle Charles knew it. Besides, Aunt Claudia wouldn't let Uncle Charles even *offer* to go.

I held my breath when the twenty of us, looking like something out of other worlds, put our feet into the smut-mass, walked into it as we would have walked into a lake.

Gradually the stuff crawled up our bodies as we walked down into Toler Draw. I couldn't feel anything getting in, but horror rose up to my heart from my feet as the smut-mass rose and rose and finally covered the eye-pieces of my helmet.

Then I had to lead the way, fumbling with my feet, while behind me all the others clung to a rope which kept us from losing one another, perhaps forever.

IV SANCTUARY OF THE AGES

I could see nothing through the eyepieces but stygian darkness. But I knew the draws as I did not know the palms of my own hands. There were sandy streambeds in each of them. I walked down the west side of Toler Draw, my unseen companions following me. There were times when I waited for the man immediately behind me to come up, bump into me. I had a horror of being lost from the others, of being alone on the deepening bottom of the smut. It would have been dreadful. As it was, it was bad enough. It did not seem to me that there was any more weight on us as we went down into night-darkness, but there must have been some. I came to the steep sides of the first draw, which led away southeastward. I dropped down into it, with a sudden sickening feeling that there might no longer be a bottom; a thought that vanished when my heavy feet struck and sank leadenly into the sand. I turned right. I felt rather than heard my helpers drop into the wash behind me.

Now I moved to the east side of the wash, held out my hand against the dirt bank, moved along, guiding myself with my hand. As nearly as I could tell there was no material resistance to our advance. We strode through the smut far easier than if it had been water; as easily as if it had been the darkness to which I likened it. I sensed opposition; the same sort of opposition, only many times stronger, one knows exists in a parent or teacher who opposes what one wishes, but says nothing about it—just sulks and opposes!

It must have taken an hour to reach the place where Norman Draw merged with Toler Draw. My left hand found it. I turned into it, memories of old terrors flooding back. Here at this place I had often stood for what seemed hours, mustering up courage to travel into Norman Draw.

I had that same reluctance now, multiplied by the years since I had been a six-year old. But I set out. I had fixed in my mind, from the microseism, just where we would face the mounded breast of the hill which we could no longer see, might never see again if we did not conquer the smut, and I held steadily on the tiring course until we reached it—and I visualized it in mind from old memory. It was in the area where badgers multiplied through the years, where literally scores of their burrows led back into the side of the hill, where mounds covered areas of fifty feet per burrow.

I faced the side of the hill, stood very still. The others came up and I knew they formed to my right and left, by the way the segments of rope pulled against the back of my diving suit.

Out of those holes, I was sure-smut was pouring like water from a big hose under high pressure! That was just a feeling I had, based on sensitivity, and a steady pushing against my body from head to heels.

I tapped the man next to me on my right. We had a fairly good set of prearranged signals. This man had a fire-drill, a new government contraption which would eat into almost any metal known as it would eat through air itself. He walked ahead and now I clung to his belt. There was no sound, but he touched me with his elbow when he started using his fire drill. And then the ground ahead of my feet became level and I knew we had started into a slope made by the fire drill.

I extended hands from shoulders. The cut into the hill was about four feet wide, plenty. And soon I had to stand on tiptoe to reach the roof. We ate back under the hill, back under the high field, almost as fast as we could walk. I felt that we had hit the microseism location right on the nose. I tapped again when my feet told me we were in the rock. Almost instantly we slanted downward at a thirty-degree angle. Where we now were we were safe from cave-ins for the moment.

When I estimated that we were perhaps four hundred feet down and five hundred feet back under the hill, I signaled for our lights expert to come forward with his equipment. Mind now, the blazing hell from the fire drill had not been felt by any of us, nor had any of us seen the flames. Nor had we felt the heat along the shaft where much of the stone must have been close to molten.

But when we stopped abysmal cold began to seep through our thick diving suits! One second and they were almost unbearably hot for their own sakes; then the coldness came in and two terrific emotions rose in me at the same time: fear and excitement.

I knew the others felt it also because we closed in to touch one another and both the fear and excitement were communicated through our contacting hands. Also, we all wished to go on and on.

My fire-drill man traveled more slowly. My lights expert had tried to pierce the gloom with his lights with utterly no effect whatever. Now, suddenly, my fire-drill man stopped, tapped me again. He stood, his tapping indicated, inside the cavern! He fumbled forward and I had a chance to marvel at the miracle of mathematics; we had struck the cavern at its base level!

The cold was even more intense. I took the lead now, feeling my way with my feet, not wishing to step into a bottomless pit. I still moved with that effortlessness by which we had made progress through the smut outside. And on a sudden hunch I moved toward the feeling of greatest cold. If the smut-entities were averse to cold, if we entered areas where it was great enough we would be free of them! So I reasoned, if a fifteen-year-old can pride himself on reasoning.

When I began to stiffen with the cold I came up solid against the acme of cold. I ran my hand over a smooth surface. My hands seemed to freeze against it. I signaled for my lights man. He came forward, switched on his light magic— and for the first time since dropping into the smut-mass we could see! I could see, there in the blackness, all of my companions. They looked like something out of Inferno and no mistake. But when we looked around us and saw into what we had come, nothing human, or made by humans, could ever again look anything but commonplace! How does one, describe something with which one has nothing to compare?

First, the cavern was vast. I knew, all of us knew how it had been formed. Ice from those ancient glaciers had, by glacier action, been wrapped up in dirt, rock, sand, and all the drippings and dregs of the great moraine; the dirt and rock had been churned, crushed, piled hill on hill, until a world of ice was incased in a world of cataclysmic earth. Then, after ages, the ice outside had receded and the dirt and rocks, miles deep all around, had preserved the ice within, like some unbelievable pig-in-a-blanket.

But what had been preserved in the ice itself?

I knew, all of us knew, that the churning I have referred to, the piling of dirt on dirt, rock on rock, hill on hill, to encase the world of ice, *had been deliberate!* We all knew it because our minds had been prepared for it. We knew it before there was any proof. The black face of ice that had been ages old when Lemuria sank beneath the Pacific, stared out at us with baleful eyes. Oh, I know how ice twinkles and stares when it reflects light, but this was different. The "eyes" were so close together, yet each orb distinct, and the balefulness so unmistakable, that I began to shiver with something that was not entirely the cold.

We were surrounded by ice. The cavern in which we stood must have been twenty acres in extent. The ice ceiling was a hundred feet overhead. In spite of the cold some sort of melting was taking place in this cavern, slowly, surely, enlarging it.

The floor underfoot was a-crawl! Water, black water, dripped from the roof, seeped endlessly from the entire surrounding wall. Maybe it came out of the floor, too. But on the floor itself, it *moved and grew!*

I knew we stood in one of the birth places, maybe the only one of the smut! The others knew it with me. We stared at one another through our eye-pieces now. The other faces were all reddish in the reflected light, strange, fearful. The stuff on the floor was not ice, but it had just been ice, and it was colder than any ice we knew on the surface. The coldness crept up our feet into our bodies. It had an added coldness, as profound as absolute zero.

I noticed an outward flow from the center of the mass on the floor. I realized that on the floor of this great mysterious cavern the drippings from roof and walls, the seepage, formed in a kind of reserve pool—and then spread slowly, inexorably outward in all directions! I knew what happened after that. Somehow it slid out under the ice, worked its way down into unfrozen soil—then moved up through the interstices of rocks, however solid, up into the clay, the sand, the gravel, then, by capillarity, the soil itself—into the roots of wheat, up to the heads where it appeared as *smut!*

But why this particular manifestation? How had *selection* been made? The choosing of just one particular field, *all* of it, but no more, indicated what Larsen had suggested: intention. But what was the entity or entities that intended?

Were we standing even now inside some laboratory of a far-off forgotten day? The ice was alive, I was sure, frozen solid through the centuries, against a set time of wakening! But what was the entity? The frozen part that we regarded as ice? Or the separate portions of it we had first regarded as smut spores or *sori* until Larsen said it was not smut?

I signaled our fire-drill man to use his apparatus on the material on the cavern floor. He blazed his flames upon it. The whole cavern, in the light, looked like some unbelievable hell. But the effect of the fire on the mass was astounding. There was instantly faster movement! The stuff on the floor, without diminishing, began to move faster in all directions, out under the ice, as if the fire gave it new life. I saw, and Larsen saw, and signaled me with his fingers against my suit, that the fire caused the material on the cavern floor to increase. Each "spore," it appeared, divided when touched by the flame, reproducing like the amoeba, by division.

Quickly my man played the flame all around the cavern wall—and before he could turn it off the moving mass on the floor, which had been no higher than our knees, rose to our shoulders! The flame, melting the ice, had released the smut and so quickly that it had almost flooded the cavern. And we had no way, down here, to reverse the process. But the flames were quickly turned off—*in spite of a sudden mental message that came to my mind—and I heard later to the minds of all the others—as if the entire ice face were pleading for more and more of the releasing flame!*

I signaled for the fire-drill man to concentrate on a stope cut straight into the ice wall.

He asked by signal if it should be about the same size as that by which we had penetrated the hillside. I nodded. He adjusted his light, played it against the ice face at a spot selected by Larsen.

The flames ate their way in, but it wasn't water that came out of the shaft behind us—it was a steady stream of smut! Our "ice" then, was not ice at all, but the material we had called "smut" frozen solid. And it was sentient. It knew who and what we were. It had known for all the ages of historic man. It communicated with us telepathically somehow! *It? They?* How could we tell? The material was immortal, that was clear—as any cellular thing that reproduces by halving itself is immortal.

We deliberately drove back into the ice face until we came to solid rock! We must have gone in a mile behind the face of the "ice." I think we all realized that we were thus traveling into the very heart of some antediluvian monster of which no record had previously come down to man in the rocks. This monster, whatever it was, was a community in itself. It was one as a community, one in each of its tiny separate entities—each of which became two at will, to add to the strength and size of the community.

A chill coursed through me as I remembered that man himself is a community—of nobody really knows how many billions of cells. This community could be some weird progenitor of man himself, easily. Else how could twenty of us—nineteen of us scientists including the greatest, Larsen—have been so sure of telepathic communication from It-Them to our brains?

The Thing welcomed the breath of the flame which released it. The dripping from the flame, from the heart of the pack, seemed almost to sing as it flowed back past us, under our feet, to the cavern, there to flow outward and upward to add to the mass which grew upon the high field, spreading in all directions across Central Washington. I could just imagine the people on the surface now, noting the increased activity of the smut-mass, wondering what dreadful things were happening to us. We were releasing more of the materials from the elder world, but we did not see how it could be helped. We had to have some idea of this or be utterly defeated at bringing it under control.

But what if the ice closed in around us, back there in that tunnel, and our fire-drill suddenly went out of condition! We must all have thought of that at once, for no sooner had realization come than we started backtracking. We could be trapped anywhere between here and the surface! And on the surface the traps were just as thickly set! There was no doubting the danger to us, to our people above, to all the neighboring counties, to the nation, for all we knew.

Nothing could destroy this entity or community of entities; but cold, if sufficiently intense, could immobilize It-Them. Cold was our answer. As we fled back through the tunnel into the great cavern I felt as if the entire pack, with millions of tiny voices, were shrieking silently after me:

"Set me free! Set me free! I will serve you always! You, too, shall be immortal!"

But there was a very human element of stupidity in It-Them, also. For if it had any consideration at all for creatures that were mortal it would certainly not have slain Lonnie Keel and the dozen other human beings the smut-mass had devoured on the surface—and then had any idea that we would listen favorably to It-Them's appeal for release. But the appeal was made. It fled after us, begging, beseeching, promising that immortality which it so plainly knew.

I did not care for its immortality, however, nor just then did my co-workers. For It-Them's immortality had kept it locked underground, like some monstrous black Prometheus chained, for ages mankind could scarcely count. Was immortality worth such restrictions?

I knew then the solution to the smutmass, a solution that was only temporary, that must be kept active to the end of man's life on earth if black Prometheus were to remain chained and thus deterred from possessing the globe.

Engineers who had worked on Grand Coulee Dam were among my nineteen coworkers and I felt sure the idea would have occurred to them also—they had used it on the east bank of the Columbia where briefly, it flowed into the north. It would work here in Norman Draw and Toler Draw. It had to, or who could say how far the doom we had released from the old moraine, in the high field above it, would eventually extend?

V. SUCH BITTER COLD

We had one very obvious and highly dangerous duty to perform before we returned to the surface. Doing it would release more and more of the queer black hellharvest, but if we didn't find out the truth it wouldn't matter much how little or extensively we freed the smut. In a short time it would possess the world anyway, limited, I supposed, only by the food it would need while "alive," while not frozen into immobility. Our duty was to find out something of the limits of the underground smut field, to check against later efforts of our seismologists.

So we started just inside the cavern, where the tunnel by which we had entered it from the surface was running almost full of the smut, and made a tunnel against the solid rock, behind the "ice," to see whether there were branching caverns—to find out, in short, whether this cavern was the only pocket of It-Them, or whether it might not be that all the land under what had once been fields of ancient ice, from side to side of the continent, was inhabited by It-Them! The stuff might never be released within the lifetime of man. It might be released everywhere simultaneously, by tomorrow morning! We must be prepared. It was our duty to take risks.

So behind the eating flames which released more and more of the ebon horror, we followed the rock face around the inside of the cavern. We learned that there were scores of branching tunnels and caverns, each ore tightly packed with the black ice!

Some sort of message, some sort of mapping job must be done to assist the seismologists. I was the only one of those twenty who could return to the surface with any chance of finding my way back. So I went out alone, sick with fear, to the surface. There I procured three sticks of dynamite, fused, capped, spoke briefly to the seismologists, did not take time to explain, and returned to my co-workers in the cavern.

In the cavern we took fresh risks, risks that one or all of us might be crushed by the falling in of the cavern roof. We set off one of the sticks of dynamite at each of three most widely separated points in the cavern. These little explosions, shaking the earth, would reach each seismograph on the surface and write its wave-record thereon. Those who knew how to read the jigglings would know, then, how far the explosion waves of each of the three had traveled to each seismograph, through what media it had traveled—whether rock, clay, sand, gravel or ice!—and a complete map could be made of the dwelling places of It-Them, across all the vast North American Moraine! Thus only could the world protect itself against what we had first known as smut.

Well, then we came out, and I waited, as a youngster should, for science itself to provide what seemed to me to be the only answer. Here it is: During the building of the Grand Coulee Dam, millions of tons of material poured into the hole where the engineers were trying to build an abutment. The material came from the hill on the eastern bank of the river. It could not be removed as fast as it slid into the pit.

So engineers had simply driven pipes into the mountainside, attached them to a special refrigeration plant—*and frozen the mountain solid!* Here, however, we must freeze the hill solid and keep it thus frozen through the ages. If ever alertness relaxed we were done!

I waited for somebody, probably Larsen, to say what we should do, after we came out of that cavern, reported to our people, to newspaper reporters and thus to the world, what we had found. Our seismologists were already studying the records of our three cavern-explosions.

Toler Draw and Norman Draw were both filled with smut when we came out.

The stuff had pushed its fighters back more than five miles in all directions during the time we were down there in the cavern.

When we had done, I waited, and Larsen, grinning at me, said: "I suppose you know the answer, kid?"

I felt shy about the whole thing. "Grand Coulee Dam," I offered, "but *you* know; it's better, coming from you!"

Well, then Larsen told them, and before that same day was ended scores of gallant engineers had gone down into the smut, down into Toler and Norman Draws, to turn the high field and all the land under it, into a gargantuan refrigerator capable of delivering nearly absolute zero cold.

It was easy to tell when they began making cold, for the smut ceased its advance. Then it began to retreat! Its retreat was faster even than its outward charge had been from the moment we began releasing it with the combined harvester, than with the fire Karl Orme had set in the wheat, than with our fire-drill in the cavern.

But not all the ebon horror got back into the cavern-sanctuary before the hillside-refrigerator was completely efficient and operative. A field of it, varying in thickness from inches to feet, covered the high field like a cooling lava flow—a constant threat, a constant reminder, to those who knew.

Scientists often stopped along the road past my Uncle's place, to take note of the ebon blanket over the now useless high field. Invariably they said to Uncle Charles, somewhat loftily:

"Volcanic action here, ages ago! That's black basalt!"

Uncle Charles always widened his eyes as with great surprise.

"I wonder," he invariably answered, "what makes 'it' so cold you can't cross it without freezing?"

They always had some learned explanation. Everybody always had explanations for everything. Only the army of seismologists which planted its seismographs across the North American Moraine offered no explanations of their work. They knew the truth would certainly be laughed to scorn.

Her skin was as white as the flowers of the great moth-orchid, her lips crimson as red blood, her eyes blazing violet, swimming with flecks of gold, and her hair beneath Trevor's hand was black and soft as silken thread.

BLACK Butterflies

by Elmer Brown Mason

A strange tale of the beautiful and the deadly . . . gorgeously illustrated by Virgil Finlay in 1949. Mason's classic story first appeared in 1916.

The Mountain Spirit

It was the obstinacy of Trevor Dillingame, the stark, sheer obstinacy and conceit of the man in his power to handle any situation, solve any jungle secret, that brought us under the shadow.

'Tis a fault of the English. Where a Scotchman is firm, an Englishman is obstinate.

Whereas a Scotchman simply realizes his powers, an Englishman puts no limit to what *he* may accomplish.

Not that I didn't like the man. Losh, who could help it from the mere good looks of him? Though I do not put undue faith in male beauties. But he was such a whale of a laddie, six feet tall, four across the shoulders, cold blue eyes, tread as light as *plandok*, the tiny mouse-deer; and big hands, that could crack a cocoanut or hold a butterfly without bruising its wings.

Butterflies were his line, and he knew as much as anyone in the world about them. I'm a cautious man and I'll go no further; he knew as much as anyone in the whole world about butterflies.

'Twas in the low swamp belt of the coast of British Borneo that it all began. We were collecting pretty nearly everything for a lot of stay-at-home scientists who could afford to have the jungle wonders sent to them to be tagged with Latin names at their leisure. It did pay, but it was hard work, dangerous work. The jungle leeches sucked blood from every uncovered inch of our bodies and our flesh was raw from mosquito bites. There were poisonous insects, snakes, and more snakes, and then the heat—moist, deadening; sapping your vitality like the final rounds of a long, long fight.

Shifting uneasily from foot to foot, and tearing away the jungle leeches that would pop onto their bare skins, three little Dyaks stood in the checkered shadows. Trevor Dillingame was bending over a great flower-stalk, around the top of which

31

were symmetrically clustered the red and black caterpillars, with their one creamy segment, of *Cethosia Hypsea*, creating a living, wriggling bloom.

A red thing sailed through the air—a bird, I thought—and settled in a low nipa palm. I saw that it was a tree frog at the very moment that a green-and-gold whiplike strand swung down from the tree-tops and caught it in it narrow jaws.

"*Chalaka, ular Tuan!*" (Very wicked snake, sir), shrieked one of the Dyaks.

From the olive green of a rattan thicket stepped out a woman, covered with wreaths of jasmine, the two wings of a coal-black butterfly pasted on her forehead. Her hands flew to the slender neck of the snake, twisted it quickly, and the head with its red prey was left between her fingers.

Dillingame stood stock still, staring at her. Laughing up into his face, she flung away the serpent's head, stripped off a jasmine garland, cast it about his neck—and was gone.

Both Trevor and I knew enough of the mythology of Borneo to realize at once that we had looked upon a *hantus*, one of the spirits that lived on the top of Mount Kina Balu and reappeared as the female priests of the country.

That was all very well; but such things can't be—they *aren't*, whether we had seen one or not; and the woman had been very beautiful.

"Yon's a bonnie lassie who favored you with the flowers," I remarked as Dillingame began to strip off the garland.

"That I leave to your Scotch susceptibility, Andy Freeman," he answered. "But did you get a good look at those butterfly wings she wore on her forehead? An eight-inch spread to each of them, and black as jet! A new species, a new genus—perhaps even a new family of Lepidoptera. What do you suppose a specimen of that butterfly would bring in Paris or London? A fortune!"

As we talked, we picked our way carefully along the back trail toward where a boat waited for us on the water of a sluggish stream that ran to the coast. We did not expect to see the Dyaks again; they had fled in wild panic, but we did hope my Chinaman would still be there and would have enough knowledge of the channel to pilot us to the sea without becoming lost in some backwater. Besides, it was getting dark, and a night in a Borneo swamp jungle is enough to make the most seasoned explorer shudder.

The boat and Chinaman were waiting, as we had hoped; but as for getting out in the darkness, Lee San positively refused to attempt to guide us. Outside of the great probability of being lost he claimed that our craft would arouse countless devils of the night by disturbing the waters.

Strange cuss, that Chinaman! He had been with me for over two years in Sumatra, Sarawak and Dutch Borneo, and never before had pretexed superstition for disobeying an order. He was unusually intelligent, too, and I had given him a large share of my confidence, and gained much interesting inside native information in return.

The Chinese are the traders of all that part of the world and know more about the Dyaks, Muruts and other tribes of Borneo than any white man.

We poled the boat out into midstream and dropped anchor, preparing to make the best of a bad situation. Fortunately there was enough dry wood on board to build a good fire on the dirt hearth so we could boil some water and attend to our countless leech wounds with ammonia. Of course the light lured hordes of blood-thirsty mosquitoes, but we stoked up on quinine (Lee preferred an opium pill) and smoked hard beneath our skeeted nets.

Sleep was impossible. Even if the heat had not put it out of the question the jungle noises would have kept a dead man awake. From a hundred yards away, as regular as the striking of a clock, a bull alligator roared out his love call; *samburs*, the big blue deer of Borneo bellowed in the distance; great fruit-bats cut the air with a mighty swish of their leather wings; and underneath all came the chorus of tragedy from the forest floor, the agonized squeal of a small rodent as it was borne in triumphant jaws, the snarl of some cat animal that had missed its spring, the cease-less snuffle of the rooting wild hogs.

"Whisky," I said to Trevor—it's bad stuff in the tropics, but the night was unendurable—and he passed the bottle.

"Quinine," he demanded, and we both took ten more grains.

In the bow of the boat Lee San's teeth began to chatter.

"What's the matter, boy?" I sang out.

"No got mo' opium," he answered.

"Come here and drink some whiskey," I ordered.

"No can," he objected—the Chinese doesn't often touch it, doesn't seem to like it—but he came down to the stern, just the same, and swallowed the big slug I had ready for him.

Silence for a long time, silence that every one of us wanted to break, but each was waiting for the other. Finally Dillingame's thoughts broke out in a torrent of words.

"Andy, how could that woman be real?—and yet you *know* she was! How did she dare grab that deadly tree-snake, that can turn and bite its own skin, and twist off his head? And why did she do it? Where did those butterfly wings come from? You know no such insect exists in lower Borneo; you know we, or others, would have found it were it here. And if it came from the mountain country, what were its wings doing in a lowland nipa swamp on a girl's forehead? I'd give all we have collected on this trip for one specimen of that black butterfly!"

"So would I," I replied, ignoring his questions, since they were unanswerable. "But it think you are on the right track. It must be a mountain species or we would have found it. Pass the whiskey."

We all had another drink. Lee did not demur this time.

"I move, unless we are down with fever in the morning, that we go back, look for the woman, and, if we find her, try to buy those wings—or at least try to discover where they came from. A black butterfly, Andy—"

"Lee savvy black butterfly," chanted the Chinaman. "You want to know, you no tell!"

"Sure not," I agreed, and the Englishman grunted an affirmation.

I shan't try to repeat Lee's exact words, for the story filled the entire night; but this is the meat of what he told us. Long before the English took over North Borneo, before Sir James Brooke came to Sarawak, even before the Dutch had seized their portion of the island, the Chinese looked upon all Borneo as their own private treasure-house. From it they exported rattan, teak, precious and semi-precious stones, and gold—quantities of gold—the source of which no Aryan nation has ever been able to discover in after years. And the power, head, moving spirit of the Chinese in those days (as now) was centered in a Tong—a Tong so mighty that it had no name.

The emblem of this Tong was a portion of a butterfly wing, never a whole wing, but just a fragment; and this fragment was always round and always black. Even now the gold that came out of British Borneo passed only through the hands of the Chinese—the Chinese that belonged to the old, old Tong that had the round piece of black butterfly's wings for emblem.

The whisky passed back and forth many times during this recital, a strange one, indeed, to come from an Oriental (they never speak of their secret societies), and Dillingame, leaning toward me, whispered:

"He's lying!"

"'Tis the whisky," I whispered back.

"No lie, no whiskey!" vehemently protested Lee San—his ears must have been devilish sharp. "China boy *pantong* (taboo)—mus' die in twenty day for makee Tong mad. No sendum body back to ancestors, jus' scatterum ashes. So no care what come. Tellum tluth!"

"Where do the butterfly emblems come from?" asked Trevor.

"Me no savvy. Way off, mebbeso. Seeum only in Blunei town."

A terrible rumpus broke out on the bank of the stream. Gruntings, howls, roars, screams. The light was just breaking, and we could dimly discern vague shapes dancing frantically about. Suddenly the sun shot over the horizon, and we saw a great python lurch into the water, leaving a crowd of big, frantically chattering long-tailed monkeys on the bank.

It rained dismally as we retraced our trail of the day before. The *mise en scène* was unchanged. The head of the tree-snake, already half decomposed, lay on the ground, but the red tree-frog was gone from between its jaws. The prickly thicket of rattan whence the *hantus* had come, and into which she had disappeared, was as impenetrable as a solid wall of barbed wire.

I lifted up my voice and called. A deer snorted near by, a flight of hornbills sawed the air with their heavy wings. No other sound broke the silence save the drip, drip, drip of the wet jungle.

Morose, and hardly believing what we had seen the day before, heavy from the night's vigil, we retraced our steps to the boat and dropped down stream.

Brunei is built on piles and roofed with thatch, and has all of twenty thousand inhabitants. A globe-trotter once called it "the Venice of the East." There is an English quarter, of course, with a resident who lives in card indexes and considers it low to have anything to do the with natives.

We were not of his favorites. He told us on one occasion that our lack of dignity in mingling with the aborigines lowered the caste of every white man in the East. Dillingame promptly chucked him into the water, and he retaliated by revoking all our collecting permits. It was a nuisance to have to forge others; and then, too, we spelled his name wrong on them. The first real government white man we met in the interior laughed at us, corrected the spelling and passed us on.

It was humiliating, though.

In the Chinese quarter, where all the business was done, they knew us well and, as near as you can gage the feelings of Orientals, liked us. We shipped all our stuff through them, and they cashed our drafts and even lent us money.

Among the Kadyans and Dyaks, in the native quarter, we were rather lords. Dillingame crumpled up all their wrestlers and astounded them with feats of strength. I told them stories in the different vernaculars.

There is absolutely no use in a white man trying to match wits with a yellow one if he wants to find out anything. I went straight to the biggest Chinaman of the lot, told him where and how we had seen the black butterfly wings, and asked him point-blank whence they came. He answered me with apparent frankness that he did not believe such an insect existed today, though it may have in the past. Goods (he did not specify what kind) that came from the mountainous country around Kina Balu often were accompanied by a fetish in the form of a black butterfly's wing, but that wing was made of paper—and to prove it, he gave me one.

This, to my mind, closed the incident.

Dillingame, who had been getting together supplies and packing our stuff for shipment, greeted me cheerfully.

"Hello, dead man," he called, "I have just been informed that anyone who sees a *hantus* is due to cash in the same quarter of the moon. One of our Dyaks ran amuck when the three got back, and was hacked to pieces by his friends; the other two have been gloriously full of arrack ever since. What did you find out about the butterfly?"

I repeated what the Chinaman had told me, taking out the paper wing and laying it before him.

I think I said before that Englishmen are obstinate. Trevor Dillingame absolutely refused to believe a word of it. He pointed out that the paper wing showed an arrangement of veins and a frenulum quite different from that of any known species of butterfly, and stoutly maintained that such a species did exist and the paper counterpart was just a typical oriental plot to throw us off. I tried to show him that there could be no reason why the Chinese would object to us sashaying all over the island after butterflies, since we always attended strictly to our own business; but he wasn't to be budged from his plot theory.

"I'm going to have that butterfly if I rake over all the mountains in Borneo," he announced, "and I'll bet you I will have it within a year—or rather that we will; because you are naturally coming along."

"You mean you *may* get it, not *will* get it," I corrected.

"I mean I *shall* get it," he insisted. And yet people say the Scotch don't understand the difference between shall and will!

Brunei is civilized in that it has one white hell where foregather the captains and mates of the trading ships, globetrotters and men who have made their pile in the black country; in short, every white who has a price. You pay your money and you get what you order. To a certain point you do as you please. Beyond that point a Malay kris ends the evening's entertainment and the tide takes you out to sea without trouble to your friends.

A Chinaman ran the place, of course. He called it the House of Unending Happiness and Delight. White men called it the Devil's Club.

Neither Dillingame nor I is a saint. We like our bit of fun as well as anyone. 'Twas to the Devil's Club we planned to go that evening; first to talk to one of the Rothschild's orchid-collecting agents, then to enjoy whatever happened along. We didn't anticipate much from the agent. He was an evil little rat of a Portuguese who bought low and, in all probability, turned in his purchases at four times what they cost him. Also he was a careful lad with the money, never known to buy a drink could he help it.

Lee San had laid out clean white clothes for us in our nipa-thatched hut, and seemed to be lingering about with something on his mind that he lacked the courage to unload. I gave him a lead, and, explaining that only nineteen days more of existence remained to him according to the sentence of the Tong, he asked for his pay covering the full period.

It's fatal to pay a Chinaman in advance, so I naturally refused and suggested, as a substitute, that he come with us into the interior, thus probably running away from his fate.

The idea of escape had evidently never occurred to him—Tongs even do their thinking for most Chinamen—and I left him to turn it over in his mind.

The entertainment furnished at the Devil's Club is rather unique. Everything starts with a good dinner, of course, and plenty of drinks. Then comes gambling on a rickety roulette wheel; fan tan, or just drinking. If none of these amusements appeals to you, you watch the show. Dyak girls, teeth blackened and ornamented with tiny gold stars let into the enamel, ears bored around the edges with holes from which dangle rings, and pendants, wave their long hands, the nails dyed to a crimson, and dance to the slow beat of the native instruments. Chinese girls, always smiling out of their slanting eyes, play toy-like banjos and never cease to wonder at European kisses. Perhaps there are wrestlers, or two sailors from rival ships put on the gloves and fight to a knockout while men from every corner of the earth stand around the ring.

These various kinds of evening, with their next morning's headaches, were old stories to us; but this evening furnished something surprisingly new. Gomez, the Portuguese, not only invited us to dinner, but actually paid for it. Then, instead of going into the back room to smoke opium, he sat out with us watching the dancing and talking about everything under the sun. 'Twas plain that the lad wanted something from us, but to save me I couldn't figure out what it was.

Finally, as the crowd thinned out, dropping into or being carried to their boats, he suggested that he accompany us to our own hut, as he had something of importance to take up with us.

Lee San set out the whiskey, and as soon as he withdrew, the Portuguese hauled a little package out of his inside pocket.

"Can't handle this alone," he remarked as he began to remove the paper wrapping, "but there should be enough in it for all three of us," and he laid a porcupine quill and a small round object, about the size of a half crown, on the table.

I picked up the transparent quill. The weight together with the color of the contents told me at once that it was filled with gold. Dillingame gave a low whistle over the round article and handed it to me. It was a kind of a locket, holding beneath its thin film of glass a round section cut from the wing of a butterfly.

"Where did you get these, Gomez?" I demanded.

"What does it matter as long as I know where the gold came from, and we can get more?"

"It matters so much that if you want us in with you, you'll have to tell us."

"I found them on the body of a Murat who had been bitten by a snake," he answered sulkily. "He told me, before he died, that he brought the gold down from the mountains each year, that there was plenty of it there."

We hadn't the slightest desire to take Gomez with us, but other considerations besides our personal feelings had to enter into the calculations. It costs like blazes to get to the back country; mainly because one has to carry all the rice for the porters, and well as everything else, and the Portuguese seemed to have lots of cash. Of course we realized the source of at least part of this wealth. Not for a moment did we believe that a single quill of gold was all that had been taken from the dead Murut, any more than we swallowed the story about the poor devil having been bitten by a snake. Gomez had no reputation save that of an excellent shot, and being death quick with a knife.

We insisted on one reservation, namely, that all entomological specimens should be our exclusive property—oddly enough it was the black butterfly that appealed to Dillingame's and my imagination even more than the prospect of gold; and then went into the project, each taking a third.

It's devilish hard getting into the interior, but it can be done by determined men who know the jungle. A couple of weeks later found us under the shadow of Kina Balu, its fourteen thousand foot summit towering high above us. The natives had not bothered us at all; indeed, we hadn't seen much of them, and our supplies were holding out splendidly.

All that day we toiled up the old course of the Tarnpassuk, collecting as we went, and we certainly did well. Everywhere were beautiful green papilos—the Saranak Beauty—and frail, black-spotted *Hestidae*, while lovely, velvety black-and-green male *brookcani* went swiftly dancing by. Also the orchids were something unbelievable; *grammatophyllums*, golden-brown spotted flowers on stout two-yard-long spikes; a greenish-yellow flowered *dendrobium*; clusters of tubular *aesclynanthus* like scarlet jewels beneath the great, leathery, aroid leaves; and the enormous moth orchids with their hundred snowy flowers.

Already we could easily see a profit on the trip from what we had gathered if we continued to do even half as well, and were all as happy as crickets.

That evening we camped on the bank of a half-dry stream, and while Dillingame and I figured out how much further we could cut down on loads for the mountain climb, Gomez washed the sands for gold—his favorite amusement, no matter where we stopped. Lee San (he had accepted my suggestion to accompany us in defiance of his Tong) was cooking our supper, and the jungle was as quiet as a high-limit poker game.

Night came quickly, as it does in the East; a black curtain rolled suddenly across the sky through which the stars would later punch their twinkling holes, and we gathered around the fire. From far off in the jungle came the bellowing of wild cattle, a flying lemur cut a straight line against the horizon across the curves of the circling bats.

Then, in the Ida'an tongue, and with the sudden crash of an orchestra, came a roaring chorus:

"Little red flames that flit so fast,
Through wet, green leaves till day is past—
Little red flames in the tree-tops shine
Where the hungry, green-gold serpents twine—

"One and all, great and small,
We carry you up the mountain tall,
Down where the jungle's hot and dim,
Under the world's far, farthest rim,
To HER, to HER
Where red waters stir,
and the lilies float
O'er the gods demure."

Weapons ready, we stepped out of the circle of the fire and stood in the shadowy edge of the jungle. The moon swept up over the tree-tops and down its silvery path filed a long procession. They were Ida'ans from the mountains, the taint of them on the breeze, and each of the fifty men was loaded down with a wicker basket whence came a volume of sound like the splashing of countless, tiny waterfalls.

Again crashed the song:

"Little red flames that feel as cool
To burning hands as the shaded pool—
Little red flames through the jungle fling
The breath of freshness while you sing—

"One and all, great and small,
Never cease your piping call,
Down where the jungle's hot and dim,
Under the world's far, farthest rim,
While you go to HER
Where the red waters stir
And the lilies float
O'er the gods demure."

"They are going to, not coming from the mountains," whispered Gomez, "so they haven't any gold. Let's stay hidden."

"Want to know what is in those baskets. They'd see our fires anyway," spoke up Dillingame, and stepped out of the shadow toward the last of the passing men.

It was an idiotic thing to do—I don't believe in hunting trouble—but I followed him, of course. The entire column halted. It was probably the first white man they had ever seen; certainly the first wearing khaki, puttees and an immaculate helmet, and I called for the *orang-kaya* (head man).

A little wizened Chinaman was pushed forward, whom I proceeded to interrogate sternly on the purpose of the expedition just as though I were a government officer.

I got away with it, of course. They were returning from a religious pilgrimage into the lowlands after having washed away their sins in a sacred stream. I said I got away with it, but not with bells on. Indeed, the Chinaman seemed somewhat inclined to interrogate me as to our destination and purpose in that part of the country, a tendency that I promptly suppressed. I also gave him orders to camp well away from our party and not to permit his men to stray in our direction.

During this conversation the fresh sound as though of running water continued to come from the baskets the natives were carrying. Trevor stepped to the nearest one and threw up the lid. It was loosely packed full of green leaves, among which sang hundreds of little red tree frogs.

Back in camp I cussed the Englishman proper for advertising our presence to the natives, and we speculated in regard to the red tree frogs. I knew the Ida'ans considered rats to a table delicacy, and the frogs might be in the same category. The strange part was that an expedition should penetrate into the lowlands to collect them—they aren't found far from the coast—and that the expedition should be in the charge of a Chinaman.

After all, it did not concern us directly, and gradually, one by one, we dropped off beneath our mosquito nets. The jungle noises blurred from separate sounds into a droning whole, I was drowsily conscious of a pair of large, bright, yellow eyes—a slow loris my brain lethargically telegraphed—and I slept.

I woke, with the first morning light, to the song of birds. The sun popped up over the horizon, and the chorus from the tree-tops increased to an ecstasy of harmony. In prompt contrast to all this joyousness came a wail of fright from behind our tents, followed by shouts of surprise and fear from the porters.

Jumping into my boots, clad only in pajamas, and an automatic in my hand, I rushed toward the sound of the disturbance. Lee San, surrounded by the Muruts, was raising his voice to high heaven and holding his upper garment away from his body—and from that upper garment fluttered a long piece of paper covered with Chinese characters and signed with a crudely inked butterfly's wing.

"Stop that fool howling," I yelled angrily, tearing away the fluttering strip that was evidently the cause of his anguish, "and tell me what this all means!"

"Lee San on'y t'lee day to live! That Tong sign. No can get 'way!" and he roared anew.

Grabbing him by the throat I choked the noise back into his gullet.

"Where did that laundry ticket come from?" I demanded.

"Pin to clo' when Lee sleep," he moaned.

I was sorry for the little Chinaman, of course; but couldn't let him go on bawling forever. It might stampede my dozen porters any minute. Naturally I surmised that one of them was in Tong employ, and had pinned Lee's sentence to him while he slept. I should have liked mightily to ferret out the guilty one, but didn't dare take the risk of the bunch quitting on me.

Pretending a wrath I was far from feeling and threatening Lee San with immediate death, I sent the men to cooking their breakfasts and then returned to my tent.

We made good progress the next two days, passing several Ida'an villages, the inhabitants of which viewed us with an uninterested stolidity that made me rather nervous, and on the second night camped just below the timber line of Kina Balu.

Gomez claimed that gold came from the western slope, but it was easier to go over the mountain than to try to thread the impenetrable jungle around its base.

We took many rare butterflies, those days, including the *Euthalia magnolia* known only from Kina Balu, another beautiful local species with a six-inch spread of velvety blackness and a broad band of pea-green across the wings; and then, just before pitching camp, I netted an entirely new species, soft gray with little squares, as though of isinglass, set in its wings, and both veination and frenulum identical with the round fragment of black wing that Gomez had shown us in the little locket.

We had out this talisman and compared the two—after which I slipped the little round thing in my pocket—and it was easy to see that we had a species for an entirely new genus; two species, if we secured the black butterfly. In spite of the rain that began to fall that night Dillingame and I were jubilant, though we could not get Gomez to enthuse—he was after more valuable game.

The altitude and cold rid us of mosquitoes and we turned in early in anticipation of a full night's sleep. Scarcely had I closed my eyes, however, when I was wide awake again and sitting up. Clear as a bell, through the darkness, came the whistle of a kite—and kites don't fly at night—to be answered from the other side of the camp by the drawling snarl of a tiger cat, followed by the unmistakable sound of a girl's laugh.

On my feet in a flash, I stole out beyond the light of the fire and lay down in the shadow, straining my eyes through the blackness. It had stopped raining and not even an insect disturbed the perfect stillness. Suddenly, to my right, a single voice broke into song—a voice so filled with contemptuous raillery that it made me grit my teeth in anger.

> "*Orang, puteh,* [stranger in our midst] what doest thou seek
> Toward Kina Balu's lofty peak
> Where the dead troop free
> 'Neath Lugundi's tree
> In the sacred lake
> Whence the spirits flee? ... "

I raised up on my left elbow and fired twice in the direction of the sound. A mocking laugh came back to me, then silence, save for the waking of the camp.

Quieting the men, I told Dillingame and Gomez not to bother me with questions that night, and, turning in, slept till daylight.

The Talisman

It was deadly cold in the morning and Lee's teeth chattered as he built our fire. I sent him over to wake the porters, only to have him back in a second, hands trembling and face ashy white.

"Come," was all he could say. "Come!"

My twelve porters lay their feet to the dead embers, and on each man's left cheek was stamped in black a butterfly's wing.

There was no holding them, of course, when they awoke and saw the mysterious emblem that had been placed on their very flesh while they slept. Furthermore the marks would not wash off—left an indelible stain that seemed to penetrate the pores of the skin. I threatened, bribed, cajoled, all in vain; and, accepting half what I had promised them for wages, my Muruts fled down the mountain.

Nice fix we were in! All our goods and chattels dumped high on the side of Kina Balu, and no one to carry them! There was only one thing to do; go back to the nearest Ida'an village and hire local carriers—and a villainous lot they proved to be when I finally managed to get ten of them at an exorbitant wage in cloth. Then it was noon before we got started again, and our nerves were on razor edge.

Lee San helped the situation by bewailing the fact that it was the last day on earth allotted to him by the Tong, and stuck so close to me that I finally lost my temper and made him lead the column.

Over the shoulder of Kina Balu the character of the country changed. Jungle grew high up a mountain slope so precipitous that we never should have been able to descend had it not been for a narrow, winding trail. There were no butterflies, the giant trees meeting overhead and shutting out the light, but never have I seen such a riot of orchids, or so many gorgeously colored birds.

My porters balked twice, demanding their wages as having gone far enough; and the second time I was forced to make good my threatening by knocking one flat. It was beastly hot and sticky, the ground fairly crawled with leeches, and the trail was cut every hundred yards by wild pig runs, along which we three times went astray.

I joined Lee San and we kept well ahead of the column, progressing downward as best we could and clearing the way. The Chinaman had recovered his spirits with the realization that sundown would see the end of his fears—Ton law considers a man dead, no matter whether he is or not, after the date for his execution has passed, and no longer molests him.

The trail became narrower and narrower. I stepped over a liana that stretched across about a foot from the ground, and turned as Lee brought down his jungle knife to sever it. There was a swish overhead and a weighted spear plunged down, entering the man's neck, piercing the length of his body through the thigh, its point going into the ground and holding him upright.

Lee San opened his mouth in an attempt to speak, his head flopped forward, and death claimed him before the words could come.

Dazed for the moment, I stood motionless, my eyes on the spear shaft along which slowly dribbled round drops of blood. A ray of sunlight filtered down from above and played over the dead man. Sable black, two feet from wing tip to wing tip, an enormous butterfly darted straight for the crimsoning spear, poising against it with swiftly fanning wings.

I grabbed with my bare hand, but it dodged, circling about my wrist, to relight on the dead man's bleeding shoulder. Again I lunged for it.

There was a rustle behind me and an arm went around my neck, flinging me flat on the trail. Beautiful as an orchid in her wreaths of fragrant jasmine, a woman caught the sable butterfly between her fingers, jumped lightly over my body, and disappeared into the jungle, while through the great tree trunks came a low, mocking laugh.

Half stunned, I stumbled to my feet, tearing away a great leech that had fastened to my lip, and the first of the porters came down the trail.

It was a trap for wild hogs that Lee San had blundered into, and I sprang two more of them, with a long pole cut for the purpose, within the next mile.

We buried the Chinaman beside the trail—tropical jungles do not admit of delay in such matters—and I certainly did feel cast down over the loss of such a good cook. Also he had been with me over two years and I was very well used to him.

Two miles farther down the trail the jungle opened up into a park of enormous teak trees with no underbrush on the forest floor; just a meadow of short grass with a stream running through the middle, on the bank of which we camped. Being completely devoid of confidence in the porters, I had all the waterproof-canvas-wrapped loads piled in a great heap, pitched the two tents, one on each side, and then the three of us matched to see who should cook. Gomez got stuck, much to his disgust; so he had to forego his customary evening's amusement of washing for gold.

Hardly had we finished our supper, and a rotten bad meal it was, when the Ida'ans appeared and asked pay for the full week I had hired them with an additional bonus to the one I had manhandled. As is always the case with natives, and inspired by arrack, they started at the top of the pitch beginning with demands and working down until they reached the pleading stage.

Their argument was based on the fact that we had not climbed Kina Balu as they expected, and as had other white men, but had led them down into the Land of Blood where the spirits stole men's souls. Their spokesman assured me that no one who went into this jungle ever came back, that it was the abode of spirits and devils who, like gigantic leeches, fed on the blood of the living.

In the end I drove them to their fire, and we turned in, agreeing to keep watch, turn by turn, during the night. Dillingame took the first period and I went promptly to sleep.

Then I began to dream. The *hantus* woman stepped out of a rattan thicket and laughed up into Trevor's face. He gathered her into his arms and bent his lips to hers, when a flock of great, black butterflies swept down, forming a cloud about them. I beat at them with my hands to reach the voice calling, "Andy! Andy!"

Someone was shaking me by the shoulder. "Wake up, for God's sake, Andy, wake up!" whispered Dillingame. "This place is enchanted!"

Outside the tent, it was light as day. A luminous mass came hurtling through the air and fell at my feet. I kicked it and a great fungus broke into a thousand pieces, each glowing with fox fire. More fungi were hurled into the open space about the camp. I rolled down several of the canvas-covered loads and we crouched behind them. The Ida'ans, near the dead fire, were standing huddled in a close group whence came no sound.

The shower of luminous fungi ceased. There was a pop like a champagne cork leaving the bottle and one of the porters staggered and fell on his face, a tiny arrow quivering in his forehead.

"Lie down, you fools!" I yelled, and pumped a bullet into the edge of the jungle. A shower of tiny arrows rattled among the packs. I picked up one and showed its point, smeared with some pitchy poison, to Trevor.

"No use staying here to be shot down like trapped hogs," he snapped. "Let's make a break for cover. Where is Gomez?"

"Here," came the little man's voice from my elbow. "We're in a tight fix, is it not?"

"We're in all of that," I answered. "Draw their fire, and after the shower of arrows, grab a pack and get into the jungle near them. I'll toss one of those flares we brought for trading where they seem thickest and we'll try to get enough to give them a permanent scare."

One of the Ida'ans rose cautiously to his knees. Came the pop of a blow gun and he went down screaming, his hands to his face. Trevor fired in the general direction whence the arrow came. A storm of the little darts rattled about us, and then we were all running, packs held before us, toward the edge of the jungle.

Safe in its shadow, I touched a match to the flare and flung it whence had come the last volley. There was a yell of fear, and we turned loose a bunch of black out-lined figures, long bamboo blow-guns in their hands. Some went down, but about twenty started across the open.

"After them, and get as many as you can," I shouted. "We've got to make this a lesson!"

Under the cover of the trees we ran, shooting as we went, until they crossed the stream and were lost in the blackness beyond.

Something stirred behind us, and Trevor jumped into the underbrush. There was a brief struggle, and then he swore.

"Gimme a light," he demanded. "I've got something queer."

I struck a taper match and held it above my head. Dillingame had two slender wrists grasped in one of his big hands, and as the flame flared higher, my eyes followed his other hand to where it was twisted in a woman's hair—the woman of the nipa swamp, snake and red tree frog, the woman who had snatched the sable butterfly from Lee San's bleeding shoulder!

Gomez switched on an electric torch and we all stood staring at her. Man, but she was beautiful! Short grass skirt, leather sandals bound halfway up her legs, the upper part of her body bare save for wreaths of jasmine. Her skin was as white as the flowers of the great moth-orchid, her lips crimson as red blood, her eyes blazing violet, swimming with flecks of gold, and her hair beneath Trevor's hand was black and soft as silken thread.

Losh, but she was beautiful as she stared back at us, her little hands twisting helplessly in the Englishman's big one, her body tensed.

Then, before we could find words, her form relaxed, her eyes flew to Trevor's face and she laughed up at him. Not a wild, hysterical laugh, just a soft, amused little one with an undercurrent of contempt in it—the sound a woman makes over a child who has done some silly thing.

Out of the corner of my eye I saw Gomez cross himself and shift forward his automatic.

"Laugh, you vixen," said Dillingame, but his eyes were not unkind. "She jabbed a knife into me and fought like a wild cat," he flung us in an aside, then turning back to her, "Do you know I ought to kill you, shoot you down in your tracks?"

Of course the woman did not understand, and again she laughed up at him, her lips curing back over her white teeth, her violet golden eyes half shut.

"*Santa Maria!*" gasped Gomez. "Let me shoot her and then we'll burn her body in the fire. Don't you see she is a hantus, a witch? She will enchant us all and the leeches will suck our bodies dry. I am afraid—me!"

"Don't be a fool," I advised gruffly, stepping in front of him, for he was fingering his pistol nervously. "Bring your captive lassie to the tents, Trevor. I'm thinking we won't be troubled with those poisoned darts while she is with us. Gomez, go over and tell the porters to keep down on the ground. If there is one of those blowgun men simply wounded, haul him in and we'll see what we can get out of him."

It had begun to drizzle. I threw wood on the fire and piled the packs in a barricade, the tents for ends. Meanwhile Trevor tied the woman's wrists together, holding the end of the rope in his own hands; nor did she resist. Gomez came back driving a small figure before him and, as it came into the firelight, I nearly yelled.

It wasn't a man, it was a beast, a human ape! There was a *sarong* around its middle but the rest of the body was naked and evenly covered with a generous growth of reddish hair, arms ending in tiny hands hung below its knees, and its head jerked from side to side with the lighting quickness of an animal while it whimpered over a wounded thigh where a bullet had creased the black skin.

The only human thing about it was its hair, which was elaborately dressed high on the head and through which were stuck several of the tiny poisoned arrows.

Suddenly it caught sight of the woman, and going down in a cringing heap, lay motionless, its face against the ground.

"Five dead," reported Gomez laconically, and took his seat as far as possible from the Englishman and his captive.

I addressed the girl in the Ida'an tongue.

"Why did you lead your slaves to kill us? Have we done you harm?"

"You come for gold as do all strangers—our gold is pledged. About that I should not care, but you take the souls of the dead, the butterflies. Not even do you respect the souls of the sacred priests that sail on sable wings!"

"Who are you that talk of souls!"

"Kratas, priestess of the Land of Blood, who knows not death, who lives forever."

"Yon lassie is wrong in her head," I said to Dillingame in English. "Let's try and find out something from the beast-man," and I heaved him to his feet.

What came next happened quicker than word can tell. Raising her hands to her lips the woman severed the cords that bound her wrists with one snap of her white teeth. Trevor caught her around the shoulders and, whirling, she bit deep into his hand.

"You'll pay for that, my girl," he snarled, gathered her into his arms, bent, and kissed her lips. One second she relaxed, clung to him, then twisted free, caught a tiny poisoned arrow from the savage's hair, drew the point in a long scratch across his back, and leaped over the packs. Trevor sprang after her just in time to slap Gomez's automatic from his hand as he fired.

A taunting laugh floated back out of the darkness.

The beast-man died from the poisoned scratch, toward morning, with many twistings and writhings. With the first light our Ida'ans disappeared up the trail and we could not catch them. They left three dead behind, victims of the poisoned arrows, and we found six beast-men in the jungle and five in the open that had stopped our bullets.

It took some time to dig a pit large enough for all those bodies, and, after we had stamped down the dirt, we sat on the packs and looked dismally at one another.

Gomez broke the silence. "Money I like it much, but if I am dead or crazy it does me no good. Let us go back as quickly as we can with what provisions our shoulders will carry."

"That's all very well for you," spoke up Dillingame, "you have a stake tucked away. Freeman and I have our all in this venture. I move we linger on and try to pick up something else. What do you say, Andy?"

"There is food for a long time," I answered judicially, "and we are more liable to be attacked on the back trail running away than if we stay boldly here. I'll not say it were best to go on, nor will I say it were best to stay, but—"

I broke off, and dived for my net. A gray butterfly of the new genus was floating just outside the barrier of packs. I caught it in midair. Then I chased another, and another till, with eleven perfect and four damaged specimens, I finally returned to the tents. Dillingame had the real luck, though. He brought in forty of them, all taken over a crimson orchid, and netted an immense Hestia besides.

As we removed our catch from the cyanide bottles and folded them, wings back to back, into envelopes before packing them away in our waterproof collecting boxes, we easily has calculated with what we already had we'd break better than square on the expedition.

Gomez was not there when we returned, but he drifted in with his gold washing pan shortly afterward, and an I-have-eaten-the-canary expression on his face.

"You found it!" I guessed at once, and could see his underlip stiffen for a lie.

"I have found traces," he answered; "it may be here, though probably in very small quantities. Anyway, I'm brave enough to stay on a little while even if you gentlemen are not."

Dillingame's face went purple, but I spoke before he could explode.

"Sure, we'll stay on. After Trevor and I have done a little more collecting we'll all turn in and pan the stream, and if there is gold we'll find it. Meanwhile let's match to see who cooks today!" And there the matter rested.

I'm a cautious man—being Scotch—and haven't been every place in the world, so I'll not say there are not collecting grounds equal to where we were, but under oath I'll swear these were the best I had ever seen.

We found no further new species of the larger butterflies, but the microlepidoptera would have kept a systematist busy classifying them for an entire year. The unnamed orchids were legion, and we took skins of two new pheasants, not to mention the Argus, Bullwer and Fireback ones; a rare yellow shrike, gorgeous red and yellow sunbirds, and a cream-white lemur. All day we were off in the jungle so interested in our own work that we paid little attention to Gomez.

Gradually it dawned on us that the Portuguese had developed a virulent grouch, wasn't even civil, and one morning when it was raining torrents, so it was impossible to leave the tents, matters came to a head. It all began by Dillingame detailing our harvest of butterflies, orchids and birds for his benefit, a cataloguing which he terminated by the statement that the next day we would join in the gold search.

Gomez promptly answered with a snarl that he'd attend to his business and it would be healthier for us to keep to ours, that we needn't be afraid he wouldn't make a fair division even though we had lured him on the trip under false pretenses and made him do all the work. And then, without the slightest warning, he jerked out his gun and barely missed the Englishman. Furious, Dillingame made a jump for him. The Portuguese fired again just as I hauled the tent pole down so the two of them were wrapped in its folds. From the outside I gathered the little man into a neat bundle of canvas. Trevor crawled from beneath, and we undid Gomez with a gun pressed to his stomach, and then tied him hand and foot.

There was no doubt he had intended to kill both of us, and he expected no gentler fate at our hands, especially after we had searched him and found fully a pound of dust in a belt strapped around his waist. There was nothing of the hero about him, and he began to whine for his life, offering the bribe of showing us the exact place he had found the gold.

I'll not deny that the Anglo-Saxon is the greatest of all races, but being one has its disadvantages at times—we talk when we should act. To save a cartridge Gomez should have had a knife stuck into him, and a savage would have applied that practical solution to his problem. White men are civilized beyond logic, however.

I sat down by the trussed-up, treacherous little rat and explained to him carefully that if he appeared at Brunei without us there would be no possibility of any explanation he might offer getting over, that he would have a mighty short time to enjoy his gold before some of our friends got him. Then we turned him loose.

Trevor kicked him once, and, according to the custom of fool Anglo-Saxons, after that we acted as though nothing had happened.

Our combined search for gold was without result. Gomez had taken his from a single pot-hole in the bottom of the creek—he showed us where. There were traces everywhere, but no place worth a second panning. The formation was unusual, the water flowing over a thin bed of sand beneath which was solid rock. The creek itself sprang from a swamp, half a mile up the mountainside, and for the two miles we followed it down, ran between high banks on which grew short grass and mighty teak or cocoanut trees exactly like the place where we were camped.

Since the immediate neighborhood had been thoroughly raked over both for specimens and gold, it seemed best to move on, and the banks of the stream offered open going without the trail danger of being ambushed or speared in a pig trap. We cached nearly everything, including the orchids and bird and animal skins, swinging them high in the air by ropes over the limbs of the immense trees, and with our butterflies (which took up little bulk), ammunition, some food, and a small pack of trading stuff, the three of us started down stream.

For three miles the character of the country did not change, and then there was an abrupt dip. The stream broke into rapids and went brawling downwards, both grass and trees disappeared from the banks, their places being taken by immense boulders, stretches of bare rock and sandy beach. Half a mile from the stream, on either side, rose the barrier of the jungle, and it was dry, broiling hot.

We progressed along the sandy beach until well into the afternoon, stopping every now and then to pan the edges of the stream, but getting no color. Before us rose a cloud of vapor that I took at first for smoke and then decided must be mist above some great waterfall.

We camped early. Wood had to be brought from the jungle half a mile away, but the ground was smooth, so we dragged an entire dead tree to the beach without much difficulty. A cool—too cool—wind sprang up at dusk, driving away the mosquitoes, and by the time it was dark we were grateful indeed for the fire.

I suppose it may seem queer to anyone who has not felt the spell of the unexplored wilderness that we should go on and on facing known as well as unknown dangers. Really it was the perfectly logical and natural thing, considering the men we were. Gomez was spurred on by his insatiable lust for gold. Dillingame and I told one another that we must have that sable butterfly; but the real reason lay in that lure, irresistible to men of our race, that Kipling so well expresses:

Something yet beyond the ranges,
Diddle, diddle, diddle come,
Something calling, something calling,
Diddle, diddle, diddle dum.

I don't remember the exact words.

After supper we sat around sleepily watching the bats swoop through the flames and listening to the roar of life from the jungle. A great beetle blundered into the fire and toppled over the ground at our feet. Dillingame and I bent over it. There was a gasp from Gomez that made us look up.

Sitting on a boulder within the circle of the firelight was Kratas, the priestess; two sable butterfly wings on her forehead; neck and bosom wreathed with jasmine, and an oblong, palmleaf-wrapped bundle between her small hands.

"Welcome, priestess of the *orang utan* (wild men)," I said, shifting my automatic well forward under my fingers. "Many times welcome, wearer of the sable wings."

She did not answer me, just sat motionless, her fearless eyes, filled with curiosity, resting on each of us in turn. Gomez shifted uneasily in his seat, Trevor picked up the floundering beetle and held it between his long nervous fingers, I slipped the strap from the trading pack.

"Do you, then, love the play 'neath the shadow of death that ye linger here, or have ye eaten of the blue root of madness?" she asked.

"Death dare not approach us," I boasted.

She seemed to accept my words as a mere statement of fact.

"And yet there was blood beneath my teeth when they sank into his white flesh," she mused, looking at Dillingame. "My lips were salty with it till his lips ravaged the taste from mine." Then, abruptly changing her tone, "I bring ye the gift that all white men crave," and she tossed the compact palmleaf bundle at my feet. "Let it be *salaamat jelan* (good-by). I bid ye go whence ye came before three suns."

"Tell her we haven't the slightest intention of leaving until we take some of those black butterflies," broke in Trevor obstinately.

"I'll tell her no such thing," was my answer, but the woman had gathered some of the meaning from the tone of his voice.

"Let him remain if he desires it more than life," she said softly, and, gliding to the Englishman, held her lips up to his.

"We, too, offer gifts," I hastened, to attract her attention, tumbling an alarm clock, gross of earrings and a bolt of pink calico out of the pack, but she did not even glance at them. Drawing her lips back from his, she laughed up into Trevor's face, and was gone into the night.

"Andy, I don't believe any man but me has ever kissed that woman," he sighed.

"Holy smoke! And who cares if a hundred had?" I demanded.

Gomez tore open the palmleaf bundle and its contents slipped to the ground— twenty hollow porcupine quills filled with gold.

"Fools we were not to keep her once we had her," he cried, gathering up the hollow tubes, avariciously. "There are probably quantities where this came from. A cord around her temples or a little fire . . . What's that for?" he howled, as Dillingame's boot caught him in the side.

In the morning, we started down stream toward the vapor that hung in the sky. I listened for the crash of falling water as we approached, but there was not greater sound than the murmur of the stream. After a mile the stream itself switched abruptly to the left while the vapor cloud rose dead ahead and close to the edge of the jungle. We were walking on solid rock and dipped in a series of remarkable symmetrical, spaced steps, so it was like going down a very shallow pyramid.

Nearer, the vapor took definite form, one thick jet going straight up into the air, and touching each side of this central column were two misty, broad, rounded clouds.

"*Santa Maria!*" gasped Gomez. "It looks like one of your cursed butterflies!"

And so it did, the body clearly defined and the wings spread out and moving in the slight breeze.

A hundred yards further on we halted in amazement. At our feet a narrow flight of stone stairs ran down into a valley, or rather an enormous amphitheatre, since it was plainly the work of a man. Half a mile broad and three-quarters of a mile long, it was sunk fifty feet deep in the solid rock. Immediately below us three springs boiled up about a central tank, springs of hot water, judging from the steam that rose and traced the butterfly in the sky. The floor was bare rock, save on the opposite side where a belt of jungle had gained a foot-hold and flourished luxuriantly.

At the end of the amphitheatre, to the left, a hundred-yard flight of easy steps led us to the plain—and, gazing in the direction, I yanked both my companions flat to the ground.

Coming down the steps was a strange procession. In the lead four bearers carried a closed litter, or palanquin, on each side of which marched attendants with long palm fronds in their hands, by means of which they created an artificial breeze for its occupant. Six men brought up the rear, muskets over their shoulders. As they reached the springs immediately beneath us, we saw that all were Chinamen.

The palanquin was placed on the ground, and curtain drawn, and out stepped a mandarin, the largest Chinaman I have ever looked upon. He must have been all of seven feet tall, very broad, and in addition, enormously fat. The attendants pitched a small tent in the stream of the springs and, after the tent flap had been respectfully held back for the big man to enter, the last of them joined his fellows in the shade thrown by the litter.

Plainly the mandarin was quite some dog and his preparation for a hot bath a real ceremony.

Before us, the giant amphitheatre for a stage, action developed like the plot on a moving picture screen. From the edge of the jungle directly across trotted out a large bull rhinoceros, its guardian angel, the Buphagus bird, flying ahead. The coolies were squatted behind the palanquin, their master still in his tent, and the great beast approached entirely unobserved.

Twenty yards from the springs, the rhinoceros bird flew back to its charge with a harsh cry of warning. The animal stood stock still for a moment, sampling the breeze; then with a squeal of rage it charged ponderously down on the empty palanquin, behind which the attendant Chinamen were sheltered from the sun.

Howling with fear, the servants fled toward the broad stairway. The horn of the furious pachyderm became entangled in the curtains of the palanquin, and it paused long enough to smash the frame to bits. The tent flap swayed back, revealing a half-naked mandarin who, taking in the situation at a glance, plunged into the tank between the hot springs. Whirling on the tent, the rhinoceros trampled it flat, then stretched its ugly head into the stream through which the figure of the immense Chinaman loomed dimly.

I rose to my feet, our heaviest rifle at my shoulder, drew a bead on the spine at the base of the short neck, and pulled the trigger.

A rhinoceros hide may stop an ordinary bullet, but it's no proof against a steel capped projectile, cut to mushroom, and fired from above. The great bulk heaved one step forward and then flattened out, stone dead, while the guardian bird circled around, still uttering its warning cry.

"Come on," I commanded, rising to my feet, "let's go down and get thanked. The Lord knows what we are in for next, the only way to find out is to keep going ahead."

We left our packs where they had dropped and climbed down the narrow stairway. The Chinaman had emerged from his forced plunge, his skin so pink as to indicate the water was slightly too hot for comfort, and, gathering up some garments from the wreck of the tent, stood ready to receive us, the dead rhinoceros at his feet.

As I approached, the size of the yellow man became more apparent. He must have weighed all of four hundred pounds, and there was something queer about his face, something horrible! To begin with a black butterfly was tattooed on his forehead, his eyebrows had been shaved, and each eye was circled by a broad ring of crimson. But it was his mouth that made the shivers run up and down my spine, for the lips had been cut away square in front, showing all his yellow, flat teeth, with two fangs, like those of a dog, at the ends. And he had no ears.

I spoke the Ida'an words of conventional greeting, and the monster mumbled their answer. Gomez and Dillingame came up behind us, and I heard the latter exclaim "My word!" Then there was a silence.

Finally the Chinaman spoke, the words hissing through his teeth.

"Whence came ye?"

I waved my hand in the general direction of the west. To tell the truth, his apparently complete absence of gratitude for preventing a rhinoceros from sharing his bath began to irritate me.

"Why came ye here?" he demanded arrogantly.

Thoroughly angry now, I jammed my hands in my pockets, determined not to answer, even by gestures. My left hand touched something round, and, feeling to see what it was, thin glass shaped beneath my fingers. A sudden inspiration came to me. I drew out the little locket I had taken from Gomez, which held the round section of black butterfly wing, and, shaking off the broken glass stepped to the dead rhinoceros and held the talisman up to the haughty mandarin standing on the other side.

Have you, perhaps, seen one of those balloons the bairns buy at fairs slowly collapse, the skin loosening, wrinkling, finally sinking into crinkled folds? That is what happened to the man before me. His eyes started from his head, his head shrank between his shoulders, and his whole, enormous body seemed to shrink, sinking in on itself. With a groan he spread his hands before his face, salaamed thrice, forehead to the ground, and his voice was a toneless whisper when he said:

"Make known thy bidding! I see the sign and am thy slave."

In The Temple

Even in after days I never fully understood why Lo Chan (thus did the mandarin name himself) caved in so utterly at the sight of the talisman. I found out before

I had been long in the Land of Blood that this same small, round locket accompanied the Murut (never a Chinaman, always a Murut) who brought the tribute of gold dust to the Tong head waiting for it on the coast.

Why, in my hands, it should have such potency, remains an unsolved problem. I evolved the theory, for want of a better one, that the breaking of the glass above the section of the black butterfly wing had some special meaning in the complicated and mysterious ritual of the Tong.

Such speculations have small significance, however. What really mattered was the fact that the mandarin recognized in the talisman a power that he feared and dared not disobey, and was, in his own words, immediately my slave.

Lo Chan stepped over the dead rhinoceros and blew a blast on a silver whistle, carved in the semblance of a dragon. The coolies reappeared at the top of the broad stairway and came timidly down to the springs. Evidently assuming that we wished to be taken to his headquarters, the Chinaman ordered his servants to pick up our packs, and himself led the way out of the amphitheatre.

It was apparent that walking was not the mandarin's favorite form of exercise, and I was rather sorry for that enormous bulk of a man toiling ahead in the burning sun, sorry as it was possible to be for anyone so utterly repulsive physically.

From the sunken amphitheatre we continued in the direction of the stream, which we struck after two miles of heavy going through sand, and then followed over a road, always sloping downward, paved with large blocks of stone, their surfaces worn as though by innumerable feet. Vegetation reappeared, gradually thickening into jungle, and in the distance rose what I took for a hill of bare rock.

The stream lost itself in wet, swampy ground on either side of the stone causeway; tree tops met overhead, shutting out the light, and we came at last to a long house of bamboo, set upon piles. Ladders admitted us beneath the thatched roof, and we were in Lo Chan's home.

Certainly that fat mandarin did not believe in discomfort. The house was no different in construction from the usual Ida'an dwelling, a single sixty-foot room with no partitions or front; but its contents were of a richness none of us had ever dreamed of. Silk rugs of brilliant colors strewed the floor; on the walls were hung embroideries heavy with gold; there were inlaid tabourets, vases as high as a man's head, and low couches heaped with pillows.

A corner, hidden behind the silver-embossed screens, held the complete paraphernalia of the opium smoker, and a great gold-and-red curtain, whence came feminine rustlings and whisperings, barred off one end of the long room.

Behind this curtain Lo Chan retired with a last profound salaam, and we were left alone.

Dillingame began to laugh. They are a feckless people, the English; I could see no joke.

"For a cautious Scotchman as you claim to be," he announced, "it seems to me you are taking big chances. That piece of butterfly's wing is a frail excuse for bossing a mandarin."

"You're a fool," stuttered Gomez, "a reckless fool to run us into this. Do you suppose for one minute that you can trust that mandarin? Do you know what the mutilation of his face means? He has been guilty of the vilest crime a Chinaman can commit; he's a parricide! Had he been a coolie he would have been burned to death. His rank saved him, but not from mutilation that all his race might know and scorn him, and he has plainly been banished to this corner of the world. Give me back that piece of butterfly wing before you get us into more trouble! It's mine, anyway!"

I think I have already said that I am a Scotchman, and therefore firm—not obstinate, firm; and once I have set myself to a certain course I am not to be turned aside. Besides, the Portuguese showed an awful cheek in trying to run matters, considering his general reputation and what we especially knew of him. I promptly told him to mind his own business, that I had brought him to the very source of the gold, and that I'd keep the talisman.

Dillingame backed me up, of course, and together we quickly silenced the vicious little runt.

With sundown came a meal the like of which we had not tasted for many a month. Lo Chan did not reappear, and we slept that night through in absolute comfort.

In the morning there was a council. Gomez urged a direct demand for gold and a quick departure. Trevor had no suggestion to make except that we do something at once. I proposed to let matters develop along their own lines, trying to pump our host without arousing his suspicions that we really hadn't the slightest idea what we were doing.

We called the mandarin in and I asked him for a report on his stewardship. Of course I had no idea what I meant, but it seemed a safe question. He answered that the coolies had been unable to wash out the usual quantity of gold, the workings were not half as rich as formerly, but that the temple tribute came in regularly every full of the moon.

Not much information in all this. The only thing I could think of was to take a look at the temple, and I ordered him on.

The wet jungle was cut by numerous stone causeways, between which I soon decided, had once been rice fields, now grown up save for occasional patches of paddy, to great trees. Everywhere were indications of a once flourishing city, stone roads, ruined houses also often of stone, and the worn surface of the rock on which we walked.

Finally the jungle opened, revealing what I had taken for an elevation of naked rock, and we halted in amazement. Built of blocks of stone, the size of which made it seem impossible they could have been moved by human hands, rose an immense, pagoda-like structure of three great stories, the topmost crowned with a single enormous block of glittering stone.

Strange beasts were carved on the over-hanging balconies, and plaques of metal hung down in clusters, tinkling musically in the slight breeze. A small pond, surrounded by a rampart of stone, its edges overgrown with white lilies, spread out in front of the temple, and the water in its center, bubbling up ceaselessly, was red as blood.

In every cranny where the tropic vegetation could find a foothold it flourished, but not even the great rending power of its growth had been able to move the enormous blocks, and bring to the ground the astonishing edifice. And there was a queer air of emptiness about it, as though it had just been deserted by a multitude that might swarm back at any moment.

Into dim coolness we entered through a lofty square portico. There was absolute silence save for two sounds—the hushed clink of the swaying metallic plaques and a muffled murmur as though of running water. The ground floor was a great bare room of solid rock, with an aperture in the ceiling opening all the way to the sky through the successive floors, and down which came a thin shaft of light. A strong ladder led up to this aperture, and towards it I pushed the mandarin. But he drew back with an exclamation of horror.

"It is not permitted!"

"Mount," I ordered, and he preceded me, obedient, though trembling.

The next story was full of vague rustlings from a floor knee deep in green foliage. Something moved at my feet, and I bent down. Seven inches long and black as jet, a thick caterpillar was eating ravenously into a camphor tree leaf.

Dillingame picked it up between his long fingers and together we examined it. Never have I looked on anything more repulsive than that twisting, worm-like creature. Unlike any caterpillar I had ever seen, it was furnished with heavy, piercing jaws—it was a flesh-eating, predacious thing that could have bitten through a finger.

"Pretty, isn't it?" commented Trevor, snapping it back disgustedly among the leaves.

At the end of the room were piled great wicker baskets whence came the sound as though of running water. We knew what those baskets held, of course; the red tree frogs from the coast. To make sure I threw back a lid. A crimson cloud floated about me as the little piping things sailed out, to fall among the leaves on the floor.

Then happened something horrible. Like lightning black caterpillars fastened their ugly jaws to the tree frogs, paralyzing them so that in a moment all were silent and still. It was plain that these joyous, crimson travelers were tid-bits indeed to the black larvae—undoubtedly brought from the coast for this purpose.

Rather shaken, I shepherded Lo Chan before us down the ladder and we hurried out into the warm sunshine. The blood-red pond with its border of snow-white water lilies heaved and bubbled as some great body swam across it barely under the water, so as to leave a swirling wake. Half running, half hopping along the causeways, bent figures sped before us. One of them swarmed up the trunk of a tree with all the agility of a monkey. Nearer, we saw that they were those same beast-men whom Kratas, the priestess, had brought down on us in the jungle.

"Let's go back to the house," urged Dillingame, "and kind of orient ourselves before we see any more horrors."

I motioned to Lo Chan to lead the way, and we retraced our steps. The Chinaman kept glancing back at me, and I knew instinctively that something was wrong—I had blundered in some detail, and he suspected I was not really what he had first taken me for.

Gomez broke out again as soon as we were alone.

"What's the use of all this waiting?" he demanded. "Why not ask the mandarin for all the gold he has, and get out of here? I'm afraid—me! There is magic all around us, black magic ... Those frightful worms!"

"Shut up and let me think," I answered crossly. "We have got to make up our minds to some definite plan of action—though I'm hanged if I know what!"

"The first thing to do is to go back and get some of those caterpillars," broke in Trevor. "I'll wager they are the larvae from which the black butterflies develop, even if predacious butterfly larvae had never been heard of before. Also I'll wager we run into Kratas before long."

The Portuguese shivered.

"I'm not going back to that place of evil," he announced decidedly, "especially if there is any chance of meeting the witch."

"Besides, we must look into that red pond and find out what that big thing swimming under water was," continued Dillingame, paying no attention to the interruption.

"Let's have a pow-wow with the Chinee first of all," I suggested, and clapped my hands to summon him.

Lo Chan emerged from behind the red-and-gold curtain, and salaamed. It may have been my imagination, but I seemed to detect that there was not quite the same degree of reverence he had shown in the past.

"I desire to look into the matter of the gold," I announced, making my statement as indefinite as possible.

"This afternoon, we will go to the diggings," and he salaamed anew.

"What's he saying?" demanded Dillingame, and I translated.

"We're going back to the temple this afternoon," the Englishman insisted obstinately. "Put off the other trip till tomorrow."

"Why not let me go with him," eagerly suggested Gomez, "while you two attend to other matters?"

For a moment I hesitated. The Portuguese was not to be trusted, and I did not know what he might hatch out against us. On the other hand, since he could speak no Ida'an or Chinese, how could he plot with the mandarin? Ashamed of my fears, I gave my consent and advised Lo Chan that only Gomez would accompany him. Again he bowed and withdrew.

Then, since the sun was at it height and it was insufferably hot, we stretched ourselves on the cold *kafang* matting for a noontime siesta.

We were not destined to visit the temple that afternoon, the next day, or the day after; nor did Gomez get to the gold diggings. After an hour's uneasy doze we woke fairly gasping for breath. The heat lay over the world like a heavy blanket, there was not a breath of air, and it was rapidly growing darker. Came a moaning in the tree tops, gradually rising to a roar. Coolies clamped heavy shutters over the open front of the house and then scurried for shelter.

The roar increased to thunder, a breath of cool wind slipped in through the loosely woven walls, and then came the rain, a solid sheet of water crashing into the ground as though hurled from above.

The coolies brought lights and, unable to make ourselves heard in the awful tumult, we settled down to wait for the end of the storm. Gomez began cooking opium pills and was soon lost in oblivion. Trevor found some rice-paper and I tried to teach him more of the Ida'an dialect (he had picked up quite a bit by himself) spelling out the words phonetically.

It rained without ceasing the next day and the next; then at sundown the storm came to an end as quickly as it had begun. The shutters were removed from the front of the house, Gomez emerged from his opium trance, and Trevor and I could hear each other speak. All ground between the stone causeways was under water and every curved leaf was a miniature fountain of silvery spray.

For half an hour we stretched our legs outside and then returned for the rest that had been impossible during the roar of the rain. The sun sank, the birds became silent, and my companions' deep breathing soon told me that they had found sleep.

From the jungle, clear and pure as a silver thread, floated a voice:

"Gone is the wind, the rain is past,
The moonlit night is here at last.
I wait, all longing, wait for thee,
Come fast, my love, come fast to me.

My skin is pale as the jasmine flower,
(Oh, haste you, love, 'tis the sacred hour!)
My breath is sweet as the *areca* bloom,
Where its purple cups in the darkness loom!"

Trevor snorted in his sleep and I stirred him with my elbow. "Wake up," I whispered. "You are being serenaded. You or that other handsome laddie, the mandarin."

"As the *epidendrum* holds the *anguska* tree,
Musk-scented, my arms shall twine 'round thee;
As the teak is held by the clinging vine,
Thus shall thy lips be held to mine!"

"It's Kratas," exclaimed Dillingame, sitting up, "and she isn't serenading that fat Chinaman, either! What did that last verse mean?"

"Leave this place as quick as you can,
I much prefer the fat Chinaman,
Or I'll have to jab a poison dart
Straight through the middle of your heart."

I translated obligingly—this love affair seemed to me to be verging on the serious.

"You're a liar," he answered promptly, and stepped out boldly into the darkness.

"Come back, you fool," I called after him. "You'll get a knife stuck into you!" But he had disappeared.

Groaning at the stark idiocy of it—Trevor had never shown himself a ladies' man before—I followed down the ladder. Somewhere in the blackness the girl laughed. My foot went off the causeway and I plumped down into the water.

Crawling out again, and cussing beneath my breath, I listened. There was no sound. Disgusted, I climbed back, shed my wet clothes and rolled up in a blanket. Again came the girl's laugh from out of the night. The ladder creaked beneath Trevor's weight and he scratched a match. Around his neck was a jasmine wreath and he held a small palm-leaf package in his hand. "Did she kiss you?" I asked him disagreeably.

"None of your business, but I couldn't get close enough to her," he growled. "She just chucked the flowers around my neck, gave me this bundle and vanished. I couldn't think of the Ida'an for 'come back' either."

In the tropics, the morning after a storm is always beautiful. The coolness still lingers, and everything is fresh green and has generally grown about a yard. We woke full of energy; even Gomez seemed to feel no ill effects from his opium debauch, and decided to carry out our original program of visiting the temple while the Portuguese accompanied the Chinaman to the gold diggings.

I was about to clap my hands to summon Lo Chan when he lurched from behind the red-and-gold curtain. Evidently opium had also been his solace for the last two days, and the effects had not worn off. At any rate, he omitted the customary salaam and began a rather heated harangue.

According to the laws of the Tong (so he said) certain privileges were due him, and I had given no intimation that I intended to grant them. For example, even if I had been sent to take his place, I should have told him at once of the manner and time of his death—it was his right. Also where was the acknowledgment of the last tribute of gold sent to the coast, and his written sentence from the Tong?

More and more inflamed by his own words and still swayed by the poppy drug, he began to wave his arms.

How did he know we hadn't stolen the black butterfly talisman? That we weren't imposters? What kept him from calling in his coolies and having us strung up by the thumbs?

This sort of talk couldn't go on, of course. The drugged man was lashing himself into a fury. I gave Dillingame a signal (he always did the fighting for both of us), and the Chinaman went down to an uppercut nicely combined with a trip.

"Dog of a parricide," I thundered, "you shall die a death unnamed, nor shall I tell you when! Who are you, scum of the earth, to question the black butterfly's wing?" and I hauled it out of my pocket.

Lo Chan got slowly to his feet and salaamed, all the fight knocked out of him.

"'Twas a madness," he mumbled. "I do my lord's bidding."

Gomez was scared to death of the big Chinaman after this outburst, but his desire to see the place whence the gold came prevailed over his fears, and away the two then went, surrounded by a guard of coolies.

The very first thing Trevor and I did when we were alone was to open the little package Kratas had given to the Englishman the night before. Inside the palm leaf wrapping was a soft piece of native cloth, which we unrolled, bringing to light two eight-inch-long cocoons, jet black, their fine silk-like threads woven as closely as a piece of linen. Dillingame split one open with the sharp blade of his knife and the pupa tumbled out on the floor.

Most pupae of butterflies make you think of angels or souls in transition. This one looked exactly like the devil disguised in the form of a dragon.

"Let's see that butterfly talisman," he demanded, and I laid it before him while he was trying to dissect out the embryonic wing. The pupa was not sufficiently developed to show wing veination, though, so he carefully replaced it in its silk cocoon and did it up with the other.

"Keep the talisman," I suggested, "and try to ask Kratas about it in the intervals of your unholy love-making."

I overhauled our weapons carefully, as became a cautious man, before starting for the temple, and we set out heavily armed. There was water on either side of the causeways and the stones beneath our feet were steaming wet. A little wind fanned the tree-tops and the whole world seemed to be a waving silver-and-green symphony.

It was not a deserted world, however, as it had been on our previous expedition. The little beast-men were trotting along the stone roads, pressing timorously to the edges while we passed, and all converging in the same direction toward the temple. They lined the rampart around the pond, no longer blood red, in which we had seen the mysterious ripple, and the square in front of the portico was one solid mass of them. There must have been two thousand of the ape-like beings, and from this great multitude came not a sound.

"Go on or hang back?" I interrogated Trevor.

"On, since we started," he answered. "Besides, they haven't even their blow-guns."

The crowd opened silently before us as we strode toward the entrance of the temple. Inside, it was as empty as when we had first visited it, save that a single, thin shaft of sunlight came down through the aperture above.

"Come on," called Dillingame, and I followed him upward. The sides being shuttered in, it was quite dark at first as we stood on the top rounds of the ladder and tried to pierce the gloom. The bar of light broadened and I saw the edge of the sun overhead. Dimly we made out that the foliage had been removed from the floor; then as the light increased, we saw the walls hung everywhere with the long, black cocoons, the resting stage into which the black caterpillars had entered.

The sun came square over the hole at the top of the temple, shining down so brightly into our eyes that we were blinded; and at the same moment came a murmur from the outside as though each member of the crowd had drawn a single, simultaneous deep breath.

"Next act. Let's see it," I suggested, and we backed down the ladder, shielding our eyes from the glare.

Along a causeway to the left, where were turned all the beast-men's faces, slowly advanced a group of strangely clad figures. Closer, we made out that they were old, old women, wrinkled, bent, tottering, clothed in strips of many-colored cloths that fluttered from their scrawny shoulders. Immediately before the temple they halted and opened out. In their midst appeared one of the beast-men, and bound to his back was the wizened Chinaman we had met leading the Ida'ans whose baskets contained the little red tree frogs.

Suddenly the old women broke into a cackling chorus:

"Pale is the pool with the silver rim,
Pale should be red,
So we send you to him.
When the sun has painted the world to gold
Pale shall be red as it was of old.

"Pale is the pool with the silver rim,
Hungry is he,
So we send you to him.
When the sun has painted the world to gold
Pale shall be red as it was of old.

Straight through the crowd came Kratas till she stood among the shrinking old hags. Catching the beast-man, who bore the Chinaman bound to his back, by the hair, she led him to the edge of the lily-bordered pool.

"Pale is the pool with the silver rim,
Waiting is he.
So go to him.
When the sun has painted the world to gold
Pale shall be red as it was of old."

Chanted the cracked voices.

The captive shrieked and struggled on the beast-man's back. With a mighty heave, Kratas sent them over the ramp into the water, their impetus carrying them beyond the border of white lilies.

The center of the pool bubbled as they sank. Up they came, something tipped with pink, something on a thick black stem pushing them half out of the water and fastening to their bodies. For a moment the miserable bound creatures were above the surface; then were drawn slowly under, the water reddening about them.

It all happened so quickly, was done so mechanically, that it was doubly horrible.

"Pretty sweetheart you have," I managed to gasp, "feeding live men to some water monster!"

Dillingame's eyes were popping from his head, but at my words his jaw set.

"Criminals, probably," he stuttered. "She was only seeing justice done—and the pool had to be red."

"Look here," I cried out in horror, "are you defending that—that witch? Have you gone crazy?"

He did not answer; his eyes were on the girl, who was coming through the scattering crowd. I plucked at his sleeve.

"Let's go from here," I begged.

I so hated, and still do hate that woman—indeed, I think she has made me hate all women—that my conscience forces me to do her justice in spite of the wrong she did me. As she stood before us smiling at Dillingame she was beautiful as a dream of Paradise, a goddess of the golden age, Eve, the first woman whence all after drew their charm. I forgot that she was a savage, forgot her beast-men had shot the harmless Ida'an porter, how she had wantonly slain one of them with the poisoned arrow; even forgot the tragedy of the two bound wretches cast to a horrible death in the water-lily-bordered pool. All I could see was that she was beautiful, desirable beyond the whole world.

Paying no attention to me, she halted not a hand's breadth from Trevor, and spoke:

"I am Kratas, priestess of the Land of Blood, who knows not death, who lives forever. The lives of all men—your life—are between my hands.

"I am Kratas, the priestess, guardian of the souls of the dead. Even the sable butterflies are beneath my law.

"I am Kratas, who guards the yellow dust all strangers desire.

"I am Kratas, all-powerful, and I come at set of sun to take you to my house as my slave and mate."

"I don't get that last part," complained Dillingame, turning to me.

"Merely a proposal that will not take 'no' for an answer," I explained. "Shall I tell the lassie you'll think it over?"

"She's very beautiful," he sighed, letting his eyes stray to her.

"The Great Lord from Afar has already a wife whom he loves," I explained hastily in Ida'an, "and *orang putehs* have but one mate."

Her arms were around his shoulders now, and she gave me one venomous backward glance.

"Her blood shall fatten hungry leeches," she hissed, "and he will forget . . . " Her lips found his.

The Price of my Freedom

Dillingame and I quarreled bitterly when we got back to Lo Chan's house. The man was mad, bewitched, and in his stark obstinacy defended himself. Hadn't he a perfect right to kiss a pretty girl if he wanted to? Hadn't she spared us when she might have wiped us out any minute? Wasn't it through her that we hoped to get the black butterfly—and gold?

There was no arguing with such a maniac, and I told him so.

Gomez came back alone, around four o'clock, and in a most disconsolate state of mind. It seems that the gold diggings were in the bottom of a dry creek and the rain had brought down an entire bluff on top of them. The little man was in despair, whined and bemoaned his fate that he had ever come with us, and declared himself ruined.

To tell the truth, we paid little attention to him. Dillingame was stretched out on one of the *kajang* mats looking exasperatingly comfortable and complacent. I was sulkily packing up our belongings at the other end of the house—and it was to me that Gomez gravitated.

The trouble with villains is that they are apt to consider the rest of the world as bad as they are, especially when it is a question of gold. Gomez proceeded to tell me that as soon as he had found out Lo Chan understood Portuguese he had pretended to conspire with him, to discover what he could. He suggested to the Chinaman that Dillingame and I be murdered, and, the piece of black butterfly wing in their possession, they grab all the gold in sight and flee to Dutch Borneo.

Lo Chan had been delighted with the murdering idea when he learned that the talisman was Gomez's property—"had to tell him that, you know"—explained the little man ingenuously—and confided to him that, without it, he would be unable to collect the tribute from the temple.

As to fleeing to Dutch Borneo, however, he did not want to because of the difficulty of transporting his three wives.

"My plan now is," the little villain continued, "to pretend to be hand-in-glove with Lo Chan, and through the black butterfly locket—which seems to be the key to the situation—hold him in check. I will let him have the talisman to collect the tribute, then we'll kill him and return to Brunei."

Fine arrangement, wasn't it? All Gomez wanted was to get the little round locket in his hands and then it would be good-by to us. I lost no time in passing all this up to Dillingame, and he lost no time in kicking the Portuguese down the ladder. It was not a diplomatic thing to do, but I couldn't altogether blame him.

We paid for it later, as you will see.

Gomez did not return, and Trevor and I picked up our quarrel where we had left off. I argued for an immediate return to Brunei; what we had already collected would show a good profit on the expedition. Further intercourse with the Portuguese was all but impossible. Dillingame obstinately stood out for waiting till we had secured a specimen of the black butterfly—in other words, until the pupae had developed in the cocoons and emerged; and added that he might trade for some more gold from Kratas—that she seemed to like him.

Seemed to like him! I should say she did! That was my main anxiety, combined with the fact that *he* "seemed to like" *her.*

We argued, if facts being presented by him can be called arguing, till nearly dark, and then we ceased speaking to each other.

Behind the gold-and-red curtain at the end of the house a woman screamed, and the sound was cut off short as though someone had grabbed her by the windpipe. Instinctively we jumped for our weapons. Without the slightest warning the curtain went down, unmasking a huddled crowd of coolies armed with muskets. I yanked Dillingame to the floor just as the house was filled with the roar and smoke of a volley.

"Got me through the shoulder," he gasped, and rolling over, turned loose with his automatic. I pumped my rifle into the thick of the smoke, and then they were upon us.

The first Chinese face that loomed up before me changed to a blur of blood beneath the butt of my gun. With my foot I slid a couch in front of us and then hauled the Englishman to his feet.

In a yellow avalanche the coolies piled over our frail barricade. Dillingame swinging a heavy tabouret, cleared the floor in front of him. I literally blew men from the mouth of my pistol. The smoke rose. I tried to slip in new shells, but there was no time. Over the motionless or squirming bodies of their companions they were upon us again. The Englishman went down, dragging a half a dozen of his assailants with him. Forced against the wall, my arms were twisted upward, a cord slipped around my wrists, binding me helpless, and my knees were pinioned.

The fight had been voiceless, just a silent striving punctuated by the firearms, till this moment, when there was a scream of deadly fear from a coolie. In the open front of the house stood Kratas, her face a mask of rage. From beneath the jasmine wreaths that clothed the upper part of her body she snatched a long knife, and, light as a butterfly, sprang over the couch to where Dillingame lay.

Three times the knife fell, dripping red after each stroke, and she rolled three dead Chinamen from the body of the unconscious Englishman. Then, with one sweep of her round arms she swung him to her shoulders, spat out some words I did not understand to the cowering coolies, and heedless of my frantic yell for help, went swiftly down the ladder with her limp burden.

The house was a shambles. There were no less than a dozen dead and wounded men lying about, not counting the three Kratas had knifed. Floor, walls, couches and overturned screens were splotched with blood, and the air was heavy with gunpowder and the smell of death.

Gently enough, though I cursed them, I was bound to a bamboo couch, a cushion even being slipped under my head to ease it. The gold-and-red curtain at the end of the room was replaced, dead and wounded were carried away, and I was left in the darkening twilight.

Not for long, however. I heard Gomez speaking in Portuguese at the bottom of the ladder.

"I hope they are both dead, damn 'em. You may take the talisman from Freeman and keep it, for all I care. Just give me a load of gold and I'll find my way down into Dutch Borneo somehow."

"True friend," purred Lo Chan, "it shall be as you desire," and they both came up the ladder.

"You turn me loose, Gomez," I roared, "or I'll beat you to death later."

"I'm going to kill you slowly as soon as I have taken away that talisman," he snarled, "you all-virtuous, heavy-handed fool!" and he began to investigate my pockets.

I shut my jaws tight and let them search me. Finally they stripped off most of my clothes and literally tore them to pieces.

"Where's that butterfly thing?" demanded the Portuguese furiously.

"I gave it to Dillingame," I answered in Portuguese so both would understand.

"Dillingame is dead, thanks to me," said Gomez, also in Portuguese. "We'll take a look at his body, Lo Chan."

"He's not dead, as you will soon find out," I interrupted. "Kratas carried him off and the talisman is with him."

"Santa Maria! That witch again!" and the little man crossed himself.

His perturbation was nothing to the terror that convulsed the mandarin's frightfully mutilated face, making it doubly hideous.

"If Kratas gets that talisman, I shall die the unknown death," he wailed to me. "Go, go at once to Dillingame Tuan and get it of him for me! I will send you from here unharmed, I swear it by the sacred black butterfly, and with all the gold three strong men can carry!"

"What of this swine?" I asked, jerking my head at Gomez. "Speak Ida'an so he may not understand."

"He shall be burnt over slow fire for your imperial pleasure, or thrown into the silver-rimmed pond. You may see him torn with hot pincers or fed living to the fire ants of the jungle ... "

"Enough," I commanded, and translated carefully into English for the Portuguese's benefit.

"Get the sable butterfly's wing and we will kill the Chinaman," he whined back at me. "You wouldn't have a fellow Christian done to death by a yellow heathen, a companion murdered in cold blood!"

"Nothing I'd enjoy more," I answered heartily. "Now, turn me loose."

On my feet, freed of bonds, I restrained myself, though with difficulty, from kicking the little man—it had brought us bad luck before. Food appeared, and with it two iron-bound chests that were humbly laid at my feet. Raising the covers I saw they were filled to the brim with raw gold-dust.

Again, his eyes on the yellow metal, Gomez began to plead that I join him in murdering the mandarin and make away with his fortune. I had just finishing translating this for Lo Chan's benefit, just so everything would be nice and friendly, when Kratas stepped in from the darkness.

Without as much as a glance at the other two men she beckoned to me, and I followed her down the ladder. Catching my hand she guided me through the shadows along the causeway. Before the red pond she stopped for a breath, and pointed.

"If he dies—you go there," she hissed.

Past the temple we went and into the black jungle. Ahead of us a voice began to sing, and the words were in English.

"They stuck him full of pins to remind him of his sins,
And still he swilled down beer and rum together.

So they cut off his fool head and filled him full of lead—
And a boy's best friend is his mother."

"He prays to his gods," sighed Kratas, dragging me on faster.

I sprang up the ladder into a torch-lit house and hurried to Trevor's side. He was tossing on a broad bamboo couch, a bandage of crushed leaves against his wounded shoulder, and his eyes hot and wild with fever. For a moment he recognized me.

"Hello, Andy, old top! Come to preserve the proprieties, hey? You're a hell of a chaperon.

"Oh, Andy married Margaret,
Oh, Andy married Jane;
He gave his name to Mary
Eloped then with Elaine . . . "

and he was in the clutch of the fever-devils again.

Thirty long anxious days Kratas and I nursed the Englishman, nursed him with the care and tenderness that a man receives only from his best friend and the woman who loves him.

Each morning Gomez appeared before the house and begged for the butterfly talisman, and each morning I cursed him and bade him be gone.

Kratas, beautiful as a dream of bliss and tender as a mother, never left the sick man's side save twice, and both times I heard the cackling chorus from the direction of the lily-bordered crimson pond.

"Pale is the pool with the silver rim,
Waiting is he,
So go to him.
When the sun has painted the world to gold
Pale shall be red as it was of old."

The thirty-first day, Dillingame's fever broke, and he knew me, reaching out his hand with a little unsteady smile. Kratas knelt beside him and her lips brushed his as light as a passing butterfly. Then he slept.

Once Trevor was on the road to recovery, his progress was rapid. In a week he was up and could walk about, though still woefully thin and white. Kratas was unceasing in her devotion and had a retinue of old women—the priestesses clad in the strange garments of strips of colored cloths—waiting on and cooking for him.

Our traps had been brought from Lo Chan's house, and I found time to do quite a bit of collecting, always in the opposite direction from the temple. I couldn't even think of that place without a shudder.

Conditions would have been ideal for a man who loved the jungle and found happiness in solving its secrets had it not been for one thing; Kratas was jealous of every word I spoke to the Englishman. He had made marvelous progress in the Ida'an tongue, and they held long conversations together, part of which Dillingame detailed to me, throwing some light on our situation.

Kratas's story of her own life was extremely simple. She calmly asserted that she was the first woman that had been put on earth, and that she would live forever.

Years ago there were many brothers of Lo Chan in the wilderness, who had built the temple and washed out great stores of gold, which were buried beneath it. Then they had all died, and for a long time there were no Chinamen. Finally Lo Chan and his coolies appeared with the black butterfly talisman to vouch for them, and had started to wash for gold.

Each full of the moon, according to the age-long custom, he was given as many quills of the precious metal as he could hold in both hands; but while in past years the dust had been collected by the beast-men, it was now drawn from the horde beneath the temple. This tribute was then sent to the coast by a Murut, who carried the round piece of butterfly's wing as a passport.

The messenger had not returned from his last trip (Gomez could have told why), but he was expected at any moment, since the time of tribute was but two days off.

In regard to the lily-bordered pool, the information was extremely sketchy. It was there dwelt the God of Blood, father of the black butterflies; but what exactly that god was, Kratas did not make clear.

"You see, Andy," Trevor explained to me a dozen times, "what we consider cruel bloodthirstiness in the girl is nothing but custom—a heritage from her ancestors. Since she has always been supreme, the life of a miserable beast-man means nothing to her. Consider for a moment how frightful it must seem to her that we catch and kill butterflies—the souls of the dead!"

He was teaching her to speak English, too; though I hardly saw the necessity of beginning with "darling" for the first noun, and "love" for the verb.

Gomez had not appeared for several days, but that morning he came to the foot of our ladder with an entirely new plan. Lo Chan had promised to send out the gold by him if the Murut did not return—"As I know well he will not," he interjected—if he could secure the black butterfly talisman, which, once recovered, Lo Chan had sworn should never again leave his hands. Instead of going to Brunei we could simply steer for Dutch Borneo, the Portuguese explained, and make away with the gold. He begged and pleaded for the talisman, but I only cursed him while Trevor laughed and tantalized him by holding it up so he might see it.

A pretty pair they made, Gomez and Lo Chan, cold-blooded murderers, both of them, and each continually plotting to destroy the other. Lo Chan's plot, in this instance, was perfectly plain to us. Gomez and his gold would never leave the Land of Blood without the black butterfly wing talisman.

That evening the three of us were sitting in the dusk, and Trevor and I were engaged in a long argument regarding the possible food plants of some new species of butterflies. Twice Kratas had spoken to the Englishman and, absorbed in what we were discussing, had not answered her.

Without the slightest warning she was on her feet with a snarl of rage.

"Offspring of the wild hog, killer of the souls of the dead," she shrieked at me, "you have dared too much! You would steal my Lord Tre-vor from me. Now you shall die. I have spoken who cannot unsay my words!"

Quick as a snake, she sprang at me, and I caught the bare blade of her knife in my left hand so it cut deep into the fingers. Dillingame threw himself upon her and I wisely retreated down the ladder. For a long time he tried to soothe her, but quite in vain. She was absolutely determined on my death—she had spoken who could not unsay her words.

Finally he got her calmed and willing to let me live for the present—and he won this concession with kisses.

My hand bled freely, the blood even soaking through a bandage, and I lay down on my bamboo couch near Dillingame with the pleasant feeling that I should probably be murdered in my sleep.

I woke at dawn to a pang of agony from my wounded hand. There was a great hole in the mosquito net and a soft black thing brushed my face.

Wide awake, as the pain increased, I looked down on a sable butterfly, a foot from wing tip to wing tip, poised above my head, its powerful jaws tearing and biting through the bloody bandage until they reached the live flesh beneath. Light as air it evaded me; them I smothered it beneath the folds of the netting, giving it that pinch every butterfly collector knows and it went limp. Marveling at the wonder of those sloe-black wings and fierce jaws, the like of which had never before been known among butterflies, I pinned it, finally, in the cyanide poison box. And it was borne in on me that this winged creature was a cannibal thing that came to human blood.

At intervals all through the next day Gomez came to our house and pleaded desperately for the talisman.

Kratas would not speak to me that day, only glared; and Trevor was plainly disturbed. At last she set out toward the temple and twice we heard the chorus that indicated another wretch had gone to the horrible unknown death in the blood-red pool. It was an anxious twelve hours, and in the evening Kratas simply sent me out of the house while she talked with Trevor.

It rained that night as it rains in the tropics, the drops coming down so that the world held no other sound but their crashing fall. I could not sleep, more than alarmed since I had not been able to get one single word alone with Trevor. Even now Kratas, awake and motionless, crouched in the dark between our beds.

Hours slipped by and suddenly I was conscious of a spot of shadow against the darkness moving silently nearer and nearer to where Dillingame slept. On my feet, I touched the girl's bare shoulder and she sprang forward as though shot from a bow.

The rain drowned all sound of the struggle and I struck a light. Gomez, his hands twisted behind his back, lay on his face, a broad-bladed knife by his side. Dillingame moaned in his sleep and the girl hastily dragged her captive within the house.

"Lo Chan sent him to murder Trevor," I shouted to her above the noise.

She nodded, her face black with fury, and quicker than a wildcat twisted the Portuguese onto his back, burying her knife in his throat. An imperative hand bade me begone, and as the match flickered out I saw her slip an earthen vase beneath the couch to catch the blood dripping from the dead man's severed jugular vein. When morning came she was still crouched by Dillingame's couch, and all our weapons had disappeared.

Not a word would Kratas let us exchange, her knife at my throat whenever I turned to the Englishman, and the sun was just rising when she led me down the ladder.

"This looks like the end of Andy Freeman," I shouted back at him.

"Kratas, if harm befalls my friend, I too, die," called Dillingame. "Here, take this, Trevor," and he flung at my feet the chamois skin bag that held the black butterfly talisman.

The same painfully silent crowd of beast-men was before the temple. Inside, the ladder to the second story had been removed and a thin shaft of sunlight came down through the hole in the ceiling, gilding a pile of porcupine quills, through whose transparent sides winked the glint of gold. The old hags with their garments of multi-colored strips of cloth filed in, the leader carrying a covered earthenware vase, which she laid at Kratas's feet. The ray of sunlight from above broadened and the priestess began to sing:

"Fill up thy hands with the golden thing.
Both hand cram-full of the dust we bring
From the secret hordes alone we know,
Stored up by the brothers long ago."

Lo Chan, his horrible features dead white, entered the temple alone and stood before the pile of porcupine quills.

"The moon is full, thy people pay,

Lord of the Pool, on this thy day,
Tribute to those who long did raise
This temple to thy glorious praise."

Through the aperture above came a solid shaft of sunlight, filling it to the edges. A sable butterfly sped down this golden stream of light; another, and then another, until the air was black with their wings. Lo Chan bent down, burying his hands among the heavy quills; and at that very moment Kratas poured the contents of the earthenware vase over his back and shoulders, soaking him from head to foot with red blood. The Chinaman straightened up with a startled cry.

First one and then a swarm of black butterflies darted upon him till his body was all but concealed beneath their quivering wings. He staggered toward the door, beating with shrieks of anguish at the monstrous flying things that fastened to his wrists, his lips, his face. The hole above vomited out a solid column of the horrible insects, and Lo Chan was smothered beneath them.

The mass of quivering wings rose from the ground, hurtled out into the sunlight. Once the man broke free and rushed toward the lily-bordered pool. Then they were on him again, whirled him in their midst above the water.

The surface broke and a pink thing protruded out into the light, a gaping pink mouth a foot broad attached to seven feet of flat, inky body that now lay on the surface—a loathsome, gigantic leech.

The butterflies raised their victim ten feet in the air, then slowly sank down with him toward the water. The pink head of the leech went blindly groping among the sable wings; then the man and butterflies together disappeared beneath the bubbling water that soon had changed to a livid pink.

For a moment they reappeared, then sank once more, and only the ripples rocking the big white lilies disturbed the calm of the blood-red pool.

"Let us go back," I begged Kratas, a great nausea coming over me.

"*You* go back to the land whence you came," she answered, "living only through my infinite mercy."

Before the bamboo house were waiting five of the beast-men loaded with my baggage. I attempted to mount the ladder, but Kratas jerked me back, and herself ascended.

"It's no use, Andy," said Trevor from above. "You have to go or die. I can not move the girl, and our weapons are gone."

"But aren't you coming?" I whispered, a great horror over me.

"No," he said. "No. It is only by staying that I bought your life. The talisman will protect you on your way out."

Behind him Kratas leaned against his shoulder and snuggled her cheek to his.

"Come back—some time," he said, looking down at me. "I sha'nt be unhappy here, but—come back—some time."

The jasmine-clad girl slipped one beautiful, warm arm around his neck and raised her face to his. Their lips met . . .

In regard to the lily-bordered pool, the information was extremely sketchy.
It was there dwelt the God of Blood, father of the black butterflies . . .

The BLACK Curtains

by G. Frederick Montefiore

Watch out, when you hear that quiet rustling . . .
first appeared in Weird Tales, *March 1925.*

Victor Stapleton, artist, seated himself opposite the gloomy black curtains that covered the folding doors separating his studio from the next room.

"I want to paint something different," he thought, "something to wake them up! Gruesome, perhaps, but with a touch of pathos and the ever-necessary feminine interest!"

It had occurred to him that gazing at certain objects which have the effect of not imposing any marked impression on the mind leaves the organ freer to roam the realms of imagination. The crystal used by the seer has no intrinsic power of revealing past or future, but the watcher, because his eyes, though open, see only the crystal's nothingness which neutralizes the immediate earthly sights, brings his mind into a receptive state for supernormal visions.

It suggested itself to the artist that those black, velvet curtains might take the place of the crystal and give him precisely that effect of staring into nothingness.

Long he sat, pondering, conjuring up fanciful scenes, mentally placing one character in juxtaposition with another of harshly opposite tendencies; raking over half-forgotten ideas of his earliest imaginings for startling subjects; now shutting his eyes completely, now through half-closed lids, allowing his sight to play upon the black curtain. But nothing came. No passion-filled, new idea swept into his brain. No grotesque fantasm, molded from life's realities, flashed before him, to be caught, analyzed and committed to tangible pigments and canvas.

His thoughts strayed from the intended picture and he began to muse idly on the man who had recently taken the next room to his. Old Mr. Fland was reputed to be a miser, and wild tales had been told of his strangling the poor relations who came to him begging for a share of his gold. Victor had not yet seen him, but the landlady had chattered, and he had once spoken a word to the old man's granddaughter, a girl of singular beauty, possessed of masses of

73

golden hair that had excited the artist's pictorial instinct. He had frequently heard the girl and the old man quarreling, and the landlady had expressed a fear that some day the miser would kill his granddaughter, as he was said to have killed his other relations. "And then," she had added tremulously, "he'll thrust her body away somewhere to get it out of his sight!"

Hours passed and the artist was about to give up his vigil, as nothing came—nothing came—Hush!

What was that?

A hand, lean and yellow, was slowly pushing its way through the black curtains.

The artist was on his feet, his eyes staring, a strange sinking sensation pervading his whole body.

Then appeared the head, the grinning, maniacal face, of a yellow and shriveled old man, blinking and leering at the artist with baleful eyes.

"I—I didn't know you were in," wheezed a voice. "You were so very quiet! I—I would like to make your acquaintance. Won't you come into my room? It is larger than yours. You are an artist, eh? I have many things of interest to an artist. I have a granddaughter! Ha!"

He chuckled in a weirdly enticing way, while a second skinny claw appeared and rubbed itself over the other one.

Victor was indignant at the intrusion, but inclined to forgive the old man because he was reputed to be half-witted. Perhaps he really did need human companionship ... besides—the granddaughter!—with hair of gold.

He followed the old man through the black curtains and into the room which the folding doors had concealed.

They sat together in a musty room breathing antiquity from every corner, before a little oil stove. One feeble gas jet sent its yellow rays down upon the miser's cheerless face. His mouth was toothless, his nose hooked and seemingly as devoid of flesh as the beak of a bird. The skin was stretched so tightly over his temples that his skull seemed to be breaking through it to summon its owner to the grave; while the cheeks were so sunken that the artist fancied, with a quaint twist of thought, that they must have encroached uncomfortably upon his mouth space.

This strange old man seemed well aware of his own shortcomings, for his eyes gloated upon the handsome face and physique of the artist.

Noting the latter's glances of distaste around the room, he laid his yellow talon on his knee and said: "Looks old and shriveled, doesn't it? Like its owner! But it has hidden beauties! There is gold hidden here! Yes, gold!"

His shrill voice arose to a shriek and he writhed in delight.

"Gold! Hidden gold! And—" (he crept over and put his dry lips close to the artist's ear) "it's yours! The gold is all yours—if you can find it!"

He wriggled back into his chair, his limbs shivering with mocking laughter at what he thought a magnificent joke ... "If you can find it!"

Then, as Victor remained silent, sickened by the atmosphere of the place, he continued briskly: "Look for it! Search for the gold! Get up! If you find it, it's yours!"

Thankful for an excuse for moving about, and shaking the horror from him, Victor arose and began the strangest search that even his Bohemian existence, spent among art treasures, antiques and grotesqueries, had ever led him into.

He opened first the top drawer of a desk, ancient and emitting an odor of decay. He inserted his hand; the light was too feeble to trust alone to sight. He withdrew it with a cry of horror, echoed by a mirthless chuckle from the old man. His touch had encountered the five hewn fingers of a human hand!

He pulled the drawer wide open.

The old man laughed. His cries rang through the room.

"Not there!" he howled. "Not that time! Some one else looked there—and you see what happened to him!"

It was true, then, as the landlady had said. This detestable old wretch murdered the people, kinfolk no doubt, who came to him for money, then concealed horrid mementoes of his deeds about this temple of his iniquities.

Victor felt that he would go insane if he remained longer in that polluted air. He stumbled toward the folding doors and his own room, which he had already made up his mind to vacate on the morrow, but the miser's ghoulish hands restrained him.

"Search for it!" he cried. "Look for my gold. It's yours—if you find it! And remember—my granddaughter!"

He tantalized the artist cunningly. He knew, and Victor knew, that he could not leave the place while thoughts of the girl and her possible danger from the fiend filled his brain.

"Search!" snarled the old man. "Find the gold!"

Victor was now searching wildly among all the rot and stench that the unhallowed place possessed. He raised a glass bowl with a hollow stem that looked like a place of concealment, and from the stem protruded the shorn lips of a man.

He dashed the bowl to fragments on the floor and fled, trembling and white, into a corner.

"Ha, ha, ha!" rasped the maniac. "Another one looked there, and see what he got! He speaks of gold no more. His lips! Ha, ha!"

"Let me go!" cried Victor, in a strange voice. "Let me go, I say! Why do you hold me in this accursed place to torture me? Let me go, I say!"

He held out his hands in supplication.

The old man seemed to have him chained to the room by an influence that drained the will from his victim.

"Find the gold!" he snarled. "Search and find." Then suddenly: "Look behind you!"

Victor turned as if galvanized. His eyes encountered a picture, its subject obliterated by grime. He tore it aside, and there in a niche in the wall a skull grinned derision at him.

Madly battering his clenched fists against the grisly piece of bone, laughing and sobbing in hideous fright, he dashed across the room. But before he reached the folding doors his frenzied eyes saw a tall, straight cupboard which he had not before observed. By some odd trick of the mind he resolved to undo his tormentor and discover his gold, even if it cost his reason. He tore at the knob of the door and immediately had the cupboard open.

Something heavy—something that had been leaning against the door, fell into his very arms. It was the body of a girl, strangely beautiful, with masses of golden hair piled high upon her head and falling in a glittering riot about her white shoulders.

She fell limply upon his chest. At first he dreaded she had met the fate of the other searchers, but gladly he felt her heart beat and knew that the warmth of life was still within her.

Eagerly his arms encircled her and he turned her around so that his eyes might better see the wonder of her beauty. Then his eyes fell to her breast, and all the horror of that night was as a frolic to the enormity of dread that seemed to freeze his soul and he saw, sticking in her bosom, a knife.

And this had been all the time he was in the room—and he had not known!

"So you've found it!" the voice of the hell-fiend wheezed from behind him. "You've found my gold? You like it? Look at it! See! On her head!"

His hideous claw touched her hair.

"Gold! All gold!"

Victor, supporting the girl with one arm, seized the handle of the knife to draw it from its human sheath. At that instant the old man uttered a peculiar, shrill whistle, the like of which he had never before heard. Immediately the door was thrown open and two men entered.

"Caught!" screamed the old man. "See the murderer! With his hand on the dagger, plunging it into her heart!"

Victor turned. The body of the girl slipped from his arm. He looked into the barrels of two automatic pistols.

"Caught!" chuckled the old man. "Caught red-handed!"

Victor, facing the guns, backed slowly through the folding door into his own room and sank inert into the armchair. A slight gust of wind caught the black velvet curtains and they fell together, leaving him in total darkness.

"Yes," he said to himself, "I think that wounded girl on the chest of the handsome young man, those two leveled guns, held by the two grim executors of the law, the grisly skull and the hideous old man grinning in the background will make an excellently gruesome but romantic picture for the jaded public taste. By Jove, I got some inspiration from sitting in the dark and staring at those old black curtains after all!"

He rose with a satisfied smile and stretched his long-cramped limbs.

"Good old curtains!" he cried aloud.

As he spoke he laughingly gave the curtains a thump. His hand went through the curtains and as he drew it back he saw that the fingers were stained red.

He tore aside the hangings, and there lolled against him the body of a young girl, the hair a piteous mass of red and ... *gold!*

"My God!" he cried. "Old Fland *did* murder his granddaughter, and thrust her body through the folding doors while I dozed and fancied! And she has been there— like that—all the time!"

A faint, dry chuckle came from behind the black curtains.

"*Nausea overcame me. I wanted to run, to escape the sight of that oozing horror, but reason came to my rescue.*

The BLACK Stone Statue

by Mary Elizabeth Counselman

Like Lugosi & Dracula, Karloff & Frankenstein, Bloch & Psycho, Mary Elizabeth Counselman & "The Three Marked Pennies" are inseparable: her most famous, oft-reprinted tale. Here's another to savor.—FJA
Weird Tales, December 1937

Directors,
Museum of Fine Arts,
Boston, Mass.

Gentlemen:

Today I have just received aboard the *S.S. Madrigal* your most kind cable, praising my work and asking—humbly, as one might ask it of a true genius!—if I would do a statue of myself to be placed among the great in your illustrious museum. Ah, gentlemen, that cablegram was to me the last turn of the screw!

I despise myself for what I have done in the name of art. Greed for money and acclaim, weariness with poverty and the contempt of my inferiors, hatred for a world that refused to see any merit in my work: these things have driven me to commit a series of strange and terrible crimes.

In these days I have often thought of suicide as a way out—a coward's way, leaving me the fame I do not deserve. But since receiving your cablegram, lauding me for what I am not and never could be, I am determined to write this letter for the world to read. It will explain everything. And having written it, I shall then atone for my sin in (to you, perhaps) a horribly ironic manner but (to me) one that is most fitting.

Let me go back to the miserable sleet-lashed afternoon as I came into the hall of Mrs. Bates's rooming-house—a crawling, filthy hovel for the poverty-stricken, like myself, who were too proud to go on relief. When I stumbled in, drenched and dizzy with hunger, our landlady's ample figure was blocking the hallway. She was arguing with a tall, shabbily dressed young man whose face I was certain I had seen somewhere before.

79

"Just a week," his deep, pleasant voice was beseeching the old harridan. "I'll pay you double at the end of that time, just as soon as I can put over a deal I have in mind."

I paused, staring at him covertly while I shook the sleet from my hat-brim. Fine gray eyes met mine across the landlady's head—haggard now, and overbright with suppressed excitement. There was strength, character, in that face under its stubble of mahogany-brown beard. There was, too, a firm set to the man's shoulders and beautifully formed head. Here, I told myself, was someone who had lived all his life with dangerous adventure, someone whose clean-cut features, even under the growth of beard, seemed vaguely familiar to my sculptor's-eye for detail.

"Not one day, no sirree!" Mrs. Bates had folded her arms stubbornly. A week's rent in advance, ye don't step foot into one o' *my* rooms!"

On impulse I moved forward, digging into my pocket. I smiled at the young man and thrust almost my last two dollars into the landlady's hand. Smirking she bobbed off and left me alone with the stranger.

"You shouldn't have done that," he sighed, and gripped my hand hard. "Thanks, old man. I'll repay you next week, though. Next week," he whispered, and his eyes took on a glow of anticipation, "I'll write you a check for a thousand dollars. Two thousand!"

He laughed delightedly at my quizzical expression and plunged out into the storm again, whistling.

In that moment his identity struck me like a blow. Paul Kennicott—the young aviator whose picture had been on the front page of every newspaper in the country a few months ago! His plane had crashed somewhere in the Brazilian wilds, and the nation mourned him and his co-pilot for dead. Why was he sneaking back into New York like a criminal—penniless, almost hysterical with excitement, with an air of secrecy about him—to hide himself here in the slum district?

I climbed the rickety stairs to my shabby room and was plying the chisel half-heartedly on my *Dancing Group,* when suddenly I became aware of a peculiar buzzing sound, like an angry bee shut up in a jar. I slapped my ears several times, annoyed, believing the noise to be in my own head. But it kept on, growing louder by the moment.

It seemed to come from the hall; and simultaneously I heard the stair-steps creak just outside my room.

Striding to the door, I jerked it open—to see Paul Kennicott tiptoeing up the stairs in stealthy haste. He started violently at the sight of me and attempted to hide under his coat an odd black box he was carrying.

But it was too large: almost two feet square, roughly fashioned of wood and the canvas of an airplane wing. But this was not immediately apparent, for the whole thing seemed to be covered with a coat of shiny black enamel. When it bumped against the balustrade, however, it gave a solid metallic sound, unlike cloth-covered wood. That humming noise, I was sharply aware, came from inside the box.

I stepped out into the hall and stood blocking the passage rather grimly.

"Look here," I snapped. "I know who you are, Kennicott, but I don't know why you're hiding out like this. What's it all about? You'll tell me, or I'll turn you over to the police?."

Panic leaped into his eyes. They pleaded with me silently for an instant, and then we heard the plodding footsteps of Mrs. Bates come upstairs.

"Who's got that raddio?" her querulous voice preceded her. "I hear it hummin'! Get it right out of here if you don't wanta pay me extry for the 'lectricity it's burnin'."

"Oh, ye gods!" Kennicott groaned frantically. "Stall her! Don't let that gabby old fool find out about this—it'll ruin everything! Help me, and I'll tell you the whole story."

He darted past me without waiting for my answer and slammed the door after him. The droning noise subsided and then was swiftly muffled so that it was no longer audible.

Mrs. Bates puffed up the stairs and eyed me accusingly. "So it's you that's got that raddio? I told you the day you come—"

"All right," I said, pretending annoyance. "I've turned it off, and anyhow it goes out tomorrow. I was just keeping it for a friend."

"Eh? Well—" She eyed me sourly, then sniffed and went on back downstairs, muttering under her breath.

I strode to Kennicott's door and rapped softly. A key grated in the lock and I was admitted by my wild-eyed neighbor. On the bed, muffled by pillows, lay the black box humming softly on a shrill note.

"*I n—n n—ng—ng!*" it went, exactly like a radio tuned to a station that is temporarily of the air.

Curiosity was gnawing at my vitals. Impatiently I watched Kennicott striding up and down the little attic room, striking one fist against the other palm.

"Well?" I demanded.

And with obvious reluctance, in a voice jerky with excitement, he began to unfold the secret of the thing inside that onyx-like box. I sat on the bed beside it, my eyes riveted on Kennicott's face, spellbound by what he was saying.

"Our plane," he began, "was demolished. We made a forced landing in the center of a dense jungle. If you know Brazil at all, you'll know what it was like. Trees, trees, trees! Crawling insects as big as your fist. A hot sickening smell of rotting vegetation, and now and then the screech of some animal or bird eerie enough to make your hair stand on end. We cracked up right in the middle of nowhere.

"I crawled out of the wreckage with only a sprained wrist and a few minor cuts, but McCrea—my co-pilot, you know—got a broken leg and a couple of bashed ribs. He was in a bad way, poor devil! Fat little guy, bald, scared of women, and always cracking wise about something. A swell sport."

The aviator's face convulsed briefly, and he stared at the box on the bed beside me with a peculiar expression of loathing.

"McCrea's dead, then?" I prompted.

Kennicott nodded his head dully, and shrugged. "God only knows! I guess you'd call it death. But let me get on with it.

"We slashed and sweated our way through an almost impenetrable wall of undergrowth for two days, carrying what food and cigarettes we had in that makeshift box there."

A thumb-jerk indicated the square black thing beside me, droning softly without a break on the same high note.

"McCrea was running a fever, though, so we made camp and I struck out to find water. When I came back—"

Kennicott choked. I stared at him, waiting until his hoarse voice went on doggedly:

"When I came back, McCrea was gone. I called and called. No answer. Then, thinking that he might have wandered away delirious, I picked out his trail and followed it into the jungle. It wasn't hard to do, because he had to break a path through that wall of undergrowth, and now and then I'd find blood on a bramble or maybe a scrap of torn cloth from his khaki shirt.

"Not more than a hundred yards south of our camp I suddenly became aware of a queer humming sound in my ears. Positive that this had drawn McCrea, I followed it. It got louder and louder, like the drone of a powerful dynamo. It seemed to fill the air and set all the trees to quivering. My teeth were on edge with the monotony of it, but I kept on, and unexpectedly found myself walking into a patch of jungle that was *all black!* Not burnt in a forest fire, as I first thought, but dead-black in every detail. Not a spot of color anywhere; and in that jungle with all its vivid foliage, the effect really slapped you in the face! It was as though somebody had turned out the lights and yet you could still distinguish the formation of every object around you. It was uncanny!

"There was black sand on the ground as far as I could see. Not soft jungle-soil, damp and fertile. This stuff was as hard and dry as emery, and it glittered like soft coal. All the trees were black and shiny like anthracite, and not a leaf stirred anywhere, not an insect crawled. I almost fainted as I realized why.

"It was a petrified forest!

"Those trees, leaves and all, had turned into a shiny black kind of stone that looked like coal but was much harder. It wouldn't chip when I struck it with a fallen limb of the same stuff. It wouldn't bend; I simply had to squeeze through holes in underbrush more rigid than cast iron. And all black, mind you—a jungle of fuliginous rock like something out of Dante's *Inferno.*

"Once I stumbled over an object and stopped to pick it up. It was McCrea's canteen—the only thing in sight, besides myself, that was not made of that queer black stone. He had come this way, then. Relieved, I started shouting his name again, but the sound of my voice frightened me. The silence of that place fairly pressed against my eardrums, broken only by that steady droning sound. But, you see, I'd become so used to it, like the constant ticking of a clock, that I hardly heard it.

"Panic swept over me all at once, an unreasonable fear, as the sound of my own voice banged against the trees and came back in a thousand echoes, borne on that humming sound that never changed its tone. I don't know why; maybe it was the grinding monotony of it and the unrelieved black of that stone forest. But my nerve snapped and I bolted back along the way I had come, sobbing like a kid.

"I must have run in a circle, though, tripping and cutting myself on that rock underbrush. In my terror I forgot the direction of our camp. I was lost—abruptly I realized it—lost in that hell of coal-black stone, without food or any chance of getting it, with McCrea's empty canteen in my hand and no idea where he had wandered in his fever.

"For hours I plunged on, forgetting to back-track, and cursing aloud because McCrea wouldn't answer me. That humming noise had got on my nerves now, droning on that one shrill note until I thought I would go mad. Exhausted, I sank down on that emery-sand, crouched against the trunk of a black stone tree. McCrea had deserted me, I thought crazily. Someone had rescued him and he had left me here to die—which should give you an idea of my state of mind.

"I huddled there, letting my eyes rove in a sort of helpless stupor. On the sand beside me was a tiny rock that resembled a butterfly delicately carved out of onyx. I picked it up dazedly, staring at its hard little legs and feelers like wire that would neither bend nor break off. And then my gaze started wandering again.

"It fastened on something a few dozen paces to my right—and I was sure then that I had gone mad. At first it seemed to be a stump of that same dark mineral. But it wasn't a stump. I crawled over to it and sat there, gaping at it with my senses reeling, while that humming noise rang louder and louder in my ears.

"It was a black stone statue of McCrea, perfect in every detail!

"He was depicted stooping over, with one hand holding his automatic gripped by the barrel. His stocky figure, aviator's helmet, his makeshift crutch, and even the splints on his broken leg were shiny black stone. And his face, to the last hair of his eyelashes, was a perfect mask of black rock set in an expression of puzzled curiosity.

"I got to my feet and walked around the figure, then gave it a push. It toppled over, just like a statue, and the sound of its fall was deafening in that silent forest. Hefting it, I was amazed to find that it weighed less than twenty pounds. I hacked at it with a file we had brought from the plane in lieu of a machete, but only succeeded in snapping the tool in half. Not a chip flew off the statue. Not a dent appeared in its polished surface.

"The thing was so unspeakably weird that I did not even try to explain it to myself, but started calling McCrea again. If it was a gag of some kind, he could explain it. But there was no answer to my shouts other than the monotonous hum of that unseen dynamo.

"Instead of frightening me more, this weird discovery seemed to jerk me up short. Collecting my scattered wits, I started back-trailing myself to the camp, thinking McCrea might have returned in my absence. The droning noise was so loud now, it pained my eardrums unless I kept my hands over my ears. This I did, stumbling along with my eyes glued to my own footprints in the hard dry sand.

"And suddenly I brought up short. Directly ahead of me, under a black stone bush, lay something that made me gape with my mouth ajar.

"I can't describe it—no one could. It resembled nothing so much as a star-shaped blob of transparent jelly that shimmered and changed color like an opal. It appeared to be some lower form of animal, one-celled, not large, only about a foot in circumference when it stretched those feelers out to full length. It oozed along over the sand like a snail, groping its way with those star points—*and it hummed!*

"The droning noise ringing in my ears issued from this nightmare creature!

"It was nauseating to watch, and yet beautiful, too, with all those iridescent colors gleaming against that setting of dead-black stone. I approached within a pace of it, started to nudge it with my foot, but couldn't quite bring myself to touch the squashy thing. And I've thanked my stars ever since for being so squeamish!

"Instead, I took off my flying-helmet and tossed the goggles directly in the path of the creature. It did not pause or turn aside, but merely reached out one of those sickening feelers and brushed the goggles very lightly.

"And they turned to stone!

"Just that! God be my witness that those leather and glass goggles grew black before my starting eyes. In less than a minute they were petrified into hard fuliginous rock like everything else around me.

"In one hideous moment I realized the meaning of that weirdly life-like statue of McCrea. I knew what he had done. He had prodded this jelly-like Thing with his automatic, and it had turned him—and everything in contact with him—into shiny dark stone.

"Nausea overcame me. I wanted to run, to escape the sight of that oozing horror, but reason came to my rescue. I reminded myself that I was Paul Kennicott, intrepid explorer. Through a horrible experience McCrea and I had stumbled upon something in the Brazilian wilds which would revolutionize the civilized world. McCrea was dead, or in some ghastly suspended form of life, through his efforts to solve the mystery. I owed it to him and to myself not to lose my head now.

"For the practical possibilities of the Thing struck me like a blow. That black stone the creature's touch created from any earth-substance—by rays for its body, by a secretion of its glands, by God knows what strange metamorphosis—was indestructible! Bridges, houses, buildings, roads, could be built of ordinary material and then petrified by the touch of this jelly-like Thing which had surely tumbled from some planet with life forces diametrically opposed to our own.

"Millions of dollars squandered on construction each year could be diverted to other phases of life, for no cyclone or flood could damage a city built of this hard black rock.

"I said a little prayer for my martyred co-pilot, and then and there resolved to take the creature back to civilization with me.

"It could be trapped, I was sure—though the prospect appealed to me far less than that of caging a hungry leopard! I did not venture to try it until I had studied the problem from every angle, however, and made certain deductions through experiment.

"I found that any substance already petrified was insulated against the thing's power. I tossed my belt on it, saw it freeze into black rock, then put my wrist-watch in contact with the rock belt. My watch remained as it was. Another phenomenon I discovered was the petrification also occurred in things in *direct contact* with something the creature touched, if that something was not already petrified.

"Dropping my glove fastened to my signet ring, I let the creature touch only the glove. But both objects were petrified. I tried it again with a chain of three objects, and discovered that the touched object and the one in contact with it turned into black rock, while the third on the chain remained unaffected.

"It took me about three days to trap the thing, although it gave no more actual resistance, of course, than a large snail. McCrea, poor devil, had blundered into the business; but I went at it in a scientific manner, knowing what danger I faced from the creature. I found my way again to our camp and brought back our provision box—yes, the one there on the bed beside you. When the thing's touch had turned it into a perfect stone cage for itself, I scooped it inside with petrified branches. But, Lord! How the sweat stood out on my face at the prospect of a slip that might make me touch the horrible little organism!

"The trip out of that jungle was a nightmare. I spent almost all I had, hiring scared natives to guide me a mile or so before they'd bolt with terror of my humming box. On board a tramp steamer bound for the States, I nearly lost my captive. The first mate thought it was an infernal machine and tried to throw it overboard. My last cent went to shut him up; so I landed in New York flat broke."

Paul Kennicott laughed and spread his hands. "But here I am. I don't dare go to anyone I know just yet. Reporters will run me ragged, and I want plenty of time to make the right contact. Do you realize what's in that box?" He grinned with boyish delight. "Fame and fortune, that's what! McCrea's family will never know want again. Science will remember our names along with Edison and Bell and all the rest. We've discovered a new force that will rock the world with its possibilities. That's why," he explained, "I've sneaked into the country like an alien. If the wrong people heard of this first, my life wouldn't be worth a dime, understand? There are millions involved in this thing. Billions! Don't you see?"

He stopped, eyeing me anxiously. I stared at him and rose slowly from the bed. Thoughts were seething in my mind—dark ugly thoughts, ebbing and flowing to the sound of that *I—n n—n n g—n n g!"* that filled the shabby room.

For, I did see the possibilities of that jelly-like thing's power to turn any object into black stone. But I was thinking as a sculptor. What do I care for roads or buildings? Sculpture is my whole life! To my mind's eye rose the picture of co-pilot McCrea as Kennicott had described him—a figure, perfect to the last detail, done in black stone.

Kennicott was still eyeing me anxiously—perhaps reading the ugly thoughts that flitted like shadows behind my eyes.

"You'll keep mum?" he begged. "Do that for me, old boy, and I'll set you up in a studio beyond your wildest dreams. I'll build up your fame as—what are you?"

His gray eyes fastened on my dirty smock.

"Some kind of an artist? I'll show you how much I appreciate your help. Are you with me?"

Some kind of an artist! Perhaps if he had not said that, flaying my crushed pride and ambition to the quick, I would never have done the awful thing I did. But black jealousy rose in my soul—jealously of this eager young man who could walk out into the streets now with his achievement and make the world bow at his feet, while I in my own field was no more to the public than what he had called me: "some kind of an artist." At that moment I knew precisely what I wanted to do.

I did not meet his frank gray eyes. Instead, I pinned my gaze on that droning black box as my voice rasped harshly:

"No! Do you really imagine that I believe this idiotic story of yours? You're insane! I'm going to call the police—they'll find out what really happened to McCrea out there in the jungle! There's nothing in that box. It's just a trick."

Kennicott's mouth fell open, then closed in any angry line. The next moment he shrugged and laughed.

"Of course you don't believe me," he nodded. "Who could?—unless they had seen what I've seen with my own eyes. Here," he said briskly, "I'll take this book and drop it in the box for you. You'll see the creature, and you'll see this book turned into black stone."

I stepped back, heart pounding, eyes narrowed. Kennicott leaned over the bed, unfastened the box gingerly with a wary expression on his face, and motioned me to approach. Briefly I glanced over his shoulder as he dropped the book inside the open box.

I saw horror—a jelly-like, opalescent thing like a five-pointed star. It pulsed and quivered for an instant, and the room fairly rocked to the unmuffled sound of that vibrant humming.

I also saw the small cloth-bound book Kennicott had dropped inside. It lay half on top of the squirming creature—a book carved out of black stone.

"There! You see?" Kennicott pointed. And those were the last words he ever uttered.

Remembering what he had said about the power of the creature being unable to penetrate to a third object, I snatched at Kennicott's sleeve-covered arm, gave him a violent shove, and saw his muscular hand plunge for an instant deep into the black box. The sleeve hardened beneath my fingers.

I cowered back, sickened at what I had done.

Paul Kennicott, his arms thrown out and horror stamped on his fine young face, had frozen into a statue of black shiny stone!

Then footsteps were clumping up the stairs again. I realized that Mrs. Bates would surely have heard the violent droning that issued from the open box. I shut it swiftly, muffled it, and shoved it under the bed.

I was at my own doorway when the landlady came puffing up the stairs. My face was calm, my voice contained, and no one but me could hear the furious pounding of my heart.

"Now, you look a-here!" Mrs. Bates burst out. "I told you to turn that raddio off. You take it right out of my room this minute! Runnin' up my bill for 'lectricity!"

I apologized meekly and with a great show carried out a tool-case of mine, saying it was the portable radio I had been testing for a friend. It satisfied her for the moment, but later, as I was carrying the black stone figure of Paul Kennicott to my own room, she caught me at it.

"Why," the old snoop exclaimed. "If that ain't the spittin' image of our new roomer! Friend of yours, is he?"

I thought swiftly and lied jauntily. "A model of mine. I've been working on this statue at night, the reason you haven't seen him going in and out. I thought I would have to rent a room for him here, but as the statue is finished now, it won't be necessary after all. You may keep the rent money, though," I added, "and get me a taxi to haul my masterpiece to the express station. I am ready to submit it to the Museum of Fine Arts."

And this is my story, gentlemen. The black stone statue which, ironically, I chose to call *Fear of the Unknown,* is not a product of my skill. (Small wonder several people have noticed its resemblance to the "lost explorer," Paul Kennicott!) Nor did I do the group of soldiers commissioned by the Anti-War Association. None of my so-called *Symphonies in Black* was wrought by my hand—but I can tell you what became of the models who were unfortunate enough to pose for me!

My real work is perhaps no better than that of a rank novice, although up to that fatal afternoon I had honestly believed myself capable of great work as a sculptor some day.

But I am an impostor. You want a stature of me, you say in your cablegram, done in the mysterious black stone which has made me so famous? Ah, gentlemen, you shall have that statue!

I am writing this confession aboard the *S.S. Madrigal,* and I shall leave it with a steward to be mailed to you at our next port of call.

Tonight I shall take out of my state-room the hideous thing in its black box which has never left my side. Such a creature, contrary to all nature on this earth of ours, should be exterminated. As soon as darkness falls I shall stand on deck and balance on the rail so that it will fall into the sea after my hand has touched what is inside.

I wonder if the process of being turned into that black rock is painful, or if it is accompanied only by a feeling of lethargy? And McCrea, Paul Kennicott, and those unfortunate models whom I have passed off as "my work"—are they dead, as we know death, or are their statues sentient and possessed of nerves? How does that jelly creature feel to the touch? Does it impart a violent electrical shock or a subtle emanation of some force beyond our ken, changing the atom-structure of the flesh it turns into stone?

Many such questions have occurred to me often in the small hours when I lie awake, tortured by remorse for what I have done.

But tonight, gentlemen, I shall know all the answers.

GRAY Ghouls

by Bassett Morgan

*I met Bassett, then an elderly lady, toward the end of her life. My
mother, about the same age, in her late 80s, accompanied me and the two
practically fell into each other's arms. I'll never forget their parting words:
"Well, before long we'll be seeing each other again".—FJA
Weird Tales, July 1927*

When there was a job to be done, especially adventurous, entailing skillful
diplomacy and undoubted peril, Tom Mansey was summoned partly because
he knew Papua as well as a white man may, partly that he seemed indifferent
to probable torture and death meted out by head-hunting savages to intruders in
hidden empires of the hinterland.

The stout official sat about a table viewing evidence which had promulgated
fresh indignation. It had been seized from the trophies of a globe-trotting curio-
hunter who parted reluctantly, indignantly from it, and spouted wrath and threats of
reprisal. It was a mummied human head no larger than a man's doubled fist, beautifully cured, furnished with balls of cat's eye chalcedony in the sockets, lips sewn in a
kissing pout. The shocking feature was its abundant and flaming red hair. Nowhere
in Papua is red hair natural to a native. The idea of a mummied head with ruddy
locks threatened the fragile foothold of white civilization on those dark flanks of a
land as treacherous as the panther it most resembles.

Mansey added the final note of nausea to the assemblage.

"A woman's head, I should say. Whether a white woman or not I don't know.
The curing might brown the skin. This hair is silky, rather fine and waved, certainly
not bleached. By the manner of lip-sewing I should say it comes from the north-
shore people. I never saw nicer work."

It was uncanny, horrid, weird, to hear him enthuse over the craft of cannibalistic savages, but his remarks were crisp when they asked him to investigate the
source of supply, take feasible measures to halt barter in heads, intimate to the most
indomitable, hellishly cunning race of blacks the earth endures, that selling human
heads to tourists was indelicate, inadvisable and immoral.

"I'd suggest right here that you'd better stop tourists buying heads. So long as they pay big money for them, the heads will be forthcoming, and since heads with Nordic-colored hair bring fatter prices, the natives will swoop down on the ports and clean out our little intrusion of white exploiters in one whirlwind of savagery run amuck. However, I'm interested. Using cat's-eye quartz for eyes is a new wrinkle that shows intelligent progress in art."

Mansey crossed the room in a weighted silence and traced a forefinger on a wall-map, traversing from the Curlews south of Sarong, then to the great island of Papua marked on the north of New Guinea.

"What white men or women have gone into here in the last decade and who's missing?" he asked of the company's clerk who had said least and done most to assist in the investigation. The clerk flipped pages of a book and wrote rapidly on slips of paper which he gave to Mansey.

With these data, Mansey set out with a power launch and a flock of Tonga boys in small outrigger proas hollowed from hardwood in a manner that has not changed since the sea spewed forth the South Sea Islands. Mansey was lightly armed. Weapons are small insurance against the peril of penetrating tribal villages of treacherous Papuasian black men, and he knew that where that ruddy-haired head was cured and fitted with quartz eyes, were intelligence and barbed cunning.

He had little information on which to base conjecture. Official files mentioned a Scotchman, Andrew Keith, who had gone native thirty years before, taken to the hinterland and never reappeared. Besides Andrew Keith, one other white man was in that locality to which Mansey was bound. His name was Homer Mullet; he had been a surgeon in London, got into disrepute and after a brief attempt to establish himself in Port Moresby, went north, evidently had luck with the natives and sent down frequently for drugs of surgical nature and new cases of instruments. His latest order was not more than six months old. With this meager information on possible sources of red hair Tom Mansey navigated the treacherous tide rips and cross currents and after weeks of tentative questioning located the lagoon where Homer Mullet was reported to have established himself as a sorcerer of greater magic than any native chieftain.

Leaving his Tonga boys and their proas outside, Mansey and a native launch man entered the reef jaws of white coral just when dawn turned the world pearl and the sea was shimmering opal. Across the lagoon were the triangular huts fringed with tinkling shells, a fire burning on the beach, cooking-pots steaming over it and the flower-decorated savages who shouted yowls of welcome. His launch churned bubbles in water clear as air, shining like green flame. Beneath were sea-gardens indescribably beautiful and menacing, tinted coral, waving fern weeds, wide-open flanges of tridacnas that can take off a man's foot if he steps into one, pretty little fish clustering and scattering like particles of an exploding glass ball. The air was hot and moist, perfumed by flowers, thick with the stench of rotting river swamp, pungent with sea-tang, the mingled scents of Papua's breasts beasts teeming with desire, unforgettable as the hells it transcended.

With a feeling of high adventure, Mansey sent the launch close to a crude causeway jutting between the nipa-thatched huts, knowing the yelps of painted, spear-pronged savages might change at a breath to cries of blood-lust and battle. His heart pounded with the spice of the thing and another discovery. Sitting in state near the fire, remaining seated while the savages danced and leaped in childlike frenzy, was the white man he sought.

A dozen black hands reached to help him to the landing-stage. The center of a swarm of rowdy young warriors hideously glorious in necklaces of human knucklebones, shark's teeth, crests of Paradise plumes, he was led to the fire and an avenue cleared down which he walked to the white man who was distinctly unornamented except by flower garlands, a collar of many strands of pearls, and pearl strings looped to his midriff.

"I'm Tom Mansey," he said, "and I suppose your name is Homer Mullet. I've been a month or two finding you to have a little talk."

"Mansey," commented Mullet without rising or offering his hand; "seems to me I've seen your name on the company's notations. Sit in for breakfast and make yourself comfortable. I'm pretty chief here, and as long as we agree you can sleep easy. There's turtle stewing and they've learned to cook it white-man fashion. It's good to hear English again. You haven't by any possibility some recent gramophone records, have you?"

Mansey had. He breakfasted on scraped coconut cream and turtle stew, a little fruit and remarkably good coffee and was patient while Mullet pumped and probed him for world news and port gossip.

He and Mullet ate alone. The crowd had dispersed to a farther fire and cooking-pot. The women were invisible in the huts. Mansey had opportunity to observe many things, a garden of sorts for that wilderness, an almost new *lagi-lagi* house for the men, and that Mullet's abundant hair curled to his shoulders but was so dark brown as to be almost black. Otherwise the renegade surgeon was a giant in stature, growing too fat and slightly insane, which Mansey expected. No white man can fight Papua. The land gets under his skull and behind his eyes. It drugs and stultifies his morale and finally kills his soul. That had evidently happened to Mullet. But his talk was rational. Mansey saw the slender, tapering fingers always playing nervously with the pearl strands, and the shifting prominent eyes. He had been a man of character and personality, a brainy intelligence, sensual-mouthed, and his good looks spoiled by a flattened nose and indulgence which over-hampered his body. "You'll stay a few days?" he asked.

"I'd like to," Mansey told him.

"You can have a house. Anything else?" Mullet's smile was suggestive and Mansey shook his head.

"The fact is I came for your help in halting the sale of heads to white tourists, if possible." Mansey told in detail the new menace which had leaped to formidable proportions and of the one ruddy-haired head which had started the rumpus.

"So you know something of heads," said Mullet, "recognized the lip-sewing and came north. They know that I'm here, and that Sandy Keith left his red-headed offspring in these hills, eh?"

"I suspected something of the sort. I suspected you."

This man was clever, also friendly. Mansey wanted that amiable feeling to continue and he had no hope of fooling Homer Mullet about his mission. Frankness might serve where guile would antagonize.

"You flatter me," said Mullet, laughing. "I start no line of devils down here, my friend. Besides, my hair isn't red."

"But the heads—" began Mansey. Mullet silenced him.

"I've no doubt my fellows do trade heads. They cure them. I can't stop that, but I have managed to put the fear o' God into them enough to confine their head-gathering to enemies and killing them outright before they begin. One thing I'll admit: there isn't a fresh one in the village. Look at the houses."

They strolled abroad and Mansey saw that the heads on display were old, rather green and misted with mold. Wooden figures carved grotesquely were plentiful. The village was clean, the houses new, there was evidence of sanitation and order unusual to natives. Yet instinct told Tom Mansey he was hot on the trail of trouble.

He was sure of it when at one hut there was a commotion and he saw a young girl struggling with older women and caught a glimpse of a head of glinting gold curled in cloudy beauty. Then amid shrieks of the women she was dragged inside and hidden. Mullet laughed.

"Bleaching a new queen," he observed. "At present I am a widower after a fashion. That shock you?"

"No." Mansey shook his head. "It isn't good for man to live alone, especially in savage lands. That new queen is a beauty."

"Six weeks in a darkened hut bleaches them like mellow ivory, and she's been kept from betel-chewing, or having her teeth filed. Making wives to order is feasible here, Mansey. Old Sandy Keith knew that."

"He is dead?" asked Mansey quickly.

"He is dead, and I inherited a lot of his troubles along with his trained apes. Sandy was quite a scientist. He was bent on learning the language of orang-outangs and had a flock of them. I have them now, nicely trained. You'll see."

Mansey was relieved at the conversational change, and puzzled. The orang-outang is a formidable simian, and he knew little about them except that they would clear the jungle in their vicinity of smaller monkeys and birds on sight. Mullet's laugh was unpleasant, yet Mansey fancied it sounded strange because laughter was not often loosed in that place. He sensed a sinister secret behind this bland talk of Mullet, and he knew instinctively that he was being entertained nicely to hide that secret, as well as Mullet's almost pathetic joy in companionship of his own race and kind.

That night he watched a dance at the *lagi-lagi* house and the ritual of initiation of young men ripe for manhood—the ritual that would enable them to take wives and heads. It was not new to Mansey, but he hated the evident relish of Homer Mullet over the stoicism of young men enduring greatly. He watched through a haze the final orgy, until satiated with strong drink and blood-lust they finally dropped inert and lay like a strange harvest of death as dawn flowed over the hills and blazed on the sea.

He went to the hut they had given him, but did not sleep. The settlement was lifeless at that hour except for a few older women at their housekeeping and cooking. He thought of the girl in the bleaching-hut who would be Mullet's queen, and was sorry for her, needlessly. He remembered that Mullet had said he was a widower at present, and during the dance in the *lagi-lagi* house he had confided drunken details of his rule and the reign of Sandy Keith.

"He lorded it, Mansey. Had several wives, and I married one of his daughters, a red-headed she-devil. She had all the beauty you'd ever find in a woman, but she was worse than native. She tried to kill me a dozen times—knives, poison, sorcery, until—"

Mullet had laughed horridly. Tom Mansey had no doubt in the world that the red-headed wife of Homer Mullet was killed, probably murdered. It was not his concern, but it sickened him. He knew that he was on the track of that forbidden traffic in heads, yet no nearer a solution of the puzzle would be presented if he tried to halt it.

That day he slept fitfully and awoke after the noon heat to find Homer Mullet astir.

Hearing his voice, Mansey looked from the hut door and saw Mullet coming down the trail of white crushed coral followed closely by a huge gray shape that loped along in the way of the great apes, paws trailing at its knees, and Mullet was talking to the creature, which seemingly answered by uncouth guttural sounds.

He hailed Mansey. "Going to take a look-see at my queen. Come along?"

It seemed diplomatic to go along and Mansey came down the notched log a little on guard because of the great ape.

"Sheba won't bother you," said Homer Mullet. "She's jealous of women but not men. I've got to get her acquainted with this girl, whom, by the way, I've named Cleo, short of Cleopatra." Mullet enjoyed the joke loudly, and the great ape showed her big teeth in a wide-mouthed grin and an uncanny cackle.

"Shut up!" yelped Mullet. The effect was magical. The ape's eyes showed shame, even grief, and she hung her head, but when Mansey looked back he thought she was snarling.

When they reached the hut where the potential queen was being bleached and beautified, Sheba the ape suddenly darted and swung to its roof-peak, and no commands of Mullet would make her descend.

"All right, you jealous old she-monk, take a look-see from up there and you'll see a real beauty. Bring out the girl!" he called to the scrawny old woman who peeped from the door.

On the roof, Sheba chattered angrily as Mullet repeated the command in native. To Mansey the experiment seemed considerable of a risk. As the child appeared in the hut doorway, Sheba showed jealousy. The girl was the prettiest Mansey had ever seen, her rounded body outlined in scarlet stain, her only covering a waist fringe of red and white blossoms.

Homer Mullet glanced at her, then beckoned to the ape on the hut roof and commanded in lurid curses, which Sheba not only ignored but chattered back her raging resentment.

"Look here," howled Mullet, "you'll come down and behave or I'll get the whip. This girl is your master-lady, hear what I say? You'll treat her nicely and none of your tricks like last time. You had your chance, you she-devil! And you made hell for everybody. You know what happened to you then, and it'll be worse next time. I'll make a crocodile of you—understand? You know how you hate water and the muggers. Well, you behave or your next incarnation will be a mugger. Now come down and kowtow."

Mansey listened in astonishment and something of fear. The she-ape was powerful enough to tear a man limb from limb, and she was roused to fury. Her eyes shot green fire, her teeth flashed and ground on themselves. The pretty little bride was gray-skinned with terror and dropped to the ground, her golden eyes a wild appeal. Mullet had been drinking heavily all night and was still drunk. His face grew purple-red, his eyes were bloodshot, the veins on his neck stood out and throbbed. But the ape defied him and in the end he snarled a command to take the girl inside, and strode off beckoning Mansey to follow to a couch by a shaded nook at the jungle edge.

There he imbibed more fermented coconut juice and gradually calmed to coherency which was no less frightful in its revelations than his exhibition of rage.

"That ape is near human. I'd say she is human. Old Keith made a study of them. I went him one better. I gave them brains. You saw that she was jealous, didn't you? Well, I'm afraid of her. Six months ago she killed my bride, another red-headed beauty like this one. I've got to prevent that, Mansey. Somehow I've got to keep her from this girl."

"Why not do away with the ape?" asked Mansey, more because some reply was expected than as a suggestion.

"I dare not. I've got seven of them trained, equipped with brains—thinking brains. They're my bodyguard. Without them I wouldn't last here. Oh, I know these blacks don't love me! I'm not that great a fool that I'd feel safe long. The she-apes are always near. You don't see them, but they don't let me out of their sight. I made a mistake with Sheba, though. Sheba was the name of that red-haired she-devil of a wife that tried to do me in. I remember telling you about her last night. Well, Sheba loved her red hair and beauty. She loved me too damn well. And God, how she hates being a monkey! But that was no idle threat about the muggers. I've never tried that, but I will. I'll make a crocodile of Sheba, so help me God, if she touches this new girl."

"Mullet, you're about as drunk as I've seen a man. Better quit that stuff or you'll be seeing monkeys," said Mansey.

Homer Mullet laughed long and loud. "You don't believe that, eh? Well, I don't blame you. But didn't you hear what they did for me in London? No? Well, I'll tell you. I took the brain of a boy dying with consumption and transplanted it to the head of a half-wit homicide. And by God, I made a success of it! And did they hail me as the discoverer of a new trail in surgery, and see as I saw, a way to empty our asylums and make use of incurables? They did not. They said I was crazy, they disgraced me. I barely escaped an asylum myself. That's why I came out here and kept my hand in. And I've done it time and time again. There was plenty of opportunity. The battles gave me subjects for experiment, and many a head is mummied and sold whose brain is still doing excellent service in a strange body. That's what I've done."

Mansey was staring at Mullet the surgeon, who gloated over his own skill. It was unbelievable, yet except for the wrath which shone in his eyes, Mullet's appearance was convincing.

"But trying the ape business was new. And possibly it was immoral. Sheba tried so many times to kill me, and one night when I was sleeping she almost got me. I struck in self-defense, stunned her and saw myself as a murderer. You may think murder a small thing to a man like me. It isn't. I've never killed. I didn't kill then. The she-ape that Keith had trained and which liked me was tearing the hut to pieces when she heard the row inside, and before I could get a gun she had snatched the body of my insensible Sheba. You won't care for details of what happened. I hadn't a weapon and I grabbed a bottle of chloroform which was handy and tried to brain the ape. The bottle broke and she was deluged. It acts quickly on them, Mansey. And something seemed to crack in my brain as I saw the unconscious ape and the dying woman. Well, the ape is Sheba. Now you know. I'm a fool not to kill her, but it's gone farther than that with me. I liked Sheba. And she cared enough for me to prevent me ever taking a second wife. More than that, she has somehow communicated to the other orang-outangs her jealous guardianship.

"I can't slaughter all the apes in the jungle, and they haunt me. Sheba has managed to people the land with gray ghouls who watch me night and day. Dante never conceived the hell of torture that I'm living through, Mansey."

In the tropic heat, Homer Mullet shivered and sweat broke cold on the forehead of Tom Mansey. Though terrific repulsion overwhelming him, he found himself sorry for the man who had made his own hell with more ingenious cunning than cannibal head-hunters could have devised for him.

"Mansey, if you could tell me a way out, I'd hang these pearls on your arm. An emperor's ransom, Mansey, for a plan to rid myself of this hell and live in peace."

Mansey was silent. The avalanche of horror had come so suddenly he could not yet grasp the thing. He assured himself it was the talk of a maniac, wildly horrible, yet in spite of reason he was convinced. And sifting through the horror was the fact of those red-haired heads drifting down to be bartered. If what Mullet said should be true, he was no nearer accomplishing what he had come to do. The authorities would not believe this tale nor could he halt the barter and trade.

"What became of the—the head—of Sheba?" he asked, licking dry lips with the tip of his tongue.

"They stole it from me. And I had made a job of that head, was rolling drunk when I did most of it. I put eyes—" "Cat's-eye quartz?" asked Mansey. Mullet nodded.

"I've got it in the boat," said Mansey. "That was the one that caused the trouble. It was nicely finished."

Mullet stared at him.

"For God's sake, hide it, Mansey. Perhaps Sheba—

He did not finish, for swinging down from tree branches overhead, the great she-ape stood before them.

Mullet ripped out an oath and added, "You heard what I was saying, you—"

Mansey fancied he heard the sound of a guttural word of speech and he leaped to his feet, ready to run for cover. The ape regarded him a moment with her alert gaze, then reached a paw, caught his shoulder and flung him, as if he were a child, at Mullet's feet.

"Better behave, Mansey," commented Mullet. "She's heard what I said. She was old Keith's daughter, remember, and he taught all of them his own tongue. If you speak French now, we might manage.

He looked at Mansey inquiringly. Mansey shook his head.

"Very little. I do comprehend 'sauve qui peut,' however, and it seems appropriate to this situation."

"A fine chance," snarled Mullet, as he looked about him. Mansey's gaze followed that survey and again he felt the chill of fear. In the thick tangle of lianas and jungle growth he caught glimpses of gray shapes watching them, swinging in grotesquely airy flight from tree to tree, a company of gray apes, the formidable "men of the woods" known to the world as orang-outangs.

"My harem," was hissed from Mullet's lips. "Each one equipped with the brains of a woman I selected as a wife, sealing her doom at the hands of this she—" The epithets he applied to Sheba were unspeakably vile. Mansey looked in apprehension at Sheba, but her eyes had not changed expression. Evidently there were a good many curses of port dives and docks not included in her knowledge of English. In place of anger, the eyes held something of the love-loyalty seen in the eyes of a faithful dog for its master. She squatted beside Mullet, took his hand and stroked it with her black paw, then held it to her cheek. Mullet jerked it away with an expression of disgust, and the great ape whimpered sorrowfully.

"You see?" snarled Mullet. "Yet we must talk. How about those gramophone records? Start a row going—"

"They're in the launch," said Mansey. "I'll get them." But when he rose, the ape caught his ankle, reaching with no apparent effort, and Mansey was jerked to the ground. Then, throwing back her head, Sheba displayed her fangs in a wide-mouthed and unmistakable grin. Mansey realized that he had walked into a trap, that only by cunning could he escape from the dread company of gray ghouls which Mullet the surgeon loosed in that jungle. Now for the first time he faced greater peril than head-hunting savages seeking trophies or glutting their unquenchable blood-lust against white intruders.

"Wait," said Mullet, then addressed the ape. "You savvy music records?" He made a circular motion with his hand and hummed a scrap of tune. "You fetchem white man proa 'longside. Savvy?"

Sheba uttered a sound from her throat and swung in swift flight through the trees. Mansey immediately scrambled to his feet and Mullet rose, but before they could take a step there was a circle of great apes hemming them in effectively. They made no attempt to touch either man, but formed a ring and marched about the two prisoners in what might have seemed a ludicrously humorous array if it had not been menacing and sinister.

"Mansey, I'm going out with you. I've got to go. God knows there isn't any other place for me—in white settlements, I mean—but I'll get to another island. They can't cross water. Oh, you can speak now! These are natives, not even very good at *beche de mer* talk. It's that devil of a Sheba who understands and communicates with the others. You heard her just now, calling them. Usually they don't come so close, but your arrival has made her suspicious, no doubt, and she doesn't want to lose me."

His laughter was mirthless and uncanny, the sound of insanity cracking in his voice. Mansey did not wonder. He felt that his own reason would not long stand the strain of this sinister surveillance. Yet what reasoning power was still uncluttered by the impasse in which he found himself, cautioned him against attempting to assist

Mullet to escape. The great ape would frustrate such an attempt, he felt sure. And there was danger in releasing a madman like Mullet on any other island, he thought. Aware that his face showed reluctance, he was again frank in speech.

"Mullet, I'm of the opinion that you can't get away, and I must. I could bring help, perhaps. I'll give you my word to do what I can, but for two of us to attempt escape, especially when you have such devoted followers, is utterly futile."

"Look here, don't you fancy for a moment you and that launch will leave this lagoon without me, Mansey. You can't, you know, unless I am willing. Even if you got to the launch, the blacks in their canoes would halt you at the reef entrance. I've had enough of this. Before you came I was making the best of it. I was content enough, only that I wanted a woman. Oh, it's my own doings! Don't think I'm shifting the blame, but at that it was something stronger than my will driving my hand to that delicate operation. If they'd let me alone in London, if they'd seen the marvel of what I'd accomplished, the greatest feat of surgery in this or any other age, I wouldn't be here and this wouldn't have happened. But they drove me out, my own race and kind. And you belong to them, Mansey. I've got a grudge, not against you, but all white men. Mansey"— his voice became quieter, more confidential in tone—"what if we'd take Sheba, you and I, and tour a few countries exhibiting the greatest marvel of the age? We'd need money, and we'd make it. I've lorded it here. I couldn't go back and grub and sweat again. But we could do that—"

"Mullet, either you talk rational or—"

"What will you do? What *can* you do except put a bullet through me, and you'd loose a hell-fury that would tear you bit by bit in rags. I've seen Sheba do that. Finger by finger, Mansey, toe by toe, handfuls of hair, eyelids—"

"Shut up, you beast!" cried Mansey.

"That gets you, eh? Well, it's true. And I'm your only protection. You've got to save me to escape alive."

"What about the natives?"

"Sheba is half native, remember, and she likes her own kind. They're safe. They're not only safe but invulnerable. When they go forth to take wives and heads, the gray apes go along and fight for them. It's a shambles when they leave, Mansey. It has one kick-back, though." Mullet laughed again and Mansey liked his curses better than his laughter. "The natives don't need to fight and they will in time lose their own initiative, their courage. Some day this tribe won't exist, but that won't come in time to save us."

"Listen, Mullet, suppose I go out and bring help, a revenue cruiser that will blast this village into nothingness as has been done before now. A few shells—"

"Shells won't reach the apes. You'd merely murder the blacks who aren't to blame. Besides, I've no assurance that you'd come back or send them. Who'd believe your story of human apes? And where would I be when they shelled the village? If

I went to the hills, the apes would go along. If I stayed here to have them killed I'd get it. What, don't you see I couldn't even kill myself if I felt like heroics to save you, because you'd have Sheba on your neck the minute I croaked? Pretty little mess, eh, Mansey? And there is no escape in the jungles or huts, none at all except to cross the water where the apes can't follow, and you're handicapped there because the natives know just what would happen to them if I'm not here to keep Sheba pacified. I did try getting away with one of my brides in a canoe and Sheba was on watch that night. She tore a *lagi-lagi* to bits, jerked the men to the shore and sent them after me in canoes. Then they gave me to understand I must not try again to escape. Oh, it's a beautiful entanglement! Here's Sheba."

The great ape dropped from overhanging tree branches and in one arm she carried Mansey's gramophone case, without which he never traveled. It was further proof of the uncanny intelligence of Sheba that she had understood Mullet's command and brought the case. She squatted and deftly unfastened the buckles of leather straps binding the oil-cloth cover, fitted the handle, opened a package of records and wound the machine. In another moment the wail of *She's My Baby Doll* rose in the hot silence. An instant later Mansey shrieked laughter of hysteric abandon, for the great she-ape was swaying from one foot to another and gazing at Homer Mullet with the amorous leer of a love-sick crone. She put out a paw to take his hand, but Mullet jerked it aside, and kicked his bare foot at her chest. Lacking his hand to fondle, she seized his foot, precipitated him on his back and cuddled the foot to her breast, laying her cheek against it and fondling each toe as mothers the world over play with toes of their babies.

"Laugh, damn you," growled Mullet. "I'll show you." He spoke in native to Sheba, who reluctantly released his foot, caught Mansey in her arms and, despite his struggles, swung to the tree branches. For all her strength the weight of a fighting man cumbered her movements and she halted her flight to hold him by both arms and shake him until his teeth rattled. Then swinging farther aloft she flung him over the crotch of a branch and dropped to earth.

From below, Mansey heard Mullet's shrieks of mirth. At that elevation he could see the village huts, the lagoon and his launch, the long reef-jaws, and ascending far down the outer beach, the smokes of fires where his Tonga boys cooked their meal. About him were the palms glittering like sabers in the sun, but the jungle was silent, bereft of the gorgeous birds of Paradise, the lorries and parakeets, the little chattering harmless monkeys. Where the great apes held court, no other jungle life lingered.

Mansey straddled the limb and considered in frantic dismay the situation in which he was placed. Reluctantly, he accepted Mullet's logic. There seemed no escape. Watching glimpses he obtained of the lagoon through swaying palms and branch plumes, he saw a dark object floating and realized with his heart racing that it was the body of his native left in charge of the boat. Evidently he had angered Sheba and she had killed him without so much as an outcry. Mansey almost envied the dead man. For the first time in his years on Papua he admitted that there were worse things than murder: far worse than the taking and curing of human heads as trade to tourists was the fitting of beast craniums with the brains of thinking humans.

Mansey looked below. The gramophone still wailed its jazz music and foolish songs. The seven great she-apes were dancing clumsily, in contrast to their lithe grace in the trees. Mullet lay prone on the mats, his naked trunk crisscrossed by strings of pearls, his arms over his eyes. Above, Mansey racked his brain to think of a plan of escape. Far off, the black crouching hills quivered in the heat, which was affecting Mansey in spite of a breeze at that elevation which did not penetrate below. He felt thirsty and faint and he knew if he should lose his grip of the tree bole, he would fall to death. His heart and blood began to pound, a throbbing which presently drummed in his ears. Then, suddenly, Tom Mansey knew he heard drums, far off, faint, inaudible to Mullet because of the grinding gramophone diligently kept going by Sheba.

Mansey knew the meaning of the drumsong of Papua, rising, falling, sinister, maddening, the voice coaxed by bare hands from bladderskins stretched over human skulls, and a new fear swooped and rode his shoulders. That drum song meant savages on the march, and it was coming nearer. He looked below and saw that the she-apes had ceased dancing and stood as if listening through the blatant jazz music to the voice of approaching peril.

In another moment, Sheba had clutched Mullet and shot him to his feet and was chattering a warning. The gramophone record died with a moan, and the drumsong rose insistent as the drone of bees, palpitant as the quivering hills. It roused sleeping natives and the huts belched savages.

They poured from the *lagi-lagi* where they had been sleeping off the night potations, arranging their plume crests as they leaped to earth, young men greedy for battle, eager for slaughter, grimly meticulous over their gaudy ornaments, proud of the fine blue lace of tattooing and blistered cicatrices obtained in agony.

Mullet looked up to where Mansey was hidden in the tree.

"Need help to get down?" he called. "Sheba will fetch you."

Mansey yelled a refusal and began to scramble down, but the great ape swung aloft before he had compassed more than a few feet of the descent. She caught the branch on which he was perched and bent it double, plucked him from his vantage and let the branch go. The crash as it flew back proved the tremendous strength of the beast-woman, and Mansey's heart missed a beat as he was swung in flying leaps and dropped on the mats, unhurt.

"Hear those drums?" began Mullet. "That means reprisal. Now Sheba and her sisters can help my fellows defend the village." He looked at Mansey, and in the bloodshot eyes of Mullet there was a meaning Mansey tried to read because neither dared utter his thoughts in the uncanny hearing of Sheba. Mullet turned to the ape.

"Good Sheba, pretty Sheba. Go after the drums, Sheba. Show the Kauloo warriors they can't fight our fellows. Take the other girls and have a good fight, old girl." He patted her shoulder, and at that careless caress the great ape fawned on him like a grateful cur that has known only kicks and abuse.

The warriors were dressing for battle in frenzied haste. They scorned to go forth to fight or die in aught but gorgeous array. And a drum-song of their own arose, one drum after another, purling the blood-rousing tempo that stirs the heart and soul of a man, tingles in his flesh, prickles on his scalp, the primal quickening call to war.

Looking at Mullet, Tom Mansey saw hope born in his eyes and thought he understood. They would be rid of the apes for a time. His own thoughts darted to the launch in the lagoon, the Tonga flotilla on the beach outside: Then as he looked seaward Mansey cursed. The Tonga boys had heard that drum-song and understood its meaning. They had no courage. They had launched their canoes, which ranged like slim dark beetles on the sun-glitter of the sea, ready to dart like arrows to safety far beyond. They hovered about the lagoon entrance evidently waiting a hail or sign from Mansey, and he was powerless to reach them.

About the cooking-fire, replenished by old men, began the war dance, and old women fetched gourds of fermented coconut wine, which was swigged by the warriors, who smacked their lips loudly and leaped into new frenzy, wild contortions, a hideous Carmagnole in which the she-apes joined, sometimes jumping to catch a tree branch and swing madly, spinning in midair like gibbet-fruit. Then at a sign from the leader, the dancers filed into the jungle, and the great apes leaped to the trees. Where had been a ferocious swarm of painted savages were only the scattered fire embers and the women gathering the empty gourds.

"Now," said Mullet. "Now is our chance. We've got the luck of fools. Get to the launch and start it, Mansey, and I'll get the girl. By God, I'd have given Sheba credit for more brains than she showed this time, but the gods are with us."

"Look here, you leave that girl behind, Mullet." Mansey's voice was stern.

"To be killed by the she-ape? What d'you take me for? Not much! I know what'll happen to every living human left in this village when Sheba comes home and finds me gone. There won't be a village. There won't be anything, Mansey, but rubbish, blood-soaked earth and bits of flesh. That girl comes. And there's no time to argue . . .

It was the one outstanding fact; they must hasten and get away. Mansey turned and ran to the landing-stage where he had been swung from the launch yesterday. He shortened her painter, dropped in and whirled the wheel. Then his heart sank. The engine was dead and a glance showed him the cunning of Sheba, for she had unscrewed every nut and bolt she could find and emptied his spare gasoline. The cans glittered at the bottom of the lagoon, when Mansey looked overside. The ape had taken time to sink them, sink every spare tool and all loose gear she could find. She had even thrust the oars, carried for emergency, into the open jaws of tridacnas, which closed on them. He leaned over, and reaching into the water, wrenched on one, but not all his strength released it. His efforts broke the blade tip and the maimed oar came up in his hands. The second one was beyond his reach.

Some minutes had elapsed in his cursory examination of the launch, but his brain was never so alert before. He thought he might use the maimed oar to scull the unwieldy craft, and stood up to summon the Tonga proas from beyond the reef, for the old men and women of the village were watching him covertly and muttering among themselves. Mansey remembered they did not want Mullet to escape for fear of the great apes' wrath. But they would probably not interfere with him. He faced a decision of saving his own life and leaving Mullet to a hell he had made for himself, or risking death in the attempt to release Mullet from horror. The choice was wrenched from him when he saw Mullet leap from the bleaching-hut to the ground with the girl on his shoulder, and Mullet's free hand clutched a big navy revolver.

Mansey saw the reason for the gun at once, and his own small automatics were in his hands. For when they saw their erstwhile white master running like a deer for the shore, there was a piercing scream from the natives left behind the war party, and they rushed to hold him on his perilous throne.

Mansey heard the man's warning cry, then the crack of his gun as he cleared a path, shooting as he ran, crashing through the out-thrust arms that would have detained him, leaving dead and dying in his wake. He had almost gained the white strip of coral beach from which the landing-stage jutted over the lagoon water, when one courageous old man threw himself headlong and Mullet tripped and crashed to earth, the girl flung from his arms and curled in a heap on the coral. In another moment, Mullet was the center of a heaving, lunging mass of blacks who tried to weight him to earth.

Mansey, in the launch, heard his fists thud on flesh, heard the thud of the gun-butt used as a club, saw black and white arms threshing like flails, then with a mighty heave Mullet was free. A triumphant yell burst from his throat and he leaped toward the shining head of the girl who lay on the sand as she had fallen, evidently knocked unconscious. That yell died in Mullet's throat and Mansey's heart missed a beat, then raced painfully. For from the quivering plumes of trees dropped a gray ghoul shape, screaming horribly in rage, and she flung herself at the white man and sent him spinning with a sweep of her long arm. It was Sheba!

With his brain in a whirl, Mansey realized that if he was ever to get away, it was the crucial moment. Yet, loosing the launch painter, he hesitated. Mullet lay prone on the glistening coral sand, and after a glance at him, Sheba had turned to the girl whose shining brush of curls turned slightly as if consciousness was just returning. One awful scream burst from her throat as the hand of Sheba encircled her throat;

then Mansey saw her bright hair through a red mist, for he realized what was going to happen, and saw from his eye corners that Mullet had rolled to his belly on the coral and was taking aim with his gun. Mansey's thoughts darted in wild speculation. Mullet would shoot Sheba, and he need not aim for the girl unless Mullet missed the ape. Otherwise—he shuddered with horror of what would happen in another moment as the hammer of Mullet's gun clicked uselessly, and Sheba, snarling horribly, picked up the girl as if she were a rag doll.

Mansey's gun cracked twice. He felt sick, revolting with nausea, for the girl's body hung limp in the ape's paws, and on her golden skin two bright soft ribbons spurted and flowed. She was beyond pain. But Mullet was creeping soundlessly, cautiously on his belly over the coral, making for the landing-stage.

Mansey loosed the painter, held the launch by his clutch of the nearest post, kept his gun aimed at the head of Sheba, trying in spite of the red mist over his sight to point for the base of her brain, afraid to risk a shot lest he should miss and she would be upon them with lightning speed.

He had time to think how marvelously the rapid-fire passing of events had shaped for this get-away. Without the sudden arrival of Sheba, the natives would have prevented their escape; and if Mansey had not insisted on bringing the girl, Sheba's attention would never have been distracted by this opportunity to glut jealous rage on her rival in the affections of Mullet. The great ape was extremely, dreadfully engrossed. Mansey tried not to see what she did, tried to believe it was a rag doll in the hands of a mischievous pet. He was bracing himself with all his will to override the violent upheaval that swept to his eyes and brain, while Mullet crept toward the launch.

Far off the drum-song was muffled, like the croon of surf on coral. Beyond the reef his Tonga boys waited. Another two minutes and Mullet would tumble into the craft. Already Mansey had braced the broken oar-tip against the planks to shove out. They must widen the water between themselves and Sheba. Mansey wondered, in a vague, darting thought, if orang-outangs could not swim, and remembered that before this trans-elementation the human body of Sheba was probably adept and strong in the water.

Mullet was on the landing-stage. Mansey heard the planks creak, but Sheba seemed to hear nothing but her own animal snarling at the dreadful task presented her. She was almost finished. Her arm swept out and held aloft something pitiful with long bright hair which she played with and stroked. Then from far out beyond the reef one of Mansey's boys hailed his master. Mansey's whole body jerked as if his nerves were strings of a puppet snatched by a crude hand.

"Marster, Marster!"

Mullet lunged as Sheba was on her feet. The launch careened crazily as he plunged in and Mansey heaved on the oar, then tried to propel the craft from the stern. One wild screech of baffled rage rang and echoed between the jungle-clad reef-prongs, and swinging the head by its long hair, Sheba sailed through the air, flung herself from the landing-stage into the water and swam after the boat.

Mullet was yelling and chattering like a madman. His gun was gone and he had seized Mansey's automatics and sent a sharp fusillade at the swimming ape. If Sheba was hit, the lead pellets did not halt her. Mansey, sculling frantically at the, stern saw her fangs bared, heard her snarls, stared in horror as his muscles cracked with the strain of propelling the tubby launch, at the long, gray, hairy ghoul which gained on them so rapidly that the boat might have been anchored for all headway they seemed to make.

A mighty lunge, and Sheba's paw caught the stern, seized the oar with which he tried to batter her off, and wrenched it from his grasp. Then Mansey threw himself on the combing as the ape's weight almost swamped them. Mullet was screaming, fighting, kicking as the paws seized him, dragged him from his clutch of the planks and hauled him, still struggling, into the sea.

For a moment there was a wild upheaval, and the clear lagoon water churned in foam that was blood-streaked. Mullet's shots had hit the she-ape, but that great body had the strength and endurance of an elephant. Yet in another moment, Mansey saw that Sheba was badly wounded, for her lips dripped redly and her eyes showed glassy.

Mullet was clasped in one arm and she tried to swim with the other. Beside the body of Mullet trailed a head with bright hair, and Mansey, helpless to avert further tragedy, sick with the shock of dread, clung to the launch combing, watching Sheba suddenly cease swimming and sink beneath the lagoon water, with Mullet in her grasp.

The ripples spread in rings, the bubbles broke. Through water clear as air, Mansey saw the gray ghoul go down, feet first, with the white man still struggling futilely. Then as the hairy gray shape parted sea-fern fronds until her foot touched a vantage by which she might have shot her body to the surface, there was a further commotion in the sea-gardens, a violent upheaval writhing below, a line of bubbles ascending, breaking soundlessly as the souls of man and she-ape escaped.

Mansey stared. He knew. Sheba's foot had touched the tinted flesh flanges of a giant tridacna and it had closed like a steel trap.

Not even in the death agony had she released her embrace of the man whom in human shape she had loved so fiercely that she took him with her to a trans-elementation far removed from reach of those bunglers who trifle with the doors of life and death.

The hot sun blazed down on a man inert, limp as a rag, lying on the launch bottom, and presently the Tonga boys who saw the launch put out, came to investigate.

They were some weeks towing the disabled launch to port, and during that time Tom Mansey recovered from a siege of sub-consciousness and fever in which he raved and fought a nightmare jungle peopled with gray ghouls. And when some time later he made a report to the authorities, it contained prophecy and prediction. "It is fairly well established that wherever the white man goes, it means elimination of the savage, not by slaughter, of course. We have subtler ways. And the higher type of skill and brains you send in, the quicker you set the death-dealing forces to work among the natives. Compared with one courageous, brainy white man, cobras, crocodiles, tigers, any of the jungle terrors are simple and innocuous. I know. As regards moneyed idiots who were promoting head barter, fine them enough and jail them. Cut off the demand and you kill the supply."

They rewarded Mansey rather well for that investigation, although in the launch bottom the Tonga boys gathered a king's ransom in pearls from strands which broke as Mullet struggled to escape death. They were rather honest Tonga boys and only thieved half of the pearls to divide among themselves, but Mansey was embarrassed. Pearls belong to the throats of pretty women, but those pearls held memories too horrid to give to a nice girl; so he is waiting to trade them to curio-hunters disappointed at a lack of mummied human heads.

Up
In SMOKE

by Tigrina

*A Colorful and COLOR FULL fantasy by a Legendary Daughter of Bilitis
and publisher of the world's first Sapphic zine, Vice Versa.—FJA*

"It's all too exasperating," Carolynne Devereaux poured out her story into the sympathetic ears of Zelda Troyer, her new and closest college chum, as they sped down Stafford Boulevard on a Saturday shopping tour in Carolynne's fleet Cadillac convertible. "I never was so humiliated in all my life—their packing me home from the de Pusters's party like that right in the middle of the evening, just because I was smoking a cigarette!"

"I don't blame you for being sore," Zelda's contralto voice chimed in. "I'd be mad as a hornet under similar circumstances. Nobody's ever objected to my smoking, but then my whole family smokes. Some parents are just too old fashioned, I guess."

"Old fashioned is putting it mildly!" Carolynne jabbed her arm out the open car window for a left-hand turn signal. "Do you realize they kept me confined to my room for two whole days as punishment, suspended my allowance, and even threatened to take away this car they just gave me for a graduation present? Of course it was about the dozenth time they've caught me smoking after they made me promise not to, but you'd think they'd understand I'm not a child any more. After all, I'm seventeen! And the lectures I've had to listen to. Oh, brother!"

Carolynne's voice burlesqued the tone of a fuddy-duddy giving a morality lecture. "'Nice girls don't smoke. It isn't moral. It isn't Christian. It's bad for your health. It lowers one's resistance to worldly wickedness.'" Carolynne's voice became normal again as she shot forth a stream of invective currently in vogue amongst the students at the supposedly elite Finishing School for Gentlewomen, from which she had just graduated.

"For the hundredth time they repeated that I, being their only daughter, got just about everything I wanted in the way of clothes, entertainment, education—oh, they went on and on through a long list—and surely I could obey them implicitly in the matter of smoking. And when I reminded them that all my friends smoked and seemed none the worse for it, they looked down their noses and said that at least *their* daughter wouldn't follow the trend of fashion like a sheep, but remain pure and unsullied, or some such words to that effect. You can bet your life that now that I'm away at college I'll do what I please!" Carolynne jammed down the brakes viciously for a red traffic light. "They don't seem to realize that this is 1947, not the middle ages."

"Perhaps it would be better to wait until you're a little older," counseled Zelda. "After all, I'm two years older than you are."

"Now don't you start in!" retorted Carolynne. "After all, I smoked constantly during the last three months of my senior year at finishing school."

Truth to tell, Carolynne admired Zelda ever since they became acquainted two weeks ago at college, and she not only aped her new-found friend in the matter of smoking, but even in the manner of her hair style.

"Did you parents make you promise again not to smoke?" asked Zelda.

"Yeah," sighed Carolynne. "Gimme a cigarette, will you?"

Zelda extended a flat silver case. Out of the corner of her eye, Carolynne noticed that the cigarettes were not the usual white cylinders, but crimson in color, matching Zelda's flame-red suit and the vermilion nail lacquer which she wore. Carolynne took her eyes off the highway a moment to inspect the interior of Zelda's case more closely.

"Why, Zelda! What kind of cigarettes are those? You and your exotic tastes! You're always blossoming out with some startling innovation!"

"Don't credit me with these," Zelda answered. "Blame Morloq. He makes them in different colors to match one's gowns."

While waiting for another traffic signal to change, Carolynne took the crimson cylinder that Zelda handed to her, eyed it speculatively, and then applied the lighter from the dashboard of her car. "Mmmm," she exhaled, "rather heavily perfumed, aren't they? Who is this Mormon you were speaking of?"

"Morloq," Zelda corrected her. "Rhymes with warlock. I first heard of him through a friend of mine. He's an odd fellow—foreigner of some sort—but indescribably handsome, with a suave, cosmopolitan manner, and just a wee dash of mystery about his personality."

Carolynne smiled. "You make him sound exciting."

"He also created individual perfumes to suit one's personality. I've had some blended for me. Surprising what he can tell you about your personality, too. Which reminds me," added Zelda, "I've got to stop by his studio on our way back to pick up my perfume. You can come in with me and I'll introduce you. He really is a most unusual character."

Morloq's small but swank studio was in the most exclusive section along Westwoodland Boulevard. A discreet sign, lettered in gold, bore the legend "Morloq— Cigarettes and Perfumes of Distinction." As Carolynne and Zelda stepped across the threshold, their entrance broke the beam of an alert electric eye, and caused the mellow note of a gong to sound, announcing their presence.

The establishment was furnished in extremely modern taste, yet with a distinctly oriental motif in the elaborate tapestry hanging, the Arabian hand-wrought lamp in a far corner, and the enormous tawny tiger skin sprawled across the floor. Carolynne was admiring the sleek pelt when a soft masculine voice behind her bade them good afternoon.

Both girls were startled. Carolynne thought that the man must have an extraordinarily cat-like tread to be able to approach them and yet not be heard. She turned quickly and surveyed the proprietor of the exotic little studio. Carolynne liked what she saw; over six feet of slim, trim masculinity, impeccably attired in a well-tailored dark business suit, topped by a handsome, smooth-shaven continence, swarthy complexion, and jet black, wavy hair. The features had a slightly oriental cast to them. He might have been in his late twenties or middle forties, but there was something in his emerald orbs which belied his youth. His eyes returned her gaze. Carolynne thought they were the greenest eyes she had ever seen.

Morloq's glance flickered toward Zelda. "Ah, Miss Troyer. You came for your perfume. I have it here." His diction was faultless, but there was a slight hesitancy between certain words and phrases.

Zelda accepted the gorgeously wrapped package that he handed to her, murmured a polite thank-you, and introduced Carolynne.

Morloq gave a slight bow of acknowledgment.

"While I'm here, I want to order some more cigarettes," added Zelda.

"They are certainly the most unique I have ever seen, Mr.—er—Morloq," Carolynne remarked, hesitating before the name, undecided whether to use the convention "Mr."

"Thank you. Would you care to try a sample while I show you two young ladies around my studio?" Morloq extended an ornate case toward Carolynne, and then toward Zelda. "Miss Troyer expressed the desire to go on a little tour through my humble establishment."

Zelda glanced at the tiny watch dial encircled with diamonds, which graced her lady-like wrist. "It's not too late just to take a look around, is it Carolynne? I wanted to last time, but didn't have time, and besides, I thought you might enjoy seeing the place, too."

Carolynne offered no objections. The exotic little studio fascinated her, and Morloq, although certainly a strange character, seemed such a charming host.

Carolynne lazily exhaled smoke from a long, emerald-hued cylinder of oriental tobacco as she and Zelda followed Morloq from show case to show case, inspecting the many cigarettes of various shapes and colors displayed therein, and listening to his lengthy but nonetheless interesting dissertation upon the qualities and origins of the different tobaccos and aromatic herbs used for special blends.

"But perhaps my perfumes might be of more interest to you," suggested Morloq, ushering the two girls into the adjoining room. Here, upon gleaming glass shelves, stood row upon row of delicate and exotic perfume flasks of every conceivable size, shape and material, some transparent, some opaque.

"This," Morloq indicated a delicately wrought silver, jewel-encrusted flacon, "contains one of my most rare and valuable scents, attar of roses, from India." His slender artist's fingers deftly whisked the jeweled top from the diminutive silver flask. A wave of heavenly scent wafted toward Carolynne and Zelda. They inhaled deeply.

"Here I have some genuine East African myrrh," continued Morloq, opening a bubble-thin glass vial, "and in this antique gold bottle is a fine and rare essence; jasmine from distant Persia."

Carolynne's head swam as she sampled the fragrance from each quaint flacon; musk, myrrh, sandalwood, jasmine, attar of roses, and other rare, oriental perfumes with unfamiliar, exotic names. She was enchanted with the rows and rows of beautiful, obviously hand wrought flasks, each one different from the rest, many of them inlaid with jewels. Espying a row of bottles as yet unexplored, she impulsively took down a little white cloisonné container, ornamented with delicate china roses.

Instantly, Morloq's suave manner changed. He almost snatched the bottle from her fingers. "Please! I must insist that you do not handle any of the bottles personally!" He replaced it, and then with a smile meant to be reassuring, continued, "Pardon, please. It is only that these bottles are antiques, so delicate, and quite irreplaceable."

"I quite understand. I'm sorry," murmured Carolynne, who wasn't sorry at all, but only annoyed at being addressed in such a brusque manner, and embarrassed because she had been rebuked in front of her girlfriend.

"Now, let me show you my most prized essence, distilled from the rare Quao Tzi flower, and first used by an ancient empress of China," resumed Morloq.

Carolynne noticed, however, that Morloq skillfully maneuvered them away from the mysterious row of bottles on the shelf where reposed the exquisite rose-bedecked cloisonné flacon.

Perhaps Morloq sensed Carolynne's annoyance at being spoken to in such an abrupt manner, for he interrupted his tour of the little shop to offer her and Zelda a rare Asiatic liqueur, claimed to be almost as fabulous an essence as his unique perfumes. Perhaps this little gesture of hospitality was an unspoken apology for his rudeness. Anyway, Carolynne preferred to think so, as she accepted his offer politely. Besides, she was pleased that Morloq had not discerned that she was still a "minor." It gave her a feeling of sophistication to join in a cocktail now and then.

The liquid had a pungent flavor as it burned a fiery course down her throat. It had quite a kick to it, too, Carolynne observed after her second glass, and heartily hoped that it would not affect her behavior.

The sound of the mellow gong, announcing someone's entrance, interrupted them. "Excuse me a moment," Morloq said. "I will return shortly."

"I think I'll go with you and order my cigarettes," said Zelda. "I forgot all about it, but I hated to interrupt your conversation with sordid business matters." Zelda whisked into the other room with Morloq.

Carolynne wandered around the room, glancing at the bottles. Funny how she couldn't quite read the labels on some of them. She had been foolish to take a cocktail when she hadn't eaten since lunch time. Then, her eyes fell on the white cloisonné bottle on the shelf, just a little apart from the others. Perhaps it was the effect of the liqueur which made Carolynne feel rebellious, which aroused her curiosity. With tipsy cunning, she softly stepped over to the shelf and took down the bottle with no disastrous results. In fact, he wouldn't even know about it!

Suddenly, the voices in the next room seemed to become louder. In her haste to replace the bottle, the top of it caught in the sleeve of her dress, was lifted from the vial, narrowly missed crashing on the glass shelf and fell harmlessly upon the soft cushioned rug, rolling under a showcase. The entire mishap had been without a sound. Carolynne breathed a sigh of relief, listened for the voices, which were not coming closer, as she had supposed, but were merely raised in volume. She quickly bent to retrieve the fallen stopper. It seemed for ages that she groped beneath the display case for the delicate bottle top, although it was actually only a matter of seconds.

When she stood upright again, her heart was pounding with excitement, and her head was whirling from having bent over in a cramped position. She reached for the cloisonné vial. Was it a trick of her befuddled senses, or did a cloudy white mist arise from it? It wafted half way across the room and then, oozing its way through a slit in the venetian blinds, escaped out into the open air.

Carolynne lifted the bottle to her nostrils, but could discern no odor of any sort. She replaced the top hurriedly, set the cloisonné bottle back in its place on the shelf, and hastened across the room to a large armchair. That liqueur must have been powerful stuff to play upon her imagination like that.

Finally her heartbeat slowed to normal. She rose deliberately and walked over toward a particularly horrible little carved idol of stone, at whose feet a few pieces of incense smoldered, in an intricately carved bowl. She had closed her eyes and was breathing in the wonderful fragrance when Zelda and Morloq returned.

"You find the incense stimulating, Miss Devereaux?"

Carolynne jumped. That was the second time that Morloq had startled her by his stealthy approach.

"A thousand pardons. I did not mean to startle you."

"You certainly are jumpy, Carolynne," observed Zelda. "What's the matter with you?"

Carolynne laughed to conceal her annoyance and embarrassment. "I guess I was carried off into a reverie by the pleasing aroma of the incense. At any rate, I didn't hear you come in again. That incense has a delightful fragrance, though I find it soothing rather than stimulating," added Carolynne, finally answering Morloq's question.

"Some people do," replied Morloq.

Carolynne was still a bit unnerved after her adventure with the cloisonné bottle, and watched Morloq carefully at first out of the corner of her eye, to see if he noticed that the flask had been molested. He appeared oblivious of this, however, and with the bottle back in the same position on the shelf, there was no reason why anyone should suspect that it had been touched.

"I can't say that I admire your taste in idols, though," Carolynne remarked, looking at the grotesque little image before whom the smoke curled and eddied upwards. "Ugly devil, isn't he?"

"Devil, yes. Ugly—well, it all depends upon one's viewpoint. Anyway, I would advise using a more respectful tone when speaking of the image. This is an effigy— the only one of its kind in the world—of Og Amankh, little-known Egyptian devil, called 'The Imprisoner of Souls,' and he is notoriously antagonistic toward those who do not show him proper respect."

Carolynne, still miffed at Morloq's previous brusque behavior toward her, replied in an irritating tone, "I suppose its age and the amount of hand carving on it must make it quite valuable as an object of art. The emeralds in its eyes alone would fetch quite a price. But it's still a hideous monstrosity as far as I'm concerned."

Carolynne regarded the diabolical statuette. Through a cloud of incense, its emerald orbs seemed to leer malevolently at her. She shuddered involuntarily, even though she knew it was merely an optical illusion, and thought to herself that had she known the statue was in the room at the time, she would never have had the nerve, under its peculiarly lifelike surveillance, to disturb the cloisonné bottle. The statuette continued to leer, as if it shared her secret.

Morloq turned to Zelda. "Some people are able to see a sort of beauty in grotesquerie. Then, too, things that are repulsive or hideous to Western eyes are not always so to those of the East."

"Oh, are you from the Orient? Frankly, I wondered about your origin," responded Carolynne, forgetting for the moment her anxiety to leave.

Morloq crossed to a chair opposite the two girls and lit one of his own brand of cigarettes. As the smoke swirled upward betwixt his tapering fingers, forming weird undulating patterns and a nebulous veil through which his green eyes regarded the two girls, Carolynne was aware of a similarity between Morloq and his heathen idol.

"I was born in Cairo, of Egyptian parents. Although I was educated in Europe, I have spent a greater part of my life in the Orient—Arabia, Egypt, India, China, even a few years in Tibet. My business takes me all over the world."

"You do not intend to stay here, then?" asked Zelda.

"Oh, I shall remain here for some time," replied Morloq, "until my—work is done."

Carolynne had just been about to ask what work he was referring to when Zelda interrupted. "Really, Carolynne, it's getting late, and I think we should be going. We don't want to miss our dinner at dear old Ivy Hall."

"You would not care to place an order for cigarettes before you go, Miss Devereaux?" suggested Morloq, hopefully.

Zelda answered for Carolynne. "Ha, that's a laugh. Her folks have just forbidden her to smoke."

Carolynne blushed crimson. Zelda's thoughtless remark had made her appear such a child.

"Oh, if I had known, I never would have offered you a cigarette, Miss Devereaux," Morloq hastily apologized.

"That's all right. I'm no longer a baby, and what they don't know won't hurt 'em," Carolynne callously replied.

Then, partly to cover her embarrassment and partly because she thought it was expected of her since Morloq had gone out of his way to show her around the studio, she said, "I will take an order of individually blended perfume, however."

Morloq's smile deepened. "That will take some time, Miss Devereaux. It should be ready next week. I can mail it to you, or perhaps you would care to call for it?"

"Better mail it," said Carolynne, "I may not get down this way again." She gave her college address.

"Don't you agree that Morloq is a fascinating creature?" asked Zelda, as they were driving toward the college.

"Yes," Carolynne thoughtfully agreed. "He's a fascinating creature. He has the same sort of fascination a snake might have for a bird."

Two days later, Zelda knocked on the door of Carolynne's room and informed her that Morloq had the perfume ready.

"What, already? But I thought he said it'd take a week."

"Well, he says he has it ready now. He phoned me about my order, and gave me the message to pass on to you. I thought maybe we could drive down this Saturday afternoon. After all, it is Saturday, and we have no classes—" Zelda seemed so excited and anxious to go that Carolynne finally relented.

Morloq greeted them cordially as they stepped through the door, and they exchanged a few polite pleasantries. Morloq indicated their packages on the desk.

"One moment, before you go," Morloq said. "I have a new blend here I would like you both to try and give me your opinion." Morloq proffered a little box lined in yellow satin, on which reposed two black-hued cigarettes.

"Oh-h-h, how exciting!" breathed Carolynne, flattered at being asked to give an opinion on one of Morloq's new blends.

"Now, you two girls just go in here where it is more comfortable," said Morloq, ushering them into the room containing the flasks of perfume, "and be seated in those easy chairs."

Carolynne half reclined in a large, cushioned chair. Morloq applied a light to her cigarette, pulled the venetian blinds closed, and said "I will be out in the other room if you want me. I must attend to my other customers too, you know."

Zelda was seated next to Carolynne, and just about to light her cigarette when she suddenly jumped up. "Say! I left my purse in the other room. I'll be back."

Carolynne, relaxed amidst the soft cushions of the easy chair, scarcely heard her. The smoke from the black cigarette was fragrant and soothing. She inhaled deeply. It tasted like jasmine smells, sweet, cloying, overpowering. She felt drained of strength, relaxed, somnolent. It was a pleasing sensation to exhale the smoke slowly from her mouth and—

Suddenly, she found herself standing in the center of the room. No, not standing, just *being* in the middle of the room. She had no sensation of bodily weight. Looking around, she perceived that Zelda has disappeared. She saw herself still half reclining in her chair, the cigarette burning itself out on a nearby ashtray. How could she be in two places at once? She looked down, and perceived her own body, white and spectral in the half-light—and something else. A thin, silver tenuous thread ran from her spectral body to the flesh-and-blood one in the chair. She should have felt horrified, and would have under normal conditions, but the effects of the cigarette made her feel giddy, irresponsible and gay. It was odd how light she felt. She took several skips and turns around the room, and the nebulous silver thread, light and pliable, adjusted itself to her every motion. Had she not seen this connecting filament, she would not even have been aware of it.

Strange how sensitive her eyes were to color. The slits of light between the venetian blinds gleamed like bands of silver. The carpet, which before had seemed merely a lovely oriental rug, now fairly glowed, *alive* with color. The figures in it seemed to dance and spin. The gold and silver and jewels of the scent bottles gleamed like liquid fire.

Carolynne began to hum a gay little tune, but ceased abruptly. The sound of her voice assumed the proportions of a hundred wailing sirens. A fly buzzing at the window pane sounded like the drone of an airplane at close range.

Undaunted by the unusual behavior of her senses, Carolynne decided to investigate the perfume bottles on the shelf. If sight and hearing were so tremendously affected, her sense of smell would probably be also. She leapt lightly onto another chair, to enable her to explore the topmost shelf, but to her amazement found she had no need of the chair as a support. She could float in mid-air! This was jolly! A little chuckle of joy welled up in her throat, but she refrained from laughing lest she be overheard. She floated lightly over the shelves, lined with row of oddly shaped bottles and flasks. Nothing there now. Surely her eyes, so keenly sensitive now to the least bit of light and color, could perceive it if there was.

Suddenly, she heard a steady beat of drums coming from outside the room. No—not drums, footsteps! Horrified, she floated down to the floor, the unstoppered cloisonné bottle clutched in her hand. She set it on the table and faced Morloq and Zelda as they entered. Perhaps they couldn't see the real Carolynne, perhaps they would see only her body in the chair. One glance at their eyes told Carolynne that this was not so, however. They were both staring at *her*, at her spectral body, and at the tell-tale cloisonné bottle on the table!

"So!" Morloq whispered, and though he whispered his voice was like thunder in her ears. "Caught with the evidence of your guilt! I missed the . . . ah . . . contents of that flask shortly after you left last time, and I knew that there was only one way the contents could have escaped. You alone were responsible for that, and I must demand reimbursement."

Carolynne tried to speak, to call to Zelda for help, to assure Morloq that she would be glad to pay for any damage done, but she was powerless to utter a sound. It was only then that Carolynne noticed that Morloq and Zelda both carried in their hands intricately plumed fans.

Zelda moved to one side of her, and Morloq to the other, and began to wave the fans in her direction. Her spectral body, smoke-like, was influenced and stirred to and fro with the air currents produced. She tried to escape, but she could not. She was helpless, wafted to and fro, to and fro, by their gentle plumed fans.

"How easily you could have avoided all this had you not been so curious," Morloq continued to whisper. "Zelda, my accomplice, lured you here for a purpose the other day. It was for this reason she left you in here alone for awhile, presumably to order more cigarettes, but actually to have a private discussion with me. But you had to be curious and open the white cloisonné bottle after I had asked you not to. Ordinarily, I would not have considered you as a . . . a . . . prospect. True, you are bad—dishonest and completely conscienceless, but you are too flighty and frivolous. You have not enough depth and character. But now I *must* accept you. You must pay for the contents of that bottle."

Carolynne tried to answer, to tell him she would pay anything, that she didn't think that there was anything in the bottle—unless he meant the milky-white vapor she thought she had seen while under the influence of the liqueur.

Morloq hissed fiercely as he gently plied his fan back and forth. "Haven't you guessed the truth yet, little fool? My black cigarettes contain magical properties. When you exhaled the smoke through your lungs, those properties also caused your 'ka,' or astral body, your soul, to issue from your body. You released a soul beyond any power to recapture when you opened the cloisonné bottle! Og Amankh, 'Imprisoner of Souls,' demands recompense. I am his high priest. All over the world I travel, gathering souls for Him." Morloq's emerald eyes glowed with fanatical fire.

"I must furnish Him with another soul in place of the one that has escaped. Quickly, Zelda! Waft her over toward the table."

Carolynne tried to fight against the current of air, but she could not.

"Good solid souls are few and far between nowadays," Morloq continued. "Yours cannot compare with the one that you liberated, but it will have to do."

Morloq deftly severed with a silver knife the tenuous filament connecting Carolynne with her physical body, made several motions with his fan, and Carolynne felt herself slowly being forced into the narrow mouth of the perfume flask.

The next day, the college students were appropriately shocked by the news that Carolynne Devereaux had been found wandering downtown, completely devoid of intelligence. There seemed to be no hope for her recovery. Zelda Troyer had ridden into town with her, but left her company soon after and could shed no light on Carolynne's activities prior to her loss of mind.

Carolynne's family was heard to remark that they couldn't understand it. Carolynne was such an intelligent, good, conscientious girl. Why, she didn't even *smoke!*

The
BROWN Moccasin

by David Baxter

*Snake's alive! I thought this was about a brown shoe 'til I read it
and discovered, as you will, it concerns a sinister serpent!—FJA
Weird Tales, February 1925*

Between banks heavily draped with long, flat slough-grass and overshadowed
by lambent-leafed cottonwoods, the greenish waters of the slow-moving creek
seemed utterly devoid of life. The Kansas sun poured a flare of somnolent
heat directly upon the flaccid bosom of the lazy stream, intensifying the shadows
behind the fringes of dry grass and making of them the only cool, damp retreat in
the whole region. There was no wind; and scarcely a ripple where the tips of the
rank, overhanging growth cut the water with an almost inaudible gurgle.

Close above the water, and close-led by his sharp-lined shadow, hovered a
silent snake doctor intently studying the sluggish current in search of any infinitesimal morsel of food that might be drifting there. His bright-blue, black-banded wings
of delicate gauze threw him into sharp contract with the rest of the drab picture.

But in the black shadows along the soggy banks, and below the murky glaze on
the surface of the water, life teemed in its mysteries and its myriad forms, giving the
lie to outward appearance.

A repulsively incongruous alligator turtle, of impregnable size and armoring,
watched with evil intent the slow but gradual approach of a school of brilliant-hued
sunfish. King of the creek was he, with his spiked coat and horn-crested helmet. He
feared no denizen of his world, and but for his massive clumsiness he would soon
have cleared it of all life but his kind, for nature had created him almost invulnerable
but had also placed restraint upon his voraciousness.

In a world where one life exists by preying upon another, this paradox must
ever be true: each inhabitant must have some protection to prevent entire extinc-
tion, and each must have some special dispensation by which he may subsist through
breaking down the protective barriers of the others.

However, beneath the edge of a tangle of drift, in the deepest part of the
torpid stream, yet another pair of glassy eyes watched with cannibalistic intentions;

117

watched for an opportunity to prey upon some weaker member of his watery do-main; watched for a lowering of the barriers; a big catfish, with bristling whiskers and slowly gaping mouth, seeming fairly a part of the snarl of roots and twigs in which he was ambushed. The sharp spines on either side of his massive head were ready for instant defense, or for slaughter, if his needs pressed him to attack the larger specimens of the water tribes. With his white belly buried in the slime and his black back blending with surrounding shadows, the marauder felt secure in his hid-ing place.

If further proof were needed to refute the appearance of lifelessness in the stagnant creek, it could be found beneath a flat ledge protruding from, and lying close to, the muddy floor of the stream. Here a mother crawfish was incessantly on guard over her large family of ever-hungry youngsters; guarding but always watch-ing for the opportunity to dash out and seize an unsuspecting minnow to throw it into the midst of the squirming multitude of claws. Her protruding eyes saw every-thing that happened in the neighborhood. Her powerful pincers were ever alert to protect her brood, or to nip the life out of an unwary prey as food for them. But in spite of her formidable armament of claws and crusty shell, in spite of her ability to scuttle backward through the water like a flash of living red light, she dared not sally forth in search of a victim while the monster "snapper" remained in the vicinity.

A slight but startling sudden splash broke the stillness of the scene.

A long, lithe body had dived from a low-hanging limb of the stunted cotton-wood tree that struggled to retain a root-hold on the steep bank. The sound was barely audible, but all of the denizens of the creek knew its portent and sought to snuggle closer in their respective dens. Even the powerful alligator turtle folded his tail and legs a big closer beneath his parasite-laden shell and drew his horrid snout back until he could scarcely see what was taking place in the dim light about him.

There was but a momentary disturbance of the surface as the brown water moccasin slipped into the water, and no waves or ripples indicated her passage along the sandy bottom near the center of the creeping current.

The swimmer was a full-grown, female water snake of the common brown type, harmless as to venom but very powerful and extremely vicious when attacked. Doubly feared by the creatures of her world because she could take to the earth, trees, or water with equal facility, bred of the water and reared of the earth as she was, and now fearfully respected by the whole animal kingdom, her younger days had been spent in a continual fight for existence.

At the age of three years and full-grown she was now a careless swimmer making her way gracefully upstream unmolested. Scarcely visible from the surface, washed clean of the dried mud with which she had disguised herself while lying on the mud-gray limb of the cottonwood, she presented a strikingly beautiful appear-ance.

After swimming several rods, she came to the silky surface for a breath of air and a survey of the surroundings; the latter for the purpose of making certain there were no lurking dangers on either bank of the creek or in the trees above it. She had learned in her younger days to be forever on guard against hidden foes, in the water, in the air, or on land. She paused to float idly a moment while trying to locate a possible source of food for which a litter of forty squirming youngsters were constantly clamoring. It frequently happened that she could obtain this food without the hours of patient waiting for a frog or fish to pass her perch on a projecting limb or log.

Momentarily, the brown-banded moccasin floated with the imperceptible current; then, with a powerful flirt of glistening tail, she proceeded more swiftly upstream, on her way to the nest of husky young ones she had already left overlong. Many of them were nearly large enough to stray off in their first adventure with the world and might leave any time now if she stayed away too long. The rest were mere waxy morsels for some of the land tribes, among which were clans of her own kin, the bull snakes and black racers.

These young moccasins were a brood of which any snake mother might be proud, strikingly marked with jet black cross-bands on a pale gray background along the body and a black spotted abdomen of dull grayish hue. When left alone they formed into one writhing knot of reptiles, as they had been taught, both for the sake of safety through intimidation and for the companionship afforded to bodily contact. The little fellows would take on the pattern and coloring of the parent later on, but now they scarcely resembled her.

Slipping through the smooth water, throwing slow, miniature rollers on each side of her course, the big female moccasin presented a picture both fearsome and inspiring. Her reddish brown body, crossed by wavy, dark brown bands on the forward portion, alternating with much broader bands of black, caused her to appear almost solid brown, in contrast with the green water. Crossed by narrow lines of yellow, the black bands glistened in the sun, fascinatingly sinuous. A narrowing of the bands on her sides, where they were separated by broad interstices of ground-color resembling an upright triangle, gave her a weird effect. On the rear portion of her body the bands broke into blotches in a series down her back, alternating with another down each side. And as the snake moved in sweeping waves through the water, her abdomen was exposed, anon, in brilliant, iridescent red and black spots.

Slipping over the surface of the creek, the female water snake held her head high out of the water as if to better her attempt to pierce the gloom beneath the cascade of dry grass; ready at the slightest alarm to dive below; ready to shoot like a sunbeam at an unsuspecting toad, should one present himself along the way.

In spite of her beautiful colors, the furtive, glittering eyes, tiny sparks of burning metal, gave the serpent a sinister aspect which threw fear into the hearts of the amphibious inhabitants and caused them to cringe further back in their dens as she passed; they knew from past experience that the brown-banded moccasin was possessed of lightning speed and a savage temper, backed by a furious fighting strength. Her somber dress, when dry or coated with mud to deceive them, inspired fear and hatred in the hearts of all the amphibious and terrestrial tribes in that region.

Her remarkable ability to flatten her head and half of her body into a thin, broad ribbon of living flesh and bone struck the frogs, toads, mice, birds and other semi-terrestrial creatures with a palsying panic of dread, chilling the courage of some who were redoubtable fighters. If anything were lacking in their fright, the big moccasin had only to emit one of her shrill hisses, like the sound of high-pressure steam.

Perhaps a hundred feet upstream, the brown moccasin suddenly shot like a flash of red light, as straight as an arrow propelled by a powerful bow, across the creek, through the shallow, beneath the grass drapery and up on the narrow mud-flat at the foot of the crumbling bank, carrying in her distended jaws the dripping, flopping body of a large sun perch. Here was food for her and food for the youngsters, aplenty!

With the still quivering fish tightly gripped in her needle fangs, the serpent crawled awkwardly over the mud-flat and up through the grassroots to where the babies were hidden, to the nest wherein she had left her family two hours ago.

But all was not well at home; even before she attained the sandy retreat, the brown moccasin sensed something wrong and wriggled desperately through the tangled undergrowth, still holding the partly swallowed perch. The sibilant rustling of her tail as it switched the dead leaves spread a tense, ominous atmosphere through the surrounding jungle. A huge beetle ceased his labors; with staring eyes a gray field mouse scampered hastily away; a speeding kingfisher sent down a raucous note of derision; the dazzling blue dragonfly skimmed the tops of the grass and weeds on soundless wings, but evidently watchful.

In the stiff sand adjoining the snake nest were innumerable footprints that told the story only too well; they said as plainly as if they had spoken that a large blue heron had feasted there, carefully picking and choosing according to his fancy.

At least half of the baby moccasins were gone completely; not more than a score remained, crawling aimlessly around the little hollow that had been their home. These seemed distraught and knew not which way to turn. The mother took in the situation at a glance, for this was not the first time that such a thing had happened to her household.

Without more ado she gulped furiously at the partially engulfed sunfish until the last of it had passed in a swollen lump though the narrows of her neck. No thought of feeding the family now, only to get away with them to some other locality as quickly as possible. As soon as the task was finished, the anxious mother set about swallowing the young moccasins, one at a time in rapid succession; in fact, so great was their anxiety to reach a place of safety that the little fellows couldn't wait their turns but crawled, two and three at a time, down the constricting throat of their mother. This had always been their custom when terrible danger hovered near, or when the parent had decided it was moving day.

When the last youngster was stowed away, the female moccasin, heavy with babies, slipped through the grass and literally fell down the eroded bank behind the dense fringe of slough-grass. Without pausing, she threw herself out into the open waters of the sun-scorched creek, where she turned her head down stream. She swam slowly, ungracefully, with never a backward glance to the scene of her multiple tragedy. Nor did her undulating sides present the attractive picture they had when she arrived. The life-filled pouch stretched the beautiful designs of her banded brown coat into grotesque, irregular shapes and almost colorless splotches.

For a mile, the laden snake swam and floated, drifted and swam, by jutting sand-bars, around low bends past other sections of grass-fringed banks. And here the same deference was granted her by the inhabitants of the region; they moved aside and permitted her to pass unquestioned, content merely to stare stolid-eyed after her.

As she floated, the brown moccasin kept her eyes roving from bank to bank in search of a place that suited her. At last she turned in at the foot of a long slope parallel to the stream and leading to a high bank overlooking the water. With much difficulty she managed to climb out upon the muddy ledge, and laboriously she made her way up the long slope.

Below lay a deep, circular pool of midnight blackness in the shade of a huge weeping-willow. High above, a startled jay screamed sarcastically. To the back, a careful rustling in the rank growth of willow sprouts indicated that some creature was cautiously withdrawing from the neighborhood. Here the tired mother snake would be fairly safe; from here she could make an instant, long dive to the depths of the pool if it became necessary to flee from terrestrial attack; and far enough from the water to be safe from amphibious enemies. Here she could disgorge her young and clean them with sundry wipings and coiling embraces.

But before the disgorging process was well under way the brown moccasin reared her flattening head in hissing anger. A peculiar, nauseating scent had been wafted to her, faint and indefinite as to source and proximity. She could not tell yet whether to fight or to flee. To be on the safe side she merely waited in silence, prepared for either event. The emanator of the odor was either a deadly enemy or food.

Soon a vigorous stirring in the dead vegetation above and beyond her caused the brown moccasin to whirl quickly in that direction.

Out of the grass and leaves squirmed a waddling, sleek, slimy creature all mottled with bright yellow spots on a satiny hide. His frog-like snout and round eyes in-

stantly branded him harmless to the tautening snake; in fact a certain air of helpless-
ness enveloped him. His stubby fingers, destitute of claw or talon, marked him an
easy victim to a determined enemy.

He ambled forth stupidly. Cocking his bright, innocent eyes first to one side,
then to the other, he approached the slowly-coiling serpent good-naturedly and with
an apparent desire to be friendly.

The brown moccasin lowered her head, while a simulated guilelessness seemed
to envelope her. She lay perfectly quiet and watched the simple-minded intruder
approach. Such an ignorant fellow! Such trusting simplicity! Why should she fear
him?

As he approached, a sinister tautening of her muscular body should have
warned him of impending danger. But the mud puppy was so trustful and innocent; he meant harm to no one and therefore thought that no one meant harm
to him.

With all of his innocence, the size and shape of the salamander denoted his
age as being past the inexperienced stage; it had been two years since he had ceased
to live entirely in the water and had taken to blundering around in the damp, soggy
places of the earth, eating nothing more exciting than flies, beetles, moths and other
small insects. His experience with danger had been manifold and he should have
known better than to waddle deliberately into this deadly peril, with his eyes open, as
it were.

Like the common toad, the *salamandria urodela* is as harmless as he is ugly. His
only method of defense is floundering. Having no teeth or fangs, he takes his food
with a long, glutinous tongue which he ejects from his mouth with incredible swiftness to engulf the insect victim. It seems these could avail him not in a life and death
struggle with a powerful serpent.

The brown moccasin merely waited for the salamander to approach within
easy striking distance, no glint of mercy in her hypnotic stare or flickering black
tongue.

The afternoon shadows were growing longer, and a bright blue snake doctor
circled above the twain like an omen, a silent witness to the coming tragedy.

The open jaws of the savage snake shot out and closed over the mud puppy's
head before he realized the significance of the vibrant hiss that accompanied the
action. A moment he lay in passive surprise, apparently acceding to the sucking
contortions of the snake.

But the salamander was not such an easy victim after all. His thick forelegs
spread wide apart in stubborn resistance to the sucking jerks of the self-enraged
reptile. All her efforts seemed useless in swallowing him farther than his braced
shoulders. Nor was the serpent, with all her sinuous strategy, able to force those
strong legs back along the spotted body far enough to make swallowing easy.

In fact, the puppy would, at times, momentarily succeed in almost tearing himself loose from the slimy cavern engulfing him; by hooking his stout toes in the corners of the snake's mouth and then lunging mightily he would nearly escape, only to lose his hold and feel the savage gulps sucking him inward again.

Unable to see, and lacerated with intense pain, the yellow-spotted creature battled nobly for his life, in utter silence save for the threshing of dry grass and dead leaves.

And so the battle raged for an hour or more, stirring up a miniature cyclone of leaves, grass and mud. It could have been likened unto a mad fight between mighty jungle beasts, where trees, shrubbery and rank jungle-grass are torn up by the roots or trodden under foot. For yards along the creek bank the two desperate creatures matted the ground vegetation. Sometimes the salamander would drag the snake. Then the snake would drag the salamander back a yard or so with vicious, jerky writhings, only to find her strength spent and feel that she was in turn being yanked and tugged in the opposite direction; with his four stuffy feet braced and his powerful tail hooked around the grass roots, the pain-maddened and fear-maddened puppy would slash the serpent along an inch at a time, meanwhile unintentionally permitting her to recuperate her waning strength.

The brown moccasin sickened of the thing. She endeavored to disgorge the threshing incubus that was overwhelming her; perhaps the squirming protests within warned her to desist. She was more than willing to comply, but, too late, she found herself unable to extricate her needle fangs from the tough skin and bone of the puppy's neck. Desperately she retched and pried. Savagely she wrenched and twisted. Desperately she flopped. But all to no avail: the serpent was securely snared in her own trap.

Then, with a last terrific backward lunge, the now thoroughly terrified water snake tore the salamander loose from his desperate foothold and threw him with herself far out over the stagnant pool at the foot of the embankment. Over and over they fell, to light with a threshing splash in the shaded waters, where their writhings notified the scavengers of the stream that a feast would soon be waiting.

With uncanny instinct the great, armored alligator turtle was already standing by, with hooked jaws agape and ready to obey the unwritten mandates of talion. A score of brilliant dragonflies swiftly circled the pool as if distraught, and an army of bead-eyed crawfish rapidly marshaled their forces.

Clusters of silver-laced bubbles leaped to the surface of the darkening water. Then the water assumed again its placid serenity.

It is said that no note of comedy ever leavens the events of wild life. But whether this is true or not, a very fat opossum, who had watched the ill-fated battle, curled his bewhiskered lips back in an unmistakably broad grin when he saw an extremely exhausted little salamander drag himself wearily out of the water and sink with drooping eyes upon the point of a sand-bar. Around his neck, like a ruffled collar, he wore the mutilated jaws of the brown moccasin. And the opossum knew that the armored alligator turtle had obeyed one of nature's immutable laws.

The
PURPLE Cincture

by H. Thompson Rich

When the deep purple falls, over creepy garden walls . . . —FJA
Weird Tales, August 1925

It was a day in midsummer, I remember. I had been tramping over the densely wooded and desolate hillside the greater part of the morning, getting with each mile farther and farther from the tawdry haunts of man and nearer and nearer the rugged heart of nature.

Finally (it must have been after noon-time) I paused and made a light lunch of the sandwiches and cold coffee I had brought with me from town, sitting on the edge of a great slab of granite rock, swept clean and smooth by ages of winds and rains and snows.

All about me was a veritable garden of great projecting rocks, jagged and broken, flat and polished, needle-like, giant flowers of earth in a thousand different forms.

Here and there a short, dwarfed pine or spruce tree struggled for a footing amid its rocky friends, and the resistless undergrowth surged up through every crack and crevice, while energetic mosses and lichens clutched at the granite walls and crept bravely up. One had a feeling of awe, as if in the presence of elemental, eternal forces. Here, I thought, if anywhere, one might commune with the voiceless void.

Suddenly my eyes chanced to fall upon a fissure in the rock to the left, and I sprang up with a low exclamation. What I had beheld was to all appearance a human skeleton!

Advancing reluctantly, yet with that insistent inquisitiveness which surrounds the dead, I bent, and peered into the fissure. As I looked, a cry escaped me. The object I beheld was indeed a skeleton—but what a skeleton! The head, the left hand, and the foot were entirely missing, nor was there any sign of them at first sight.

Thoroughly fascinated by the morbid spectacle, I began a search for the missing members, and was finally rewarded by unearthing the head some twenty feet away, where it lay half buried in the soft loam of decayed vegetation and sifted chole. But a painstaking and minute hunt failed to reveal the missing hand and foot.

I was successful, however, in finding something immeasurably more important—a manuscript. This I found by the side of the mangled skeleton.

It consisted of several pages of closely written material, in a small pocket notebook, which fact, in connection with the partial shelter afforded by the crevice where the body lay, doubtless accounts for its preservation through the years that have passed since its owner met his hideous fate.

Picking up the notebook with nervous fingers, I opened it and turned the damp and musty pages through, reading it at first hastily, then slower and more carefully, then with a feverish concentration—as the awful significance of the words was riveted into my brain.

The writing was in a man's cramped agitated hand, and I give it to you just as I read it, with the exception of the names and places, and a few paragraphs of vital scientific data—all but a few words at the very beginning and end, where the manuscript had been molded into illegibility by the gradual action of the weather. Here follows:

"——as strange. I had a sense of apprehension from the start, a vague, indescribable feeling of doubt, of dread, as if someone, something, were urging me out, away, into these sullen hills.

"I might have known. The law of retribution is as positive as the law of gravity. I know that now. Oh irony!

"But I was so sure. No one knew. No one could know. She, my wife, heart of all, until the end. And the neighbors, her friends, never. She had merely pined away. No one dreamed I had poisoned her. Even when she died, there was no thought of autopsy. She had long been failing. And had I not been most concerned? None in the little town of ——, but who sympathized with me. And I mourned. Oh, I mourned! So it was that she paid the price of her infamy. Ah, but revenge never was sweeter!

"And he? Oh, but I despised him—even as I had formerly admired him, even as I had once loved my wife—so I despised him. And despising him, I killed him—killed him, but with a poison far more subtle than that I had used to destroy my wife—killed him with a poison in effect so hideous, so harrowing, that I can scarcely think of it without sickening even as I write.

"The poison I inculcated into his veins was a germ poison—a disease I, a physician of no small repute, had discovered and bred—a disease I had found existed only in a particular and very rare species of virulent purple and orange-banded spider—the genus—— [Here follow in the original manuscript seven paragraphs of elaborate scientific data, of no particular interest to the average reader, but of incalculable import to the scientific world. These paragraphs I have omitted from this account for very significant reasons, but I hold them open to scientific examination at any time, and as I have said before, I will

welcome investigation by reputable scientists]—a disease which was responsible for the extreme rarity of this particular species.

"By careful investigation I was able to learn the exact manifestation and workings of the disease—which by their frightful ravages upon the system of the unfortunate victim fairly appalled me.

"By segregating and breeding diseased members of this particular species of
spider, I was able to produce the disease in the young in its most virulent form. You
can well imagine the care I used in handling these spiders, to prevent infection.
Briefly, the symptoms were as follows: The spider about to be stricken apparently
first experiences a peculiar numbness of the first left foreleg, to judge from its inability to use or move the affected member. A day or so later the leg, which in a
healthy condition is a dull brown, turns a pale, sickening shade of yellow, which
deepens rapidly until it has taken on a flaming orange hue. Then, in a few hours, a
deep, vicious-looking blue cincture, or band, appears just at the first joint of the
affected member. This cincture rapidly deepens to purple, which seems somehow to
sear its way into the flesh and through the bone, so that in a surprisingly short time
the whole leg is severed at the joint where the cincture has been.

"The spider then appears to regain its normal condition of health, which it
maintains for about a week; then once again the hideous disease manifests itself, this
time in the left feeler, or antenna, which in turn becomes yellow, then orange, where-
upon the same blue cincture appears and deepens to purple; then, in about the same
period of time as in the case of the leg, the antenna drops off, seared as if by hellish
flame.

"Once again the spider appears to regain its health; then in about a week the
whole *head* of the stricken insect turns slowly yellow, then orange; then the cincture
appears—and as a last manifestation, the head is seared off in flaming agony—and
the spider dies in horrible convulsions.

"That, briefly, is the process—as I was able to note after weeks and months of
tireless research and observation.

"So what more perfect punishment for the man who stole from me my wife,
while pretending to be my friend?

"Loving her as I did, I had not the heart to kill her in this hideous way; so I put
her to death with a painless and insidious poison.

"But for —— I had no mercy. In fact I gloated as I worked over my vile and
diseased spiders, breeding them together until I was convinced that I had the germs
of the disease in its most virulent form. Even then I was not sure what their effect
would be on a human being—but that much at least I must hazard.

"So having finally made all my preparations, I invited him to my house and
placed one of the diseased spiders upon his forehead one night as he slept.

"It must have bitten him, for he awoke with a cry, and I had barely time to close his door and get back to my room before I heard him rise and turn on the light.

"The he called me, and I came to him, burning with a fiendish satisfaction. 'Something has bitten me, horribly,' he said. 'I feel as if I were going to be ill.'

"I managed to reassure him by telling him that it was very likely nothing but one of our uncommonly large mosquitoes, and he returned to bed.

"But he did not sleep. All night I heard him moaning and tossing. And in the morning he was very pale.

"'I do not know what is the matter with me,' he said, and I thought he looked at me queerly, 'but I feel as if a little rest would do me good. I feel choked. I think I will pack up my knapsack and go off to the hills for the weekend. Want to come?'

"I longed to go with him, to see the dread disease work, but I feared its deadly contagion, and was anxious to get him away before I myself became contaminated. So I said no—and he went.

"That was the last I ever saw of him—but once.

"He went away, as he had promised, and he seemed apparently well—all except the curious little inflamed spot on his forehead, whose significance I knew so well.

"He went away—and he failed to come back. Days passed, and there came no word from him. People began inquiring. It was odd that he should have left no address. His business suffered.

"Weeks went by—and no word. Search parties were sent out. The river was dragged. The morgues of near-by cities were searched. And all the while I laughed. For who would think of turning to those far-off hills?

"And yet, as the days went by, I found myself turning to them again—wondering, wondering, wondering. I grew nervous, agitated. I got so I couldn't sleep.

"Finally, on a day in late summer (it was the 8th of August—a date I shall never forget!) I packed a few things and set off. In search of him? God knows. I tried to tell myself not—but at any rate I found myself strangely, magnetically drawn to those distant somber hills—and thither I went.

"It was one of those gorgeous mornings that only August can produce. And the exhilarating air would have lifted my spirits, but instead I walked along depressed, and the knapsack strapped to my shoulder served only to intensify the feeling.

"In spite of all I could do, I found my mind reverting to the hideous revenge I had wreaked on my wife and her lover, and for the first time repentance stole in upon me.

"I walked along slowly, and it was well toward noon before I left the beaten road and started at random off over the hills, following a narrow and little-used path.

"Progress now became doubly slow and painful, leading often up steep inclines and hard descents, with the aspect momentarily becoming more and more rugged, as I left the lower hills and climbed toward the mountain.

"By this time, however, I had got a kind of exhilaration sought in vain during the earlier hours of the morning, and climbed on and on, glad to free body and mind thus of the poison of brooding and lassitude. I would return to the town at night and take supper at one of the small inns that abounded thereabouts. This would give me back some hours yet before I turned back. For the time being, the thought of searching for ———— was forgotten. I had freed my mind of him entirely.

"Presently the path I had been following branched, and the right half narrowed into an all but obliterated trail, leading up a laborious slope. Forcing my way over dry, snapping underbrush and under low-hanging spruce boughs, occasionally startling an indignant partridge from its hidden nest, often put to a wide detour to avoid some hazardous gully cut deep by centuries of spring and autumn freshets, I at last emerged upon a small, circular clearing, evidently the work of some lone woodchopper.

"Here I sat down, tired by the climb, and refreshed myself with a sandwich from my knapsack. Then I pushed on to the summit, pausing frequently to examine some uncommon species of insect life with which the hills abounded.

"So much was I enjoying myself and such scant notice of time did I take, that sunset came upon me unawares and I found myself, with darkness settling in on all sides with a startling rapidity, still on the summit of the mountain, with a good three-mile descent before me. Indeed, the prospect was not altogether a cheering one and I reproached myself for my heedlessness. But I had found a species of spider for which I had searched for months; so, somewhat reassured by its precious body in a pill-box in my pocket, I started down.

"In spite of my best speed, however, night shut in on me before I had made one quarter of the return, leaving me to grope the rest of the way in utter darkness, with not even the light of a dim star to go by. Vague fear awoke within me, but I shielded my eyes and stumbled to the bottom, sliding, falling, clutching here and there at some projecting tree-limb to check my headlong descent. Finally, torn and disheveled and shaking, I emerged upon the clearing. Pausing only for breath, I plunged on into the dark. Fear was growing—growing—that peculiar fear of the dark which is the heritage of those who have taken human life.

"What was that? Something lay gleaming queerly ahead, with a dull phosphorescent glow. I stooped and picked it up—and flung it from me shuddering. It was the skeleton of a human foot!

"I groped on, my every heartbeat choking at my throat. All of a sudden I came forcefully against a barrier of rock. I tried to feel my way around it, to get beyond it, but could not. It seemed continuous, a solid wall that would not let me by. Had I fallen into a trap in the darkness? Terrified, I turned—and there lay something else gleaming with that same weird phosphorescent glow! Sick with terror and dread, half fearing what it might be, I sprang on it and picked it up—*picked it up*—the rotting hand of a human being! With a stifled gasp I flung it from me, reeled, tripped though some vines and fell swooning.

"When I came to myself, I struck a match and looked about me. Its feeble flame revealed a pair of damp, rocky walls, low and vaulted. I was in some sort of cavern.

"Later on I crept out, collected an armful of sticks, brought them back, and soon had a fire started. By its light I observed that the rear of the cave was still in darkness, and judging that it must extend back indefinitely, I gave my attention to my immediate surroundings—when with a shock I saw, directly in front of me, a granite slab. On it lay several loose sheets of manuscript, scrawled wildly on odd scraps of paper.

"With a prophetic dread I bent forward and gathered the loose sheets together. Holding them near the fire, I peered closer. Then I think a cry must have escaped me. The writing was in ——'s hand, curiously scrawled and scraggy, but still recognizable.

"So fate had brought me to my victim!

"For the rest, there is little more to say. I am doomed as I deserve, even as he was doomed. His words speak all that can be spoken. They follow:

April 4th—*I had meant to spend only the week-end in these hills, yet here I am, after two weeks—still here, and suffering the pains of hell. What has come over me I cannot imagine. And yet—can I not? I am not so sure? Perhaps—perhaps —— has in some devilish way managed to poison me. He is insanely jealous. He thinks there was something between his wife and me. Verily I believe he harassed her to death on the subject. And, having thus brought her to her grave, he wishes to send me there.*

Perhaps he will succeed—if it is true, that in some fiendish way he has got some of his germs into my blood. That bite, at his house that evening. I am not so sure. It was a most unusual bite. It seemed upon the instant to sour all my blood.

And yet, if he accomplishes my death, how vain it will be—for as God is my witness I swear I never harmed his wife. We were the best of friends, nothing more. And she loved him with a wholeness, a passion that any but a man maddened by groundless jealousy must at once have seen.

How he has wrecked his life! A mind so brilliant—and yet, with her dead, a closed room.

However, I may be wrong. I will wait. By the symptoms I will know. I write this down, for I must do something.

April 5th—*It is he now, his hellish work. I am sure of it. Today my left leg, which for two weeks has felt positively numb, turned a sickening yellow, from the ankle down, which began at once to deepen, until it now flames orange! And oh! the pain is hellish! Yes, I am sure it is ——'s work. But I will still withhold judgment.*

April 6th—Today a deep, virulent blue cincture has appeared just at the ankle of the affected leg. What a hellish contrast to the orange!

It is ——. I am sure now. Oh, what a fiend!

April 7th—The cincture has deepened to purple, and seems to cut into the very flesh. It seems sometimes as if the pain would drive me mad.

April 8th—My flaming foot dropped off tonight, seared at the ankle by the purple cincture, and I flung it outside the cave. I wonder. Perhaps I may yet live to return to the world. Ah, I will be avenged for this!

May 23rd—I am cursed, cursed! Today, just as I was beginning to believe the hellish thing had left me, it returned, this time in my left hand. Oh, I can see it all: tomorrow and the next day and the next, for just two weeks, my hand will be numb; then will come that frightful yellow; then the orange; then—then the purple cincture!

Curse the man who discovered this hellish disease—and turned it into me! I could tear him limb from limb. Oh, I pray to return. I would go now, yet I fear my malady is of a vilely contagious nature. I have not the heart to menace a whole community, perhaps a whole nation, perhaps humanity itself—merely to avenge myself on one man.

June 6th—I was right! This morning I awoke with my hand that death yellow. Oh, it is too regular, too certain—too cruelly certain!

June 9th—Thank God! My hand is gone—out there where my foot went. It happened tonight. Perhaps I may yet return! Perhaps I may yet be avenged. I wonder.

July 21st—Doomed! That fearful numbness again—this time in my head. I cannot think— I cannot write—I can scarcely breathe. Oh, the pain—the pain ——

"Here it ended in a sputter of ink. Trembling in every limb, filled with a horror and anguish and remorse no man can know, spellbound by the awful tale those few sheets told, I sat there motionless.

"So I had been wrong. Oh, my jealousy, my insane jealousy! As I sat there, all desire of life suddenly left me, and I thrilled with joy at the remembrance of the hand and foot I had come upon, outside the cave. They were his. I had touched them. I was contaminated with the dread disease.

"What was that? I listened, straining every nerve. From the back of the cave had come a sound.

"Five minutes passed—ten—fifteen (I was oblivious of time)—but it was not repeated. Slightly I relaxed my aching nerves and tried to think. Already I fancied I could feel the fearful poison of the diseased spider working in my veins.

"Suddenly the significance of that last entry in ——'s diary burst upon me, and I sat shivering as under a sudden deluge of icy water. *'July 21st.'* Two weeks more would make it *August 5th,* and three days more would bring it to—*August 8th!*

" 'Great God!' I cried aloud, 'tonight is the night!'

" *'Yes, tonight is the night!'* echoed a sepulchral voice from the cavern's inner darkness.

"In an agony of dread I looked, and the blood within me paled to water at the sight that met my gaze. Something—*something with but a single hand and foot*—emerged from the shadows of the back of the cavern and began to come forward, leaning heavily upon a rough staff for support.

" 'Stay back—*stay back!* For the love of God!' I shrieked. But the terrible thing came on and on, and the awful eyes fastened themselves upon my person and suddenly recognized me—and it smiled a hideous smile.

"When it drew nearer, I could see that all above the shoulders flamed orange, while around the neck a livid purple cincture seemed actually to be searing its way into the flesh.

" 'This is your revenge,' it spoke. 'And this is mine,' raising the hellish stump of its mutilated left arm and panting heavily at me: 'My suffering is over—but yours is all to come. And to the bodily pains of hell will be added the mental tortures of hopeless remorse—knowing your wife was innocent. With that I curse you.'

"Even as it spoke, the eyes rolled out of sight behind horrible lids, the tongue protruded itself in flaming agony, and the whole head, suddenly severed at the neck, thudded on the cavern floor.

"I came to my feet with a mad cry, that, shattering the silence beyond the deepest shadows, swelled up in a thousand echoes, from the wail of a soul in torment to the screech of a crucified demon. Then I rushed headlong out.

"For the rest ——"

The last page was illegible, as the first had been, worn and corroded by the slow action of years of decay.

I put the notebook slowly in my pocket and sat there thinking, sickened and awed by the astounding manuscript.

Again I went over to the skeleton there in the fissure. Now I understood why the hand and foot were missing, and why I had found the head many feet from the body.

There it lay, mute evidence that the retribution was complete.

The VIOLET Death

by Gustav Meyrink

Gustav Meyrink introduced us to the "man of clay"
in his popular novel "The Golem".—FJA
Weird Tales, July 1935

A day or two before Pompejus Jaburek died in the hospital in Lucknow, he called the head nurse, entrusted to her a bulky envelope which he had been keeping under his pillow, and urged her, after his death, to see that its contents were given as wide publicity as possible. She might turn it over to the Government, to the press—she would know better than he how it could be made widely known. He had no doubt that the information contained in it was profoundly important—at least it was extremely strange and curious—and the only reason why he had not told his whole story when he had first got back to civilization and safety was that he was afraid of being tempted to betray a secret which might do the world incalculable harm. Well—she would understand what he meant when she had read his story, and after all, the delay was not important, since he was growing so much weaker that he knew he could not live a great deal longer. And when he died, carrying the secret with him, the danger would be over, at least the danger of any harm for which he should be responsible, and only the strange and perhaps valuable information would remain.

Pompejus Jaburek was a nondescript southeast European who had been a servant of the British explorer Sir Roger Thornton. The most remarkable thing about him was that he was as deaf as a post—he had told the nurse once that he had gone stone-deaf as a child and had never heard a sound since—but that he was so expert at lip-reading that in a good light he could talk to you for hours, so easily and intelligently that you would have had no suspicion of his deafness if it had not been for the careful, singsong tone that all deaf persons acquire, like the extraordinary cautious step of a blind man. Aside from this, his English was perfect.

He had been brought to the hospital from somewhere off to the north, two or three months before, in a very dilapidated condition, with a bad wound in his foot, and apparently with his mind clean gone. He had recovered his faculties in time, and

133

had grown so much better that he was able to sit up in bed and write, industriously, for hours—hence the manuscript which he was bequeathing to the hospital—but although he talked intelligently and sometimes rather freely, his eyes glittered with terror when anything was said about his relations with Sir Roger, and he would cut the discussion short with a curt declaration that he was sure the English explorer would never be seen again. And since no one was sure that Pompejus Jaburek was entirely sane, no one pressed him for an explanation. He wasted away from what seemed to be the effects of a slow poison, and one morning did not awaken.

His manuscript, written in spite of great weakness and distress of mind, was almost impossible to decipher and was full of gaps and inconsistencies. But its drift was approximately as follows:

Somewhere up on the Tibetan frontier, Sir Roger Thornton had been visited by a Tibetan "Sannyasin" or penitential pilgrim, on his way to Benares. Sir Roger had a profound respect for the Sannyasin. He knew that they are pretty sure to be intelligent, and that they are filled with an earnestness that makes them entirely honest. He did not know why the Sannyasin told him the story of the strange Tibetan colony in the isolated valley, but he had seen and heard so many mysterious things in his contacts with this strange race that nothing he heard about them surprised him. He knew that they hate the Europeans and that they cherish magic secrets with which they hope some day to destroy them. But Sir Hannibal Roger Thornton was one of the bravest men who ever lived, and he determined at once to see with his own eyes whether this colony possessed the magical powers which the Sannyasin imputed to them.

Sir Roger had a group of Asiatic guides and servants with him, but he knew that they were superstitious and cowardly, and that they would be entirely useless on such an expedition as this. So he touched his deaf Balkan lieutenant with his stick, and he told him in detail all that he had learned from the Tibetan ascetic.

Some twenty days' journey from their camp, in a side valley of the Himavat, which had been so carefully described to him that he could go directly to it, it appeared that there was a very curious bit of territory. It was a tiny valley, and on three sides of it the mountains rose almost perpendicularly, so that there was no entrance or egress except from the fourth side, and the fourth side was very strangely cut off by gaseous exhalations which rose constantly from the spongy earth, and which were so deadly poisonous that any living being which tried to cross would be almost certain to be suffocated and never reach the other side. In the ravine itself, which was reported to be in dimensions perhaps half a dozen miles each way, lived a little tribe, in the midst of the most luxuriant vegetation, a tribe belonging to the Tibetan race, wearing a characteristic pointed red cap, and worshiping a Satanic being in the form of a peacock. This devilish being, in the course of the centuries, had taught the tribe a potent black magic, and had transmitted secrets to them which were capable, in time, of changing the face of the earth. Thus, they had perfected a kind of melody, which if properly executed would destroy the strongest man in an instant . . .

Pompejus grinned sarcastically.

Sir Roger explained to him that he had thought out a way of passing the poison-gas region with the help of diving-helmets and reservoirs of compressed air, and that he was sure there would be no serious difficulty about reaching the valley in this way. Pompejus Jaburek nodded approval, and rubbed his dirty hands together delightedly.

The Tibetan pilgrim had told the exact truth. The two Europeans reached a spot where the strange ravine was plainly visible, with its marvelous vegetation; and between it and them stretched a yellow-brown, desert-like girdle of loose, friable earth, not more than a mile wide, and cutting the marvelous valley completely off from the rest of the world.

The exhalations which rose incessantly from the girdle of desert were pure carbonic acid gas. Sir Roger Thornton climbed a little hill and studied the situation very carefully. Then he decided to cross the poisonous belt the next morning. The diving-outfits which he had ordered from Bombay worked perfectly.

Pompejus carried two repeating rifles and various other articles which his chief deemed necessary.

An intrepid Afghan adventurer who had first thought of accompanying the two had flatly refused to go along when he had learned that the black art was involved. He had remarked that he was perfectly willing to crawl into a tiger's den, but that he declined to embark on an enterprise which might imperil his immortal soul. So Sir Roger and Jaburek constituted the expeditionary force.

The copper helmets glittered in the sun. The poison gas crept out of the spongy soil in numberless tiny bubbles. Sir Roger had set out at a rapid, swinging gait, so that there would be no danger that the supply of air would be exhausted before the gas-zone was passed. The mountain-backed valley in front of the two floated and swayed before the eyes of the invaders like the bed of a moving brook. The sunlight had a ghostly green tinge and colored the distant glaciers—the "Roof of the World"— with its gigantic profile, like a wonderful landscape of death.

Sir Roger and Pompejus had passed the arid belt, had stepped out on the beautiful green turf, and with the help of a match or two had convinced themselves that good oxygen was present at every distance from the ground. Then the two removed their diving-outfits.

Behind them the wall of gas wavered like a strangely tenuous stream. The air was filled with a heady perfume, like the odor of amberia blossoms. Gleaming, party-colored butterflies as big as your hand, with markings these white men had never seen before, sat on the silent flowers with their wings spread wide, like open conjurers' books.

The two, several steps apart, moved toward the little wood which cut off their view of the main part of the valley ...

Sir Roger gave his deaf servant a sign—he was sure he had heard a noise. Pompejus lifted the trigger of his gun ...

They skirted the little forest, and came out on a broad meadow. A quarter of a mile from the wood, they saw perhaps a hundred men, evidently Tibetans, all topped with pointed red caps, and drawn up in a semicircle. They must have had wind of their visitors' coming, and they were ready to receive them. Sir Roger and his servant walked intrepidly, abreast of each other, but several feet apart, toward the waiting phalanx.

These Tibetans were dressed in the sheepskin coats which are the usual garb of the race; but as the Europeans came nearer to them they were startled by the unearthly ugliness of all the faces, which were naturally hideous and were moreover distorted by expressions of violent loathing, hatred and malice. They allowed the two to come very near them; then all at once, in perfect unison like one man, at a signal from their leader they all raised their hands and held them tight against their ears. Then they all shouted something at the top of their voices.

Pompejus Jaburek looked toward his master for instructions, and brought his gun into position, for the strange maneuver of the group seemed to presage some hostile intention. But what he saw as he glanced at Sir Roger drove every drop of blood from his heart.

About the Englishman a trembling, floating garment of gas had formed, like that which the two had traversed a short time before. Sir Roger's form began to lose its contours, as if it had been attacked by the gas and were disintegrating under its influence. The head seemed to grow pointed; then the whole mass began to sink into itself as if it were dissolving, and on the spot where a few moments before the big, athletic Englishman had stood, nothing was visible any longer but a clear violet cone like a great lump of colored sugar ...

Deaf Pompejus was seized with an impulse of mad rage. The Tibetans continued to scream, and with his uncanny skill at lip-reading, he noticed that they were uttering the same word or phrase again and again. His anger seemed to have given him a clairvoyant clearness of intelligence, and his lips began to form the sound which he saw on all those ugly lips in front of him ...

Suddenly their leader sprang out before them, and they all stopped yelling and took their hands away from their ears. Like panthers they all rushed at Pompejus. The deaf man began to fire into the mob like a madman with his repeating rifle. This stopped them a moment.

Then, obeying some mysterious impulse, he began to bawl at the company the syllables which he had learned from their lips. He had caught the thing perfectly, and he bellowed it with his mighty lungs like a whole army shouting a war-cry.

He grew dizzy, everything went from dim and dark before him. The earth began to sway under his feet, and he came near falling. But the feeling of dizziness lasted only a few seconds, and his mind and his senses cleared again.

The Tibetans had disappeared—disappeared exactly as his master had done—and in their place he saw a great number of the little violet cones.

Their leader was still alive. His legs were already transformed into a bluish paste, and the upper part of his body was shrinking away. It seemed as if his substance was being digested in a great transparent or invisible stomach. This man did not wear a red cap like the others, but an elaborate head-dress like a bishop's miter, in which yellow, living eyes could be seen moving to and fro . . .

Jaburek stepped up to the creature and struck him on the head with the butt of his rifle, but his enemy still had the strength to hurl a sickle-shaped weapon at him and wound him in the foot . . .

The victor stood and looked about him. No living thing was visible anywhere on the plain . . .

The odor of amberia blossoms had grown so intense that it was almost suffocating. It seemed to be given out by the violet cones, which Pompejus now examined with some care. They were almost entirely uniform, and all consisted of the same clear violet gelatinous slime. Since the Tibetans had moved forward to surround him, Pompejus could not distinguish the remains of Sir Roger from the other violet pyramids.

Mad with rage, Pompejus crushed the pitiful substance of the half-dissolved leader under his heavy heels; then he made his way back to the edge of the green island. The copper helmets lay shining in the sun . . . He pumped one of the reservoirs full of air and started back across the gas-zone. He struggled over the strip of desert, his head buzzing with confusion, grief and horror. The ice-topped giants of the Himalayas towered toward heaven—what cared they for the pain and perplexity of a poor deaf vagabond who had lost his best friend and who would have gone to eternity in the same moment with him if it had not been for the accident of his deafness? . . .

"The knife the fellow threw was poisoned," Pompejus had traced painfully at the end of his manuscript, "but I think I might have worked the poison out of my system if I hadn't grieved so at the death of Sir Roger, and especially if I had not been tormented all the time by the fear that I should blurt out the awful word some time or other and exterminate a whole roomful, or a hallful, or a streetful, of innocent victims. The crazy thing rings in my head all the time and I can't forget it. But I am so near the end now that I think the world is safe from me. And when I die, the danger will be past. The word will die with me—"

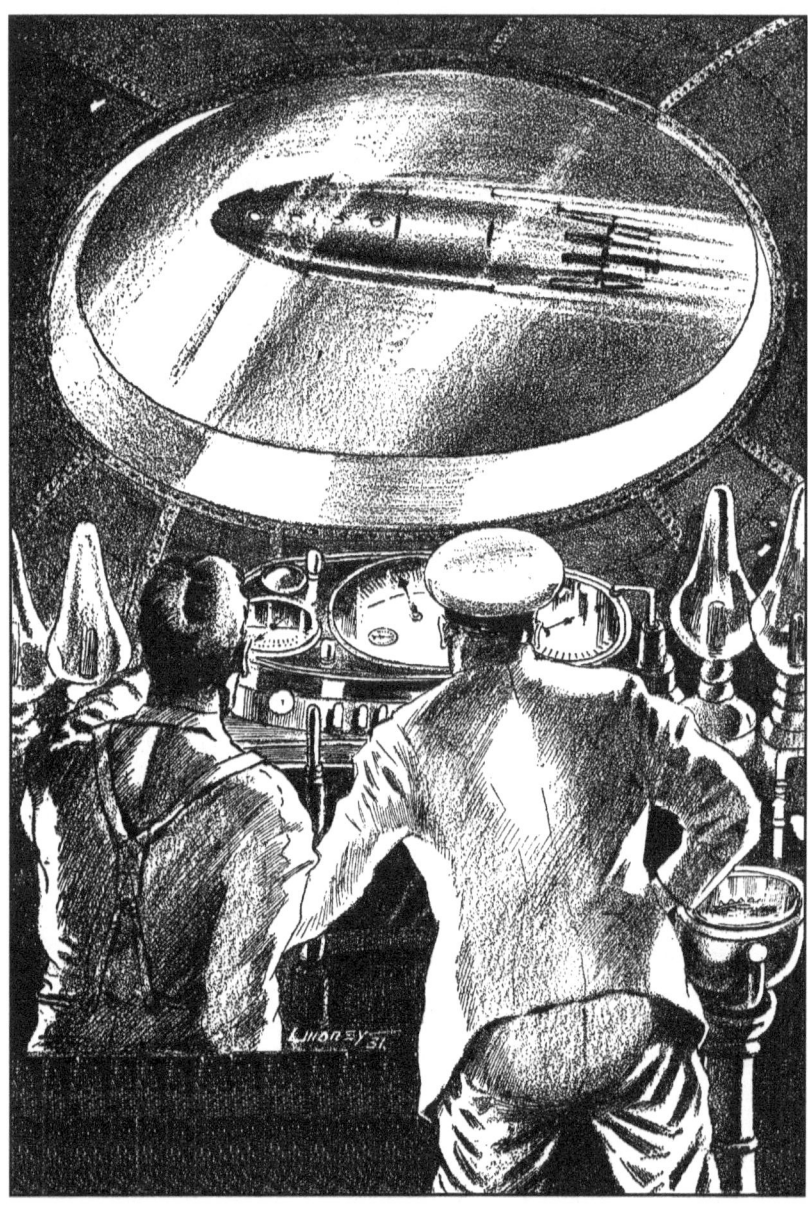

*And then they saw the Rocket VII through the thick glass of the observation port.
Streaking across the black velvet of the heavens . . . in the direction of Theophilus.
Her forward rocket tubes were belching yellow flame, yet she hurtled on as if the
reaction against the expanding gases was of no avail.*

Once in
a BLUE Moon

by Harl Vincent

Harl Vincent (Schoepflin) gave me my first manuscript in the late 20s.
I befriended him as an adult and attended his funeral.—FJA
Amazing Stories Quarterly, Winter 1932

L ike the alchemists of ancient days who sought to transmute baser metals into gold and silver our scientists of the twenty-first century have labored for three decades in the hope of producing lunium in their crucibles. They have analyzed the metal with infinite care and precision and have mixed its constituent elements under every conceivable combination of pressure and temperature. Yet their efforts have met with failure. The natural alloy found on Earth's moon seems impossible of duplication in their laboratories.

The remarkable properties of the moon metal were brought to light in 2017, after Philip Meta returned from that first rocket trip which was sponsored by the Smithsonian Institute. He brought with him a sample of the strange blue metal and, quite by accident, experimenters discovered that certain high-frequency electrical impulses imparted to it the powerful gravity force which has since been used in lifting and propelling our vessels of the air and of space. Then followed the rapid broadening of man's knowledge and attainments that came with the contacts he was enabled to establish with other inhabited planets.

There is no need that the men of science produce synthetic lunium; the mining of the natural substance has now become a well-organized industry, and vast quantities of the material are daily removed from the so-called rays of the moon's surface and transported to Earth, Mars and Venus in huge freighters of the ether whose construction was made possible by the use of the blue metal.

But the early adventurers and prospectors faced great hardship and untold danger in making the trip from Earth in the crude rocket ships of the day. Many of those who reached the moon did not return to tell of their experiences; many others missed their destination entirely and were lost in the trackless void of outer space.

And we, who so calmly enjoy the benefits brought to mankind by the universal use of the moon metal, are prone to forget the difficulties which beset those early pioneers. There were strange tales that came to our ears, conflicting stories and most of them incredible. In the increasing rush of modern civilization we gave them little heed. And returning voyagers soon ceased speaking of their adventures.

There came the time when the moon presented to us an entirely new face, the satellite having turned completely over on its axis during a single night. It was a nine days' wonder to the layman, but scientists were glib in explaining the phenomenon by natural causes, although there were many dissenting opinions among them. This, too, was forgotten in a short time, and the world went merrily on. It was far more interesting to speculate on the financial and educational gains to be realized from the contemplated alliances with the peoples of other worlds.

The true story of what happened in the ancient hidden world of Luna has never before been told and is only made public at this time through the finding of the diary written by one of the terrestrial participants who recently died. In its essentials the story has been confirmed by other survivors of the expedition. Whether the diarist was strictly accurate in his account is of little moment; the take makes good reading, and the fact remains that Luna *did*, on June 6, 2019, completely reverse her position in the heavens with respect to earth. And, be it known, astronomers are yet disagreeing as to the precise nature of the disturbance which brought about the change. It is the way of scientists.

This, the diary's story, likely will leave them still at odds.

Moon Rocket IV lay just south of the great crater of Tycho, within less than a half mile of the broad ray of lunium, which extended to the southeast in the direction of the Doerfel Mountains. Her main cargo compartments were nearly filled with huge ingots of the blue metal that was so greatly desired by a world gone suddenly mad over the idea of interplanetary travel. Those who had financed the vessel's construction were sure to reap handsome profits on this, her second voyage.

Captain Wallace James was at the eye-piece of the telescope in the observation dome at the vessel's nose. The glass was trained on the great white-mottled green globe that hung low in the lunar sky. Earth! A quarter of a million miles away; infinitely remote it seemed and at the moment so utterly desirable a berth for the Rocket IV. A wave of nostalgia gripped the captain and he vowed under his breath that this was his last voyage outside the atmosphere of Terra.

"Reporting the approach of Rocket VII, sir." Clark Peters, his optophone operator and auxiliary pilot, broke in on his meditations.

"Close by, Pete?" The captain turned guiltily from the eye-piece of the refractor, making desperate efforts to compose his features.

"A thousand miles out and coming in fast. Too fast, I'd say."

Young Peters, wiry, lanky Kansan, with huge hands and feet, stood there awkwardly with thumbs hooked in his suspenders. Deep concern was in his long, solemn countenance.

"*How fast?*" The captain drew in a quick breath; this was to be another case of a hopeless rescue attempt, he feared.

Pete, though hardly past thirty, was the veteran of a half dozen South American revolutions and of many times that number of hairbreadth escapes from sudden and horrible death. Easy-going and fearless, he was ordinarily unmoved in the face of danger of any sort. But he was sick of digging mangled, exploded remains of his compatriots from the twisted wreckage of rockets. They all were.

"Well, I don't know now," the operator drawled, his tense look relaxing somewhat. "They should be in sight by this time. And maybe it isn't as bad as I thought."

Captain James swung the telescope around and searched the heavens in the direction indicated by Peters. "Who's master of the vessel?" he mumbled.

"Their optophone man didn't say. And a funny thing, too, no image came through on the disc. Transmitting operator said his image projector was out of whack—generator burned out or something."

"You think they were hiding something?" The captain did not look up from the eye-piece, but his voice was brittle.

Moon Rocket VII had been constructed and launched by a group of shady financiers, he well knew.

"Don't know as I'd go so far as to say that," Peters replied with calm deliberation. "But—"

"Here she comes!" the captain exclaimed excitedly. "Rocket-tubes flaming, but hardly slowing her down. Plug in on the opto, Pete."

Whatever the doubt regarding the Rocket VII, she was a ship in distress and their duty was clear.

The optophone purred gently as Pete closed the switch, then emitted the hollow, empty sound of an open ether wave. "Ahoy, Rocket VII!" he called into the disc. "Rocket IV asking if you are in need of help."

"What in the devil could you do if we were?" the optophone snarled in return.

"Well, I don't know now," Pete commenced slowly.

"To hell with them!" the captain roared, interrupting, "if that's the way they feel." He turned jerkily from the telescope and his face was purple when he glared into the disc of the opto.

No image was there to return his savage stare.

Clark Peters smiled his slow, disarming smile. When Pete grinned *that* way, Captain James knew he was riled and riled plenty.

And then they saw the Rocket VII through the thick glass of the observation port. Streaking across the black velvet of the heavens she was, and heading northwest over Tycho, the great lunar crater, in the direction of Theophilus. Her forward rocket tubes were belching yellow flame, yet she hurtled on as if the reaction against the expanding gases was of no avail.

"With your permission, sir, I'd like to follow them," Pete offered. He switched off the optophone as he spoke, and his grin had crystallized into an ominous thing that had no mirth in it.

Captain James looked out over the earth-lit lunar landscape in the direction the unfriendly vessel had taken. He hated to risk the lives of any of his crew, Pete's especially. But the strange actions of the Rocket VII demanded investigation.

"Very well, Pete," he agreed finally. "But the miners are all out working the ray. You'll have to take the kid along—Downey, I mean. And old Saunders, though I'm afraid he'll not be much good to you."

"Okay, sir; they'll do." Pete nodded grimly and was gone.

Moon Rocket IV was the first of her kind to be equipped with a lunium-hulled tender. It was the only form of light craft which could navigate over the moon's surface. Airplanes and helicopter planes were useless on account of the absence of an atmosphere. But the slender, torpedo-bodied blue ship, provided by the owners of Rocket IV, could rise swiftly above the tallest lunar spire when her lunium plates were negatively energized and made speedy progress forward under the tremendous blasts from her single swiveled rocket-tube astern.

Clark Peters had conceived a deep affection for the little vessel and had christened her the "Hornet" when first he heard the spiteful, high-pitched hum of her frequency converters. The name had stuck.

Pete faced Morton Saunders in the airlock that berthed the "Hornet." Saunders was a character and not at all as useless as the captain had indicated. Probably fifty or fifty-five years of age, he was totally bald, but his square face was set off with re-markable bristling brows and mustache of unbelievably deep red hue. A conceited ass in the eyes of the miners, but he'd been places and seen things in his day. And he was a crackerjack electrician.

"Mort," Pete was saying, "Cap is sending us out after a ship that only now came in from home. Rocket VII. She went overhead like a streak and was lost in the direction of Theophilus."

"Huh," Saunders exclaimed with a grimace. "Another crackup?"

"Don't know as I'd go so far as to say that," Pete answered slowly. "Maybe yes, maybe no. She's a queer bird, Mort; turned us down when we hailed her. And the optophone man didn't show his face."

"Huh! Nice, friendly folks, I'd say. We'll have to put 'em in their place. You and I, Pete—"

"You sent for me, Mr. Peters?" a respectful voice broke in from the inner door of the lock.

"Slim" Downey, a light-haired lad in his early twenties, stood there uncertainly, and Pete eyed him contemptuously. One didn't address any man as "mister" on board the Rocket IV—excepting the captain. Downey was a stowaway and there was considerable mystery as to the history of his immediate past. General opinion in the miner's mess had it that he was a fugitive from justice. "Yellow Kid," they called him. Certain it was that he acted jumpy, scared of everything and everybody. But at times there would come into his mild blue eyes a gleam of intense feeling that belied his meek demeanor.

"I did," Pete snapped. "Bolt home the inner door, kid."

"We—we're going out in the 'Hornet,' Mr. Peters?" the lad faltered, paling swiftly.

"Right. What's wrong with you—no guts? And listen, I'm not *Mister* Peters either—get that?" Pete glowered, baiting the lad.

Downey flushed as swiftly as he had paled and a fierce glitter shot out from beneath his quickly narrowed brows. "I get you—Pete," he said in edgy tones. And then he turned jerkily to the bolts of the door clamps.

Pete hooked his thumbs in his suspenders and grinned at Saunders. "May make a man of him, Mort—this expedition," he whispered.

"Huh!" Saunders sniffed disdainfully and tugged at his fiery mustache. "In my humble opinion, the boy is a—"

But Downey had finished his task and now whirled to face the two older men. "I'm with you," he said unexpectedly. "Let's go."

Pete stared in amazement. The flush still mantled the youngster's smooth cheeks and his chin was raised. But the cold fire was dying out of the pale blue eyes. They were mild once more and dropped before the fixity of Pete's regard.

"All right, kid, we go," Pete growled. "And make it snappy." His gaze, puzzled now, did not leave the slim figure as the Yellow Kid scrambled through the entrance port of the "Hornet."

With the "Hornet's" atomic motors running at full speed, the turning gear that projected from her nose made quick work of unscrewing the circular outer port of the airlock. There was the swift hiss of escaping air as the hinged door swung outward, the shrill note of the frequency-converters within, and the little vessel raised lightly from her cradle. Pete pressed the rocket-tube control and, with the staccato barking of the blasts astern, they shot out into the frigidity and semi-darkness of the long lunar night.

"Slim" Downey crouched by one of the floor ports of the control room as Pete drove the "Hornet" out over the huge crater of Tycho at top speed. He was utterly appalled by the altitude and by the swift rush into the desolate wastes of the cold satellite, Pete thought. Mort Saunders was in the motor compartment, starting their oxygen apparatus.

They lunged out over the towering serrated rim at the far edge of the crater and drove along above the mile-wide streak of cobalt blue—that was a lode of pure lunium—the great moon ray that extended the entire distance from Tycho to Theophilus. What enormous wealth would be his who might convoy but a small fraction of that vast deposit to Earth!

Pete searched the horizon with the telescope, but could make out nothing to indicate where the Rocket VII had landed, if indeed it had landed. In the mellow earth-light the moon's rugged contours stood out against the diamond-studded ebony of the firmament in sharp relief, barren and forbidding, yet softened somehow by the thick dust of ages that lay like a vast blanket over all.

Pockmarked and scarred, lonely and mysterious as a graveyard, cooled to a temperature one hundred degrees below zero during the long night of more than fourteen earth-days, and heated to near the boiling point during the equally long lunar day, there were still optimists of Terra who made bold to predict that the god-forsaken satellite would one day become a vast hive of industry and be peopled by hundreds of thousands of Earth's workers. Clark Peters was not one who believed them. A prospecting trip was one thing, with every hope of a quick return to civilization; permanent residence was quite another matter.

A grotesque dark blot spread along the rim of a small crater ahead of them, then was lost astern as they sped past directly overhead, all that was left of Moon Rocket III! Pete saw that young Downey had risen from his crouching position at the floor port and was eyeing him intently. The lad was chalky white and his lips trembled.

"Tha-that was a wreck, wasn't it?" he babbled.

"Well, I don't know now," Pete drawled. "Seems to me it's better called a tomb. Used to be Rocket III, that mess, and there are some ninety-odd corpses spread around down there."

"Good Lord!" Downey fell gloomily silent for a moment, then turned on the pilot in sudden panic. "Where are we headed?" he demanded.

Pete grinned. "Who knows?" he replied with aggravating calm. "Perhaps for another such tomb. At any rate, we're hunting another ship—Rocket VII. She came over from home ten minutes before we set out."

Downey yelled in what seemed like utter demoralization. "No, no!" he screeched. "Not that, man! You don't know—" And then he wound his slender fingers around Pete's wrist, fingers that gripped like steel.

Astonished, the pilot loosed the controls and tore his arm free.

"What the devil!" he roared. "You yellow cur—"

And then Clark Peters found he had a young wildcat on his hands.

"You can't!" Downey was jabbering. "Not Rocket VII. You can't—I won't let you."

A sharp-knuckled fist caught Peters behind the ear with painful force. The frantic youth squirmed in under Pete's arms before the amazed pilot was able to stop him. The lad was tugging at the controls, snarling like an animal at bay, staring wild-eyed. There was but one thing to do and Pete did it.

Lashing out with a huge fist, he doubled the boy up with a swift blow to the solar plexus. Not his usual hard-driven punch, but enough. The Yellow Kid slumped to the floor plates, moaning and gasping.

Careening violently, the "Hornet" headed madly toward the surface. Pete dove for the controls and endeavored to right her. But in that instant they swooped down into the deep chasm of a rill. Pete caught a momentary glimpse of this vast gulf that was swallowing them up, a yawning abyss into whose depths the "Hornet" plunged. Murky blackness enveloped them.

And the motors stopped with a despairing, trailing whine.

Mort Saunders blundered into the control room. "Huh!" he exploded. "Machinery's dead. I swear I did everything, Pete; no one could—"

He broke off grunting as he collided with the wriggling, whimpering thing that was Slim Downey. Pete heard him swear softly in the hollow silence and Stygian gloom.

The emergency lights flashed on then, illuminating the control room with their dim soft glow. Their batteries, at least, had not failed them. And Pete switched on the forward searchlight, sending forth its dazzling beam into the blackness of the pit.

Slim Downey yelled then, coughing painfully. "No, Pete, not the lights! They'll see us. Turn them off."

"You shut up!" the pilot snapped. Pete had thought there was a moving mass down there in the depths.

"Oh, God!—you've *got* to listen." Downey was dragging himself to his knees; his teeth chattered uncontrollably.

Pete growled savagely, continuing with his search of the depths. The "Hornet" was dropping with swift acceleration into a seemingly bottomless pit that was fully a half mile across. Utterly helpless she was, her atomic motors paralyzed by some strange force that surrounded them.

"In my opinion," Saunders was saying, "the boy knows something. I'd do as he says, Pete."

"I'll say he knows something!" Pete had caught the gleam of a huge steel cylinder down there; Rocket VII, without a doubt. And the big rocket ship was dropping even faster than they. He pulled on the switch and once more darkness closed in about them.

He reached for Slim Downey, saw a violet corona discharge crackling as his fingers closed in on the trembling arm. The very air of the control room was electrified.

The youngster moaned as Pete's grip dug into his yielding flesh. "Let up, Pete," he whined. "I *do* know something."

"Spit it out then!" Pete relaxed his grip somewhat.

"It's a—a big job of Aleck Carter's. His men were here before on the first trip of Rocket VI. There's a world inside here, Pete, and it's peopled with ghastly little devils that Carter wants to hook up with. Keep the lights off, for God's sake. We may get away."

"A hidden world!" Pete gasped. "How do you know?"

"Never mind. I know, all right—" Slim blubbered as Pete's fingers dug deeper. "Carter put me on Rocket IV," he moaned then. "I won't do his dirty work, though—damned if I will. You're the boss, Pete. I'll do anything you say, see if I don't."

"I'll see that you *do*," Pete grated, shoving the lad away in disgust. So Aleck Carter was mixed up in this thing! His minions had found their way even here and were planning some new deviltry that would involve humanity still deeper in his toils. Carter, with his billions in wealth, would buy an entire civilization, good or bad, to serve his own ends.

"Huh!" Saunders blurted out of the darkness. "A likely story. You and I, Pete, will get at the truth of it when we—"

"When we crash? You're optimistic, Mort."

"There won't be any crash," Slim broke in eagerly. "This force of the pit will—"

And then, as if to belie his words, the "Hornet" struck heavily on the starboard side amidships. She rolled over and pitched the three men in a scrambling heap, then slid nose down along a gentle declivity, bouncing and careening over the rough surface. There was a ripping screech below as her landing gear was torn loose and she pitched over on her nose, coming to rest at an angle of about forty-five degrees.

"Well, I don't know now," Pete drawled. "This seems *almost* like a crash to me."

His cheek was pressed to the icy glass of one of the floor ports and the wriggling weight of Mort Saunders lay across his shoulders. But there was no hiss of escaping air; the lunium hull of the staunch vessel was unpunctured.

Rosy light streamed in through the ports and they saw they were in an enormous cavern where Rocket VII stood solidly on her base, nose skyward and unharmed. The "Hornet" lay on a slope several hundred yards away, partly submerged in the powdery surface and hidden from the lower portion of the great rocket ship.

Mort Saunders pointed to the instrument panel. "We're ten miles below the surface, Pete," he exclaimed. "And, in my humble opinion, the pit has an atmosphere of some sort. Look at the manometer."

The outside pressure was indicated at about seventeen inches of mercury, not much lower than that on the mountain tops of Terra. If this was air in the pit, they would be able to venture outside without their bulky Metz suits and oxygen helmets. The temperature was much higher than on the surface, showing as 48 degrees Fahrenheit.

Pete whistled. "*This* will be something to write home about," he remarked. "What next, I wonder."

"You—you're not leaving the 'Hornet'?" Slim Downey asked.

"Nothing else but," he said cheerfully, "and you're coming with us, my boy. Here, Mort, we'll have to use the lead boots."

He had started toward the airlock where the heavy equipment needed in the moon's low gravity was stored, when there came the gentle rising purr of the atomic motors. The paralyzing effect of the pit had been released or "turned off." Quickly Pete threw the starting lever forward and the purring died off into silence.

"You could leave at once—" Slim Downey began.

"Not on your life! We'll see this thing through, now we're here. Step lively, boy."

"You're the boss," the lad replied meekly. But his eyes did not meet those of the big man who stood menacingly over him.

With the lead-soled boots strapped to their feet, they dragged themselves out from the artificial earth-gravity of the "Hornet's" interior, dropping one at a time to the thick dust of the lunar cavern floor. A sound of clanking machinery and the shouting of many voices came from beyond the knoll where the rocket ship reared its great bulk.

A curious sense of light-headedness came to Clark Peters with the breathing in of the thin, sharp air. His vision was distorted in the wavering roseate light. Young Downey had slipped to his knees and was wriggling his way to the top of the knoll.

"Stay where you are," Pete called out cautiously. "And no signals to your friends, either." Suddenly it had come to him that there was more to the Yellow Kid than he had thought.

The young fellow halted, crouching, and grinned over his shoulder. "You're the boss, Pete," he replied. But there was a new courage in his slightly superior smile, the courage of desperation and of a dark knowledge that was his.

Pete fingered the cold tube of the bullet projector he carried. He had taken care that only Mort and himself were thus armed, and with more than a hundred rounds of the ultranite ammunition in the possession of each, he was confident of their ability to cope with almost any situation. But he was darkly suspicious of young Downey.

Scrambling to the side of the strangely metamorphosed youngster, he raised his head to peer out over the vast floor of the cavern. Mort Saunders, with much puffing and grunting, drew himself alongside.

A scene of intense activity centered about the five massive pillars of Rocket VII's base. Queer, stunted creatures, thousands of them it appeared, were clustering there before a massive mechanism that was being lowered from the crane arm of the rocket ship. Impossible pigmy beings that stood erect on two legs, bodies covered with iridescent scales, long arms dangling. Globular, hairless heads of chalky white, with bulging eyes and cavernous, scarlet mouths. And twenty or thirty Terrestrials in this midst, fraternizing with the ugly monstrosities!

"A rummy lot, in my opinion. Huh!" There was utter loathing in Mort Saunders' much-used exclamation. That "huh" of his was capable of expressing his every mood and reaction.

Pete's blood froze in his veins at the sound of a demonical shriek that rose unexpectedly from the lips of Slim Downey. He clapped an enormous paw over the crazy youngster's mouth and shook him violently.

"Idiot!" he hissed. "You'll have them on us like a pack of wolves."

Things happened all at once when Slim's yell rang out in the huge open space at the pit bottom. There was a bedlam of shouting over by the rocket ship, unintelligible, gulping screeches of the moon-men and hoarse curses in vivid English. A muffled explosion sounded from behind the great vessel and a swirling cloud of faintly luminous green vapor rose swiftly, forming itself into an immense shimmering bubble that closed down over the scene. Rocket VII and the polyglot pack at its base were completely enclosed.

And Slim Downey developed muscles of steel and the agility of a cat. Like a coiled spring suddenly released, he popped out from beneath Pete's swiftly flung bulk, leaving the amazed pilot to sprawl in the thick dust. And then he was sprinting toward the shining green bubble.

"Damned little rat!" Saunders snarled. "That's enough for you." He raised his bullet projector and fired from the hip.

"Mort, don't!" Pete struck upward at the slender weapon, his arm deflecting the tube just as the propelling ray spat forth.

The explosive bullet went wide of its mark and an appalling crash echoed in the pit as its energy was expended harmlessly on the rubbery surface of the green vapor dome. The mighty force of the ultranite charge would have shattered a monolith, yet the gleaming bubble merely shivered under the impact, changing its smooth contour not at all.

Slim Downey tossed back a tantalizing laugh.

And now three globular objects burst out from the hemisphere of green; solid metallic shapes, apparently about four feet in diameter, drifting unsupported through the rare air of the lunar pit, coming swiftly in the direction of the knoll and floating waist high above the cavern floor. Still laughing crazily, young Downey flung himself on the nearest of the spheres and was immediately absorbed into the body of the uncanny thing. Just melted into its embrace and was swallowed up bodily as if the thing were a ball of jelly.

It might have been the disappearing act of a vaudeville magician. The weird globe changed not one whit in size or appearance, but halted its progress and hovered there in midair as if awaiting its fellows, which continued in their deliberate movement toward the remaining two Terrestrials.

Mort Saunders went berserk, firing rapidly from his bullet projector. Ear-shattering reverberations echoed in the cavern as ultranite charges exploded in swift succession against the spheres. But the drifting globes only came on the faster, their surfaces unmarred and undeterred in their ghastly purpose.

"Run for it, Mort!" Pete shouted, wheeling about to suit his own action to the words. "Quit shooting; they're too close."

He groaned as Saunders staggered and fell. One of the spheres was upon the older man in an instant. With a sucking, whistling sound the sturdy body was merged with its mysterious substance. Gone; vanished, Mort had, as Slim had vanished. Like water absorbed by a sponge.

Unreasoning fear had Pete in its grip. It was as if his feet were rooted to the spot. A nightmare! His voice, when he essayed a yell of unalloyed terror, died chokingly in his parched throat. Then the clammy metal of the third sphere enwrapped him.

The rosy light of the cavern was dimmed. Flame-shot blackness was in Pete's vision. Frigid, unyielding metal congealed about him. Icy fingers of steel twisted in his vitals and he knew no more.

Consciousness returned swiftly and painlessly. Clark Peters sat up on the hard floor he found under him and took in his surroundings with unbelieving eyes. He was in a great circular hall of many tall columns and with a high arched ceiling that glowed with the rosy light they had seen in the pit bottom. The air was fresh and warm. Mort Saunders lay close by, still unconscious, but breathing normally and with good color in his cheeks.

A quick search apprised Pete of the fact that they were without their weapons.

"Your companion will recover shortly," a voice sounded in his ears. No, it was *not* a voice; a mental impression more accurately. There had been no sound in the vast chamber.

Looking swiftly around him, Pete saw one of the spheres like those which had captured them. Certainly they were made of gleaming blue-white metal, yet they were possessed of miraculous powers of locomotion and of other qualities that made it certain they were not ordinary mechanisms of human manufacture. These things had *brains*. This one was resting on a tripod made of a multicolored translucent material like stained glass.

"I suppose *that's* what talked to me," Pete muttered foolishly.

"You have guessed the truth, Earth-man," came the quick mental response. "And you may speak freely that which is in your mind. Or speak not at all, if you choose. We may communicate regardless. And the Great Ones of Luna have commanded me to enlighten you."

Pete hooked his thumbs in his suspenders and regarded the metal globe curiously. After this experience, nothing he might see within this mad satellite or on its surface would surprise him.

"There are still more surprising things," the mental reply flashed back. The eerie globe needed only his thoughts, not his speech.

And thought-images flickered across Pete's mind in swift succession, after the fashion of a panoramic motion picture. Rather they flashed as shimmering light-images on the surface of the mysterious sphere. He saw that Mort Saunders had drawn himself erect and was staring goggle-eyed, plucking nervously at the bristles of his red mustache. Mort was seeing the same things, getting the same reactions as was Pete.

Under the sphere's strange telepathic influence, the hall of the many columns faded away in blue mists and was gone. It seemed they were drifting freely in space then, Pete and Mort and the shimmering globe, hovering in the enormity of a cosmos where three other objects, three suns of indigo hue, bathed them in eerie light that altered all things in their perceptions.

They were deep in the moon's interior, their minds were informed, hundreds of miles beneath the surface. Earth's satellite was hollow! And the three suns lighting the blue realm were huge masses of lunium, charged with the sub-electronic forces and mind-energies of ancient Luna, possessed of powers far greater than those of the insignificant Lesser One which had been detailed as the mentor and guard of the Earth-men. The Terrestrials were in the presence of the Great Ones of a blue moon, in a realm unknown to the science of Earth.

Many puzzling things were made clear to Pete and Mort. The old uncertainty of astronomers as to why the moon always presented the same side to the mother planet was explained away. The hollowed-out heart of Luna, a cavity some twelve hundred miles in diameter, is concentric with the outer surface. But the Great Ones, enormous gravity masses in the Earth-moon system, hovered constantly near the huge lunium deposits in the inner wall that was nearest the mother planet. Luna's center of gravity being thus offset a considerable distance from its mathematical center, Earth's powerful attraction acted more strongly on the heavy side, keeping the same face of the satellite always in view. As a round-bottom, weight-loaded toy stands erect, so the moon maintained its position with respect to earth.

Millions of years older than Earth's civilization, the original inhabitants of Luna had taken to the inner region when the atmosphere outside thinned out and had escaped. Evolution through subsequent ages made of them the complex, atomic structure now represented by the spheres which seemed to the Terrestrials only like globes of polished metal. These metal balls, the true Lunarians, were capable of existence without an atmosphere and without food. But there were the pigmy folk, cave-dwellers primarily and much lower in the evolutionary scale, and the Great Ones had decreed that these be cared for until the end of time. The Lesser Ones were their guardians and protectors.

And then had come the minions of Aleck Carter, stumbling accidentally into the great shaft which connected with the inner regions. The omniscient Great Ones envisioned their coming and sent the sub-electronic energies into the pit to break their fall. And there at the bottom of the pit, the pigmy folk had made friends with the first Terrestrials they had ever seen.

But the Great Ones and the Lesser Ones were suspicious of these visitors who had come to trade the bounty of the mother planet for their own vast deposits of lunium.

"Trade!" Pete blurted out the unnecessary words. "What can Aleck Carter offer in trade? How can he hope to acquire a monopoly of the metal which is so plentiful on the moon's surface?"

If a smooth metallic sphere can shrug its shoulders, this Lesser One did that very thing—mentally.

"You shall judge for yourselves," its unspoken message came. "We go to the abode of the pigmies."

Again there was the confusing sense of change. The blue mists came and advanced before them in tiny weaving wisps, then coalescing into shapes that were gigantic yet familiar in form. An endless vista of blue columns appeared before them, and they set foot on solid ground. The Lesser One drifted before them as they walked.

"Are we awake, Mort?" Pete whispered.

"In my humble opinion we're not," Saunders returned. "Or else we are both quite hopelessly dotty. This business of the big ones and the little ones is too much—"

"No, Mort, look! There's Aleck Carter himself."

The avenue of blue pillars had opened out into a great amphitheatre where hundreds of the pigmy folk were gathered about the machine which had been taken from Rocket VII. And in their midst was Carter, the man who was possessed of more ill-gotten wealth and vicious commercial influence than any man in the history of Earth—bossing a gang of Terrestrials, riggers and mechanics, as if he were an ordinary foreman!

It all came to Pete then in a flash of understanding. Carter was reaching out for new worlds to conquer. If he could manipulate matters so as to obtain exclusive control of the supply of lunium, he alone of all humans would be able to traffic with the Martians and Venerians and with whatever races there might be found on other planets of the solar system. But to have risked the rocket trip itself; it was incredible.

"Huh!" Saunders grunted. "The old boy has let himself in for something *this* time. Look at him; his chest is puffing up like a pouter pigeon's. And he's yelling himself hoarse."

"This Terrestrial plans to move Luna to Earth and has promised the pigmy folk everything which is available there," came the mental advice of their attending sphere. "Everything, comfortable homes, fresh air in abundance for their weakened lungs, food for their primitive stomachs."

"What!" Pete shouted. "He's crazy. It can't be done; the tides of Earth would submerge the land. There would be—"

"Only too well are these things known to the Great Ones." There was dignity and patience in the unspoken voice of the Lesser One. "A vast cataclysm would result were this Terrestrial to succeed in his mad purpose. His own scientists should be able to tell him these things."

"Certainly, certainly," Saunders sputtered. "I myself, with my—huh—extensive knowledge of electricity and other natural forces might enlighten him. If he would listen."

"Electricity?" The mental reaction of the sphere was questioning. "That is the force the Terrestrial is using. It is unfamiliar to us and we would know of its nature."

Mort Saunders floundered hopelessly in the effort to explain. But it was apparent that the Lesser One gathered from his chaotic thoughts that which his rebellious tongue was unable to put in words.

"An elementary form of energy we have not developed." the sphere commented wordlessly. "Our own sub-electronic energy is greatly superior. But there are possibilities in this force, and we would guard against the evil that might arise from these possibilities."

"Then why not step in and put a stop to the thing?" the query rose to Pete's lips. "Surely the Great Ones are powerful enough."

"Yes," the Lesser One assented. "But you forget, Earth-man. The pigmies have their own minds in the matter. It is not permitted that we interfere with them or assist them unless they call upon us for help."

"It might be too late when they do," Pete growled. He had no idea as to what deviltry Carter was planning, but knew from past performance that it boded no good to the strange inhabitants of Luna—nor to his own world.

"That is true, Earth-man, and is the reason we have brought you here with your friend. The Great Ones approved of you and bid me work to the end that you might be enlisted in their service."

"You—you mean to try and forestall Carter's plans?" Pete asked incredulously.

"That is the plea of the Great Ones."

Plea! These incomprehensible brain machines and energy sources of the blue realm were capable to forcing their will on Earth, man and pigmy alike. They had superhuman power over ordinary matter and were disseminators of unknown forces that could be as destructive as ten thunderbolts in one, yet they chose to plead with him and Mort. Pete could not bring himself to believe his senses.

"Huh!" Mort Saunders exclaimed. "We can do it, Pete. We'll show Carter and his gang. *We'll—*"

"Don't know as I'd go so far as to say that," Pete drawled. "You have an exalted opinion of yourself, Mort, and of me. But we can try."

Some unexplainable force radiated by the expectant Lesser One was permeating his being, buoying him up. Fantastic as were his surroundings, mysterious as were the activities of the Lunarians and of Carter, his old Earth spirits and courage were returning. In Aleck Carter and his gang of hirelings there was a tangible inimical force; these could be fought with their own guile and weapons. And in the Great Ones and the Lesser Ones there were powerful friends.

"We can try," Pete repeated softly. And the light of battle was in his eyes.

Mort Saunders grinned and tweaked his mustache apologetically.

A bright glow illuminated the surface of the Lesser One. In its approving telepathic reply there was exultation. And, quite as if the sphere had reached out with invisible arms to hand them over, their bullet projectors were restored to their hands. The Terrestrials gaped in amazement.

But the feel of the cold tube was comforting in Pete's hands. He fingered the weapon lovingly.

"You will likewise learn of the Dark Ones of Luna," came from the sphere. And there was sinister meaning in the telepathic flash.

Pete thought instantly of Slim Downey.

"No," came from the Lesser One. "The Dark Ones are of our own realm. The Terrestrial youth was returned to his fellows. His thoughts were not wholly good, although at first the Great Ones were inclined to approve of him. And so he was sent to rejoin his former associates."

With that information imparted, their attending sphere melted into the blue shadows of the great pillars and was gone. Pete and Mort stood there alone, gazing each into the puzzled eyes of the other.

"Illusions?" Mort whispered hesitantly.

"No, siree. Brain cases, these spheres, and *real;* impregnable housings of the most remarkable intellects in the universe. Superhuman minds with godlike emotions, and endowed with supernatural powers. All-seeing, all-knowing, all ... oh, dammit, I'm talking like a preacher. You know what I mean."

"Yes." Mort Saunders turned toward the amphitheatre as in a daze. "But there's nothing supernatural about them," he argued. "It's only that they know of forces we can't comprehend. They—"

A whirring sound rose up from Carter's mechanism and they saw the pigmy folk scatter and draw away from the devil-machine of the Earth-men. Mort and Pete ran swiftly down the sloping floor into the arena.

Unnoticed by Carter and his crew, and unmolested by the excited pigmy folk, they wormed their way through the press and drew near to the scene of action. And then they saw that the floor was of transparent crystal. Beneath them yawned the great cavity of the blue realm, infinitely vast and mysterious. The enormous globes that were the Great Ones hovered over there in all their majesty and silent watchfulness like heavenly bodies in a cosmos *within* this strange world of ancient Luna. Living, thinking mechanisms of slumbering potentialities.

Carter's machine rested on skids that partly bridged the crystal floor. It was a ponderous thing and incorporated a mighty atomic power plant and two huge beam transmitters. There were frequency converters as well, like those of the "Hornet," but vastly larger than hers.

"Lord!" Pete gasped, "the fool means it. He intends to energize the main lunium deposit."

"No—see there!" Mort returned. "The projectors are trained on the Great Ones themselves."

It was true; Carter's crew was preparing to send twin beams of ionized air across the gulf to carry the energizing frequencies to the very bodies of the Great Ones.

Thunderstruck, Pete stood undecided. They were in the shelter of a column where the blue light from below struck up to mingle with the rosy illumination of the high arches above. Of course they might ruin Carter's machine with their ultranite bullets—easily. But their own lives then would be forfeit. Even if they could overcome Carter's gang there were the pigmies to be dealt with. Thousands of them would stream in from the labyrinth of passageways; tens of thousands. And besides, Pete wasn't sure of his ground; he saw Mason and Thornbill over there by the machine, and Zimmerman—three of Earth's greatest men of science, whom Carter's gold had bought. Surely these men could not be contemplating a move that meant disaster on Earth.

His indecision was ended by a warning cry from Mort; a strangling horror-filled yell that caused Pete to whirl suddenly, crouching with his bullet projector in hand.

Behind them, a monstrous, black creature stood staring with red saucer-eyes; an object like a huge football poised on a single support that was more like the stem of a plant than the limb of an animal. Yet this thing was undoubtedly of the animal class—and intelligent.

One of the Dark Ones of Luna!

Pete pressed the release of his bullet projector, but, even as the propelling ray sped forth, the creature was covered with a shroud of green vapor such as that which had enclosed Rocket VII. The ultranite charge exploded with a deafening crash, but made no impression on the green armor. And a quavering wail of terror rose up from the throats of the thousands of pigmies. The great amphitheatre was in instant confusion.

A sharp mental command came then from out the green cloud; an order that carried with it the compulsion of a nameless force. Pete's grip on the bullet projector was loosened, struggle though he might, and the weapon clattered to the floor. He was rooted to the spot, his limbs trembling and muscles paralyzed. Mort Saunders had slumped to the base of the column, a quivering nerveless heap in the blast of energy that radiated from the Dark One.

With a twang like that of a snapped violin string, the green vapor disrupted, and the Dark One trailed off swiftly across the arena, its single supporting member drawing up within the mass of the black ovoid as a terrapin withdraws its limbs into its shell. Drifting in mid-air as the Lesser Ones did, the weird shape hovered in the midst of Carter's crew when it came to rest.

Others of the eerie creatures converged on the scene and the shoutings of the pigmy multitude rose high and menacing. Aleck Carter had leagued himself with the Dark Ones of Luna.

Desperately Pete set his will to the task of unbending his cramped fingers. Muscles refused his bidding and his knees gave way beneath his stiffened body. He crumpled helplessly to lie on his face, staring into the depths of the blue moon, his numbed lips framing wordless supplication to the Great Ones.

And everywhere about him were the pigmies; cold scaly hands pawed at him and rolled him over. Vacant bulging eyes peered into his own; cavernous mouths of scarlet jabbered. He struck out feebly and to no avail. There was not the strength of an infant in his puny blows.

It was all over; they were carrying him and Mort to the center of the arena, to Aleck Carter and the Dark Ones.

Next they knew they were lying bound before a small rostrum near which Carter's machine had been set up. From it they could see that tier upon tier of balconies surrounded the arena, mounting into the high arches of the amphitheatre as far as the eye could follow. And these balconies groaned under the weight of the pigmy folk that crowded them.

It was a place of ceremonial; a temple. And Aleck Carter was in his element as he faced the multitude from the rostrum, one of the Dark Ones hovering at his side. The eyes of a world were upon him.

Pete knew that his strength was returning. His muscles answered to his bidding once more, but the bonds of the pigmies held fast.

"Huh," he heard Mort whisper. "Old Carter's putting on quite a show."

Pete grinned. Saunders was all right, and so was he. If only they could free themselves. Carter had paid them scant attention; he was too deeply engrossed in the matter at hand, and confident that his bodyguard could handle these interfering snoopers if the pigmies and the Dark Ones could not. He was secure in his newly established position of power.

Silence fell in the huge gathering place when a mental message of the ugly swaying mass, that seemed to be leader of the Dark Ones, swept out over the assemblage.

"The power of the Great Ones is at an end," it conveyed. "The gods of Terra have kept their word and have brought their chief god with his machine to carry the ancient world of Luna to the land of happiness and plenty—"

"It's a lie!" a voice screamed from near the machine.

"Thornhill!" Pete gasped. "He's rebelling."

The scientist, purple of face, was struggling with one of Carter's huskies, trying to make his way to the platform. They saw his arms raised high, and his clenched fists threatening the man whose dominance of so much of Earth's enterprise, was now reaching out here into the depths of the blue moon.

Aleck Carter's flabby jowls quivered with rage; his basilisk eyes flashed fire. "Away with him!" he roared, "We'll have no traitors alive here."

They saw the gray-haired scientist go down. There was a flash and a report, the gunmen drawing back as the disintegrating charge of an atomic projector found its mark. The body of Earth's most renowned physicist, who had made the mistake of bowing to the will of Aleck Carter, was a squirming, bloated thing on the crystal floor. Then, in a puff of incandescent vapor, it had vanished.

But Carter was shaken; his ponderous frame sagged as the gulping yells of the pigmies rolled out over the arena a vast screaming roar of amazed protest. The god-beings of Terra were not invulnerable.

"Thus perish those who oppose the chief god of our benefactors," the Dark One's voiceless message came instantly. "Keep to your places, pigmy folk, and observe the overthrow of the Great Ones."

Carter brightened and raised his arm in a signal to his men as the Babel of pigmy voices was stilled in superstitious awe. And a shrill note of vibrant energy rose up from the throbbing machine.

Looking down into the blue cosmos, Pete saw the streaking light-pencils that stabbed out from the beam transmitters. Hundreds of miles beneath them a vast halo of white brilliance closed in on the Great Ones and caused them to draw together in a swift huddle. The crystal floor vibrated madly under the energy reaction and Luna's outer shell was set quivering.

Succeeding events came with confusing swiftness.

The Great Ones, each a sphere of about seventy-five miles diameter, sent out long streamers of indigo flame and backed away from the man-made energy that attacked them.

Carter was shouting like a gleeful fiend; dancing like a lunatic there on the rostrum. And the telepathic voices of the Dark Ones were ghoulishly exultant. The Great Ones were retreating before the blasts of the Earth-gods' machine.

A whining chant came up from the pigmy folk, a mad cadence of superstitious, religious fervor. The sound was awe-inspiring in its immensity, ghastly in its triumphant emotion.

And then, as the Great Ones baffled ineffectually against Aleck Carter's forces, the blue abyss beneath the crystal floor became alive with swirling forms that gleamed blue-white in the darkening realm. The Lesser Ones, legion in number, darting hither and yon in a panic of uncertainty.

A slender figure detached itself from the group at the machine and came running swiftly to the captives.

"Slim!" exclaimed Pete, "Slim Downey."

"Yes," the lad sobbed. "I couldn't stand it. Know what this means? Carter's figuring on throwing the whole damn moon out into space where Earth's rocket ships can't reach it. He's energizing the Great Ones themselves—they're mostly lunium—and the major deposits of the raw metal, to force the moon out from Earth's attraction."

"What!" Pete yelled. Slim was working at his bonds with a knife and one arm was free. "*Out*, you say?"

"Yes, out. Not in toward Earth, as he told the Dark Ones and the pigmies—he's too smart for that. *Out*. He'll control all the lunium then, and be able to deal with the other planets without competition. Don't you see? He was going to kill all of you on Rocket IV; I was his spy there. And the pigmies, he'll kill. Pete, I'm afraid; I don't want to be shot into space—God knows where. He's crazy."

"I'll say he is." Pete stretched and worked his arms and legs to limber them up. "Here, give me that knife."

He took it from the trembling lad and sawed rapidly at Mort's bonds. "Get that, Mort?" he whispered.

"Sure did; the kid's coming clean." Mort was free in a moment.

"W-what are you going to do?" Slim was blubbering.

"*You* do it!" Pete demanded. His eyes bored into Slim's.

White-faced and trembling, the boy stared. Then, quick as a flash, he streaked away toward the machine and flung himself into the main control switch—bodily. Pete and Mort ran after him, yelling.

There was a bellow of rage from Carter. Agonized cries from the pigmy folk. And despairing mental outbursts of the Dark Ones. Pete was fighting Carter's gang now, back to back with Mort. Desperately slugging, unmindful of the consequences. And the high reaches overhead were suddenly filled with gleaming forms of the Lesser Ones, doing battle with flashing energies as the Dark Ones sought to get away.

Pandemonium broke loose in the balconies. Luna lurched sidewise and threw the combatants in milling, struggling heaps.

The rest was confusion. Pete saw Otto Zimmerman scramble to the rostrum and jump astride Aleck Carter's shoulders, throttling him with his hairy paws grimly and efficiently. The German scientist was one more rebel—a game one.

He saw Mort, dragged away from him, fighting like a demon—saw him pick up one of Carter's huskies bodily and fling him into the mob. Slim Downey's body was smouldering over there in the flaming switch of the frequency converter. But the great machine still sang its song of vast energies unleashed; on a different note now—Slim's sacrifice had changed the characteristic of the emanations.

All was chaos in the blue abyss. The Great Ones were swinging around in a wide arc that was carrying them ever nearer.

Overhead, the Lesser Ones were victorious. One by one the Dark Ones vanished in blue vapor puffs until all were destroyed. In the balconies, the pigmy folk were kneeling; a new chant had arisen, and in its wailing note was supplication, and dread of the wrath of the Great Ones. Their ages-old faith had returned.

Otto Zimmerman had joined Pete now. Together they beat off a half dozen of Carter's maddened brutes. Mort flung himself into the tangle, cursing vividly. Blindly, desperately, the three fought.

And then there was a new lurching of Earth's satellite, a general swaying and crunching and grinding of the space about them. Only half conscious of what transpired, Peters knew there were many of the Lesser Ones about them. They were rushed out of dark passages and through rose-lit vistas of blue columns, hustled from the melée by the spheres.

Now they were again in the pit bottom where Rocket VII and the "Hornet" lay waiting. There was much activity of the Lesser Ones, and a flow of liquid blue metal came in to close off the opening which led to the inner realm. Dozens of the blue-white globes converged on the great rocket ship, invisible energies crackling in their midst, and she melted down swiftly to join the blue torrent which already was congealing to seal off the ancient world within.

Urged on and assisted by the friendly Lesser Ones, they boarded the "Hornet" and soon were rising speedily out of the pit. And all was darkness and mystery beneath them.

But a majestic voice came out of the depths, a voice that was strong in the consciousness though it sounded not in the ears. It told them all was well in the blue realm; told them the conspirators were no more; told them Luna's surface was free to those of Earth who might come in search of its treasures. They, the Great Ones, the Lesser Ones, and the pigmy folk, would remain inside until the end of time. The adventure was ended.

Clark Peters sucked in his breath sharply when the "Hornet" shot up out of the pit and over the crater's rim. The blazing sun greeted them. It was a wonderful thing to see.

"Himmel!" Otto Zimmerman exclaimed, "Earth iss gone; der sun iss here. Id vos Downey's act. Hiss body shorted der energy, made it negatiff. Ven der Great Vuns mofed der shall followed, und der moon turned completely ofer, nicht wahr? Now ve alvays see der odder side from Earth—alvays."

Mort Saunders wrinkled his brow and tugged at his fiery lip ornament. Figuring it out, Mort was. Pete laughed, then sobered on the instant.

"We'll not speak of the Great Ones." he breathed. "Or of any of it—about the blue realm, I mean."

The others agreed vociferously. No one would believe them, not in a million years. And besides, there was something—perhaps that majestic voice; perhaps Slim's deed—which bid them keep silence. And so the story has been a secret these many years, coming to light only with the unearthing of Clark Peters' diary.

Peters will be remembered as the hero of the "Hyperionic" disaster a year ago. He it was who saved eighteen passengers of the ill-fated space liner from certain death in the lava pools of Mercury ere he succumbed to his own burns and injuries. Of him no more need be said.

Otto Zimmerman is an old, old man who smiles and nods agreement when asked to confirm the tale of the diary.

But Mort Saunders, older still, and his once fiery hirsute adornments now white as the driven snow, is more specific. Certain of the personal details about Pete that the diarist omitted, he will be perfectly willing to tell.

"Huh!" he has said, "Pete didn't record the half. In my humble opinion, it was *he* who saved the Great Ones. True? Of course it's true; go ahead and print it if you want to. Nobody will take any stock in it but Captain Wallace James.

"And he won't believe it either."

Queer, stunted creatures, thousands of them it appeared, were clustering there before a massive mechanism that was being lowered from the crane arm of the rocket ship. Impossible pigmy beings that stood erect on two legs, bodies covered with iridescent scales, long arms dangling. Globular, hairless heads of chalky white, with bulging eyes and cavernous, scarlet mouths. And twenty or thirty Terrestrials in this midst, fraternizing with the ugly monstrosities!

The BLUE Room

by Gordon Philip England

. . . an uncanny feeling, don't be fooled. First appeared in
Weird Tales, November 1936.

Pollock scowled. His long, slender fingers, adeptly manipulating the euchre deck, betrayed a degree of nervous tension. He wished that Creighton and Duquette, at the table opposite, would hold their tongues. Ever since the two had entered the 77 Club half an hour before, they had been chattering like magpies. And the tommyrot they were spouting hindered him from concentrating upon his game of solitaire.

But, despite Pollock's wishes, the conversation at the other table continued unrelentingly.

The big, blond Englishman bent forward, his steel-blue eyes boring the fascinated black ones of the swarthy-faced little Frenchman. His voice was solemn:

"Yes, Duquette, I used to doubt, myself—but that was before I leased Doom Manor. After living there awhile, the most pronounced skeptic would be convinced."

Duquette nodded sober agreement.

"True, *mon ami*. I myself was skeptical until I saw your so-horrible Blue Chamber. But, after viewing it, and studying the records, only a fool would remain incredulous. *Moi*, Joseph Napoleon Duquette, I am no coward. Without fear of contradiction, I assert that I am as brave as the next fellow. Yet—name of a green monkey!—I would not sleep in that room—not for all the wealth of India."

Creighton blew a reflective smoke ring.

"And I don't blame you. A pity for Adams that he couldn't have been as discreet! Sad case, Adams. I really almost hated to take his money, after what happened. But a bet's a bet."

"Yes, certainly. Besides, Adams will not miss the two hundred pounds. He is still in the sanitarium, is he not?"

Creighton flipped his cigarette stub into an ash-tray. His voice grew reminiscent.

"He must be; I haven't heard of his being released. When we found him he was

161

a raving maniac. You could hear his screams from within the cottage, quarter of a mile away. I have always believed it was after the sixth shot that he went mad."

Duquette twirled his wax-ended black mustache.

"Ah, yes. And his automatic was empty, you say?"

Creighton made a silent sign of affirmation.

"But of course," Duquette shook his head gravely, "to attempt to shoot an apparition is the height of imbecility. For against a specter, you comprehend, bullets are useless."

"Of course. But Adams was a skeptic, you know. More—he was a dead shot. He had absolute faith in his ability as a marksman. And—to do him justice—he must have kept his nerve well up until the last. Six of the bullet holes in the wall are within a small radius, at about the height of a woman's heart. It was only the seventh, last shot, that went wild. That is why I think it was after the sixth that he cracked."

"Doubtless you are correct. Well, as you marked, *mon ami*, it was a sad business. At least, however, Adams' fate has had a salutary effect upon other unbelievers. No one has taken you up on the bet again, I understand."

Creighton's laugh was scornful.

"No fear. No one would have the nerve."

By now Pollock was distinctly annoyed. Suddenly, he threw down his cards and sprang to his feet. He strode wrathfully across to the other table.

"Look here," he began hotly, "I couldn't help hearing your conversation. Now, let me introduce myself. I'm Jimmy Pollock. And I kick every black cat out of my way, walk under ladders regularly, smash thirteen mirrors a year just for luck—and spill salt at least once a week. What I mean, gentlemen, I don't believe in disembodied spirits, apparitions and such balderdash. If this chap Adams you were gassing about shot seven times at your dashed spook and registered seven misses, he must have been a rotten shot. There never was a ghost yet that a bullet wouldn't kill!"

Creighton and Duquette exchanged significant glances; then the former addressed the interrupter frigidly:

"Let me be sure that I understand you, my friend. You say you are a skeptic. A disbeliever in returned spirits?"

Jimmy Pollock thrust out his hard, lean jaw aggressively.

"Ghosts are bunkum!"

"A large statement, and one you'll find it difficult to prove. Well, put up or shut up!"

"Eh?" Pollock blinked at him.

"Put up or shut up," repeated Creighton. He drew a hand from his pocket and threw down on the table a two-hundred pound note. "If you're ready to back up your boast, cover that. My friend Duquette here will hold the stakes."

Pollock drew out his own billfold. He extracted a matching note and fingered it tentatively.

"What are the terms of the bet?" he rasped.

"The same as with Adams," explained Creighton. "You will arrive at Doom Manor at eleven next Friday night. It will be, I may mention, Friday the thirteenth. But, of course, as you are not superstitious, that little item won't interest you. You will, upon arrival, accompany me to the Blue Room, and after you have examined it thoroughly I shall lock you in. There will be a portable telephone connected with Jasmine Cottage, and Duquette or myself will be ready to answer a call at any time. You will have no light except the moon-rays filtering in through the iron-barred window partly raised, so that if you start to scream as Adams did, we can hear you at the cottage.

"I'll give you a .45 automatic containing seven cartridges. If you remain in the room overnight without calling or phone for help, and come out at six the next morning alive and well, you win the wager. If, however, you summon assistance, go off your head, or are found dead, you forfeit your stake . . . Well, how about it? Are you game?"

Pollock thought for a moment. Creighton noticed his hesitation. He laughed contemptuously.

"Oh, of course, if you're afraid—"

Pollock cut in sharply: "Afraid? Don't make me laugh. Of course I'm not."

He slapped down his note upon Creighton's, then added another. "If you're not afraid yourself, Creighton, cover that. I'd like to get back what you took from poor Adams, as well . . . Right! Now, bring on your spook!"

At five minutes to eleven on the following Friday night, Creighton and Duquette stood on the porch at Jasmine Cottage staring down the drive. Creighton broke the silence:

"You think he'll really come?"

Duquette nodded with conviction.

"Oh yes, he has nerve enough, I think . . . Everything is prepared?"

"I think so . . . Oh look, car lights! That must be our friend now."

Then Creighton uttered an exclamation.

"Oh yes, I forgot. The automatic. I put it away after filling the magazine this afternoon, you know—in the top left-hand drawer of my desk. Better run up and get it, while I welcome our ghost hunter."

"*Bon.* I will join you at the manor-house."

So while Creighton went out to greet Pollock, the little Frenchman hurried up to his friend's room for the pistol. Without troubling to snap on the switch, he felt his way across the desk, opened the drawer, and took out the automatic. With a grunt of satisfaction, he pocketed it.

Bounding down the stairs, Duquette hastened up to the manor-house, where he found the other two men awaiting him.

"Well," said Creighton, "I think we are ready. Shall we inspect the room immediately?"

"Suits me." Pollock was laconic.

Creighton silently led the way up some stairs. At the end of the corridor lay the Blue Room. He snapped on the single light.

"Well, here we are," he observed briskly.

Pollock glanced about him. The room—a fairly large one—contained a large four-poster bed, beside which was a small stand holding the telephone. Upon a side wall opposite the bed hung a hideous full-length picture depicting a bloody-handed spectral figure in the act of strangling a child. This horrible painting might have shaken the nerves of the superstitious, but to the skeptic appeared merely disgusting.

"The johnny that perpetrated that atrocity," he remarked caustically, "must have had a bad case of the D.T.s . . . I suppose the books go with it."

As he spoke, Pollock stepped across to a well-filled, built-in book-case. He glanced carelessly at a few of the titles. All were decidedly suggestive. *Uncanny Yarns, Tales of Wandering Spirits, The Headless Cavalier*—and the like.

At random Pollock pulled out a book (it was *Bedtime Tales*) and opened it. The first words to catch his eye were these:

The screams continued for some minutes, while the terrified servants battered frantically at the heavy oaken door, then died into a faint but no less horrible gibbering. When finally the domestics broke in they found their master squatting in the chimney-corner mouthing imbecilities. So white had grown his hair—raven-black an hour before—that they scarcely recognized him. But it was his forehead that held their attention most. Across it was the imprint of a woman's blood-stained hand. It—"

Pollock snapped the book shut and returned it to the shelf. From behind him sounded the lugubrious voice of Creighton:

"Perhaps, Mr. Pollock, you are unacquainted with the history of the Blue Room. Doom Manor, so tradition says, was owned five hundred years ago by Sir Austin Fairholm. The knight married a girl named Ann Fenriss, whose mother was reputed to have been a witch. On her wedding night Ann, in a fit of insane jealousy, strangled Sir Austin as he lay asleep; then, cheating the hangman, hanged herself inside this clothes closet." Creighton pointed to a gaping empty doorway at the farther end of the room. "If you will step inside, you will see the large steel hook in the rafter overhead. It was from that they found the body suspended."

Creighton's voice sank to a hollow whisper:

"Every night, between midnight and dawn, the apparition is said to appear. If by any chance anyone is asleep in the bed, the specter strangles him, then hangs itself from the hook, where it remains until daybreak."

Pollock forced a laugh.

"A female strangler, eh? Say, it looks as if I'll get my money's worth."

Creighton and Duquette looked at him solemnly, without speaking. Their expressions were so unpleasant that, in spite of himself, the skeptic knew a moment's uneasiness. He covered his momentary qualms with another laugh.

"Well, if you have finished with your childish exhibits, suppose we get down to business." He drew an official-looking document from his breast pocket. "Here, if you two will just witness to this, please. Nothing like having everything regular, you know."

"Why, what's this?" Creighton took the paper suspiciously. Coolly Pollock explained:

"Oh, just a little formality. Merely a statement of the terms of the wager, and your promise that if my bullets do any mischief I shall not be held responsible. I want you to understand, gentlemen, that if I do see any unknown moving object in this room tonight I will shoot. Any human being who tries impersonating your lady strangler will do so at the risk of his own skin!"

Creighton smiled.

"No fear, Mr. Pollock. I can see that you are a determined—although sadly mistaken—young man. And neither my friend nor myself has any intention of serving as a pistol target. No, no, my dear fellow, if you are visited by an apparition tonight, I can guarantee that it will be genuine specter. And if you want to blaze away at it, why, go ahead. Your bullets won't have much effect, though, I'm afraid. You can see where Adams' went."

He waved his hand meaningly toward a number of bullet-holes in the wall opposite them. Pollock's gaze followed thoughtfully. He noted that, as Creighton had observed at the London club, the seventh bullet had gone wild. Involuntarily he shuddered, but quickly recovered.

"Well, then, if you'll just sign, please."

"Oh, by all means, by all means." Hastily, Creighton scrawled his signature; then Duquette followed suit. Pollock took back the paper, waved it in the air to dry the ink, then nodded with satisfaction and slipped the folded document into his pocket.

"Thank you very much, gentlemen. Well, I think I'm ready, then. But—hold on a minute. What about that gun?"

"Duquette will give it to you before we leave," assured Creighton. "But first, another small formality. You're not allowed matches, you know, nor other means of making a light. Just to make certain that you haven't accidently overlooked any such forbidden articles, you won't object to our searching you?"

They searched very thoroughly, finding no matches, but unkindly confiscating an efficient cigarette-lighter; then they stood back, smiling.

"Well," growled the skeptic, "I hope you're satisfied. And now, one question, please. Suppose I shoot this dashed apparition—and kill it? What shall I do then?"

Creighton smiled superiorly.

"My dear fellow, you *can't* shoot a ghost. It simply isn't done, you know."

Pollock's answering smile was unpleasant.

"No? Well, gentlemen, I am a sure shot, and if an apparition shows itself, I will shoot to kill. In the eventuality that I am successful, what am I to do?"

"Oh, in that case," returned Creighton airily, "you can call us on the phone and inform us. But, if you do so, in order to win the bet you'll have to produce your victim."

"Fair enough . . . Here, what are you doing with that light?"

For Creighton was coolly starting to unscrew the electric bulb.

"Wait!" snapped Pollock sharply. "I want that gun!"

Duquette flashed faultlessly white teeth.

"A thousand pardons, *monsieur.* I had almost forgotten." He drew the pistol from his pocket with a flourish. "A most efficient weapon, complete with a fresh clip of cartridges." He tendered the automatic with a mocking bow.

"Fair enough," repeated Pollock, pocketing the pistol with an air of supreme contentment. "Well, then, gentlemen, I needn't detain you any longer. See you in the morning."

The skeptic heard the grate of the key in the lock, the click of the bolt, then a sound of retreating footsteps. After that there was nothing but ominous silence.

As he turned to go over to the bed, Pollock's gaze fell upon the picture. With a startled exclamation, he leapt back.

Little wonder the ghost-hunter was startled. The forms in the portrait had undergone a horrifying transformation. Hideous under the electric light, they were a hundred times more so in darkness. An unearthly light seemed to emanate from the picture faces, and the eyes of the ghost strangler glowed like balls of flame.

For some moments Pollock gazed at the ghastly figures in horrified fascination; then, suddenly, he laughed shakily.

"By Jove, that surely fooled me for a minute," he admitted to himself frankly.

"Of course, though, the explanation's simple. Those beauties touched up the figures with some kind of phosphorescent paint . . . No wonder that poor devil Adams went mad!"

Now that he understood the trick, the picture did not seem so terrifying; so, turning his back upon it, Pollock went over to the bed. He sat down upon it and waited.

Minutes passed. Pollock caught himself listening. Of course any apparently spiritual manifestation this night would be the work of human agencies. On the other hand, there was something he distinctly disliked about the whole atmosphere of the place. He never had fancied such ancient houses much, anyway. A great deal must have happened here since the building had been erected. Could that story about the female strangler be true? Of course it might be. Horrible things of such a nature had occurred in other houses in medieval times, so why not in Doom Manor?

Something stirred and groaned in a corner of the room. Pollock held his breath and waited. Presently he heard a strange, rustling sound. It seemed to come from the clothes closet.

The skeptic drew out his automatic and pointed it toward the empty doorway. But now all was still again.

Pollock clutched his gun tighter and waited. Five minutes passed ... ten ... fifteen. But nothing moved again. The ghost-hunter laughed mirthlessly.

"I must have been just hearing things. There wasn't anything."

Then he started. As if to belie his assertion, he heard the thing again. But this time the apparition grew more versatile. After uttering a hollow groan, it clanked a chain.

Then again, all was silent. Pollock cursed softly.

"By the lord Harry," he exclaimed, his voice oddly shrill and tremulous, "I'm going to have a look in that closet!"

Resolutely, Pollock groped his way over to the doorway. Pistol in hand, he stood a few feet from the entrance, waiting for the thing to show itself. But all remained silent as the tomb.

The skeptic waited a few moments longer, then cautiously advanced. Something was in that clothes closet. Either that, or else his imagination had been tricking him. He went closer to that empty, gaping doorway. Still no sound. Then he crept over and peered in. He saw nothing. Growing bolder, he stepped into the closet and felt about it.

But the closet was empty!

The very emptiness of the place unnerved the skeptic. His groping hand came in contact with the steel hook. Its feel sent an involuntary shudder through him. All at once, the closet seemed alive with horrors from the past.

"Ugh," shuddered Pollock, "I don't much like the feel of this place. Maybe the girl did hang herself here ... I'm going back to bed."

He was only half-way there when the thing groaned again. He whirled about and made a rush for the closet, only to find it empty again.

Once more the ghost-hunter retreated to the four-poster. Before long came the noise of the clanking chain, then again that ominous, nerve-racking silence.

Pollock was beginning to feel desperate.

"Look here," he called, trying to make his voice sound stern and authoritative, and feeling miserable; "I don't know who's making that unholy row, but you'd best not let me see you. You poke your ugly spook face out of that clothes closet—and I'll pump you full of lead!"

After that, no further sounds issued from the closet. Half an hour crawled by, but the thing did not return again.

Pollock began to feel complacent. "That's fixed them," he thought. "They realize I'm a dangerous man and mean business. Well, since they've gone away, I'll see if I can't get a bit of sleep."

Slipping the automatic under his pillow, the skeptic pulled up a blanket over him, and shut his eyes. At first the remembrance of the happenings of the night kept him wide awake, but gradually he grew drowsy. Presently he slept . . .

Exactly how long Pollock slept he couldn't have told, but suddenly he awoke. His eyes popped open. Horror-stricken, they fastened upon something in the center of the room.

It was a tall, white figure. As it glided forward toward the bed its chain clanked harshly. Then slowly it stretched out its arms. Its long, slender fingers clenched and unclenched, working nervously.

The apparition glided closer. By the phosphorescent glow emanating from the picture, and the pale moon-rays shimmering between the window bars, the man in the bed could see it with horrible distinctness. Its hands continued to weave the air in that hideously suggestive fashion, then the creature bent, as if about to spring.

Now convinced that this was not a nightmare but an awful reality, Pollock went into action. His hand slid beneath his pillow, drawing out the automatic. He sat up and pointed it. Although icy fingers of dread seemed clutching at his heart, his hand was steady as a rock.

"See here," the sound of his own voice startled him, "you'd better scram. I'm a dead shot, I am. Just one step nearer, mister ghost, and you're a dead spook. Dead as a leg of mutton!"

But the ghostly intruder did not appear frightened. It clanked its chain menacingly, and the long fingers continued those suggestive choking gestures. Again the thing prepared to advance.

Pollock's voice was a hoarse croak:

"For the last time, now. I'm warning you!"

Unheeding, the apparition glided forward.

Pollock pulled the trigger.

A realistic scream ripped the air. The thing sprang upward, then hit the floor with a resounding thud. It lay sprawled in a silent, huddled mass.

Pollock stared incredulously. The thing remained motionless. The skeptic uttered a cry of exultation.

"By the lord Harry," he shouted, "I've killed the ghost!"

Cautiously, he slipped one foot to the floor, then the other. After all, the spook might be shamming. He advanced with still greater caution. He poked the mass gingerly with his toe. It had a horrible feel, soft and yielding.

With a scream, the ghost-killer leapt back. He grabbed for the telephone.

A moment more, and he was ringing the cottage. A Gallic voice answered mockingly:

"Are you there? So, *mon ami*, you have had enough."

"Is that you, Duquette?" yelled Pollock. "Come on over, for God's sake! I've shot the ghost!"

He heard a startled French oath, then the click of the receiver.

Presently came the sound of running feet. The key grated in the lock and Duquette bounced in, a flashlight in his hand.

At sight of the huddled shape on the floor, he recoiled in horror.

"*Mon Dieu!*" he screamed.

Pollock snatched the flashlight from his trembling hand. By the rays of the electric torch he saw what lay there: a white sheeted figure, with a chain about its waist, and a slit-eyed hood over its head. The upper part of the front of the sheet was ominously red. A trickle of crimson oozed through a hole in the cloth.

With hands as shaky as Duquette's own, Pollock pulled off the masking hood, revealing the face of Creighton. The dull, glassy eyes stared up at the ghost-killer unseeingly.

Pollock felt suddenly sick. He reeled to his feet, his face twitching.

"The fool!" he said brokenly. "Why did he do it? I warned that I'd shoot."

Duquette was shaking like a man with ague.

"But it is impossible," he whispered hoarsely. "You cannot have killed him, *monsieur*. The bullets were blanks."

Pollock stared at him in amazement; then his face hardened. He was beginning to understand. On a sudden thought, he turned the light toward the closet. A glance showed him the truth. A portion of the back wall was slid aside, disclosing a secret passage.

"So it was all a trick!" he exclaimed contemptuously. "That conversation at the club was staged for my benefit. You swine planned to treat me as you had Adams, then to fatten on my money."

Then a puzzled look crept into Pollock's eyes.

"But—I still don't understand one thing. Those bullets in the wall. Surely, Adams couldn't have missed *every time?*"

Duquette was still staring at his friend's corpse. He answered mechanically:

"But those were blanks, also, *monsieur*. The bullet-holes? Bah! We fired those shots *after* we had taken Adams from the room."

Again the Frenchman gazed amazedly at the body. As if to convince himself, he put his fingers to the wound; then, as he felt the blood, sprang back as though struck by an adder.

"But yes. He is dead, of a certainty. Name of a dog, but it is incredible! I myself saw him load the gun with blanks. Permit that I examine it, *monsieur.*"

Silently Pollock handed over the weapon. Duquette inspected it unbelievingly.

"But yes. These are real bullets. Yet—*I saw him fill the magazine with blanks.*"

Wonderingly, the Frenchman turned the gun over in his hands. Suddenly, his face went white as milk. His legs gave way, and he sat down heavily upon the floor.

Pollock caught him roughly by the shoulder and shook him vigorously.

"Here," he exclaimed, "what's the matter, man? What is it?"

Duquette's eyes held unfathomable horror. When he spoke, his words reflected that expression.

"Listen, *monsieur.* Tonight, before you came, Creighton sent me up for the gun. It was in the left-hand drawer of his desk."

"In the left-hand drawer?" Pollock repeated the words uncomprehendingly.

Suddenly Duquette laughed—a mirthless, hysterical laugh.

"But yes, *monsieur* . . . Creighton had two .45 automatics of the same make, with only the serial numbers different. This one must have been in the *right-hand* drawer. *In the dark I made the mistake!*"

The Weird
GREEN Eyes of Sari

by Margaret McBride Hoss

"Those soft and limpid green eyes" . . . you'll be "Sari" when you "sea" your worst fears realized! First appeared in Weird Tales, March 1925.

Since man first reared himself upright on his two legs and looked at the stars, the sea and the things of the sea have worked strange enchantments upon that inward part of him he calls his soul. I have known many men whom the sea has regenerated. Like the boom of the Almighty, sweeping away rottenness and filth, the salt wind sometimes blows clean the secret places of the soul. On the other hand, I have known many men whom the sea has cursed. Back to the land that spawned them it tosses them with queer tormenting kinks in their souls, kinks destined never to be ironed out by anything save the impartial hand of death. But only once have I known the sea, or a thing that crept out of the sea, to steal the soul from the body of a man.

In a modest coast town, tucked unobtrusively away in the southeast corner of the map, Philip Sanborne and I grew up together. Our green apples, our marbles, our dreams and our lickings all lacked savor unless we shared them one with the other. First as a kid and later as a man, I admired Phil inordinately. He was easily the best man I have ever known. Not the pious sort of good, you understand: never went near a church, proclaimed his faults and hid his virtues, and in particularly lurid moments made use of a vocabulary as picturesque and colorful as that of any pirate who ever scoured the seven seas. But he was innately clean and selfless and square; he couldn't have been any other way even had he tried.

He was beautifully built, broad shouldered, narrow hipped, with hair of that attractive, glinting blondness that shines like precious metal in the sun. In appearance he might have been one of the blue-eyed heroes of the old Norse sagas, a hardy sea rover worshiper of Odin and the great god Thor come down from Valhalla; but, as a matter of fact, Phil was indifferent to the sea. Always clever with his hands, he built a squat, friendly little house that he adored and puttered over endlessly. He lined it with books and framed it with flowers; he cluttered it with quaint outlandish furniture carved in his leisure moments; he saturated it with pipe smoke and peopled

171

it with the dreams that come to a man when he is young and a little lonely. Most of these dreams bore the quiet gray eyes and thoughtful face of the one girl in whom Phil ever evinced more than a passing interest—Mary McKee.

My wife and I were more than ordinarily fond of Mary and we were genuinely distressed when the years slipped by with nothing definite coming of their friendship. The pitiful truth was that Mary cared more than Phil. Hers was the steady, unswerving love of a woman, whose heart once given cannot be recalled at will. I think there were times when she tried desperately to call it back into her keeping, for the heart of Mary was a prize that was coveted by more men than one; but Phil's it was in the beginning and Phil's it stubbornly remained.

How or where Phil came under the spell of Sari Threnow's shoal-green eyes, I don't know. There was something terrible and at the same time infinitely pathetic about his passion for her; it worried and tore at him like a vindictive live creature determined to leave him neither mental peace nor surcease from bodily longing. She was lovely to look at, but there was an intangible something about her beauty that I hated. I never looked at her without crushing down an itching, maniacal desire to twist her long yellow hair about her pale throat and . . .

I am not naturally subject to homicidal seizures, either, I assure you! At the same time, I was heartily ashamed of that desire. Later, I cursed myself sick for throttling it.

Her mode of dress was so startling that it deserves mention. Always she was garbed in silvery, shimmering, exquisite stuffs, fashioned with an odd pointed effect trailing in back, and her only ornaments were strands of pearls that vied with her skin in whiteness. When she and Phil were together, the presence of others was seemingly regarded as a nuisance to be escaped as quickly and expeditiously as possible. When Phil was busy, she came often to see my wife, Nancy, and two vertical lines of worry etched between Nancy's eyes were the invariable sequels to her visits. Now Nancy has no kinship with the damp, lachrymose type of female who drips tears merely for the pleasure she derives thereby, and when I came home one evening and found her crying, the incident left me unpleasantly shaken.

"Don't mind me, Bob," she said, dabbing at her eyes and attempting a watery smile. "Sari Threnow just left. There is something about that woman that puzzles and frightens me. It isn't anything she says, because she never says anything at all—just sits and watches me. Oh, you can't imagine! My tiniest move never escapes her weird green eyes. She is absorbingly interested in the way I wash my dishes, sweep my house, comb my hair and darn your socks. She behaves like a visitor from another planet, who, ignorant of the ways of women, tries to learn by heart the things that women do. Oh, I know what I'm saying sounds ridiculous! And more ridiculous still is my creepy feeling of certainty that she wants something, wants it so terribly she would move heaven itself to gain it. It isn't love and it isn't money or any of the things a normal woman craves—it's something incredible—something she is working night and day to take away from Phil. It frightens me."

My bland demeanor was far from being a true index to my feelings, for I recalled with a shiver of disgust the emotions that a sight of Sari Threnow never failed to evoke in me.

"You're letting your imagination run away with you, dear," I soothed. "If she's after anything poor old Phil could give, he'd hand it over and be pathetically grateful to her for taking it.

"A material something, yes. But it isn't a question of that."

Nancy's quiet conviction silenced the protest that rose to my lips.

"Do you think she loves Phil?" I asked after an uneasy pause.

My wife made a surprising answer.

"I think she tries, but she doesn't know how."

"Fiddlesticks!" I replied. "I'm going to see Phil tomorrow and tell him that her visits here must come to an end."

But I never did.

That very night Sari Threnow vanished as suddenly and mysteriously as she had appeared. I pictured her flitting like some exotic bird of passage to some fairer region; she wasn't a Mary McKee—one man couldn't hold her long. Might lucky for Phil, too, I mused. Of course he'd be hard hit for a while—but time is a marvelous healer of wounds.

I trailed over town searching for him. I wanted to drag him home to one of Nancy's hot, savory dinners. I wanted to keep him with me while I wrangled about the morals of the Patagonians, enlarge upon the utter inadequacy of charlotte russe as a dessert—anything to keep him from brooding over his ill-starred slavery to a woman's green eyes and white, white skin.

When the day passed and I found no trace of him, I was worried. Then the second day dragged by, a replica of the first, I was frantic. When the third day ushered in a troop of crawling rumors, I was beside myself. Of course it was inevitable that a woman of Sari Threnow's personal appearance should be conspicuous. Phil's infatuation for her, too, was public property. The thing that damned Phil was this: her silvery clothes and her priceless pearls, left intact, offered to the village mute testimony that her going had been neither regular nor premeditated. I got my first clue of Phil's whereabouts from a rum-soaked piece of human driftwood who claimed to have seen him wandering, hatless and disheveled, among the sand dunes.

"Hanted he looked for sure, sir," he mumbled, blinking his bleary eyes at me. "For all the world like the ghost of the pore, pretty lady he murdered wouldn't give him no rest. All he done was stare out at the sea like he was listenin' for somethin'—listenin' for somethin'. It's hanted he is for sure!"

It was among the dunes that I finally found him. At first I couldn't believe it was Phil. He was changed—terribly. His eyes were the eyes of a man struggling vainly to understand some nameless horror that had befallen him; the selfsame look was doubtless in the eyes of the first fallen angel when he felt the barriers of hell closing around him. He stared at me in a curious, groping fashion as if I were some stranger whose identity had eluded him.

"For God's sake, what's the matter?" I pleaded.

"I with I knew," he answered dully. "I—wish—I—knew."

I fairly hurled my next question at him.

"Where is Sari Threnow?"

He made a little, impotent gesture toward the sea.

"D'you mean she's drowned?" I cried.

It seemed centuries before Phil replied.

"No. There are some things you can't drown."

"Cut out the riddles," I begged. "Back in the village they're saying you murdered Sari Threnow. Of course I know that's nonsense. But I'm here to find out what happened."

"The village can say what it damn pleases and if I told you the truth you wouldn't believe me. Go away and leave me alone, Bob."

"Of course I'm not going," I said quietly. "Sit down, Phil! Quit prowling around staring at the sea! You make me as nervous as a cat. Cigarette?"

He took one, not from a desire to smoke, but because he wanted something to twist with his fingers, and he seemed tormented by some inner restlessness that drove him to continual bodily movement. As he talked, I knew his mind was not on what he was saying; there was a hushed expectancy in his attitude that brought back the words of the bit of human driftwood with maddening persistency: "Listenin' for somethin'—hanted he is for sure!"

"You'll think I'm crazy, Bob," Phil began. "Maybe I am, but I don't think so— yet. From the first time I looked into Sari Threnow's green eyes, I was like a man possessed. There was a mystery and an elusiveness about her that maddened me almost as much as the clinging persistence with which she drew me to her—a persistence that gave me a horrible sensation of being caught in a net and smothered—a net woven of her soft yellow hair."

He broke off sharply.

"Did you hear anything, old man?"

"Nothing but the wind," I said. "Go on."

"She was obsessed by a strange passion for the sea. That last night, we were walking on the beach and she tilted her face toward me in the moonlight and I—I'd never touched her before, you understand—I crushed her in my arms and kissed her. And Bob" (his voice shook), "her lips tasted salty and they were cold and clammy to the touch like the belly of a fish. As they clung to mine, I swear I felt them drawing something holy from me, something that, to lose, takes all the color and meaning from life and leaves it only an empty horror. Then she slipped from my arms like water and I saw—so help me God!—that she was a thing with a tail like a fish. She laughed at me as she dived into the sea—and this holy thing she stole from me went with her. You know the tale the old women tell of mermaids who come out of the sea to seek for a soul from men like . . ."

"What utter drivel!" I croaked.

I was having difficulty controlling my vocal cords.

"Why, it's monstrous—you're just plain—"

Here my speaking apparatus deserted me entirely.

"Crazy!" rasped Phil savagely. "Go on and say it! Listen—wasn't that someone calling?"

I felt the goose flesh rising in tiny prickles on my skin as I asked a question whose answer I already knew.

"Who is it you're listening for, Phil?"

"That—thing—with a tail like a fish. Sometime—I'll hear it call—out there in the depths of the sea. Then, who knows? I may gain back my—soul."

"See here," I fumed, "I've heard all I can stand of this! Some decent food and a hot bath will work wonders with you. You're going home with me."

Phil turned his face toward the sea. It was as if already he had forgotten I was there. I dragged him to his feet, ignoring the dangerous glitter that flared into his blue eyes at my touch on his arm.

"You're going home with me," I repeated.

A quirk that fell short of being a smile twisted one corner of his mouth.

"An army mule is a tractable fairy compared to you, Bob. But remember this. I'm coming back. And I'm coming alone!"

For five restless days and as many nights he tramped the shore of the sea. He ate almost nothing and he slept only when outraged nature snatched him into short periods of dream-harried oblivion. The sixth night, he heard the call for which he waited—but it was no Sari Threnow, after all, who gave back the soul to the body of Philip Sanborne. A frantic pounding at my door in the black rain-lashed hours of the early morning jerked me into instant wakefulness. Pulling on a perfunctory array of clothes as I ran, I stumbled downstairs and shot the bolt. I don't know whom I expected to find, but assuredly not Mary McKee. She was drenched to the bone; her flimsy dress was whipped to ribbons by the gale; and the only spot of color on her face was a great, livid bruise on her cheek.

"Hurry," she gasped. "I'm afraid Phil is dead—dead, I tell you! He's lying in his motor boat down at the wharf. Hurry!"

Phil's limp form was a dead weight as I bore him home through the storm; there was the faintest flutter of breath in his nostrils and that was all.

It was while we waited his return to consciousness that Mary said, "Of course you're wondering what happened. Most of it is meaningless, garbled blur to me, but I'll try to tell you. With the coming of the wind and the rain, I had a strange presentiment that some evil thing of the sea menaced Phil. I think it's because I love him so much that I knew. I've always loved him, you know—always—" Mary's low voice trailed off in a sagging diminuendo as if flattened into nothingness by the weight of unbidden memories. Quick tears brimmed Nancy's eyes.

"And then, dead?" Nancy prompted gently.

"Of course I thought of Phil's motor boat," resumed Mary, "so I hurried down to the wharf. I got there as he was putting out to sea. I begged him to stay with me, but he didn't hear a word I said. I was crazy with fright. I clung to him but he shook me off and once he even—"

Mechanically, one of her hands touched her bruised cheek. At Nancy's cry of pity, she flamed, "Don't you dare blame Phil for that! In his right mind he'd die sooner than strike a woman! I managed to crawl into the boat and then things went hazy. When my head cleared, I realized that we were headed toward the open sea. Phil steered by sound rather than direction, though—he kept listening—listening. Oh, it was horrible! The boat bobbed around like a cork gone mad. I knew I'd have to do something, and that soon. I pawed around in the blackness (Phil always leaves his tools pitched helter-skelter) and as luck would have it I found a big monkey-wrench—a horrid, murderous thing. Clutching it, I crept toward him on my hands and knees. It seemed the only way out. Just as I was ready to—to—he crumpled up in a heap, flabby as a rag doll. I didn't touch him. I'll swear to that! I'm a good sailor, but God only knows how I ever made land. But I'm afraid it wasn't any good after all. Phil wants to die.

As if to bear witness to the truth of her words, Phil's eyes opened. Accusingly they probed Mary's stricken face.

"You dragged me back to face life without a soul," he whispered. "I'll never forgive you—never. Please go away quietly where I'll never have to look at you again."

Then he turned his face to the wall and lay there for long hours without moving. Never for the tick of a second was he free from the tormenting thought that he had lost his soul. His former restlessness gave way to an apathy far more alarming. He did not sleep unless under the influence of an opiate. Physically, he was sound enough, although unbelievably weakened from exposure, under-nourishment and worry, but mentally he was a wreck.

"I'm an obscene, unspeakable thing, Bob," he would mutter, "a man without a soul, haunted by eyes green as the treacherous shoals that lie at the edge of the sea—greedy green eyes forever laughing at me and the tang of salt in my mouth. God!"

Day or night we never left him; at 3 o'clock in the morning came my time to relieve Mary. The fourth morning, instead of greeting me with her usual tired little nod and slipping away to bed, she faced me with her head thrown back and her shoulders squared. She was a gallant fighter, was Mary!

"Phil is dying by inches. But I won't let him die! I won't! Bob, you're pretty much of a heathen, but even a heathen prays to the gods he fashions. If you'd try it might help me."

In a shadowy corner of the room I waited and shivered as if with the ague. To my distorted fancy, Phil's face, as stark as the face of a corpse, floated in the eerie pool of light spilled by a pale boudoir lamp. I gave a great gasp of relief when Mary bent over him; the face of Mary was the face of life incarnate. The poised serene beauty of it brought an ache to my throat.

"Philip, dear," I heard her plead, "listen to me carefully. If a kiss can take away the soul from the body of a man, surely, surely a kiss can give it back to him! That is only reasonable, isn't it? If some evil thing has robbed a man of his soul, I know the kiss of the woman who loves him can help him find it again. The love kiss of a woman can bring anything—anything—to a man if he will only believe—and believe hard enough."

I hid my face in my hands as her head drooped toward him, for there are some things it is sacrilege to watch. There came a long, long silence; then softly, slowly as if from an infinite distance I heard Phil's voice.

"Your eyes, Mary—I'm glad God made them gray and kind as the smoke that curls upward from a man's hearth-fire. If you'll kiss me again—I think—I think—I can go to sleep."

Twenty-four hours later, he woke and shouted for his clothes; he grew incensed when they were not immediately forthcoming and nursed a sense of injury because Nancy refused to cook him a porterhouse smothered in onions.

When he and Mary were married, he carried her away to a pleasant little sun-baked town in western Kansas, and they have a husky young hopeful now whom they call Bob. If one is disposed to accept literally his parents' glowing accounts of their progeny, Bob is a paragon of all the childish virtues. He has only one peculiarity; he cannot bear the sight of a fish, and a body of running water sends him into paroxysms of terror.

The GREEN Monster

by Arthur Macom

Bet your college days were never this exciting! The ultimate in the absent-minded professor . . . first appeared in Weird Tales, July 1928.

As I passed beneath the dense shadow of Bremlin Tower it seemed that the whole world had suddenly become a place of creeping phantoms, half visible in the heavy fog that hung about me. The complete quietude of the quadrangle palled upon my distraught nerves like the aftermath of an opiate. My feverish imagination created hideous powers in every corner of the old stone cloister that skirted my path. Then, through the curtain of darkness about me, the chimes in the tower rang out with muffled tone. It was only a matter of a few minutes before I should be in the house of my professor, yet I dreaded with unreasoning fear the thought of keeping my path. Nor could I explain the sensation. But the lights of the professor's house loomed before me; I should be there at once.

I knocked hastily upon the huge oaken door. Presently there came the sound of approaching footsteps, falling softly on the carpets within. I was surprised at the suddenness with which the door was swung open.

"Ah! Good evening, Boreau," the professor greeted me. "I have been expecting you." He glanced at me with an oddly significant air. I trailed him back into his tiny study, where he designated my chair before the remnants of a log fire. For several minutes he stood, staring at me like a cat watching a sparrow. Whatever may have been the purpose of this brief examination, he seemed to be satisfied as he sat down, facing me at an angle. At last the silence was broken by his low-pitched voice.

"Perhaps you are wondering why I have asked you here tonight?"

The inquisitiveness of my expression was his answer. Again he fell into a profound quiet. There, in the hush of the old house, with the weird atmosphere of the whole evening, I could not restrain my moody thoughts. The flitting shadows of the log fire danced grotesquely upon his long face, changing its shape and mine with every moment. His white beard was visible and invisible by turns. His eyes, too, affected by the play of changing light, gleamed sardoni-

179

cally through the dusk or faded into mysteriously gloomy pits. The spell was again broken by the professor's voice.

"Boreau," he stated, "I have an experiment." I nodded. "You have heard my theory of the concentration of thought? Doubtless it will be better if I go over it briefly, since this experiment is based upon its principles. This is my assumption."

He paused momentarily to collect his thoughts. I leaned forward eagerly, knowing that the professor's opinion was considered authoritative upon the subject.

"The theory of hypnosis holds that a person may easily be convinced of any being or state of being while he is in the hypnotic trance. Under such conditions he can actually perceive with all of his senses the being suggested by the person who has hypnotized him. This part of the theory is incontestable."

As I did not question him, he continued in a dull, ponderous monotone:

"A number of the savants have a still more advanced belief—to which I admit that I subscribe—that if the state of hypnosis has been deep enough, the subject will be open to a number of post-hypnotic influences. That is, when the subject has been awakened from the actual state of hypnosis, the beings which he has been led to see or to feel while under the influence will recur in his ordinary existence. He will hear voices or see apparitions which a person who has not been in the same state cannot hear or see. Furthermore, he will in all probability give some logical reason for his sensations, or at least some acceptable data which will substantiate his statements. Yet he does not know that these are merely the result of the suggestions of the operator, nor is he aware that he had ever experienced them before. In other words, they exist as phantoms of his own brain, which can be dispelled only at the will of the operator who has instilled them."

The professor paused, quietly observing the doubtful expression on my face. I could not see what he was driving at, yet the vague feeling of uneasiness returned to trouble me with renewed insidiousness. The silence became unbearably ominous, and I hastened to ask further questions.

"And exactly what, professor, is the aim of this experiment?'"

"This: I shall deliver in these rooms a lecture to a selected group of students. I shall tell them that there exists in this locality a certain apparition which I have seen. I have chosen a list which, I feel sure, includes only those who will be open to the power of my suggestion from my mind. By this experiment we shall determine whether this last premise of mine is actually true, whether these men will encounter the hallucination which I shall picture."

For a moment he seemed to consider giving me some further detail of his plan, but he evidently thought better of it.

"There is," he continued, "a still more fantastic premise, born of the brains of Oriental philosophers—yogis—which holds that the human mind can actually restrain, arrest, destroy, or create matter; but there is no reliable evidence to support this theory, and I have absolutely no faith in it. You may forget it, since it has no part in this experiment."

I stared at the professor in nervous astonishment. The whole scheme seemed fraught with unforeseen dangers. Yet I could not help feeling complimented that he should have told me in advance.

"Then, professor," I asked, "what is it that you wish me to do?"

I confess that I questioned him with a certain temerity, for I had no desire to become deeply involved in so mysterious an affair. The professor stared into the fire with half-closed eyes. At first I thought he had not heard me. I was mistaken.

"Boreau," he answered, casting off his mantle of silence, "you must gather in this room the men on this list by 10 o'clock tomorrow night. If they question you, tell them that you know absolutely nothing about it."

He shot me a look of warning.

"And remember, Boreau, that you must not listen to my lecture. I shall want you in the room, but if you need me, the result will be disastrous to the success of the experiment. If you feel an impulse to believe me, throw it off! I shall need you as a witness."

The tone of his voice revived my uncanny mood. The professor had risen from his chair, indicating that the interview was at an end. After murmuring my good-byes, I hastened from the house.

The day following this strange conversation found my mind filled with forebodings. I had invited the men to come to the professor's house and had maintained complete silence regarding the nature of the meeting. But in spite of my confidence in the professor's judgment, the unearthly nature of the affair had played havoc with my peace of mind.

When the appointed hour arrived, I knocked upon the professor's door. From where I stood I saw that the students had come before me. They were standing in groups of three and four, babbling disconnectedly of what might possibly occur. One of them, a certain Hallmark who was in several of my classes, called out to me from across the room.

"Hullo there, Boreau!" He hurried over to grasp my hand. Then, while I was greeting my fellow students, he whispered in my ear with an inquisitive voice: "The professor left a note for you to come immediately to his study. He was not here when we came in. And say—what's up? D'you know?"

"Not yet, Hallmark," I lied glibly.

"Darn funny he doesn't show up to say hello," he whispered. "Prof's putting on too much mystery for me!"

"He is!" I called over my shoulder, for I was on my way to the professor's study.

I found him sitting at his desk.

"You are on time," he said.

"Yes," I replied. "You wanted me?"

"Yes, Boreau. Take them into the drawing-room. The lights will be off but they can find chairs. Tell them I shall be in at once. And remember"—he laid his hand upon my shoulder with an air of gravity—"you must not believe a word that I say. The cause of science can be materially advanced tonight if you obey me. Remember: don't listen!"

"I won't," I muttered to myself as I returned to the guests.

It was a matter of minutes before I had them seated in the darkened room. The curtains had been drawn, so that there was no light except at the front, where a single beam came through a small pane.

The hum of excited conversation was suddenly interrupted by the creaking of the door. Immediately the head of the professor appeared in that single ray of light. His body was draped in some black cloth, so that his sardonic face seemed to be floating about in the darkness, from which it stood out with eerie definiteness. His eyes darted this way and that until the whispering of the men had died down to a tense hissing of breath between their teeth. Then he began to speak without any apparent change of his features.

"My friends," he murmured heavily, "it is a pleasure to have you here tonight. But you must not be nervous; you must lean back in your chairs. Lean back in your chairs—and rest. Rest! I have something to tell you but you cannot understand me if you are nervous or excited. You must rest . . . rest . . . rest!"

The breathing of the men became placid as his words affected them with their gentle persuasiveness. From somewhere outside the room came a low booming sound like the thud of a distant drum. It was warm in the darkness, and I felt a comfortable sensation of drowsiness settling over me.

"That is better," continued the professor. "Now you are quiet. Now you will listen to me. You rest . . . you no longer doubt me!"

The distant booming continued, keeping a sort of rhythm with the professor's gentle voice.

"This thing which I shall tell you is strange . . . strange. Yet you know me," his voice rambled on, "and you shall believe me. What I tell you is true and you believe me. Your minds are at rest with themselves and all shall be as I say that it shall! You believe me!"

The voice, the booming, the warmth of the room, the darkness, all seemed to lull my mind into a shadowy trance, and through the darkness I could feel the tingling of some unknown potency. I felt that I would believe the professor; but while my spirit seemed at peace, far off in the subterranean channels of my intellect I knew that something was wrong. The sensation lay dormant before the rhythm of the distant drum and the deathlike darkness. The professor droned on.

"I have seen a Thing moving about in the darkness . . . a strange and fearsome

Thing. First I saw it by the cloisters, covering in the shadows there. I have seen it again, creeping along by the wall of the great Tower. It seemed like a luminous mist, like an aura in the dusk. While I stood there watching it, it glided away, like a phantom back from the grave."

His voice trailed off into the darkness about him. The booming sound seemed to have blended with the pulsing warmth, yet I could not feel that there was much warmth. Even the professor's head, limned against the darkness by that single beam of light, seemed to have fused with the void surrounding him. All consciousness receded from me; I thought that I stood in the shadows of the cloisters with the dim outline of the Thing somewhere in the dusk before me. Then a voice came back from unfathomable distance.

"It towered above me like some monster jinni from the past. It was entirely green, with trailing shadows of green hanging from its mighty form. And its eyes, great balls of fire gleaming through the night, glared at me with murderous hatred. There was unutterable wickedness in those fiery orbs, wickedness that would have mocked me even as it slew me. When it turned upon me it reached out gigantic talons, groping in the ghoulish twilight for my throat. Then I fled from those haunted cloisters, fled before the Thing that would have slain me even as it would slay you. Oh beware! Beware of the Thing in the cloisters that will strangle you with its hideous talons. And do not look into its flaming eyes, for it will fasten you down with its tensity until it can tear the breath from your throat!"

Perspiration broke from my brow. I was seized with a fit of violent trembling. My throat seemed dry and swollen, as though I had felt the terrific clutch of those murderous hands. Fear ran through my heart and burrowed deep into the hidden recesses of my soul; for I knew I should meet this fiend incarnate, this hideous monster that transfixed its victims with gleaming eyes, to tear open their throats with its ghastly talons. My mind could not tell me where I was; I dreaded lest I was standing beside that haunted cloister where this Thing stalked in its deathly course. In vain I strove to move; I was paralyzed by fear of the unknown.

Then from afar came the voice of the professor, piercing the wall of my trance. The cloister, the Tower, seemed to totter in the gloom and go reeling off into a vague mist. All became a chaos as I went whirling through imaginary space at a tremendous velocity. Again came the voice, this time much nearer to me.

"Boreau! Boreau! Awaken! This is the professor!"

The giddiness left me as my senses began to clear, and I saw the professor standing before me in the dark. I gazed at him bewilderedly.

"I told you not to listen," he said, speaking sharply. "I warned you! Now stand here—and do not listen again!"

My mind was now quite clear: I understood that I must have fallen into a deep trance, for I was once more aware of the monotonous booming and the sultry room. The professor had glided back into the solitary beam of light. His voice continued, yet now I did not heed what he said, but strained to the sound of tense breathing in the room. Again that ponderous voice:

"Watch for this Thing when the night has come, and such demons are stalking about. Even now I feel the glare of those terrible eyes, boring into my back with their incarnate hatred. Even now I dread to glance over my shoulder, lest its fearsome arms should come stretching through the darkness toward me."

With a tremendous effort the professor forced himself to turn his head up into that beam of light. As he stared into the distance his calm features began to distort themselves with a look of unspeakable terror. His mouth sagged open; his eyes, dilated, seemed to bulge from their sockets. He flung his black-robed arms into the light above him as though to ward off some menacing gesture.

"Look!" he moaned weirdly. "It is there. Its talons are reaching at my throat! Its eyes . . . how fiendishly they gleam in the darkness! Beware of it! Flee from it! It is the Green Monster!"

There came a scrambling of feet, a falling of chairs. Someone, overcome with hysterical fear, screamed wildly. The darkness pulsated with the trembling of human bodies. The rampant horror of that moment was indescribable . . . yet I had seen nothing!

"It is gone," cried the professor loudly, this time in his natural voice. "Awaken, my friends." Then, turning toward me, he called out, "Lights, Boreau, quickly!"

In the dazzling rays of the electric lamp he stood before us as the professor whom we knew in the classroom, having cast aside his black draperies. The guests were sprawling in their chairs in all stages of stupefaction. Some of them stared before them with the effect of that horrible moment stamped on their faces. Some held their heads between their hands as though awakening from a bad dream. Others shuddered, fingering their throats nervously. All were dazed.

The professor continued to command them to awaken until the spell began to wear off. Then he commenced to read rapidly and calmly from a manuscript. The paper was absolutely irrelevant, and I could not restrain an exclamation when he ended without mentioning the singular events of the evening. His conduct bore an astounding similarity to that which he affected in closing his ordinary classroom lectures. At the end, the guests arose, talking complacently on various topics. In a few minutes they began to saunter casually from the house.

I hastened to approach the professor, intent on asking him to explain their peculiar behavior. He must have read my question in my eyes, for as I neared him he whispered to me:

"Not tonight, Boreau. Come in the morning—and good-night!"

At the door I joined Hallmark, and together we started across the campus. Outside of a few trivial remarks we said nothing at all until we reached my door, when he spoke in a casual voice.

"Dry old lecture tonight, wasn't it?" he yawned lazily. "When he acted so queerly about telling us to sit back and rest I thought we were in for something interesting. I fell asleep . . . pretty darn dry . . . glad I woke up in time to say good-bye."

My stare must have disturbed him a bit, for he turned back into the night.

"Well . . . see you tomorrow," he said. "Me for the sheets!"

"Good-night," I managed to utter.

And to think that only fifteen minutes before I had seen him shuddering with fear! Could he remember nothing of what had happened?

I sat in my room for some minutes before the possibility of it could soak into my head. Undoubtedly the whole affair was strange beyond description. I went to sleep with my brain a whirling mass of doubts, fears and perplexities.

The next morning I sat through my classes with a maze of questions running through my mind. I could not understand the sudden transition from a state of abject fear to one of complete ignorance. Nor could I understand how I had allowed my mind to slip from my control, sweeping me into those peculiar and terrifying illusions which I had undergone. Why the professor had gone about this experiment in such an odd way was baffling. Why were all the lights off except that single beam in the front of the room? Why had the professor affected that unusual tone of voice? The heat, the strange booming sound, the garb of the professor—all of these were beyond my understanding.

When the last class was over I hastened to the professor's with these questions on my tongue. I found him sitting in his office, busily writing in a memorandum book. He greeted me laconically, waved me into a chair and continued until he had finished his writing. At last he turned toward me.

"Well, Boreau, what do you think of it?" he asked.

"Why, professor, I am completely at sea."

The tone of my voice must have forecast the state of my mind, for the professor, smiling faintly, settled back to answer the flood of questions which he knew I would ask. I lost no time in discussing the general scene, but plunged immediately into the mystery.

"First of all," I asked, "why did your pupils act so queerly when they had completely come to? They did not seem to realize that only few moments before they had been frightened out of their wits. In fact, Hallmark remarked that he had never heard such a dry lecture in his life. He said that he had fallen asleep soon after you started, and could remember nothing until the end."

"Naturally," he laughed.

I did not understand.

"They remembered nothing because they had been in a deep hypnotic state," he explained. "When I called them into their consciousness they assumed that they had been asleep, since they could remember nothing of what had occurred."

He grinned at my amazement.

"But I remember it all!" I exclaimed.

The professor waved the remark aside.

"Certainly, Boreau. I saw that you, too, in spite of my warning were falling into the same state. I hastened to call you back before you had seen the Green Monster. Does that explain the matter?"

I thought this point over for a minute. It seemed that I had caught the professor in a mistake, for, if they remembered nothing upon regaining consciousness, where could the experiment lead to? I put this question to him in a rather triumphant manner.

"Boreau! Boreau!" he cried; "do you forget everything I tell you? I explained that I predict they will suffer from hallucinations caused by post-hypnosis. That is, they will actually see the Green Monster as I have described him, only they will not realize that they are under a foreign influence. If he does appear to them, it will seem to be for the first time. This, Boreau, is the entire experiment. We have only prepared our elements; the reaction, if there is to be one, should ensue."

I was crestfallen at my lack of memory, yet my mind was not at peace.

"But, professor, do you mean to tell me that these visions may continue indefinitely? In that case, you will have done the men a great harm, for they would always be haunted by the Green Monster; and that, I confess, would be a horrible existence. I know, for I almost saw him myself!"

"Oh no," he explained; "I can destroy this hallucination at any time by putting them into the hypnotic state and removing the idea. Then, too, if something should happen that my mental powers failed, the vision would recede, since it exists only in their minds through the directing force of mine!"

This prepared an ultimate solution to the matter. When I asked about the darkness, the solitary beam of light, the dull sound and the heat, the professor explained that these were mere accessories to hypnosis, externals which facilitated his task. Yet now that I had smoothed the mechanical doubts from my mind, I found that my vague uneasiness refused to disappear. I dared not mention this to the professor, since he would have laughed at my groundless presentiment. I paused for a final question.

"Then do you believe the experiment will succeed?" I asked.

"It is still a little early to come to any conclusion," he answered, "yet I believe that within the next few days we shall hear of some strange apparitions in the neighborhood of the Tower or the cloisters. Of course," he added, "the matter is entirely problematical. I cannot be sure that they really accepted my suggestion, nor shall I know until we have heard several rumors about the school. But something should happen soon, if my theory is correct."

Again I felt that sensation of uneasiness. The professor had turned to his writing, completely unaware that I was still in the room.

Several days passed in which I heard nothing more of the matter. I began to believe that, after all, the professor had failed to produce any of the effects he had anticipated. I saw a great deal of the men who had been there that night, yet never did I mention the matter nor signify that I remembered anything of the lecture. I fell into the routine of college life. My uneasiness passed away.

About a week later I was standing in front of my house when Hallmark came walking by. He called in a casual voice, asking if I wanted to walk by the library, and, since I recalled that I had certain research work to do, I accepted, glad of the companionship.

The night was much like that on which I had first gone to the professor's house. A dense fog had settled down over us like a blanket, so that we could not see around us for more than twenty feet. There was a faint wind in the pine trees, which, with the dripping of the water from the limbs above, gave the night a somber tone. Here and there in the gray mist a light glowed dully. All about us was a sullen quiet; our feet crunched harshly upon the graveled path. Hallmark and I, somewhat depressed by the singular hush, walked along without speaking. Then Hallmark whispered:

"That's the cloister, isn't it? I can't make it out from here."

There was nothing unusual in his voice, yet his words sent a faint tingle through my body, recalling, as they did, the professor's warning.

"Yes," I answered; and then, "Why do you ask?"

"Oh, I don't know," he returned; "just wondered."

We went on, and since it was closer to the library by way of the cloister, we headed for the spot. I stifled whatever misgivings I might have had, for I knew that is was merely a suspicion that prompted them. We entered the cloisters just as the chimes were beginning to toll the hour. It was 10 o'clock. "About this stuff I've got to dig up." I thought to myself. "I'll need a Schneider & Greve's, and I'd better glance through Hudson while I'm here."

The crunching of our feet on the gravel intruded on my reverie with an ominous sound and I was recalled to my surroundings. Suddenly I felt Hallmark's grip tighten convulsively on my arm.

"Look, Boreau!" he muttered tensely. "There by the second arch!"

He stopped dead-still, rooted to the spot. I looked. There was nothing but the eddying fog, moving in a fantastic sort of way. Hallmark's fingers were digging sharply into the biceps of my arm. I glanced at the man; his face was screwed into a look of doubt and perplexity. But even as I watched him his face began to twist into a picture of agony.

"It's coming here, Boreau! God! What is it? Boreau!"

Still I saw nothing!

"What is coming?" I whispered, for I was frightened in spite of my senses.

"Look! Boreau!" he screamed. "This way . . . run!"

He strove futilely to move from his tracks.

"Those blazing eyes!" he shrieked. "Run! Oh God . . . it's got me . . . help! Help!"

His voice died in his throat as if some monstrous hand had throttled him as he screamed. His eyes seemed to bulge from his head, and his mouth hung open with seeming torment. Even as I stared at him he fell to the ground with a low, hideous moan. Yet I saw nothing!

I set my teeth into my lips and forced myself to bend over the form of my friend. With an agony of self-restraint I picked him up and fled into the library.

The doors were open, so that I was able to dash in. At the sound of my frightened cries and Hallmark's piteous moaning a crowd swept around us and strove to bring Hallmark to his senses.

"What's happened to him?" someone cried.

All eyes turned toward me. I looked at them with a frightened glance. I could not find my tongue; my palate was parched and dry; my senses reeled.

"I—I don't know," I managed to utter. "He saw something in the cloisters and fell beside me. He is—"

My explanation was cut short by a jumbled flow of words from Hallmark's mouth.

"It was green . . . all green," he moaned, thickly, "with trailing shadows of green. God! It's got me, Boreau! Run—"

His voice trailed off again in a dismal muttering. I stared at him aghast. Those were the professor's words! Trailing shadows of green! I had not foreseen this, nor could I believe I knew its cause. For a moment I thought I should hurl my secret at the throng, but by clenching my nails until they dug into the flesh of my palms I managed to restrain myself. The crowd was whispering excitedly, half frightened by Hallmark's condition and my own dismay.

Someone cut in with an authoritative tone: "He's coming around now."

Hallmark had opened his eyes, and was staring at us in wild amazement.

"Is it gone?" he whispered, tensely.

"What was it?" asked the person with the authoritative voice.

"The . . . the . . . Thing . . . the Green Monster . . . it nearly got me—"

His voice broke into a sob; the man was completely unnerved. The professor's words again!

With the aid of a few of the crowd I carried him home, and there I left him, piteously nervous. And that night I dreamed of terrible green talons reaching for my throat, and all through my sleep ran the monotone of Hallmark's piteous sobbing.

The morning paper carried a short account of Hallmark's "Mysterious Encounter." There was nothing definite to the matter: he had seen (so the story ran) a monstrous green thing slithering toward him through the fog. Its eyes had seemed to bore into his very soul, filling him with an unreasoning fear of his giant unknown. Then, as Hallmark had said, it had fastened gruesome talons into his throat, after which he knew nothing until he was revived in the library. The paper mentioned that a Mr. Boreau, who had been with him at the time of the alleged encounter, had absolutely denied having seen anything, although he, too, had confessed that he had felt that inexplicable panic. The article ended with an attempt at editorial satire, commenting upon "those who flee from imaginary bugaboos!" Hallmark was suspected of some nervous disease or a great prankishness—with emphasis on the latter. Poor fools!

With the news in my hand I rushed to the professor's house. He was sitting in his study, the scene of the first terrible night, grimly reading the first result of his unusual experiment. His lips were curved in a satisfied smile; he gloated in his triumph.

"Professor," I cried, "you must destroy this evil hallucination!"

The professor looked amazed. "But, Boreau—it is succeeding!"

"If you had seen Hallmark's face! If you had been there, professor," I pleaded, "you would not ask for reasons. The man's nerves were shot to pieces. I have never seen such terror!"

The thought of poor Hallmark sent cold shivers coursing up and down my spine. I could say no more, but only stare at the professor in vain entreaty. He looked coldly at me.

"Boreau, I am disappointed in you. I do not propose," he continued, "to allow this scourge to run on for long. But there must be several occurrences to substantiate the experiment. In a week's time the need will have passed, and I shall release them from their condition."

There was nothing I could do. I must remain a party to the experiment until the professor chose to terminate it. He alone could solve the situation; I was powerless. I felt a revulsion from my former admiration for him. This was too cold-blooded, too completely cruel. The thought that Hallmark might go through the experience again caused me to shudder. I bowed as politely as I could and left the house.

The week succeeding was one of the utmost horror. Six different men, all members of that memorable séance, had seen the Green Monster in the darkness. After twilight the voices of all were hushed or stilled, for in all of them dwelt the fear of this terrible thing. Out of every corner its hideous eyes seemed to stare with murderous glance at passers-by. Grim terror stalked rampant where once had been peace and youthful happiness. And the men, who at first had been ashamed of their fears, had begun determining a hurried exodus from the accursed spot.

I could not go near the professor; the very thought of him filled me with loathing. When I watched the havoc he had wrought in the minds of my comrades, I burned with a singular bitterness, all the more intensified by the knowledge that I was helpless to prevent it. I dared not approach him. Then the catastrophe occurred. I was in my room, trying to solve a knotty problem in one of my courses, when I heard the chill night air suddenly rent with terrific screaming. My muscles were temporarily paralyzed; I knew that the Green Monster had appeared again. The screams died off into the darkness and were superseded by violent yells for help, which all the time came closer to my room. I was terrified into action. I rushed pell-mell into the hall, where I found a group of men, all of them staring at each other in dreadful anticipation.

"Come quickly," I cried; "let us help him! The Green Monster has appeared again!"

Their faces writhed in ill-suppressed anguish, but they ran swiftly at my side. We dashed out of the door into the darkened street, flying toward those terrible yells as fast as our legs would carry us. Then, a few hundred yards from the cloister, we met them!

Three men were dragging between them the collapsed body of another. I rushed to their side. Upon their stricken faces I saw the stamp of the monster.

"What has happened?" I shouted, my tongue beyond control.

"The Green Monster . . . we saw it . . . all of us! And it got Bob, here."

I stared at them aghast. I bent over the prostrate body to give assistance.

God! What was this? This was unbelievable! There was a trickling of blood at the nose. His eyes seemed about to burst from his head; the lips were literally shredded by the champing of his teeth. My reason seemed to totter with the horror of it all. He was dead! Strangled by the Green Monster! So this was the experiment!

"Dead!" I screamed.

A low moan went up from his comrades. The crowd fell back, offering no aid, saying nothing, only stunned by the catastrophe.

"Take him home!" I shrieked, almost hysterically.

Without another word I turned and ran toward the professor's house. The light was still burning in the studio. It would not have mattered had it been otherwise, for I should have torn him from his bed had he been there. I did not knock; I rushed headlong into the study. The professor sat before me with a smile on his cruel lips. He looked at me amusedly.

"Has the Green Monster appeared again?" he laughed.

"It has!" I cried, panting with the intensity of my hate. "It has appeared again, and this time it has slain a man! Strangled him with its monstrous talons, as you said it would."

The professor's face went a pasty white. He stared at me like a man possessed. I knew that the fear of the monster had come over him, too. I gloated in the consternation of that look. Then his expression changed to one of determination; he set his jaws grimly.

"Sit down, Boreau," he commanded. "Tell me about this."

"The Green Monster has appeared again," I shouted. "It was seen by three other men at the same time, and it has strangled Bob Huntingdon. I saw him after it was done!"

For a minute the professor seemed to be working at some idea. Then he leaped to his feet.

"Boreau, this is terrible! Had I foreseen this I would never have started this experiment." His words came hard and fast. "The concentrative power of the minds of the university has created it. Their wills, their rampant fears, have gotten beyond control. Where before it was only a hallucination, it is now a reality! Run, Boreau, and gather all of those who were at the lecture before. It is a matter of life and death, for at any minute the living fantasy may seize upon one of them—or anyone now!"

I turned and fled, but as I ran I heard the professor muttering, "I had not foreseen this. I have heard of the creation of material forces through the exercise of the mind—a Hindoo, a yogi theory—yet I had thought it a fantastic myth . . . a myth—"

His voice was beyond my hearing as I rushed toward the quadrangle.

In fifteen minutes I had collected the majority of his former guests about me, and the others, convinced of the all-importance of the request were hastening toward the professor's. As we neared the place we saw that the lights were off. From somewhere on the place came that ominous booming sound. I noticed the shades of the study had been drawn.

As we put our feet within the door we heard a sudden scream, a wild cry for help. So great was our excitement that we dashed back into the study without pausing.

My companions fell back against the door, paralyzed by the vision before them. There, under that solitary beam of light, lay the professor, while over him loomed that hideous Monster I had heard described. I felt the fiendish hate of his glance as he stared at the dying professor with those fierce eyes of his. As I stood there he began to glide through the gloom toward me. I was frozen with horror. The perspiration broke from my brow, blinding me with its scalding sting. Even as I thought it would fasten its tremendous fingers into my throat, the professor rose from the floor in a semi-crouch.

"Boreau," he moaned, "it shall not touch you! It has broken my neck. I am dying, and when I die it will disappear forever!" he gulled a knife from his garments.

I believe he had anticipated the attack upon himself. The Monster leaped to snatch the knife from his hand—too late! The professor sank back upon the floor, and even as he did so, the green Thing faded into the shuddering dark.

"Lights!" I cried. "For God's sake put on the lights!"

Someone found them. We stood in the study with only the dead professor before us. I turned to my companions in the doorway.

"Let us go," I sobbed. "The professor is dead, and the Green Monster is gone forever."

Blindly groping in the clear light, I staggered from the unholy spectacle. Somehow I reached my room. Then, in the still fearsome night hours which the shadow of the monster seemed to inhabit even now, I wrote a full report of the professor's terrible experiment; I expressed that, with the death of the professor, his power over the minds of his unfortunate subjects had passed away, and with that the power the Green Monster. Morning came, and the sun cast a cheerful beam over my fast whitening hair.

The Man in the GREEN Coat

by Eli Coulter

I met Eli Colter late in her life. I don't know what her real name was but I seem to remember the Colter came from the gun, a colt.—FJA
This story appeared in Weird Tales, August 1928

rant Thorpe lounged comfortably in a big easy chair and looked across at Myron Tobin, his host. They two were alone in the big library of Tobin's palatial home, smoking a sociable cigar and drinking an after-dinner cocktail before the massive fireplace. Tobin saw the unveiled curiosity in the gray eyes of Grant Thorpe, and he had an idea he knew the cause of it. But he said nothing. He turned his gaze on the leaping flames in the grate and continued smoking in silence. Thorpe was bluntly outspoken. When his curiosity began to ride him hard enough he should come out with it baldly.

Thorpe was mulling over in his mind the thing that had aroused his curiosity. There had been a large and impressive reception in Tobin's huge house that evening, and after the departure of the guests Thorpe and his host had gravitated naturally to the library with their liquor and cigars. The two men had been friends for twenty years, but for eight years they had seen nothing of each other. When they had parted eight years before, Thorpe had gone to Egypt on a little private business of his own. He had left the United States harboring not a little concern over his old friend Myron Tobin.

Tobin, at that time, was decidedly down on his luck, which was nothing at all unusual for Tobin. He hadn't a cent in the world, and he had as little prospect for the future as he had money. He had ever been very much of a dreamer, cherishing the hope of sometime stumbling upon a formula, concerning no matter what, that would bring him wealth, set the world by the ears and make him famous. He had fiddled along ineffectually with chemicals and metals, accomplishing precisely nothing. Thorpe had bade him good-bye rather sadly. He liked Tobin. He hated leaving him poverty-stricken with hunger, lean with futile hopes, but too stubbornly wedded to his dreams to desert them for any more practical method of achieving wealth and fame. But he knew Tobin. So he shook his hand, sighed, shrugged and went on his way.

And eight years later Thorpe returned from Egypt, to find Tobin as wealthy and famous as he had ever painted himself in his wildest visions. Tobin had found his formula, and it had set the world by the ears right enough. No one knew what it was, and no one was ever likely to know. It was guarded rigidly. But it had brought him fabulous wealth, and the very secrecy attached to it had served to thrust Tobin's name willy-nilly into the notice of the world.

But it was nothing of this that had aroused Thorpe's curiosity. That which had caught and held Thorpe's attention and puzzled him to the point of irritation was a man. Tobin had a host of moneyed and influential friends. The house had been full of them that evening. But among them, moving about and making himself at home with an ease of manner that was distinctly noticeable, was the mysterious man who had held Thorpe's eye and baffled his brain.

He was a small man, with a thin, dried-up body and a great knob of a head as ugly and repellent as the head of a mummy. His long, narrow eyes as hard as granite and as gray, seemed to be everywhere at once. His lank, drab hair fell over his forehead continually, in a peculiarly offensive fashion. He was conspicuous in the throng of correctly dressed men and women for the fact that he wore a bright green coat that fell to his knees. Thorpe could not have told what other garments clothed the man. Shirt, vest, trousers and shoes were rendered unworthy of notice by that spotted and worn vivid green coat.

The guests paid no attention to him, and he paid none to them. Thorpe had seen a few people address politely perfunctory remarks to him. He had made no reply; in fact, he did not speak at all. He moved in and about among the rest of the guests with an oddly proprietary manner, as though he belonged there. He gazed upon the magnificent appointments of the room, the statuary, the murals on the walls, the great shining grand piano, with an air of personal pride in them.

But the most conspicuous thing about him was his absorption in Tobin's strikingly beautiful wife. Whenever his long, hard eyes fell upon her, his ugly face lit with a passion of worship as intense as it was unmistakable. Thorpe frowned upon it, inwardly. He wondered if it were possible that Tobin was unaware of the violent affection lavished upon his wife by the man in the green coat. But no, he couldn't be. Impossible. And Thorpe resented it. It was unlike Myron Tobin to allow anything like that to be so blatantly paraded before his guests and under his eyes. There was something hidden about it that made Thorpe uneasy. He moved restlessly in the chair and asked bluntly:

"Who is the man in the green coat?"

Tobin had been waiting for that question. He knew the explanation would have to come to Thorpe. That he conceded, in view of their years of long close friendship. So far as anyone else was concerned, those who didn't like the man in the green coat could go to the devil. And they could stay away from Tobin's house. His guests and associates had long since learned to tacitly ignore the man's presence. But Thorpe was different. Tobin wanted Thorpe to know.

"Have you ever looked up the word 'gratitude' in the dictionary, Grant?" Tobin asked softly. "To the man in the green coat I owe everything I am and have today. He comes and goes as he will. I never know when to expect him, never can tell when he may suddenly walk in and greet me with that flashing smile of his. Did you notice his smile? How it changes and softens his face? He knows how welcome he is; knows that no matter who is here, no matter what I am doing or what the hour, the door is always open to him and his place in my home unquestioned and assured forever. You may have noted, too, that he never speaks. He is dumb.

"After you left the United States for Egypt, I was deucedly down in the mouth. Not new for me, eh? But it was worse than ever with you gone. Nothing seemed to go right. Not that anything ever had. But then, I was always expecting it to, and your companionship had always helped me to keep my own faith. I got moody when I didn't have you to spill all my grief to any more. I took to going out by myself for long walks in the woods. I didn't know then what was directing me. I do now. So will you before I'm done talking.

"The way I went habitually led down an old road winding off into the trees and seemingly going nowhere. Every time I went I followed it a little farther. And I came finally one day to a clearing in the depth of the forest, surrounding an old deserted house. I stopped short in surprise. You know how old deserted houses have always held a fascination for me. I stood and stared at this one. It was an ancient building, almost covered with vines, half hidden under huge elm trees. But it was still in a fair state of preservation, although I could see it had been abandoned for a long time. Its doors and windows were still intact, and not a pane was broken.

"There was an air of mystery about it. Perhaps there is always that about deserted houses. I guess there is. But there was a different tone here. The mystery in the air was sinister, warning. I didn't just like it. I was drawn to it. I stood there trying to analyze that sinister atmosphere. It was so powerful as to be almost tangible. It seemed to pervade even the trees. Then I noted an odd thing. The place lacked that shroud of mold, of disintegration and decay that seems indigenous to abandoned habitations. Everything was flourishing there.

"The trees were monstrous, healthy and green. The weeds and grass that had claimed the clearing, had grown wildly over everything, were virile, alive. There could never have been flowers in that place, for there were none left to tell the tale, and they couldn't have died there. You couldn't imagine anything *dying* there. Nothing was tumbled down but the old picket fence enclosing the house, yard and elms. Nothing was out of place but the old gate dragging in the rank weeds on one rusty hinge.

"Drawn by something irresistible—curiosity, interest; call it what you will, it was stronger than I was—I turned in the gate and approached the house. I went up on the porch and tried the front door. It was locked. I tried the two front windows. They were locked also. I descended from the porch and started around the house, making my way with difficulty through the grass and wild vines. Every window and door opening into the house was locked, and I could see nothing of the interior through the thick folds of the curtains drawn close across the windows and dusty panes.

"I decided I might as well leave with my curiosity unsatisfied, and turned to go, when I noticed an odd enclosure in the yard quite a way to the rear of the house. It, too, was surrounded by a picket fence, but this fence was in better repair than the other. It was plain to be seen that it had been put up years later than the fence surrounding the yard. The space it enclosed was perhaps eight by ten feet, and was hidden from me at that distance by brush and vines.

"My interest aroused afresh, I walked toward it. And when I reached that fence I stopped a good deal shorter than I had done when I first sighted the house, for squarely in the center of that enclosure was a grave. It had been there a long time, and I couldn't help thinking to myself that it seemed decidedly out of place. It simply wasn't conceivable that *anything* should die there. Yet, there was the grave. The earth was sunken in on top, and the plain granite headstone was stained and covered with moss. I could see there was some kind of inscription on the stone, but the moss rendered it illegible. The gate in this fence hung squarely. I passed through it, leaned over the stone and scraped the moss away. I read this:

Here lies the body of Lona Bennares.
Nobody knows and nobody cares.

"That inscription itself was odd enough to arrest attention. But still more arresting was the fact that the two lines had not been placed there by the same hand. The first line was in script, beautifully chiseled by expert fingers. The second line had been crudely printed, and had been done with some blunt and unsuitable instrument. I scraped the moss from the entire face of the stone, but nothing else was there. No date—nothing. Only those two strange lines. I stood there puzzling over it for a long time. But conjecture was useless. I could make nothing of it, of course, and I turned for the second time to go away. But as I rounded the corner of the house I halted in my tracks.

"Somebody was coming in the front gate. It was the man in the green coat. He saw me standing there, gave me a sharp, scrutinizing look, as though he were measuring me, then averted his eyes and walked up the steps to the front porch. He took a key from his pocket, unlocked the door and went in, leaving it open behind him. Actuated by a curiosity whose control was far beyond my capacity, I followed him up the steps and peered through the door at him.

"To my astonishment the house was fully furnished. Carpets on the floor and pictures on the walls were exactly now as they had been left. The chairs scattered about were in the careless array of chairs lately used. Yet dust was over everything. It was a long time since anyone had lived there. The thought struck me that the whole place had the look of having been forsaken hurriedly, at the instigation of some compelling impulse—or fear. I wondered if the house and grounds belonged to the man in the green coat. He certainly acted as though they did.

"He must have known I was watching him, I thought, but he paid no attention to me. He had removed some small books from his pocket. Note-books they were. He selected from them one with a mottled gray cover, and went to an old desk in a corner of the room. He opened the desk, removed some faded papers from its central drawer, sat down at the table by the window and began to compare the papers with notes in the gray book. He was after some specific thing, and it didn't take him long to find it. He gave a little nod of satisfaction, got to his feet, replaced the papers in the desk, closed it and thrust the note-book back into his pocket with the others. Then he came briskly toward the door.

I made no attempt to conceal myself. I wanted him to see me. I wanted to force him to speak to me. I stepped aside as he emerged from the house and paused to lock the door behind him. He glanced at me but made no offer to speak. My curiosity had me in a strangle-hold by this time, and I wasn't going to let him get away from me so easily.

"How do you do?" I said politely.

"Without looking at me, he pulled one of the books from his pocket, tore out a page, scribbled something on it, thrust the paper abruptly into my hand and hurried down the steps. Completely mystified and astonished, I looked at the sheet of note-paper. On it he had written, 'I am dumb. How do you do?'

"In spite of myself I grinned. Evidently my presence there was of no concern to him. I chuckled as I crumpled the paper in my hand and thrust it into my pocket. But it was enormously curious still, and I knew that my curiosity would never let me rest until I learned what important notes the man in the green coat kept hidden in that old desk in that deserted house out in the trees, miles from anywhere. I turned to glance after the man in the green coat. He was just disappearing down the old road beyond the picket fence.

"With a sneaking feeling of meddling in something that was none of my business, I decided to go to the nearest village and see what I could find out about that forsaken house and the man in the green coat. I lost no time in getting there. There is always one man in a small village who is very apt to know more about everybody in the village than they themselves know—the postmaster. Acting on that premise I headed for the dinky post-office, housed in a little one-story frame building down the main street. Besides being the post-office, it was drug store, candy store, and grocery store combined, and it was presided over by a tall, lank individual with a cadaverous face and deep-set near-sighted eyes. He greeted me with the curiosity and interest a stranger is accorded in a small village and asked me what I would have. I said I was hungry from a long walk, which was pretty much the truth, and would take some cheese and crackers and eat them there if he didn't mind. He was loquacious enough, and was only too glad to have someone about whom he could talk to a standstill.

"I mentioned casually that it was just possible I might buy a place in the village and come to live there—if I found the villagers to my fancy. That was enough to launch him into the family history of every inhabitant, save one. He did not mention anyone by the name of Bennares. I had to get him started in that direction somehow, so I said I had been hiking over the countryside to see how it would suit me. From which it was easy to lead up to the deserted house in the woods.

"The postmaster glanced at me with a slightly startled expression, then he said rather shortly, 'That's a pretty good place to stay away from, Mister. You couldn't hire a soul in this town to set foot in that yard. That place was owned by Sam Bennares some years ago, and still is for all I know. I'm certain nobody else wants it. Sam deserted it after his girl Lona died.'

"He halted a moment, as though not having any intention to let his tongue run away with him. He shot me a shrewd, appraising glance, as though wondering how much he'd better tell. I asked him half jestingly if the place was haunted. That fired his pride in what was perhaps the village's one authentic legend. He answered darkly, trying to be very mysterious.

"'It's haunted, right enough, but not by the spirit of Lona Bennares. By another kind of spirit, Mister. The spirit of something hidden and ugly. Lona died under funny circumstances.'

"He halted again, and after waiting patiently for a moment, I prodded him on.

"'Yes? How so?' I asked. 'What was the cause of her death?'

"'That's what nobody knows.' The postmaster scowled and leaned toward me confidentially. 'There was something mysterious and secretive about it, Mister. Sam was a doctor, and it was him that tended her and him what signed the death report. She died uncommon sudden, that's what. One day we seen her here on the street as live as anybody, and the next day she was dead. Sam give out her funeral notice, but he kept the coffin closed and wouldn't let nobody see the body. Then, instead of burying her in the churchyard by her mother as was right and proper, he got a permit and buried her in his own back yard. There wasn't a thing to which we could rightly point a finger and <lay no suspicion of foul work on anybody.

"'But all of us begun to remember queer things. We remembered that for the last week or two Lona has acted like she was scared of something. And we remembered, too, that when she was in town the day before she died she wasn't ailing. No sir, not none. She was just as well as she'd ever been. Sam put up a picket fence around her grave. Next thing we knew, Sam was gone. And he never come back, only once a year. Folks think he comes to visit the grave, that there's something on his conscience. He never has nothing to say to anybody, and he always goes right away again. He ain't showed up lately, though. Not for about three years.'

"'Yes, I think I've seen him,' I put in. 'He wears a bright green coat, doesn't he?'

"'No.' The postmaster stared at me, an odd look in his near-sighted eyes. 'So you seen *him*, eh, Mister? H'm, he's as bad as Sam. The fellow that wears the green coat is an inventor, an old crony of Sam's. Awful queer fellow he is. He lived there with Sam for about a year before Lona died so sudden. Folks always thought he was pretty much in love with Lona, but he was ugly as sin and you couldn't imagine her as fancying the man in the green coat. Lona was right pretty. When Sam went away, the fellow in the green coat went with him. Folks have seen him around these parts once in every few months ever since. But what him and Sam find so interesting around that old house, unless it's Lona's grave, is more than anybody can figure.

"'I'm telling you, Mister, there's something mighty queer about the whole business. If one of them two men didn't have something to do with Lona's death, I'm a poor guesser. One of them made away with her, that's what everybody thinks. But they's no way to prove it. Look here, Mister. If that girl died all right and proper, and they wasn't nothing ugly about it, why wouldn't Sam open the coffin? Why wouldn't he let nobody see her? And if he had any good reason for not letting nobody see her, why didn't he come out with it? But, no sir, nothing like that. Sam just refused to let anybody look at the body and shut up like a clam, and he looked so funny and mad-like that everybody was afraid to ask him any questions. Even I was. And I'm mighty cur'us, Mister. When I'm afraid to ask anybody questions, you can bet there's something wrong.'

"'Yes, I imagine so.' I returned dryly. 'It certainly does look as though you had a real first-class mystery here. But if I decide to buy in the village, I assure you your mystery will not deter me in the least.'

"I had finished my crackers and cheese. I had gotten from the postmaster about all the information I was likely to get, so I bade him good-bye and took my leave.

"You can easily see that my curiosity, already uncomfortably active, would now be rendered almost unbearable. I simply had to find out why those two men kept coming back in that old house, and what they were after. And, if possible, which of them had killed the girl, if the postmaster was right in his sinister insinuation. I watched the house in the woods for several days, intending to spy upon the man in the green coat and follow him into the house. I had no idea what I would do when I got there. I was simply determined to get into that house. But the man in the green coat did not reappear, and I couldn't stand it any longer. I took a bunch of pass keys and tried the front door. To my surprise, though I don't know why I should have been surprised, I had no trouble turning the lock.

"I entered the house, locked the door behind me and went directly to the old desk. I knew exactly which drawer he had opened, and I pulled it out. There lay the papers which the man in the green coat had been comparing in his note-book. I picked them up with a good deal of eagerness.

"What do you think I found, Grant? You'd never guess in a million years. I found a formula for transmuting all base metal into gold—everything from lead to steel. I read it over carefully. It was written in a stilted hand, and it did not bear the name of any person. But it was easily legible, and I studied it minutely with growing interest. So this was the thing that brought those two men back to the old house so persistently. Had it anything to do with the strange death of Lona Bennares? I decided right then and there to determine just what value the formula had; I copied it in a note-book of my own, replaced the papers in the desk drawer exactly as I had found them, and let myself out of the house.

"For the next two weeks I spent every waking moment experimenting with that formula. I tried it on a half-dozen metals, but the result was always the same. It transmuted the metal all right, to some strange composition infinitely finer, of a dirty greenish yellow—but not to gold. Then, unexpectedly, what little gray matter I have got on the job and I saw what was wrong. The formula lacked one important ingredient. I sat in my chair scowling at it, wondering if there were some other copy of that formula more complete. Perhaps all the formula papers worked out by the man in the green coat were not in that one drawer. I kicked myself for an ass, for not going through the whole desk, but I consoled myself with the knowledge that I could easily enough go back to the house the next day.

"And I guess I don't need to tell you that I was there as soon as it became daylight. I searched that old desk from top to bottom, but there were no other papers in it concerning the formula. I slammed all the drawers shut, peevishly, and stood there scowling at the old desk, wondering if that one lacking ingredient was hidden somewhere in the house. If so, was that the thing the two men were trying to find? Which one of them hid it, and which knew where it was? Or had the man who had hidden it forgotten where he put it?

"I started at the plausibility of a sudden thought. Maybe it was the girl who had hidden it. The postmaster said the ugly little inventor had been in love with her, and that she was rather pretty. I could picture her rather easily. A light-headed, vain little small-town belle, who might find the attention of the man in the green coat very obnoxious. I could picture her spying upon the inventor, and upon her father who inevitably would have become interested in the marvelous formula concocted by his old crony. I could see her gloating over the discovery of that one important ingredient which the inventor doubtlessly had omitted purposely from the written formula.

His reason for omitting it would be very clear. He was taking no chances of anyone's stealing that formula, not even trusting his old friend and host.

"I could see Sam Bennares spying, too, trying to discover where the man in the green coat kept notes on that missing ingredient. I visioned the girl locating its hiding-place, and changing the notes to some place she alone knew, then by a sly word here and there setting the two men at each other, causing the inventor to suspect that her father had stolen the notes, egging her father to indignant denial. And her motives, also, would be very clear. A right pretty small-town belle would go farther than that to engineer a quarrel between the two men, inveigle her father into ordering the inventor out of his house, and so rid herself of the presence of a man whose attentions were offensive to her. And it might very well have been that she had failed in her design, drawn their combined anger down on herself, and paid for her meddling with her life.

"Having settled this in my own mind as being a very reasonable hypothesis, I began trying to conjecture as to which would be the most likely place for the girl herself to hide the notes. But there I was baffled. My understanding of women was precisely nil. About the only thing I could do was search the entire house. I had just decided to give the whole day to that search, and began it immediately, when I heard the door open behind me.

"Startled, I whirled to face the door. There stood the man in the green coat.

"Oddly enough, he did not seem at all surprised to find me there. He smiled slightly, that strange smile that so lights his ugly face, and I had an uncomfortable feeling that *he* had been spying upon *me*. That he had known I was there all the time. I'll go farther than that. I felt that for some obscure reason he had been waiting and watching, hoping that my curiosity would bring me back there.

"He stood and eyed me for a moment, then, while I stood staring at him inanely, he took out one of his note-books, rapidly scribbled something on a page, tore out the page, laid it on the table, turned around and walked out of the house. I stood gazing after him, wondering what the deuce he was up to, then stepped over to the table and looked at the scribbled message. And I felt my eyes nearly pop out of my head. This is what he had written:

Lona Bennares is not dead. Buried in that grave is a hundred thousand dollars gold, transmuted from lead. Leave it alone. Lona was put out of the way by her father. The story is too long to tell here. I have been waiting and watching for someone like you. If you will seek Lona out, and free her from her living death in the asylum at Wentworth, I will give you the complete formula for transmuting base metal to gold. You will thereby become wealthy, with an absolutely unlimited supply, and at your death will add to the world's scientific discoveries. I must request that you keep the formula secret as long as you live. Too common knowledge of it would be disastrous. No answer is necessary. I will be watching to see what you do.

"Well, you may be able to imagine faintly how I felt. If the queer old inventor had told the truth, I was a mile off my hypothesis. If there was a hundred thousand dollars worth of transmuted gold in that grave, no wonder both of the two men kept watch on that house. But why in the devil did Bennares go to such extremes to make it appear that the girl had died, to put her out of the way and bury that gold, presenting it as her body? And why did the inventor let him get away with it? And why should he want to put the girl out of the way, anyhow? The mysterious muddle was getting worse every minute, and I decided to waste no more time in vague hypotheses. I began to wonder what I was going to do about that note.

"I read it again and roamed about the room scowling and thinking it over. For a moment, I will admit, I toyed with the idea of digging that hundred thousand dollars out of that grave and ducking out of the country, but on second thought was ashamed of myself for it. If the queer old crank in the green coat was telling the truth, and if he really had completed and proved that formula, and if he would keep his word and turn it over to me for merely finding some way of releasing the girl, there was no question as to the course I should pursue. *If!* But what the devil would he do with the girl, granted that she was in the asylum, alive and well, and I could succeed in getting her out? That, however, was none of my business. But if he really had such a formula, why pass it on to me? Of course, he would have it, too, and he demanded that I keep it secret. I figured he must think a lot of that girl.

"Well, of course, it was inevitable that I should take him up. The prospect of owning that formula, of reaching all in a breath my lifelong desire, was too great a temptation. I got out of there, carrying the note in my pocket, and seeing that the house was securely locked behind me.

"Wentworth was little less than a hundred miles away. I was there before noon the next day. I went directly to the asylum, representing myself as a visitor, but admitting confidentially to the superintendent that I was looking for an old friend who had disappeared seven years ago. Lona Bennares had been 'dead' for seven years. The superintendent told me he had but three inmates who had been there that exact length of time, two women and a man. The man wasn't to be considered, and the first of the two women to which he took me was immediately eliminated by her white hair and seventy years of age. The moment I laid eyes on the other woman, I began to put some credence in what had been said by the man in the green coat. I thought of what the postmaster had said—that she was a right pretty girl. I would have liked to knock him down. And yet she was exactly the type that would be so designated by a small-town fellow with no standards by which to judge.

"I suppose that nothing short of yellow hair, doll features and china blue eyes could have appealed to him as beauty. Who could have expected him to realize any proper appreciation of her tall, erect, goddesslike figure? Features that, with the high rounded forehead, deep-set black eyes, slender Roman nose, finely curved mouth and pointed chin above the long, slim neck, would have driven Raphael post-haste to his palette and brushes. No wonder the man in the green coat had been mad about her. He, at least, was not without standards. But I looked in her face, and temporarily I was as dumb as the inventor. What should I say to her, and how should I begin? The superintendent addressed her as Miss Jane, and told her that I was merely one of their infrequent visitors. She looked at me intently, holding herself in a kind of calm dignity and with an inscrutable expression worthy of the Mona Lisa. But very clearly in her eyes I saw a sadness, a deep, settled despair. Whether or not she was Lona Bennares, she was obviously a very beautiful woman of about my own age, without hope, without desire to live. The resignation mingling with the despair in her deep eyes vouched for the fact that rebellion had long since withered and died within her.

"I turned abruptly to the superintendent and asked to be allowed to talk to her alone. He hemmed and hawed a bit, stared first at her, then at me, protested that it was somewhat irregular, but finally acceded grudgingly to my request. He said, as though to warn me that any collusion with her would be impossible, that she was dumb, and could answer no questions I might intend to ask her. Then he went out and left me alone with her. Dumb—dumb! Why was everybody dumb? She stood looking at me with a slight expectancy, and I was fudging around for some diplomatic opening. But I could find none.

"Finally, I blurted out, baldly: 'Are you Lona Bennares?'"

"There was no perceptible change of expression on her face, but I felt that something moved in her eyes. I stepped closer to her and lowered my voice.

"'Listen,' I said. 'I am here as a friend. I had not heard that you were dumb. Are you?'

"Still there was no change of expression. The black eyes stared back at me unwinking. But now I was certain of the expectancy there, and it was growing. I went on swiftly.

"'If you are Lona Bennares, and can signal to me, and will do so, in answer to my questions, it may be that I can get you out of here,' I said. 'I have not come impelled in any way by curiosity, nor with the intent to meddle in your affairs. I come only to be of assistance, if that assistance is desired. I was sent by the man in the green coat.'

"And then indeed did her expression change, so suddenly that it startled me. Her eyes widened, incredulously, mirroring an unmistakable flash of fear. She backed from me abruptly, staring, then suddenly dropped into the one chair in that cell-like room and burst into tears.

"I was utterly nonplused. Had I done the wrong thing in mentioning him? That swift fear in her eyes was a thing about which there could be no doubt. I wondered, with a startled sense of uneasiness, if it were the man in the green coat who was responsible for her being here. Yet if that were so, what was it that drove him now to seeking her release? And I pondered over something that had puzzled me before. Why didn't he try to accomplish her release himself? But I had no time to be standing there wasting precious moments in hopeless conjecture. I knew well enough that the superintendent would not leave me alone with her any too long. So I stepped closer and ventured to lay a sympathetic hand on her shoulder.

"'Please listen,' I urged, striving to draw her attention. 'What is it you fear? I will be frank with you. I realize that I am an utter stranger, but you have no cause to doubt my motives in seeking you out. I repeat, I come as a friend. I don't know any too much about this affair myself, but I will tell you what I do know, since I believe it is your right. I happened to make the acquaintance of the man in the green coat. He told me about you, and claimed that your father had put you here to get you out of the way. He offered me a pretty big reward if I would come here and get you out. That is all there is to it. I am here. I know nothing more, nor do I need to know. If you are unjustly incarcerated in this place, any man with a grain of humanity would do his utmost to secure your release, reward or no reward. As a matter of fact, having been of service to you would be reward enough. There, I have laid my cards on the table. I can do nothing more unless you choose to co-operate with me.'

"She had controlled her tears, but that was the only change in her attitude. She still sat with her head bowed in her hands, not paying the least attention to the touch of my fingers on her shoulder. Feeling uneasy, baffled, I dropped my hand, stepped back a pace and stood looking down at her.

"Was it possible after all that she was mad? Was the man in the green coat mad? I began to suspect it. Yet hers were not the eyes of mad woman. I frowned, annoyed at the time that was passing, wondering what step to take next. Then, she suddenly raised her head and looked at me. No, those were not the eyes of a mad woman. Many expressions mingled there for me to read. Confusion, wonder, grief, hope, suspicion and fear—but not madness. And then to my utter astonishment she spoke.

"'No, I am not dumb—any more. I am Lona Bennares, yes. I am not known here by that name. Lona Bennares is dead.' She halted there, with a grimace of bitterness, then asked abruptly: 'When and where did you see the man in the green coat?'

"All doubt of that man had left me the moment she spoke. Whatever his motives in wanting her released, whether they were selfish or altruistic, he had told me the truth concerning her whereabouts, and I had a swift intuition that he had told me the truth all the way. I stepped closer to her again, and my blood hammered in my heart. Oh yes, I was gone, all right. Head over heels. Had been from the moment I stepped in the doorway of her cell-like room and looked in her face. I answered her question eagerly.

"'I saw him yesterday, in the old deserted house where you used to live. I stumbled on the place several days ago, and saw him going in there. I also saw him comparing notes in a book he carried in his pocket to some papers in that old desk in the front room. That aroused my curiosity. I went back to the house, got in with a pass key and looked at those papers. You'll know what I found. I'll admit I was wildly excited about it. I copied the formula and tried it out, but it lacked one important ingredient, as you must also know. I went back there again to see if he had left any notes containing the ingredient. He came in while I was there, wrote this note, left it on the table, and walked out.'

"The strange fear in her eyes grew, wavered and grew again as I talked. As I withdrew the note from my pocket, unfolded it and handed it to her, she cried out strangely, and shuddered even as she accepted it. Then her eyes glued to it, unbelieving, and she looked up at me with an incredulous stare as she returned it and spoke.

"'Yes, I believe you. I *must* believe you. I don't understand. But that is unquestionably his handwriting. This is a terrible place for a sane woman. I wonder at myself that I *am* sane after everything that has happened. The superintendent will be back any minute. I must talk quickly. My father and the man in the green coat quarreled over the formula. Father wanted it. The inventor would not give it to him. He said it would not be good for him, that he was not a big enough man to handle it. They came to blows. Father proved that he would stop at nothing to get the formula. When I was asleep, he injected into my veins some strange fluid that would render me dumb for five or six years. Then he brought me here. He represented me as his sister, and placed me here under the name of Jane Allen. Then he devoted all his time in an effort to procure that full formula. Two years ago he was found dead in his laboratory. News of it reached me, and I gave up all hope of ever leaving this place. There is much more I could tell you. There is neither time to do so now, nor wisdom *in* doing so.'

"'Your father rendered you dumb by the use of something injected into your veins?' I interrupted, struck with a sudden thought. 'Then—was the man in the green coat—?'

"'Yes,' she interrupted in turn. 'He was made dumb by the same process. He refused to give my father the name of the missing ingredient, to *tell* him, I should say, since he had never written it down. And my father injected into his veins that hideous fluid. I fear—I fear that my father must have become something of a fiend, mentally unbalanced by the visions of what that formula could bring a man. He could regulate the period of dumbness he inflicted by the strength of the injection. He only intended making me dumb for a few years, but I heard him tell the man in the green coat that he was making him dumb forever. He said that if he would not tell him that missing ingredient, he would see that no other man ever got it. The man in the green coat had taken a vow never to write it down.'

"She ceased speaking, and I stood lost in thought for a moment. If he was rendered dumb forever, the man in the green coat would be compelled to break his vow and write that ingredient's name down for me. Or had he some idea whereby he hoped to break that long silence of his? That passed through my head more in a sense of detached curiosity than anything else.

"I was on the point of speaking to her again, when I heard the superintendent returning. I said, hastily, under my breath, 'Trust me, Miss Bennares, if you can trust a stranger after those nearest to you have treated you so inhumanly. I haven't time to say more. I shall go to the man in the green coat, and see what he has to suggest. I'll see you again as soon as possible.' Then I heard the steps drawing nearer, and I raised my voice to a casual, perfunctory remark. 'I'm sorry you can't speak, Miss. But I guess you wouldn't know anything about my friend, anyway, I fancy you wouldn't remember.'

"'She remembers nothing,' the superintendent put in, suavely, with something of satisfaction on his face. 'I told you it would do no good to talk to her. If you care to come along with me, we have a very interesting case down the hall a few doors.'

"I wanted to tell him that I wasn't interested in anything else in the world right then but Lona Bennares, and I wanted to knock his impudent tongue down his throat. But I had to keep my mouth shut and follow him out of there, knowing that Lona's eyes were following me, half frantically, afraid to hope, desperately trying to keep herself from hoping. Once down the hall with him, I studied him and tried to estimate the likeliest way of reaching him. He was inclined to be suspicious of everyone, which might have been natural to a man in his place. I don't know. But he was also one of those men whose vanity is rather easily touched. And when he asked me if he hadn't called the turn about the uselessness of talking to Lona, I lied like a trooper.

"'Yes, you certainly did,' I admitted, and I didn't have to dissemble in putting on a long face, either. I felt gloomy enough inside. 'She doesn't know me at all— showed not the least sign of recognizing me. So I pretended to be looking for someone else, to avoid exciting her. But she is the girl I was trying to find. We were to have married, years ago. I left the United States on business, and when I came back she had disappeared. I've been looking for her ever since. I found her—here.'

"'Well, now, I want to know!' He looked at me sympathetically, and wanted to see what else I was going to say. I didn't leave him wondering long.

"'Yes,' I said, with the idea of planting a few seeds where they would flourish and do the most good. But what I said now was true enough. 'It's very sad for me to find her this way, and sadder still to think of leaving her here. You're a man of discernment, you can see that. And I imagine you must be a man with a great deal of influence in the right quarters. Couldn't you use that influence to help me get her out and into my personal care?'

"'No. No, sir, Mister, I can't. I'm sorry.' And I believe he really was. My flattery had hit home, exactly as I intended it should, and he thawed to me, his voice half apologetic as he went on in explanation. 'You see, it's like this. When her brother brought her here he seemed very much upset and grieved over her condition. He paid her keep here for six months, and came back once or twice to see her. The last time he came we had quite a long, confidential talk. I could see that merely the sight of her was too much for him. He told me he didn't think he could stand to come back again. So he gave me a perfectly enormous sum of money, on the written agreement we were to care for her here until her death, and under no conditions allow anyone at any time to take her out. So you see, I am duty bound to fulfill my obligation. That Mr. Allen has since died in no way lessens my duty toward him or Miss Jane. But I *can* appreciate your position. And I say again—I'm sorry.'

"Well, that was that. Old Sam Bennares had certainly sewed the whole thing up. And he'd sewed it tight. It looked like a blank wall to me. I want to tell you, Grant, I packed a pretty heavy heart as I walked out of the asylum and headed back to the old deserted house to keep my rendezvous with the man in the green coat.

"As I half expected, he was waiting there for me when I arrived the next afternoon. And the expression of my face must have been rather glum, for he scrutinized me sharply, waved me to a chair, scribbled something on a paper and thrust it in front of my face. I read: 'Don't be so down-hearted. There's always some way out of everything. You've seen her. What did you find?'

"'Yes,' I admitted calmly, rather wearily. 'I've seen her, and she admitted her identity to me. But apparently that's about all the good it'll ever do—just my having seen her.' And then I went on to recount to him, verbatim, all that had passed between Lona and me, and between the superintendent and me.

"He listened with a perfectly stoical face until I had finished. He had taken a chair facing me. And then he sprang to his feet and began pacing back and forth across the room, his face livid with rage. I watched him in silence, wondering if there were any possible way out for Lona. Then suddenly he turned and darted out of the room, into the rear of the house, and I heard him running pell-mell up the stairs to the rooms overhead. I heard him scurrying around up there, and very shortly he came tearing back down again at the same breakneck pace. He raced into the room and, before my wondering eyes, he planked down on the table a small bottle half-filled with some milky brown fluid, and a small hypodermic syringe. He pulled his indispensable note-book from his pocket, tore out a leaf, and began writing on it with feverish haste.

"I waited in silence, watching him; this time his message seemed rather lengthy. When it was finished he made no move to give it to me, but backed from the table, and stood perfectly motionless, his strange eyes darting back and forth from the note he had written to the objects on the table, and to me. After a long moment his gaze glued to mine, and if I ever saw desperation, hope and supplication in human eyes, I saw them then in his. He made a queer little half-threatening gesture, darted by me and rushed out of the house.

"I sat there and stared at that bottle and syringe like a fool, half afraid to go and see what he had written. But my eagerness and my own desperate desire for action were stronger than my fear. I got abruptly to my feet, stepped to the table and bent to read the note:

There is only one way out. She is right. Sam grew to be a terrible fiend. He was my friend, and I would have let him have the formula if he had been a bigger man, and if I hadn't known for what purpose he wanted unlimited wealth. He was dabbling in black magic; he had the house littered with potions and serums. Lona never knew what they were. Had I given him that formula I would have loosed a destroying fiend on the world. He is gone now, driven to a far plane, and held there by the reaction of his own dark sorcery. We can forget him. But some of his own evil knowledge may now be the thing that will make possible a solution for us to this tangle.

You have seen Lona, and your face tells me that you have loved her, even as I have done. She could never care for a hideous thing like me. Even my attempts at kindness were repellent to her. It seems irony now that it should rest solely upon me to release her from that horrible prison into which her fiend of a father put her. But all I ask of eternal life is to be allowed the privilege of doing that thing. And no reward is too great for the man who will aid me. If I could see her free, see her your contented and beloved wife, as I know you are seeing her already in your imagination, I would be content.

Here, then, is what you must do. To get her out of there, we must have her die temporarily. In that bottle is a solution Sam distilled. Injected into the veins, it produces a coma that so closely simulates death that no physician can tell it from death. You must get to her secretly, inject this into her arm, and the next day go to see her. You will be told she is dead, and you must claim the body. But you must get her away quickly. She will wake from the coma in thirty-six hours. This is what remained of the same fluid Sam used to place her in a state of coma when he took her away. In the name of God, I ask you to act.

"I backed from the table with an involuntary shiver as I finished reading what had been written by the man in the green coat. I had to hold on to myself rigidly, that I might consider it sanely. I was repelled by it, yet I was touched by it, too. Touched by his devouring and hopeless passion for her, and his honest realization of his own repugnant appearance. I thought of his little dried-up body, his great mummylike head, his hard gray eyes and ugly features—and I thought of her. Yes, I could pity him. But it was going to take all the will-power I possessed to drive myself to do the thing he asked.

"And yet I knew it was the only way we should ever get her out of there; I knew now how utterly selfless was his motive toward her. Loving her as he did, he asked only to see her released from what must be torture to her sensitive spirit. To procure her release, he could contemplate seeing her the wife of another man, could even be contented at the sight. That, if I knew anything about it, was a brand of love to which I could take off my hat. I knew even as I stood there that I would do as he asked. But a thousand things ran through my mind and turned me cold as I contemplated it. Suppose the solution might be weakened or changed after standing all these years. Suppose it would not send her into a coma. Suppose it would send her into a coma from which she would never wake. Even as reason argued, eternal sleep would be infinitely better than the living death she now knew. Whatever the chances, ghastly as they were, I had no choice. It was the one way open to me, and I must take it.

The next night, well after 11 o'clock, I stealthily approached the asylum. I blessed the crescent moon that gave me barely enough light to get my bearings, yet left enough of shadow to conceal me effectually, as I stood looking up at the grim building. It was entirely dark. Everyone within it was long since asleep. Fortune favored me in one thing. Her room was on the ground floor. When I had finally located it, I slipped warily up to the window and tapped on the bars. I dared not make too much noise. And I had about despaired of waking her when I finally heard a stir in the room, and saw her face gleaming whitely at me from within. The window was partly open, and I placed my mouth close to the bars as I spoke to her. When she saw it was I, I heard her give a little indrawn breath of relief. Rapidly I explained to her what had taken place, and what had been proposed by the man in the green coat. I added my plea to his, and told her then and there that I asked no greater privilege than to free her and make her my wife.

For a long time she was silent, and I wondered what was going on in her mind. . . . Then she abruptly slipped the window up a little farther, and held her arm close to the bars. It was I who caught my breath then. I've never been a coward, but it took all the courage I had to fill that needle with that unknown solution and raise it toward that white arm. The drive of the needle must have hurt her, but she gave no sign. And if I ever prayed in my life, I was certainly praying desperately as I drove that plunger home. She gave a little gasp and backed from the window, and I turned and stumbled away like a blind man.

"I don't think I care to try to describe the rest of that night, Grant. In Peking there is an edifice called the Temple of Seventeen Hells. By the time morning came I think I could have told the Chinese how to build a temple of twice seventeen hells. I didn't know what I had done, nor how it would end. I was, still like a blind man, trusting desperately in the word of the man in the green coat.

"By daylight, my nerves in rags, I found myself pacing restlessly about in a grove perhaps a mile from the asylum. It was all I could do to control my fevered impatience, and the moments dragged like hours. Along near noon I turned my steps toward the asylum. When I presented myself, the moment I looked into the superintendent's face, I knew the desperate plan had succeeded in part at least. He sighed regretfully, greeting me before I had a change to speak.

"'I have sad news for you, my friend,' he said. 'The young lady died very suddenly last night. She hadn't been ailing that we know of. The doctor says that her heart simply stopped.'

"I don't know how I retained enough of coherence to go ahead with things. Certainly I had no need to simulate shock and grief. I was feeling upset enough without any dissembling. And, barring a little red tape, I had no trouble in getting him to allow my claiming the body.

"There was no doubt in my mind as to where I should take her. To the old house, of course, till she revived and we could make plans for the immediate future. It was ghastly business for me, driving a closed car up to the side door, and with his aid, carrying her out to the car. She was so cold and white, so utterly lifeless in appearance, that I was ridden by panic lest she should be really dead.

"I managed somehow to exist through that long drive away from Wentworth to the old house in the woods. I drove steadily, but not too swiftly, and reached my destination along about 10 o'clock that evening. The man in the green coat was there waiting for me, with a single light burning and the shades drawn. I wish you could have seen the way his face lighted up when I carried her in and placed her on the old divan beyond the desk. He could not speak, and I had no desire to do so. There was nothing to be said, anyway. Each of us understood the other. Strangely— yet not so strangely after all, perhaps—I was beginning to feel a genuine affection for the queer little man in the green coat. In a tense, racking silence we sat there all night, guarding her and waiting. Daylight came, but still we sat there, unmoving. As the hours dragged by and noon approached, each moment seemed more unbearable than the last.

"The hands of my watch had just passed 12, when she stirred slightly and opened her eyes. She looked up at me, and then her gaze went on to the man in the green coat. She started, shrank back, and cried out.

"'You!' she gasped. Then her eyes darted to me. 'I don't even know your name,' she said to me. 'You forgot to tell me. But unless I'm very mad indeed, my prayers are answered and that awful nightmare is over. How can I ever be grateful enough to you?'

"'More to him than to me,' I answered, nodding to the ugly little man who was worshiping her with his eyes. 'If it hadn't been for him—'

"I didn't finish the sentence. But she knew what I meant. She winced; her eyes traveled to him and then back to me.

"Her next words were little more than a whisper. 'When you first came to me—oh, what is your name? How can I talk to you properly when I don't know your name?'

"I told her what it was. She thanked me and went on. 'As I started to say, Mr. Tobin, when you first came to me there and said he had sent you, I thought *you* were the mad one. But I guess I can sum it all up when I say I was so desperate that I would have taken any chance for release that presented itself, even when it came through a man who was mad.'

"'And that is why you were afraid?' I put in quickly, in a flash of enlightenment. She nodded soberly. 'But why,' I asked, 'should you think I was mad?'

"'Because—the man in the green coat is dead.' Her eyes were on him, wide and staring. 'My father killed him, in a rage, because he would not give up the formula. It is his body that is buried out there in the yard, was buried there seven years ago.'

"She saw the shock and disbelief in my eyes and turned to him. 'Isn't it so?'

"He nodded.

"'Shall I tell him everything?' she asked, and he nodded again.

"'That was why my father put me away. He knew I was horrified, sickened by what he had done. He was afraid I'd tell. He rendered me dumb so I couldn't tell. Then he put me in the madhouse, where, if I attempted to write down what I knew, my keeper would only pity me and consider that I was where I belonged. Certainly had I attempted to write the truth it would have seemed mad enough to the average person. In the grave with him my father buried for safe keeping a large amount of gold made by the formula. He came back from time to time and carried it away, knowing well enough the villagers would stay away from here. He gave a large part of it to the superintendent of the asylum to insure my being kept there. I think there is nothing more to tell.'

"And, Grant, there is little more for me to tell you. You have seen my wife. You know the position I have attained through my secret formula. You have seen him. You will understand now why my house is open to him no matter when he chooses to come, and no matter who is here."

As Tobin ceased speaking, Thorpe sat staring at him with horrified eyes. His blanched face and startled expression were evidence of the shock he had received as Tobin's story had drawn to a close. He drew a long breath, and shook his head, like a man who can in no wise credit what he has heard.

"Do you mean to tell me," he demanded, "that the man in the green coat, the man I saw here this evening, is a *ghost?*"

"You may call him what you will," Tobin answered quietly. "Ghost, disembodied spirit, or materialized astral being. I only know what I have told you. I only know that he has been dead for fifteen years—that he came back from beyond the grave, God knows at what cost—to pass on to me information that only he could give. I only know that he was the means of rescuing my wife from a living death. No matter who or what he is, he has shown me more than one priceless formula. He has shown me what ingredients it takes to make a noble man, a gentleman unafraid. And that's enough for me."

The Eighth
GREEN Man

by G. G. Pendarves (Gladys Gordon Trenery)

When you're green with envy, seven is not always your lucky number!
First appeared in Weird Tales, March 1928.

"D angerous road, huh!" Nicholas Birkett slowed down and frowned at the battered old signpost. "I'll take a chance, anyhow!"

"I should try another road," I said abruptly.

"But this one leads right down to the valley, and will save at least ten miles round."

"It's a dangerous road—very dangerous," I answered, with the conviction growing fast within me that the signpost gave only a faint inkling of the deadly peril it guarded.

Birkett stared at me, his big brown hands resting on the steering wheel. "What d'ye know about the road, anyhow?" he asked, his round blue eyes blank with amazement. "You've never been this way in your life before!"

I hesitated. My name is famous in more than one continent as that of an explorer, and I had recently achieved an expedition across the Sahara Desert which had added immensely to my fame. In fact, it was my lecture on this expedition, given in New York, that had brought about my friendship with Nicholas Birkett. He had introduced himself and carried me off to stay with him at his country estate in Connecticut, in a whirlwind of enthusiastic interest and admiration.

How could I make my companion understand the shuddering fear that gripped me? I—Raoul Suliman d'Abre—to whom the face of Death was as familiar as my own.

But it was not Death that confronted us on that road marked "Dangerous" . . . something far less kind and merciful!

Not for nothing am I the son of a French soldier and an Arab woman. Not for nothing was I born in Algeria and grew up amidst the mysteries and magic of Africa. Not for nothing have I learned in pain and terror that the walls of this visible world are frail and thin—too frail, too thin, alas! For there are times—there are

213

places when the barrier is broken . . . when monstrous unspeakable Evil enters and dwells familiarly amongst us.

"Well!" My companion grew impatient, and began to move the car's nose toward the road on our left.

"I'm sorry," I answered. "The truth is . . . it's a bit difficult to explain . . . but I have my reasons—very strong reasons—for not wishing to go down this particular road. I *know*—don't ask me how—that it's horribly dangerous. It would be a madness—a sin to take that way!"

"But look here, old chap, you can't mean that you . . . that . . . that you're only imagining things about it?" His face was quite laughable in its astonishment.

I was frightfully embarrassed. How explain to such a rank materialist as Nicholas Birkett that instinct alone warned me against that road? How make a man so insensitive and practical believe in any danger he could not see or handle? He believed in neither God nor Devil! He had only a passionate belief in himself, his wealth, his business acumen, and above all, the physical perfection that went to make his life easy and pleasant.

"There are so many things you do not understand," I said slowly. "I am too old a campaigner to be ashamed of acknowledging that there are some dangers I think it foolhardy to face. This road is one of them!"

"But what in thunder do *you* know of the damned road?" Birkett's big fresh-colored face turned a brick-red in his angry impatience. Then he cooled down suddenly and put a heavy hand on my knee. "You're ill, old chap? Touch of malaria, I suppose! Excuse my being so darned hasty."

I shook my head. "You won't or can't understand me. The truth is that I feel the strongest aversion from that path, and I beg you not to take it."

Birkett looked me in the eye and began to argue. He settled down to it solidly. I had nothing to back my arguments except my intuition, and such a flimsy nothing as this he demolished with his big hearty laugh and a heavy elephantine humor that reduced me to a helpless silence.

Opposition always narrowed Birkett down to one idea, that of proving himself right; and at last I said, "This is more dangerous for you than for me. I am prepared . . . I know how to guard myself from attack, but you—"

"That settles it," he interrupted, gripping the wheel and shooting forward with a jerk. "I can look after myself." His cheerful hello echoed hollowly as the car dived into the leafy roadway under a branching archway of trees.

- 2 -

Birkett became more and more boisterous in his mirth as we sped along, for the road continued smooth and virtually straight, descending in a gentle slope to the Naugatuck valley.

"Dangerous road!" he said, with a prolonged chuckle; "I'll bet a china orange to a monkey that sign means a good long drink. Look out for an innocent little roadhouse tucked away down here. Dangerous road! I suppose that's the latest way of advertising the stuff."

It was useless to remonstrate, but I noticed many things I didn't like along that broad leafy lane.

No living creature moved there—no bird sang—no stir of wings broke the silence of the listening trees—not even a fly moved across our path.

Behind us we had left a world of life, of movement and color. Here all was green and silent. The dark columns of the tree-trunks shut us in like the massive bars of prison.

Shadows moved softly across the pale, dusty road ahead; shadows that clustered in strange groups about us; shadows not cast by cloud or sun or moving object in our path, for these shadows had not relation to things natural or human.

I knew them! I knew them, and shuddered to recognize their hateful presence.

"You're a queer fellow, d'Abre," my companion rallied me. "You'd waltz out on a camel to meet a horde of yelling, bloodthirsty ruffians in the desert, and thoroughly enjoy the game. Yet here in a civilized country, you see danger in a peaceful hillside! You certainly are a wonder!"

"*Inshallah!*" I murmured under my breath. "It is more wonderful that man can be so blind!"

"Are you muttering curses?" Birkett showed white teeth in a flashing grin at my discomfiture. "I suppose it's the Arab half of you that invents these ghosts and devils. Life in the desert must need a few imaginary excitements. But in this country it needs something more than imagination to produce a really lively sort of devil. Something with a good kick to it."

Suddenly, ahead of us, the trees began to thin out, and we caught a glimpse of a low white building to our left. Birkett was triumphant.

"What did I tell you?" he cried. "Here I am leading you straight to a perfectly good drink, and you sit there blabbing of death and disaster!"

He stopped the car before a short flight of mossy steps; from the top of them we stood and looked at the house, glimmering palely in the dusky shade of many tall trees.

A flagged path led from where we stood to the house—a straight white path about fifty yards in length. On each side of it the tall, rank grass, dotted with trees and shrubs, stretched back to the verge of the encroaching forest. And within this spacious, park-like enclosure, the distant house looked dwarfed and mean—a sort of fungus sprouting at the foot of the stately trees.

Birkett, undeterred by the menacing gloom of the whole place, cupped his hands about his mouth and gave a joyful shout, which echoed and died into heavy silence once more.

"Not expecting visitors," he grinned. "This is a midnight joint, I'll wager. Come on."

At that moment we saw a sign at our elbow—a freshly painted sign—the lettering in a vivid luminous green on a black background. It read:

"*THE SEVEN GREEN MEN.*"

- 3 -

"Seven Green Men, hey! Don't see 'em," said Birkett, moving up the pathway. I followed, looking round intently, every nerve in me sending to my brain its warning thrill of naked, overwhelming terror crouching on every hand, ready to spring, ready to destroy us body and soul.

Then, suddenly I saw them! . . . and my heart gave a great leap in my body. They faced us as we approached the house, their grim silhouettes sharp and distinct against the white roadhouse behind.

The Seven Green Men!

"Gee!" said Birkett. "Will you look at those trees? Seven Green Men! What d'you think about that?"

In two stiff rows before the house they stood, each one cut and trimmed to the height of a tall man. Their foliage was dense and unlike that of any tree or shrub I had seen in all my wanderings. A few feet away, their overlapping leaves gave all the illusion of metal, and seven tall warriors seemed to stand in rank before us, their armor green with age and disuse.

Each figure faced the west, presenting its left side to us; each bared head was that of a man shaved to the scalp; each profile was cut with marvelous cunning, and each was distinct and characteristic; the one thing in common was the eyelid, which in every profile appeared closed in sleep.

And when I say *sleep*, I mean just that.

They could awaken, those Seven Green Men!. . . they could awaken to life and action; their roots were not planted in the kindly earth, but thrust down deep into hell itself.

"The Seven Green Men! Well, what d'you think of that for an idea?" And my companion planted his feet firmly apart, clasped his hands behind his broad back, and gazed in puzzled admiration at the trees. "Some gardener here, d'Abre! I'd like to have a word with him. Wonder if he'd come and do a bit of work like that for me? A few of these green fellows would look fine in my own place. Beats me how the faces are cut so differently; must need trimming every day! Yes, I'll say that's some gardener!"

I put my hand on his arm.

"Don't you—can't you see they're not just trees? Come away while there's time, Birkett." And I tried to draw him back from those cursed green men, who, even in sleep, seemed to be watching my resistance to them with sardonic interest. "This place is horrible . . . foul, I tell you!"

"I came for a drink, and if these green fellows can't produce it, I'll pull their noses for them!" His laugh rang and echoed in that silent place. As it died, the door of the inn was opened quickly and a man stood on its threshold.

For a long moment the three of us stood looking at each other, and my blood turned to ice as I saw the great massive figure of the innkeeper. Most smooth . . . most punctilious and deferential in manner as he summed us both up, gaged our characters, our powers of resistance, our usefulness to him in the vast scheme of his infernal design.

He came down the flagged path toward us, passing through the stiff, silent rank of the seven green men—four on one side of the path, three on the other.

"Good morning, sirs, good morning! How can I serve you?" His high, whispering voice was a shock; it seemed indecent issuing from that gigantic frame, and I saw from Birkett's quick frown that it grated on him too.

"If you've got a drink wet enough to quench my thirst, I'd be mighty glad," answered my friend, rather gruffly. "And about lunch . . . we might try what your green men can do for us!"

Our host gave a long snickering laugh, and glanced back at the seven trees as though inviting them to share the joke.

He bowed repeatedly. "No doubt of that, sir! No doubt of that! If you'll come this way, we'll give you some of the best—the *very* best." His whisper broke on a high squeak. "Lunch will be served in ten minutes."

I put a desperate hand on Birkett's arm as he began to follow in the wake of the innkeeper.

"Not past *them*, not past *them!*" I urged in a low voice. "Look at them now!"

As we approached, the trees seemed to quiver and ripple as though some inner force stirred within their leafy forms, and from each lifted eyelid a sudden flickering glance gleamed and vanished.

Beneath my hand I felt Birkett's involuntary start, but he shook me off impatiently. "Go back, if you like, d'Abre! You'll get me imagining as crazy things as you do, soon." And he stalked on to the house.

- 4 -

"Enter, enter, sirs! My house is honored!"

Unaccountably, as we passed the threshold my horror gave place to a fierce determination to fight—to resist this monstrous swollen spider greedy to catch his human flies.

Power against power—knowledge against knowledge—I would fight while strength and wisdom remained in me.

I waved away the proffered drink.

"No, nothing to drink," I said, watching his smooth pale face pucker at this first check in the game.

"Surely, sir, you will drink! You will not refuse to pledge the luck of my house!

You are a great man—a great leader of men; that is written in your eyes! It is a privilege to serve so distinguished a guest."

His obsequious whispers sickened me, and I gathered my resources inwardly to meet the assault he was making on my will.

When I refused not only to drink, but even to taste a mouthful of the unique lunch provided, a sudden vicious anger flickered in his pale, cold eyes.

"I regret that my poor fare does not please you, sir." he said, his voice like the sound of dry leaves blown before a storm.

"It is better for me that I do not eat," I answered curtly, my eyes meeting his as our wills clashed.

For a long, terrible minute the world dropped from under me: existence narrowed down to those malicious eyes which held mine. I held on with all the desperation of a drowning man tossing in a dark sea of icy waters—torn, buffeted, despairing, at the mercy of incalculable power.

With hideous, intolerable effort I met the attack, and by the mercy of Allah I won at last; for the creature turned from me and smoothly covered his defeat by attending very solicitously to Birkett's needs.

I relaxed, sick and trembling with the price of victory.

I had fought many strange battles in my life; for in the East, the Unknown is a force to be recognized, not laughed at and despised as in the West. Yet of all my encounters, this one was the deadliest, this evil, smiling Thing the strongest I had known in any land or place.

Must Birkett's strength go to feed this insatiable foe who battened on the race of men?

I shuddered as I watched him sitting there, eating, drinking, laughing with his host; his whole mind bent on the pleasure of the moment, his will relaxed, his brain asleep; while the creature at his side served him with hateful, smiling ease, watching with cool, complacent eyes as his victim let down his barriers one by one.

In his annoyance with my behavior, Birkett prolonged the meal as long as possible, ignoring me as I sat smoking and watching our host as intently as he watched us.

Anxiously I wondered what the next move in this horrible cat-and-mouse game would be; but it was not until Birkett rose from the table at last that the enemy showed his hand.

"It's a pity you can't be here on Friday night, sir! You'd be just the one to appreciate it. One of our gala nights—in fact the best night in the year at the *Seven Green Men*. You'd have a meal worth remembering that night. But I'm afraid they wouldn't let you in on it.

"Why not?" demanded Birkett, instantly aggressive.

"I beg your pardon, sir, but you see it's a very special night indeed. There's a very select society in this neighborhood; I don't suppose you've so much as heard of it: *The Sons of Enoch.*"

"Never heard of 'em." Birkett's tone implied that had they been worth knowing, he *would* have heard of them. "Who are they? Those seven green chaps you keep in the grounds—eh?"

A cold light flashed in the innkeeper's eyes; and my own heart stood still, for the flippant remark had been nearer the truth than Birkett guessed.

"It's a society that was founded centuries ago, sir. Started in Germany in a little place on the Rhine, run by some old monks. There are members in every country in the world now. This one in America is the last one to be formed, but it's going strong, sir, very strong!"

"Then why the devil haven't I been told of it before?"

"Why should you know of all the hole-and-corner clubs that exist?" I interposed. The innkeeper was probing Birkett's weakest part. How well—oh, how truly the smiling, smooth-spoken devil had summed up my poor blundering friend!

"It'll be a society run for the Great Unwashed!" I continued. "You'd be a laughing-stock of the neighborhood if it got out that you were mixed up with scum of that sort."

"There is much that your great travels have not taught you, sir," answered the innkeeper, his sibilant speech savage as a snake's hiss. "The members of this club are those who stand so high, that as I said, I fear they would not consent to admit you even once to their company."

"Damn it all!" Birkett interrupted irritably. "I'd like to know any fellows out here who refuse to meet *me*. And who are you, curse you, to judge who can be members or not?"

Our host bowed, and I caught the mocking smile on his thin lips, as the fish rose so readily to his bait.

I poured ridicule on the proposition and did all I could to turn Birkett aside, but to no avail. Opposition, as always, goaded him to incredible heights of obstinacy; and now, half drunk and wholly in the hands of that subtle devil who measured him so accurately, the poor fellow fairly galloped into the trap set for him.

It ended with a promise on our host's part to do all in his power to persuade the *Sons of Enoch* to receive Birkett and perhaps to make him a member of their ancient society.

"Friday night then, sir! About 11 o'clock the meeting will start, and there's a midnight supper to follow. Of course I'll do my best for you, but I doubt if you'll be allowed to join."

"Don't worry," was Birkett's valedictory remark. "I'll become one of the *Sons of Enoch* on Friday, or I'll hound your rotten society out of existence. You'll see, my jolly old innkeeper, you'll see!"

And as we left the grounds, passing once more the Seven Green Men, their leaves rustled with a dry crackle that was the counterpart of the innkeeper's hateful, whispering voice.

- 5 -

Our drive homeward was at first distinctly unpleasant. Birkett chose to take my behavior as a personal insult, and, being at a quarrelsome stage of his intoxication, he kept up a muttered commentary: "... insulting a decent old bird like that ... best lunch I ever had ... damned if I won't ... Sons of Enoch ... what's going to stop me ... be a Son of Enoch ... damned interfering fellow, d'Abre! ..."

He insisted on driving himself, and took such a roundabout way that it was two hours later when we saw New Haven in the distance. Birkett was sober by this time and rather ashamed of his treatment of a guest. He insisted on pulling up at another little roadhouse, *The Brown Owl*, run by a New England farmer he wanted me to meet.

"You'll like the old chap, d'Abre!" he assured me, eager to make amends for his lapse. "He's a great old man, and can put up a decent meal. Come on, you must be starving."

I was thankful to make the acquaintance of both old Paxton and his fried chicken ... and Birkett's restored geniality made me hopeful that after all he might not prove obdurate about repeating his visit to the *Seven Green Men*.

Old Paxton sat with us later on his porch, and gradually the talk veered round to our late excursion. The old farmer's face changed to a mask of horror.

"The *Seven Green Men! Seven*, did you say? My God! ... oh, my God!"

My pulse leaped at the loathing and fear in his voice, and Birkett brought his tilted chair down on the floor with a crash. Staring hard at Paxton, he said aggressively, "That's what I said! *Seven!* It's a perfectly good number; lots of people think it's lucky."

But the farmer was blind and deaf to everything—his mind gripped by some paralyzing thought.

"Seven of them now ... *seven!* And no one believed what I told 'em! Poor soul, whoever it is! Seven now ... Seven Green Men in that accursed garden!"

He was so overcome that he just sat there, saying the same thing over and over again.

Suddenly, however, he got to his feet and hobbled stiffly across the veranda, beckoning us to follow. He led us down the steps to his peach orchard behind the house, and pointed to a figure shambling about among the trees.

"See him ... see him!" Paxton's voice was hoarse and shaken. "That's my only son, all that's left of him."

The awkward figure drew nearer, approaching us at a loping run, and Birkett and I instinctively drew back. It was an imbecile, a slobbering, revolting wreck of humanity with squinting eyes and loose mouth, and a big, heavy frame on which the massive head rolled sickeningly.

"My only son, sirs!"

We were horribly abashed and afraid to look at old Paxton's working features.

"He was the *Sixth* Green Man . . . and may the Lord have mercy on his soul!"

The poor afflicted creature shambled off, and we went back to the house in silence. Awkwardly avoiding the farmer's eye, Birkett paid the reckoning and started for his car, when Paxton laid a detaining hand on his arm.

"I see you don't believe me, sir! No one will believe! If they had done so, that house would be burnt to the ground, and those trees . . . those trees— those green devils with it! It's *they* that steal the soul out of a man, and leave him like my son!"

"Yes," I answered. "I understand what you mean."

Paxton peered with tear-dimmed eyes into my face.

"You understand! Then I tell you they're still at their fiend's game! My son was the *Sixth* . . . the *Sixth* of those Green Men! Now there are *Seven!* They're still at it!"

- 6 -

"How about staying on here and having another swim when the moon rises?" I said, apparently absorbed in making my old briar pipe draw properly, but in reality waiting with overwhelming anxiety for Birkett's reply.

It was Friday evening, and no word had passed between us during the week of the Seven Green Men, or Birkett's decision about tonight.

He was sitting there on the rocks at my side, his big body stretched out in the sun in lazy enjoyment, his half-closed eyes fixed on the blue outline of Long Island on the opposite horizon.

"Well, how about it?" I repeated, after a long silence.

He rolled over and regarded me mockingly.

"Anxious nurse skillfully tries to divert her charge from his naughty little plan! No use, d'Abre; I've made up my mind about tonight, and *nothing's* going to stop me."

I bit savagely on my pipe-stem, and frowned at an offending gull which wheeled to and fro over the lapping water at our feet.

As easily could a six-month-old baby digest and assimilate raw meat so could Birkett's intellect grasp anything save the obvious; nevertheless I was impelled to make another attempt to break down the ramparts of his self-sufficient obstinacy.

But I failed, of course. The world of thought and imagination and intuition was unknown and therefore non-existent to him. The idea of any form of life, not classified and labeled, not belonging to the animal or vegetable kingdom, was simply a joke to him.

And old Paxton's outbursts he dismissed as lightly as the rest of my arguments.

"My dear chap, everyone knows the poor old fellow's half mad himself with trouble. The boy was a wild harum-scarum creature always in mischief and difficulties. No doubt he *did* go to a midnight supper at the *Seven Green Men*. But what's that got to do with it? You might as well say if you got sunstroke, for instance, that old Paxton's fried chicken caused it!"

- 7 -

"You don't mean to say that you're coming too?" asked Birkett, when, about 10:30 that night, I followed him out of doors to his waiting car.

"But of course!" I answered lightly. "You don't put me down as a coward as well as a believer in fairy-tales, do you?"

"You're a sport anyhow, d'Abre!" he said warmly. "And I'm very glad you're coming to see for yourself what one of our midnight joints is like. It'll be a new experience for you."

"And for you," I said under my breath, as he started the engine and passed out from his dim-perfumed garden to the dusty white highroad beyond.

A full moon sailed serenely among silvery banks of clouds above us; and in the quiet night river and valley, rocky hillside and dense forest had the sharp, strange outlines of a woodcut.

All too soon we reached the warning sign, "Dangerous Road," and passed from a silvery sleeping earth to the stagnant gloom of the tunnel-like highway.

But hateful as it was, I could have wished that road would never end, rather than bring us, as inevitably it did, to that ominous green-and-black sign of our destination.

The sound of a deep rhythmic chant greeted us as we went up the steps, and we saw that the roadhouse was lit from end to end, not with the mellow, welcoming radiance of lamp or candle, but with strange quivering fires of blue and green, which flickered to and fro in mad haste past every window of the inn.

"Some illumination!" remarked Birkett. "Looks like the real thing to me! Do you hear the *Sons of Enoch* practicing their nursery rimes? Coming, boys!" he roared cheerfully. "I'll join in the chorus!"

As for myself, I could only stare at the moonlit garden in horror, for my worst fears were realized, and I knew just how much I had dreaded this moment when I saw that the seven tall trees—those sinister devil-trees—were gone!

Then I turned to see the huge bulk of the innkeeper close behind us, his head thrown back in silent laughter, his eyes smoldering fires above the ugly, cavernous mouth.

Birkett turned too, at my exclamation and drew his heavy eyebrows together in a frown.

"What the devil do you mean by creeping up on us like that?" he demanded angrily.

Still laughing, the innkeeper came forward and put his hand familiarly on my friend's arm. "By the Black Goat of Zarem," he muttered, "you are come in a good hour. The *Sons of Enoch* wait to receive you—I myself have seen to it—and tonight you shall both learn the high mysteries of their ancient order!"

"Look here, my fine fellow," said Birkett, "what the deuce do you mean by crowing so loud? I've got to *meet* these minstrels of yours before I decide to join them."

From the house came a great rolling burst of song, a tremendous chant with an earth-shaking rhythm that was like the shock of battle. The ground rocked beneath us; gathering clouds shut out the face of the watchful moon; a sudden fury of wind shook the massed trees about the house and grounds until they moaned and hissed like lost souls, tossing their crests in important agony.

In the lull which followed, Birkett's voice came to me, low and strangely subdued: "You're right, d'Abre! This place is unhealthful. Let's quit." And he moved back toward the steps.

But the creature at our side laughed again and raised his hand. Instantly the grounds were full of shifting lights, moving about us—hemming us in, revealing dim outlines of swollen, monstrous bodies, and bloated features which thrust forward sickeningly to gloat and peer at Birkett and me.

The former's shuddering disgust brought them closer and closer upon us, and I whispered hastily, "Face them! Face them! Stamp on them if you can, they only advance as you retreat!"

Our host's pale, smiling face darkened as he saw our resolution, and a wave of his hand reduced the garden to empty darkness once more.

"So!" he hissed. "I regret that my efforts to amuse you are not appreciated. If I had thought you a coward"—turning to Birkett—"I would not have suggested that you come tonight. The *Sons of Enoch* have no room for a coward in their midst!"

"Coward!" Birkett's voice rose to a bellow at the insult, and in reaction from his horror. "Why, you grinning white-faced ape! Say that again and I'll smash you until you're uglier than your filthy friends here! No more of your conjuring tricks! Get on to the house and show me these precious Sons of yours!"

I put my hand on his arm, but the blind anger to which the innkeeper had purposely roused him made him incapable of thought or reason, and he shook me off angrily.

Poor Birkett! Ignorant, undisciplined, and entirely at the mercy of his appetites and emotions—what chance had he in his fatuous immaturity against our enemy? I followed him despairingly. His last chance of escape was gone if he entered that house of his own free will.

"The trees are gone!" I said in a loud voice, pulling Birkett back, and pointing. "Ask him where the trees are gone!"

But as I spoke, the outlines of the *Seven Green Men* rose, quivering in the dimness of the garden. Unsubstantial, unreal, mere shadows cast by the magic of the Master who walked by our side, they stood there again in their stiff, silent ranks!

"What the deuce are you talking about?" growled Birkett. "Come on! I'll see this thing through now, if I'm hanged for it."

I caught the quick malice of the innkeeper's glance, and shivered. Birkett was a lump of dough for this fiend's molding, and my blood ran cold at the thought of the ordeal to come.

- 8 -

Over the threshold of the house! . . . and with one step we passed the last barrier between ourselves and the unseen.

No familiar walls stood around us, no roof above us. We were in the vast outer darkness which knows neither time nor space.

I drew an Arab knife from its sheath—a blade sharpened on the sacred stone of the Kaaba, and more potent here than all the weapons in an arsenal.

Birkett took my wrists in his big grasp and pointed vehemently with his other hand. In any other place I could have smiled at his bewilderment; now, I could only wish with intense bitterness that his intellect equaled his obstinacy. Even now he discredited his higher instincts; even here he was trying to measure the vast spaces of eternity with his little footrule of earthbound dimensions.

Our host stood before us—smiling, urbane as ever; and, at his side, the *Seven Green Men* towered, bareheaded and armor-clad, confronting us in ominous silence, their eyes devouring hells of sick desire!

"My brothers!" At the whispered word, Birkett stiffened at my side and his grip on my arm tightened.

"My brothers, the *Sons of Enoch*, wait to receive you to their fellowship. You shall be initiated as they have been. You shall share their secrets, their sufferings, their toil. You have come here of your own free will . . . now you shall know no will but mine! Your existence shall be my existence! Your being my being! Your strength, my strength! What is the Word?"

The *Seven Green Men* turned toward him.

"The Word is thy Will, Master of Life and Death!"

"Receive, then, the baptism of the initiate!" came the whispered command.

Birkett made a stiff step forward, but I restrained him with frantic hands.

"No! No!" I cried hoarsely, "Resist . . . resist him."

He smiled vacantly at me, then turned his glazed eyes in the direction of the whispering voice again.

"No faith defends you . . . no knowledge guides you . . . no wisdom inspires you. *Son of Enoch*, receive your baptism!"

I drew my dagger and flung myself in front of Birkett as he brushed hastily past me and advanced toward the smiling Master. But the *Seven Green Men* ringed us in, stretching out stiff arms in a wide circle, machine-like, obedient to the hissing commands of their superior.

I leapt forward, and with a cutting slash of my knife got free and strode up to the devil who smiled, and smiled, and smiled!

"Power is mine!" I said, steadying my voice with hideous effort. "I know you . . . I name you . . . Gaffarel!"

- 9 -

In the gray chill of dawn I stood once more before the house of the *Seven Green Men.*

The dark woods waited silent and watchful, and the house itself was shuttered, and barred, and silent too.

I looked around wildly as thought and memory returned. Birkett . . . Birkett, where was he?

Then I saw the trees! The devil-trees, stiff, grotesque, and menacing in their armor, silhouetted against the white, blank face of the roadhouse behind.

The *Seven Green Men!*

Seven . . . no . . . there were *eight* men now! I counted them! My voice broke with a cry as I counted and recounted those frightful trees.

Eight!

As I stood there sobbing the words . . . eight . . . eight . . . eight! over and over, with terror mounting in my brain, the narrow door of the inn opened slowly, and a figure shambled out and down the path toward me.

A big, heavy figure that mouthed and gibbered at me as it came, pouring out a steam of meaningless words until it reached my feet, where it collapsed in the long dewy grass.

It was Birkett—Nicholas Birkett! I recognized the horrible travesty of my friend at last, and crept away from him into the forest, for I was very sick.

The sign was freshly painted as we passed it coming out, much later, for it was long before I could bring myself to touch Birkett, and take him out to the waiting car.

The sign was freshly painted as we passed . . . and the livid green words ran:

"THE EIGHT GREEN MEN."

When the GREEN Star Waned

by Nictzin Dyalhis

I know nothing about the exotically named Dyalhis except that he was a Brit. His name suggests to me a misspelling of Nicotine Dialysis. Fall, now, under the spell of his Green Star!—FJA
This story first appeared in Weird Tales, April, 1925

Ron Ti is our greatest scientist. Which is to say that he is the greatest in our known universe, for we of the planet Venhez lead all the others in every attainment and accomplishment, our civilization being the oldest and most advanced.

He had called a meeting of seven of us in his "workshop" as he termed his experimental laboratory. There came Hul Jok, the gigantic Commander of the Forces of Planetary Defense; Mor Ag, who knew all there was to know about the types, languages, and customs of the dwellers on every one of the major planets; Vir Dax, who could well-nigh bring the dead to life with his strange remedies, powders, and decoctions; Toj Qul, the soft-spoken, keen of brain—the one Venhezian who could "talk a bird off the bough," as the saying goes—our Chief Diplomat of Interplanetary Affairs; and Lan Apo, whose gift was peculiar, in that he could unerringly tell, when listening to any one, be that one Venhezian, Markhurian, or from far Ooranos— planet of the unexpected—Lan Apo could, I repeat, tell whether that one spoke pure truth or plain falsehood. Nay, he could even read the truth held back, while seemingly listening attentively to the lie put forward! A valuable man—but uncomfortable to have about, at times!

Lastly, there was myself, whose sole distinction, and a very poor one is that I am a maker of records, a writer of the deeds of others. Yet, even such as I have names, and I am called Hak Iri.

Ron was excited. That was plain to be seen in the indifferent, casual manner he displayed. He is like that. The rest of us were frankly curious, all but that confounded Lan Apo. He wore a faintly superior smile, as who should say: "No mystery here, to me!"

Ron stood before a huge dial. Now this is not a record of this invention, but a statement of the strange adventure in which we seven figured because of the events called to our attention by means of that wonderful device, so I shall not attempt its full description, merely saying that it was dial-formed, with the symbols of the major planets graven on its rim at regular intervals, and from the center there swung a long pointer, just then resting at a blank space.

"Listen," commanded Ron, and swung the pointer to the symbol of our own world.

Instantly there broke forth in that quiet room all the sounds of diversified life with which we Venhezians are familiar. All six of us who listened nodded comprehension. Already our science knew the principle, for we had long had dials that surpassed this one, apparently; for ours, while attuned to our planet alone, could, and did, record every event, sight, or sound thereon, at any distance, regardless of solid obstacles intervening. But this dial—it bore the symbols of all the inhabited worlds. Could it—?

Ron swung the indicator to the symbol of Markhuri, and the high-pitched uproar that immediately assailed our ears was characteristic of that world of excitable, volatile-natured, yet kindly people.

Planet after planet, near and far, we contacted thus, regardless of space, until Ron swung the pointer to the symbol of Aerth.

And silence was the result!

Ron's look was significant. It spoke volumes. One and all, we looked into each other's faces, and read therein reflected the same anxiety, the same apprehension which we each experienced.

That something was radically wrong with our neighbor, everybody already knew, for many years before the green light of Aerth had become perceptibly dimmer. Little attention, however, had been paid at first, for, by interplanetary law, each planet's dwellers remained at home, unless their presence was requested elsewhere. And no call had come to us nor to any other world from Aerth; so we had put it down to some purely natural cause with which, doubtless, the Aerthons were perfectly capable of coping without outside help or interference.

But year by year the green light waned in the night skies until finally it vanished utterly.

That might even have been due to atmospheric changes, perhaps. Life, even, might have become extinct on Aerth, so that no one lived to hold communication with anyone on any of the other inhabited worlds of the Planetary Chain, but it was hardly likely, unless the catastrophe was instantaneous; and in that case it would needs be violent. Anything so stupendous as that would have been registered at once by instruments all over the universe.

But now—this invention of Ron Ti's placed a remarkably serious aspect upon the question. For, if Aerth still occupied its old place—and we knew beyond doubt that it did—then what lay behind this double veil of silence and invisibility?

What terrible menace threatened the universe? For whatever had happened on one planet might well occur on another. And if Aerth should perchance be wrecked, the delicate balance of the universe would be seriously shaken, might even be thrown out completely, and Markhuri, so near the sun, go tumbling into blazing ruin.

Then horror upon horror, until chaos and old night once more held sway, and the unguessed purposes of the Great Mind would be—

Oh, but such thoughts led to madness! What to do? That course alone held fast to sanity.

"Well?" demanded Hul Jok, the practical. "What are *you* going to do about it Ron?"

"It is a matter for the Supreme Council," replied Ron, gravely. "I propose that we seven obtain permission to visit Aerth in one of the great Aethir-Torps, bearing credentials from the council and explaining why we have trespassed, and, if possible, try to ascertain if this be a thing warranting interference or not."

Why record the obvious? When such as Ron Ti and Hul Jok make request to the Supreme Council, it is from necessity, not for amusement. And the council saw to it in that aspect, and granted them free hand.

We started as promptly as might be.

The great Aethir-Torp hurtled through space in smooth, even flight, Hul Jok in command. And who better fitted? Was he not our war prince, familiar with every device known for purposes of offense and defense? Surely he whose skilled brain could direct whole fleets and armies was the logical one to handle our single craft, guide her, steer her, and, if need arose, fight her!

With this in mind I asked him casually yet curiously: "Hul Jok, if the Aerthons resent our inquiry, and bid us begone, what will you do?"

"Run!" grinned the giant, good-humoredly.

"You will not fight, should we be attacked?"

"Hum!" he grunted. "That will be different! No race on any planet may boast that they have attacked an Aethir-Torp of Venhez with impunity. At least," he added, decisively, "not while Hul Jok bears the emblem of the Looped Cross on his breast!"

"And if it be pestilence?" I persisted.

"Vir Dax would know more about that than I," he returned, shortly.

"And if—" I recommenced; but the giant released one hand from the controls, and clamped his great thick fingers on my shoulder, nearly crushing it.

"If," he growled, "you do not cease chattering when I am on duty, I shall most assuredly pitch you out through the opening of this conning tower into space, and there you may start on an orbit of your own as a cunning little planet! Are you answered?"

I was. But I grinned at him, for I knew our giant; and he returned the grin. But he was quite right. After all, speculations are the attempts of fools to forestall the future. Better to wait, and see reality.

And as for surmises, no one could have possibly dreamed any such nightmare state of affairs as we found upon our arrival.

A faint, dull, but lurid reddish glow first apprised us that we were drawing near our destination. It was Aerth's atmosphere, truly enough, but thick, murky, almost *viscous*, like a damp, soggy smoke.

So dense it was, in fact, that it became necessary to slow down the speed of the Aethir-Torp, lest the intense friction set up by our passage should melt the well-nigh infusible plates of Berulion metal of which our Aethir-Torp was built. And the closer we drew to Aerth's surface, the slower we were obliged to proceed from the same cause.

But finally, we were gliding along slowly, close to the actual surface; and, oh, the picture of desolation which met our eyes! It happened that we had our first view where once had stood a great city. Had stood, I say, for now it was but tumbled heaps of ruins, save here and there still loomed the shape of a huge building; but these, even, were in the last stages of dilapidation, ready to fall apart at any moment.

In fact, one such did collapse with a dull crashing roar, merely from the vibrations set up by the passing of our Aethir-Torp—and we were a good half-mile distant when it fell!

In vain we sounded our discordant *houtar*, no sign of life could we discern, and we all were straining our eyes in hopes. It was but a dead city. Was all Aerth thus?

Leaving behind this relic of a great past, we came to open country. And here the same deadly desolation prevailed. Nowhere was sign of habitation, nowhere was trace of animate life, neither bird, nor animal, nor man. Nor anywhere could we discern evidence of cultivation, and even vegetation of wild sorts was but little to be seen. Nothing but dull, gray-brown ground, and sand-colored rocks, with here and there a dingy, grayish-green shrub, stunted, distorted, isolate.

We came eventually to a low range of mountains, rocky, gloomy, and depressing to behold. It was while flying low over these that we for the first time saw water since we arrived on Aerth. In a rather wide valley we observed a narrow ribbon of sluggish, leaden-hued fluid meandering slowly along.

Ron Ti, who was then at the controls, brought our craft to a successful landing. This valley, especially near the stream banks, was the most fertile place we had thus far seen. There grew some fairly tall trees, and in places, clumps and thickets of pallid green bushes as high as Hul Jok's head, or even higher. But tree trunks and bushes alike were covered with dull red and livid purple and garish yellow fungi, which Vir Dax, after one look, pronounced poisonous to touch as well as to taste.

And here we found life, such as it was. I found it, and a wondrous start the ugly thing gave me! It was in semblance but a huge pulpy *blob* of a loathly blue color, in diameter over twice Hul Jok's height, with a gaping, triangular-shaped orifice for mouth, in which were set scarlet fangs; and that maw was in the center of the bloated body. At each corner of this mouth there glared malignant an oval opaque, silvery eye.

Well it was for me that, in obedience to Hul Jok's imperative command, I was holding my Blastor pointing ahead of me; for as I blundered full upon the monstrosity it upheaved its ugly bulk—how, I do not know, for I saw no legs nor did it have wings—to one edge and would have flopped down upon me, but instinctively I slid forward the catch on the tiny Blastor, and the foul thing vanished—save for a few fragments of its edges—smitten into nothingness by the vibrations hurled forth from that powerful little disintegrator.

It was the first time I had ever used one of the terrific instruments, and I was appalled at the instantaneous thoroughness of its workings.

The Blastor made no noise—it never does, nor do the big AK-Blastors which are the fighting weapons used on the Aethir-Torps, when they are discharging annihilation—but that nauseous ugliness I had removed gave vent to a sort of bubbling hiss as it returned to its normal atoms; and the others of our party hastened to where I stood shaking from excitement—Hul Jok was wrong when he said it was fear!—and they questioned me as to what I had encountered.

Shortly afterward, Hul Jok found another one and called us all to see it, threw a rock the size of his head at it, hit it fairly in the center of its mouth; and the rock vanished inside and was apparently *appreciated*, for the nightmare quivered slightly, rippled a bit, and lay still. Hul Jok tried it with another rock, but had the mischance to hit his little pet in the eye—and *seven* Blastors sent that livid horror to whatever limbo had first spawned it! And it was above our heads in the air, hurtling downward upon us when we blew it apart! Lightning scarcely moves swifter! Even Hul Jok was satisfied thereafter, when encountering one, to confine his caresses to pointing his Blastor and pressing the release stud, instead of trying to play games with it.

But that was, after all, the sole type of life we found in that valley, although what the things fed upon we could not then ascertain, unless they devoured their own species.

We found others like them in another place—blob-things that could not be destroyed by our Blastors: and we saw, too, what they were fed with. But that in its proper place!

We spent some time here in this valley, but then, finding nothing new, we again took to our craft and passed over the encircling mountains, only to find other mountains beyond, also other valleys.

At length we came to a larger valley than any we had before seen. This was, rather, a plain between two ranges, or, to speak more accurately, a flat where the range divided and formed a huge oval, to re-unite and continue as an unbroken chain farther on.

And here we again landed where a grove of trees gave concealment for our Aethir-Torp in case of—we did not know—anything! But upon us all there lay a heavy certitude that we were in a country inimical to our very continuance of existence.

Why? We could not tell that, yet each of us felt it, *knew* it, and, to some extent, feared it—for the bravest may well fear the unknown. It was Mor Ag who had spoken the word which guided our actions for some time past.

"Were Aerth inhabited as we understand the word," he had said, sententiously, "the great city we saw would be no ruin, but teeming with life and activity, as was the custom of the Aerthons before the light of the Green Star waned. So, if any be still alive, it is in the wilderness we must seek them. Wherefore, one place is as another, until we learn differently."

How utterly right he was, speedily became manifest.

The pit-black murk of night slowly gave way to the pallid wan daylight wherein no actual sunlight ever shown, and as we gathered up our Blastors and other impedimenta, preparatory to setting forth, Toj Qul raised a hand in warning.

There was no need for speech. We all heard what he did. I think the dead must hear that infernal, discordant din every time it is sounded. Describe it? I cannot. There are no words.

When our ears had somewhat recovered from the shock, Vir Dax shook his head.

"O-o-o-f-f-f!" he exclaimed. "To hear *that* very often would produce madness! It is agony!"

"Perhaps," growled Hul Jok. "But I have already gone mad because of it— gone mad with curiosity! Come along!"

He was commander. We went, leaving our Aethir-Torp to care for itself. But never again were we thus foolish.

We proceeded warily, spread out in a line, each keeping within sight of the next. The noise had come from the north side of the flat, and thither we directed our steps. Well for us that we were hidden by the trees and bushes!

As one we came to a sudden halt, drew together in a group, staring amazed, incredulous, horrified.

We were at the very edge of the high-bush, and before us was open space clear to the foot of the towering cliff-walls, which rose sheer to some ten times the height of a tall male.

Half way up this there stuck out a broad shelf of rock, extending completely across the face of the cliff from the western end to the eastern, and at regular intervals we could perceive large, rectangular openings, covered or closed, by doors of some dully glinting, leaden-hued metal.

And all the space between the edge of the bush-growth and foot of cliff was occupied by the same sort of loathly monstrosities as we had previously encountered! There they lay, expectant, apparently, for their attentions were seemingly concentrated upon the shelf of rock high in the air above them.

A door close to the western end opened and a procession emerged therefrom. At last we had found—

"Great Power of Life!" ejaculated Mor Ag profanely. "Those beings are no Aerthons!"

And he was right. Aerth never had produced any such type as we then beheld!

They had faces, and they had not faces! They had forms and they were form-less! How may I describe that which baffles description? We are accustomed to concrete, cohesive, permanent types of form and faces, and these were inchoate! Never in any two moments were their aspects the same. They were elongated, con-tracted, widened, expanded. At one moment the lower parts of one of these beings would apparently vanish while the upper parts remained visible, and again, condi-tions were reversed. Or a front aspect faded instantaneously, leaving but the rear section visible, only to promptly reverse the phenomenon. Or the left side disap-peared leaving the right side perceptible, then—but picture it for yourself! I have said enough!

It made me dizzy; it provoked Mor Ag because he could not name them! It enraged Hul Jok, inflamed him with desire to attack the whole throng, shatter them—why, he could not have told, but looking at them made him feel that way.

Ron Ti was mildly curious; Vir Dax frantic with ambition to study such be-ings—deliver *me* from the curiosity of such as Vir Dax, his methods of study!

Only Toj Qul and Lan Apo remained unperturbed: Toj Qul because he is a diplomat, therefore in no wise startled or amazed at, or by, anything. And Lan Apo was contemptuous, for as he looked at them, any race thus shifting as to bodily aspect must inevitably be shifty as to minds, and he had naught but contempt for a liar of any sort. Strange argument, strange stimulus to courageousness, yet perhaps as good as any!

Only one permanency had these beings—and even that fluctuated. They were of a silvery color, and they were black, of that blackness which is blacker than black. Later, we learned what manner of beings these were, and whence they came to afflict Aerth with their presences.

They formed in a row well back from the shelf-edge and then, from out the same door from which they had emerged, came another procession, or rather, a rout of rabble. These were, as Mor Ag at once asserted, unmistakable Aerthons. But how had that once wise and mighty race fallen! For these men were little better than brutes. Naked, round-shouldered, bowed of heads, cringing, shambling of gait, matted as to hair, and bearded—the males, at least—and utterly crushed, broken, dispirited!

It had long been a proverb on all the inhabited planets, "As beautiful as the Aerthon women;" but the females we were then beholding were, if anything, more abject, more deteriorate, than the males.

Many things became apparent to us who stared at these poor unfortunates. Very evidently, some *things*, from some *where*, had enslaved, debased, that once mighty race who were, or had been, second to none in all the universe—and this, *this*, was the result.

Hul Jok shifted his feet, stirred uneasily, growling venomously deep in his throat. Despite our giant's ferocious appearance, his heart was as a little child's or like that of a girl, gentle, tender, and sympathetic where wrong or oppression dared rear their ugly heads. And here, it was all too apparent, both those pitborn demons had been busily at work.

The rabble of Aerthons halted at the very edge of the shelf, grouped together, about equidistant from either end of the long line of the Things we could not name. And as the Aerthons stood there, the animate abhorrences on the ground fixed their malignant eyes upon the wretched creatures, the triangular mouths gaped wide, and from all that multitude of loathly blobs came beating against our shrinking, quivering, tormented eardrums that same brain-maddening discordance we had previously heard, even before we left the Aethir-Torp.

Of a sudden the Things standing behind the Aerthons ceased *flickering*, became fixed as to forms, although the change was anything but an improvement. For, although they became in shape like other living, sentient, intelligent beings, their faces bore all evil writ large upon them.

Acquaint yourself with all depravity, debauchery, foul indecency ever known throughout the universe since the most ancient forgotten times, multiply it even to the Nth power, limitless, and then you have not approximated their expressions!

Personally, even beholding such aspects made me feel as if, for eons uncountable, I had wallowed in vilest filth! And it affected the others the same way, and we knew, by our own experience, what had befallen the Aerthons!

Had such foul things once gained foothold on the great central sun, even the radiant purities of that abode of the perfected would have become tainted, polluted by a single glance at such unthinkable corruptiveness!

They, the Things, slowly raised each an arm, pointed at one Aerthon in the group. He, back to them as he was, quivered, shook, writhed, then, despite himself he slowly rose in the air, moved out into space, hung above the *blobs* that waited, avid-mouthed. The Aerthon turned over in the air, head down, still upheld by the concentrated wills of the Things that pointed . . .

Breathless, my eyes well-nigh starting from my head at sheer horror of what must in another moment befall, I stared, waiting the withdrawal of the force upholding the wretched Aerthon.

Half consciously, I saw Hul Jok's Blastor swing into line with the poor shrieking victim, and, just as he commenced dropping toward those triangular, gaping, hideous, orifices which waited slavering, saw him vanish—and silently blessed Hul Jok for his clemency and promptitude.

Then, momentarily, we all went mad! Our Blastors aimed, we pressed the releases, and swept the line of Things. And, to our aghast horror, nothing happened. Again and again we swept their line—*and they were unconscious that aught was assailing them!* The deadly Blastors were impotent!

Ron Ti first grasped the situation.

"These things are not 'beings'—they are but evil intelligences, of low order, crafty, vile, rather than wise! They are of too attenuate density—the vibrations of disintegration cannot shatter, but pass unfelt through their atomic structures! We can do naught save in mercy slay those poor Aerthons, and destroy those foul corruptions waiting to be fed."

We did it! It was truest kindliness to the Aerthons. Yet, despite the seeming callousness of our deed, we knew it for the best. And one thing it proved to us—low as the Aerthons had sunk, they had not fallen so far from their divine state but that in each the silver spark that distinguishes the soul-bearers from the soulless was still present. For as each body resolved back to the primordial Aethir from whence it was formed, the silver spark, liberated at last, floated into air until in distance disappeared. Then we turned our attentions to the blob-things.

But even as we smote the filthy Things, we noted that the strange beings on the rock-shelf had grasped the fact that a new phase of circumstance had entered into Aerth's affairs. They stood, amazed, startled, bewildered for a space of perhaps a minute, then passed into activity with a promptitude well-nigh admirable.

Several of them calmly stepped from the rock-shelf into the air and came hurtling toward us. In some way they had sensed our direction. In no time, they hovered above us, descended, and confronted us.

One, evidently of importance among his fellows, made articulate sounds, but we could not understand. Nor did we wish to! For with such as those, there can be but one common ground—unrelenting war!

And so, again and again we tried the effect of the Blastor, and as previously, found them impotent. I caught Hul Jok's eye. He was fairly frothing at the mouth with wrath—literally.

The Things, close by, seemed to emanate a vibration that was abhorrent, stultifying. Little by little I felt a silent but urgent command to start toward the foot of the rocky cliff. Unthinkingly I took a step forward, and Hul Jok's mighty arm slammed me back.

"I can feel it too," he snarled at all six of us. "But," he thundered sternly, "I command you by the Looped Cross itself, that you stand fast! 'Tis but their *wills!* Are we babes, that we should obey?"

Suddenly—I laughed! Obey the wills of such as these? It was ridiculous. Answering laughter came from the rest of the party. Hul Jok looked approvingly at me.

"Well done, Hak Iri!" he commended. "The Looped Cross thanks you—the Supreme Council shall give you the right to wear it, for high courage, for services rendered!"

And he had promised me our planet's supremest gift, highest honor—for laughter! Yet, though I say it, perhaps the service was not so trivial after all. For there is, in the final analysis, no weapon so thoroughly potent against evil as laughter, ridicule!

To take evil seriously is to magnify its importance; but ridicule renders its venom impotent, futile. Try it, you who doubt—try it in your hour of utmost need!

The Things became all black, no silvery tints remaining. One attempted to seize me, thrust me in the desired direction. Something—I had not known that it lay dormant in me—flamed into wrath. My hand closed, became a hard knot, my arm swung upward from my side with no volition on my part, and my fist drove full into the face of the Thing—left a horrible blank orifice which slowly filled into the semblance of a face again. The thing emitted a strange sobbing, gasping squawk of pain.

"Aho!" shouted Hul Jok, gleefully. "They may not be shattered nor slain, but— they *can* be hurt!" And he swung his Blastor up as a truncheon and brought it down full on the head of the nearest. The stroke passed through the Thing as through soft filth, yet that Thing, evidently having enough, rose hurriedly into air and sped to safety, followed by the rest.

"Back to the Aethir-Torp" commanded Hul Jok, and we retreated as swiftly as legs would take us. And, at that, we did not arrive there first.

To our dismay, we found it in possession of a horde of those Things. They were all over it, even inside, and worse still, all about it on the ground were Aerthons, a great crowd of them formed in solid masses, all facing outward, bearing in their hands long shimmering blades of brightly glinting metal, sharp as to points, with keen cutting edges.

"Swords," gasped Mor Ag. "I had thought such weapons obsolete on Aerth ten thousand years ago! Ware points and edge!"

"*Hue-hoh!*" shouted Hul Jok. "The Blastors, quick!"

Oh, the pity of it! I know that tears streamed from my eyes before it was finished. Ron Ti was equally affected. Hul Jok himself was swearing strange oaths, and, had it not been for Lan Apo, I doubt if we had had the necessary fortitude to go through with the ghastly affair. But as the silver sparks floated upward, a smile, almost beatific, came upon his set, white face.

"But they are rejoicing!" he cried out to us who grieved even while we smote. "I can feel their gratitude flowing to us who give them release from a life that is worse than death. They are glad to depart thus painlessly!"

And thereafter, we sorrowed no more.

The Aerthons were almost all disposed of when Mor Ag shouted: "Catch one or more of those slaves—alive! I would question—"

Hul Jok leapt forward, caught one by the wrist, wrenched his blade from his hand, slammed him against the hull of the Aethir-Torp, knocking him limp, threw him to us; and dealt likewise with another.

Meanwhile our Blastors played unrelentingly, and presently there were no more of the unfortunate Aerthons to be seen. Yet, the Things who, through sheer will-force alone, had compelled the Aerthons to face annihilation—for they could not fight; the Blastors slew from far beyond reach of sword-blade or hurled rock—those things still held our Aethir-Torp. Surely, Our Lady of Venhez kept them from guessing that they had but to slide the stud atop one of the great AK-Blastors from the white space to the black one, and we—ugh! Well for us that there was no Lan Apo among them to catch our thoughts.

A long while afterward, we found that they were acquainted with the principle of the AK-Blastors—and I can only account for their not using those on us by the supposition that they wished to capture us alive in order to gratify their fiendish propensities, so refrained from slaying us, willing to go to any lengths rather than do so, for the dead can in no wise be made to suffer!

We drew back, shaking from excitement and from the strain induced by their evil minds, or wills, beating on us, for, though they could not make us obey, still that force they directed was almost solid in its impact. Our craft was still in their possession, and we were standing on open ground, and sorely perplexed as to how we were to regain possession of the Aethir-Torp.

Hul Jok, war prince, solved our dilemma. He grasped a young tree, thick as his wrist, tore it from the ground, broke it across his knee—

"Club!" he grunted. "Our million-year-ago ancestors used such on Venhez. There are records of such in the Central War Castle!"

Hurriedly he prepared one for each of us, talking as he wrought.

"They can *feel*," he growled, "for all that they may not be slain. Very well! We will beat them from the Aethir-Torp!"

And that is precisely what occurred. On Venhez I had, at times, worked with my hands, for the sheer delight of muscle movement. But never had I dreamed what actual hard work was until that hour, during which, club in hand, we stormed our own craft, until at last, we stood watching the last of the Things as they rapidly passed through the air toward their cliff-abode—all but one, which we had finally cornered alone in a compartment into which it had strayed from the rest. We hemmed it about, beat it with our clubs until it cringed from the pain. Then Ron Ti thrust his face close to its face. . . .

We caught Ron's idea, added our wills to his, overbore that of our captive. It became confused, bewildered, shifted from silver to black, to silver again, the black became dull, smoky, the silver paled to leaden hue. The Thing crouched, palpitant with fear waves, manifest in dim coloration!

"We have learned enough!" declared Ron Ti solemnly. "Back to Venhez! This is a matter for the Supreme Council, as I feared even before we started. Here we cannot cope with conditions: we seven are too small a force. Back to Venhez!"

"Nay," Hul Jok demurred. "Let us remain and clean Aerth of this spawn!" And he indicated the captive Thing with a contemptuous gesture of his foot.

But Vir Dax added his voice to that of Ron Ti; and I—I was eager to go—to stay—I knew not which. The others felt as I did. Both courses had their attractions—also their drawbacks. For myself, I fear me very greatly that I, Hak Iri, who have ever held myself aloof from all emotions of violence, desiring clear mind that I might better chronicle the deeds of others—I fear, I say, that in me still lives something of the old Hak Iri, my remote ancestor who, once in the Days of Wildness of which our minstrels still sing, made for himself a name of terror on all Venhez for his love of strife.

But Mor Ag really settled the argument.

"We have this—Thing," he declared. "It must be examined, if we would learn aught of its nature, and that must be done if we hope ever to cope with such as it has proved to be in structure"(here an unholy light shone transient in the keen, cold eyes of Vir Dax), "and," continued Mor Ag, "we can, while on the return to Venhez, learn what has actually happened to Aerth from the two Aerthons——"

"One Aerthon!" interrupted Vir Dax. "The other died. Hul Jok knows not his own strength!"

He bent over, examined the living Aerthon and promptly brought him back to consciousness. Mor Ag spoke to him. The Aerthon brightened a trifle as he became assured we meant him no harm. He brightened still more when he observed that we held captive one of his former masters.

Then the thing caught the Aerthon's eye, and Lan Apo hastily turned to Hul Jok.

"It were well to confine this—where the Aerthon may not win to it," he warned emphatically. "Otherwise the will of the Thing will compel the enslaved fool to assist it to escape, or work us harm in some manner!"

We left the captive Thing in the little room, fastened the sole door, and Hul Jok retained the ward-strip which alone could unlock it again. The Aerthon said something to Mor Ag, who smiled and patted him on the shoulder, reassuringly.

"He thanked us for putting it beyond his power to obey——"

He broke off to ask the Aerthon another question, then gasped.

"Dear Mother of Life!" he ejaculated. "*The Things are from the dark side of the Moun, Aerth's satellite!*"

"*Avitchi!*" he exclaimed, and added another word: "*Hell!*"

We knew not his language—that is none save Mor Ag, but we all caught his meaning. He referred to the abode of evil, as it was understood on Aerth.

We would have questioned the Aerthon farther through the medium of Mor Ag, for we all were intensely curious, but just then that occurred which put an end to questioning and served, likewise to hasten our departure from this sorely afflicted planet.

A crackling, sizzling hiss of lightning and a terrific crash of thunder—the world, so far as we were immediately concerned, all one blinding glare of violet-tinted light—and the great Aethir-Torp rocked under the impact.

"Aho!" shouted Hul Jok. "What now?" And he dashed to one of the lookout openings just as another levin-bolt struck.

We joined him, and one glance was enough. All about us and above us were swarming great iridescent globes, and it was from these that there now came incessant streaks and flashes of lightning—powerful electric currents.

Our commander leapt into the conning tower, the others of us sprang, each to his station at one of the AK-Blastors, of which our craft mounted 6, and we promptly left the ground.

In a manner of speaking, we had little to fear, for the metal Berulion, of which the Aethir-Torps are built, could in no wise be harmed by lightning, nor could we who were inside be shocked thereby. But some parts of the controlling mechanism might have been seriously disarranged by the jarring concussions, and, besides, it was no part of our natures to submit tamely to attacks from any source.

With a *swoosh* we shot into the air and Hul Jok headed the sharp pointed nose of our great fighting cylinder straight into the thick of the shining globes that swooped and floated and swirled about and above us. Their thin walls gave them no protection against our impact, and we shattered them as easily as breaking the shells of eggs.

With the AK-Blastors we could and did shatter some of the globes which we failed to ram, but the vibrations of disintegration from these had no more effect upon the occupants of the globes than did the little hand Blastors previously—and Hul Jok fairly stamped in rage.

"Ron Ti," he exclaimed wrathfully, "your science is but a fraudulent thing! We mount your improved model Blastors purported to slay aught living, disintegrate anyone, and now——"

His anger well-nigh choked him.

"Content you," soothed Ron. "If we come again to Aerth——"

"If we come again to Aerth," Hul Jok asserted grimly, "Aerth will be *cleaned*, or I return no more to Venhez! But," he went on, imperatively, "you must find that which will destroy those Lunarions. We shattered and rammed their foolish globes, from which they play with powers of thunder and lightning, but them we might not harm. They did but float, insolent, safely down to Aerth!"

"We have one Lunarion upon whom to experiment," suggested Vir Dax meaningly.

"Ay," snapped Hul Jok. "And I look to you and Ron Ti to produce results! See to it that you fail not!"

I have known the giant commander since we were children together, but never had I seen him in such a mood. He seemed beside himself with what, in a lesser man, I should have classed as humiliation, but I realized, as did the others that it was merely that in him the dignity of the Looped Cross had been proffered insult, amounting well-nigh to defeat, and that to him the Looped Cross, emblem of our planet, was a sacred symbol, his sole object of adoration; and his high, fierce spirit was sore, smarting grievously and could in no wise be appeased until, as he himself had phrased it, "Aerth was clean!"

We had formally made report to the Supreme Council and had handed over to them, for disposal, both the Aerthon and the Lunarion we had brought back with us. And the Supreme Council in their wisdom, had commanded Mor Ag and Vir Dax to examine and question the Lunarion, with me to make records of aught he might say—but he would say naught, seemingly taking fiendish delight in baffling us.

The Aerthon, whose name was Jon, had told Mor Ag, while we were on our homeward flight, all that was known as to the conditions on Aerth. Here is no space to record it all, but briefly it was as follows:

Centuries ago, the Aerthons, divided into nations, warred. A mighty empire, hoping to dominate the planet, attacked a little country as a commencement. Another and larger nation hastened to the rescue of its tiny neighbor. A great island kingdom was drawn into the fray. A powerful republic overseas took hand in the matter; so ended the strife.

But rather than ending warfare, it did but give fresh incentive for inventions of deadly devices. Someone found that the element—metal—gold, had strange qualities, previously unguessed. Another discovered that gold could be produced synthetically, to use Aerth terminology. But the producing was by drawing it from out the storehouse of the universe, the primordial Aethir, wherein, dormant, are all things objective and subjective. And the drain on the Aethir opened strange doors in space, which heretofore, by fiat of the Great Wisdom, had been fast sealed.

Scientists of a great race, Mongulions, made too free use of the Aethir, hoping in their turn to subjugate the races of the West. Because of the vibrations set up in their labors, they made easy passage from Aerth to Moun. And on the dark side of the Moun dwelt a race of fiends, soulless, beyond the pale of the Infinite Mercy, who moved about to keep the Moun's bulk always between them and the hated light of the Sun. These had ever hated Aerth and its dwellers, for once they had inhabited that fair planet, until they became too wicked and they, and the Moun, broken from its parent Aerth by Almighty wrath, had been set apart in the sea of space. The Moun, although circling ever about its parent planet revolved never on its axis, so had one side turned ever toward Aerth; and these Lords of the Dark Face, in their eon-old hate, saw chance, at long last, to regain their lost world, upon which they looked with envy when the lunar phases brought them during the dark of the Moun to the side facing Aerth. In their Selenion globes they invaded Aerth, availing themselves of the openings the Mongulions had unwittingly established.

Aided by these unholy powers of evil, the Mongulions had dominated, even as they had planned, all other races, reduced them to conditions of abject servitude, and were in turn subjugated by the Lords of the Dark Face, through sheer will-energy alone.

So, reduced to conditions wherein they were less than beasts, the Aerthons had remained, prey to their fiendish conquerors, subjected to such treatments as even now, while I write, sicken my soul within me to think of, and are unfit to describe, for why afflict clean minds with unnecessary corruption?

Only those who have heard that Aerthon's story can conceive of what had, for ages, taken place in the ghastly orgies of the Lunarions—and we who did hear will never again be quite the same as we were before our ears were thus polluted.

So utterly abhorrent were conditions on Aerth that our Supreme Council decreed that such must be abolished at any cost. Not the planet, but the state of affairs prevailing. For they feared that the very Aethir would become putrescent, and moral degeneracy reach eventually to every planet of the Universal Chain!

But that, again, involved every planet in the matter. So they, the council, sent out invitation to all other planets for conference. Then came delegates from them all. They talked, they discussed, debated, consulted—and that was all.

Hul Jok, the practical, violated interplanetary etiquette, finally.

"Talk!" he shouted, rising from where he sat with the other Venhezians. "What does talk do?" We be no nearer than when we started. Since none can offer helpful suggestions, hear me! I am War Prince of Venhez, not a sage, but I can say that Ron Ti, if allowed sufficient time, can find that which will slay these Lunarions—all of their evil brood, and *that* is what is needed! Leave the matter to us of Venhez!"

A gravely genial delegate from Jopitar rose in his place.

"Oh you of Venhez," he said in his stately courtly speech, "your War Prince has spoken well! Since Ron Ti is acknowledged greatest of inventors in any world, he has but to demand, and if we of Jopitar can place aught at his disposal to further his investigations, he has but to communicate with us, and what we have is at his disposal!"

One by one, delegates from all the planets confirmed the Jopitarians' proffer, repeating it for those whom they represented. And one delegate, a huge red-hued, blue-eyed being, went even farther, for, springing to his feet, he thundered: "But if there is to be actual affray, we of Mharz demand that we participate!"

Hul Jok strode forward and slapped the Mharzion on the shoulder.

"Aho!" he laughed. "One after my own heart! Brother, it is in my mind that the crafts and fighters of all the planets will be needed before this matter is ended!"

It seems cruel, I know, but what else was there to do? From then on, that captive Lunarion was subjected to strange, some of them frightful, tests. Poisons and acids Vir Dax found had no effect upon him. Cutting instruments hurt, but failed to injure permanently. Already we knew that the Blastors—deadliest weapons known on any planet—were ineffective.

Ron Ti was at his wits' end! Two of our Venhezian years passed and all to no progress. Then a girl solved for him the one problem he was beginning to despair of ever solving for himself.

He had a love—who of all Venhez has not?—and she entering fully into his ideals and ambitions with that sweetly sympathetic understanding none but a maid of Venhez can bestow, had free access at all times to his workshop, wherein he toiled and studied for planetary benefit.

And she, one day seeing his distress at bafflement in his researches, saying naught, withdrew, returning shortly bearing in her arms her chiefest treasure, an instrument of many strings from which she proceeded to draw sweet strains of music, hoping thus to soothe his perturbed mind.

There came a wondrously sweet strain recurring in her melody and the first time it sounded the Lunarion winced. Repetition of the strain made him *howl!* And realization came to Ron Ti in one blinding flash of lightlike clarity.

"Harmony!" he shouted, rejoicing. "The blob-thing is discordant in its essential nature.

Never a maid of all Venhez was so proud just then as that love-girl of Ron Ti's. She had, at last, produced some sort of impression on the fiend, made it suffer grievously. So over and over she played that selfsame strain, and, ere many minutes had passed, the Lunarion fell prone, writhing in anguish, howling like a thing demented.

"Enough, Alu Rai: Ron bade her after watching the captive's misery for a space. "You have rendered the universe a service! Now depart, for I would think. Herein lies the secret of the weapon which will purge an afflicted world of its woe!"

It was a mighty fleet which started for Aerth on that never-to-be-forgotten expedition of rescue and reprisal. Practically speaking, all the craft were of similar appearance, for the Aethir-Torps had long been conceded to be the most efficient type for inter-spacial voyaging. Even the Aerthons had used them before they were subjected, and Jon the Aerthon stated that the Lunarions had a large fleet of them housed away in readiness against the day when they might desire to win to other worlds. But, he likewise told us, until the Lunarions had exhausted Aerth's resources, they would remain there, and for Aerthly voyaging in air, their Selenion globes were more satisfactory to them, moved by will-force as they were, than the great Aethir-Torps which were managed by purely mechanical means.

Naturally the Aethir-Torps from the different planets varied slightly, as, for example, those of Venhez had the conning towers cylindrical in shape and placed midway from nose to stern; the noses sharply pointed, sterns tapering to half the size of the greatest diameter—that of the waist of the craft; our Ak-Blastors were long, slender, copper-plated. The Aethir-Torps from Mharz were lurid red in color; blunt of nose; rounded as to stern; with short thick Ak-Blastors; their conning towers were well forward of the middle; octagonal in shape. But why amplify? Surely the Aethir-Torps of each planet are familiar to the dwellers of all the other planets.

And, of course, each craft bore the symbol of its home world. The Mharzions bore the Looped Dart in gold, even as we of Venhez painted upon the nose of ours the Looped Cross—but the symbols of the worlds are too well known to require description.

Ron Ti and Hul Jok had full authority over the entire squadron, although the war-commanders from all the worlds fully understood the carefully laid plans of aggression. And all the Aethir-Torps, in addition to the Ak-Blastors, now mounted before their conning towers a new device consisting of a large tube, much like an enormous *houtar*, terminating at the snout-end in five smaller tubes.

It was black night when Aerth was reached. And it was not until the sickly, wan daylight broke that actual operations commenced.

Spreading out, we quartered the air until the great oval flat showed plain. It was our good luck that it was our own craft which was the first to come above it, and, as we identified it, Hul Jok's eyes glowed in wrathful joy—if such an emotion may be thus contradictorily described. He caught Ron Ti's eye and nodded.

Ron Ti, obeying, threw over a lever. A most dreadful and terrific din shook the air with its uproar. From afar to the northward came a similar bellowing howl. Then from the eastward the same sound reached our ears, being replied to, a moment or so later, by the signal from the distant west. And from the southward came the answering racket, and we knew that all Aerth's surface was under surveillance of one or more of the Aethir-Torps comprising the Expeditionary Fleet.

Slowly, deliberately, we began circling above that infernal ovoid valley. But after that one hideous, bellowing howl, the tubelike arrangements before the conning towers changed their tones and from them came the same wondrously sweet, heart-thrilling, soul-shaking strain of melody as that which Alu Rai, the love-maid of Ron Ti, had produced to the exquisite torment of our captive Lunarion.

Over and over the strains were played, and still nothing happened. The idea was Ron Ti's and I began to wonder if in some manner he had miscalculated. Suppose it did not affect all the Lunarions alike? In that case not only would the expedition be doomed to failure, but the name of Ron Ti would become subject for many a jest on many a world! And we of Venhez must, perforce, walk with bowed heads!

But Ron Ti was smiling, and Hul Jok's fierce face bore an expression of confident, savage expectancy, and I—I waited, curious, hopeful still.

So swiftly that we could barely see it, an iridescent globe spun through the air, rising diagonally from the cliff-base, shooting straight at our Aethir-Torp. A touch of Ron Ti's hand, and the strain of music sounded even louder, clearer, sweeter.

The globe, when within a quarter of a mile, shot straight upward, discharged a terrific, blinding flash of chain-lightning against our craft, followed by a second and even more intense discharge—and still the sweet strain of harmony was all our reply.

The globe swooped until it nearly touched us—and I slid forward the stud on the AK-Blastor behind which I stood.

The Lunarion bubble was not more than a hundred feet away at that instant, and, like a bubble, it vanished incontinently. As ever, for all that we could shatter their Selenion globes, those demonical Lunarions themselves we could not disintegrate, or, so we deemed then, and I know that I said wrathful profanities in my impotent disappointment.

But Hul Jok grinned and Ron Ti nodded reassuringly to me, saying consolingly: "Wait!"

Well, I waited. What else could I do? But by this time the same game was going on all over Aerth. Wherever the Lunarions had abode, the strains of melody were driving them into a frenzy of madness, and they came swarming forth in their globes, hurling lightning-flashes at our Aethir-Torps, which might not thus be destroyed.

Yet, in a way, honors were even, for if they could not damage our Aethir-Torps, neither could we do aught but blow their globes into nothingness, while they themselves did but flee through the air back to their abodes, unharmed by the vibrations of the Ak-Blastors.

And in this manner, for three days and nights the futile warfare continued, and by morning of the fourth day I doubt if there were left to the Lunarions a single Selenion globe. At least, for two days and nights more, we none of us saw any. Yet, during those two days and nights, we continually played the music over and over and over until all Aerth vibrated from the repetitional sound-waves.

But on the next morning following, we had clear proof that the Lunarions had had all that they could endure of suffering. An Aethir-Torp, of a far different model than any we were acquainted with, shot into the air with incredible speed, and catching a craft of Satorn unawares rammed it in mid-air, completely wrecking it—only to be shattered into dust in its turn by the Ak-Blastors of a Mharzion Aethir-Torp. The crew of the ill-fated craft we could not save, but they were amply avenged ere long.

It happened that we witnessed this ramming, and Mor Ag shouted his surprise.

"But that Aethir-Torp, despite its speed, is of an age-old model," he affirmed excitedly, and Hul Jok nodded agreement.

"Their vibrations are too long and too slow wave-lengths to affect the modern Berulion metal of which we now build our fighting craft!" he chortled.

And so it was later proved to be.

We could very easily have shattered their old-model crafts, taking our own good time therefore, but to what avail? It would leave us with the same old problem. The Lunarions, with their levitational powers, would descend safely to the ground, and would still inhabit Aerth, over-running it like the evil vermin that they were.

But the far-thinking brains of Ron Ti and Hul Jok had laid out a carefully evolved plan, and aside from continuing to drive the Lunarions mad with the hated music and evading further collisions with their Aethir-Torps (no light task, either, considering their speed) we of the expedition refrained from using our Ak-Blastors until the Lunarions must have come to the very conclusion that our master-strategists desired them to reach eventually—that in some manner we had exhausted our vibratory charges.

At last, one morning we were made the object of a concerted attack. From all points came hurtling those old-style Aethir-Torps, and we—we fled from before them! Finding that their old-model Ak-Blastors had little or no effect on us, protected as we were by the Berulion plates, they fell back on their levin-bolts and these they hurled incessantly, until they, as well as we, were well out of Aerth's atmosphere, and into the great Ocean of Aethireal Space.

But ever we played that same maddening music, and it acted as a powerful incentive to hold them to the pursuit, for they had lost all caution in their rage. And ever, as we fled from before them, we laughed.

And at last, some five million miles from Aerth's surface we turned upon them! Stretched out in a long, curved line, we awaited their coming, and as they came within our range, every Aethir-Torp commenced whirling about as if on a traverse axis, presenting one moment the nose, next a side, then the stern, and again the other side, and once more the stern or prow, in this manner giving play to all six Ak-Blastors-the forward on<one>, the two on each side, and the one pointing to rearward.

And the Lunarions, although heretofore we might not injure them, were soon without protection, their Aethir-Torps shattered, left exposed to the deadly chill of outer space, and their forms, loose though they were in structure, subjected to the awful pressure of the inelastic Aethir!

It compressed their bodies as if they had been density itself. And having no defense, they instinctively drew close to each other—the Aethiric pressure did all that was necessary.

They were jammed into a single mass, and *then* we played upon that with the Ak-Blastors until that mass, too, became as nothing!

Only from that blank space where the fiends, the Lords of the Dark Face, had been, floated in all directions a shower or swarm of dull red sparks, which, even as we watched, slowly flickered and burned out in the depths of Abysmal Night!

Ron Ti bowed his head in reverence to that great Power which had permitted us to be the instruments of Its vengeance, signing in the air before him the Looped

Cross symbol of Life.

"As I suspected," he said, gravely, "they were soulless. They had naught but form and vitality, mind and will—life of the lower order, non-enduring. The red sparks proved that—and even those have burned out, resolved back into the sea of Undifferentiated Energy. Our work is ended. Let Aerth work out its own rehabilitation. That wondrous race of Aerthons will soon rear the foundations of an even greater civilization than their world has ever before known."

The
YELLOW Sign

by Robert W. Chambers

Who makes YOU "think of a disturbed grub in a chestnut"?
Watch out for unfamiliar faces in this tale from Chambers' collection,
"The King in Yellow", first published in 1895.

Along the shore the cloud waves break,
The twin suns sink behind the lake,
The shadows lengthen
In Carcosa.

Strange is the night where black stars rise,
And strange moons circle through the skies,
But stranger still is
Lost Carcosa.

Songs that the Hyades shall sing,
Where flap the tatters of the King,
Must die unheard in
Dim Carcosa.

Song of my soul, my voice is dead,
Die thou, unsung, as tears unshed
Shall dry and die in
Lost Carcosa.

Cassilda's Song in *The King in Yellow*.
Act 1. Scene 2.

I. BEING THE CONTENTS OF AN
UNSIGNED LETTER SENT TO THE AUTHOR

There are so many things which are impossible to explain! Why should certain chords in music make me think of the brown and golden tints of autumn foliage? Why should the Mass of Sainte Cécile send my thoughts wandering among caverns whose walls blaze with ragged. masses of virgin silver? What was it in the roar and turmoil of Broadway at six o'clock that flashed before my eyes the picture of a still Breton forest where sunlight filtered through spring foliage and Silvia bent, half curiously, half tenderly, over a small green lizard, murmuring: "To think that this also is a little ward of God!"

When I first saw the watchman his back was toward me. I looked at him indifferently until he went into the church. I paid no more attention to him than I had to any other man who lounged through Washington Square that morning, and when I shut my window and turned back into my studio I had forgotten him. Late in the afternoon, the day being warm, I raised the window again and leaned out to get a sniff of air. A man was standing in the courtyard of the church, and I noticed him again with as little interest as I had that morning. I looked across the square to where the fountain was playing and then, with my mind filled with vague impressions of trees, asphalt drives, and the moving groups of nursemaids and holiday-makers, I started to walk back to my easel. As I turned, my listless glance included the man below in the churchyard. His face was toward me now, and with a perfectly involuntary movement I bent to see it. At the same moment he raised his head and looked at me. Instantly I thought of a coffin-worm. Whatever it was about the man that repelled me I did not know, but the impression of a plump white grave-worm was so intense and nauseating that I must have shown it in my expression, for he turned his puffy face away with a movement which made me think of a disturbed grub in a chestnut.

I went back to my easel and motioned the model to resume her pose. After working awhile I was satisfied that I was spoiling what I had done as rapidly as possible, and I took up a palette knife and scraped the color out again. The flesh tones were sallow and unhealthy, and I did not understand how I could have painted such sickly color into a study which before that had glowed with healthy tones.

I looked at Tessie. She had not changed, and the clear flush of health dyed her neck and cheeks as I frowned.

"Is it something I've done?" she said.

"No,—I've made a mess of this arm, and for the life of me I can't see how I came to paint such mud as that into the canvas," I replied.

"Don't I pose well?" she insisted.

"Of course, perfectly."

"Then it's not my fault?"

"No. It's my own."

"I'm very sorry," she said.

I told her she could rest while I applied rag and turpentine to the plague spot on my canvas, and she went off to smoke a cigarette and look over the illustrations in the *Courier Français.*

I did not know whether it was something in the turpentine or a defect in the canvas, but the more I scrubbed the more that gangrene seemed to spread. I worked like a beaver to get it out, and yet the disease appeared to creep from limb to limb of the study before me. Alarmed I strove to arrest it, but now the color on the breast changed and the whole figure seemed to absorb the infection as a sponge soaks up water. Vigorously I plied palette knife, turpentine, and scraper, thinking all the time what a séance I should hold with Duval who had sold me the canvas; but soon I noticed that it was not the canvas which was defective nor yet the colors of Edward. "It must be the turpentine," I thought angrily, "or else my eyes have become so blurred and confused by the afternoon light that I can't see straight." I called Tessie, the model. She came and leaned over my chair blowing rings of smoke into the air.

"What *have* you been doing to it?" she exclaimed.

"Nothing," I growled, "it must be this turpentine!"

"What a horrible color it is now," she continued. "Do you think my flesh resembles green cheese?"

"No, I don't," I said angrily, "did you ever know me to paint like that before?"

"No, indeed!"

"Well, then!"

"It must be the turpentine, or something," she admitted.

She slipped on a Japanese robe and walked to the window. I scraped and rubbed until I was tired and finally picked up my brushes and hurled them through the canvas with a forcible expression, the tone alone of which reached Tessie's ears.

Nevertheless she promptly began: "That's it! Swear and act silly and ruin your brushes! You have been three weeks on that study, and now look! What's the good of ripping the canvas? What creatures artists are!"

I felt about as much ashamed as I usually did after such an outbreak, and I turned the ruined canvas to the wall. Tessie helped me clean my brushes, and then danced away to dress. From the screen she regaled me with bits of advice concerning whole or partial loss of temper, until, thinking, perhaps, I had been tormented sufficiently, she came out to implore me to button her waist where she could not reach it on the shoulder.

"Everything went wrong from the time you came back from the window and talked about that horrid-looking man you saw in the churchyard," she announced.

"Yes, he probably bewitched the picture," I said, yawning. I looked at my watch.

"It's after six, I know," said Tessie, adjusting her hat before the mirror.

"Yes," I replied, "I didn't mean to keep you so long." I leaned out of the window but recoiled with disgust, for the young man with the pasty face stood below in the churchyard. Tessie saw my gesture of disapproval and leaned from the window.

"Is that the man you don't like?" she whispered.

I nodded.

"I can't see his face, but he does look fat and soft. Someway or other," she continued, turning to look at me, "he reminds me of a dream,—an awful dream I once had. Or," she mused, looking down at her shapely shoes, "was it a dream after all?"

"How should I know?" I smiled.

Tessie smiled in reply.

"You were in it," she said, "so perhaps you might know something about it."

"Tessie! Tessie!" I protested, " don't you dare flatter by saying you dream about me! "

"But I did," she insisted; "shall I tell you about it?"

"Go ahead," I replied, lighting a cigarette.

Tessie leaned back on the open window-sill and began very seriously.

"One night last winter I was lying in bed thinking about nothing at all in particular. I had been posing for you and I was tired out, yet it seemed impossible for me to sleep. I heard the bells in the city ring ten, eleven, and midnight. I must have fallen asleep about midnight because I don't remember hearing the bells after that. It seemed to me that I had scarcely closed my eyes when I dreamed that something impelled me to go to the window. I rose, and raising the sash, leaned out. Twenty-fifth Street was deserted as far as I could see. I began to be afraid; everything outside seemed so—so black and uncomfortable. Then the sound of wheels in the distance came to my ears, and it seemed to me as though that was what I must wait for. Very slowly the wheels approached, and, finally, I could make out a vehicle moving along the street. It came nearer and nearer, and when it passed beneath my window I saw it was a hearse. Then, as I trembled with fear, the driver turned and looked straight at me. When I awoke I was standing by the open window shivering with cold, but the black-plumed hearse and the driver were gone. I dreamed this dream again in March last, and again awoke beside the open window. Last night the dream came again. You remember how it was raining; when I awoke, standing at the open window, my night-dress was soaked."

"But where did I come into the dream?" I asked.

"You—you were in the coffin; but you were not dead."

"In the coffin?"

"Yes."

"How did you know? Could you see me?"

"No; I only knew you were there."

"Had you been eating Welsh rarebits, or lobster salad?" I began laughing, but the girl interrupted me with a frightened cry.

"Hello! What's up?" I said, as she shrank into the embrasure by the window.

"The—the man below in the churchyard; he drove the hearse."

"Nonsense," I said, but Tessie's eyes were wide with terror. I went to the window and looked out. The man was gone. "Come, Tessie," I urged, "don't be foolish. You have posed too long; you are nervous."

"Do you think I could forget that face?" she murmured. "Three times I saw the hearse pass below my window, and every time the driver turned and looked up at me. Oh, his face was so white and—and soft? It looked dead—it looked as if it had been dead a long time."

I induced the girl to sit down and swallow a glass of Marsala. Then I sat down beside her, and tried to give her some advice. "Look here, Tessie," I said, "you go to the country for a week or two, and you'll have no more dreams about hearses. You pose all day, and when night comes your nerves are upset. You can't keep this up. Then again, instead of going to bed when your day's work is done, you run off to picnics at Sulzer's Park, or go to the Eldorado or Coney Island, and when you come down here next morning you are fagged out. There was no real hearse. That was a soft-shell crab dream."

She smiled faintly.

"What about the man in the churchyard?"

"Oh, he's only an ordinary unhealthy, everyday creature."

"As true as my name is Tessie Reardon, I swear to you, Mr. Scott, that the face of the man below in the churchyard is the face of the man who drove the hearse!"

"What of it?" I said. "It's an honest trade."

"Then you think I *did* see the hearse?"

"Oh," I said, diplomatically, "if you really did, it might not be unlikely that the man below drove it. There is nothing in that."

Tessie rose, unrolled her scented handkerchief, and taking a bit of gum from a knot in the hem, placed it in her mouth. Then drawing on her gloves she offered me her hand, with a frank, "Good-night, Mr. Scott," and walked out.

II.

The next morning, Thomas, the bellboy, brought me the *Herald* and a bit of news. The church next door had been sold. I thanked Heaven for it, not that being a Catholic I had any repugnance for the congregation next door, but because my nerves were shattered by a blatant exhorter, whose every word echoed through the aisle of the church as if it had been my own rooms, and who insisted on his r's with a nasal persistence which revolted my every instinct. Then, too, there was a fiend in human shape, an organist, who reeled off some of the grand old hymns with an interpretation of his own, and I longed for the blood of a creature who could play the doxology with an amendment of minor chords which one hears only in a quartet of very young undergraduates. I believe the minister was a good man, but when he bellowed: "And the Lorrrrd said unto Moses, the Lorrrd is a man of war; the Lorrrd is his name. My wrath shall wax hot and I will kill you with the sworrrd!" I wondered how many centuries of purgatory it would take to atone for such a sin.

"Who bought the property?" I asked Thomas.

"Nobody that I knows, sir. They do say the gent wot owns this 'ere 'Amilton flats was lookin' at it. 'E might be a bildin' more studios."

I walked to the window. The young man with the unhealthy face stood by the churchyard gate, and at the mere sight of him the same overwhelming repugnance took possession of me.

"By the way, Thomas," I said, "who is that fellow down there?" Thomas sniffed. "That there worm, sir? 'E's night-watchman of the church, sir. 'E maikes me tired a-sittin' out all night on them steps and lookin' at you insultin' like. I'd a punched 'is 'ed, sir—beg pardon, sir—"

"Go on, Thomas."

"One night a comin' 'ome with 'Arry, the other English boy, I sees 'im a sittin' there on them steps. We 'ad Molly and Jen with us, sir, the two girls on the tray service, an' 'e looks so insultin' at us that I up and sez: 'Wat you looking hat, you fat slug?'—beg pardon, sir, but that's 'ow I sez, sir. Then 'e don't say nothin' and I sez: 'Come out and I'll punch that puddin' 'ed.' Then I hopens the gate an' goes in, but 'e don't say nothin', only looks insultin' like. Then I 'its 'im one, but, ugh! 'is 'ed was that cold and mushy it ud sicken you to touch 'im."

"What did he do then?" I asked, curiously."

'Im? Nawthin'."

"And you, Thomas?"

The young fellow flushed with embarrassment and smiled uneasily. "Mr. Scott, sir, I ain't no coward an' I can't make it out at all why I run. I was in the 5th Lawncers, sir, bugler at Tel-el-Kebir, an' was shot by the wells."

"You don't mean to say you ran away?"

"Yes, sir; I run."

"Why?"

"That's just what I want to know, sir. I grabbed Molly an' run, an' the rest was as frightened as I."

"But what were they frightened at?"

Thomas refused to answer for a while, but now my curiosity was aroused about the repulsive young man below and I pressed him. Three years' sojourn in America had not only modified Thomas' cockney dialect but had given him the American's fear of ridicule.

"You won't believe me, Mr. Scott, sir?"

"Yes, I will."

"You will lawf at me, sir?"

" Nonsense!"

He hesitated. "Well, sir, it's God's truth that when I 'it 'im 'e grabbed me wrists, sir, and when I twisted 'is soft, mushy fist one of 'is fingers come off in me 'and."

The utter loathing and horror of Thomas' face must have been reflected in my own for he added:

"It's orful, an' now when I see 'im I just go away. 'E maikes me hill."

When Thomas had gone I went to the window. The man stood beside the church-railing with both hands on the gate, but I hastily retreated to my easel again, sickened and horrified, for I saw that the middle finger of his right hand was missing.

At nine o'clock Tessie appeared and vanished behind the screen with a merry "Good-morning, Mr. Scott." When she had reappeared and taken her pose upon the model-stand I started a new canvas much to her delight. She remained silent as long as I was on the drawing, but as soon as the scrape of the charcoal ceased and I took up my fixative she began to chatter.

"Oh, I had such a lovely time last night. We went to Tony Pastor's."

"Who are 'we'?" I demanded.

"Oh, Maggie, you know, Mr. Whyte's model, and Pinkie McCormick—we call her Pinkie because she's got that beautiful red hair you artists like so much—and Lizzie Burke."

I sent a shower of spray from the fixative over the canvas, and said: "Well, go on."

"We saw Kelly and Baby Barnes the skirt-dancer and—and all the rest. I made a mash."

"Then you have gone back on me, Tessie?" She laughed and shook her head.

"He's Lizzie Burke's brother, Ed. He's a perfect gen'l'man."

I felt constrained to give her some parental advice concerning mashing, which she took with a bright smile.

"Oh, I can take care of a strange mash," she said, examining her chewing gum, "but Ed is different. Lizzie is my best friend."

Then she related how Ed had come back from the stocking mill in Lowell, Massachusetts, to find her and Lizzie grown up, and what an accomplished young man he was, and how he thought nothing of squandering half a dollar for ice-cream and oysters to celebrate his entry as clerk into the woollen department of Macy's. Before she finished I began to paint, and she resumed the pose, smiling and chattering like a sparrow. By noon I had the study fairly well rubbed in and Tessie came to look at it.

"That's better," she said.

I thought so too, and ate my lunch with a satisfied feeling that all was going well. Tessie spread her lunch on a drawing table opposite me and we drank our claret from the same bottle and lighted our cigarettes from the same match. I was very much attached to Tessie. I had watched her shoot up into a slender but exquisitely formed woman from a frail, awkward child. She had posed for me during the last three years, and among all my models she was my favorite. It would have troubled me very much indeed had she become "tough" or "fly," as the phrase goes, but I never noticed any deterioration of her manner, and felt at heart that she was all right. She and I never discussed morals at all, and I had no intention of doing so, partly because I had none myself, and partly because I knew she would do what she liked in spite of me. Still I did hope she would steer clear of complications, because I wished her well, and then also I had a selfish desire to retain the best model I had. I knew that mashing, as she termed it, had no significance with girls like Tessie, and that such things in America did not resemble in the least the same things in Paris. Yet, having lived with my eyes open, I also knew that somebody would take Tessie away some day, in one manner or another, and though I professed to myself that marriage was nonsense, I sincerely hoped that, in this case, there would be a priest at the end of the vista. I am a Catholic. When I listen to high mass, when I sign myself; I feel that everything, including myself, is more cheerful, and when I confess; it does me good. A man who lives as much alone as I do, must confess to somebody. Then, again, Sylvia was Catholic, and it was reason enough for me. But I was speaking of Tessie, which is very different. Tessie also was Catholic and much more devout than I, so, taking it all in all, I had little fear for my pretty model until she should fall in love. But *then* I knew that fate alone would decide her future for her, and I prayed inwardly that fate would keep her away from men like me and throw into her path nothing but Ed Burkes and Jimmy McCormicks, bless her sweet face!

Tessie sat blowing rings of smoke up to the ceiling and tinkling the ice in her tumbler.

"Do you know, Kid, that I also had a dream last night?" I observed. I sometimes called her "the Kid."

"Not about that man," she laughed.

"Exactly. A dream similar to yours, only much worse."

It was foolish and thoughtless of me to say this, but you know how little tact the average painter has.

"I must have fallen asleep about 10 o'clock," I continued, "and after awhile I dreamt that I awoke. So plainly did I hear the midnight bells, the wind in the tree-branches, and the whistle of steamers from the bay, that even now I can scarcely believe I was not awake. I seemed to be lying in a box which had a glass cover. Dimly I saw the street lamps as I passed, for I must tell you, Tessie, the box in which I reclined appeared to lie in a cushioned wagon which jolted me over a stony pavement. After a while I became impatient and tried to move but the box was too narrow. My hands were crossed on my breast so I could not raise them to help myself. I listened and then tried to call. My voice was gone. I could hear the trample of the horses attached to the wagon and even the breathing of the driver. Then another sound broke upon my ears like the raising of a window sash. I managed to turn my head a little, and found I could look, not only through the glass cover of my box, but also through the glass panes in the side of the covered vehicle. I saw houses, empty and silent, with neither light nor life about any of there excepting one. In that house a window was open on the first floor and a figure all in white stood looking down into the street. It was you."

Tessie had turned her face away from me and leaned on the table with her elbow.

"I could see your face," I resumed, "and it seemed to me to be very sorrowful. Then we passed on and turned into a narrow black lane. Presently the horses stopped. I waited and waited, closing my eyes with fear and impatience, but all was silent as the grave. After what seemed to me hours, I began to feel uncomfortable. A sense that somebody was close to me made me unclose my eyes. Then I saw the white face of the hearse-driver looking at me through the coffin-lid—"

A sob from Tessie interrupted me. She was trembling like a leaf. I saw I had made an ass of myself and attempted to repair the damage.

"Why, Tess," I said, "I only told you this to show you what influence your story might have on another person's dreams. You don't suppose I really lay in a coffin, do you? What are you trembling for? Don't you see that your dream and my unreasonable dislike for that inoffensive watchman of the church simply set my brain working as soon as I fell asleep?"

She laid her head between her arms and sobbed as if her heart would break. What a precious triple donkey I had made of myself! But I was about to break my record. I went over and put my arm about her.

"Tessie dear, forgive me," I said; "I had no business to frighten you with such nonsense. You are too sensible a girl, too good a Catholic to believe in dreams."

Her hand tightened on mine and her head fell back upon my shoulder, but she still trembled and I petted her and comforted her.

"Come, Tess, open your eyes and smile."

Her eyes opened with a slow languid movement and met mine, but their expression was so queer that I hastened to reassure her again.

"It's all humbug, Tessie, you surely are not afraid that any harm will come to you because of that."

"No," she said, but her scarlet lips quivered.

"Then what's the matter? Are you afraid?"

"Yes. Not for myself."

"For me, then?" I demanded gayly.

"For you," she murmured in a voice almost inaudible, " I—I care for you."

At first I started to laugh, but when I understood her, a shock passed through me and I sat like one turned to stone. This was the crowning bit of idiocy I had committed. During the moment which elapsed between her reply and my answer I thought of a thousand responses to that innocent confession. I could pass it by with a laugh, I could misunderstand her and reassure her as to my health, I could simply point out that it was impossible she could love me. But my reply was quicker than my thoughts, and I might think and think now when it was too late, for I had kissed her on the mouth.

That evening I took my usual walk in Washington Park, pondering over the occurrences of the day. I was thoroughly committed. There was no back out now, and I stared the future straight in the face. I was not good, not even scrupulous, but I had no idea of deceiving either myself or Tessie. The one passion of my life lay buried in the sunlit forests of Brittany. Was it buried forever? Hope cried "No!" For three years I had been listening to the voice of Hope, and for three years I had waited for a footstep on my threshold. Had Sylvia forgotten? "No!" cried Hope.

I said that I was not good. That is true, but still I was not exactly a comic opera villain. I had led an easy-going reckless life, taking what invited me of pleasure, deploring and sometimes bitterly regretting consequences. In one thing alone, except my painting, was I serious, and that was something which lay hidden if not lost in the Breton forests.

It was too late now for me to regret what had occurred during the day. Whatever it had been, pity, a sudden tenderness for sorrow, or the more brutal instinct of gratified vanity, it was all the same now, and unless I wished to bruise an innocent heart my path lay marked before me. The fire and strength, the depth of passion of a love which I had never even suspected, with all my imagined experience in the world, left me no alternative but to respond or send her away. Whether because I am so cowardly about giving pain to others, or whether it was that I have little of the gloomy Puritan in me, I do not know, but I shrank from disclaiming responsibility for that. thoughtless kiss, and in fact had no time to do so before the gates of her heart opened and the flood poured forth. Others who habitually do their duty and find a sullen satisfaction in making themselves and everybody else unhappy, might have withstood it. I did not. I dared not. After the storm had abated I did tell her that she might better have loved Ed Burke and worn a plain gold ring, but she would not hear of it, and I thought perhaps that as long as she had decided to love somebody she could not marry, it had better be me. I, at least, could treat her with an intelligent affection, and whenever she became tired of her infatuation she could go none the worse for it. For I was decided on that point although I knew how hard it would be. I remembered the usual termination of Platonic liaisons and thought how disgusted I had been whenever I heard of one. I knew I was undertaking a great deal for so unscrupulous a man as I was, and I dreaded the future, but never for one moment did I doubt that she was safe with me. Had it been anybody but Tessie I should not have bothered my head about scruples. For it did not occur to me to sacrifice Tessie as I would have sacrificed a woman of the world. I looked. the future squarely in the face and saw the several probable endings to the affair. She would either tire of the whole thing, or become so unhappy that I should have either to marry her or go away. If I married her we would be unhappy. I with a wife unsuited to me, and she with a husband unsuitable for any woman. For my past life could scarcely entitle me to marry. If I went away she might either fall ill; recover, and marry some Eddie Burke, or she might recklessly or deliberately go and do something foolish. On the other hand if she tired of me, then her whole life would be before her with beautiful vistas of Eddie Burkes and marriage rings and twins and Harlem flats and Heaven knows what. As I strolled along through the trees by the Washington Arch, I decided that she should find a substantial friend in me anyway and the future could take care of itself. Then I went into the house and put on my evening dress for the little faintly perfumed note on my dresser said, "Have a cab at the stage door at eleven," and the note was signed "Edith Carmichel, Metropolitan Theater, June 19th, 189—."

I took supper that night, or rather we took supper, Miss Carmichel and I, at Solari's and the dawn was just beginning to gild the cross on the Memorial Church as I entered Washington Square after leaving Edith at the Brunswick. There was not a soul in the park as I passed among the trees and took the walk which leads from the Garibaldi statue to the Hamilton Apartment House, but as I passed the churchyard I saw a figure sitting on the stone steps. In spite of myself a chill crept over me at the sight of the white puffy face, and I hastened to pass. Then he said something which might have been addressed to me or might merely have been a mutter to himself, but a sudden furious anger flamed up within me that such a creature should address me. For an instant I felt like wheeling about and smashing my stick over his head, but I walked on, and entering the Hamilton went to my apartment. For some time I tossed about the bed trying to get the sound of his voice out of my ears, but could not. It filled my head, that muttering sound, like thick oily smoke from a fat-rendering vat or an odor of noisome decay. And as I lay and tossed about, the voice in my ears seemed more distinct, and I began to understand the words he had muttered. They came to me slowly as if I had forgotten them, and at last I could make some sense out of the sounds. It was this:

"Have you found the Yellow Sign?"

"Have you found the Yellow Sign?"

"Have you found the Yellow Sign?"

I was furious. What did he mean by that? Then with a curse upon him and his I rolled over and went to sleep, but when I awoke later I looked pale and haggard, for I had dreamed the dream of the night before and it troubled me more than I cared to think.

I dressed and went down into my studio. Tessie sat by the window, but as I came in she rose and put both arms around my neck for an innocent kiss. She looked so sweet and dainty that I kissed her again and then sat down before the easel.

" Hello! Where's the study I began yesterday?" I asked.

Tessie looked conscious, but did not answer. I began to hunt among the piles of canvases, saying, " Hurry up, Tess, and get ready; we must take advantage of the morning light."

When at last I gave up the search among the other canvases and turned to look around the room for the missing study I noticed Tessie standing by the screen with her clothes still on.

"What's the matter," I asked, "don't you feel well?"

"Yes."

"Then hurry."

"Do you want me to pose as—as I have always posed?"

Then I understood. Here was a new complication. I had lost, of course, the best nude model I had ever seen. I looked at Tessie. Her face was scarlet. Alas! Alas! We had eaten of the tree of knowledge, and Eden and native innocence were dreams of the past—I mean for her.

I suppose she noticed the disappointment on my face, for she said: "I will pose if you wish. The study is behind the screen here where I put it."

"No." I said, "we will begin something new;" and I went into my wardrobe and picked out a Moorish costume which fairly blazed with tinsel. It was a genuine costume, and Tessie retired to the screen with it enchanted. When she came forth again I was astonished. Her long black hair was bound above her forehead with a circlet of turquoises, and the ends curled about her glittering girdle. Her feet were encased in the embroidered pointed slippers and the skirt of her costume, curiously wrought with arabesques in silver, fell to her ankles. The deep metallic blue vest embroidered with silver and the short Mauresque jacket spangled and sewn with turquoises became her wonderfully. She came up to me and held up her face smiling. I slipped my hand into my pocket and drawing out a gold chain with a cross attached, dropped it over her head.

"It's yours, Tessie."

"Mine?" she faltered.

"Yours. Now go and pose." Then with a radiant smile she ran behind the screen and presently reappeared with a little box on which was written my name.

"I had intended to give it to you when I went home to-night," she said, "but I can't wait now."

I opened the box. On the pink cotton inside lay a clasp of black onyx, on which was inlaid a curious symbol or letter in gold. It was neither Arabic nor Chinese, nor as I found afterwards did it belong to any human script.

"It's all I had to give you for a keepsake," she said, timidly.

I was annoyed, but I told her how much I should prize it, and promised to wear it always. She fastened it on my coat beneath the lapel.

"How foolish, Tess, to go and buy me such a beautiful thing as this," I said.

"I did not buy it," she laughed.

"Where did you get it?"

Then she told me how she had found it one day while coming from the Aquarium in the Battery, how she had advertised it and watched the papers, but at last gave up all hopes of finding the owner.

"That was last winter," she said, "the very day I had the first horrid dream about the hearse."

I remembered my dream of the previous night but said nothing, and presently my charcoal was flying over a new canvas, and Tessie stood motionless on the model-stand.

III.

The day following was a disastrous one for me. While moving a framed canvas from one easel to another my foot slipped on the polished floor and I fell heavily on both wrists. They were so badly sprained that it was useless to attempt to hold a brush, and I was obliged to wander about the studio, glaring at unfinished drawings and sketches until despair seized me and I sat down to smoke and twiddle my thumbs with rage. The rain blew against the windows and rattled on the roof of the church, driving me into a nervous fit with its interminable patter. Tessie sat sewing by the window, and every now and then raised her head and looked at me with such innocent compassion that I began to feel ashamed of my irritation and looked about for something to occupy me. I had read all the papers and all the books in the library, but for the sake of something to do I went to the bookcases and shoved them open with my elbow. I knew every volume by its color and examined them all, passing slowly around the library and whistling to keep up my spirits. I was turning to go into the dining-room when my eye fell upon a book bound in yellow, standing in a corner of the top shelf of the last bookcase. I did not remember it and from the floor could not decipher the pale lettering on the back, so I went to the smoking-room and called Tessie. She came in from the studio and climbed up to reach the book.

"What is it?" I asked.

"'The King in Yellow.'"

I was dumfounded. Who had placed it there? How came it in my rooms? I had long ago decided that I should never open that book, and nothing on earth could have persuaded me to buy it. Fearful lest curiosity might tempt me to open it, I had never even looked at it in book-stores. If I ever had had any curiosity to read it, the awful tragedy of young Castaigne, whom I knew, prevented me from exploring its wicked pages. I had always refused to listen to any description of it, and indeed,

nobody ever ventured to discuss the second part aloud, so I had absolutely no knowledge of what those leaves might reveal. I stared at the poisonous yellow binding as
I would at a snake.

"Don't touch it, Tessie," I said; "come down."

Of course my admonition was enough to arouse her curiosity, and before I
could prevent it she took the book and, laughing, danced away into the studio with
it. I called to her but she slipped away with a tormenting smile at my helpless hands,
and I followed her with some impatience.

"Tessie!" I cried, entering the library, "listen, I am serious. Put that book away.
I do not wish you to open it! " The library was empty. I went into both drawing-
rooms, then into the bedrooms, laundry, kitchen, and finally returned to the library
and began a systematic search. She had hidden herself so well that it was half an
hour later when I discovered her crouching white and silent by the latticed window
in the store-room above. At the first glance I saw she had been punished for her
foolishness. "The King in Yellow" lay at her feet, but the book was open at the
second part. I looked at Tessie and saw it was too late. She had opened "The King in
Yellow." Then I took her by the hand and led her into the studio. She seemed dazed,
and when I told her to lie down on the sofa she obeyed me without a word. After a
while she closed her eyes and her breathing became regular and deep, but I could not
determine whether or not she slept. For a long while I sat silently beside her, but she
neither stirred nor spoke, and at last I rose and entering the unused store-room took
the yellow book in my least injured hand. It seemed heavy as lead, but I carried it
into the studio again, and sitting down on the rug beside the sofa, opened it and read
it through from beginning to end.

When, faint with the excess of my emotions, I dropped the volume and leaned
wearily back against the sofa, Tessie opened her eyes and looked at me.

We had been speaking for some time in a dull monotonous strain before I
realized that we were discussing "The King in Yellow." Oh the sin of writing such
words,—words which are clear as crystal, limpid and musical as bubbling springs,
words which sparkle and glow like the poisoned diamonds of the Medicis! Oh the
wickedness, the hopeless damnation of a soul who could fascinate and paralyze
human creatures with such words,—words understood by the ignorant and wise
alike, words which are more precious than jewels, more soothing than Heavenly
music, more awful than death itself.

We talked on, unmindful of the gathering shadows, and she was begging me to
throw away the clasp of black onyx quaintly inlaid with what we now knew to be the
Yellow Sign. I never shall know why I refused, though even at this hour, here in my
bedroom as I write this confession, I should be glad to know what it was that prevented me from tearing the Yellow Sign from my breast and casting it into the fire.
I am sure I wished to do so, but Tessie pleaded with me in vain. Night fell and the
hours dragged on, but still we murmured to each other of the King and the Pallid

Mask, and midnight sounded from the misty spires in the fog-wrapped city. We spoke of Hastur and of Cassilda, while outside the fog rolled against the blank window-panes as the cloud waves roll and break on the shores of Hali.

The house was very silent now and not a sound from the misty streets broke the silence. Tessie lay among the cushions, her face a gray blot in the gloom, but her hands were clasped in mine and I knew that she knew and read my thoughts as I read hers, for we had understood the mystery of the Hyades and the Phantom of Truth was laid. Then as we answered each other, swiftly, silently, thought on thought, the shadows stirred in the gloom about us, and far in the distant streets we heard a sound. Nearer and nearer it came, the dull crunching of wheels, nearer and yet nearer, and now, outside before the door it ceased, and I dragged myself to the window and saw a black-plumed hearse. The gate below opened and shut, and I crept shaking to my door and bolted it, but I knew no bolts, no locks, could keep that creature out who was coming for the Yellow Sign. And now I heard him moving very softly along the hall. Now he was at the door, and the bolts rotted at his touch. Now he had entered. With eyes starting from my head I peered into the darkness, but when he came into the room I did not see him. It was only when I felt him envelop me in his cold soft grasp that I cried out and struggled with deadly fury, but my hands were useless and he tore the onyx clasp from my coat and struck me full in the face. Then, as I fell, I heard Tessie's soft cry and her spirit fled to God, and even while falling I longed to follow her, for I knew that the King in Yellow had opened his tattered mantle and there was only Christ to cry to now.

I could tell more, but I cannot see what help it will be to the world. As for me I am past human help or hope. As I lie here, writing, careless even whether or not I die before I finish, I can see the doctor gathering up his powders and phials with a vague gesture to the good priest beside me, which I understand.

They will be very curious to know the tragedy—they of the outside world who write books and print millions of newspapers, but I shall write no more, and the father confessor will seal my last words with the seal of sanctity when his holy office is done. They of the outside world may send their creatures into wrecked homes and death-smitten firesides, and their newspapers will batten on blood and tears, but with me their spies must halt before the confessional. They know that Tessie is dead and that I am dying. They know how the people in the house, aroused by an infernal scream, rushed into my room and found one living and two dead, but they do not know what I shall tell them now; they do not know that the doctor said as he pointed to a horrible decomposed heap on the floor—the livid corpse of the watchman from the church: "I have no theory, no explanation. That man must have been dead for months!"

I think I am dying. I wish the priest would—

YELLOW
Imagicide

by Brad Linaweaver

Here's a tale for all those readers who feel the "sense of wonder" was lost somewhere along the way! Unlike many of the authors in this anthology, Brad hails from the near side of World War II and is still erupting volcanically with a youthful sense of wonder, actively publishing both fiction and non-fiction.

They started by outlawing that "ugly neologism," sci-fi. Very few people at the time noticed what was happening within the science fiction field. After all, the nationalization of all commercial art was the main issue; and what was going on inside one genre was happening on a larger scale in what was euphemistically called the mainstream. All sorts of labels and pet names went by the wayside that first week of the new edicts.

One of the most popular science fiction writers of the time issued a stunning *pronunciamiento* before committing suicide. Theoretically, his argument went, none of this should be happening. The computer revolution was supposed to have rendered impossible the centralization of authority. "No one will ever have a strangle-hold on imagination!" he assured his readers. He put his faith in the cypherpunks, the resourceful inheritors of the cyberpunk tradition. The Internet, virtual reality, spread spectrum . . . all these were magic words of power to him, promising new vistas of personal freedom for those with the wit to see and understand.

The idea was that in record time there would be no monopoly on information; and the media centers of the world would lose their power. Why, if teenagers could create their own three-dimensional, interactive worlds at the push of a button, they didn't have to rely on the movies or music videos that someone else would give them. They could create their own.

The only trouble was that the author's utopian projections had not reckoned on the SS (the Systems Soldiers in their canary yellow uniforms) and their ability to invade any program that was not approved. In this, the authorities had a surprising amount of assistance from the younger generation that proved somewhat deficient in the imagination department and didn't know what to do with all the new technology. Clearly, guidance was needed.

Guidance was provided when the Educational Authority was given control over popular entertainment. The nationalization of commercial art was the inevitable result.

Within the genres, a number of writers thought they could fight the new edicts with a united front. The world famous author, who wrote the *pronunciamiento*, had entertained the rather hopeful idea that government officials would need to bring in outsiders to take over science fiction; and that the lack of specialized knowledge of the field would defeat their purpose. He was most adamant on one point: "The fans won't support something just because it has SF on the label. They don't fill their shelves with travel guides to San Francisco! They won't buy a name brand just to keep collections complete. They're too smart for that, I tell you!"

Whatever the merit of his views on fans, he did not bring his analytical skills to the subject of his fellow professionals. No one was more surprised than he when certain prominent members of science fiction writer organizations volunteered to help in the transition to the New Order. But he didn't stay around long enough to see the ultimate outcome. Before he died, he left a note apologizing for his deep weariness, but still concluding on an optimistic note: "I am sure that one day someone of stature will avenge the world of imagination."

Meanwhile, back at the politically correct dictatorship, all fiction henceforth was to be socially responsible. Science fiction seemed to catch the brunt of the new policy in many ways. Heroic stereotypes and monstrous adversaries were considered a distraction from the purity of extrapolation, and they were associated with the banished term, "sci-fi," anyway. So without a single disintegrator beam fired, whole armadas of star ships were swept away. Anything that overly excited the adolescent mind was condemned. It was easy enough to single out sexual material or brute violence as culprits (and neither escaped the watchful eye of the authorities) but intellectual stimulation could be more dangerous than the sensual.

The mind itself had to be straightened out. The more fanciful aspects of science fiction were exiled to the same realm as undisciplined fantasy—and so the time machines were loaded onto the magic carpets and shipped off. Then Faster-than-Light drive took up company with reincarnation. And intelligent robots joined vampires in dusty oblivion.

By the time the housecleaning was over, there wasn't a whole lot left. Science fiction had been purged of much of its fiction. Alternate History had been eliminated because of a new ruling against recursive characters. Besides, history was the most dangerous kind of fiction.

Very few writers were still practicing the craft, but those who were doing the current work had been producing material before the new epoch dawned upon the earth. Finally, the few magazines that remained became one magazine. The anthologies became one anthology. And then the unforgettable moment arrived when all novels became one novel. In the end, there were only five writers of the new science fiction. Despite the limitations of the form, they managed to produce millions of words annually.

Not very much happened in their stories. Only one extrapolation was allowed in any given work, regardless of length. And a very strange thing happened. Although science hadn't been forbidden, as had been the case with fantasy, there was less and less science every year. One computer bulletin board offered a prize to the first reader who could find any scientific extrapolation in the year's installment of *The Novel.* Before the authorities closed down that particular BBS, the author responded with an e-mail: "Science is subjective," she wrote, "unless it serves objective social harmony."

Another of the five working writers had made the same sort of observation about characterization, a good indication of the restrictions these creators labored under. Yet, somehow, they continued pouring out millions of words. They were pros. Of course, no one read much anymore in the United States. In science fiction, a few thousand read *The Novel.* Only a few hundred hardened fans read *The Magazine.* Times were bad for legitimate, authorized, high-minded, acceptable SF. Maybe no one was really happy except for The Reviewer, the one fan who did all the reviews of all five writers for his Education Authority approved publication, *The Column.* The five writers took turns receiving an award from this fan every single year, given out at The Convention. The festivities were held in Washington, D.C. They'd moved it there after terrorists eliminated New York City.

Meanwhile, millions of Americans were reading sci-fi! On diskettes. On paper. Over the phone lines. The SS had bragged that no black market could exist in their America—so it seemed pretty clear that the day of liberation was at hand. A computer genius, an expatriate American living in Germany, bragged that he could defeat anything the American SS came up with. His was the holy crusade of the cypherpunks, back for round two. The United States of Europe had become home to many Americans, and those interested in imaginative fiction had congregated around the Ackermuseum in Berlin.

The computer wizard had known the proprietor of the museum personally. They were part of a group that relocated to the bracing freedom of Europe when tyranny extinguished the rocket's glare of American liberty. Now they had a plan to ignite the imagination that must still slumber in their native land.

No government propaganda campaign could stand up against the old classics of Hollywood (and new productions as well) being projected with giant holographic, 3-D images, anywhere, anyplace, anytime. And as a final extra touch, the first test of the new technology would carry a personal meaning for those who had betrayed The Sense of Wonder.

The five writers were attending The Convention in Washington. The Reviewer was doing his usual job as toast master. One hundred and thirty-three really serious fans were attending the awards ceremony. Most of them hadn't read the year's installment of *The Novel*. But most of them had read at least something in *The Magazine*. The Best Editor trophy was about to go to the usual computer program, *Eddead*, and the Reviewer was already holding the freeform Jell-O sculpture encased in an ecologically acceptable—and therefore melting—block of ice.

Accepting for the computer program was a writer who insisted he didn't write this junk, but who managed to show up at The Convention anyway. He was putting on a pair of gloves in anticipation of receiving the award that, whatever its intrinsic absurdities, still represented that most important of all extrapolations: money in a bank account.

No sooner was the block of ice in the writer's gloved hands, than he dropped the thing. A thousand little white shards spread across the floor, leaving the ugly blotch of gelatin spinning around as if Dr. Frankenstein had dropped an organ in haste to get away from something. Something terrible. Something like the apparition outside the window.

The writer recognized what he saw. He turned yellow . . . and he screamed; this writer who didn't write "childish twaddle," as he sometimes referred to sci-fi in his more charitable moments, knew a lot more about the field than its current five practitioners. The five were blessed with total ignorance of its history even before the Education Authority had decided to fix everything in sight. The Reviewer and the ex-SF writer were both probably familiar with an old Heinlein classic, *Sixth Column*. The five didn't have a clue.

But everyone who saw a five-hundred foot tall Forrest J Ackerman would never forget it. Nor the ringing words he was speaking, first in Esperanto, then in English translation. The sound came booming out of the sky as if all the thunder of Mount Olympus had been gathered in this one spot. And these were the words:

"Sci-fi *is* my high!"

The
GOLDEN Whistle

by Eli Colter

This is a story of "mind blowing" good vibrations along with some unexpected alien overtones. First published in Weird Tales, January 1928.

The picture on the wall? Yes, gentlemen—that is Suelivor. And the strange orna-ment hanging above it? Ah—that ornament has a strange history! I first saw Suelivor in Japan, a number of years ago. It was evening, and I stood idly absorbing the beauty of a full-blooming cherry tree. The tong-tong of a temple gong was in my ears, the blaze of the sunset sky was in my eyes. Aimless philosophic hypotheses were entertaining my thoughts. My heart was hushed by the atmosphere surrounding me, in tune with the fantastic and weirdly romantic. It was a fitting moment in which to come into contact with Suelivor.

I heard footsteps behind me, but I did not turn. I was uninterested in human personalities just then, and I continued gazing dreamily at the cherry tree. I say I *heard* footsteps. Rather should I say I was conscious of them. They were so queerly light, so unlike a normal footfall that I felt an inner start when, in the next instant, their odd character communicated itself to my absorbed consciousness. Still, I did not turn. But I went unaccountably tense, listening, sensing that queer footfall. The steps paused behind me and I was conscious of someone's curious gaze boring into my back.

I knew from the weight of those strange footsteps that the intruder into my solitude was a man, but I ignored his pause and stare as I had ignored his approach. And though he received from me no invitation either of word or look, he abruptly advanced a pace or two until he stood beside me. Sharply conscious that I was in the presence of something alien, something as fantastic as my surroundings, I held my-self tensed, waiting. Presently he spoke. I answered vaguely, in kind. His remark to me had been vague.

There ensued a persistent silence between us. Seeing that he was as stubbornly noncommittal as I, after a long moment I turned my head and scrutinized him deliberately. I was glad he was an Occidental. I was tired to death of the sight of slant-eyed miniature males. But there my pleasure in his presence ended. I did not like him. There was something sinister in him which repelled and chilled; something more sensed than caught by the eye.

He was broad and high, set up like a well-balanced ship. His soft hat raked the evening sky like a full-bellied sail. His eyes were as clear, deep and green-brown as the water of the open sea at early twilight. His mouth was firm and straight, without a curve. A queer mouth it was; sensuous, cruel, at once hard and tender, above a squared, determined jaw. I knew then that I should place him instantly if I ever saw him again, though it be ten thousand miles away in the crush of a moving restless crowd. And I did.

I first saw *her* in the State of Georgia. She was walking slowly along a flat country road on the outskirts of a town. A light rain had fallen but a few hours before, and as the dusk deepened, a cool damp veil spread over the bayous and fields of young cotton. The fireflies had begun their nocturnal peregrinations, sailing over china trees and water oaks like vagrant sparks emitted from some unseen chimney. I had paused by a wide, fertile field, impressed by the weird beauty of the evening.

She approached along the way I had come, and having reached a position in the road directly opposite me, she paused also and stood looking into the cotton field where the fireflies were circling thickly. I glanced at her appraisingly from the corner of my eye. She blended so concordantly with the scene before her. She was a weirdly beautiful woman.

Her uncovered hair was black. Her face was without a vestige of color save for the heavily reddened lips. Her posture, the unconscious regal poise of her head, the grace of her movements, all gave eloquent evidence of an atmosphere and an environment of culture. She stood there with the grace of a tall and slender young tree on a hill crest at sunset. For a moment she gazed at the fireflies, then passed on. And I saw that her eyes (for she turned them full on me as she went by) were so black that one could not distinguish pupil from iris, and that they were blank with an odd emptiness, deep with an unspeakable pain. I knew then that I should recognize her again instantly, also through any space of time, in any place or circumstance. And I did.

I saw them together long afterward, at the parting of the ways. The slim young tree had been stripped of its leaves and branches, so that it poised on the hill crest a stark signpost of grief, poignant example of what life can do to a human being when the dreams go to smash. And the well-balanced ship had lost its rudder, to go sailing ruthlessly, doggedly on, terrible example of what may happen to a firmly built vessel when the cargo has been looted from the hold, the sails unfurled to a high wind, and there is no hand to guide it from the rocks.

I entered the café because I was chilled to the bone, and the warmth of the glittering interior was irresistibly inviting. And because the proprietor was a friend of mine, after a fashion. And because I like the service, the cuisine and the music. I had been wandering the streets for an hour, breasting the gusty blasts and cold fog of San Francisco. I was ready to rest. I went down the stairs slowly, wishing that something would happen. I think I was lonely.

I took a seat at my customary table and leaned back in my chair, looking idly about. I felt curiously empty. Not in the stomach, but in the heart. The waiter approached with his customary greeting. I gave him a light order. He grinned, bowed obsequiously and stalked with a deal of majesty to the rear of the café.

My thoughts went flowing aimlessly on. I had found nothing of sufficient interest to halt them or turn them into another direction. I focused my gaze, finally, on the raised stage, slightly to my right. It was, for the moment, bare. Hanging across the stock background drop were the dull gray curtains which habitually remained closed during the entertainers' intermissions. But as my order was set down before me, the gray curtains parted and slid to each side of the stage, disclosing not the garishly painted scene I was accustomed to viewing, but another curtain that delighted my senses. It was one solid wall of shimmering cloth of gold. The orchestra began a subdued throbbing of mellow chords. I sat up, at that, keenly instinct with pleasure and surprise. I knew the chords.

Then from behind the gold curtains came another sound, a sound I shall always remember, shall always hear, as I heard it then. It was a whistle. High and clear, but never shrill. It was round and full, a liquid sound, a golden sound, like nothing else I have ever heard. There came to me the strange fancy that the gleaming sound added luster to the curtains through which it emanated. Sense-enthralled by the indescribable beauty of its vibration, I held my breath as I listened. Wailing and calling, it slid smoothly over the exquisite melody of Schubert's *Serenade,* like an unbelievably pure-toned ocarina. A hush had settled over the café, and it obtained until the threnodic tones had sobbed to the perfect close, ending on one long, round and shining note.

A storm of applause eddied to a mighty crescendo and shook the room. I waited, breathless. The applause persisted, demanding. The gold curtains swayed and parted to allow a woman to pass through them. She advanced only a step or two, and halted to stand motionless, facing us.

Her hair formed a sharply defined black triangle, framing her colorless face in startling contrast against the shimmering background. From breast to feet she was swathed in a single fold of jade-green silk. The silk was rendered stiff and heavy by a great black dragon embroidered down the front of it; cunningly embroidered, so that the reptile's head rested on her heart, its claws clasped her shoulders, and its sinuous tail wound around her feet and trailed on the floor. In her weird beauty and fantastic robing she looked like some old Chinese wood carving come to life.

But I, perversely, after the first astounding glance, saw her not at all. I saw only a cloud of fireflies in a damp field of young cotton, and black eyes blank with emptiness, deep with pain.

She pursed her heavily reddened lips ever so slightly. The muted orchestral chords throbbed again, other chords now, and the unearthly whistle rose again in the lilt of Rubinstein's *Melody in F.* As the last note died away the gray curtains closed over her, like gray waters covering some bright thing from the farthest reaches of light. And though the applause rose thunderously, she did not return.

I sat in a spell as the applause died away and the hum of disjointed conversation once more claimed the atmosphere. Every nerve in my body was vibrating tumultuously to the call of that golden whistle. I sat like a man in a dream, staring at the senseless gray curtains, oblivious of my untouched luncheon, when a voice said suddenly, almost in my ear:

"I say—did you ever hear anything like that in your life? We come a long way to meet again. From Japan to San Francisco."

I turned abruptly, like a man stung, feeling an actual physical pain in all my nerves as his harsh voice broke the exquisite vibration of the harmony that held me.

I turned to see him standing there beside me, his sensual cruel mouth compressed into a vibrant line, his green-brown eyes burning with unleashed fire. And the forbidding atmosphere of the man, which I had felt so keenly upon our first chance meeting in Japan, was unexpectedly clear and unmistakable.

The brig was a pirate ship! The skull and crossbones flew from the masthead. Uncontrollably I shivered, before I could get a grip on my aversion to his presence. I greeted him rather curtly, with an unwelcome sense of uncanny premonition inhibiting any cordiality courtesy might have demanded. He ignored my brusqueness. In fact, I knew that he was oblivious of it. He wasn't thinking of me at all. Save as how he might make use of me, perhaps. He seated himself across from me without waiting for an invitation to join me. No doubt he divined that none would be forthcoming.

"You know her?" he asked, gesturing toward the stage.

I shook my head, shaken with an utterly senseless rage that this sinister being should even have looked upon her. I said that I did not know her, but I certainly intended to. He looked at me queerly, as though he had heard the warning in my words, and said coolly, "I'll introduce you after a while."

Impudent, that! Yet, when I asked abruptly if he knew her, he also shook his head and answered with something of amused surprise: "No, never saw her before. But I know Jeremy Falleaux." I nodded understanding. Falleaux owned the café.

I turned to my neglected luncheon, wishing that he would take himself off. But he obviously had no such intention. Grudgingly I suggested an order for him. He declined anything to eat, remarking that he was not hungry. That was a lie. But he sat there watching me with his disconcerting, burning eyes, sharing my bottle readily enough, totally unconscious of what excellent liquor was going down his throat, absent-mindedly asking all manner of queer questions. Personal questions. He volunteered no information, and finally I spoke my thought rather impatiently:

"Well, that all may be interesting to you perhaps. Where I've been, what I've done, am doing or intend to do. But what of yourself? You're essentially of the sea, I should say. What's your ship? And where to you go from here?"

"The sea?" He smiled, and I almost stared. I had not seen his smile before. It was cruel, sinister, evil, in accord with his cold exterior. He went on smoothly: "The sea! Good Lord, no! Whatever made you think that? I've crossed it enough, sailed it enough—but I'm not *of* it. I'm only—only an explorer."

I set aside my glass and looked him up and down. The lie was so apparent, so uncalled for. He might just as well have said, "I don't care to tell you." I let it pass. If he wasn't of the sea no man ever was. As cold, as immutable, as implacable, as cruel, harsh and devastating as the sea. I didn't intend letting him get totally away with evasion, though. I followed the line he threw out.

"Yes? What do you explore?"

"The universe," he said evenly, smiling again at my start of surprise. "Through the unfathomable law of vibration. It's a bit difficult for me to estimate time by Earth laws, I've been covering so much space. But I'd say I've been here about twenty years. Prior to that I spent a hundred years or so on Jupiter. I arrived there from Betelgeuse."

I gripped myself to control a shiver. Not for a moment was I insane enough to think him mad. I had known from the first time I saw him that he was not an ordinary human personality. He read the expression on my face.

"Thanks," he said dryly. "Anyone else would have immediately judged me a lunatic. I knew you wouldn't. Otherwise I shouldn't have ventured to answer you truthfully. I travel by the law of vibration, as I told you. There are different vibratory systems. I follow the vibration of tone, melody. I don't know how old I am, or how long I've been going on, on, exploring—hunting for something. Needless to say, I haven't found it yet. At least, I'm not sure I have."

His eyes turned covertly to the curtained stage. I wanted to choke him to death where he sat. But I knew no human fingers of flesh could ever throttle the life from that columnar neck. Suddenly he went on speaking, deliberately forcing a change in my current of thought.

"Do you know a great deal about the theory of vibration, Dr. Johns?" I shook my head, staring at him. How the devil did he know who I was? He grinned impudently, as though he could see into my brain, and answered to my mental query. "Oh, everyone knows you, Doctor. But we were discussing vibration. Or rather, *I* was talking about it. You indicate that you are not intimately conversant with the theory. Surely you are aware of the steps science has made in that direction on your planet Earth! Surely you know that the right vibration properly projected will put out a candle's light. And what man doesn't know that the perfect vibratory tone, sustained over a bridge, will cause that mighty structure to vibrate in answer, and sway? I assure you, were that tone sustained long enough it would cause the bridge to continue swaying in a ever wider arc until it toppled down. Think of it! A powerful massive thing of steel girders and riveted plates, razed by the thin tone of a violin string! And these are only the elemental stages, the ABC's of the great law of vibration."

"I suppose you'd say all our science is in the elementary stages," I cut in sarcastically.

"It certainly is," he agreed, with a slight smile. "I admit, though, that you've had some workers who accomplished quite a bit. Some of them reached the fringes of the real laws themselves. You had a philosopher and psychologist who went after vibration pretty heavily. Yet, he didn't get so far, considering what there is to know. Vibration! Why, you live, work and have your being by vibration! The planets are held in space and the sun feeds the universe with fire—by vibration. And by that same law of vibration the planets could be blown to oblivion and the sun put out forever!"

"You seem to know a lot about it," I said, considering his statements slightly vehement, to say the least.

"Yes, I do—and I'm not exaggerating," he retorted shortly. "I'm not even scratching the surface of the subject. Your psychologist, he rather scratched the surface. He tried to get down to concrete facts. His physical theory was drawn from certain speculations as to the nervous action."

"You're speaking of Hartley?" I interrupted.

"Surely." He nodded, and his green-brown eyes played over me curiously. "The theory is that before sensation exists, the mind is a blank. By growth from simple sensations those states of consciousness which appear most remote from sensation come into being. Hartley held that sensation is the result of vibration of the most minute particles of the medullary substance of the nerves. To account for which he postulated a subtle elastic ether. Starting from a detailed account of the senses, or, I should say, from the phenomena of the senses, he tried to show how all the emotions might be explained by the law of vibration."

"*Tried* to show?" I queried, pointedly.

"Well, he didn't prove so much, concerning what there is to prove. It's a pity he didn't live longer, a pity for the Earth. I venture to say he could have accomplished enough to turn a new leaf in history if he had been granted an extended period of time. However, he's working on, where he is. It doesn't matter a great deal."

"Well, he wasn't so far off, was he?" I leaned over the table toward him, fascinated in spite of my aversion to him, interested intensely as I always have been by any learned technical discussion of theory or hypothesis—or fact.

"Oh, he was right, of course," he answered vehemently. "*All* right—but he didn't go far enough. All voluntary action is the result of a firm connection between motion and sensation, and on the physical side between an idea and motor vibration. Pleasure is merely the result of moderate vibrations, pain the result of vibrations so violent as to break the continuity of the nerves. Even Hartley sounded that deep. But the law of vibration is illimitable. Why, man alive, your body's atoms are held together by vibration. By sounding the right tone or tones I could blow you into a million atoms that it would take ten million years to reassemble."

"And by the same token, a man sounding the right tones could blow *you* into atoms," I retorted, a trifle vindictively. I was astonished at his sudden pallor, the instant flash of terror in his green-brown eyes. He caught himself, and his color returned, his eyes went stone-hard and ice-cold, as he answered:

"Quite true. But no one ever will. My vibration is beyond the determining and comprehension of any Earth man. I've been over at least a thousand planets in the last million years or so, and I shall keep going till I find the thing I seek. But that is neither here nor there. I could blow this whole globe to atoms were I so minded. I am not so minded. It would take too long to find the right vibration. I have something more important to do. More important to me, at least. To find the thing for which I search. I shall draw it to me by that same law of vibration—when I find it. You are finished with your luncheon?" he broke into his own discourse abruptly, observing me. "Let's get on."

Although I was eager to be rid of him, I was perversely just as eager to keep track of him, now that I had obtained a glimpse into what manner of thing he was. I threw off my feeling of repulsion as best I might, rose from the table and followed him out. At the entrance of the café he asked me to wait for him, and turned to disappear up the three steps leading into Jeremy Falleaux's private office. I waited impatiently, stung with depressing premonition of evil, yet grimly determined to see it through so long as he was within *her* vicinity.

Shortly he returned to say that she would receive us in her dressing room. I nodded, finding nothing to reply, and we went around to a side door back of the stage. We entered the door, traversed a long, narrow hall and came to another door. Hers. It was closed, and he rapped lightly. At her answering "Come in" he threw open the door and motioned me to precede him.

She reclined on a long, green couch, facing us, propped on one elbow against a great black cushion. The ebony dragon twisted around her like some prehistoric monster in the throes of unendurable agony, as she rose to a sitting posture. My eyes plunged to her face hungrily. The black eyes were still empty, but the pain was gone. There was instead a peculiar quality of receptivity, as though she waited breathless for some monumental thing to happen.

She glanced at us, and spoke to him: "Mr. Falleaux said you wished to see me?"

"Yes." He stood immobile, looking at her, devouring her with his blazing eyes. "Allow me to present my good friend, Dr. Emile Johns. Madame Falleaux, Doctor."

Madame Falleaux! Jeremy's wife? And—"his good friend." His insolent presumptuousness was almost admirable. He certainly knew who I was, all right.

The black dragon waved a protesting claw as she leaned forward and extended her hand. I stepped to the couch and took her fingers. They were quite cold. Nerves, I said to myself.

"Ah, Doctor! One is delighted!" Her words were manifestly sincere. And then, I saw her eyes. "There is only one Emile Johns! I need not ask if you are he. Perhaps I too may some day dare claim your friendship. It is well to have a great surgeon on one's list. *Non?*" I shook my head, smiling at her. "*Mais Oui!*" she insisted, adding softly, "They sometimes sever the soul from the body without great inconvenience to either." I knew what she meant. I said so.

As for him, he stood there with his hands folded together behind him looking hard at her with never a word. She obeyed his gaze, finally, saying, with a queer inflection in her throaty tone: "And you, *M'sieu?*"

"I?" I caught the driving power of that strange, sinister being in the one word. I had an uncomfortable sense of wishing I had killed him before he came into her presence. He'd hurt that woman. She knew it, too. Such hurts a surgeon might give his soul to heal, finding himself pitifully helpless, his skill utterly impotent when it was most needed. He proceeded with glib, swift speech. "I'm an explorer. My name— Henteli Suelivor. It—it's a wonderful thing you have in your throat."

She smiled. It was a wide smile that showed her exquisitely set teeth, but failed to touch her somber eyes. Already she was fighting him. I did not like that smile.

"You think so?" she answered him, almost insolently. "Some do. I do not know whether or not I care that you should have that opinion. Won't you be seated. And you, Doctor?"

Suelivor dropped his powerful frame lightly into a chair by the door. Deliberately I seated myself by her on the couch. I took one of her long, white fingers in mine, and studied it a moment before I spoke. Jove! It was *cold*. Like a hand of one chilled—by fear. I wanted to let her know I would be standing by.

"The fireflies still play in the cotton fields of Georgia," I said. I did not raise my eyes, but I felt her gaze upon me. Her voice broke out with spontaneous delight that was patently unassumed.

"Oh ho! So it is you! I thought your face was familiar. Well indeed! After all these years. No—not so many. Only five. And you remembered!"

"And *you* remembered!" I retorted, gently laying the white hand on its mate. "That's the surprising thing. I couldn't forget. No man could."

"You met her five years ago?" Suelivor abruptly cut into the conversation. "You didn't tell me that!"

"No." I wondered if he could read my thoughts now. "No. I didn't tell you. Why should I? Besides, there was nothing formal in the meeting. It was a thing of chance. I had no idea she would recall it."

"Dr. Johns," she interrupted smoothly, "it is always the privilege to meet men of professional eminence. Me, I am lucky. Very lucky this night. A world-renowned surgeon and a—an explorer." Her eyes darted at Suelivor, piercing, probing. *"Voilà!"* She rose to her feet, spreading her white hands in a deprecating gesture. "I fear I tire of this room. If you would be kind enough to wait outside till I have shed my dragon? *Non?* I shall then be pleased to entertain you in my home this evening."

Wordlessly we got up and quitted the room to comply with her request. Silence lay between Suelivor and me as we waited outside her door. I tried to ignore him, but I felt his eyes on me in the shaded light, mocking, dissecting. In an incredibly short space of time she joined us, wrapped in a long velvet cloak as black and shadowy as her hair. Not a word was said till we were seated in the long, black car awaiting her at the curb.

"You know," she volunteered, as the car swung away to the hill facing the bay, "I'm an explorer, too. I've been seeking something for ten years. Me—I haven't found it yet." I sat still, hushed, startled. Almost Suelivor's exact words!

"Just what are you hunting?" he asked levelly.

"Oh, M'sieu Suelivor! That was so terribly obvious. But really, I wasn't baiting. I shan't tell you, you know. If you discover it for yourself, that is your business. If you can't—that is my business. My—my search, it answers for my being in the café tonight. I dare that Jeremy to let me whistle there for a week. He nearly had the apoplectic fit. But he finally gave in. That Jeremy, he knows Felice Falleaux. His brother who died a year ago was my husband."

Ah—*not* Jeremy's wife! I closed set teeth on a sigh of relief. Merely his brother's widow. Suelivor did not answer, and she did not speak again until we had reached her house. While we discarded our wraps in the wide hall she gestured to the great, magnificently appointed rooms.

"Be it ever so humble there's no place like home," she said mockingly, and rang for a servant. She ordered something light to eat, and left us to ourselves temporarily.

Suelivor walked up to a huge bronze copy of Rodin's *Thinker* and stood staring at it in a peculiar attitude of waiting. I wanted him to know that I was fully sensible of the duel between us. I said to his back: "Just what are you exploring, Suelivor? If you didn't find it on a thousand other planets, how do you hope to find it here? What the devil are you trying to find?" He stiffened for a shocked second.

"Myself." His tone was as hard as lignum-vitae.

"Why?" I probed. He stood perfectly still, but he didn't answer. He hadn't time. She came in the door at that moment. But then, he hadn't intended to anyway.

"You're not a thinker," she said at him, quite without sarcasm. "Come over here and sit down, and eat good cheese and drink good beer with two other explorers."

I shot her a surprised glance, and she smiled slightly. I don't think he ever deceived her for one moment, from the very first. But she was a fighter. She was ready to put up a battle for the thing she wanted, and she thought he had it. She merely didn't know *what* he was.

He turned to face her with a relieved sigh, and that queer, cruel smile of his. Things had been getting too tense in him for comfort. Somehow, in that instant, I felt an unexplainable sense of pity for him. He was going to be hurt, too. And she knew that, also—*while he did not.*

She had donned a loose robe, a black, unshining thing, a long chain of carved jade was twisted through her black hair, and one great, five-petaled jade flower lay on her breast. The severity of her gowns would have sentenced another woman to downright ugliness, but for her they were the epitome of art.

Suelivor seated himself by the little table whereon the servant had laid out cheese sandwiches and beer. He plunged headlong into an aimless conversation, and again refused to eat. I am certain he never did eat. But how the man could drink!

She countered easily as he talked, ignoring his insatiable consumption of beer. I knew that he was fencing, warding off any intent of hers to probe her purpose or thought, and that she was doing precisely the same thing. Dumb, I listened silently, watching, sensing every slightest change in the charged atmosphere. He was not for her, that unholy fiend. He was something out of space, cold, sinister, devouring and inimical. She was gloriously of the Earth, warm, pulsing with the hot blood of life, fit only for the heights of love and ecstasy. He—even his blood was cold! She was not for him! In a mad chaos of grim determination I listened to them talk.

Desultory talk it was, about nothing and everything over which you would least expect those two to wage conversation. They did not dare express their thoughts. Neither did they succeed in concealing them any too well. Yet, I did not feel at all *de trop.* I knew too well they both wanted me there.

Finally that infelicitous evening wore away, and we two men rose to take our leave. She said to us: "Well, gentlemen, I am nearly always home. This evening finished the engagement at the café."

Suelivor looked keenly into her face. "You desire that we call again?"

"I do." She smiled—at *me.*

"Do you like music?" he asked irrelevantly.

"I do. Very much indeed."

"You wish us to come together?" Suelivor pressed, indelicately. "Or—singly."

"Oh, it does not matter, so that you come." And though her smile was for me, her words were for him. I knew it quite well. So did he.

He answered, "We will do so—singly."

I ignored his rudeness, looking levelly into her eyes. There I saw the thing I wanted to know. "Yes," I said.

I went the next night. She received me with a cool gladness that delighted me and chilled me. There was not any thought behind it, thought for me. Her thought was with Suelivor.

"He comes later, this evening," she said, as I followed her into the room. "You would do something for me, and not ask the embarrassing question?" Her black eyes held mine intently, and I winced at that breathless hush in them. How frantically she was waiting—waiting. For *what?* I hadn't the least idea. I was a fool—but I hadn't.

"Of course," I returned quietly.

"Then—here. See, it is the closet of which no one knows. The storybook secret passage." She stepped to a great mural, depicting a cathedral with a mighty door under a rose window. She plunged some lever on the window and the door slid back to show a small room, perhaps eight by ten, beautifully appointed, containing a comfortable couch and a big easy chair. A table between the two was heaped with books and magazines. "There—I ask you to sit and wait every night when he comes. See—from this side the door opens, so." She beckoned me into the secret room and I followed.

From the wall depended a heavy silk cord. She gave it a slight jerk and the door slid into place. She jerked it again and the door opened. I nodded and looked at her inquiringly.

"See—the wall—it is sound-proof. No one can hear you even if you should shoot a gun in here. Nor can you hear anything said or done in the next room. But I will know you are here. I shall feel safe. Some day—I may need to have the friend close."

I did not think of anything to say. Anything I could have replied would have been so obvious to her. The knocker on the outside door rang, and her face set into oddly expressionless lines as she turned to me.

"There—M'sieu Suelivor. I go. You wait here. There is much to read. You will not be lonesome?"

I shook my head. I was dumb that night. She went out and left me alone in that room, closing the secret door after her. She was right. The room was sound-proof—*to all sounds of ordinary vibration.* I dropped into the big chair and picked up a book. I couldn't read. I sat there thinking unwholesome thoughts regarding the thing called Suelivor.

I must have been sitting there half an hour when I heard a sound in that sound-proof room. It came from the room where they were. Music. He had asked her if she liked music. But if that was music, then I am God, Christ and the Devil all rolled into one! I shrank back in my chair, listening to it. Its indescribable vibration cut through the sound-proof wall as easily as though that solid partition of matter were thin fog. I shivered at the power of that high, wailing sound. I had no idea of what manner of instrument made it. There is nothing on this Earth to which to liken it.

It was not of this Earth. It was, like him, out of space. Something implacable, sinister, yet at the same time fascinating, luring, compelling. Were one touched by that vibration, he would break down the wall of China to follow it. But, strangely, it touched nothing in me. I heard it, I felt it playing over me like electric ice—but it did not touch me. I thought I knew why, instantly. He was seeking the thing that had driven his unhuman being through countless years and over measureless miles—but apparently nothing of it was in me. Frantically I crouched there and prayed that it was not in her.

I don't know for what an eternity I endured that wild music—well, I have to *call* it that, at least. We have no other word. That's what he called it. I held myself in a stoical numbness, inviolate to that torture. Then suddenly the sound ceased. There was silence. And I was back in the solid, reassuring atmosphere of the world we know, breathless as though I had been hurled through space and left utterly shaken by the rapidity of my transit.

The silence endured for another eternity. Then suddenly the door slid back and she appeared to face me. I sprang to my feet, toward her. Her face was bewildered, but it held no fear.

"That so strange man is gone," she announced casually. "He played for me. Such music I never heard. He did not talk much. He has so little talk. But he play. *Mon Dieu,* how he play!"

"What did he play?" I asked, striving to attain the same casual attitude she assumed. I knew she did not feel it. Something impelled me not to tell her I had heard that strange wild music through the sound-proof wall. She frowned, shrugged lightly, and smiled as she motioned me to enter the other room.

"A whistle. Strange conceit, M'sieu Doctor. A golden whistle. He tell me that is what I have in my throat." She laughed aloud as she manipulated the door back into place. "A long pole of shining gold, it is. Like a flute. He—he play the weird music. I feel it inside of me. But it says nothing. You and I—let us talk, *M'sieu.*"

I sat there and talked with her for better than an hour. We talked of sane, commonplace things. We avoided further mention of Suelivor. But neither of us was thinking of anything else. Yet how vastly different were our thoughts! I looked at her, and thought of him. Sacrilege! Blasphemy! But I couldn't help it. I had to find some way of protecting her. He would come again, many times. He would play for her again that unholy wild music. And not always might she say truly that it said nothing! I was cold to the heart when I bade her good-night and walked out.

That impossible situation went on for three weeks. Every night he came, and sat and played that wild, insistent music on that golden whistle. And slowly but surely that persistent vibration began to speak to Felice. But he was not so wise as he thought. It began to speak, but it did not say the thing he wanted it to say. It was to me it called, and I began to fear. Gradually I began to have a feeling of being drawn from my body toward him as he played there beyond that sound-proof wall. The night my senses swam and I was unconscious when she opened the door, I knew something must be done, and quickly. He was feeling some response to that vile music of his, and he thought it came from her.

It was then I thought of Ahmbodie, and cursed my stupidity for not thinking of him before. Ahmbodie was a mystic with wildly unbelievable powers, living across the bay in Oakland. He did not display his powers for the satisfaction of public curiosity. He was wealthy, independent to the point of rudeness, and lived a secluded, studious life in which he pursued his investigations into other worlds. To his friends he talked, and for his friends he employed every ounce of his capacities when he found those friends in trouble or distress. I was his friend. I went to Ahmbodie. He received me with a polished courtesy and a warming welcome that froze into shocked dismay when he got a good look at my face. I knew I had changed. It was as though I had shrunken away, not by any such means as merely growing emaciated. Shrunken, as though numberless electrons of those composing my flesh had been by some hideous means extracted from my body.

"What has happened to you?" Ahmbodie demanded tersely, forcing me into a chair and bending to stare into my face. "I know! That damnable music from space! I have heard it. I am in tune."

"You have heard it—clear over here?" I sat up in my chair, staring at him incredulously. "Through the noise of traffic—clear across the bay—above the blare of the ferry-boats?"

"I am in tune," he repeated, fixing me with his fathomless black eyes. "Where is it? Who plays? Who brings that ungodly sound into a sane world? I suspect! Who?"

"A man named Suelivor," I answered wearily. "He—"

"Suelivor!" Ahmbodie interrupted sharply, and his dark face paled as he gripped my arm. "I thought it must be he. I have been watching him, sounding him for fifteen years. Sailing the sea, always on the sea. Last month I lost trace of him. And he is there! Only across the bay. Tell me what he does there, quickly."

Concisely and swiftly I gave him an account of the last three weeks. His face darkened with an exalted anger, the anger of a god blasphemed, and when I finished my recital he exclaimed loudly:

"You must get for me that golden whistle! You must bring it to me. We must drive him from this Earth. We have no housing space for such as he! Go, Emile! You shall not say it can not be done! You shall bring me that whistle!"

"I'll get it, somehow," I said grimly, thinking of Felice as I got to my feet. "But for God's sake, Ahm, what is it he seeks? What is it he goes from planet to planet trying to find?" Ahmbodie paled again slightly at my vehement cry, but he answered without hesitation.

"His soul."

"His *soul!*" I gasped, shrinking from the import of those two words.

"Exactly," Ahmbodie corroborated. "His soul. He hasn't any. Don't you understand, Emile? He is one of the soulless ones. One of those born in the outer darkness, denizens of space, knowing no laws and no God, spawn of the devil. He exists, feeds, drives on and devours by the terrible law of vibration. Few of them have the intelligence he has acquired through centuries of study and restless search. He knows no sensation but emptiness and pain. That wild music brings him the only relief he can find when it touches some soul even remotely in tune and draws something toward him. If he could draw another soul from another body into his, he would become mortal, know mortal joys and feel mortal delights. That is what he seeks. Another's soul to warm his cold blood. He has sought it in women—knowing women's souls are finer, easier to bring in tune. He has found what he sought in you. And we must act quickly or that fine etherous thing will leave you and answer his call."

"It has begun to leave me already?" I cried, shaken.

"The atoms are loosed and quivering around you, ready to follow that vibration that has shaken them," Ahmbodie confirmed, eyeing me steadily. "You must get me that golden whistle."

"What will you do with it?" I demanded. "He can make another."

"Ah—but it will take him a thousand years!" Ahmbodie smiled. "That vibration he produced is the result of centuries of tireless effort. Such as he knows no failure, no discouragement and no fatigue. But I—I have been working like mad to find his vibration, been working for fifteen years. Ever since I first located his unholy presence on the Earth. At night I leave my body in sleep, and go to him, standing over him. I never know where he is, but vibration takes me to him. And I have come near enough his vibration that six or seven hours over that evil whistle will change the course of his ways. Bring it!"

I left Ahmbodie and hurried back to Felice. She had been for several evenings kindly concerned over my altered appearance. I had evaded any excuse for it, save that I was weary from overwork. Now I told her candidly that the music which had left her untouched, so far as reaching the thing he sought, had pierced to me through the sound-proof wall, had racked me and shaken my nerves. I dared not even intimate what vital part of me was menaced. Nerves! I had to speak to her in sane terms of this everyday world. She had no least idea of the thing Suelivor was. I told her I wanted her to get the whistle for me that I might take it home and examine it. She agreed with a lack of protest that surprised me. But it developed that she was curious to touch and examine the thing herself.

That evening she persuaded him to leave off playing and talk to her. He complied, ungraciously, she told me afterward, and I knew why. He was avid for the possession of the soul that had begun to answer him—impatient at the least delay. But, thinking that soul lay in her, he cannily considered it wisest not to pique her. She begged to keep the whistle till he came again. Secure in his knowledge of its invincibility to any puny meddling of hers, he finally capitulated, yielding to her pleading. And that night when she opened the door to me after he was gone, she laid in my hand that ungodly golden whistle. I thanked her with wild gratitude, and left her in almost indecent haste. I went straight to Ahmbodie.

He received the golden, flutelike thing with quivering eagerness, almost snatching it from my hands, turning it over and over in his fingers and gazing at me intently with his piercing black eyes. He handed it to me suddenly.

"Blow it," he commanded.

I shivered, but there was something so significant in his tone that I put it to my lips and expended my breath through it. It emitted no least sound. I gaped, but Ahmbodie gave me a meaning smile.

"You see? No one but Suelivor can play that devilish thing. You are prompt. When does he return to see Madam Felice again?"

"Tomorrow night." I stared at the whistle as I returned it to Ahmbodie. "I'll come for that thing along about 5 o'clock."

"Good!" Ahmbodie's eyes gleamed. "That gives me at least sixteen hours to work. I shall see no sleep this night. Come for it tomorrow, late afternoon. And I promise you, my friend, when it again comes into your hands you shall play it. But never let him touch it again! Now be off, and let me get to my task."

"But you will work yourself ill, into a frenzy!" I protested.

"What a human thing to say!" Ahmbodie smiled reprovingly. "Aye, I shall no doubt work in a very terrible frenzy, for hours that will bear a strain of which you cannot even conceive. But—there is a human soul at stake! I have lived to protect and benefit human souls, Emile. And if I can bring to bear all my exhaustive research, all my tireless effort, all my capacity, understanding and power to save one human soul this night, to drive from the environs of the Earth so menacing a thing as that spirit of the outer darkness, then no moment of my life has been in vain. What though I *give* my life in that last stupendous culmination of achievement— sacrifice my little breath in the merciless driving of my utmost capacities? Man alive, where is your sense of values? If I succeed, a human soul has been saved from Satan's spawn to the god who gave it!"

"But, that—that whistle," I groped. "How can any mighty power lie in that fragment of polished metal?"

"My dear Emile!" Ahmbodie spoke slowly, striving to impress me with what he was saying, smiling at me patiently. "The potencies of the law of vibration are beyond conception. There is no sounding the wonders that may be accomplished by a fine understanding, an expert and delicate wielding of that law by a master hand; and there is no grasping the hideous cataclysm that may be wreaked by that same law if it be manipulated by a malignant being who has attained understanding of it. I work with it beneficently, for the betterment of mankind and the glory of God. Suelivor juggles it with malevolent ruthlessness of the havoc he produces, caring only to achieve his selfish desires. Emile—there rises tonight a battle royal between the powers of light and the emissary of darkness, construction against destruction! Go, and leave me to my labor. Go praying that God is all-powerful still!"

And I—I bowed my head and walked out of his door with my hat in my hands, praying that his gallant life might not be forfeit.

There was little sleep for me that night. I rolled and tossed restlessly in my bed, following Ahmbodie in spirit through his frenzied hours of striving. I rose with the dawn and paced my room for hours more, unable to eat or contain myself in anything like tranquility, wondering how valiant Ahmbodie was faring, hoping desperately that his power was equal to the great emergency. When I could endure my room no longer I went out and paced the streets. I lived in a fever of agonizing suspense until it was time to take the ferry-boat across the bay.

It was with a sense of unutterable relief that I looked into Ahmbodie's face when he himself opened his door to me. I stepped in eagerly, grasped his arms and gazed into his eyes.

The result of those long, terrible hours of straining application was written on every feature. His face was haggard, worn and furrowed with lines of weariness. His eyes were sunk into his head. His whole body drooped with utter exhaustion. But there was in the sunken eyes an exultant gleam of triumph. He had come to the supreme struggle of his mystical, weird activities. He had given something vital of himself in that task. Something had gone out of him—something *vibrant*. But I knew instinctively that it would renew itself. And I felt inarticulately that his exaltation over the fact that he had not failed, that he had accomplished whatever obscure thing he intended, was high reward for all it had cost him. But what was the thing he sought to do?

Ahmbodie read my puzzled thought and spoke quietly: "When you play it to Suelivor, you will know. I do not wish to tell you. I am not too certain myself. I set a high goal. I may have fallen short. But I at least accomplished something. Without doubt I refined that vibration to such an extent that it will drive him a million miles hence. I am eager to know just how great a thing I have achieved. I shall wait in impatience for your report. Here."

He slipped his hand into the pocket of his heavy velvet lounging-robe as I dropped my own hands to my sides. He extended toward me the object of his long interval of endeavor. I looked into his face, thinking of the night, as I felt that whistle again in my hands. It was in no whit changed in looks, but Ahmbodie placed it in my fingers with a solemn warning.

"Blow it not until you stand in his presence. But if you would save your soul from a fiend, blow it then! And blow it until he is gone from the surface of this Earth! He will writhe in torture, he will call to his comrades for help, but nothing can save him from banishment if you hurl that vibration at him till he is gone! I have come near enough sounding him for that. And I may in sixteen short hours have done the thing it would take him a thousand years to do. You see, my friend, I have a soul. Go, now. Go, to save yourself and others from the pestilence of his presence. And when it is over, come back and tell my how you fared."

He waved aside my efforts at expressing my gratitude, and I hurried down to take the ferry across the bay. I felt as though I carried in my pocket enough dynamite to blast the Earth. I knew no peace till I stood in the big room beside Felice, and told her that I wished to keep the whistle, to take it with me into that sound-proof room. She stared, puzzled, but she assented finally out of trust in, and concern for me. When we heard Suelivor knock at the door I hastily entered the secret room, and she went to admit him.

I gave them time to get into that room and be seated and enter in conversation. Then I pulled the silk cord that operated the door and took the golden whistle from my pocket. Noiselessly the door slid back, and I saw them. He sat with his back toward me, and she stood facing him.

"Where is the whistle?" he was asking.

"Oh, I shall get it for you presently," she answered, watching him, some unfathomable emotion burning in her black eyes. "Always you play, never you talk. It is that I want you to talk to me, to tell me of these great countries that you so much explore."

He sprang to his feet and took a step toward her. She moved back, instinctively, paling.

"I shall not tell you!" His voice was harsh, and he leaned toward her menacingly. "Have you forgotten the things I have told you already? You know what I seek! And you can give it to me, and you will not!"

"Very dramatic and romantic!" Felice drew herself up proudly, and her black eyes smoldered. Her voice barely escaped a sneer. "You know nothing about me after all! Go on, *M'sieu,* and explore! You'll never find the thing you seek. Because you are going away from it every mile you travel! As for me—oh, me—*je suis—la femme—a huis clos! Comprennez vous?"* She didn't mean the thing he really sought; she didn't know. Yet how merciless a truth she spoke.

"No!" Suelivor's voice rose in a bitter cry. "Neither do you. You *think* you do.

But you don't understand at all. You don't know anything about me. And I only know I'm in hell!"

Almost there was something human in that cry. Swiftly I lifted the whistle to my lips. Felice's black eyes caught sight of me, attracted by the motion of my hand, and leaped to my face. I stared back at her. I decided the rest of my existence in that look. And even as I drew my breath to blow that unholy whistle, Suelivor saw her gaze and wheeled to face me. He saw the whistle at my mouth, and he screamed, a hideous, terrible sound like nothing human. I never saw such hideous pain on any man's face as flashed into his then. I never want to see it again. Frantically I hurled my breath into that dumb tube of gold.

There rose from it a melody so sweet, so delicate, so holy and heaven-born that I shook in the flood of peace that descended to fill to throbbing ecstasy that great room. Felice's black eyes widened, and her face went still in a kind of awe. Suelivor writhed and twisted, and his scream went out in a diminishing moan that died in a futile whimper. Felice turned her gaze to him, but I blew steadily on. I knew nothing of manipulating the keys of that instrument. I could only blow into it. And I knew the unearthly achievement of Ahmbodie as that unutterably sweet melody rose ever more clearly and claimed the air.

But Suelivor! He twisted and squirmed like a man under torture, striving to spring toward me. He could not move from there. That holy melody held him bound to that spot. Then wild things began to happen. He began to glow and burst into atoms by fragments. That was the most ungodly sight ever witnessed by any man. First his feet went, glowing as though a fire were lit in the flesh, bursting into minute particles that shimmered like pulverized glass shot through with prismatic light. The particles quivered for an instant, gyrating as though in the path of a whirlwind, then disappeared like sparks extinguished in a cold blast. Next his legs went, his thighs, the lower part of his trunk.

It was Felice who screamed then. She sprang back with her hands held out before her as though she would shield her eyes from some unbearable horror. But I played steadily on, grimly, inexorably, knowing that the God of Justice stood at my elbow and would not let me cease.

I played. And even though my hand was unshaken as it held that avenging tube of gold, the soul I was fighting to save shook at the awful power of that thin, sweet vibration. A delicate, dulcet sound so mighty in its cosmic force that it disintegrated and drove apart the atoms that thing in the shape of a man had accrued and welded together: drove them back, shattered and blown to the five black winds of the outer darkness from which they had come. With a paean of gratitude flooring me for the stupendous achievement of Ahmbodie, I played.

Suelivor's trunk was gone, his arms. Only his distorted, rage-convulsed face hung gargoyle-like in the air, like some fantastically lighted, grotesque lantern. Then it, too, shattered in a thousand gleaming atoms, glowed for a moment a malignant red, and went out. And I knew what Ahmbodie had done, what he had hoped he had done. He had found Suelivor's exact vibration in those years he had worked, and prayed for this to come to pass when I played the whistle he had transformed— played it in the presence of that unspeakable being from the outer darkness.

And yet for a moment I played on, feeling the music of the spheres about my head, loth to hear that holy melody die away. Felice stood staring at the spot where Suelivor had been, soothed by the melody in spite of her shock, quieted to something resembling coherency. Then I dropped my hand and slipped the whistle into my pocket. There was silence. Silence profound, not of the Earth.

"Oh, Emile!" Felice broke the hush with a cry, not looking at me, still staring at the oddly luminous void in the air where Suelivor had stood. "*Mon Dieu!* What have you done? What is this? Am I mad? Do my eyes see? What was he? Emile—Emile! *Mon coeur—tout est flétri—pour toujours!*"

"No!" I denied. "Such hurts a surgeon might give his soul to heal! No—not forever. Time—you know time. And Henteli Suelivor was nothing human. Don't ask me what he was!"

I dragged myself to the window-ledge and dropped wearily to a seat, but she remained standing, motionless, her face dead-white, her eyes still averted from me.

"Time! Time!" she mocked. "The great doctor speaks of time! But what of *love?* Do you not know that it is love I have been seeking, Emile? Do you not know love? *Have* you not known it?" And now she turned toward me, with a swift, angry little gesture of rebellion, her eyes flaming. "Me—I thought to know it, Emile. And now he is gone. When I saw you there in Georgia I was searching for it. Always I have searched. It has been a gorgeous hunt. Big game, eh, Emile?"

Her bitter smile cut me. Hysterics and tears I should have been able to hold in control. But there were no tears, no frantic cries. She did not even seem to consider the fact that I was responsible for his going. Neither as man nor surgeon did I like that smile. No. Even now, even after what she had witnessed, she had not least idea of what manner of thing had been Suelivor. She did not contemplate that. She was racked, crushed with her false sense of loss. But how to persuade her that it *was* false?

"Emile!" I started at the repressed vehemence in her voice. "I tell you. *Oui.* I tell you all. Only, my friend—I need you now. Don't go away from me. Don't ever go away from me!"

"I won't." That was a promise. She knew I was incapable of breaking it, too. She looked at me sharply, as a man dying of thirst might stare at a water-flask— which he feared was empty.

"*Merci,* Emile! See, I have lived for love, Emile. Lived to find it. Oh, not this light, light thing so many call love. But that thing which goes so deep we cannot find its roots; that thing which goes so high we can not find its topmost branches; that thing which is so wide it possesses us utterly, makes of us both the king and the slave. You know such love, Emile? He—Henteli Suelivor, he could have given it! But he would not! There was something missing, Emile. Such a mind he had! Brains enough to run a world. Such a huge thing he was, powerful, like a fighter. One loves big men, Emile!"

I smiled to myself, wryly. Suelivor had been two inches shorter and ten pounds lighter than I! And I was no imbecile. Was I not acknowledged the greatest surgeon of the world? Love! Love from that cold, bloodless being? God—what I could have given her! I clamped my teeth grimly. Her voice went on, pinched with pain.

"And the fire he had. It was enough for ten men. But he turned it all to his furious music. He—you know he said he was an explorer. You know what he explored? The realms of harmony! You know for what he sought? A cool companion to play with him that so violent music! *Sacré!* What did I care for his wild music! I wanted him!"

I put my two hands together and held on to myself. So *that* was what he had told her! Anything, any flimsy excuse to retain access to her presence till he had drawn the soul from her body and left her cold and still in death. But is was not *her* soul he had touched with his satanic vibration. He had not reached her *soul* at all. Had he irrevocably claimed her *heart?* The heart he did not want. The heart I would have given my life to make my own! I sat in dumb silence. I did not yet dare trust my tongue.

"Love!" She laughed, a laugh that made me wince. "Love was not for him, Emile. You knew that, didn't you? I did not. I thought he had it. He shook me so. When he came into this room he brought light with him. The very air was alight with glory and desire. I felt as though a sharp electric glow were playing over me. When he spoke, a thousand little bells went ringing in my heart. And he knew it, Emile! He knew I loved him, and he traded on that love to come here and play his wild music. What—what did he hope to gain? Oh, I don't understand—but I hate him! Do you hear? I hate him!"

I hated only the pain in her face; the pain that choked me to silence and rendered me furious at my own impotency. Neither surgeon's brains nor surgeon's knives—but what of a surgeon's love? If in the zenith of her shock and misery her violent nature swung to hate him, if that heart wheeled on the rebound—was there hope for me?

Her voice sank to a weary, patient resignation: "I am glad that I will never see him again, Emile. Such a wild, terrible thing—such a horrible way to go. Me—I do not understand what you did to that whistle. I do not understand how it could blast him and touch us not at all. But I care not how he went—I am glad he is gone. I hate him, I tell you! Love! I laugh! All my life I wait, I live, I hope for love. It come—like a blinding star in a black cave—and it go, leaving only hate. I live for love—and I get this! I laugh at him. At me. At love. He didn't know what the word meant. No man does!"

"Some do!" I bit in, hard-gripped. *"Some do!"*

"I wonder!" She stared at the vehemence of my cry, her eyes wide upon me. "If he could not know—how could any man know?"

"Don't!" I cried, almost at the limit of my endurance. "He was not human. He was evil—evil that can not exist in struggle against the vibration of a holy melody. Even you may have followed false gods!"

"False gods! What do you mean, Emile?" She leaned toward me where she stood, and I saw that more and more her mind, her thought, her being was turning to me. "Oh—Emile!" Suddenly all the fury died out of her. Her shoulders drooped. She spread her hands toward me in a gesture of appeal. "Emile—did you ever know what it means to love anyone so much that if that one touch you, you hurt with happiness? Did you ever love anyone so much that wanting them made you faint-hearted and weak-kneed? Did you ever love anyone so much that that one was like a scorching fever in your veins, that when that one was absent your life was gone, that you would sell your soul and body to the devil just to have that one to hold and love till love was satisfied—forever? Oh, Emile—did you?"

"Yes!" I cried out, under torture. "Good God, yes! That's how I love you!"

"Emile!" The hands that had been clasped across her breast dropped limply. Her black eyes stared wider, wider, and she leaned nearer me in stunned silence. And after a little while she whispered tensely, "Oh—my friend, not so! My Emile—not so!"

"It is so! It *is* so!" I gripped the edge of the window-seat and stared back into her eyes. Was it possible he had not claimed her heart at all? Merely shaken it with his unearthly vibration, confused her and turned her senses? I rushed on. "False gods, Felice! You have been following false gods. That was not love! That was only the glittering mirage of an archfiend in human trappings. This is love—here. Here! You have been so blinded by the nearness of a sputtering star of hell that you could not see the great sun itself just beyond!"

"Emile!" She stepped close to me, and I went down on the knees that refused to bear me up, burying my face in her gown and clasping her with my arms. She was very still and I knew that she felt me shaking—shaking.

"Have you been that blind?" I raised my face. "So blind that you did not know? From the first time I saw you down there by the cotton field in Georgia my own dream has been of finding you again and making you mine forever!"

"Have I found it?" She leaned down and placed her hands on my shoulders with a grip that astonished me by its intensity. A high light broke into the empty depths of her black eyes. "Emile—have I found it? Here—waiting patiently under my own roof while I was misled by—false gods?"

Emotion flooded me, dizzying with promise. I knew then that the heart had not gone astray after all. Shaken, dazzled by a mirage, but mine. Mine all the while—even now coming home to me. Her hands drew at me, but I had hard work getting to my feet. My silly knees had no will to bear me up. I succeeded by great effort, and she held me off, staring at me.

My blood leaped exultantly. No longer were the black eyes empty. They were glowing with a blinding light. She stared at me as a man dying of thirst might stare at an empty water-flask, suddenly, miraculously brimming with clear, cool water. I stood motionless, searching her eyes for the thing I must see. And suddenly it was there. Home! The dazzled, wounded, bewildered heart had come home.

"Oh, Emile! Have I found it?" And her arms went around my neck in surrender.

I broke, then. I'd held it in too long. I think I kissed her. I can't be sure. I only know my arms went around her, possessing her utterly. This was Earth! Cool, sane, warm, beloved Earth. Green Earth, pulsant with spring, swept clean of the last vestige of that sinister denizen from the outer darkness. And in the flood of mad desire that overwhelmed me, shaking me to the depths, there ran the steady current of an unfailing, abiding love. She knew very well she had found it!

Sometimes even yet, I pause in my happiness to think of Suelivor. And almost I pity him. I keep that picture to remind me how near we are to unseen, unhallowed things. I wonder if somewhere he has reassembled by the aid of his kind the atoms that were his body, and gone on to yet another planet, seeking. I see him standing broad and high on the deck of a ship, his longing insatiate, consuming, his cruel mouth drawn into a bitter line, his green-brown eyes searching the empty sea as he flies recklessly into the weather. Or is he shattered forever?

The whistle? Ah, yes, there it hangs. To remind me that Light must ever triumph over Darkness. No one will ever play it again. Ahmbodie has seen to that. That holy melody is not yet for this Earth. But—there is another whistle. Hush—listen, do you hear it? My wife, gentlemen. Is there another sound like that anywhere? So round—so golden! You will pardon me, *non?* Every night she whistles me from my office to the garden. I go.

The
GOLDEN Chalice

by Frank Gruber

Frank Gruber was a famous detective novelist in his day. I had the pleasure of meeting him in his mansion in Bel-Air, California.—FJA
Weird Tales, July 1940

The cup was made of gold, no question about that. It was about four inches tall and weighed pretty close to a pound. I didn't know of any other metal that would have made the cup weigh as much, even though the thing didn't look like gold. But I guess that was because it was so old.

It looked like it had been buried in the ground for a long time and was pretty battered and dented. It wasn't a big haul. We'd be lucky to get three hundred for it from Opdyke. He'd make maybe two hundred profit on it, by melting it down and selling it to the government as old gold, at thirty-five dollars an ounce.

We'd turned in pretty late the night before and it was almost noon before we got up. I dug the cup out from under the bed and was looking it over and thinking that I was a damn fool for taking such chances for a lousy hundred and fifty—my share of the split.

Benny, on the other hand, was pretty chipper. He wasn't used to big money and all he'd done to earn his share was keep a lookout outside the place, while I went in and did the dirty work.

"Not bad, Jim," he cackled. "It couldda been more, but this ain't bad at all."

I looked around the room I was sharing with Benny. It was about eight feet by ten and contained a bed with springs that sagged almost to the floor, two chairs, a cheap dresser and a row of nails in the wall that served as a clothes closet. Benny paid four dollars a week for the room. The one I'd had up the river—with bars on the door and window—had been just as cheerful.

I said to Benny: "We'll get some clothes and some good food and have a couple of parties. We'll be broke in a week. Then what?"

"Then we'll crack another safe," he replied promptly. "There're some swell joints on Long Island and . . ."

That was when the knock came on the door. I never saw a man change his color as quickly as Benny did. One minute he'd been cocky as a Jungle Shawl fighting rooster, the next his face looked like sour dough and he was shivering like a man who's just been pulled out of the river.

I took a couple of quick steps toward Benny. "Thought you said no one knew where you lived?" I hissed at him.

Benny's teeth chattered as he shook his head. "They—they don't! That's why . . . you s'pose it's—the cops?"

Well, it could be. But I didn't think so. We'd made a clean getaway the night before. I said to Benny: "Maybe it's your landlady?"

The knock on the door was repeated, two quick knocks, then three spaced further apart. I jerked my head at the door and moved toward it.

Benny called out: "Who is it?"

A quiet sort of voice answered. A man's voice. "Open up, I want to talk to you." Benny wasn't shivering, now; he was shaking like a young sapling in a Kansas twister. For my own part I took a quick look out of the window. I saw that it opened on a dead air shaft. There was no retreat that way, and I cursed Benny for being such a fool as to rent a room without a hole by which he could escape.

Well, there was nothing to do but open the door. I slipped back the bolt and jerked open the door. I expected a cop. Maybe he was a cop. But he didn't look like one.

He was tall, about six feet, well built, but still looked kind of lean. He was in his early thirties and rather dark complexioned.

I hardly took in his features though, because of his eyes. They were large and dark and there was an expression in them that I can't describe—except that when I looked into them I was . . . scared! I admit it and I don't scare easy.

He was smiling.

"May I come in?" It wasn't the tone a cop usually uses.

I moved back into the room and shot a quick look toward the bed. Benny had had sense enough to throw a blanket over the gold cup. But when I looked back at the stranger his eyes were on the bed. He'd closed the door behind him.

He said: "You'll have to take it back." He couldn't see the gold cup; for that matter he couldn't have known that Benny and me were the ones who stole it.

I began edging around him, so that he was partly between Benny and myself. I said: "What're you talking about? Take what back?"

He shook his head and smiled. "The golden chalice—I guess you'd call it a cup. You'll have to take it back to Alfred Halleck."

Benny chirped up, then. He said: "Sure," and went to the bed. He stooped over, put his hand under a pillow and came up with a .32 caliber automatic. I blinked. I hadn't known that Benny had a rod. He pointed it at the stranger and snapped: "Up with 'em, Copper! You're not pinching us—not today!"

I was looking at the stranger. He didn't seem worried. He was still smiling, only

. . . the smile was a kind of sad one. I had a funny feeling down around where my stomach's supposed to be.

"I'm sorry," the stranger said, "you'll have to take it back."

Benny sneered. "There's some rope in the top drawer, Jim. Tie his hands. My room rent's up today, anyway. We'll just leave him here."

I got the rope, but I wasn't feeling so good. The gun in Benny's hand—I've done a lot of things in my time; I've been up the river, but I never carried a gun. I didn't believe in guns. Sure, I'm a safecracker—a burglar. But I take my chances. I try not to get caught, but if I am—that's my hard luck. I take the rap. But I don't ever want any murder rap. All the fellows I ever knew who carried guns wound up with murder raps.

The stranger put his hands behind his back. I wound the rope around his wrists, then he stretched out on the bed and I finished up by tying his feet. I did a good job of it. I wanted enough time to take the cup to Opdyke, get my split and leave. I wanted no more of Benny.

Benny got the cup from under the blanket, wrapped it in a towel, then rolled the whole thing inside an old newspaper and tied a piece of string around it.

We were ready to leave the room when the stranger spoke again. He said: "Take it back. Take it back, Benny Potter and Jim Vedder."

I didn't think about that until we were outside of Benny's rooming house. Then it struck me. No one, aside from Benny, knew my name. I'd only got out two days ago. I'd come straight to Benny's room and had been out of it only once, the night before when we took the trip up to Fox Meadow in Scarsdale and cracked the safe.

Benny lived on Christopher Street. We walked east to Sixth Avenue, then turned north. After a block or two, Benny said, "Let's stop in here and get a glass of beer."

I was willing. My throat was kind of dry. The saloon didn't look like much, but beer's beer no matter where you get it. We went in. It was the middle of the morning and the place was deserted except for the bartender and one customer who stood in front of the bar, with his back toward us.

"Two beers," Benny said, before we even got to the bar.

Then the man at the bar turned around. It was The Stranger. The man we'd left in Benny's room, tied hand and foot.

He looked right at me and this time he wasn't smiling. The temperature of the cafe seemed suddenly to get ten degrees colder and I know that the short hairs stood straight up on the back of my neck.

He said: "You'll have to take it back." I was pretty shocked by the sight of him, but Benny looked like he was going to faint. His mouth was opening and closing like that of a fish taken out of the water. I backed to the door and that broke the spell on Benny. He gave a hoarse yell, whipped out the .32 automatic and rushed backwards, like a prize-fighter backing away. He was in such a hurry he missed the door and banged against the wall.

He made it the second time and I was only one jump behind him. Out on Sixth Avenue we rushed to the next corner, which was 11th Street, turned right and didn't stop until we were almost up to Fifth. We stopped then just because we were out of breath. We both looked back, but The Stranger wasn't in sight.

"Gawd!" panted Benny Potter. "How did he get loose from those ropes and beat us to that saloon?"

"He couldn't have done it," I told Benny. "We went there straight from your room, by the shortest way. And, anyway . . . how did he know we were going to turn into that very saloon? We didn't know it ourselves until we saw the sign."

Benny's eyes almost popped out of his head. "That's right!" he gasped. "He couldn't have known we'd go in there—unless he guessed!"

I didn't say a word. I was still feeling cold, despite the long run I'd just had and I don't think the short hairs on my hackle had gone down. Up the street a little ways was a delicatessen shop, with a newspaper stand in front of it. I plunked down two cents and picked up a morning newspaper. It was on the front page, a picture with the caption: "Holy Grail Stolen." Below the head were three lines, reading: "Burglars last night blew the safe in the home of Alfred D. Halleck, noted archaeologist, and took the famous golden chalice which has been the subject of much controversy since Halleck brought it to America three years ago. Page 3, for further details."

I turned to Page 3. The story went on:

"Burglars last night dynamited the safe of Alfred D. Halleck's Fox Meadow estate and stole the golden chalice that was the sensation of the New York World's Fair. Professor Halleck returned from Asia Minor three years ago with the golden cup that has since been called the Holy Grail. Professor Halleck claimed to have found the cup while excavating near Antioch. Scientists, religious leaders and archaeologists have become divided in two camps as to the authenticity of the cup. Professor Halleck's group claims the cup is undoubtedly of first century manufacture and from its description and the location where it was found believe it is the original chalice used by Christ and his disciples during the Last Supper . . .

There was more, but that was as far as I read. I couldn't see more of the print. All I could see was the face of The Stranger. Swarthy, tall, in his early thirties . . . Once, when I was broke and it was snowing outside I spent an entire after afternoon in the Public Library. I was looking through an encyclopedia and came across a number of pictures supposed to be of old religious paintings found in the Catacombs near Rome. One of the pictures was supposed to go back to the first century. It showed a tall, well-built man in his early thirties, a swarthy man, with a prominent nose and a beard.

The stranger didn't have a beard . . . but I knew now why he looked familiar.

I gave the paper to Benny and let him read it. He snorted: "Imagine those suckers paying money to see this thing at the World's Fair. Well, Grover Whalen's going to be disappointed this season, because this cup won't be there. It'll be melted down and . . ."

"No," I said, "it won't be melted down. We're taking it back."

Benny stared at me. "Are you crazy? After the trouble we went to get it? Hey— snap out of it. Opdyke lives over here on Fourth Avenue. He'll haggle around a little, but he'll come across with three hundred. Two-fifty at the least."

"The cup goes back to Fox Meadow," I told Benny. "It's—an antique. It's worth a lot more than three hundred."

"All the more reason then!" Benny cried. "We'll show this to Opdyke—kick the price up on him."

All of a sudden I got mad. I grabbed Benny's arm and twisted him around. "You fool, don't you see? Halleck values this cup. It's worth a lot to him—a lot more than three hundred. All right, we'll sell it back to him."

Benny's eyes lit up. "Say, that's an idea. Maybe he'll go a grand for it. It says here he thinks it's a religious piece. Well, if he thinks so much of it he ought to go a grand. He's got the dough. That place of his cost a lot. We'll hold him up for a grand. Come on—we'll grab a train out to Scarsdale and get it over with. We'll break in on him and make him come across with the dough, before we turn over the cup. Otherwise he might call the cops . . ."

We took a bus on Fifth Avenue and rode up to Forty-second, then walked across to the Grand Central. Inside we bought two one-way tickets to Scarsdale and looked up the train schedule. One was listed to leave in twelve minutes. I didn't like the idea of waiting around the waiting room, so gave Benny the high-sign and headed for the washroom, on the lower level.

To kill time we got up on a couple of high seats to get our shoes shined. Benny got his shined first, then the bootblack got on mine. It was timing things pretty close. When he finished with me, it was two minutes to train time. I paid for the shines and headed for the door. It opened before I got to it and—The Stranger came in!

Benny let go altogether this time. He yelled to high heaven and he got so scared he dropped the cup that was wrapped in the towel and newspaper.

Me, I just stood and stared at The Stranger. I guess I'd still be standing there looking at him, if he hadn't stooped and picked up the package. He held it out to me, smiled and said:

"Take it back, Jim Vedder."

He left me holding it, turned and then walked out. Benny recovered then. "What—what do you make of that, Jim?" he cried.

I said: "We're taking it back, Benny. Come on!"

The gateman was just about to close the gate when we got to it. I grabbed a newspaper from a stand next to the door, threw down a nickel and scooted inside. We ran to catch the last car of the train, just as it was starting.

We got seats in the rear and I spread out the newspaper. It was the noon edition of an evening paper. The story was still on the front page. But there were some new angles to it. First of all, Alfred D. Halleck was offering a reward of $1,500 for the safe return of the Golden Chalice, as he called it. And *No Questions Asked.*

In an adjoining column was an interview of Halleck, made by one of the paper's reporters. Halleck was pretty worked up by the thing. He was offering a reward, he said, but he didn't really expect to get the Golden Chalice back. That was because he didn't think that ordinary burglars had blown his safe. He suspected the job had been done, or hired done, by a certain wealthy collector of *objets d'art*, who'd been bothering him for the last three years, trying to make Halleck sell the Golden Chalice. The collector, Halleck said, had offered him $50,000 for the cup and when he'd still refused to sell it, had threatened to steal it from him.

Halleck wouldn't tell the reporter the collector's name, but the reporter was a smart lad. He'd checked up back in the office and had gone to ask a Mr. August Messerschmidt, who lived on Park Avenue in New York, if he had any comment to make. Mr. Messerschmidt was a well-known collector of *objets d'art*. The reporter didn't come right out and say that Messerschmidt was the man who'd made the offer and threat to Halleck, but any kid could figure out the answer. Anyway, Messerschmidt had thrown the reporter out on his ear.

Benny was reading over my shoulder. When I put down the paper he took it from me and ripped out the page. He began folding it up.

I said: "What're you going to do with that?"

He didn't answer right away. The conductor had come along, collected our tickets and put a couple of slips in the slot on the back of the seat ahead of us. When he had gone away, Benny said:

"This Messerschmidt's a crook. He wants that cup any way he can get it. I've heard of guys like him. There's a fella in Philadelphia, collects pictures. He's got a million dollars worth of them and no one ever sees them but himself, because half of them have been swiped. This Messerschmidt'll go twenty-five g's. We'll get off at the 125th Street Station."

I wondered why I'd ever tied up with Benny Potter. With what had happened to us in the last hour . . . I said to him: "No, we're going to Scarsdale. The cup goes back to Halleck. We take whatever reward he gives us and we let it go at that."

"Are you crazy?" Benny yelped. "The most he'd give is fifteen hundred and the chances are four in five he won't give us anything but a houseful of cops. We're not going anywhere near Fox Meadow. We're getting off at the first stop and taking this to Park Avenue. That guy Messerschmidt's a bigger crook than we are.

That's why he'll come across . . . Gimme the cup! "

He reached for it and I shifted it to my left arm, against the window. With my right hand I slapped down his reaching paw.

He gave me a dirty look, then slumped down in his seat. He didn't say a word until the train pulled into the 125th Street Station. Then he suddenly got up. "All right, Jim, if that's the way you want it—"

His hand went to his hip and came back with the .32 automatic. I'd forgot all about him having it. There'd been too much on my mind.

I looked into his eyes and knew that he was going to take the cup from me if he had to shoot to get it. But I knew, too, that I wasn't going to give it to him.

I shook my head. "You can't, Benny. You . . ." I broke off and made a sudden dive for him. Even as I moved I knew I couldn't make it. Benny's finger was going to tighten on that automatic.

It thundered. But I didn't feel any shock or pain. I landed in the aisle on my hands and knees, twisted around and looked up at—The Stranger!

Benny was looking at him, too. And all of a sudden he yelled and headed for the door.

The train was already moving, the door was closed, but Benny tore it open. I climbed to my feet, started back for Benny and then I heard a yell that I'll hear to my dying day. It was Benny.

There was a lot of commotion, then. People yelled, the conductor pulled the cord and the train stopped and backed to the station.

Benny . . . Benny was dead.

The 125th Street Station is in the heart of Harlem, it's up in the air, like an elevated and the station platform is about three feet above the tracks. When Benny jumped the train was already beyond the platform. Benny, had landed on the ties, fell forward on to the next track . . . just as another train pulled in on that track.

I didn't wait around. There were a half dozen policemen around and questions were going, to be asked—questions I didn't want to answer. I took a subway train back to the Grand Central, I bought another ticket far Scarsdale and took the first train.

In Scarsdale I took a taxi to Alfred Halleck's house in Fox Meadow. I went to the front door of the house.

I didn't ring the bell. I didn't have to, because the door opened before I got to it. It was opened by—The Stranger. I wasn't surprised. Not by then. In fact, I would have been surprised if the door had been opened by anyone *but* The Stranger.

He smiled at me, in a pleased sort of way and said: "I'm glad you brought it back. Will you come in, please?"

He led the way to a library, opened the door for me and said: "Mr. Halleck!" Halleck sitting behind a teakwood desk, looked up at me, said: "Yes?"

I walked across the room and put the package on the desk in front of him. "I brought back the Golden Chalice."

His eyes popped wide open and he grabbed the package and tore the newspaper from about it. When he stripped off the towel and saw the cup, perspiration came to his forehead. He said: "Thank God!"

Then he looked at me. "Do you mind telling me . . . I know, I said no questions asked and this is not going to go any further . . . did you steal it, or are you returning this for someone?"

I told him. "I stole it. I'm sorry. You can call the police."

He looked at me in a funny sort of a way. "The police?" he repeated. "I'm not going to call them. I'm too glad to get this back. And here . . ." He opened a drawer and pulled out a thick stack of bills. "And here's the reward—fifteen hundred dollars."

I shook my head at him. "No, I don't want any reward. Not money. But you can do something. Tell me . . . who is the man who brought me into this room?"

He blinked. No one brought you into this room. You came in yourself." "But there was a man with me. He-he opened the door and brought me to the room. He announced your name."

"You said my name," Halleck replied. "And you came in by yourself. There isn't another man in my house. Besides ourselves only the cook in the kitchen . . . a middle-aged woman."

I stole it and returned the Golden Chalice six months ago. Alfred Halleck gave me a job. I'm working for him, now. I'm a sort of handy-man around his place and I'm going with Mr. Halleck on his next trip to Asia. He knows all about me.

All except what I did, the day after I returned the Golden Chalice. I wanted to get some things off my mind and I took the train back to Grand Central. In the washroom on the lower level, I went up to the bootblack. Before I could say anything he grabbed up a couple of big brushes and backed away.

"Don't you bother me, Mister, I'll call the police!" he yelled.

I shook my head at him and put a dollar bill on one of the seats. Then I took three steps away from it. "That dollar's yours," I told him, "if you tell me exactly what you saw here yesterday when I had my shoes shined."

The bootblack looked at the dollar and then at me. He shook his head, mumbled in his throat, then said: "Well, sir, you and the gent'man with you had a couple drinks too many I guess. You started for the door, then all of a sudden you got to talking and yelling and then you bust out of the door like you'd seen a ghost."

I nodded. "You're sure there wasn't another man here at the time—a man who'd just come in the door?"

The bootblack took another step back. "No, sir, there was only the two of you. And myself. That's all there was in here . . . no more."

I went out, took the Fifth Avenue bus and rode down to the Village, then walked to the cafe on Sixth Avenue where Benny and I had gone for a glass of beer and encountered The Stranger.

The bartender recognized me right away and reached for a bung-starter. "Get out of here!" he snarled at me. "I don't want no hop-heads in my place."

"I'm sorry," I said, "but would you mind telling me exactly what happened here yesterday?"

His eyes rolled, but he said, "I'll tell you. You and some other dope came in here, yelled for a drink, then started cutting up, pretending there was someone else here, that you were afraid of. That partner of yours had it particularly bad . . ."

"I guess he did. But you're sure there wasn't anybody else in here at the time—a tall, dark complexioned man?"

"There wasn't no one else in here," the bartender said, grimly. "There hadn't been anyone in for a half hour until you dopes came along . . .."

There was a lot of stuff in the papers for awhile about the Golden Chalice. Mr. Halleck gave it out, that it had been sent back to him, anonymously. The papers wouldn't believe that; they claimed it hadn't been stolen in the first place, that it was a publicity stunt on Halleck's part.

That started up another bunch who claimed that the Golden Chalice was a fake. All of them admitted that it was old and that Halleck might even have dug it up in Asia Minor, but the chances of it's being the Golden Chalice were about one in eighteen billion. They're still arguing about it. I don't say anything. Because I *know*.

The sides of the cañon were shaggy and rough, beyond anything I had ever seen. Huge boulders, hundreds of feet in diameter, were imbedded in them. The bottom also was strewn with similar gigantic rocks.

The Girl
in the GOLDEN Atom

by Ray Cummings

*In 1919 All Story Weekly published this first, novella version, of
this classic. It inspired an entire sub-genre of Sci-Fi/Fantasy
devoted to exploration of the realms of the infinitesimal*

AUniverse in an Atom
"Then you mean to say there is no such thing as the *smallest* particle of matter?"
asked the Doctor. "You can put it that way if you like," the Chemist replied.
"In other words, what I believe is that things can be infinitely small just as well as
they can be infinitely large. Astronomers tell us of the immensity of space. I have
tried to imagine space as finite. It is impossible. How can you conceive the edge of
space? Something must be beyond—something or nothing, and even that would be
more space, wouldn't it?"

"Gosh," said the Very Young Man, and lighted another cigarette.

The Chemist resumed, smiling a little. "Now, if it seems probable that there is
no limit to the immensity of space, why should we make its smallness finite? How
can you say that the atom cannot be divided? As a matter of fact, it already has been.
The most powerful microscope will show you realms of smallness to which you can
penetrate no other way. Multiply that power a thousand times, or ten thousand times,
and who shall say what you will see?"

The Chemist paused, and looked at the intent little group around him.

He was a youngish man, with large features and horn-rimmed glasses, his rough
English-cut clothes hanging loosely over his broad, spare frame. The Banker drained
his glass and rang for the waiter.

"Very interesting," he remarked.

"Don't be an ass, George," said the Big Business Man. "Just because you don't
understand, doesn't mean there is no sense to it."

"What I don't get clearly—" began the Doctor.

"None of it's clear to me," said the Very Young Man.

The Doctor crossed under the light and took an easier chair. "You intimated you had discovered something unusual in these realms of the infinitely

small," he suggested, sinking back luxuriously. "Will you tell us about it?"

"Yes, if you like," said the Chemist, turning from one to the other. A nod of assent followed his glance, as each settled himself more comfortably.

"Well, gentlemen, when you say I have discovered something unusual in another world—in the world of the infinitely small—you are right in a way. I have seen something and lost it. You won't believe me, probably." He glanced at the Banker an instant. "But that is not important. I am going to tell you the facts, just as they happened."

The Big Businessman filled up the glasses all around, and the Chemist resumed:

"It was in nineteen ten that this problem first came to interest me. I had never gone in for microscopic work very much, but now I let it absorb all my attention. I secured larger, more powerful instruments—I spent most of my money"—he smiled ruefully—"but never could I come to the end of the space into which I was looking. Something was always hidden beyond—something I could almost, but not quite, distinguish.

"Then I realized that I was on the wrong track. My instrument was not merely of insufficient power, it was not one thousandth the power I needed.

"So I began to study the laws of optics and lenses. In nineteen thirteen I went abroad, and with one of the most famous lens-makers of Europe I produced a lens that I hoped would give me what I wanted. So I returned here and fitted up my microscope that I knew would prove vastly more powerful than any yet constructed.

"It was finally completed and set up in my laboratory, and one night I went in alone to look through it for the first time. It was in the fall of nineteen fourteen, I remember.

"I can recall now my feelings at that moment. I was about to see into another world, to behold what no man had ever looked on before. What would I see? What new realms was I, first of all our human race, to enter? With furiously beating heart, I sat down before the huge instrument and carefully adjusted the eye-piece.

"Then I glanced around for some object to examine. On my finger I had a ring, my mother's wedding ring, and I decided to use that. I have it here." He took a plain gold band from his little finger and laid it on the table.

"You will see a slight mark on the outside. That is the place into which I looked."

His friends crowded around the table and examined a scratch on one side of the band.

"What did you see?" asked the Very Young Man eagerly.

"Gentlemen," resumed the Chemist, "what I saw staggered even my own imagination. With trembling hands I put the ring in place, looking directly down into that scratch. For a moment I saw nothing. It was like a person coming suddenly out of the sunlight into a darkened room. I knew there was something visible in my view, but my eyes did not seem able to receive the impressions. I realize now they were not yet adjusted to the new form of light. Gradually, as I looked, objects of definite shape began to emerge from the blackness.

"Gentlemen, I want to make clear to you now—as clear as I can—the peculiar aspect of everything that I saw under this microscope. I seemed to be inside an immense cave. One side, near at hand, I could now make out quite clearly. The walls were extraordinarily rough and indented, with a peculiar phosphorescent light on the projections and blackness in the hollows. I say phosphorescent light, for that is the nearest word I can find to describe it—a curious radiation, quite different from the reflected light to which we are accustomed.

"I said that the hollows inside of the cave were blackness. But not blackness— the absence of light—as we know it. It was a blackness that seemed not empty, but merely withholding its contents just beyond my vision.

"Except for a dim suggestion of roof over the cave, and its floor, I could distinguish nothing. After a moment this floor became clearer. It seemed to be— well, perhaps I might call it black marble—smooth, glossy, yet somewhat translucent. In the foreground the floor was apparently liquid. In no way did it differ in appearance from the solid part, except that its surface seemed to be in motion.

"Another curious thing was the outlines of all the shapes in view. I noticed that no outline held steady when I looked at it directly; it seemed to quiver. You see something like it when looking at an object through water—only, of course, there was no distortion. It was also like looking at something with the radiation of heat between.

"Of the back and other side of the cave, I could see nothing, except in one place, where a narrow effulgence of light drifted out into the immensity of the distance behind.

"I do not know how long I sat looking at this scene; it may have been several hours. Although I was obviously in a cave, I never felt shut in—never got the impression of being in a narrow, confined space.

"On the contrary, after a time I seemed to feel the vast immensity of the blackness before me. I think perhaps it may have been that path of light stretching out into the distance. As I looked, it seemed like the reversed tail of a comet, or the dim glow of the Milky Way, and penetrating to equally remote realms of space.

"Perhaps I fell asleep, or at least there was an interval of time during which I was so absorbed in my own thoughts I was hardly conscious of the scene before me.

"Then I became aware of a dim shape in the foreground—a shape merged with the outlines surrounding it. And as I looked, it gradually assumed form, and I saw it was the figure of a young girl, sitting beside the liquid pool. Except for the same waviness of outline and phosphorescent glow, she had quite the normal aspect of a human being of our own world. She was beautiful, according to our own standards of beauty; her long braided hair a glowing black, her face, delicate of feature and winsome in expression. Her lips were a deep red, although I felt rather than saw the color.

"She was dressed only in a short tunic of a substance I might describe as gray opaque glass, and the pearly whiteness of her skin gleamed with iridescence.

"She seemed to be singing, although I heard no sound. Once she bent over the pool and plunged her hand into it, laughing gaily.

"Gentlemen, I cannot make you appreciate my emotions, when all at once I remembered I was looking through a microscope. I had forgotten entirely my situation, absorbed in the scene before me. And then, all at once, a great realization came upon me—the realization that everything I saw was inside that ring. I was unnerved for the moment at the importance of my discovery.

"When I looked again, after the few moments my eye took to become accustomed to the new form of light, the scene showed itself as before, except that the girl was gone.

"For over a week, each night at the same time I watched that cave. The girl came always, and sat by the pool as I had first seen her. Once she danced with the wild grace of a wood nymph, whirling in and out of the shadows, and falling at last in a little heap beside the pool.

"It was on the tenth night after I had first seen her that the accident happened. I had been watching, I remember, an unusually long time before she appeared, gliding out of the shadows. She seemed in a different mood, pensive and sad, as she bent down over the pool, staring into it intently. Suddenly there was a tremendous cracking sound, sharp as an explosion, and I was thrown backward upon the floor.

"When I recovered consciousness—I must have struck my head on something—I found the microscope in ruins. Upon examination I saw that its larger lens had exploded—flown into fragments, scattered around the room. Why I was not killed I do not understand. The ring I picked up from the floor; it was unharmed and unchanged in any way.

"Can I make you understand how I felt at this loss? Because of the war in Europe I knew I could never replace my lens—for many years, at any rate. And then, gentlemen, came the most terrible feeling of all; I knew at last that the scientific achievement I had made and lost counted for little with me. It was the girl. I realized then that the only thing I ever could care for was living out her life with her world, and, indeed, her whole universe, inside an atom of that ring."

The Chemist stopped talking and looked from one to the other of the tense faces of his companions.

"It's almost too big an idea to grasp," murmured the Doctor.

"What caused the explosion?" asked the Very Young Man.

"I do not know." The Chemist addressed his reply to the Doctor, as the most understanding of the group. "I can appreciate, though, that through that lens I was magnifying tremendously those peculiar light-radiatons that I have described. I believe the molecules of the lens were shattered by them—I had exposed it longer to them that evening than any of the others."

The Doctor nodded his comprehension of this theory.

Impressed in spite of himself, the Banker took another drink and leaned forward in his chair. "Then you really think that there is a girl now inside the gold of that ring?" he asked.

"He didn't say that necessarily," interrupted the Big Business Man.

"Yes, he did."

"As a matter of fact, I do believe that to be the case," said the Chemist earnestly. "I believe that every particle of matter in our universe contains within it an equally complex and complete a universe, which to its inhabitants seem as large as ours. I think, also, that the whole realm of our interplanetary space, our solar system and all the remote stars of the heavens are contained within the atom of some other universe as gigantic to us as we are to the universe of that ring."

"Gosh!" said the Very Young Man.

"It doesn't make one feel very important in the scheme of things, does it?" remarked the Big Business Man dryly.

The Chemist smiled. "The existence of no individual, no nation, no world, nor any one universe is of the least importance."

"Then it would be possible," said the Doctor, "for this gigantic universe that contains us in one of its atoms, to be itself contained within the atom of another universe, still more gigantic than it is, and so on."

"That is my own theory," said the Chemist.

"And in each of the atoms of the rocks of that cave there may be other worlds proportionately minute?"

"I can see no reason to doubt it."

"Well, there is no proof, anyway," said the Banker. "We might as well believe it."

"I intend to get the proof," said the Chemist.

"Do you believe all these innumerable universes, both larger and smaller than ours, are inhabited?" the Doctor asked him.

"I should think probably most of them are. The existence of life, I believe, is as fundamental as the existence of matter without life."

"How do you suppose that girl got in there?" asked the Very Young Man, coming out of a brown study.

"What puzzled me," resumed the Chemist, ignoring the question, "is why the girl should so resemble our own race. I have thought about it a good deal, and I have reached the conclusion that the inhabitants of any universe in the next smaller or larger plane to ours probably resemble us fairly closely. That ring, you see, is in ourselves. The same forces control it that control us. Now, if the ring had been created on Mars, for instance, I believe that the universes within its atoms would be inhabited by beings like the Martians—if Mars has any inhabitants. Of course, in planes beyond those next to ours, either smaller or larger, changes would probably occur, becoming greater as you go in or out from our own universe."

"Good Lord! It makes one dizzy to think of it," said the Big Business Man excitedly.

"I wish I knew how that girl got in there," sighed the Very Young Man, looking at the ring.

"She probably didn't," retorted the Doctor. "Very likely she was created there, the same as you were here."

"I think that is probably so," said the Chemist. "And yet, sometimes I am not at all sure. She was very human." The Very Young Man looked at him sympathetically.

"How are you going to prove your theories?" asked the Banker, in his most irritatingly practical way.

The Chemist picked up the ring and put it on his finger. "Gentlemen," he said, "I have tried to tell you facts, not theories. What I saw through that ultramicroscope was not an unproven theory, but a fact. My theories you have brought out by your questions."

"You are quite right," said the Doctor, "but you did mention yourself that you hoped to provide proof."

The Chemist hesitated a moment, then made his decision. "I will tell you the rest," he said.

"After the destruction of the microscope, I was quite at a loss how to proceed. I thought about the problem for many weeks. Finally I decided to work along another altogether different line—a theory about which I am surprised you have not already questioned me."

He paused, but no one spoke.

"I am hardly ready with proof tonight," he resumed after a moment. "Will you all take dinner with me here at the club one week from tonight?" He read affirmation in the glance of each.

"Good. That's settled," he said rising. "At seven, then."

"But what was the theory you expected us to question you about?" asked the Very Young Man.

The Chemist leaned on the back of his chair.

"The only solution I could see to the problem," he said slowly, "was to find some way of making myself sufficiently small to be able to enter that other universe. I have found such a way, and one week from tonight, gentlemen, with your assistance, I am going to enter the surface of that ring at the point where it is scratched!"

Into The Ring

The cigars were lighted and dinner over before the Doctor broached the subject uppermost in the minds of every member of the party.

"A toast, gentlemen," he said, raising his glass. "To the greatest research Chemist in the world. May he be successful in his adventure tonight."

The Chemist bowed his acknowledgment.

"You have not heard me yet," he said smiling.

"But we want to," said the Very Young Man impulsively.

"And you shall." He settled himself more comfortably in his chair. "Gentlemen, I am going to tell you, first, as simply as possible, just what I have done in the past two years. You must draw your own conclusions from the evidence I give you.

"You will remember that I told you last week of my dilemma after the destruction of the microscope. Its loss and the impossibility of replacing it, led me into still bolder plans than merely the visual examination of this minute world. I reasoned, as I have told you, that because of its physical proximity, its similar environment, so to speak, this outer world should be capable of supporting life identical with our own.

"By no process of reasoning can I find adequate refutation of this theory. Then, again, I had the evidence of my own eyes to prove that a being I could not tell from one of my own kind was living there. That this girl, other than in size, differs radically from those of our race, I cannot believe.

"I saw then but one obstacle standing between me and this other world—the discrepancy of size. The distance separating our world from this other, is infinitely great or infinitely small, according to the viewpoint. In my present size it is only a few feet from here to the ring on that plate. But to an inhabitant of that other world, we are as remote as the faintest stars of the heavens, diminished a thousand times."

He paused a moment, signing the waiter to leave the room.

"This reduction of bodily size, great as it is, involves no deeper principle than does a light contraction of tissue, except that it must be carried further. The problem, then, was to find a chemical, sufficiently unharmful to life, that would so act upon the body cells as to cause a reduction in bulk, without changing their shape. I had to secure a uniform and also a proportionate rate of contraction of each cell, in order not to have the body shape altered.

"After a comparatively small amount of research work, I encountered an apparently insurmountable obstacle. As you know, gentlemen, our living human bodies are held together by the power of the central intelligence we call the mind. Every instant during your lifetime your subconscious mind is commanding and directing the individual life of each cell that makes up your body. At death this power is withdrawn; each cell is thrown under its own individual command, and dissolution of the body takes place.

"I found, therefore, that I could not act upon the cells separately, so long as they were under the control of the mind. On the other hand, I could not withdraw this power of the subconscious mind without causing death.

"I progressed no further than this for several months. Then came the solution. I reasoned that after death the body does not immediately disintegrate; far more time elapses than I expected to need for the cell-contraction. I devoted my time, then, to finding a chemical that would temporarily withhold, during the period of cell-contraction, the power of the subconscious mind, just as the power of the conscious mind is withheld by hypnotism.

"I am not going to weary you by trying to lead you through the maze of chemical experiments into which I plunged. Only one of you"—he indicated the Doctor—"has the technical bases of knowledge to follow me. No one had been before me along the path I traversed. I pursued the method of pure theoretical deduction, drawing my conclusions from the practical results obtained.

"I worked on rabbits almost exclusively. After a few weeks I succeeded in completely suspending animation in one of them for several hours. There was no life apparently existing during that period. It was not a trance or coma, but the complete simulation of death. No harmful results followed the revivifying of the animal. The contraction of the cells was far more difficult to accomplish; I finished my last experiment less than six months ago."

"Then you really have been able to make an animal infinitely small?" asked the Big Business Man.

The Chemist smiled. "I sent four rabbits into the unknown last week," he said.

"What did they look like going?" asked the Very Young Man. The Chemist signed him to be patient.

"The quantity of diminution to be obtained bothered me considerably?. Exactly how small that other universe is, I had no means of knowing, except by the computations I made of the magnifying power of my lens. These figures, I know, must necessarily be very inaccurate. Then, again, I have no means of judging by the visual rate of diminution of these rabbits, whether this contraction is at a uniform rate or accelerated. Nor can I tell how long it is prolonged, or the quantity of the drug administered, as only a fraction of the diminution has taken place when the animal passes beyond the range of any microscope I now possess.

"These questions were overshadowed, however, by a far more serious problem that encompassed them all.

"As I was planning to project myself into this unknown universe and to reach the exact size proportionate to it, I soon realized such a result could not be obtained were I in an unconscious state. Only by successive doses of the drug, or its retardant about which I will tell you later, could I hope to reach the proper size. Another necessity is that I place myself on the exact spot on that ring where I wish to enter and to climb down among its atoms when I have become sufficiently small to do so. Obviously, this would be impossible to one not possessing all his faculties and physical strength."

"And did you solve that problem, too?" asked the Banker. "I'd like to see it done," he added, reading his answer in the other's confident smile.

The Chemist produced two small paper packages from his wallet. "These drugs are the result of my research," he said. "One of them causes contraction, and the other expansion, but an exact reversal of the process. Taken together, they produce no effect, and a lesser amount of one retards the action of the other." He opened the papers, showing two small vials. "I have made them as you see, in the form of tiny pills, each containing a minute quantity of the drug. It is by taking them successively in unequal amounts that I expect to reach the desired size."

"There's one point that you do not mention," said the Doctor. "Those vials and their contents will have to change size as you do. How are you going to manage that?"

"By experimentation I have found," answered the Chemist, "that any object held in close physical contact with the living body being contracted is contracted itself at an equal rate. I believe that my clothes will be affected also. These vials I will carry strapped to my armpits."

"Suppose you should die, or be killed, would the contraction cease?" asked the Doctor.

"Yes, almost immediately," replied the Chemist. "Apparently, though I am acting through the subconscious mind while its power is held in abeyance, when this power is permanently withdrawn by death, the drug no longer effects the individual cells. The contraction or expansion ceases almost at once."

The Chemist cleared a space before him on the table. "In a well-managed club like this," he said, "there should be no flies, but I see several around. Do you suppose we can catch one of them?"

"I can," said the Very Young Man, and forthwith he did.

The Chemist moistened a lump of sugar and laid it on the table before him. Then, selecting one of the smallest of pills, he ground it to powder with the back of a spoon and sprinkled this powder on the sugar.

"Will you give the fly to me, please?"

The Very Young Man gingerly did so. The Chemist held the insect by its wings over the sugar. "Will someone lend me one of his shoes?"

The Very Young Man hastily slipped off one of his shoes.

"Thank you," said the Chemist, placing it on the table with a quizzical smile.

The rest of the company rose from their chairs and gathered round, watching with interested faces what was about to happen.

"I hope he is hungry," remarked the Chemist, and placed the fly gently down on the sugar, still holding it by the wings. The insect, after a moment, ate a little.

Silence fell upon the group as each watched intently. For a few moments nothing happened. Then, almost imperceptibly at first, the fly became larger. In another minute it was the size of a large horse-fly, struggling to release its wings from the Chemist's grasp. A minute more and it was the size of a beetle. No one spoke. The Banker moistened his lips, drained his glass hurriedly and moved slightly farther away. Still the insect grew; now it was the size of a small chicken, the multiple lens of its eyes presenting a more terrifying aspect, while its ferocious droning reverberated through the room. Then suddenly the Chemist threw it on the table, covered it with a napkin, and beat it violently with the shoe. When all movement had ceased he tossed its quivering body into a corner of the room.

"Good God!" ejaculated the Banker, as the white-faced men stared at each other. The quiet voice of the Chemist brought them back to themselves. "That, gentlemen, you must understand, was only a fraction of the very first stage of growth. As you may have noticed, it was constantly accelerated. This acceleration attains a speed of possibly fifty thousand times that you observed. Beyond that, it is my theory, the change is at a uniform rate." He looked at the body of the fly, lying inert on the floor. "You can appreciate now, gentlemen, the importance of having this growth cease after death."

"Good Lord, I should say so!" murmured the Big Business Man, mopping his forehead. The Chemist took the lump of sugar and threw it in the open fire.

"Gosh!" said the Very Young Man. "Suppose when we were not looking, another fly had—"

"Shut up!" growled the Banker.

"Not so skeptical now, eh, George?" said the Big Business Man.

"Can you catch me another fly?" asked the Chemist. The Very Young Man hastened to do so. "The second demonstration, gentlemen," said the Chemist, "is less spectacular, but far more pertinent than the one you have just witnessed." He took the fly by the wings, and prepared another lump of sugar, sprinkling a crushed pill from the other vial upon it.

"When he is small enough I am going to try to put him on the ring, if he will stay still," said the Chemist.

The Doctor pulled the plate containing the ring forward until it was directly under the light, and everyone crowded closer to watch; already the fly was almost too small to be held. The Chemist tried to set it on the ring, but could not; so with his other hand he brushed it lightly into the plate, where it lay, a tiny black speck against the gleaming whiteness of the china.

"Watch it carefully, gentlemen," he said as they bent closer.

"It's gone," said the Big Business Man.

"No, I can still see it," said the Doctor. Then he raised the plate closer to his face. "Now it's gone," he said.

The Chemist sat down in his chair. "It's probably still there, only too small for you to see. In a few minutes, if it took a sufficient amount of the drug, it will be small enough to fall between the molecules of the plate."

"Do you suppose it will find another inhabited universe down there?" asked the Very Young Man.

"Who knows," said the Chemist. "Very possibly it will. But the one we are interested in is here," he added, touching the ring.

"Is it your intention to take this stuff yourself, tonight?" asked the Big Business Man.

"If you will give me your help, I think so, yes. I have made all arrangements. The club has given us this room in absolute privacy for forty-eight hours. Your meals will be served here when you want them, and I am going to ask you, gentlemen, to take turns watching and guarding the ring during that time. Will you do it?"

"I should say we would!" cried the Doctor, and the others nodded assent.

"It is because I wanted you to be convinced of my entire sincerity that I have taken you so thoroughly into my confidence. Are those doors locked?" The Very Young Man locked them.

"Thank you," said the Chemist, starting to disrobe. In a moment he stood before them attired in a woolen bathing-suit of pure white. Over his shoulders was strapped tightly a narrow leather harness, supporting two silken pockets, one under each armpit. Into each of these he placed one of the vials, first laying four pills from one of them on the table.

At the point the Banker rose from his chair and selected another in the farther corner of the room. He sank into it a crumpled heap and wiped the beads of perspiration from his face with a shaking hand.

"I have every expectation," said the Chemist, "that this suit and harness will contract in size uniformly with me. If the harness should not, then I shall have to hold the vials in my hand."

On the table, directly under the light, he spread a large silk handkerchief, upon which he placed the ring. He then produced a teaspoon, which he handed to the Doctor.

"Please listen carefully," he said, "for perhaps the whole success of my adventure, and my life itself, may depend upon your actions during the next few minutes. You will realize, of course, that when I am still large enough to be visible to you, I shall be so small that my voice may be inaudible. Therefore, I want you to know, now, just what to expect.

"When I am something under a foot high, I shall step upon that handkerchief, where you will see my white suit plainly against its black surface. When I become less than an inch in height, I shall run over to the ring and stand beside it. When I have diminished to about a quarter of an inch, I shall climb upon it, and, as I get smaller, will follow its surface until I come to the scratch.

"I want you to watch me very closely. I may miscalculate the time and wait until I am too small to climb upon the ring. Or I may fall off. In either case, you will place that spoon beside me and I will climb into it. You will then do your best to help me get on the ring. Is all this quite clear?"

The Doctor nodded assent.

"Very well, watch me as long as I remain visible. If I have an accident, I shall take the other drug and endeavor to return to you at once. This you must expect at any moment during the next forty-eight hours. Under all circumstances, if I am alive, I shall return at the expiration of that time.

"And, gentlemen, let me caution you most solemnly, do not allow that ring to be touched until that length of time has expired. Can I depend on you?"

"Yes," they answered breathlessly.

"After I have taken the pills," the Chemist continued, "I shall not speak unless it is absolutely necessary. I do not know what my sensations will be, and I want to follow them as closely as possible." He then turned out all the lights in the room with the exception of the center electrolier, that shone down directly on the handkerchief and ring.

The Chemist looked about him. "Good-by, gentlemen," he said, shaking hands all around. "Wish me luck." And without hesitation he placed the four pills in his mouth and washed them down with a swallow of water.

Silence fell on the group as the Chemist seated himself and covered his face with his hands. For perhaps two minutes the tenseness of the silence was unbroken, save by the heavy breathing of the Banker as he lay huddled in his chair.

"Oh, my God! He *is* growing smaller!" whispered the Big Business Man in a horrified tone to the Doctor. The Chemist raised his head and smiled at them. Then he stood up, steadying himself against the chair. He was less than four feet high. Steadily, he grew smaller before their horrified eyes. Once he made as if to speak, and the Doctor knelt down beside him. "It's all right, good-by," he said in a tiny voice.

Then he stepped upon the handkerchief. The Doctor knelt on the floor beside it, the wooden spoon ready in his hand, while the others, except the Banker, stood behind him. The figure of the Chemist, standing motionless near the edge of the handkerchief, seemed not unlike a little white wooden toy, hardly more than one inch in height.

Waving his hand and smiling, he suddenly started to walk and then ran swiftly over to the ring. By the time he reached it, somewhat out of breath, he was little more than twice as high as the width of its band. Without pausing, he leaped up and sat astraddle, leaning over and holding to it tightly with his hands. In another moment he was on his feet, on the upper edge of the ring, walking carefully along its circumference toward the scratch.

The Big Business Man touched the Doctor on the shoulder and tried to smile. "He's making it," he whispered. As if in answer the little figure turned and waved its arms. They could just distinguish its white outline against the gold surface underneath.

"I don't see him," said the Very Young Man in a scared voice.

"He's right near the scratch," answered the Doctor, bending closer. Then, after

a moment, "He's gone." He rose to his feet. "Good Lord! Why haven't we a microscope!" he added.

"I never thought of that," said the Big Business Man. "We could have watched
him for a long time yet."

"Well, he's gone now," returned the Doctor, "and there is nothing for us to do
but wait."

"I hope he finds that girl," sighed the Very Young Man, as he sat chin in hand
beside the handkerchief.

The Banker snored stertorously from his mattress in a corner of the room. In
an easy-chair near by, with his feet on the table, lay the Very Young Man, sleeping
also.

The Doctor and the Big Business Man sat by the handkerchief conversing in
low tones.

"How long has it been now?" asked the latter.

"Just forty hours," answered the Doctor, "and he said that forty-eight hours
was the limit. He should come back at about ten tonight."

"I wonder if he *will* come back," questioned the Big Business Man nervously.
"Lord, I wish *he* wouldn't snore so loud," he added irritably, nodding in the direction
of the Banker.

They were silent for a moment, and then he went on: "You'd better try to sleep
awhile," he said to the Doctor. "You're worn out. I'll watch here."

"I suppose I should," answered the Doctor wearily. "Wake up that kid; he's
sleeping most of the time."

"No, I'll watch," repeated the Big Business Man; "you lie down over there."

The Doctor did so while the other settled himself more comfortably on a
cushion beside the handkerchief, and prepared for his lonely watching.

The Doctor apparently dropped off the sleep at once, for he did not speak
again. The Big Business Man sat staring steadily at the ring, bending nearer to it
occasionally. Every ten or fifteen minutes he looked at his watch.

Perhaps an hour passed this way, when the Very Young Man suddenly sat up
and yawned. "Haven't they come back yet?" he asked in a sleepy voice.

The Big Business Man answered in a much lower tone. "What do you mean—
they?" he said.

"I dreamed that he brought the girl back with him," said the Very Young Man.

"Well, if he did, they have not arrived," answered the Big Business Man. "You'd
better go back to sleep. We've got six or seven hours yet."

The Very Young Man rose and crossed the room. "No, I'll watch a while," he
said, seating himself on the floor. "What time is it?"

"Quarter of three."

"He said he'd be back by ten tonight. I'm crazy to see that girl."

The Big Business Man rose and went over to a dinner-tray, standing near the door. "Lord, I'm hungry. I must have forgotten to eat today." He lifted up one of the silver covers. What he saw evidently encouraged him, for he drew up a chair and began his lunch.

The Very Young Man lighted a cigarette. "It will be the tragedy of my life," he said, "if he never comes back."

The Big Business Man smiled. "How about *his* life?" he answered, but the Very Young Man had fallen into a reverie and did not reply.

The Big Business Man finished his lunch in silence and was just about to light a cigar when a sharp exclamation brought him hastily to his feet.

"Come here, quick, I see something." The Very Young Man had his face close to the ring and was trembling violently.

The other pushed him back. "Let me see. Where?"

"There by the scratch; he's lying there; I can see him."

The Big Business Man looked and then hurriedly woke the Doctor.

"He's come back," he said briefly; "you can see him there." The Doctor bent down over the ring while the others woke up the Banker.

"He doesn't seem to be getting any bigger," said the Very Young Man; "he's just lying here. Maybe he's dead."

"What shall we do?" asked the Big Business Man, and made as if to pick up the ring. The Doctor shoved him away. "Don't do that!" he said sharply. "Do you want to kill him?"

"He's sitting up," cried the Very Young Man. "He's all right."

"He must have fainted," said the Doctor. "Probably he's taking more of the drug now."

"He's much larger," said the Very Young Man, "look at him!"

The tiny figure was sitting sideways on the ring, with its feet hanging over the outer edge. It was growing perceptibly larger each instant, and in a moment it slipped down off the ring and sank in a heap on the handkerchief.

"Good Heavens! Look at him!" cried the Big Business Man. "He's all covered with blood."

The little figure presented a ghastly sight. As it steadily grew larger they could see and recognize the Chemist's haggard face, his cheek and neck stained with blood, and his white suit covered with dirt.

"Look at his feet," whispered the Big Business Man. They were horribly cut and bruised and greatly swollen.

The Doctor bent over and whispered gently, "What can I do to help you?" The Chemist shook his head. His body, lying prone upon the handkerchief, had torn it apart in growing. When he was about twelve inches in length he raised his head. The Doctor bent closer. "Some brandy, please," said a wraith of the Chemist's voice. It was barely audible.

"He wants some brandy," called the Doctor. The Very Young Man looked hastily around, then opened the door and dashed madly out of the room. When he returned, the Chemist had grown to nearly four feet. He was sitting on the floor with his back against the Doctor's knees. The Big Business Man was wiping the blood off his face with a damp napkin.

"Here!" cried the Very Young Man, thrusting forth the brandy. The Chemist drank a little of it. Then he sat up, evidently somewhat revived.

"I seem to have stopped growing," he said. "Let's finish it up now. God! How I want to be the right size again," he added fervently.

The Doctor helped him extract the vials from under his arm, and the Chemist touched one of the pills to his tongue. Then he sank back, closing his eyes. "I think that should be about enough," he murmured.

No one spoke for nearly ten minutes. Gradually the Chemist's body grew, the Doctor shifting his position several times as he became larger. It seemed finally to have stopped growing, and was apparently nearly its former size.

"Is he asleep?" whispered the Very Young Man.

The Chemist opened his eyes.

"No," he answered. "I'm all right now, I think." He rose to his feet, the Doctor and the Big Business Man supporting him on either side.

"Sit down and tell us about it," said the Very Young Man. "Did you find the girl?"

The Chemist smiled wearily.

"Gentlemen, I cannot talk now. Let me have a bath and some dinner. Then I will tell you all about it."

The Doctor rang for an attendant, and led the Chemist to the door, throwing a blanket around him as he did so. In the doorway the Chemist paused and looked back, with a wan smile, over the wreck of the room.

"Give me an hour," he said. "And eat something yourselves while I am gone." Then he left, closing the door after him.

When he returned, fully dressed in clothes that were ludicrously large for him, the room had been straightened up, and his four friends were finished with their meal. He took his place among them quietly and lighted a cigar.

"Well, gentlemen, I suppose that you are interested to hear what happened to me," he began. The Very Young Man asked his usual question.

"Let him alone," said the Doctor.

"Was it all as you expected?" asked the Banker.

It was his first remark since the Chemist returned.

"To a great extent, yes," answered the Chemist. "But I had better tell you just what happened." The Very Young Man nodded his eager agreement.

"When I took those first four pills," began the Chemist in a quiet, even tone, "my immediate sensation was a sudden reeling of the senses, combined with an extreme nausea. This latter feeling passed after a moment.

"You will remember that I seated myself upon the floor and closed my eyes. When I opened them my head had steadied itself somewhat, but I was oppressed by a curious feeling of drowsiness, impossible to shake off.

"My first mental impression was one of wonderment when I saw you all begin to increase in size. I remember standing up beside the chair, which was then half again its normal size, and you"—indicating the Doctor—"towered beside me as a giant of nine or ten feet high.

"Steadily upward, with a curious crawling motion, grew the room and all its contents. Except for the feeling of sleep that oppressed me, I felt quite my usual self. No change appeared happening to me, but everything else seeming growing to gigantic and terrifying proportions.

"Can you imagine a human being a hundred feet high? That is how you looked to me as I stepped upon that huge expanse of black silk and shouted my last good-by to you!

"Over to my left lay the ring, apparently fifteen or twenty feet away. I started to walk toward it, but although it grew rapidly larger, the distance separating me from it seemed to increase rather than lessen. Then I ran, and by the time I arrived it stood higher than my waist—a beautiful, shaggy, golden pit.

"I jumped upon its rim and clung to it tightly. I could feel it growing beneath me as I sat. After a moment I climbed upon its top surface and started to walk toward the point where I knew the scratch to be.

"I found myself now, as I looked about, walking upon a narrow, though ever broadening curved path. The ground beneath my feet appeared to be a rough yellowish quartz. This path grew rougher as I advanced. Below the bulging edges of the path, on both sides, lay a shining black plain, ridged and indented and with a sunlike sheen on the higher portions of the ridges. On the one hand this black plain stretched in an unbroken expanse to the horizon. On the other, it appeared as a circular valley, enclosed by a shining yellow wall.

"The way had now become extraordinarily rough. I bore to the left as I advanced, keeping close to the outer edge. The other edge of the path I could not see. I clambered along hastily, and after a few moments was confronted by a row of rocks and boulders lying directly across my line of progress. I followed their course for a short distance, and finally found a space through which I could pass.

"This transverse ridge was perhaps a hundred feet deep. Behind it and extending in a parallel direction lay a tremendous valley. I knew then I had reached my first objective.

"I sat down upon the brink of the precipice and watched the cavern growing ever wider and deeper. Then I realized that I must begin my descent if ever I was to reach the bottom. For perhaps six hours I climbed steadily downward. It was a fairly easy descent after the first little while, for the ground seemed to open up before me as I advanced, changing its contour so constantly that I was never at a loss for an easy downward path.

"My feet suffered cruelly from the shaggy, metallic ground, and I soon had to stop and rig a sort of protection for the soles from a portion of the harness over my shoulder. According to the stature I was when I reached the bottom, I had descended perhaps twelve thousand feet during this time.

"The latter part of this journey found me nearing the bottom of the cañon. Objects around me no longer seemed to increase in size, as had been constantly the case before, and I reasoned that probably my stature was remaining constant.

"I noticed, too, as I advanced, a curious alteration in the form of light around me. The glare from above (the sky showed only a narrow dull ribbon of blue) barely penetrated to the depths of the cañon's floor. But all about me there was a soft radiance, seeming to emanate from the rocks themselves.

"The sides of the cañon were shaggy and rough, beyond anything I had ever seen. Huge boulders, hundreds of feet in diameter, were imbedded in them. The bottom also was strewn with similar gigantic rocks.

"I surveyed this lonely waste for some time in dismay, not knowing in what direction lay my goal. I knew that I was at the bottom of the scratch, and by the comparison of its size I realized I was well started on my journey.

"I have not told you, gentlemen, that at the time I marked the ring I made a deeper indentation in one portion of the scratch and focused the microscope upon that. This indentation I now searched for. Luckily I found it, less than half a mile away—an almost circular pit, perhaps five miles in diameter, with shining walls extending downward into blackness. There seemed no possible way of descending into it, so I sat down near its edge to think out my plan of action.

"I realized now that I was faint and hungry, and whatever I did must be done quickly. I could turn back to you, or I could go on. I decided to risk the latter course, and took twelve more of the pills—three times my original dose."

The Chemist paused for a moment, but his auditors were much too intent to question him. Then he resumed in his former matter-of-fact tone.

"After my vertigo had passed somewhat—it was much more severe this time—I looked up and found my surroundings growing at a far more rapid rate than before. I staggered to the edge of the pit. It was opening up and widening out at an astounding rate. Already its sides were becoming rough and broken, and I saw many places where a descent would be possible.

"The feeling of sleep that had formerly merely oppressed me, combined now with my physical fatigue and the larger dose of the drug I had taken, became almost intolerable. I yielded to it for a moment, lying down on a crag near the edge of the pit. I must have become almost immediately unconscious, and remained so for a considerable time. I can remember a horrible sensation of sliding headlong for what seemed like hours. I felt that I was sliding or falling downward. I tried to rouse but could not. Then came absolute oblivion.

"When I recovered my senses I was lying partly covered by a mass of smooth, shining pebbles. I was bruised and battered from head to foot—in a far worse condition than you first saw me in when I returned.

"I sat up and looked around. Beside me, sloped upward at an apparently increasing angle, a tremendous glossy plane. This extended, as far as I could see, both to the right and left and upward into the blackness of the sky overhead. It was this plane that had evidently broken my fall, and I had been sliding down it, bringing with me a considerable mass of rocks and boulders.

"As my senses became clearer I saw I was lying on a fairly level floor. I could see perhaps two miles in each direction. Beyond that there was only darkness. The sky overhead was unbroken by stars or light of any kind. I should have been in total darkness except, as I have told you before, that everything, even the blackness itself, seemed to be self-luminous.

"The incline down which I had fallen was composed of some smooth substance suggesting black marble. The floor underfoot was quite different—more of a metallic quality with a curious corrugation. Before me, in the dim distance, I could just make out a tiny range of hills.

"I rose, after a time, and started weakly to walk toward these hills. Though I was faint and dizzy from my fall and the lack of food, I walked for perhaps half an hour, following closely the edge of the incline. No change in my visual surroundings occurred, except that I seemed gradually to be approaching the line of hills. My situation at this time, as I turned it over in my mind, appeared hopelessly desperate, and I admit I neither expected to reach my destination nor to be able to return to my own world.

"A sudden change in the feeling of the ground underfoot brought me to myself; I bent down and found I was treading on vegetation—a tiny forest extending for quite a distance in front and to the side of me. A few steps ahead a little silver ribbon threaded its way through the trees. This I judged to be water.

"New hope possessed me at this discovery. I sat down at once and took a portion of another of the pills.

"I must again have fallen asleep. When I awoke, somewhat refreshed, I found myself lying beside the huge trunk of a fallen tree. I was in what had evidently once been a deep forest, but which now was almost utterly desolated. Only here and there were the trees left standing. For the most part they were lying in a crushed and tangled mass, many of them partially embedded in the ground.

"I cannot express adequately to you, gentlemen, what an evidence of tremendous superhuman power this scene presented. No storm, no lightning, nor any attack of the elements could have produced more than a fraction of the destruction I saw all around me.

"I climbed cautiously upon the fallen tree-trunk, and from this elevation had a much better view of my surroundings. I appeared to be near one end of the desolated area, which extended in a path about half a mile wide and several miles deep. In front, a thousand feet away perhaps, lay the unbroken forest.

"Descending from the tree-trunk I walked in this direction, reaching the edge of the woods after possibly an hour of the most arduous traveling of my whole journey.

"During this time almost my only thought was about the necessity of obtaining food. I looked about me as I advanced, and on one of the fallen tree-trunks I found a sort of vine growing. This vine bore a profusion of small gray berries, much like our own huckleberries. They proved similar in taste, and I sat down and ate a quantity.

"When I reached the edge of the forest I felt somewhat stronger. I had seen up to this time no sign of animal life whatever. Now, as I stood silent, I could hear around me all the multitudinous tiny voices of the woods. Insect life stirred underfoot, and in the trees above an occasional bird flitted to and fro.

"Perhaps I am giving you a picture of our own world. I do not mean to do so. You must remember that above me there was no sky, just blackness. And yet so much light illuminated the scene that I could not believe it was other than what we would call daylight. Objects in the forest were as well lighted—better probably than they would be under similar circumstances in our own familiar world.

"The trees were of huge size compared to my present stature: straight, upstanding trunks, with no branches until very near the top. They were bluish-gray in color, and many of them well covered with the berry-vine I have mentioned. The leaves overhead seemed to be blue—in fact the predominating color of all the vegetation was blue, just as in our world it is green. The ground was covered with dead leaves, mold, and a sort of a gray moss. Fungus of a similar color appeared but of this I did not eat.

"I had penetrated perhaps two miles into the forest when I came unexpectedly to the bank of a broad, smooth-flowing river, its silver surface seeming to radiate waves of the characteristic phosphorescent light. I found it cold, pure-tasting water, and I drank long and deeply. Then I remember lying down upon the mossy bank, and in a moment, utterly worn out, I again fell asleep."

Lylda

"I was awakened by the feel of soft hands upon my head and face. With a start I sat up abruptly; I rubbed my eyes confusedly for a moment, not knowing where I was. When I collected my wits I found myself staring into the face of a girl, who was kneeling on the ground before me. I recognized her at once—she was the girl of the microscope.

"To say I was startled would be to put it mildly, but I read no fear in her expression, only wonderment at my springing so suddenly into life. She was dressed very much as I had seen her before. Her fragile beauty was the same, and at this closer view infinitely more appealing, but I was puzzled to account for her older, more mature look. She seemed to have aged several years since the last evening I had seen her through the microscope. Yet, undeniably, it was the same girl.

"For some moments we sat looking at each other in wonderment. Then she smiled and held out her hand, palm up, speaking a few words as she did so. Her voice was soft and musical, and the words of a peculiar quality that we generally describe as liquid, for want of a better term. What she said was wholly unintelligible, but whether the words were strange or the intonation different from anything I knew, I could not tell.

"Afterward, during my stay in this other world, I found that the language of the people resembled English quite closely, so far as the words themselves went. But the intonation with which they were given, and the gestures accompanying them, differed so widely from our own that they conveyed no meaning.

"The gap separating us, however, was very much less than you would imagine. Strangely enough, though, it was not I who learned to speak her tongue, but she who mastered mine.

The Very Young Man sighed contentedly.

"We became quite friendly after this greeting," resumed the Chemist, "and it was apparent from her manner that she had already conceived her own idea of who and what I was.

"For some time we sat and tried to communicate with each other. My words seemed almost as unintelligible to her as hers to me, except that occasionally she would divine my meaning, clapping her hands in childish delight. I made out that she lived at a considerable distance, and that her name was Lylda. Finally she pulled me by the hand and led me away with a proprietary air that amused, and, I must admit to you, please me tremendously.

"We had progressed through the woods in this way, hardly more than a few hundred yards, when suddenly I found that she was taking me into the mouth of a cave or passageway, sloping downward at an angle of perhaps twenty degrees. I noticed now, more graphically than ever before, a truth that had been gradually forcing itself upon me. Darkness was impossible in this new world. We were now shut in between narrow walls of crystalline rock, with a roof hardly more than fifty feet above.

"No artificial light of any kind was in evidence, yet the scene was lighted quite brightly. This, I have explained, was caused by the phosphorescent radiation that apparently emanated from every particle of mineral matter in this universe.

"As we advanced, many other tunnels crossed the one we were traveling. And now, occasionally, we passed other people, the men dressed similarly to Lylda, but wearing their hair chopped off just above the shoulder line.

"Later, I found that the men were generally about five and a half feet in stature, lean, muscular, and with a grayer, harder look to their skin than the iridescent quality that characterized the women.

"They were fine-looking chaps these we encountered. All of them stared curiously at me, and several times we were held up by chattering groups. The intense whiteness of my skin, for it looked in this light the color of chalk, seemed to both awe and amuse them. But they treated me with great deference and respect, which I afterward learned was because of Lylda herself, and also what she told them about me.

"At several of the intersections of the tunnels there were wide open spaces. One of these we now approached. It was a vast amphitheater, so broad its opposite wall was invisible, and it seemed crowded with people. At the side, on a rocky niche in the wall, a speaker harangued the crowd.

"We skirted the edge of this crowd and plunged into another passageway, sloping downward still more steeply. I was so much interested in the strange scenes opening before me that I remarked little of the distance we traveled. Nor did I question Lylda very often. I was absorbed in the complete similarity between this and my own world in these general characteristics, and yet its complete strangeness in details.

"I felt not the slightest fear. Indeed the sincerity and kindliness of these people seemed absolutely genuine, and the friendly, naïve manner of my little guide put me wholly at my ease. Toward me Lylda's manner was one of childish delight at a new-found possession. Toward those of her own people with whom we talked, I found she preserved a dignity they profoundly respected.

"We had hardly more than entered this last tunnel when I heard the sound of drums and a weird sort of piping music, followed by shouts and cheers. Figures from behind us scurried past, hastening toward the sound. Lylda's clasp on my hand tightened, and she pulled me forward eagerly. As we advanced the crowd became denser, pushing and shoving us about and paying little attention to me.

"In close contact with these people I soon found I was stronger than they, and for a time I had no difficulty in shoving them aside and opening a path for us. They took my rough handling all in good part; in fact, never have I met a more even-tempered, good-natured people than these.

"After a time the crowd became so dense we could advance no more. At this Lylda signed me to bear to the side. As we approached the wall of the cavern she suddenly clasped her hands high over her head and shouted something in a clear, commanding voice. Instantly the crowd fell back, and in a moment I found myself being pulled up a narrow flight of stone steps in the wall and out upon a level space some twenty feet above the heads of the people.

"Several dignitaries occupied this platform. Lylda greeted them quietly, and they made a place for us beside the parapet. I could see now that we were at the intersection of a transverse passageway, much broader than the one we had been traversing. And now I received the greatest surprise I had had in this new world, for down this latter tunnel was passing a broad line of men who obviously were soldiers.

"The uniformly straight lines they held; the glint of light on the spears they carried upright before them; the weird but rhythmic, music that passed at intervals, with which they kept step; and, above all, the cheering enthusiasm of that crowd, all seemed like an echo of my own great world above.

"This martial ardor and what it implied came as a distinct shock. All I had seen before showed the gentle kindliness of a people whose life seemed far removed from the struggle for existence to which our race is subjected. I had come gradually to feel that this new world, at least, had attained the golden age of security, and that fear, hate, and wrong-doing had long since passed away, or had never been born.

"Yet here, before my very eyes, made wholesome by the fires of patriotism, stalked the grim God of War. Knowing nothing yet of the motives that inspired these people, I could feel no enthusiasm, but only disillusionment at this discovery of the omnipotence of strife.

"For some time I must have stood in silence. Lylda, too, seemed to divine my thoughts, for she did not applaud, but pensively watched the cheering throng below. All at once, with an impulsively appealing movement, she pulled me down toward her, and pressed her pretty cheek to mine. It seemed almost as if she were asking me to help.

"The line of marching men seemed now to have passed, and the crowd surged over into the open space and began to disperse. As the men upon the platform with us prepared to leave, Lylda led me over to one of them. He was nearly as tall as I, and dressed in the characteristic tunic that seemed universally worn by both sexes. The upper part of his body was hung with beads, and across his chest was a thin, slightly convex stone plate.

"After a few words of explanation from Lylda, he laid his hands on my shoulders near the base of the neck, smiling with his words of greeting. Then he held one hand before me, palm up, as Lylda had done, and I laid mine in it, which seemed the correct thing to do.

"I repeated this performance with two others who joined us, and then Lylda pulled me away. We descended the steps and turned into the broader tunnel, finding near at hand a sort of sleigh, which Lylda signed me to enter. It was constructed evidently of wood, with a pile of leaves, or similar dead vegetation, for cushions. It was balanced upon a single runner of polished stone, about two feet broad, with a narrow, slightly shorter outrider on each side.

"Harnessed to the shaft were two animals, more resembling our reindeers than anything else, except that they were gray in color and had no horns. An attendant greeted Lylda respectfully as we approached, and mounted a seat in front of us when we were comfortably settled.

"We drove in this curious vehicle for over an hour. The floor of the tunnel was quite smooth, and we glided down its incline with little effort and at a good rate. Our driver preserved the balance of the sleigh by shifting his body from side to side so that only at rare intervals did the side-runners touch the ground.

"Finally, we emerged into the open, and I found myself viewing a scene of almost normal, earthly aspect. We were near the shore of a smooth, shining lake. At the side a broad stretch of rolling country, dotted here and there with trees, was visible. Near at hand, on the lakeshore, I saw a collection of houses, most of them low and flat, with one much larger on a promontory near the lake.

"Overhead arched a gray-blue, cloudless sky, faintly star-studded, and reflected in the lake before me I saw that familiar, gleaming trail of star-dust, hanging like a huge straightened rainbow overhead, and ending at my feet."

The Chemist paused and relighted his cigar. "Perhaps you have some questions," he suggested.

The Doctor shifted in his char.

"Did you have any theory at this time"—he wanted to know—"about the physical conformation of this world? What I mean is, when you came out of this tunnel, were you on the inside or the outside of the world?"

"Was it the same sky you saw overhead when you were in the forest?" asked the Big Business Man.

"No, it was what he saw in the microscope, wasn't it?" said the Very Young Man.

"One at a time, gentlemen." The Chemist laughed. "No, I had no particular theory at this time—I had too many other things to think of. But I do remember noticing one thing which gave me the clue to a fairly complete understanding of this universe. From it I formed a definite explanation, which I found was the belief held by the people themselves."

"What was that?" asked the Very Young Man.

"I noticed as I stood looking over this broad expanse of country before me, one vital thing that made it different from any similar scene I had ever beheld. If you will stop and think a moment, gentlemen, you will realize that in our world here the horizon is caused by a curvature of the earth below the straight line of vision. We are on a convex surface. But as I gazed over this landscape—and even with no appreciable light from the sky, I could see a distance of several miles—I saw at once that quite the reverse was true. I seemed to be standing in the center of a vast shallow bowl. The ground curved upward into the distance. There was no distinct horizon line, only the gradual fading into shadow of the visual landscape. I was standing, obviously, on a concave surface, on the inside, not the outside of the world.

"The situation, as I now understand it, was this: According to the smallest stature I reached, and calling my height at that time roughly six feet, I had descended into the ring at the time I met Lylda several thousand miles, at least. By the way, where is the ring?"

"Here it is," said the Very Young Man, handing it to him. The Chemist replaced it on his finger. "It's pretty important to me now," he said, smiling.

"You bet!" agreed the Very Young Man.

"You can readily understand how I descended such a distance, if you consider the comparative immensity of my stature during the first few hours I was in the ring. It is my understanding that this country through which I passed is a barren waste— merely the atoms of the mineral we call gold.

"Beyond that I entered the hitherto unexplored regions within the atom. The country at that point where I found the forest, I was told later, is habitable for several hundred miles. Around it on all sides lies a desert, across which no one has ever penetrated.

"This surface is the outside of the Oroid world, for so they call their earth. At this point the shell between the outer and inner surface is only a few miles in thickness. The two surfaces do not parallel each other here, so that in descending these tunnels we turned hardly more than an eighth of a complete circle.

"At the city of Arite, where Lylda first took me, and where I had my first view of the inner surface, the curvature is slightly greater that that of our own earth, although, as I have said, in the opposite direction."

"And the space within the curvature—the heavens you have mentioned—how great do you estimate it to be?" asked the Doctor.

"Based on the curvature at Arite, it would be about six thousand miles in diameter.

"Has this entire inner surface been explored?" asked the Big Business Man.

"No, only a small portion. The Oroids are not an adventurous people. There are only two nations, less than twelve million people altogether, on a surface nearly as extensive as our own."

"How about those stars?" suggested the Very Young Man.

"I believe they comprise a complete universe similar to our solar system. There is a central sun-star, around which many of the others revolve. You must understand, though, that these other worlds are infinitely tiny compared to the Oroids, and, if inhabited, support beings nearly as much smaller than the Oroids, as they are smaller than you."

"Great Caesar!" ejaculated the Banker. "Don't let's go into that any deeper!"

"Tell us more about Lylda," prompted the Very Young Man.

"You are insatiable on that point," said the Chemist, laughing. "Well, when we left the sleigh, Lylda took me directly into the city of Arite. I found it an orderly collection of low houses, seemingly built of uniformly cut, highly polished gray blocks. As we passed through the streets, some of which were paved with similar blocks, I was reminded of nothing so much as the old jingles of Spotless Town. Everything was immaculately, inordinately clean. Indeed, the whole city seemed built of some curious form of opaque glass, newly scrubbed and polished.

"Children crowded from the doorways as we advanced, but Lylda dispersed them with a gentle, though firm, command. As we approached the sort of castle I have mentioned, the reason for Lylda's authoritative manner dawned on me. She was, I soon learned, daughter of one of the most learned men of the nation and was—hand-maiden, do you call it?—to the queen."

"So it was a monarchy?" interrupted the Big Business Man. "I should never have thought that."

"Lylda called their leader a king. In reality he was the president, chosen by the people, for a period of about what we would term twenty years; I learned something about this republic during my stay, but not as much as I would have liked. Politics was not Lylda's strong point, and I had to get it all from her, you know.

"For several days I was housed royally in the castle. Food was served me by an attendant who evidently was assigned solely to look after my needs. At first I was terribly confused by the constant, uniform light, but when I found certain hours set aside for sleep, just as we have them, I soon fell into the routine of this new life.

"The food was not greatly different from our own, although I found not a single article I could identify. It consisted principally of vegetables and fruits, the latter of an apparently inexhaustible variety.

"Lylda visited me at intervals, and I learned I was awaiting an audience with the king. During these days she made rapid progress with my language—so rapid that I shortly gave up the idea of mastering hers.

"And now, with the growing intimacy between us and our ability to communicate more readily, I learned the simple, tragic story of her race—new details, of course, but the old, old tale of might against right, and the tragedy of a trusting, kindly people, blindly thinking others as just as themselves.

"For thousands of years, since the master life-giver had come from one of the stars to populate the world, the Oroid nation had dwelt in peace and security. These people cared nothing for adventure. No restless thirst for knowledge led them to explore deeply the limitless land surrounding them. Even from the earliest times no struggle for existence, no doctrine of the survival of the fittest, hung over them as with us. No wild animals harassed them; no savages menaced them. A fertile boundless land, a perfect climate, nurtured them tenderly.

"Under such conditions they developed only the softer, gentler qualities of nature. Many laws among them were unnecessary, for life was so simple, so pleasant to live, and the attainment of all the commonly accepted standards of wealth so easy, that the incentive to wrongdoing was almost non-existent.

"Strangely enough, and fortunately, too, no individuals rose among them with the desire for power. Those in command were respected and loved as true workers for the people, and they accepted their authority in the same spirit with which it was given. Indolence, in its highest sense the wonderful art of doing nothing gracefully, played the greatest part in their lives.

"Then, after centuries of ease and peaceful security, came the awakening. Almost without warning another nation had come out of the unknown to attack them.

"With the hurt feeling that comes to a child unjustly treated, they all but succumbed to this first onslaught. The abduction of numbers of their women, for such seemed the principal purpose of the invaders, aroused them sufficiently to repel this first crude attack. Their manhood challenged, their anger as a nation awakened for the first time, they sprang as one man into the horror we call war.

"With the defeat of the Malites came another period of ease and security. They had learned no lesson, but went their indolent way, playing through life like the kindly children they were. During this last period some intercourse between them and the Malites took place. The latter people, whose origin was probably nearly opposite them on the inner surface, had by degrees pushed their frontiers closer and closer to the Oroids. Trade between the two was carried on to some extent, but the character of the Malites, their instinctive desire for power, for its own sake, their consideration for themselves as superior beings, caused them to be distrusted and feared by their more simple-minded companion nation.

"You can almost guess the rest, gentlemen. Lylda told me little about the Malites, but the loathing disgust of her manner, her hesitancy even to bring herself to mention them, spoke more eloquently than words.

"Four years ago, as they measure time, came the second attack, and now, in a huge arc, only a few hundred miles from Arite, hung the opposing armies."

The Chemist paused. "That's the condition I found, gentlemen," he said. "Not a strikingly original or unfamiliar situation, was it?"

"By Jove!" remarked the Doctor thoughtfully. "What a curious thing that the environment of our earth should so effect that world inside the ring. It does make you stop and think, doesn't it, to realize how those infinitesimal creatures are actuated now by the identical motives that inspire us?"

"Yet it does seem very reasonable, I should say," the Big Business Man put in.

"Let's have another round of drinks," suggested the Banker. "This is dry work!"

"As a scientist you'd make a magnificent plumber, George!" retorted the Big Business Man. "You're about as helpful in this little gathering as—as an oyster!"

The Very Young Man rang for a waiter.

"I've been thinking—" began the Banker, and stopped at the smile of his companion. "Shut up!" he finished. "That's cheap wit, you know!"

"Go on, George," encouraged the other, "you've been thinking—"

"I've been tremendously interested in this extraordinary story"—he addressed himself to the Chemist—"but there's one point I don't get at all. How many days were you in that ring do you make out?"

"I believe about seven, all told," returned the Chemist.

"But you were only away from us some forty hours. I ought to know, I've been right here." He looked at his crumpled clothes somewhat ruefully.

"The change of time-progress was one of the surprises of my adventure," said the Chemist. "It is easily explained in a general way, although I cannot even attempt a scientific theory of its cause. But I must confess that before I started, the possibility of such a thing never even occurred to me.

"To get a conception of this change you must analyze definitely what time is. We measure and mark it by years, months, and so forth, down to minutes and seconds, all based upon the movements of our earth around its sun. But that is the measurement of time, not time itself. How would you describe time?"

The Big Business Man smiled, "Time," he said, "is what keep everything from happening at once."

"Very clever," said the Chemist, laughing.

The Doctor leaned forward earnestly. "I should say," he began, "that time is the rate at which we live—the speed at which we successively pass through our existence from birth to death. It's very hard to put intelligibly, but I think I know what I mean," he finished, somewhat lamely.

"Exactly so. Time is a rate of life-progress, different for every individual, and only made standard because we take the time-duration of the earth's revolution around the sun, which is constant, and arbitrarily say: "That is thirty-one million five hundred and thirty-six thousand seconds."

"Is time different for every individual?" asked the Banker argumentatively.

"Think for a moment," returned the Chemist. "Suppose your brain were to work twice as fast as mine. Suppose your heart beat twice as fast, and all the functions of your body were accelerated in a like manner. What we call a second would certainly seem to you twice as long. Further than that, it actually would be twice as long, so far as you were concerned. Your digestion, instead of taking perhaps four hours, would take two. You would eat twice as often. The desire for sleep would overtake you every twelve hours instead of twenty-four, and you would be satisfied with fours hours of unconsciousness instead of eight. In short, you would soon be living a cycle of two days every twenty-four hours. Time then, as we measure it, for you at least would have doubled—you would be progressing through life at twice the rate I am through mine."

"That may be theoretically true," the Big Business Man put in. "Practically, though, it has never happened to anyone."

"Of course not, to such a great degree as the instance I put. No one, except in disease, has ever doubled our average rate of life-progress, and live it out as a balanced, otherwise normal existence. But there is no question that to some much smaller degree we all of us differ one from the other. The difference, however, is so comparatively slight, that we can each one reconcile it to the standard measurement of time. And so, outwardly, time is the same for all of us. But inwardly, why, we none of us conceive a minute or an hour to be the same. How do you know how long a minute is to me? More than that, time is not constant even in the same individual. How many hours are shorter to you than others? How many days have been almost interminable? No, instead of being constant, there is nothing more inconstant than time."

"Haven't you confused two different issues?" suggested the Big Business Man. "Granted what you say about the slightly different rate at which different individuals live, isn't it quite another thing, how long time seems to you? A day when you have nothing to do seems long, or, on the other hand, if you are very busy it seems short. But mind, it only *seems* short or long, according to the preoccupation of your mind. That has nothing to do with the speed of your progress through life."

"Ah, but I think it has!" cried the Chemist. "You forget that we none of us have all of the one thing to the exclusion of the other. Time seems short; it seems long, and in the end it all averages up, and makes our rate of progress what it is. Now if any of us were to go through life in a calm, deliberate way, making time seem as long as possible, he would live more years, as we measure them, than if he rushed headlong through the days, accomplishing always as much as possible. I mean in neither case to go to the extremes, but only so far as would be consistent with the maintenance of a normal standard of health. How about it?" He turned to the Doctor. "You ought to have an opinion on that."

"I rather think you are right," said the latter thoughtfully, "although I doubt very much if the man who took it easy would do as much during his longer life as the other with his energy would accomplish in the lesser time that had been allotted to him."

"Probably he wouldn't," said the Chemist, "but that does not alter the point we are discussing."

"How does this apply to the world in the ring?" ventured the Very Young Man, somewhat timidly.

"I believe there is a very close relationship between the dimensions of length, breadth, and thickness, and time. Just what connection with them it has, I have no idea. Yet, when size changes, time-rate changes; you have only to look at our own universe to discover that circumstance."

"How do you mean?" asked the Very Young Man.

"Why, all life on our earth, in a general way, illustrates the fundamental fact that the larger a thing is, the slower its time-progress is. An elephant, for example, lives more years than we humans. Yet a fly is born, matured, and aged in a few months. There are exceptions, of course; but in a majority of cases it is true.

"So fundamental is this fact that the same condition holds with the heavenly bodies. Mercury, smallest of the planets, travels the fastest. Venus, slower, but faster than earth, and so on throughout the solar system.

"So I believe that as I diminished in stature, my time-progress became faster and faster. I am seven days older than when I left you day before yesterday. I have lived those seven days, gentlemen, there is no way of getting around that fact."

"This is all tremendously interesting," sighed the Big Business Man, "but not very comprehensible."

Strategy and Kisses

"It was the morning of my third day in the castle," began the Chemist again, "that I was taken by Lylda before the king. We found him seated alone in a little anteroom, overlooking a large courtyard, which we could see was crowded with an expectant, waiting throng. I must explain to you now, that I was considered by Lylda somewhat in the light of a Messiah, come to save her nation from the destruction that threatened it.

"She believed me a supernatural being, which, indeed, if you come to think of if, gentlemen, is exactly what I was. I tried to tell her something of myself and the world I had come from, but the difficulties of language and her smiling insistence and faith in her own conception of me, soon caused me to desist. Thereafter I let her have her own way, and did not attempt any explanation again for some time.

"For several weeks before Lylda found me sleeping by the river's edge, she had made almost a daily pilgrimage to that vicinity. A maidenly premonition, a feeling that had first come to her several years before, told her of my coming, and her father's knowledge and scientific beliefs had led her to the outer surface of the world as the direction in which to look. A curious circumstance, gentlemen, lies in the fact that Lylda clearly remembered the occasion when this first premonition came to her. And in the telling, she described graphically the scene in the cave, where I saw her through the microscope." The Chemist paused an instant and then resumed.

"When we entered the presence of the king, he greeted me quietly, and made me sit by his side, while Lylda knelt on the floor at our feet. The king impressed me as a man about fifty years of age. He was smooth-shaven, with black, wavy hair, reaching his shoulders. He was dressed in the usual tunic, the upper part of his body covered by a quite similar garment, ornamented with a variety of metal objects. His feet were protected with a sort of buckskin; at his side hung a crude-looking metal spear.

"The conversation that followed my entrance lasted perhaps fifteen minutes. Lylda interpreted for us as well as she could, though I must confess we were all three at times completely at a loss. But Lylda's bright, intelligent little face, and the re-sourcefulness of her gestures, always managed somehow to convey her meaning.

The charm and grace of her manner, all during the talk, her winsomeness, and the almost spiritual kindness and tenderness that characterized her, made me feel that she embodied all those qualities with which we of this earth idealize our own womanhood.

"I found myself falling steadily under the spell of her beauty, until—well, gentlemen, it's childish for me to enlarge upon this side of my adventure, you know, but— Lylda means everything to me now, and I'm going back for her just as soon as I possibly can."

"Good for you!" cried the Very Young Man. "Why didn't you bring her with you this time?"

"Let him tell it his own way," remonstrated the Doctor. The Very Young Man subsided with a sigh.

"During our talk," resumed the Chemist, "I learned from the king, that Lylda had promised him my assistance in overcoming the enemies that threatened his country. He smilingly told me that our charming little interpreter had assured him I would be able to do this. Lylda's blushing face, as she conveyed this meaning to me, was so thoroughly captivating, that before I knew it, and quite without meaning to, I pulled her up toward me and kissed her.

"The king was more surprised by far than Lylda, at this extraordinary behavior. Obviously neither of them had understood what a kiss meant, although Lylda, by her manner, evidently comprehended pretty thoroughly.

"I told them, as simply as possible to enable Lylda to get my meaning, that I could, and would gladly aid in their war. I explained, then, that I had the power to change my stature, and could make myself grow very large or very small in a short space of time.

"This, as Lylda evidently told it to him, seemed quite beyond the king's understanding. He comprehended finally, or at least he agreed to believe my statement.

"This led to the consideration of practical questions of how I was to proceed in their war. I had not considered any details before, but now they appeared of the utmost simplicity. All I had to do was to make myself a hundred or two hundred feet high, walk out to the battle lines, and scatter the opposing army like toys."

"What a quaint idea!" said the Banker. "A modern *Gulliver.*"

The Chemist did not heed this interruption.

"Then like three children we plunged into a discussion of exactly how I was to perform these wonders, the king laughing heartily as we pictured the attack on my tiny enemies.

"He then asked me how I expected to accomplish this change of size, and I very briefly told him of our larger world, and the manner in which I had come from it into his. Then I showed the drugs that I still carried carefully strapped to me. This seemed definitely to convince the king of my sincerity. He rose abruptly to his feet, and strode through a doorway to a small balcony overlooking the courtyard below.

"As he stepped out into the view of the people, a great cheer arose. He waited quietly for them to stop, and then raised his hand and began speaking. Lylda and I stood in the doorway, out of sight of the crowd, but with it and the entire courtyard plainly in our view.

"It was a quadrangle enclosure, formed by the four sides of the palace, perhaps three hundred feet across, packed solidly now with people of both sexes, the gleaming whiteness of the upper parts of their bodies, and their upturned faces, making a striking picture.

"For perhaps ten minutes the king spoke steadily, save when he was interrupted by applause. Then he stopped abruptly, and turning, pulled Lylda and me out upon the balcony. The enthusiasm of the crowd doubled at our appearance. I was pushed forward to the balcony rail, where I bowed repeatedly to the cheering throng.

"Just after I left the king's balcony, I met Lylda's father. He was a kindly-faced old gentleman, and took a great interest in me and my story. He it was who told me about the physical conformation of his world, and he seemed to comprehend my explanation of mine.

"That night it rained—a heavy, torrential downpour, such as we have in the tropics. Lylda and I had been talking for some time, and, I must confess, I had been making love to her ardently. I broached now the principal object of my entrance into her world, and, with an eloquence I did not believe I possessed, I pictured the wonders of our own great earth above, begging her to come back with me and live out her life with mine in my world.

"Much of what I said, she probably did not understand, but the main facts were intelligible without questions. She listened quietly. When I had finished, and waited for her decision, she reached slowly out and clutched my shoulders, awkwardly making as if to kiss me. In an instant she was in my arms, with a low, happy little cry.

"The clattering fall of rain brought us to ourselves. Rising to her feet, Lylda pulled me over to the window-opening, and together we stood and looked out into the night. The scene before us was beautiful, with a weirdness almost impossible to describe. It was as bright as I had ever seen this world, for even though very heavy clouds hung overhead, the light from the stars was never more than a negligible quantity.

"We were facing the lake—a shining expanse of silver radiation, its surface shifting and crawling, as though a great undulating blanket of silver mist lay upon it. And coming down to meet it from the sky were innumerable lines of silver—a vast curtain of silver cords that broke apart into great strings of pearls when I followed their downward course.

"And then, as I turned to Lylda, I was struck with the extraordinary weirdness of her beauty as never before. The reflected light from the rain had something of the quality of our moonlight. Shining on Lylda's body, it tremendously enhanced the iridescence of her skin. And her face, upturned to mine, bore an expression of radiant happiness and peace such as I had never seen before in a woman's countenance."

The Chemist paused, his voice dying away into silence as he sat lost in thought. Then he pulled himself together with a start. "It was a sight, gentlemen, the memory of which I shall cherish all my life.

"The next day was that set for my entrance into the war. Lylda and I had talked nearly all night, and had decided that she was to return with me to my world. By morning the rain had stopped, and we sat together in the window-opening, silenced with the thrill of the wonderful new joy that had come into our hearts.

"The country before us, under the cloudless, starry sky, stretched gray-blue and beautiful into the quivering obscurity of the distance. At our feet lay the city just awakening into life. Beyond, over the rolling meadows and fields, wound the road that led out to the battle-front, and coming back over it now, we could see an endless line of vehicles. These, as they passed through the street beneath our window, I found were loaded with soldiers, wounded and dying. I shuddered at the sight of one cart in particular, and Lylda pressed closer to me, pleading with her eyes for my help for her stricken people.

"My exit from the castle was made quite a ceremony. A band of music and a guard of several hundred soldiers ushered me forth, walking beside the king, with Lylda a few paces behind. As we passed through the open streets of the city, heading for the open country beyond, we were cheered continually by the people who thronged the streets and crowded upon the housetops to watch us pass.

"Outside Arite I was taken perhaps a mile, where a wide stretch of country gave me the necessary space for my growth. We were standing upon a slight hill, below which, in a vast semicircle, fully a hundred thousand people were watching.

"And now, for the first time, fear overtook me. I realized my situation—saw myself in a detached sort of way—a stranger in this extraordinary world, with only the power of my drug to raise me out of it. This drug you must remember, I had not as yet taken. Suppose it were not to act? Or were to act wrongly?

"I glanced around. The king stood before me, quietly waiting for my pleasure. Then I turned to Lylda. One glance at her proud, happy little face, and my fear left me as suddenly as it had come. I took her in my arms and kissed her there before that multitude. Then I set her down, and signified to the king I was ready.

"I took a minute quantity of one of the drugs, and as I had done before, sat down with my eyes covered. My sensations were fairly similar to those I have already described. When I looked up after a moment, I found the landscape dwindling to tiny proportions in quite as astonishing a way as it had grown before. The king and Lylda stood now hardly above my ankle.

"A great cry arose from the people—a cry wherein horror, fear, and applause seemed equally mixed. I looked down and saw thousands of them running away in terror.

"Still smaller grew everything within my vision, and then, after a moment, the landscape seemed at rest. I kneeled now upon the ground, carefully, to avoid treading on any of the people around me. I located Lylda and the king after a moment; tiny little creatures less than an inch in height. I was then, I estimated, from their viewpoint, about four hundred feet tall.

I put my hand flat upon the ground near Lylda, and after a moment she climbed into it, two soldiers lifting her up the side of my thumb as it lay upon the ground. In the hollow of my palm, she lay quite securely, and very carefully I raised her up toward my face. Then, seeing that she was frightened, I set her down again.

"At my feet, hardly more than a few steps away, lay the tiny city of Arite and the lake. I could see all around the latter now, and could make out clearly a line of hills on the other side. Off to the left the road wound up out of sight in the distance. As far as I could see, a line of soldiers was passing out along this road—marching four abreast, with carts at intervals, loaded evidently with supplies; only occasionally, now, vehicles passed in the other direction. Can I make it plain to you, gentlemen, my sensations in changing stature? I felt at first as though I were tremendously high in the air, looking down as from a balloon upon the familiar territory beneath me.

"That feeling passed after a few moments, and I found that my point of view had changed. I no longer felt that I was looking down from a balloon, but felt as a normal person feels. And again I conceived myself but six feet tall, standing above a dainty little toy world. It is all in the viewpoint, of course, and never, during all my changes, was I for more than a moment able to feel of a different stature than I am at this present instant. It was always everything else that changed.

"According to the directions I had received from the king, I started now to follow the course of the road. I found it difficult walking, for the country was dotted with houses, trees, and cultivated fields, and each footstep was a separate problem.

"I progressed in this manner, perhaps two miles, covering what the day before I would have called about a hundred and thirty or forty miles. The country became wilder as I advanced, and now was in places crowded with separate collections of troops.

"I have not mentioned the commotion I made in this walk over the country. My coming must have been told widely by couriers the night before, to soldiers and peasantry alike, or the sight of me would have caused utter demoralization. As it was, I must have been terrifying to a tremendous degree. I think the careful way in which I picked my course, stepping in the open as much as possible, helped reassure the people. Behind me, whenever I turned, they seemed rather more curious than fearful, and once or twice when I stopped for a few moments they approached my feet closely. One athletic young soldier caught one of my buskins, as it hung over my instep close to the ground, and pulled himself up hand over hand, amid the enthusiastic cheers of his admiring comrades.

"I had walked nearly another mile, when almost in front of me, and perhaps a hundred yards away, I saw a remarkable sight that I did not at first understand. The country here was crossed by a winding river running in a general way at right angles to my line of progress. At the right, near at hand, and on the nearer bank of the river, lay a little city, perhaps half the size of Arite, with its back up against a hill.

"What first attracted my attention was that from a dark patch across the river which seemed to be woods, pebbles appeared to pop up at intervals, traversing a little arc perhaps as high as my knees, and falling into the city. I watched for a moment and then I understood. There was a siege in progress, and the catapults of the Malites were bombarding the city with rocks.

"I went up a few steps closer, and the pebbles stopped coming. I stood now beside the city, and as I bent over it, I could see by the battered houses the havoc the bombardment had caused. Inert little figures lay in the streets, and I bent lower and inserted my thumb and forefinger between a row of houses and picked one up. It was the body of a woman, partly mashed. I set it down again hastily.

"Then as I stood up, I felt a sting on my leg. A pebble had hit me on the shin and dropped at my feet. I picked it up. It was the size of a small walnut—a huge boulder six feet or more in diameter it would have been in Lylda's eyes. At the thought of her I was struck with a sudden fit of anger. I flung the pebble violently down into the wooded patch and leaped over the river in one bound, landing squarely on both feet in the woods. It was like jumping into a patch of ferns.

"I stamped about me for a moment until a large part of the woods was crushed down. Then I bent over and poked around with my finger. Underneath the tangled wreckage of tiny tree trunks, lay numbers of the Malites. I must have trodden upon a thousand or more, as one would stamp upon insects.

"The sight sickened me at first, for after all, I could not look upon them as other than men, even though they were only the length of my thumb-nail. I walked a few steps forward, and in all directions saw swarms of the little creatures running. Then the memory of my coming departure from the world of Lylda, and my promise to the king to rid his land once and for all from these people, made me feel again that they, like vermin, were to be destroyed.

"Without looking directly down, I spent the next two hours stamping over this entire vicinity. Then I ran two or three miles directly toward the country of the Malites, and returning I stamped along the course of the river for a mile or so in both directions. Then I walked back to Arite, again picking my way carefully among the crowds of the Oroids, who now feared me so little that I had difficulty in moving around without stepping upon them.

"When I had regained my former size, which needed two successive doses of the drug, I found myself surrounded by a crowd of the Oroids, pushing and shoving each other in an effort to get close to me. The news of my success over their enemy had been divined by them, evidently. Lord knows it must have been obvious enough what I was going to do, when they saw me stride away, a being four hundred feet tall.

"Their enthusiasm and thankfulness now was so mixed with awe and reverent worship of me as a divine being, that when I advanced toward Arite they opened a path immediately. The king, accompanied by Lylda, met me at the edge of the city. The latter threw herself into my arms at once, crying with relief to find me the proper size for her world once more.

"I need not go into details of the ceremonies of rejoicing that took place this afternoon. These people seemed little given to pomp and public demonstration. The king made a speech from his balcony, telling them all I had done, and the city was given over to festivities and preparations to receive suitably the returning soldiers.

The Chemist pushed his chair back from the table, and moistened his dry lips with a swallow of water. "I tell you, gentlemen," he continued, "I felt pretty happy that day. It's a wonderful feeling to find yourself the actual savior of a nation."

At that the Doctor jumped to his feet, overturning his chair, and striking the table a blow with his fist that made the glasses dance.

"By God!" he fairly shouted. "That's just what you can be here to us."

The Banker looked startled, while the Very Young Man pulled the Chemist by the coat in his eagerness to be heard. "A few of those pills," he said in a voice that quivered with excitement, "when you are standing near enemy country, and you can kick the houses apart with the toe of your boot."

"Why not?" said the Big Business Man, and silence fell on the group as they stared at each other, awed by the possibilities that suddenly opened up before them.

I Must Go Back!

"The tremendous plan for the salvation of their own suffering world through the Chemist's discovery occupied the five friends for some time. Then laying aside this subject, that now had become of the most vital importance to them all, the Chemist resumed his narrative.

"My last evening in the world of the ring, I spent with Lylda, discussing our future, and making plans for the journey. I must tell you now, gentlemen, that never for a moment during my stay in Arite was I once free from an awful dread of this return trip. I tried to conceive what it would be like, and the more I thought about it, the more hazardous it seemed.

"You must realize, when I was growing smaller, coming in, I was able to climb down, or fall or slide down, into the spaces as they opened up. Going back, I could only imagine the world as closing in upon me, crushing me to death unless I could find a larger space immediately above into which I could climb.

"And as I talked with Lylda about this and tried to make her understand what I hardly understood myself, I gradually was brought to realize the full gravity of the danger confronting us. If only I had made the trip out once before, I could have ventured it with her. But as I looked at her fragile little body, to expose it to the terrible possibilities of such a journey was unthinkable.

"There was another question, too, that troubled me. I had been gone from you nearly a week, and you were only to wait for me two days. I believed firmly that I was living at a faster rate, and that probably my time with you had not expired. But I did not know. And suppose, when I had come out on to the surface of the ring, one of you had had it on his finger walking along the street? No, I did not want Lylda with me in that event.

"And so I told her—made her understand—that she must stay behind, and that I would come back for her. She did not protest. She said nothing—just looked up into my face with wide, staring eyes and a little quiver of her lips. Then she clutched my hand and fell into a low, sobbing cry.

"I held her in my arms for a few moments, so little, so delicate, so human in her sorrow, and yet almost superhuman in her radiant beauty. Soon she stopped crying and smiled up at me bravely.

"Next morning I left. Lylda took me through the tunnels and back into the forest by the river's edge where I had first met her. There we parted. I can see now, her pathetic, drooping little figure as she trudged back to the tunnel.

"When she had disappeared, I sat down to plan out my journey. I resolved now to reverse as nearly as possible the steps I had taken coming in. Acting on this decision, I started back to that portion of the forest where I had trampled it down.

"I found the place without difficulty, stopping once on the way to eat a few berries, and some of the food I carried with me. Then I took a small amount of one of the drugs, and in a few moments the forest-trees had dwindled into tiny twigs beneath my feet.

"I started now to find the huge incline down which I had fallen, and when I reached it, after some hours of wandering, I followed its bottom edge to where a pile of rocks and dirt marked my former landing place. The rocks were much larger than I remembered them, and so I knew I was not so large, now, as when I was here before.

"Remembering the amount of the drug I had taken coming down, I took now twelve of the pills. Then, in a sudden panic, I hastily took of the others. The result made my head swim most horribly. I sat or lay down, I forget which. When I looked up I saw the hills beyond the river and forest coming toward me, yet dwindling away beneath my feet as they approached. The incline seemed folding up upon itself, like a telescope. As I watched, its upper edge came into view, a curved, luminous line against the blackness above. Every instant it crawled down closer, more sharply curved, and its inclined surface grew steeper.

"All this time, as I stood still, the ground beneath my feet seemed to be moving. It was crawling toward me, and folding up underneath where I was standing. Frequently I had to move to avoid rocks that came at me and passed under my feet into nothingness.

"Then, all at once, I realized that I had been stepping constantly backward, to avoid the inclined wall as it shoved itself toward me. I turned to see what was behind, and horror made my flesh creep at what I saw. A black, forbidding wall, much like the incline in front, entirely encircled me. It was hardly more than half a mile away, and towered four or five thousand feet overhead.

"And as I stared in terror, I could see it closing in, the line of its upper edge coming steadily closer and lower. I looked wildly around with an overpowering impulse to run. In every direction towered this rocky wall, inexorably swaying in to crush me.

"I think I fainted. When I came to myself the scene had not greatly changed. I was lying at the bottom and against one wall of a circular pit, now about a thousand feet in diameter and nearly twice as deep. The wall all around I could see was almost perpendicular, and it seemed impossible to ascent its smooth, shining sides. The action of the drug had evidently worn off, for everything was quite still.

"My fear now left me, for I remembered this circular pit quite well. I walked over to its center, and looking around and up to its top, I estimated distance carefully, then I took two more of the pills.

"Immediately the familiar, sickening, crawling sensation began again. As the walls closed in upon me, I kept carefully in the center of the pit. Steadily they crept in. Now only a few hundred feet away! Now only a few paces—and then I reached out and touched both sides at once with my hands.

"I tell you, gentlemen, it was a terrifying sensation to stand in that well (as it now seemed) and feel its walls closing up with irresistible force. But now the upper edge was within reach of my fingers. I leaped upward and hung on for a moment, then pulled myself up and scrambled out, tumbling in a heap on the ground above. As I recovered myself, I looked again at the hole out of which I had escaped; it was hardly big enough to contain my fist.

"I knew, now, I was at the bottom of the scratch. But how different it looked than before. It seemed this time a long, narrow cañon, hardly more than sixty feet across. I glanced up and saw the blue sky overhead that I knew was the space of this room above the ring.

"The problem now was quite a different one than getting out of the pit, for I saw that the scratch was so deep in proportion to its width that if I let myself get too big, I would be crushed by its walls before I could jump out. It would be necessary, therefore, to stay comparatively small and climb up its side.

"I selected what appeared to be an especially rough section, and took a portion of another of the pills. Then I started to climb. After an hour the buskins on my feet were torn to fragments, and I was bruised and battered as you saw me. I see, now, how I could have made both the descent into the ring, and my journey back, with comparatively little effort, but I did the best I knew at the time.

"When the cañon was about ten feet in width, and I had been climbing arduously for several hours, I found myself hardly more than fifteen or twenty feet above its bottom. And I was still almost that far from the top. With the stature I had then attained. I could have climbed the remaining distance easily, but for the fact that the wall above had grown too smooth to afford foothold. The effects of the drug had again worn off, and I sat down and prepared to take another dose. I did so—the smallest amount I could—and held ready in my hand a pill of the other kind in case of emergency. Steadily the walls closed in.

"A terrible feeling of dizziness now came over me. I clutched the rock beside which I was sitting, and it seemed to melt like ice beneath my grasp. Then I remembered seeing the edge of the cañon within reach above my head, and with my last remaining strength, I pulled myself up, and fell upon the surface of the ring. You know the rest. I took another dose of the powder, and in a few minutes was back among you."

The Chemist stopped speaking, and looked at his friends. "Well," he said, "you've heard it all. What do you think of it?"

"It is a terrible thing to me," sighed the Very Young Man, "that you did not bring Lylda with you."

"It would have been a terrible thing if I had brought her. But I am going back for her."

"When do you plan to go back?" asked the Doctor after a moment.

"As soon as I can—in a day or two," answered the Chemist.

"Before you do your work here? You must not," remonstrated the Big Business Man. "Our war here needs you, our nation, the whole cause of liberty and freedom needs you. You cannot go."

"Lylda needs me, too," returned the Chemist. "I have an obligation toward her now, you know, quite apart from my own feelings. Understand me, gentlemen," he continued earnestly. "I do not mean to place myself and mine before the great fight for democracy and justice being waged in this world. That would be absurd. But it is not quite that way, actually; I can go back for Lylda and return here in a week. That week will make little difference to the war. On the other hand, if I go to Europe first, it may take me a good many months to complete my task, and during that time Lylda will be using up her life several times faster than I do. No, gentlemen, I am going to her first."

Two days later the company met again in the privacy of the club-room. When they had finished dinner, the Chemist began in his usual quiet way.

"I am going to ask you this time, gentlemen, to give me a full week. There are four of you—six hours a day of watching for each. It need not be too great a hardship. You see," he continued, as they nodded in agreement, "I want to spend a longer period in the ring world this time. I may never go back, and I want to learn, in the interest of science, as much about it as I can. I was there such a short time before, and it was all so strange and remarkable. I confess I learned practically nothing.

"I told you all I could of its history. But of its art, its science, and all its sociological and economic questions, I got hardly more than a glimpse. It is a world and a people far less advanced than ours, yet with something we have not, and probably never will have—the universally distributed milk of human kindness. Yes, gentlemen, it is a world well worth studying."

The Banker came out of a brown study. "How about your formulas for these drugs?" he asked abruptly; "where are they?" The Chemist tapped his forehead smilingly. "Well, hadn't you better leave them with us?" the Banker pursued. "The hazards of the trip—you can't tell, you know—"

"Don't misunderstand me, gentlemen," broke in the Chemist. "I wouldn't give you those formulas if my life and even Lylda's depended on it. There again you do not differentiate between the individual and the race. These drugs are the most powerful thing for good in the world today. But they are equally as powerful for evil. I would stake my life on what you would do, but I will not stake the life of a nation."

"I know what I'd do if I had the formulas," began the Very Young Man.

"Yes, but I don't know what you'd do," laughed the Chemist. "Don't you see I'm right?"

They admitted they did, though the Banker acquiesced very grudgingly.

"The time of my departure is at hand. Is there anything else, gentlemen, before I leave you?" asked the Chemist, beginning to disrobe.

"Please tell Lylda I want very much to meet her," said the Very Young Man earnestly, and they all laughed.

When the room was cleared, and the handkerchief and ring in place once more, the Chemist turned to them again. "Good-by, my friends," he said, holding out his hands. "One week from tonight, at most." Then he took the pills.

No unusual incident marked his departure. The last they saw of him he was sitting on the ring near the scratch.

Then passed the slow days of watching, each taking his turn for the allotted six hours.

By the fifth day, they began hourly to expect the Chemist, but it passed through its weary length, and he did not come. The sixth day dragged by, and then came the last—the day he had promised would end their watching. Still he did not come, and in the evening they gathered, and all four watched together, each unwilling to miss the return of the adventurer and his woman from another world.

But the minutes lengthened into hours, and midnight found the white-faced little group, hopeful yet hopeless, with fear tugging at their hearts. A second week passed and still they watched, explaining with an optimism they could none of them feel, the non-appearance of their friends. At the end of the second week they met again to talk the situation over, a dull feeling of fear and horror possessing them. The Doctor was the first to voice what now each of them was forced to believe. "I guess it's all useless," he said. "He's not coming back."

"I don't hardly dare give him up," said the Big Business Man.

"Me, too," agreed the Very Young Man sadly.

The Doctor sat for some time in silence, thoughtfully regarding the ring. "My friends," he began finally, "this is too big a thing to deal with in any but the most

I was awakened by the feel of soft hands upon my head and face. With a start I sat up abruptly; I rubbed my eyes confusedly for a moment, not knowing where I was. When I collected my wits I found myself staring into the face of a girl, who was kneeling on the ground before me. I recognized her at once— she was the girl of the microscope.

careful way. I can't imagine what is going on inside that ring, but I do know what is happening in our world, and what our friend's return means to civilization here. Under the circumstances, therefore, I cannot, I will not give him up.

"I am going to put that ring in a museum and pay for having it watched indefinitely. Will you join me?" He turned to the Big Business Man as he spoke.

"Make it a threesome," said the Banker gruffly. "What do you take me for?" and the Very Young Man sighed with the tragedy of youth.

* * *

And so today, if you like, you may go and see the ring. It lies in the Museum of the American Society for Biological Research. You will find it near the center of the third gallery, lying on its black silk handkerchief, and covered with a glass bell. The air in the bell is renewed constantly, and near at hand sit two armed guards, watching day and night. And as you stand before it, thinking of the wonderful world within its atoms, you well may shudder at your infinite unimportance as an individual and yet glow with pride at your divine omnipotence as a fragment of human life.

On his desk there reposed an instrument comprising a disc of silvery gray metal,
framed in darker gray, and mounted vertically upon a base of similar material. This
instrument was Roy's private videophone . . . His number was repeated again. This
time, not in the accustomed voice of the operator; but in a low, sweet and compelling
feminine one. A voice of gold, thought Roy, . . .the voice, though far away, was clear,
and it certainly was beautiful. The most beautiful voice he had ever heard . . .

The GOLDEN Girl of Munan

by Harl Vincent

Engineer Harl Vincent (Schoepflin) published many vigorous stories such as this, to much acclaim in the pages of Argosy, Amazing Stories and Astounding Science Fiction in the years before WW II. This tale of scientifiction wonder appeared in the June 1928 issue of Amazing Stories.

H ad you been present in a certain studio apartment in New York City at ten o'clock in the evening of January 16th, in the year 2406, you would have witnessed a surprising series of events. As it happened, Roy Hamilton was alone in his studio when the thing occurred which altered his entire life and led up to the historic destruction of Munan.

An unusually handsome man in artist's smock, his hair a tousled dark mass, his jaw set, and his black eyes snapping with determination, Roy alternately sat at his writing desk for a few minutes at a time, then paced the floor in impatient annoyance. This procedure was repeated again and again, his impatience rapidly increasing.

On his desk there reposed an instrument comprising a disc of silvery gray metal, framed in darker gray, and mounted vertically upon a base of similar material. This instrument was Roy's private videophone, and it was the calls from it of a voice repeating, "NY-19-635," that occasioned his numerous returns to it. As he returned and answered his number, a face would appear in the disc and inform him in a monotonous voice that no success could as yet be reported on his call. Each time this was a signal for his renewal of the nervous pacing and muttering, accompanied by further rumpling of his hair.

It was preposterous! Here he had been trying for two hours to get a connection with one of his patrons in Paris. Constant reports there had been that something was wrong with the continental video. Pity that the Terrestrial Videophone Company couldn't keep their confounded voice and vision ether waves working, he thought angrily. Or whatever kind of waves they were! Roy was no scientist.

His number was repeated again. This time, not in the accustomed voice of the operator; but in a low, sweet and compelling feminine one. A voice of gold, thought

Roy, as he dashed to the instrument. Surprised, he did not view the usual clear-cut image in the disc; but, as through a dense veil, an extremely indistinct vision met his gaze. The features of the girl could not be discerned. Possibly she was beautiful; possibly not. At any rate, the voice, though far away, was clear, and it certainly was beautiful. The most beautiful voice he had ever heard, it seemed.

"Mr. Hamilton, I must speak rapidly. We have probably upset the entire video system in thus attempting to get you. No doubt the connection will not remain for long," she spoke.

"You know me?" Roy replied, astonished. "I am sure that I have never had the pleasure of hearing your voice before."

"Please, please listen," begged the voice. "There is no time for explanations. What I have to say is of world importance and it may never again be possible to establish this contact."

"All right, lady. Go ahead," said Roy, though he had not the slightest idea as to what was coming.

"Remember from your history, the consolidation of the Powers in 1950?" asked the golden voice. "Remember the two thousand undesirables, sent away on the steamship *Gigantean?* The *Gigantean* which never returned, and from which no word ever came back to the world?

"The Terrestrial Government and the world at large thought they were well rid of a bad lot. But the *Gigantean* was not lost. Neither were the two thousand reactionaries; men and women from all walks of life. The ship eventually reached one of the uncharted islands of the Pacific, where the passengers landed and took up their abodes.

"With materials from the ship, they established their homes. With the machinery from the vessel, one of the scientists of their number did wonderful things. Soon he discovered means of producing a wall of neutralizing vibrations completely surrounding the island. This wall prevented and still prevents the approach of any visitors from the outside world, since under its influence all electrical and mechanical vibrations are entirely stopped. Thus no aeros have ever been able to reach the island, which they called Munan, and the secret has been preserved for four centuries and a half.

"Four hundred and fifty years they have multiplied and now number over a million persons. Many deadly secrets are in the hands of those, whom I must call my people, much as I hate to do so. The lust for revenge has been handed down from generation to generation and now they are prepared. The date has been set when a hundred thousand men will set forth to devastate and conquer the entire outside world, where peace and happiness have reigned these hundreds of years. With them will be carried the deadliest of weapons ever conceived by man, and these are of such nature that it is utterly impossible for your unprepared billions to combat them.

"I cannot dwell on the miseries of Munan. But a pitifully small group of us, mostly women, are against this move and we must prevent it. We have selected you, partly because of your own vitality and athletic prowess, partly because of your close friendship with Professor Nilsson. He, your greatest scientist, we believe will be able to avert this catastrophe, if anyone can.

"But you must both come to Munan. We are sure you will do this, as we have learned of the characters of both through the one spy we have been able to get through to the outside. Think of the utter destruction of probably three-quarters of your inhabitants, which you may be able to prevent.

"We have set the date for your arrival and at the appointed time we will contrive an accident which will temporarily remove the neutralizing wall and permit you to land on Munan. Convince Professor Nilsson of the extreme necessity of this and come in a fast aero. Win, and your reward will be the everlasting gratitude of the world. Fail, and your fate will be no worse than had you refused."

Here followed minute directions as to the exact location of Munan. Busy with pencil and paper, Roy barely had time in which to set down the latitude and longitude; also other necessary information, including the time and date when they would be expected. No sooner had he finished that the dim features and the golden voice faded from his video completely. He was left cold and trembling.

The soft pleading voice lingered in his mind to the exclusion of all else. He tried to picture the girl. Her vision had been terribly blurred, sometimes fading almost entirely from view. The voice, though! That told him that she must be young, lovely, tender. Ever a sentimentalist, he visioned more his meeting with this girl than he did the seriousness of the mission. Instantly, he decided that he would go.

"NY-19-635," spoke the humdrum voice of his videophone operator, "something has been wrong with the video for two hours and a half. The past half-hour it has been absolutely dead all through the terrestrial system; something never before experienced. However, all is well now and you may have your Paris connection."

"Oh, hang the Paris connection!" was Roy's reply. "Give me NY-20-325 right away."

"Hello, Roy," almost instantly responded the deep masculine voice of his friend, as the face of Professor Nilsson appeared in the disc, "what in the world are you calling about at this hour, and what are you so pale and mussed up over? Have you seen a ghost?"

"Maybe I have, Prof; but if I did, it was a ghost with a wonderful voice and such a story to tell as has never been heard before. This is serious. Can you come right over?"

"Well, seeing that it is you, my boy, and seeing that you look so ill, I will do it. But you know that I cannot remain for long."

"You may stay longer than you think, when you hear what I have to tell you."

"Maybe so; maybe not. At any rate, expect me in ten minutes. I am worried about you."

The voice and face of his dearest friend and advisor vanished, and Roy proceeded to remove his paint-bedaubed smock and brush his hair, so as to present a somewhat better appearance when the professor arrived. Observing his reflection in the glass over his dresser, he saw that he did indeed look shaky.

II.

By the time the professor arrived, Roy was in a much calmer mood, and was seriously going over the information he had jotted down. His friend rushed in, and when he looked at Roy he laughed aloud in relief.

"Well, you certainly look better. What happened to you, anyway?" was his greeting.

"Prof, when I tell you this story, you are going to be as hard hit as I was. Here; what do you make of this?" he said, handing over the paper on which his notations had been made.

"Why, Roy, this is the definite location of some place or other in terms of latitude and longitude. Also, I see the date February first, and the notation 'two A.M. Washington time.' Something about green beacons, too. Where did you get this and what does it mean?"

"That's my own handwriting, and I'll tell you in a minute how I came to write it. In the meantime, sit down and make yourself comfortable for a long talk."

"Roy, have you an atlas around this old workshop of yours?" asked the professor. He seemed suddenly to take more interest in the paper. "I believe this location is out in the uncharted wastes of the ocean somewhere."

"If it is, it will be pretty good proof of what I have to tell you," was the retort.

Roy produced the atlas and the professor at once turned to a double-page map of the western hemisphere.

"Just as I thought," he muttered. "Look here, Roy, are you spoofing me or what? There is not even an island within a thousand miles of this spot, and it is at least that far off any of the transoceanic aero lanes."

"Then it shows that I wasn't dreaming. Sit tight and listen to this yarn," said Roy, as they pulled their chairs close to the table.

With the golden voice softly whispering in his consciousness, Roy told his story. The professor listened intently; never interrupting, but occasionally starting in surprise, occasionally nodding as if in confirmation. Almost word for word, Roy repeated the plea of the girl as it had come to him, and when he had finished, the professor sat silent for several minutes, evidently deep in thought.

"Funny," he finally said, "I have always thought there was something mysterious about the disappearance of the *Gigantea*. You know she was the last one of the old floating ocean liners. When the Powers got together away back there in the middle of the twentieth century, and formed the Terrestrial Government, with headquarters in Washington, there still remained a group of widely scattered radicals, who were against the consolidation. They did not believe that war was actually made forever impossible by the many irresistible weapons which science had developed. They fought disarmament and the consolidation bitterly, and stirred up much discord. Finally, in desperation, the Terrestrial Government rounded up the ring-leaders in various parts of the world, put them on the *Gigantea* and told them to go wherever they pleased, but to never appear near any inhabited coast on pain of destruction, by means of beam energy, of the ship and themselves. With the abolishment of all surface travel on land and sea, and the establishment of the beam lanes uniting all countries with innumerable aero connections, this seemed easy. The only logical course for the exiles was exactly that which was explained by your mysterious voice. I am inclined to believe the whole story."

"I am, too," said Roy, "and I also think that we ought to see this thing through."

"Good for you, my boy. And I am with you to the end." They gripped hands.

Reaching for the paper on which Roy had scribbled the instructions, the professor again scanned it closely. "What is this about two green beacons?" he asked.

"The voice said that we were to land between two such lights when we reach Munan," answered Roy, "and that we could not possibly made a mistake about it, since all of the regular landing stages in Munan are lighted by white beacons at night. She said that they would have the green ones especially prepared for our arrival, and in a safe place."

"Strange that no one has discovered this hiding place in these hundreds of years," mused the professor. "But I suppose that fact that it is so far off the regular lanes of aero travel explains it. That, together with the fact that anyone who might by accident have reached it, never could have returned to tell the tale. Think, though, of how much spying on us they have been able to accomplish in all those ages. Quite naturally their civilization will be as far advanced as our own. They may have made even greater scientific advances than we, if that island has good natural resources. According to history, a number of eminent scientists were originally among them and the descendants of these would undoubtedly have obtained still further knowledge."

"Well, how about getting some sleep?" said Roy, with a yawn, "I am all worn out and tomorrow is another day. Shall we start making our preparations at once?"

"We certainly shall, as we have only a little over two weeks in which to get ready. Your suggestion about the sleep is a good one though, and I am going home. Good thing we are both bachelors and able to decide for ourselves. Well, good night, my boy. See you in the morning."

The professor was gone and Roy betook himself to bed.

III.

During the succeeding two weeks Roy and the professor were very busy indeed. Many things there were to be accomplished, and they dared take no one into their confidence. One of the most important items was to provide for some means of warning the world in case their mission should be unsuccessful. This was done by writing a complete record of the affair and the part they intended to take in it, sealing the records and depositing them with a bank president who was intimately known to the professor. They left instructions that the packet was to be opened only in case it was not called for in person on the fifteenth day of February at noon. They had two weeks from the time of their start in which to save mankind! And mankind had only five days from that period in which to save itself, if they failed! The date set by the Munanese was the twentieth.

This detail satisfactorily arranged, they applied themselves to the task of making ready for the journey to Munan. On the third day after the mysterious disarrangement of the videophone system, which was still the main topic of conversation and conjecture by the experts, the professor took Roy with him to his laboratory.

"Roy," he said, "I have a big surprise for you. One that I did not intend to make public at once. Possibly I shall never be able to publish it now. But it is going to serve us admirably in our present dilemma."

"We sure do need any help that can be obtained from your discoveries. I hope that you have something that will save the day," Roy said, as they entered the laboratory building.

"At least," said the professor, "we have here the vehicle which is going to carry us to Munan swiftly and safely. Whether it will bring us back, remains to be seen."

Leading the way to a large room on the second floor, he commenced removing the canvas cover from what resembled the hull of a small submarine boat of the early twentieth century. As the cover was completely withdrawn, there was revealed a cigar-shaped metal body about sixty feet long and fifteen feet in its largest diameter. This did in some way resemble the archaic under-water craft.

"This is a big surprise, my boy," the professor stated, "and we are going to have time to test it thoroughly before starting on the big adventure. This is an aero, the like of which has never before been constructed.

"Unlike the standard aeros mine does not depend upon beam energy for its motive power. Had we to rely upon the regular thing, we should be in a bad way for the job at hand. No existing beam could be used, since none are set for the proper direction. Thus we should have been compelled either to construct our own beam transmitter, for which there would not be time, or to take the Thomas Energy Company into our confidence and arrange for them to provide our power.

"My aero utilizes stray electronic energy as the old time sailing vessels used the winds of the ocean. But here we obtain both lifting force and propelling power from the losses of the regular energy beams. Of course you know that there are some losses in our standard beam transmission systems. These are very slight, but are constantly building up a supply of stray impulses, completely filling the earth's atmosphere envelope and extending far out into space. This storage of energy will continue as long as it remains unused, and until my discovery there was no means of tapping this huge reservoir. In the meanwhile all space is gradually filling up with these stray electrons, which are merely chasing each other about at terrific speed but producing no useful energy.

"The most important part of my discovery is a peculiar metal alloy which has the property of absorbing this potential energy and converting it into useful forms. If the use of this form of energy ever becomes universal, the present stored supply will eventually become exhausted. When this occurs, the use of the stray impulses will have to be reduced to a total amount not exceeding the usable losses of the regular energy systems. We have no free energy here and never will have. We are merely increasing the efficiency of the present energy systems."

They entered the aero, which was provided with a tiny galley, a small but perfectly equipped dining salon, a cabin having sleeping accommodations for twelve persons, and the control room which also contained the propelling machinery. Storage compartments, refrigerating and heating equipment and ballast filled the spaces between the rectilinear walls and floors and the curvilinear outer shell. Roy exclaimed at the luxury of the appointments as he followed the professor through the cabin and into the control room.

All of the propulsion machinery and the controls were housed in a cubicle in the bow which was not over twelve feet square. In the center of this, mounted on a heavy pedestal, was a sphere about two feet in diameter. For all the world this reminded Roy of one of the globes used during his school days in the study or the geography of the earth and other planets. The sphere was constructed of metal having a purplish tinge and its surface was covered with fine corrugations. Two small driving motors were in evidence, and the sphere was so mounted as to permit its axis to be swung into any angle with relation to the longitudinal axis of the cigar-shaped vessel. Mounted upon a pair of encircling rings and so arranged that its position with relations to the sphere could be varied at will, was a truncated cone about a foot long and six inches in diameter at the large end. This object was constructed of the same purplish metal and its axis was directed toward the contour of the sphere tangentially.

In the front of the room was the control platform. Two or three control levers, a periscope arrangement for obtaining unobstructed vision in all directions, and a glass case containing the navigating instruments completed the equipment of this pilot house.

"Is this all there is to it, Prof?" asked Roy.

"Absolutely all," replied the Professor. "Simple, is it not? Let me explain it to you briefly so that you will understand something of the operation of the aero which is to carry us on our mission.

"You have observed the sphere and the conical object trained upon it. Both are of adamite, the alloy which I mentioned. When in operation, the sphere is protonically charged, and the truncated cone of adamite collects the electrons, taking them from their regular orbits and redirecting them in a continuous stream against whichever portion of the sphere it is pointed at. If you remember your ancient history, you will recall that in the early twentieth century a vessel for travel on the ocean surface was invented by one Flettner. This vessel obtained its driving force from the winds by means of two large vertical rotors on the deck. In much the same way as these forces, we utilize the stray electronic energy to drive our aero.

"Our sphere may be rotated on its axis in any plane. The electron collector may be directed upon its surface at any angle. By proper adjustments of the angles and the speed of rotation of the sphere, we obtain both lifting power and propulsive force. The direction and speed of our vessel is determined by the force transmitted to its hull through the pedestal. This force is the resultant of the angles and velocities, and its direction and magnitude may be varied at will. We are not limited in this resultant force as was Flettner. He was dealing with winds of low velocity, whereas we are utilizing an electron stream with a velocity of 186,000 miles a second.

"The speed attainable by our aero is limited only by the density of the atmosphere and the temperature we can bear in our cabins. I have found that about six hundred miles per hour is as fast as I want to travel at ordinary altitudes, since at much greater speed the room temperature becomes somewhat uncomfortable, even with the refrigeration system in operation. This is due to the friction of the atmosphere on the hull. Of course at greater altitudes, the air density decreases and the speed may be proportionally increased. Were we to proceed outside the atmosphere, we should be able to approach the velocity of light, if we so desired."

This partial, but lucid, description was fairly well understood by Roy, and he was utterly astounded by what he had seen and heard. It seemed so absurdly simple that he wondered why it had not been thought of centuries ago. And what a storehouse of this energy must now be in reserve, he thought, after the centuries during which these stray impulses had been accumulating.

With the inspection of the *Pioneer*, as the professor had named his machine, completed, they went ahead with plans for the trip. It was agreed that Roy should gather and store in the *Pioneer*, all clothing, foodstuffs and the like which would be required, while the professor was to spend his time in stocking the aero with the scientific needs of the expedition.

The succeeding nine days were spent in making these preparations, and in making two trail trips in the *Pioneer*, the aero performing beautifully on both occasions. An important feature of the trail trips was Roy's instruction in the operation of the aero. He learned easily, and was pronounced a finished pilot at the end of the second journey.

All was in readiness on the twenty-eighth of January and the two men contemplated the results of their labor with satisfaction. Roy had provided several changes of raiment for both; tropical and arctic regalia being included, in case of their being taken far from their course and making a forced landing in some rigorous climate. Condensed, but appetizing food and drink had been provided in sufficient quantity for a two months trip in case so long a time was found necessary for some unforeseen reason. All such supplies had been carefully stowed away in the rear compartments of the *Pioneer.*

The professor had installed oxygen apparatus on board the *Pioneer* in case of the necessity of entering high altitudes. He had packed away, in various compartments, numbers of scientific instruments. The purposes of these were unknown to Roy, but the professor assured him that many might be found necessary. Stores of chemicals and of laboratory equipment for chemical experiments were included. The professor also had taken a number of odd weapons from his extensive collection. Some of these he said were very effective, regardless of the ancient source. In addition to these, he told Roy, there were weapons of his own devising, which might prove a great surprise to the Munanese, should it become necessary to use them.

With this work completed, the professor set about plotting their course. He proved to be no mean navigator. To be on the safe side, he figured on an average speed of four hundred miles an hour. Their course as laid out, passed directly over New Orleans and measured almost exactly seven thousand miles from New York. It therefore behooved them to leave seventeen and a half hours in advance of the time set by the girl for their arrival. This meant that the start would be made at eight thirty in the morning of January thirty-first, and arrangements were made accordingly.

In the short time intervening, the two were occupied in straightening our their personal affairs so that all would be in order in case of their failure to return. This was a comparatively simple matter for each, since neither had any immediate relatives to be concerned over.

Finally the morning of the fateful day arrived, bright and clear but very cold. At a half hour before the appointed time, both men were at the laboratory.

The sliding roof had been opened over the *Pioneer* and all was in readiness. With the interior of the aero comfortably heated, both men sat in the control room watching the minute hand of the chronometer as it approached the time of eight thirty. Minutes seemed hours and neither spoke.

At last the time was at hand, and the professor was at the controls. Precisely on the minute, he turned the switch which started the sphere revolving, and adjusted its angle with reference to the cone, which was pointed directly upward beneath the sphere. Without a sound, the *Pioneer* arose vertically, gathering speed as the revolutions of the sphere became faster and faster. They were off!

IV.

When the needle of the altimeter registered four thousand feet, the professor changed the angles of the sphere and cone, headed in a southwesterly direction, and settled down to a steady speed of four hundred miles an hour.

At eleven eighteen by the chronometer they passed over New Orleans, and by eleven forty were headed out across the Gulf of Mexico. At one thirty in the afternoon they were leaving the southwest coast of Mexico and passing over the broad expanse of the Pacific. The professor now turned the controls over to Roy, instructing him to keep the helm so adjusted that the needle of the inductor compass continued to point to the vertical mark. The altimeter was to be kept at four thousand feet while the professor when astern for his lunch.

Roy took the controls with enthusiasm. He could not understand the professor's matter-of-factness, though he could understand his hunger, as neither had stopped for breakfast. Roy was beginning to feel the pangs of hunger himself. They were more than five hours out now; practically a third of their journey had been completed. As time passed, the impression left in Roy's mind by the golden voice which had brought about this trip, became stronger and stronger. The rich, mellow tones of this voice seemed to ring in his ears, drawing him on. Something within his consciousness told him that he was going to his destiny. Reckless of the future, this thought grew on him until he began planning all sorts of things. But these were happy thoughts; somehow he had no thought of the dangers to be encountered, nor of the fact that his own life and those of countless billions of his fellow-men depended on the success of this expedition.

His meditations were cut short by the return of his friend, who announced that he was feeling much better after a hearty lunch. Relinquishing the control, Roy suddenly realized that he was even hungrier than he had thought, and betook himself to the miniature saloon for his own lunch. He found that the professor had kindly prepared an appetizing meal for him. An atomic percolator on the table was busily preparing steaming hot coffee for him, and he shouted his thanks through to the professor before he sat down to eat. The meal was piping hot and delicious. He returned to the controls much refreshed.

By now it was four p.m. by the chronometer; their journey was nearly half over. As Roy peered at the periscope reflector, noting that nothing but the tumbling surface of the Pacific was visible in all directions far below them, the professor startled him with a remark:

"Well, we will not be running into darkness for hours yet, but if my weather sense is correct, we are going to encounter a storm very soon."

"What," exclaimed Roy, "no darkness for hours? Why, it is after four o'clock now, and these are the shortest days of the year."

"Yes. Four o-'clock, Washington time," said the professor, dryly, "but you must remember that we have been traveling away from the sunset hour. We shall not see nightfall for four hours or more, if my dead reckoning is correct. At two a.m. tomorrow by our time, we shall be in Munan. There it will be only ten p.m. of today's date."

"Right. I never thought of the difference in time, Prof," was Roy's response, "but look at the periscope. Isn't that a storm coming up, way ahead of us?"

"Yes, that must be the one I smelled," the professor responded, "but the *Pioneer* has nothing to fear. We shall simply go up over it, and I hope that by the time we reach Munan, the storm will have passed. In fact, I know it will, because such storms usually cover a comparatively small area, although they travel rapidly. However, their speed is as nothing compared with ours, and even if it is traveling in the direction of Munan, we shall far outdistance it."

With that the professor manipulated the controls, and the altimeter at once showed the increase in altitude. Six thousand, eight, ten, twelve thousand feet and there it stopped.

"There is no real need of rising further, as we shall be well above the storm now," said the professor. "But I would like to test out the oxygen apparatus, so we are going up further. I shall be compelled to correct my reckoning on this account, but that will not be difficult, and if we lose any time, it can be quickly made up by increased speed."

Closing one valve and opening another, the professor pulled back the altitude control; the cone swung way around to a new position, and the *Pioneer* shot skyward at an angle of about forty-five degrees.

"That is what those railings around the operating platform are there for," laughed the professor, as Roy swung about and wildly grabbed for one to keep his balance. "Better strap yourself into the seat beside mine here, as we may do a little more of this sort of thing before we return to a lower level."

Roy complied, as the professor adjusted his own strap. A slight hiss told of the functioning of the oxygen apparatus, and Roy glanced at the altimeter. Already it showed forty thousand feet, and was mounting rapidly. Their speed was tremendous; fifty thousand feet a minute now by the 'rate of rise' indicator. At their angle, this meant over eleven hundred miles an hour, air speed. Fifty, seventy, one hundred, two, three, four hundred thousand feet read the altimeter and there was the *Pioneer* restored to an even keel. Roy took a deep breath. It was becoming very cold, but the professor had already turned on the atomic heat and soon the control room returned to normal temperature.

"I must provide for thermostatic control of the room temperature, when I get the time," spoke the professor, more to himself than to Roy, "but our oxygen supply seems to function perfectly anyhow. We are far outside the upper limits of the atmosphere now, and we have been for several minutes."

"Everything seems to work to perfection," was Roy's only reply, as the descent started at a reduced speed.

When they had finally returned to their altitude of four thousand feet, the storm was far astern, but they could see from the turbulent surface of the ocean that it had been a serious squall. The professor again gave over the controls to Roy and disappeared astern. He returned soon and announced that they were but slightly off their course and somewhat ahead of their time schedule, rather than behind. Making a minor correction in the setting of the compass, he told Roy that he wanted to lie down for a short while to get a little rest, and returned to the cabin.

Roy had plenty of time in which to think while the professor rested, and as the distance to Munan became rapidly less, he thought more and more on the seriousness of their mission. Still the voice which had brought them kept intruding on his consciousness. He began to believe that there was some thought transference connected with this, for he simply could not shake off the impression of the voice. It was now somewhat different than when he had heard it over the video; then it had been sad and pleading; now it was confident, cheering. But it retained the charm, the golden quality which had first interested and captivated him.

When the professor returned, night had long since fallen and only a few hours of the trip remained. He advised Roy to get some sleep himself, saying that he would remain at the controls anyway until they had landed. Roy was too excited, however, and occupied the seat at the professor's side for the rest of the journey.

At last only a half hour remained and soon, directly ahead, they made out a faint speck of light which grew rapidly in size until it was finally discerned as the lights of a city in the distance. Again the *Pioneer* arose until an altitude of about fifteen thousand feet was attained. All lights were extinguished, with the exception of the small ones in the instrument case, and soon they were directly over Munan. The time was exactly two by their chronometer as the vertical descent commenced, and in a few seconds they made out the outlines of the island.

The city itself occupied only a small portion of the island's surface. The remainder of its area was in darkness, with the exception of scattered groups of lights which probably marked the locations of farms and mines. Shortly, they located two tiny spots of green light in one of the darkest spots on the island.

"Your friend certainly kept her word," said the professor, as he maneuvered the *Pioneer* to a position directly over the two green beacons, which appeared to be about three hundred feet apart. "The neutralizing wall must have been out of service all right, and there are the green beacons as big as life."

Swiftly, but without a shock at landing, the *Pioneer* dropped between the two guiding lights and came to rest as the professor opened the switch.

V.

With his pulses beating madly, Roy rushed to the manhole, which was the only exit, as well as entrance to the *Pioneer*. He desired to be the first to set foot on the soil of Munan, but the professor stopped him as he began to unfasten the clamping bolts.

"Not so fast," warned the professor. "We are not sure whether we will be met by friend or foe. Possibly the enemy has learned of your friend's plans and has only allowed us to land so as to make away with us before our world can be warned again. We had better go out armed. Better to die fighting, if we have to die. And if we are met by friends, it will do no harm."

"Professor, you are always right," admitted Roy, as the professor went to the locker where he had stored his weapons.

He returned at once with two small pistol-like contrivances, one of which he thrust into Roy's hand.

"This," he said, "is a very ancient weapon. In fact, this device is one of those which contributed in bringing about the conference of the Powers in 1950, resulting in the disarmament and consolidation of the various peoples of our world. This device <projects the disintegration ray which immediately destroys entirely any animate object at which it is directed. Just press this little button and the ray shoots forth, but be sure you have it pointed in the right direction. I am sure that this is just as effective now as it ever was, but we do not know what sort of weapons we may have to combat here. But I suppose we are as well prepared as we can be, under the circumstances."

The arm was examined curiously by Roy, who had never seen one before, except in the museum.

Unbolting the manhole cover and swinging it open, the professor courteously allowed Roy to leave first, knowing that he was extremely anxious for this honor. They stepped forth into the darkness—even the green lights were now extinguished. Cautiously they left the *Pioneer* and advanced into a clearing which was dimly visible by the faint light from what few stars were out. Weapons in hand, they waited breathlessly.

Suddenly a voice spoke, clear, sweet, compelling. Roy's heart seemed to leap and turn over in his body. It was the golden voice of his dreams, and very softly it spoke the words of welcome which he would never forget.

"Dear, brave strangers from The Outside. I was sure you would come. Roy, I have been sending my thoughts out to you for the better part of twelve hours. Several times we were almost *en rapport*, never quite. Professor, I know you will not fail in this great undertaking. I thank both of you with the deepest gratitude. Follow me to our hiding place, where we shall meet the rest of my group and find a haven for your aero, and rest for yourselves."

While speaking, the girl of the golden voice approached the two until finally she stood beside them. By this time their eyes had become more accustomed to the darkness, and they made out the dim outlines of a small figure, evidently cloaked in some dark material. The features could not be discerned even when she stood directly before them, but the voice of their welcomer thrilled them both.

She grasped Roy's hand, and at its touch his body tingled from head to foot as from an electric shock. Surely the possessor of this tiny and delicate, although firm, hand needed assistance and protection, he thought as they were led in silence towards the edge of the clearing, where the tree-tops were faintly visible against the almost black sky. As they neared these trees there was a slight rustle ahead of them, and a masculine voice spoke out in a very low tone:

"Is all well, Thelda?"

"All is well, Ramon. You may light your torch," she replied, and with that there was a click and the beams of a hand light revealed the way ahead through the forest.

For a short way they traversed a heavily wooded space and soon, after emerging from the woods and climbing a slight grade in the open, approached the base of a sheer vertical cliff of stratified rock. Feeling along an entirely smooth and unmarked section of this wall, Ramon, their guide, soon found the depression for which he was searching. At his touch, a section of the solid stone swung back, revealing the entrance to a long, unlighted passage. They entered and silently the stone door swung behind them. With the way lighted only by the beams from Ramon's torch, they followed a winding passage for a considerable distance and finally reached a large circular cavern, which was so brilliantly lighted as to dazzle them temporarily.

Their guide led them directly to a large council table, around which were seated some thirty people, only about six of them were men. As they reached the group, all eyes were focused on the strangers, but Roy's eyes were only for the girl at his side. She threw off her cloak as she turned to the council table, and there stood revealed in her transcendent beauty. Even the professor gasped; Roy stood spellbound.

Although small in stature, her slimness and the erectness of her carriage gave her the appearance of greater height. Vibrant with life, her face was turned partly towards Roy, so that he was enabled to study the perfect profile intently. Fluffy red-gold hair seemed a fitting halo for the piquant oval of ivory creaminess which was her face. Large, golden brown eyes, wide set beneath perfectly arched brows, with their expression of sadness and innocent appeal, belied the firmness of the small chin, the sauciness of the very slightly upturned little nose, and the sweet promise of the rosy lips, now barely parted in excitement.

The words of her presentation of them to the assembly were unimportant to Roy's ears; the voice and the girl herself held him in a trance. To him she became the "Golden Girl" at once. Her mellow voice; her golden coloring; the beautiful spirit revealed by her spoken thoughts; all contributed to this impression. Thelda, her name might be; but in Roy's innermost thoughts she would always remain the "Golden Girl." Then and there he resolved that, whatever the cost, he was going to win this girl for his wife and take her from this terrible island to his own home.

"People," she spoke to the assembled listeners, "these are the two of whom we learned so much through the visit of Thandar to 'The Outside.' This man," turning to Roy, "is Roy Hamilton, to whom I made my plea on the night when we disrupted the videophone system of The Outside. This man," nodding in the professor's direction, "is Professor Nilsson, the famous scientist of The Outside, in whom we have placed our hopes. Both, as we all know, are brave, courageous men, and I am sure that our confidence has not been misplaced. May the Supreme Power, in which we few of all Munanese believe and trust, be their guide and protector."

Thelda then sat at the head of the council table, and her glance met Roy's. A slow flush heightened her beauty and told Roy that his feelings were at least partly returned. Frankly the eyes of each appraised the other.

A handsome and imposing man, who sat at Thelda's right, arose and addressed the strangers:

"Gentlemen, I am Landon, Thelda's chief advisor," he spoke. "Our dear leader has brought about your coming to us. Like her, we cannot convey to you adequately our gratitude for your noble response to our appeal. We thank you in the name of mankind, which is ignorant of the fate with which it is threatened. For ourselves we care not. Many of those here may lose their lives in this undertaking. One lost his life tonight in contriving the power house accident which closed off the neutralizing wall for a half hour to permit your entrance. We have terrible powers to combat; but we feel sure that, with the help of you two, we shall succeed. After you have obtained the rest which you so badly require after your arduous journey, I shall again call the council together and our entire problem will be placed before you. Our workmen have, by this time, transported your aero to an adjoining cavern, and we believe that you will find yourselves more at home in your own quarters than in any we could provide. We shall now disband until tomorrow and allow you to return to your aero."

With Landon's conclusion, all members arose from the council table and crowded around the two strangers, introducing themselves, and overwhelming Roy and the professor with thanks and with wishes for a good night's rest. These people were a remarkably striking looking lot; the men were physically very powerful and of classic and dignified features; the women, though slightly smaller in stature than those of the outside world, were far more beautiful, with a loveliness that was almost ethereal in character. None could compare with Thelda though; and, as he and the professor were led to another passage by Ramon, Roy kept his eyes on her until she was lost to his view.

They found the *Pioneer* reposing on the floor of another huge cavern similar to the first. Ramon explained that an opening to the outer atmosphere had been provided at the top of this cavern and that this was of sufficient size, though hidden by underbrush which grew at the top of the cliff, to permit of easy entrance and exit for their aero. How the *Pioneer* had been transported to this spot, he did not explain. This cavern was unlighted, and they were left at the manhole of the aero in darkness as Ramon departed with his torch.

Entering and flooding the *Pioneer* with its own light, they soon disrobed and, without further discussion, sank into the deep sleep of utter exhaustion.

VI.

Roy awoke at one, by his watch; nine o'clock in the morning by Munan time, he remembered, and set his timepiece back accordingly. Finding the professor still asleep, he dressed quietly so as not to disturb him and set forth to investigate his new surroundings. He stepped out from the *Pioneer* and found the cavern in which she reposed dimly alight from a circular opening high overhead, though which the light of day was admitted, and through which it would be necessary to guide the aero when they left. He returned for a pocket torch, and started down the passage through which they had entered this cavern. When he reached the large council chamber, he found it as brightly lighted as previously. On the far side of the cavern he observed a sort of raised dais on which there was a smaller table than that about which the company had assembled the previous night; also several easy chairs, one of which was occupied by none other than the Golden Girl, who was busily engaged with several books and a large map. At<#the> sight of her beautiful head bent over her work, his heart again behaved unaccountably, and he approached silently, almost reverently.

When within a few feet of the dais, he spoke. "Good afternoon, fair lady. Or rather I should say, 'good morning.'"

Somewhat startled, for she had been so absorbed in her work, that she did not notice his approach, she raised her head. When she saw who it was, she smiled and replied, "Good morning, Roy. I hope that you are new refreshed after a good sleep. And you must not mind my use of your given name. That is our custom. You are to call me Thelda, too."

Again, when their glances met, there was that indefinable something which passed between their minds and told both that a close bond existed. Each was momentarily confused, but Roy seated himself, as Thelda motioned him to a chair beside her own, and soon the embarrassed feeling passed. They found themselves at once discussing seriously the object of the trip from The Outside, as the outer world was spoken of in Munan. Roy was full of eager questions concerning Munan itself, and Thelda launched forth into a discussion of the subject nearest and dearest to her heart.

It seemed that Thelda had been the only daughter of one Paul Serano, who had been the leader of the small group of thinkers who were opposed to the designs of the Munanese against The Outside. He had been working on plans for frustrating these designs for ten years. Thelda's mother had died at the time he first conceived these plans, and Thelda herself had been but ten years of age when this occurred. A few months before the call to Roy and the professor, Serano had been apprehended by the Zar in an attempt to obtain certain information regarding the exact nature of the plans for the conquest of The Outside, and had been summarily executed. This left Thelda an orphan, hunted by the Zar; and the group of faithful adherents to her father's beliefs had made her their leader in his stead. Despite the fact that she was only twenty, she was well qualified to lead them, because she was not only greatly loved by the group, but she had worked with her father constantly since the conception of his idea and was more familiar than any of the others with that which had been accomplished. She was compelled to live in apartments connected with this underground refuge, as were several others of the group, to escape the hand of the all-powerful Zar. Luckily, however, most of the group were not known by the agents of the Zar as being non-adherents. These were enabled thus to live normal lives in the city, and ten or twelve of them were in the employ of the Zarists, endeavoring to get all information possible. Thelda's father had been a scientist of repute in Munan; the only scientist in the group; and with his demise the group had become desperate, for it was necessary to combat the designs of the Munanese by means of Science. This had necessitated the sending of an emissary to The Outside, which was accomplished with considerable difficulty. The emissary had returned with knowledge of the professor and of his friend, Roy. The call to New York had followed.

By the time Thelda had reached this point in her narrative, the two were joined by the professor. Soon the party was augmented by the arrival of Landon and two of the women members of the group, who were known as Zora and Merna. Zora was a very beautiful woman of possibly forty years of age; nearly that of the professor, thought Roy, as he noted from the corner of his eye that she and the professor had engaged in earnest conversion.

Thelda and Landon decided that it was not necessary to call a meeting of the council, but that the entire situation could be discussed immediately among themselves. Landon was requested to give to the two strangers the entire story in as few words as possible. This being agreeable to all present, the six proceeded to the council table, where a map of the island and city of Munan had been laid out.

Roy and the professor examined this map closely, noting that the island was roughly elliptical in shape, about seventy miles in length and about thirty miles across the widest point. On the map, surrounding the island at a distance of some five miles from the coast, was a broad red line which Landon explained represented the neutralizing wall. The city itself occupied only one end. The rest of the island, which was of volcanic origin, consisted of part mountain and part level land, a small portion of which was covered by forest. The caverns were located almost exactly in the center, and were under the surface of a mesa-like projection of the largest mountain, which was known as Leyris.

"Friends from The Outside," commenced Landon, "there is much to be done within the next twenty days, if the designs of our accursed people are to be circumvented. For this reason I am going to make my story as short as possible.

"Beginning with the founding of Munan and leading up to the present time, I need not tell you much more than Thelda reported over your videophone system. That conversation was very difficult of attainment, for none of us fully understand the operation of the apparatus which Paul had perfected for this very purpose before his death. However, we did paralyze the terrestrial video system as you know, and Thelda did get her message through.

"Munan was conceived in hatred, and the descendants of those original two thousand have handed down that hatred of The Outside, which gradually intensified through the ages. In each generation there would be a few who, like ourselves, were born with the love of mankind in their hearts, but as quickly as these were discovered by the Zar they were killed off in cold blood. Thus, by a process of enforced evolution, there was developed a race of cold-blooded creatures who call themselves men and women, but who are in actuality, fiends incarnate. There has been practically no internal strife, because the Munanese has a single-track mind. His venom is all directed against The Outside. Such is the power of evolution. Our group is entirely different. In all evolution there are reversions to types, which types may have been remotely located in the roots of the family tree. We are those reversions; thank the Supreme Being. We were born with love in our makeup instead of hate, and none of the early training could remove this love.

"Zar Taled the fourth, our present despotic ruler, decided about fifteen years ago that the time for the conquest of The Outside was nearing: he set the date for February twentieth, 2406. Meanwhile all efforts of the inhabitants, excepting those in pursuits necessary for the business of living, such as food preparation and the like, have been expended in preparation for the great event.

"The time is approaching rapidly and all is in readiness. Ten thousand aeros have been constructed; each is capable of carrying ten men and a cargo of ten tons. These are stored under heavy guard in the Zar's arsenal directly on the other side of Leyris. They are the product of the not-to-be-despised scientists of Munan, and are very speedy and powerful. The secret of their motive power is known only to a trusted few; but we do know that it is from an inexhaustible source. These aeros, like your own, have no external wings or propelling mechanism. Unlike the *Pioneer*, though, they are provided with an impregnable means of defense and a horrible and inescapable offensive weapon. They can be made invisible! The mines of Munan have yielded metals and chemical elements unknown to The Outside, and from these our chemists have compounded a substance similar in consistency to the house paint of ancient days. This substance, when applied to its surface, renders the metal munium invisible. The Zar's aeros are constructed of munium and will be painted with this compound. Thus the aeros and all they contain will be absolutely non-existent as far as human vision is concerned. What avail would any of the energy beams of The Outside be against an attacker who could not be seen?

"The offensive weapon is also a product of our chemists. It is a highly concentrated liquid which has the property of completely disintegrating any object with which it may come in contact, excepting only the metal crysinum. The ingredients of this liquid are found only in Munan and are extremely rare, even here. Two hundred years have been spent in accumulating a sufficient supply and storing it away in crysinum containers. One drop of this liquid on the *Pioneer* would utterly destroy it and all within it. A crysinum bomb weighing less than one hundred pounds, dropped from the sky on your city of New York, would entirely destroy it with all of its inhabitants, and all within a radius of thirty miles besides. Do you see why we warned you and sent for you?

"The centuries old plan of the Munan is this: On the day appointed, ten thousand aeros, rendered invisible, are to set forth. Each aero will carry a crew of ten men and a cargo of two hundred of the crysinum bombs. Two thousand of the aeros are to head for the North American division, two thousand to the African division, two thousand to the European division and so forth. Each fleet is to spread out over its particular area, destroying the principal cities and industrial centers. No quarter is to be given; in fact none could be asked, since the inhabitants would not have the slightest idea of the cause of the destruction, nor where to sue for quarter. After the wanton destruction of all the great cities and probably eighty per cent of the population of the globe, the Munanese intend to take possession and start the foundations of a new civilization in accordance with their own ideas.

"The small group you saw in this chamber when you arrived, with a few workmen who were taking care of your aero, and your two selves, are all that stand between The Outside and this dreadful catastrophe. Possibly we shall fail; but we have every confidence in you. Professor, as the only man who can avert the holocaust; and in you, Roy, as a valiant supporter of our cause and of the professor in his part of the work. That is all."

VII.

At the finish of Landon's talk, Thelda had bowed her head into her arms, which had been folded before her on the table. Roy sat in stunned silence, while the professor drummed nervously on the table top with his fingers, staring at Landon all the while. Finally the processor started shooting rapid-fire questions at Landon, and Thelda straightened up with interest, though her eyes were brimming with tears. Roy wanted then, more than anything in the world, to take her in his arms; to comfort her and cheer her. He had the utmost confidence in the professor's wizardry.

"Landon," asked the professor, "you say these invisible aeros are stored in an arsenal directly across and on the other side of this mountain?"

"Yes, that is correct, Professor, but this arsenal is under heavy guard, you must remember," replied Landon.

"Have you any samples of the metal crysinum and of the deadly liquid with which the bombs are filled?"

"We have several articles constructed of crysinum but the liquid has never been seen by any of us. In fact, so great is the secrecy surrounding the production of this liquid that the chemists engaged in the work have been kept isolated by the

several Zars for centuries. The secret has been handed down through the generations of this one family, who have all been chemists."

"Have you knowledge of the exact location of the storage vault of the crysinum
bombs, Landon?"

"We have suspicion that they are stored in caverns similar to these, under the
arsenal on the other side of Leyris. Even now, one of our number who is employed
in the arsenal, is investigating this very point. She may be discovered as a spy at any
time and executed. When Doreen, for that is her name, joins us, you may question
her yourself, Professor."

"Very good, Landon. Now you might enlighten me on just one more point.
You say that Paul Serano, before his death, had developed the equipment with which
you paralyzed the video and made the call to Roy. Is that equipment still in existence?"

"It is, Professor. It is located in a smaller cavern only a few steps from here. I
will show it to you."

At this the professor arose and followed Landon through another winding
passage, up a flight of steps cut into the stone, and to a small compartment fitted
out as a workshop. As he examined the various mechanisms in this room, some
completed, others only partly so, he commented to Landon regarding the stone
steps that they had just mounted. These were considerably worn as if by long usage,
and Landon gravely explained that the caverns had been the refuge of similar fugitives for centuries.

"It is a pity that Paul could not have lived to complete his wonderful work,"
remarked the professor in admiration, as he examined some of the results of Serano's
labor, "but I do see a faint glimmer of hope here. For one thing, here is a beam-
transmitter not unlike some of our own, and after I master its workings, we may be
able to find a good use for it."

When they returned to the council chamber, several others of the group had
arrived, and the professor sat at the table and addressed them:

"Friends, I do not want to seem officious," he said, "but I believe it will be to
the advantage of all concerned if you will give complete authority to me over all
activities of the group from now on. I see a vague basis for hope, but our work must
be done with the greatest care, or failure will be the result. Will this be agreeable?"

Thelda answered at once, "Indeed it will, Professor. I am sure that all here will
agree now, and I can vouch for the rest. We trust you implicitly and I, for one, feel
encouraged already. Do the rest of you here consent?"

There was a chorus of assent, and the professor asked at once, "Where is
Doreen, the lady member, who, you stated, was employed at the arsenal?"

Doreen and the professor drew aside to a settee and conversed animatedly for
several minutes. Roy saw that Zora watched this procedure closely, and he chuckled
to himself. When the professor returned to the council table, he stated that he would

like to have some private conversation with Roy. Not that he had any secret plans, he explained, but that he wanted Roy's advice on something he had in mind before putting it to the test. Naturally there was no objection, so he and Roy retired to Serano's workshop.

"Roy," he said as they entered the room, "this is even more serious than I had contemplated, and although I have an idea forming in my mind already, there is one big obstacle which may block the successful carrying out of the plan. The young lady I just spoke with told me that she is confident that the supply of the deadly liquid and of the crysinum bombs is in one greater chamber immediately beneath the arsenal. She has, however, been unable to locate this chamber, and is now fearful of entire failure, since she has been under more or less suspicion for several days. It is absolutely necessary that I obtain a sample of this liquid; also that the precise location of the supply be determined. One possibility is suggested by another statement of Doreen's. She told me that Pietro, the commander in charge of the arsenal—a man with a viciousness of disposition not exceeded by any of the Munanese—has a soft spot in his heart for Zora, who is employed in the Zar's palace as tutor to his children. She suggests that, through Zora, this information might be obtained."

The professor flushed as he repeated the last words, much to Roy's secret delight. "Well, how do you think this could be arranged?" asked Roy.

"By the usual power of woman over man," he replied. "The trouble in this case is that Zora has repulsed him for years. Besides, she is under constant surveillance in the daytime, when in the Zar's household. I hesitate to approach her on the subject, as I consider her a very high type of woman and she might seriously resent the suggestion. What do you think?"

"But," Roy answered, "we are all in this thing to the bitter end, and I am sure that she, as well as any of the other, will do anything that might be necessary. I can see your interest in this admirable woman—as you, no doubt, can see mine in the glorious Thelda. But we must not think of personal preferences now. My advice is to put it up to her at once."

They reentered the council chamber, and the professor called Thelda, Zora, and Landon aside to talk over the matter. To his surprise, Zora did not oppose the plan, although she made it plain how repugnant it was to her to be compelled to change her attitude with respect of Pietro's suit. She felt, however, that she would be able to act the part. Knowing how important such a move might be, she did not hesitate. It was decided that she would return to her duties and again take up her normal life in her city apartment, using her own judgment as to the best means of ensnaring Pietro and inveigling him into a disclosure of the desired information. It was with the deepest regret that the professor completed the arrangements and, as a final precaution, he provided Zora with one of their ancient hand weapons and taught her how to use it. Zora felt that at least a week would be required for her work, and the portion of the group which was assembled bid her good-bye and good luck when she left. The professor accompanied her to the end of the passageway and did not return for some little time. What took place between them at this parting will never be recorded. But when he returned, he seated himself at the council table with the most serious mien he had displayed since their arrival.

VIII.

After Thelda, Landon, Roy, and the professor had partaken of a satisfying luncheon in Thelda's apartments, they returned to the council chamber. The professor and Landon repaired to Serano's workshop where they spent the afternoon, thus leaving Roy and Thelda together. This suited Roy exactly, and did not seem to be unpleasant to Thelda, either. She spent the time showing him through the various connecting caverns of the underground refuge, and the several luxurious living compartments which had been hollowed from the solid rock. The permanent dwellers were mostly in their living quarters and Roy became better acquainted with these during the several visits they made. More and more was he impressed with the beauty and sweetness of the women in the group. They far outshone the beautiful women of The Outside, not only in physical perfection but in mentality as well. He soon observed that much of their conversation was perfunctory, and seemed to be only a medium of establishing contact for an actual interchange of thoughts. When he remarked about his, Thelda informed him that thought transference among the group was a common accomplishment; that it was a development of their own mentalities and was not shared by the Munanese in general. This amazed Roy and to him accounted for some of the sensations he had had of hearing the golden voice when he was still thousands of miles from Munan. What if Thelda was not reading his thoughts? If she were she must already know that he loved her. It must be then, that she was not unreceptive, since her actions were very friendly, even affectionate. True, this might be due to her gratitude to the two strangers for their response to her plea for assistance. Try as he would he could obtain no inkling of what was in the mind to which his own must be almost an open book. But his resolve to win this glorious creature did not abate in the slightest degree.

That night when the council assembled, Zora, Doreen, and Ramon were missing. They had anticipated the absence of the courageous Zora, but the non-arrival of the other two caused considerable uneasiness in the group.

Thelda, in calling the meeting to order, advised the members of what had been done thus far. Unanimous approval was given of the acceptance of the professor's leadership, and of what he had already accomplished. The professor then arose and addressed them:

"Dear people. I am not ready as yet to give you any real hope; but I can say that my research thus far has been successful, and that if your dear comrade, Zora, succeeds in her mission, out hopes will be strong indeed. The time is very short, but there is nothing which can be done outside of that which is now being attempted. It will be necessary for Roy and myself to remain hidden away here with those of you who are already forced to reside here permanently. I know that this will gall the adventurous spirit of my friend from The Outside, but it is absolutely imperative, for if either of us ventured forth into Munan and were recognized as strangers and captured by the Zar's police, all of our plans would be brought to naught.

"This afternoon, with the aid of Landon, who provided me with samples of metal crysinum, I have learned several things of value. As you know, crysinum is as transparent as crystal, as hard as steel, and as light as aluminum. Today I have, in your deceased leader's workshop, succeeded in making a chemical analysis of this metal, also in determining its electrical and mechanical properties. I have also constructed several vessels from this material: retorts, beakers, test tubes, for use in analyzing the deadly fluid when we obtain a sample. The most important work of the afternoon was the construction of a receptacle of crysinum which may be used for obtaining the required sample with safety. This receptacle must be placed in Zora's hands at once, and I would like to have a volunteer to carry it to the city without delay."

Two-thirds of the assembly volunteered at once, and the professor chose the young woman Allayne and the man Theron to accompany her. Both were residents in the city and, so far, had not been under suspicion. Allayne was well acquainted with the location of Zora's apartment, and Theron was physically well able to protect her from any ordinary danger she might encounter. When these two left, the professor continued:

"What we would like to do is to obtain one of the crysinum bombs from the Zar's storage vault, load it and out<our> entire group into my aero, rise vertically ten or fifteen thousand feet and destroy this island by dropping the deadly bomb from the aero. The group could then proceed to The Outside at leisure, since the destruction of the city and its power houses would forever remove the neutralizing wall. Unfortunately, this is impossible, since the size and weight of one of the bombs is entirely too great to permit its successful removal from the heavily guarded secret storehouse. Our next best hope is to obtain a small sample of the compound, with the idea that I shall be able to determine some means of destroying the entire supply from a distance. That is the reason for Zora's distasteful assignment, and that is why I have sent Allayne and Theron with the crysinum receptacle. Let us have hope."

When the professor finished, there was a babble of excited voices. All seemed pleased with his progress and all were considerably encouraged. As the evening wore on, the uneasiness over the continued absence of Ramon and Doreen increased. Surely some misfortune must have overtaken both. All that could be done was to hope and pray that they had not been apprehended; that the safety of the remainder of the group had not been endangered by their capture, if captured they had been.

It was very later when Theron and Allayne returned, and their report confirmed the worst fears of the group regarding the missing members. Doreen had been arrested in the arsenal and executed by the Zarist troops, after being tortured savagely in an effort to learn of the whereabouts and identity of her accomplices. The brave girl had steadfastly remained silent and finally died a noble martyr to the cause she had espoused. Ramon had been killed outright by a police officer, when he was discovered in an attempt to carry away some records from the administrative offices of the Zar's "Council of Five," where he was employed. In sadness was this news received by the group. The report of the successful meeting with Zora did little to cheer them up. As yet Zora had been able to do nothing; the turmoil caused by Doreen's discovery made it unthinkable to approach Pietro in any way.

For several days Roy was in a miserable state of mind. The professor spent practically all of his time in the workshop, and Roy felt absolutely useless as an adjunct to the group. What made him feel still worse was the fact that he was being studiously avoided by Thelda. She addressed him pleasantly enough when he saw her, it was true. But he found it impossible to engage her in conversation alone. She always made some excuse to get away, and the little intimate talks in which they had engaged on the first day could not be repeated. After the fifth day he became morose and uncommunicative, spending the greater part of his time in the *Pioneer*. Little as he saw of the professor, he spoke very little to him when he did see him.

Finally the professor, busy as he was, noticed this, and took Roy to task one night when he returned to his sleeping quarters. "Roy," he said, "do not let this thing break your spirit. What is tormenting you anyhow?"

"Well, for one thing," was the response, "I am about as much use around here as two tails would be to a dog. Why was I ever chosen for this expedition?"

"That is not the only trouble with you my boy. Do not think that I am unaware of your love for the little leader of this group. And do not feel discouraged at her actions. The little girl is aware of your feelings towards her, and is only taking some time to make up her mind as to what to do about you. I have observed her closely several times, and am confident that your feelings are reciprocated and that all will be well. Give her a little time, and do not give up hope. As to your uselessness; what is anyone else in the group doing? Outside of my own efforts, in which I do not now need your help, the only other work for the cause is being done by Zora. I am becoming much worried at her silence. We have only slightly over a week left. So forget your grouch, my boy. Get a good night's sleep, and you will feel better in the morning.

Acting upon the professor's advice, Roy turned in. In the morning he stepped out of the *Pioneer* with more confidence than he had felt in several days. If he could only get out into the sunshine, he knew that he would feel different.

IX.

Meanwhile Zora had been having her troubles. She dared not approach Pietro directly, for this would be certain to arouse his suspicion. Instead, she carried on her work in the Zar's household as usual. Evenings, attired in the most attractive gowns and looking her absolute best, she frequented the hotel, where she knew that Pietro was accustomed to dine. On the third evening he encountered her in the lobby and stopped at once. A change in expression came over his cruel face, the admiration and tenderness in his demeanor made him appear, for the moment, almost human. As he addressed her, Zora did something she had not done for years. She greeted him civilly and with a half smile. Thus encouraged, Pietro begged her to dine with him. Not wishing to overdo her part, she refused, but after an hour's insistent plead-ing on his part, she compromised and agreed to meet him for dinner the following evening. With triumph in his eyes, Pietro left her. She returned to her apartment, there to do a little gloating on her own part. It had not been a bad night's work, she thought.

The following evening Zora appeared at Pietro's hotel, ravishingly gowned, and a picture of mature beauty from the top of her exquisitely coiffured head to the soles of her modishly shod feet. Pietro was speechless with admiration at first, but eventually recovered his equanimity and proudly led her to his table in the dining room.

Dinner was a success. Zora was friendly, but not too much so. Pietro was as if enchanted by his companion's nearness. He was exultant, too and pressed his advan-tage to the utmost. He begged her to accompany him to the opera after dinner, but she refused. She cleverly turned the conversation to the subject nearest and dearest to his vain soul; his high position in Munan, and the arsenal of which he had com-plete command. Zora feigned great interest when he boastingly told of the impor-tance of his work, and, insinuatingly, she flattered him until, in his vanity, he finally offered to take her to the arsenal and show her through it. This was the identical thing for which Zora had maneuvered, but she did not display too great enthusiasm and consented to visit his stronghold the next evening only after considerable per-suasion from him. Pietro informed her that he could do her no greater honor; that he was risking his position, perhaps even his life, in thus violating the strict order of the Zar that no outsider was ever to be admitted to the arsenal. He thought that, in thus impressing upon her the risk he was running for her sake, she would reward him by further softening in her attitude towards him. Little did he realize the pur-pose behind her acceptance of his offer. Little did he realize that he had been tricked into making this offer.

Next night Zora appeared at the hotel as usual, but this time she had with her and hidden in her clothes, the hand weapon which the professor had given her, as well as the crysinum receptacle which he had sent. After dining with Pietro she was taken to a small aero, which left from a landing stage on the roof of the hotel. In a few minutes they had reached the gates of the arsenal, where they were stopped by two huge guards who menaced them with leveled weapons. At a curt word from Pietro, they lowered the weapons and allowed the two to pass, muttering disapproval. With a growl, Pietro warned them to be silent, on pain of death, and with that they entered.

Now was Zora's opportunity, and she used all of the feminine wiles at her command to further put the braggart at her side under her spell. She succeeded admirably, for Pietro took her from one end of the arsenal to the other, explaining to her eager ears all that was seen. Finally they had completed their inspection of all the buildings on the surface and Zora's heart fluttered wildly as they neared a blank metal wall at the far end of the remotest building. Hesitating for a moment as they faced the wall, Pietro was about to turn around and leave. Something had told Zora that the secret for which she had searched was hidden behind that blank wall, and for a moment she leaned her body close to Pietro, the fragrance of her breath on his face, her eyes bright with expectancy. With a shrug of decision, Pietro took a small instrument from his pocket and placed it close to the metal wall. There was a stream of crackling blue fire between the instrument and the wall and suddenly, before their eyes, the partition had vanished, disclosing a spiral of steps cut into the solid rock and leading downward. He produced a light and again presented the instrument to the point where the metal wall had shut off. Again the crackling flame and the wall was in place, closing them off completely from the room they had just quitted.

As they descended the winding steps Zora counted them carefully while Pietro was informing her, with the greatest solemnity, of the unheard of privilege she was being accorded. Only five persons in all Munan knew of the whereabouts of this hiding place, he told her. Only the Zar and he were in possession of means of entry, and his life would surely be the penalty were the Zar to learn of this visit. In convincing words, Zora assured him that she would never divulge the fact of the visit to a soul in Munan, making the mental reservation that the professor was not of Munan, therefore that she could tell him without breaking this promise. After counting one hundred and thirty-two steps, Zora followed Pietro into a huge cavern similar to their own council chamber but much larger. Here were stored the nearly two million crysinum bombs, and a vat of the liquid which they contained. Here was the chance for which Zora had worked. She must not fail! Pietro told her of the terrible effectiveness of the bombs, and of the difficulty in producing the liquid content. With the fanatical fluency of the Zarist, he expanded upon the conquest of The Outside which was so soon to come.

While he talked, his greedy eyes devoured her and suddenly, with no warning, he had leaped to her like a wild animal and, extinguishing the light he carried, had her in his arms and was crushing her to him with brutal strength. Zora struggled frantically and finally squirmed into a position where she was able to withdraw the professor's weapon from the folds of her gown. Breathlessly she held it against

Pietro's writhing body and pressed the button. There was a purple flare which lighted the entire cavern momentarily, and Zora lost consciousness!

X.

The eighth day had passed and still no word from Zora. The group was becoming panic-stricken and the professor, although deeply worried and heartsick himself, was endeavoring to calm and reassure them. For three days the members of the group who lived in the city had been unable to learn of Zora's whereabouts. She had not been seen, either at her apartment or at the Zar's palace during that time. Further than this, it had been reported this last day that Pietro has disappeared, and the authorities were at this moment searching for him. A strange woman had been seen to enter the arsenal grounds with him, but neither had been observed to leave. Possibly, even now, the authorities were searching underground passages for the two. The situation never had seemed more serious.

Roy had been avoiding Thelda for several days, as she had avoided him, though it hurt him greatly to do this. Now, in this hour of darkness, she turned to him for comfort and he was overjoyed. They were seated apart from the remainder of the group in solemn conversation, when all were startled by the shrill cry of a feminine voice from the passage and Zora, haggard, worn, and bedraggled, burst in upon them. Thrusting a small metal cylinder into the professor's hand, she cried, "Here is the sample," and collapsed in a heap at his feet. Tenderly he lifted her limp body and, in sudden abandon, pressed his lips to hers. Realizing that he had betrayed himself, he flushed to the roots of his hair, relinquished her to the women, and rushed off to the workshop with the crysinum cylinder which she had handed to him.

No time was to be lost as the excitement in the city might well lead to their detection. Frenziedly the professor worked in the laboratory, with Roy and Landon drafted as assistants. At last Roy was doing something to help and he was happier than he had been since the first day. Soon Thelda came to the workshop with Zora, who had been revived by the kind administrations of the women of the group. With a fond glance at the professor, who returned it with some embarrassment, she told her story:

"Professor, you must go right ahead with your work," she started, "for I am a hunted woman now and there is a chance that we may be discovered, though I am pretty sure that I left no trace in coming here. It was necessary for me to dispose of seven Munanese with your marvelous weapon, but as they are utterly destroyed, leaving no tell-tale bodies, the chances that my escape can be traced are fairly remote. If no others saw me, we are safe."

With great rapidity, she told her story up to the point where she had struggled with Pietro in the underground storeroom. All listened intently while the professor proceeded with his first test of the deadly fluid.

Great was the care with which he handled the small cylinder which Zora had brought. He spread on the floor a sheet of crysinum about four feet square, then directed Roy and Landon to bring him as large a loose stone as they could carry from one of the passageways. The two men struggled back with a block of stone between them which must have weighed close to two hundred pounds. This they deposited on the sheet of crysinum in the center of the room. All stood aloof at the professor's bidding as, carefully, he allowed one drop of the precious liquid to fall on the surface of the rock. As it struck, there was a slight puff of yellow vapor at the point of contact. They watched in astonishment as the vapor quickly surrounded the stone with a venomous sputtering. Immediately the rock began to shrink in size and, in less time than it takes to tell, the large piece of solid granite had completely vanished, leaving not a trace on the surface of the glistening crysinum sheet.

The onlookers let forth a simultaneous gasp as the last of the rock disappeared, looking at each other in wondering realization that the properties of this fluid had not been exaggerated in the slightest degree. Zora, as soon as she had recovered from the surprise of the sight, continued with her story, and the professor when on with his experiments:

"When I recovered consciousness in the underground chamber, I realized that I had lain there for a long time. Now I know that it was for nearly seventy-two hours. I remembered what had occurred. Hearing no sound, I felt around for Pietro's body, but could not find it. However, I found his torch and, as it flooded the cavern with light, I saw that there was no body in sight. Near the spot where I had lain in a coma, I found all of the metal articles his pockets had contained, including the instrument with which he had obtained entrance to the spiral stair. I could not then understand what had become of him—whether he was still alive and had left of his own accord, or whether his dead body had been removed by others. At any rate, I did not forget what I had come for and, advancing to the open vat of the deadly liquid, I filled the little crysinum cylinder carefully.

"Then I appropriated the instrument which had belonged to Pietro and cautiously crept up the spiral stair. When I reached the metal wall, I listened intently, but could hear no sound. Placing the instrument near the wall, as I had seen Pietro do, I located a small switch or push-button on its side. This catch I pressed. As had occurred when we entered, the crackling flame appeared and the wall vanished. I stepped into the room through which we had passed, and found it deserted. It was still night and I extinguished Pietro's light. With a palpitating heart, I traversed the length of the building and stepped into the open air. Keeping in the shadows as much as I could, I finally came to the gates without having been discovered. My problem now was to get out, and I racked my brain for some means of doing so. Only the two guards were in sight and they paced to and fro before the locked metal gates. Finally I tiptoed close to the bars and addressed the nearest guard softly. He drew over to the gate, and I tried to convince him that Pietro had sent me out alone. He called the other guard at once and both leveled their weapons at me. There was nothing for me to do but point your weapons at each in turn and press the button. As a purple ray shot forth twice in rapid succession, both bodies stiffened, emitted a purple aura for a moment, and disappeared into thin air as we have just seen that stone vanish. Now I understood what had become of Pietro and I was glad—glad. It is horrible to feel that way, but I could not help it.

"Luckily the nearest guard had been very close to the gate, for, with his disintegration, there fell to the ground the bunch of keys which had swung from his belt. These were within my reach and, thrusting my arms through the bars, I obtained them and let myself out, re-locking the gates behind me. As I ran down the hill from the arsenal, I plumped straight into the arms of four of the Zar's police. Eluding them, I continued at the greatest speed of which I was capable. Apparently they wanted to capture me alive, for they did not discharge their weapons. The first gained on me, then the second and third, and in turn I was forced to dispose of them with the disintegrating ray. I had become exhausted, but I kept on running until I reached the entrance to our retreat. I thought that I had lost my fourth pursuer but, just as the stone swung aside for my entrance, he crept up on me from the underbrush. That was when you heard me scream. Luckily, I was able to get the professor's weapon into action again and I disposed of him as I had of the others." She shuddered at the memory of the wholesale slaughter.

All were much excited over this story, especially the professor, but the two women left at once so as to permit the professor and his two assistants to continue with their work.

Zora's narrative was later repeated to the assembled council, who now numbered but nineteen, excluding the three men who were hard at work. Several had been killed that day in the city, during the excitement which followed the discovery of Pietro's disappearance and of the open entrance to the secret vault under the arsenal. The disappearance of the two guards and four of the Zar's police had given the impression that a great conspiracy was under way, and the Zar was executing suspects right and left. The professor would indeed have to hurry.

XI.

Two days and three nights the men worked almost incessantly, alternating between the workshop and the *Pioneer* and only obtaining occasional snatches of sleep. During this period none of the group dared leave their hiding place. Thelda and Zora became constant companions. Before long, both had admitted privately their love for the two strangers from The Outside. Thelda ruefully thought of her avoidance of Roy and the reaction which it had produced. She had done that after the first day for the reason that his thoughts had told her of his love, and she had not been sure of herself. Now she realized that she loved this young man and could never live without him. But she was no longer able to bring his thoughts to her mind, for there was now a misunderstanding between them. She lived in constant dread that her treatment had killed the love which had at first existed. Zora's feelings were of a much calmer nature. She was serenely confident, and happy in the love which she felt sure was returned.

In the meantime, Roy was much too busy to have constant thought of Thelda but, strangely, the golden voice intruded itself upon his consciousness at the most unexpected times. Success had crowned their efforts, and on the morning of the third day, the three tired men burst forth into the council chamber with a shout of triumph which brought all members of the group on a run.

"Folks, we have the solution," the professor exulted loudly. "Listen. Get all of your belongings together at once and carry them aboard the *Pioneer*. We are all going to The Outside to finish our lives in peace and happiness. And we will destroy this miserable island as we leave."

There was a shout of joy as all gathered around to hear the details. At that moment there was a crash at the entrance to the main passageway. Their retreat had been discovered by the Zarists!

"No time for explanations now, people!" cried the professor. "Get everything you wish to take with you and stow yourselves away on the *Pioneer* immediately. The entrance stone is some ten feet thick, and should resist their efforts for a long enough time to permit our escape. Evidently they have not learned the secret of opening the door. But hurry."

The group scattered in all directions as the crashing at the entrance continued with increased violence. Soon there was the sound of automatic rock drills from the passage, but all, except the three men, were already aboard the *Pioneer*. With a sudden terrific jar and a yell from the attackers, the stone door came down and they swarmed through the passageway. Roy, Landon and the professor had remained behind to see that all reached the aero safely. As they retreated towards the passage leading to the chamber in which the *Pioneer* rested, the enemy streamed into the council chamber in great numbers. Roy and the professor shot forth the purple rays from the hand weapons time after time, bringing down many of the Zarists and temporarily stopping the rush. Landon recklessly hurled himself into the massed troops and was down at once. Seeing that nothing could be done to save poor Landon, Roy and the professor ran for the aero and just had time to get the entrance manhole bolted from the inside when the attackers entered the second chamber. In a flash the professor was at the controls and the sphere started revolving as the enemy swarmed around the aero. With a great rush, the *Pioneer* arose, straight as an arrow, for the circular opening far overhead and they were in the sunshine, rising at terrific speed.

XII.

When the altimeter indicated thirteen thousand feet, the professor turned the controls over to Roy, instructing him to keep the *Pioneer* hovering in its present position. He pulled a lever which uncovered all the portholes in the bottom of the aero, and as he rushed back to the salon, he cried to all of the excited group to watch the scene below through the glass covered openings. All complied immediately, kneeling on the floor about the several windows. The professor uncovered a small mechanism which had been installed in the salon, and started manipulating its controls as he peered through the telescopic sight.

"Watch Leyris now, folks," he shouted, and as they turned their eyes in that direction, there was a hum from the machine which the professor was operating. A faint ray, like a beam of sunlight which might have been reflected from a mirror, shot earthward, striking exactly at the last building of the arsenal, which could be seen as a small object far below.

Immediately there came a violent upheaval at that spot and a heavy yellow vapor poured forth from the point at which the ray had been directed. This yellow vapor crawled swiftly over Leyris like an octopus surrounding its prey, and the mountain melted away beneath their eyes as had the stone in Serano's old workshop. The vicious yellow vapor continued to pour forth as from the crater of a volcano, and all in its path went the way of the mountain.

Munan was overtaken by the fate it had decreed for The Outside. None could escape. No quarter could be asked. None could have been given. No pity stirred the breasts of the little groups watching in awe-struck silence.

When the vapor reached the city, tall buildings sank into the yellow turbulence like pillars of ice under undermined by boiling water. The population could be seen swarming into the ocean like a rippling massed formation of army ants. In five minutes all that remained of Munan was a seething mass giving the appearance of ebullient sculptural. This rapidly disappeared into the depths of the Pacific, leaving in its wake a foaming swirl which drew down with it the last of the survivors.

Gone were the invisible aeros. Gone were the deadly fluid and the supply of crysinum bombs. Gone was the race which hated the world with so great an intensity that this same fate had been planned for billions of innocent and unsuspecting victims. Gone were the results of centuries of misdirected mental and physical effort. The Outside was saved!

The various groups around the portholes reacted suddenly; some jumped to their feet and shouted for joy, others among the women sobbing in hysterical relief. Slowly the professor arose from the ray generator and looked for Zora. She came to him immediately and thanked him with tear-dimmed eyes, and the others crowded around, embracing him in their joy and praising him as the deliverer of mankind and of themselves from a most terrible fate. After what they had just witnessed, they could visualize more clearly than ever the awful destruction which had been prepared for The Outside, and their thankfulness knew no bounds.

Disengaging himself, the professor addressed the group, which was crowded into the little salon:

"Dear friends, we have accomplished what we started out to do. We should be grateful to the Supreme Being who has aided his humble servants in saving the world at the expense of Munan, the accursed. There are only twenty-one of us left now, with poor Landon gone. Though we are somewhat crowded for sleeping accommodations, you will be able to make yourselves fairly comfortable on board the *Pioneer* for the comparatively short journey ahead. With your consent we intend to return to New York in the shortest possible time. The neutralizing wall has now left us forever, along with the island of Munan, and we can depart unhindered. We shall arrive at our destination in twelve hours. Afterwards I will tell you the story of our labors for the past few days and how this destruction was accomplished. For the present, suffice it to say that, in the experiments with crysinum and the deadly liquid, I discovered that a stream of electrical impulses of a definite frequency would cause a reaction between the fluid and the enclosing metal which would start the destructive action and render the metal no longer resistant. The rest was easy, since we had available the small beam transmitter which had been constructed by your deceased leader. This I was able to modify so as to produce the required frequency, a ray of which you saw projected to the spot which Zora reported as the location of the supply of crysinum bombs.

"Now tell me; do you all wish to return with us to our home and there take up peaceful lives as inhabitants of our world, which nevermore will be 'The Outside' to you? Or had you rather be landed in some other location less thickly populated? Roy and I have both grown to love you all during the short time we have known you and we hope to have you always near us."

Enthusiastically, all decided to make the city of the strangers' choice their own future home, and to remain together as a group, at least until such time as they had become accustomed to the new order of things. In little knots they gathered on the several settees in the salon and cabin, there to discuss plans for the future, which, for the first time in their lives, seemed bright.

XIII.

The professor proceeded to the control room, where he found Ray anxiously awaiting him.

"Well, it is all over, my boy, and our dear old world is saved," said the professor in a tired voice. "Let me have the controls and we will start for home at once. If all goes well, we will be there in time to get to our own familiar beds by midnight, Washington time. Do you realize that it is now only eight a.m. Munan time? That attack on our retreat was intended as a surprise at dawn. Fortunately none of our number had been able to sleep on account of the excitement and all could thus prepare quickly."

"Yes, I noticed the time before we left," replied Roy, who was still shaken up because of the destruction of Munan which he had witnessed in the periscope. "But, professor, I do think that you should get some rest at once. You know you not only worked harder, but had considerably less sleep than poor old Landon or myself these past few days. You must be worn out."

"I am pretty well exhausted, Roy," he responded, "but another twelve hours will do no harm. Besides, I feel a personal responsibility for those dear people we are taking back with us. You may relieve me at the controls if you wish, but I want to be here all the time. I would not sleep now if I could."

He took the controls from Roy and headed for home, bringing the speed of the *Pioneer* to nearly six hundred miles an hour. Softly Roy closed the door as he left.

Seeking out Thelda, he found her alone in the tiny galley, examining the cooking utensils with deep interest.

"I knew that you would come to me, Roy," she whispered as he closed this door also and sprang to her side. "Oh, my dear, why have you been so blind, and why have I been so uncertain? Your mind spoke to mine long before you had even reached Munan, long before I had even seen you. I knew then that you were destined to love me. I think that I have loved you myself ever since I first heard your voice, which was over the videophone."

"Thelda, dearest. My wonderful—golden girl," was all that Roy could say, as he folded her yielding body to him and their lips met in the first kiss. No further words were necessary—their minds were now in close communion and to each was revealed the perfect sincerity and deep affection of the other.

The *Pioneer* sped swiftly toward what was now to be the home of both. There, high above the Pacific, as Roy and Thelda continued in their embrace, the sturdy aero carried another happy pair.

Forward, in the control room, the professor had just turned his beaming face to gaze into Zora's adoring eyes. They smiled in complete understanding, and two more pairs of lips met in a kiss of real love.

Executing a Pirouette in ORANGE

by Brad Linaweaver

Bran Linaweaver is a multi-talented young award-winner who has cleverly contrived to incorporated Lon Chaney Sr. and H.G. Wells into two of his stories.[See, also, "Yellow Imagicide".]—FJA

"Why do I always anticipate disaster? I don't want to live through it beforehand!"

Many times he'd listened to the desperation in her voice. His agony did not diminish. Flipping on his kindly doctor expression, he half-lectured, "You have imprinted bad experiences. Now you expect them."

They were at the bottom of a well. The well was made of plastalloy and was perpetually alight with an off-pink color. A small circle of blue was the sky above them, made more distant by the filtered lens. Although they had ample room on their big, round bed inside the bigger circle of the well, they felt closed in by the sameness of the surroundings, as indeed they were.

"I know I've used this service a lot," she said; as he looked at the chart with the number of her treatments standing at 13. "One shouldn't. . ." Her voice tapered off.

"One shouldn't what?" He could make his voice stern. "Depend!" she nearly shrieked. He nodded. A passing mark. The well hummed as treatment began.

"Now, a little free association is called for. We start with what you do. You've been a teacher how long?"

She was hurt. "That's not fair."

"Of course you don't remember. That is as it should be." He never liked himself during this stage. He smiled at her. She didn't smile back. That was good. It proved that she needed 14.

"So, let's hear the first thing that comes into your mind when I say . . . apples!" With the mention of the word came an appropriate fragrance. The well had just been outfitted with all the latest touches.

"Teacher."

He volunteered another fruit: "*Oranges.*"

"Scurvy."

Time to shift gears, he thought, and came out with: "Teaching."

"Shit," was her swift reply. He silently thanked the identi-odor for being linked to his words alone. The well stopped humming; started playing violin music from some obscure concerto.

"An interesting association,"he commented lamely. The good old days of withholding evaluation from patients were long gone. Prudence could no longer be master over the "shrinks" now that they had the machine, or it had them.

"What did I say?" She looked genuinely puzzled, as if she couldn't remember, and after more than ten treatments, maybe she couldn't. There were unexpected holes in the pattern.

Patting himself on top of his bald head, he leaned back against a pillow, the better to contemplate the blue disc above. "You equated education and excrement— or at least the training that passes for 'education' in our cautious institutions. Belphegor would approve."

Pulling the sheet up around her small breasts, she shook her head. "I hate it when you do that."

"What?"

"You're doing it again. First you leave me hanging with a name I've never heard of, but acting as if I should. Now you're playing the innocent. Next you'll . . ."

He cut her off with a laugh. "Leave what's *next* to me." They lay there in silence for a while, listening to music. He reached under the sheet, and played in a desultory fashion with her right nipple. She would not be distracted.

"Belphegor," he finally got on with it, "was a demon of many specialties. He was as brooding a scholar as any solemn monk, such was his concern for knowledge. And as others in the profession will attest, a suitable offering could be made to him in heaps of dung." The disgust on her face was also a good sign. She didn't really want to think about it; which meant that she was already trying to forget; which meant that she'd be more attuned to what lay in store.

Silence returned. This time they cultivated it. When the music stopped, there was no encore.

He'd made up his mind that she would have to resume the dialogue, and she accepted this. After all, she was paying.

When she spoke, it was the sound of a little girl lost in a dark wood: "Sometimes I'm afraid that I'm giving up my life, piece by piece. Shouldn't I be trying to hold onto it?"

That was his cue, if he'd ever heard one: "That depends on whether you want to hold onto unhappiness." He'd hate himself later for going through with the treatment, but when had that ever stopped him?

She climbed out of bed, and her warm feet on the soft, compliant floor, triggered new responses in the well. The light dimmed, the warmth increased.

"No one would go through as many treatments as you have who didn't want to be happy."

"Why must I *forget?*" She wanted to sound angry, but her voice was toneless.

"Remembering will make you sad."

"I'll bet you always say that."

"That's something you can't know," was his answer. She looked like the pale women who used to haunt bus stations in the days before tube travel made it more difficult to study strangers, each locked into private miseries. She sighed at him in exasperation, and he noted again how her green eyes were her best feature. They had been what first attracted him so very many years ago.

"Let's finish it," suggested the woman, his patient, his old flame who had forgotten.

"Say aloud what troubles you."

From the manner of her presentation—brows knitted, voice tense, body language a threat to all and sundry—he concluded that she had rehearsed. "I have enemies on the faculty," was how it began. "I have no idea if they are enemies I've had before . . . but they are certainly after me now!" As she named names, the well trembled at the emotions released. How paranoia tickled plastalloy when it was geared to the machine.

She went on and on: "Since I'm aware of who dislikes me, I can't be at ease around them. That would be asking too much. The turn of a head, a chance remark, the gaping emptiness of a room that was occupied right before I enter . . . it affects the way I act in the little minutiae of the day. The events cling together and grow like coral! They stifle me! I want to start over again. Please give me another chance. My mind must be purged!"

There were pictures on the wall of the well. They were the pictures she needed to see. She might not have her old dreams any longer, but the well did.

White-capped mountains in high, cold air; flat, featureless deserts; gray-silted craters on the moon; and, finally, black space, without even a glint of starlight. These images were clean for her.

"Lie down," he ordered, but his voice was soft. "I'll hold you." She hesitated, but the bed was inviting and he *was* her therapist. Sex was a calculated part.

He stroked her hair, massaged her neck, drew her hand to him. She was only half there, a few mechanical gestures of masturbation augmenting the hypnotic patterns of the womb they occupied. The wires in the well, as veins in a living body, pulsed with constant support.

A voice was whispering, "Forget, forget . . ." and she couldn't tell if it was the machine or the therapist who spoke. The lights all around, the sounds from underneath, and the perfume in the air prepared her to do more than listen—she absorbed.

"To remember the cause of a trauma is not necessarily to overcome it. We used to be in the business of selling fragmented understanding, when what our customers wanted all along was a narcotic. The point was to clear the road of unwanted debris so that the patient could get back on the job. Anything else is a waste of time. *Memory* is *insanity*."

There was a rocking motion in the bed, a cradle at the bottom of an Orange hole. Down there where they can't find you, out of the scary, blue world.

"We don't want people to become comfortable with their pain. A thorn is to be found, extracted, thrown away! There is no past. There is no present. There is only the future of idle daydreams—which fantasies we choose for you. We know what you want."

Then the voice repeated the same message, more or less, in French, her other language. Mustn't allow for denials hidden in another tongue.

When a thin beam of light came down from the top of the well and touched her brain, it was over. 14. All quiet on the downward end.

He was smelling perspiration, she was tasting metal, and the well was glowing in the aftermath of their satisfaction. It was forbidden that they converse now in any but the most banal pleasantries. This they did with conviction, and the smiles that they held for each other were unchangingly tiresome so that when she had been lifted out of the well by the nurse-tentacle, they both felt a great release as they relaxed into private frowns. She carried hers all the way home. Below, he allowed himself the luxury of anger. He wanted to put an end to its gnawing insistence by leaping from the bed and breaking the quivering structure of the well, well, well! How he cursed. It was indestructible, so far as his bare flesh was concerned. Exercises in futility were his recreation. Wrenching his foot with a final kick, he settled for a drawn-out scream, a howl of identity.

He asked for the file. His voice was the well's to obey. Information flashed on the wall space directly in front of the bed.

Sure enough, two of the names she had mentioned were there—chronic patients themselves. He'd even treated one a while back. Although his memory was intact, there were still too many names for easy recall.

"Oh, Janice," he whispered, placing his hand on the gentle valley where she had lain beside him. "Why did it happen?"

He was granted remorse. Others saw it as the price he paid for his position; he held tightly to it as compensation.

While awaiting his next patient, he let his mind wander. In the state he was in, a path was quickly trod—a destination swiftly reached.

He had been her assistant. Although one of many, he'd been a notable talker and worrier. That contributed to the relationship, such as it was. Their first serious disagreement had been over the extent to which The Institute planned to use the new technique of the mind-wipe. He thought that there should be limits placed on the wells, his nickname for the mass produced therapy wombs.

It was perhaps not surprising that as the inventor, she had argued for the widest possible application. At the time, she had no inkling of the nervous breakdown that was crouching in the shadows, waiting for her a mere year down the line. When part of a good mind dies, what is left finds the loss unbearable. For her, this meant the first treatment. For him, it meant the special guilt that only comes with survival.

She gave up her patent to become a patient. Her name was stricken from the records. Eventually her co-workers were "wipes" themselves, except for him. He guarded his position as her permanent therapist, as he guarded his memory.

What wisdom he possessed was derived from a sober understanding of The Institute. Those who owned the wells did not brook any criticism. Predictably they did not desire that the inventor recover her memory. They could not risk her advancing a different point of view.

His task was clear. He was to keep her happy. In return, they let him keep himself . . . down to the last tantrum.

At the bottom of the orange well, it was always warm. He waited for more souls descending to his and the machine's smooth embrace.

The ORANGE God

by Nat Schachner

Nat Schachner wrote the first "Thought-Variant"
tale for Astounding Stories.—FJA
Astounding Stories, October 1933

The Baghdad-Calcutta mail was less than an hour out of Peshawar when the storm came. It was inexplicable—this storm. One moment ten thousand square miles of Indian plain and shaggy, snow-humped Himalayas seethed under a copper sun; the next, a wall of darkness swept out of the east, blotting out sky and mountain and plain as though they had ceased to exist. The fast-flying ship seemed suspended in a lightless void; the spinning earth beneath was gone; the sun above erased. Even the motor's familiar roar was oddly hushed in the sudden quiet.

"Damn!" said Saunders, the pilot, and groped for the light switch. The instrument panel glowed into feeble illumination, as if it, too, were oppressed by the blackness. Two heads bent over simultaneously to stare at the gauges. Saunders, leathery and dour from too much solo flying, and Ward Bayley, the American passenger from Peshawar for the last leg of the trip.

"Queer, isn't it?" muttered Saunders, startled, but not yet afraid, as he jerked the plane upward in an attempt to clear the strange pall. The instruments seemed to be working all right.

But Bayley's face showed white in the dim, reflected glow.

"Not scared, are you?" asked Saunders, his voice edged with contempt. "We'll get out of it soon." He opened the throttle another notch.

"A little," the American admitted calmly. "I've heard rumors about this from the hill tribes on the Tibetan border; that's why I was in a hurry to reach Calcutta to consult with—"

The instrument board blanked out suddenly; the motor sputtered once and died. The plane did not seem to be moving; all around was black nothingness. Saunders swore and wrestled with the controls.

"Look!" came Bayley's voice.

Far in the distance, a million miles away, it seemed, a tiny pinprick of light stabbed the world. It danced up and down, like a pith ball on a jet of water; then it, too, went out. A moment later it reappeared, steady and fixed; and as the fascinated watchers strained aching eyeballs, it elongated swiftly like a traveling rocket, straight up, and up, and up—a shaft of orange light that flamed clear-etched in the void, cut off beneath where the earth might be if the earth still existed, and extending upward to an infinitude where alien universes once had form and substance.

Saunders was afraid now, horribly so. He could not see his companion. The plane, the world, had come to an end in everything but that endless column of light.

"God!" It was his only word. Bayley did not speak at all. He crouched grimly in the cockpit, waiting.

Then came the storm.

The ship was caught in a blast of overwhelming sound. It whirled and whirled around in dizzying circles, while the two men held on with a grip of death. The keel shuddered once, and the rudderless plane leaped forward, faster and faster, until the tremendous acceleration pressed unbearably upon the limbs and hearts of the crouching pair. The invisible wind screamed and howled; the plane fell faster and ever faster, straight for the motionless shaft of fire.

How long it lasted, Bayley was never to know. It might have been minutes, or hours, or days, even. The plane took a final great leap, and was immersed in the orange glare. A split second of dazzling comprehension, a strange look of exaltation on Saunders's prosaic face, and darkness again as the ship hurtled clear. Bayley tried to hold on to what he had seen, what he had understood, but the plane was dropping now, and the memory fled into the pit of his stomach. There was a quick, ripping sound, a crash, and Bayley's head collided violently with something hard.

He awoke—it might have been seconds later, it might have been hours—with a sharp pain in his left shoulder, and a dull throb to his head. His eyes opened unsteadily, and saw—nothing. The orange pillar of flame was gone, the storm was over; only blackness and thick silence brooding over chaos. He moved. There was jagged hardness beneath, rock and splintered fragments of the plane. Twinges of fire streaked through his shoulder.

"Saunders!" he called weakly. The sound of his voice drummed in his ears. There was no answer. The pilot was dead, or still unconscious. Bayley closed his eyes wearily against the unbearable dark. Something rustled, something dry and crackly. He forced his lids open again. Nothing! The sound ceased.

A shriek tore jaggedly through his failing consciousness, cleared his head of the groping pain like a douche of cold water. He thrust himself upright with a superhuman effort. The shriek was repeated. A woman's voice in the last extremity of terror! The clogging veil split open in a long gash, revealing a mountainside in weird half light. A girl crouched against a huge rock, her hand outthrust in an agony of horror, every limb instinct with unutterable fear. Her face could not be seen.

She shrieked a third time, and Bayley staggered to his feet, ripping his side unheeded against a jutting strut. He took a wavering step forward, when the walls of the darkness rushed soundlessly together, blotting out mountainside and girl and the accents of horror as if they had never been. The world was void of light and movement once again.

Bayley stood rooted.

"Saunders!" he shouted, and the sound mocked him. Was he, Bayley, dead, too, and all this but a dream of the beyond? Terror flooded him; strange terror he had never known in a long, adventurous life. Something made a stealthy *pad-pad* close by. He started to run, stumbling, crashing, in the impenetrable blackness. The *pad-pad* behind him quickened and grew in intensity. He was being pursued. He ran on blindly. They were gaining on him. He tried a last desperate spurt, and his foot slipped. He was falling. He thrust his arms out wildly, caught at a projection, swung precariously a moment, and lost his hold. Down again into chaos, until something came up with a thud, and the blackness without gushed into his brain.

When Bayley recovered consciousness it was night—normal, natural night, with stars and a dim sliver of moon overhead. A great thirst tormented him; his left shoulder was stiff and caked, and his head ached oddly. He tried to move, and almost went toppling into the abyss. One leg was dangling clear. Clawing awkwardly, he managed to pull himself back to safety. For a moment he lay panting; then he looked cautiously.

He was perched amid the rotted roots of a tree that had long since whirled into the tremendous depth below. It was a sheer precipice; the feeble starlight disclosed no bottom. Bayley shuddered as he thought of what might have happened had he not caught in the matted roots. He looked upward.

The lip of the cliff slanted backward from where he lay, not more than fifteen feet above. He had not fallen far. The slope could be negotiated. Slowly, painfully, he pulled himself up over the roots, testing each hold with infinite caution, pausing when a stone dislodged beneath his unwary feet to hear the sound of its thud at the bottom of the gorge. But no smallest noise came up through the still night. At last he stood at the top, disheveled, clothes slashed and torn, blood caked stiff.

What had happened? Where was he? Where was Saunders? It had been noon when they left Peshawar; now, by the stars, it seemed close to midnight. What had caused that strange, weird storm, that supernatural column of light? He had been pursued, too. Did those invisible padding feet belong to animals or men? The girl, disclosed a moment by a rift in the black curtain, and swallowed up forever—what did it all mean? The questions beat furiously through his mind and evoked no answers.

Force of habit dictated his next move. All his life he had wandered in the outplaces of the world, amid strange tribes and savage customs, and caution was second nature to him. He dropped quickly behind a huge boulder that teetered on the edge, so that no hostile eye could spy him in the shimmer of the stars. Now he was able to take stock of his surroundings.

He was on the outthrust of a huge mountain, perched seemingly at the edge of the world. The ground descended slightly away from the cliff, then rose again in a long slope of a thousand feet, and ended abruptly in a towering granite wall, whose top was lost in the thin darkness. All around, to north, east, and south, tumbled mountain range on range, higher, more breathtaking than the Himalayas themselves. To the west, however, there was nothing; a pool of blackness that disclosed neither land nor sea.

Bayley shivered. There was only one range of mountains in the entire world that compared with this—the fabulous, sinister, almost unknown Gangi Mountains of northern Tibet. That meant that they had been swept a thousand miles east and north, over the Himalayas themselves, into a land of jealous seclusion, of strange lama rites, of unknown horrors. He would never get out alive!

His searching eyes raked the rumpled terrain of the shallow valley. There was nothing—no sign of the wrecked plane or of Saunders. A black cloud passed suddenly over the horned moon; its shadow raced gigantically over the valley, straight up the precipitous slope on the other side. Bayley's gaze followed it involuntarily. In spite of his caution, a low exclamation escaped him.

Something was moving in the heart of the shadow, a confused, wavering blob that seemed to be climbing the long slope. The cloud over the moon veered sharply to the east, and the obedient ground shadow moved with it. A procession disclosed itself momentarily—a long, threadlike movement of toiling doll figures. They were carrying something. Almost at the same time, toward the westerly slope, another group dissociated from the shadows, converging at an angle with the first. They, too, were carrying a burden. Then the cloud shifted back again; and the streaking shadow made one vast blob on the mountainside, blotting out all sight and sound in darkness as palpable as that first weird storm.

But Bayley had seen enough. It was not merely the processions. There had been something else. High up on the precipitous wall, the focal point of the converging parties, his eye had caught a light, a steady pin-prick of orange flame that seemed to emanate from the black mouth of a cave. The heart of the mystery of the night's strange, untoward events was there.

Bayley felt grimly for the gun under his torn, dirtied jacket. It was still in its holster, unharmed in the smash. He stepped out from the shadow of the protecting rock, and started down into the valley, gliding from rock to rock with the practiced ease of an Indian on the trail, careful to make no sound in his passage, merging indistinguishably with the blurred outlines of the rubbly slope. Whatever unholy mess was brewing, he was going to be present. There was Saunders, the pilot—he had been monosyllabic and dour enough, offended at the American the Peshawar officials had thrust upon him, but he was a white man. There had been the girl, too.

Her face had been hidden, but he was sure she was no Tibetan. Those stories of the frightened hill tribes came home to roost now; tales of strange rites and of a stranger god whom the lamas were worshiping in the hidden recesses of innermost Tibet.

He was past the valley now, and climbing steadily. There was no further sign of the two weird processions, but the orange flame gleamed steadily far above. The moon was gone; the cloud was spreading and blotting out the stars one by one. An hour of tortuous climbing brought him to the end of the trail. The granite wall of the mountain loomed perpendicularly overhead, a smooth, towering *massif,* unscalable, insurmountable. The unwinking flame had snuffed suddenly out.

Bayley searched desperately about. He must find a way in a hurry, before the shadows crept on him. Where had the processions gone; how had they scaled the tremendous cliff? There was not even a single hold on that smooth, vertical surface. The blackness was closer now, coming up in a wall of dead lightlessness. A last swift, despairing glance, and Bayley was engulfed. He seemed suddenly bodiless; a floating brain in a sea of nothingness.

But before the last sightless blotting out, he had seen something. Two huge boulders like giant guards at a portal, and a black hole that yawned between. It was only a dozen feet away, and he was facing it.

Without hesitation, he started forward, right arm extended, eyes closed to avoid the uncanny dark. Pebbles made odd noises beneath his feet. Then his outstretched arm hit with a thud. He felt around the smooth stone. He was on the verge of the opening. He paused a moment, cursing the fact that he had no flash. How deep was the orifice; was it a sheer drop or a path? There was no way of telling.

Bayley took a deep breath and inched his way in. It descended, but gently. A cold wind was blowing steadily outward. He kept close to the invisible side of the tunnel. It was going upward now. The wall seemed to angle sharply, and far ahead was a pale glimmer. There was a orange tinge to it. Bayley sucked his breath in with a gusty murmur, made sure his gun was easy-sliding in its holster.

There was light enough now to move a little faster. But the American redoubled his caution. He crept slowly along the wall. There was something artificial about its smooth, unbroken surface, about the well-worn condition of the path beneath.

The orange glow ahead grew stronger in intensity. There was movement beyond, and a confused murmur of sound. Bayley had his gun out, and his caution increased. He seemed but a shadow creeping along the wall. The flaming orifice ahead expanded; the murmurs took on shape and form. A chanting pulsed and fell. Drums throbbed in staccato unison.

Luckily the wall curved slightly as it reached the opening. Bayley threw himself down flat and wriggled forward, keeping to the curve. The sounds grew louder, and the wall glowed brighter. He inched his head warily around the bend, his gun extended a bit, ready to shoot at the first cry of alarm. The scene sprang full-orbed into view.

Bayley almost cried out, though his life hung by a thread. Never in all his wanderings had he come across such a sinister, blood-chilling sight.

The great cavern, hollowed out to the shape of a perfect hemisphere, was aglow. Seated in concentric circles, like an audience in a stadium, were hundred of Tibetans, lamas by the red robes of them, all facing inward toward the center, their dark faces aflame with the fires of fanaticism. Within the inner circle weaved a dance, red-clad figures swaying and drumming on tiny drums. A lama in a yellow robe, emblematic of a high order, face uplifted, back to Bayley, was chanting, *"Om mani padme hum hri!"* Bayley recognized that much; it was the sacred sentence of Lamaism.

But it was not the yellow lama, the drummers, or the crowded priests, that drew his startled gaze. It was the figure in the very center, the cynosure, the point of adoration of the assembled monks. Bayley had all he could do to stifle the shriek that rose to his lips, to control his limbs from jerking upright and carrying him in a mad race from that cavern.

A huge globe of crystal poised lightly on the ground. It was hollow, thin-walled, like a bubble. Within its clear depths, at the very center, unsupported, floated a figure. It was not a man. Bayley was positive of that—yet it held some vague resemblance to the human form. The body was elongated, and deep-orange in color. Sinuous appendages that might have been arms and legs hung limply down. The head was round and bald, and Bayley caught two round, unwinking orbs staring straight outward. The eyes, if eyes they were, were not malign. On the contrary, their unscrutable depths seemed filled with passionless wisdom, with infinite knowledge. Bayley had seen plenty of the leering, hideous idols the Tibetans worshiped in their religion. This was indubitably none of them. And it was *alive!*

The sphere glowed outwardly with a colorful iridescence, and immediately behind was the opening to the outer world through which Bayley had first noticed the flame.

Three figures lay bound on the ground before the globe. Bayley was just able to see them through a gap in the serried ranks. At the risk of discovery, he raised his head. His heart gave a great bound. One of them was a naked Tibetan, browned and dirty, his scrawny limbs trembling uncontrollably against the cords. The second was Saunders, his clothes in tatters, a red gash across his forehead. His dour Scotch features were more sullen than ever, eyes upturned to the great living idol. The third was a woman—the girl who had shrieked on the mountainside. She, too, was bound, prone on the ground. She was dressed in mannish clothes, breeches and puttees, and she wore a leather jacket. Her profile was pale and pure. A strand of glossy black hair escaped from under a close leather cap. She was not shrieking now, but Bayley caught a glimpse of even teeth clenched over a lower lip before he sank back to his hiding place.

The American's first impulse was to turn and run; his second to open fire. The first was rejected even before it was fully formed; the second was suicidal, and could achieve nothing. Yet something hideous was about to take place; of that he was sure. Wild thoughts flashed through his brain of that strange figure in the globe, of the weird ceremony.

But before he could evolve any plan, the chanting ceased; the drums stoppped their monotonous throb. A hush fell over the cavern. The figure did not move, yet Bayley had a horrible intuition that it was speaking. Queer sounds beat within his mind; the tongue, the language, was unknown. It was not Tibetan; it had no counterpart on earth. Yet the Tibetan lama seemed to understand. He snapped out orders. Two red-clad natives stepped forward. They lifted the captive Tibetan, their countryman, high above their heads, while he struggled and twisted in his bonds. Bayley could see him plainly now. His hollow, dark features worked convulsively, foam dribbled from his lips, and scream after scream ripped through the stillness.

The supporting natives suddenly loosed their hold, and the unfortunate captive remained suspended in mid-air. His struggles ceased; he was rigid. The eyes of the sphere being turned to him. To Bayley, crouched and panting, there seemed a cool understanding in their depths. A bubble formed around the suspended Tibetan, a thin-walled globe. The light glowed stronger. It beat out of the opening into the void! Bayley had seen a star a moment before. Now a column of light extended out and up—to infinity.

The sphere with its enclosed prisoner trembled and moved. It slid out along the orange column, as though it were a greased way. Higher and higher it fled, until it was a tiny speck in the glow; then it disappeared. Bayley again had that wild impulse to flee. This was not of the world of men and natural forces. But he was held, taut, cold, senses attuned like a fine violin.

The girl was being lifted!

She did not struggle. But, as she was turned in the movement, her finely chiseled face disclosed to Bayley blue-black eyes, large with repressed fear. A thoroughbred! Saunders, the dour, hard-bitten Scotsman, lapsed from his sullen silence— violently. He heaved at his bonds, his tongue loosened with a flow of hard, sulphurous profanity that would have warmed Bayley's heart under any other circumstances.

"Leave that girl be, you heathen swine!" he barked.

No one paid any attention to him; least of all, the orange creature of the globe.

The girl was halfway up when Bayley went into action. He flung himself erect, took careful aim, and shot at the great sphere. The roar of the .44 crashed, echoing through the cavern. Bayley raced forward, gun in hand.

At once the great sphere went black, and the entire cavern plunged into thick darkness. Bayley had a quick glimpse of startled lamas clambering to their feet. Then he was in the thick of a press of shouting, milling, sweating, invisible bodies.

Left elbow stiffly advanced, gun clubbed, Bayley plunged on his way, straight for the spot where he had last seen the sphere and the bound victims. Cries of alarm gave way to screams of pain as he battered a path through the shaken mob. Hands clutched at his invisible progress, but he shook them off, and the gun butt rose and fell with deadly precision. Then he was through into a clearing. He stopped short. This must be the circle that had held the sphere. He groped around, finger on trigger for another shot. Back and forth he ranged in the blackness, arm blindly extended, while the clamor around rose to a solid roar of rage. A torch flamed in the distance. It was moving swiftly up the passageway. He must work fast before the light came, before the enraged lamas could locate him.

But the sphere was gone! There was no question about it. He ran in quick circles, and found nothing but thick darkness. The torch was nearing, bobbing and flickering with the speed of its carrier. Forgetting the mystery of the sphere, Bayley thrust desperately at the ground. He must free the girl first; then Saunders. But where was the girl? He was sure she had fallen somewhere around this particular spot, but his frantic groping disclosed nothing.

Just then the runner with the flaming wood burst into the cavern. A howl of triumph rose from a hundred throats. There was a rush of fantastic red figures to the area of illumination. Then the torch commenced bobbing forward. Its smoky illumination cast but a feeble light of long, flickering shadows, and the blood-lusting lamas who crowded in its wake seemed like a pack of demons on the trail of a damned soul. It wouldn't take long to discover the intruder.

The girl, like the sphere, had disappeared. Bayley paused. He could not orient himself to Saunders. Seconds were precious now. A voice came up almost at his feet.

"Whoever you are, devil or man," it said in angry tones, "cut these cords so I can die with my fists going."

Bayley grinned and bent over, his hand questing. A large, wriggling body was underneath. He whipped out his penknife, flipped open the blade, clashed at interminable cords.

"Hurry, man!" the invisible voice expostulated. "They're coming fast."

Bayley sliced the last knot just as the searching, sooty flare caught at his bent form. The lamas saw him almost simultaneously. A howl of frenzied execration burst from the Tibetans. Arms upraised, they rushed forward. Steel glittered in brown fists.

Bayley ripped frantically, tugged Saunders to his feet. The pilot could hardly stand, so weak was he from the long confinement.

"Got a gun?" the American whispered fiercely. Saunders nodded. The sweat was pale on his brow, but he got at it somehow. His voice grew stronger.

"Let the beggars have it!" he shouted.

The two guns flamed together. Steel-jacketed death tore through the massed onrushing ranks; the heavy slugs slammed and crashed through half a dozen brown-skinned bodies. The roars of hatred mingled with screams of pain and the groans of the dying.

"Think we can fight our way through the passage?" Saunders grunted as they fired again.

"Not a chance," Bayley said. "We'd be sliced for sure. Watch out! Here they come!"

The lamas had recovered from the first shock and were coming with a deadly rush. The long, keen knives gleamed wickedly in the uncertain light.

Bayley had had experience with religious fanatics before.

"Can't stop them now," he said to Saunders as they pumped bullets into the compact mass as fast as triggers could jerk. Gaps appeared and filled up almost immediately. Suddenly the Scotsman stopped.

"No more bullets," he said casually. "It's been a pleasure to meet you. Good-by."

Bayley had two bullets left. The lamas were almost on them. He could hear the whistling of their breaths, see the glare of their eyeballs. The knives were plunging downward. Saunders had his gun clubbed, ready to sell his life as dearly as possible.

Bayley took a last careful aim and fired. In the background, the bearer of the torch howled dismally, and the smoking wood dashed to the ground, scattered sparks, and was extinguished. The cavern was in pitch darkness again.

"This way, Saunders," Bayley shouted, and threw himself sideways. A knife ripped down through his coat. Something red-hot seared his side, and warm fluid ran in a smear. The next instant he was the center of a struggling, howling mass. Luckily, in the dark no one knew his neighbor. The lamas were slashing at each other indiscriminately. Bayley tried to break through the weaving horde, but there was another rush, and he was borne backward, fighting desperately with fist and gun butt.

Back and back he went, ducking, weaving, feeling sudden stabs of pain as knives slashed at him and skinny hands gashed with razor sharp nails. There was cold air on his back, a steady, strong wind. Bayley knew what that meant; his brow beaded with sudden horror. He tried to smash his way clear, but a solid wall of flesh pressed him remorseless back.

Far away he heard a cry. It sounded like Saunders's voice, shouting words that were indistinguishable. Then something struck him—the concerted heave of fifty lamas. He was hurled back. His left foot tried to plant itself, found nothing. The wind was cold and dawn-fresh on his brow. Bayley staggered, clutched desperately. Then both feet went over, and he was falling. He had been pushed out of the cave opening, high up on the smooth, perpendicular wall of the mountain.

Saunders found himself separated from the American almost immediately as the light crashed out. He heard Bayley's shout to follow him, but he was in the middle of as pretty a dog fight as he had ever experienced during the War. He smashed out with fist and gun, heard the grunts of pain, felt a knife wound in his shoulder, broke clear and dashed for what he thought was the direction of the tunnel.

He ran headlong into a wall, and the breath was knocked out of him. To the other side he heard the thuds and shouts of battle. He groped along, trying to find the path, when something gave way suddenly. He called out Bayley's name just as the wall opened. He found himself thrown into an irregular chamber in the rock, dimly illuminated with unseen light. Saunders shook his head and came to his feet with a bound. The wall had glided smoothly into position behind him. He was cut off from Bayley.

A whistling sound made him turn around sharply, and duck at the same time. That saved his life. A knife blade ruffled his hair with the speed of its flight, and ground with a dull thud into the wall beyond.

The lama in the yellow robe was standing close to a fat, obscene, pot-bellied idol that represented the Tibetan's degraded caricature of Buddha. He gibbered foul phrases as he plucked frantically at his sleeve, where another knife lay hidden.

Saunders's eyes slid past him to the mysterious girl, sitting rigidly upright on a cushioned dais next to the idol. She was not bound, and her eyes were open, but they had the peculiar stare of a person under the influence of drugs. Saunders's gaze jerked back to the lama. His arm was bent back! It held a knife.

The pilot raised his gun.

"Drop it," he said sharply. The gun was empty, and Saunders knew it.

The bluff worked, but in surprising fashion. The steel blade clattered to the ground, and the lama moved like a striking snake. He scooped up the immobile girl with one hand; the other went behind him. The Scotsman jerked forward with a cry of alarm, but it was too late. The huge belly of the idol swung open on hinges, disclosing a hollow interior. The Tibetan monk glided backward in a single flowing motion, the girl in his arms, and the idol closed with a brazen clang.

Saunders came crashing into a metallic, rounded idol just as mocking laughter floated hollowly up to him. He glared at the obscene visage, raised a huge fist to crash into its stomach, but withheld his blow. He would only break his hand. There must be a button concealed somewhere on the bulging belly.

He was fumbling clumsily when another sound burst on him. He whirled. The secret entrance from the greater cavern was open, and a horde of red lamas came pouring through.

The air rushed upward as Bayley fell through the void. He knew it was a good thousand feet to the long, irregular slope beneath, yet he felt strangely calm. Events of over three decades of existence flashed through his mind as he dropped. The exploration of hitherto unknown portions of Afghanistan and the Gobi; the acclaim of learned societies; the last trek out of Nepal; the rumors of the god that had come to Tibet; the determination to seek him out after consulting with a learned friend in Calcutta who knew all the intricacies of Lamaism; the courteous air official at Peshawar; the dour pilot, glum at the thought of flying company; and—the girl he had seen twice.

It was on the thought of her that he felt the sudden slackening of his speed. He looked upward. The orange sphere dazzled against the pale dawn light; the stars were burning low. Even as he looked, a cylinder of flame darted down toward him. It caught him in mid-flight, spun him round and round. Then he felt himself come to a breaking halt, hesitate, and start to rise again. He was being lifted through the air toward the waiting globe.

Marian Temple came dizzily out from under the influence of the drug. By a tremendous effort of will she managed to force open leaden eyelids. She found herself lying in a luxuriously furnished room, the walls of which were covered with Ispahan carpets of intricate weave. The floor was piled thick, and the odor of incense hung dense in the chamber. At the farther end the yellow lama, his back turned, was engaged in mixing something in a brass mortar with a stone pestle.

The girl tried to rise, but the leaden weight of lethargic limbs held her down. She closed her eyes again to clear her head, then reopened them. Life was slowly flowing back into her numbed body.

The past twelve hours had been filled with horrors. Her lovely face, with the eyes that had been the toast of New York, was pallid now, drawn with fine lines of unending terror. From the time that their round-the-world plane had been drawn into the mysterious black storm over southern Siberia, she had not known a moment's peace.

This, she reflected bitterly, was the result of trying to be different. Bored to tears by the dull sound of New York's gaiety, she had snatched at Maxton's offer to take her as the first passenger on a globe-girdling trip. The papers had featured it— "Society Girl Seeks New Thrills."

She had them. Poor Maxton was dead under the crashed plane. The fantastic figures in red had risen out of the earth to seize her; the strange column of flame beat around her. The rest was mounting terror! The weird rites; the god in the crystal; the bound figures beside her; the sudden appearance of the white man. Then the battle—a bony arm lifting her, the sweetish capsule pressed between her lips, and unconsciousness.

She felt better now. She moved a leg cautiously, and the warm blood raced through it. She glanced around the room. The four walls stared back, unrelieved by door or other opening. Still, there must be one. The lama's back was still turned. She looked wildly around. There was no weapon handy. Yes, there was!—a small ointment jar of exquisite workmanship that stood on a pedestal at the head of her couch.

The girl slowly reached over for it, trying to make no sound. The grind of the pestle in the mortar filled in the rhythm of her movements. With infinite care she raised herself, raised the fragile jar. She hurled it.

As the missile left her fingers, the monk dodged suddenly. The precious vase thudded into a rare Ispahan, shivered into a thousand fragments. Yellow ointment streaked the reddish surface of the rug.

The lama whirled around, a scornful sneer on his brown parchment face. The skin was tight and smooth over high cheek bones; the lean, high nose was quite unlike the usual squatness of the Tibetans. His black eyes flashed commandingly. There was a knife in his hand.

In despair the girl looked around for another weapon.

"I shall have to kill you if you persist," the monk spoke surprisingly. "See!" He raised the keen blade and made a significant gesture across his throat.

The girl fell back.

"You speak English?" she panted.

He bowed mockingly. "Among many other tongues. I saw every move you made in here." He pointed to a tiny mirror set in the wall directly above the mortar.

Marian Temple stood erect. If the man knew English, then—

"What do you wish of me?" she asked. "If it's ransom, my people will pay—"

The lama interrupted scornfully. "Ransom! Ha! What do I need with that trash? Bits of gold that you Westerners kill and lie and cheat over!"

The girl was forgetting her terror in her curiosity.

"You've killed, too," she said pointedly.

"Yes, but for a different, a holier purpose. For power! Power over all men—the only real thing in a world of illusions."

"Why was I taken captive, then?" Marian asked.

The yellow monk smiled grimly.

"You will be the instrument of my power," he said.

She stared at him aghast. He did not seem insane.

"How?"

He threw up an arm.

"The Buddhas of Lamaism are outworn. Every lamasery has one; there is no merit in them. You are beneath one now. Can he breath, or speak, or move? He is but an idol of wood and precious metal. I—I shall set you up, a warm, breathing, living goddess. You will be decked in gorgeous robes and gems. You will smile. The people will see—and adore."

Marian Temple tried to envisage herself as a goddess. Somehow she felt an odd sense of relief.

"Then the strange being in the crystal was just a mummery?" She breathed freely. That scene had lain like a hidden pool of terror in the back of her mind. "The whole ceremony was a fraud?"

The change in the lama astounded her. The arrogant, ambitious monk shrank fearfully away; his features worked horribly. There was a light froth on his lips.

"He—he was a god!" The words burst from him unwillingly. He was suddenly shrunken and old.

"Nonsense." Marian tried to put a positiveness into her voice that she did not feel.

The yellow lama glared at her. For one awful second she thought he was going to plunge the knife into her bosom. Then the words flowed.

"He came from above, I tell you, clothed in the globe and in light. Here to our monastery. The red monks bowed. I refused, and he struck me down. He ordered us to do his bidding. He spoke no language, yet I understood. I hated the god, but I dared not disobey."

Suddenly he laughed, mockingly, horribly.

"You are right," he told the terrified girl. "He is not god; he is but some mummery. The white man's bullet destroyed him." He advanced sardonically. "Goddess! You shall be worshiped, and I shall be the power in the land!"

The girl shrank back as far as she could. He came closer; she could feel his rapid breathing.

It commenced as a rumble and ended in an ear-splitting crash that sounded as if the mountain had been split asunder. The room heaved and rocked; the carpets fell violently off the walls. Luckily Marian was already flat against the wall; she was thrown, but not badly hurt. The yellow monk, however, was caught in mid-stride. He lay huddled against the farther side. The contents of the mortar, a greenish powder, spilled over his immobile face. Blood trickled slowly from the left eye.

The roaring ceased. The room trembled once more, as though the mountain had given itself a final shake, and there was silence.

The girl arose unsteadily, panting. Now, if ever, was her chance to escape. She took one step forward when a voice slashed through her brain. It was no outward sound, yet it said commandingly, imperatively: *"Come!"*

There was no denying the summons. She felt an irresistible impulse to obey. Her feet started to walk mechanically. The body of the lama rose slowly, rigidly, the green poison flecking his lips. It moved forward with deliberate, rigid steps. He was dead—she was sure of that—the eyes were the eyes of a dead man, and the pallor of the face was a corpse pallor. Yet the dead man heard and obeyed!

She may have screamed. She was not quite certain of just what took place. The horror mercifully blotted out part of her memory. But she, too, went ahead, in back of the dead monk. Without a falter, he ascended a winding passageway, the girl directly behind. He pressed unerringly on the right spring within the hollow of the idol. The brazen belly opened outward, and they passed through—the dead man and the live girl.

The chamber of the idol was a veritable devil's caldron. The mountain-quake had sent huge fragments of ceiling rock thudding to the ground. The Buddha's head had broken off jaggedly at the neck, and the lolling, painted face leered wickedly up at them. But it was the procession that startled the girl almost out of her hypnotic obedience.

The red monks were marching. The living, the wounded, the dead; with faces rigid, with movements like mechanical dolls, they filed toward the opening that led to the great cavern where the god had been. In the very center of the strange procession strode Saunders, as rigid and as staring as any. He was bleeding from a dozen wounds. The lamas had not seized him without a struggle, and his dour face was set and hard. There was no flicker of recognition in his eyes.

The girl tried to faint, but a driving force impelled her on. Dead men walked along with her, corpses that moved their limbs up and down with regular tread. The living were but little better.

"If only I could faint and shut out all these horrors!" she moaned repeatedly— and walked ahead with steady pace.

They were through the orifice, streaming into the great cavern. The place was ablaze with orange light, and in the center, lightly poised, rested the great sphere. Within its bubble sheerness floated the god, the strange, elongated being with limp appendages and round, bald head. His eyes, Marian decided, had lost their inscrutability; there was a hint of weariness about them.

But more startling even than this was the sight of the stranger, the white man who had attacked the god and the lamas just as she was about to be sacrificed. He was standing close to the huge globe, nonchalantly, pistol in had, and *grinning!* Yes, in the midst of that chamber of horrors he was grinning. A likeable grin, thought Marian, the hypnotic power almost gone from her. He was tall, weathered, and lean.

The lamas, corpses and pseudo-corpses, dropped heavily to the ground, and bobbed at once to sitting positions. The girl found herself constrained downward, next to the lama in the yellow robe. The glare in his eyes was fixed, the green poison on his lips, meant for others, had served as Nemesis. She shuddered and tried to move away, but could not.

Then the god spoke. Again there was no outward sound; the bald head did not move, nor were there any lips from which speech could issue; but the girl heard and understood plainly. There was the feeling of immense boredom.

"People of earth," he said, "insects of a tiny speck in the great void—of all the inhabitants on planets and suns, you are the dullest, the slowest witted, the least important. Sharkis will not thank me for the specimens I have returned for his curiosity. I am going. An infinity of worlds and an eternity of time await me; the very thought of your existence will be lost in the vastness. Sharkis will remember you no longer on my return. Farewell!"

The sphere glowed into a flame of orange, and the being within rotated once, slowly. Marian noted suddenly that Bayley's grin had not left him; that the gun was still in his hand.

A long, fiery cylinder extended outward like a released jack-in-the-box, through the orifice into the outer world—up through unimaginable distance to alien universes.

The sphere commenced whirling, slowly at first, then faster and faster. The strange being within was but a blur of movement. Then the rotating sphere commenced to slide up the path of light piercing the sky like a flaming sword. Out it fled into the early morning, where men toiled in the accustomed fields and women went about their homely household tasks; up the shining path through the pale-blue of dawn sunshine, until it was only a mote of shining dust in infinity. Then it was gone. The alien being was on his far-wandering travels again.

Within the cavern, as the ambassador from Sharkis spurned the earth from under him, there was an indescribable confusion. The strange hypnosis departed suddenly, and the upheld dead went limp, sprawling into loose-limbed heaps—corpses. The odor of corruption rose like a miasma.

The living rubbed their eyes, and were suddenly awake. A united susurrus of terror burst from the lama's throats, and with one movement they cast themselves prone on the rocky floor.

"The devil was with us!" they cried, and groveled in fear.

Bayley was striding toward the girl.

"Thank heavens you are safe," he said fervently. "I'm Ward Bayley."

"I—I'm all right," she gasped, with a little shudder. "My name is Marian Temple. Please—let's get out of this horrible nightmare."

"If we can," he answered grimly. His eye roved over the prostrate horde—the dead and the living.

"Saunders!" he shouted.

A figure tried to rise, and collapsed. Bayley was there in three steps, the girl right behind him. He caught the pilot in his arms. He was bleeding profusely.

"Not hurt much," muttered the Scotsman feebly, and fainted.

Bayley spurned a prostrate monk with his foot. His gun pointed threateningly. The lama sprang to his feet. Bayley spoke rapidly in Tibetan. The red one nodded and answered in short, explosive gasps. He was respectful. The others were rising now, staring at the three white people, but making no move.

"It's all right," said Bayley to the girl. "They think we're heroes. We've saved them from the devil. Come!"

He threw the large figure of the pilot easily across his shoulder, and followed the monk. The girl walked at his side, pulling away involuntarily each time they passed a dead lama. The other monks trailed after at a respectful distance.

Through many winding passages they went, illuminated by the flare of smoky torches, until they came to the monastery at the foot of the mountain.

There, for several weeks, they rested, while Saunders tossed in delirium, and

Bayley had his own wounds dressed. The lamas tended all three with great care; they had routed the devil himself.

When at last Saunders was well enough to travel, the monks escorted them to the border of Tibet in a closed vehicle. No white man, they insisted, had ever set foot in this forbidden territory before; there were sights and sounds to drive them mad if they came upon them unprepared. Bayley smiled thinly, and did not protest.

In the jolting half light of the shrouded cart, Saunders did an unusual thing. He betrayed curiosity.

"What," he asked, "did you do to the being in the sphere to compel his departure from the earth?"

Bayley grinned.

"It was simple," he explained. "So simple as to be almost incredible. Remember when I took a shot at him and the globe disappeared?"

The girl nodded. It had saved her life, or, rather, levitation to an unknown universe.

"I only nicked a piece out of the substance of the sphere. When the lamas had forced me over the precipice, the ambassador from Sharkis was overhead. He was foolish enough to pick me up; thought I was a good specimen to send back to his master."

The girl was listening with parted lips. Her breathing came fast.

Bayley went on: "I found myself enclosed in a tiny sphere, filled with a peculiar fluid, not air, not liquid, but strangely exhilarating. The great globe was alongside, and the orange one stared out at me. I was desperate. Might as well die now as later, I thought, and, pulling my gun, I shot deliberately through my own enclosure, directly at the larger one."

Saunders said: "Gosh, what a chance you took!"

"It was the only way," Bayley answered simply. "The bullet drilled clean. I felt the rush to rarefied cold air into my chamber. But I watched the other. Something had happened. There was fear, actual fear, in the orange one's eyes. He seemed to struggle. The hole in his sphere plugged up almost at once, but I had seen enough.

"I pointed the gun threateningly, and said aloud, in English, that I could repeat the performance indefinitely. He understood, somehow, for there came to me a plea for mercy. I granted it on conditions. I learned afterward that guns were unknown elsewhere in the universe; that in spite of his almost supernatural powers, he feared a hole in his sphere."

"Why?" asked the girl.

"Our atmosphere was poison to him. The little whiff he got before he was able to plug it up almost killed him."

They rode along a while in silence.

Then Bayley chuckled softly.

Saunders stared at him glumly. His face was normal again; that is, dour and suspicious.

"What's the joke?" he demanded.

"I just remembered," said Bayley. "That pot-shot I took at the orange one was my last bullet. My gun was empty."

From this picture, used as the cover of the February 1930 issue of Air Wonder Stories (now merged into Wonder Stories) the prize stories were to be written. We see the strange-looking men, encased in some metallic suits, rising in hordes from metal spheres in the ground. They have established some sort of communication with the strange-looking ship. In the distance float two heavenly bodies—suns, or moons or planets.

$300.00 PRIZE CONTEST
FEBRUARY 1930 AIR WONDER STORIES

Mr. Miller is a student at Union College, Schenectady, N. Y., and is a "collector" of science-fiction themes, culled from his studies and from general conversations.

FIRST PRIZE $150.00
Awarded to
THE RED PLAGUE

By
P. SCHUYLER MILLER
302 So. Ten Broeck St.
Scotia, N. Y.

Wonder Stories provided the "image" (above) and invited readers to compose a story to accompany the illustration. Young Mr. Miller's prize-winner was "The Red Plague," for which he was awarded $150 "depression" dollars.

The
RED Plague

by P. Schuyler Miller

Readers of Hugo Gernsback's July 1930 Wonder Stories were informed that
college student P. Schuyler Miller (who went on to become one of the most popular
science fiction writers and personalities of all time) had won first prize for an
original story based on the accompanying illustration. Wonder Stories editors
said "Our readers will agree, we believe, that the use of the cover picture
was quite ingenious." We're sure that you will too!

A low, circling range of crumbling red cliffs hem in a tiny valley in the heart of the desert—a pale green speck in a sea of red sand. At their base, a great cavity in the cliff-face gapes black, set about with little black and red cubicles of baked mud or sheet iron. The valley itself is a scant half mile in diameter, a dot lost in the red waster, but in its center rise tall slim domes of silvery white, two hundred feet or more in height and a fourth as much in diameter, reflecting the blinding rays of the setting sun. About their base clusters a little, restless smudge of black, ebbing and flowing about the three broad vanes and interset jets of each great machine, resting on the base of white concrete that fills the center of the valley. High above, in the cloudless sky, a scattered swarm of gnats drone dully through the flickering haze beneath the deep blue heavens, where already dozens of stars are rivaling the brilliance of the setting sun.

Darkness, spangled with silver and set with gems of blue and red and gold, falls suddenly, with no blaze of twilight, over the crimson desert. In the little cubicles near the cave, in many of the tiny black openings of the silver towers, lights blink into being. From the valley floor rise circling shafts of light, white or golden or red, that bathe the silver towers and stab up into the star-spangled night. From their bosom, the droning gnats are spiraling down to the valley floor, to spew forth lesser blots of black figures that join the silent throng in the center of the valley, now drawn back from the base of the three silent domes of white metal.

Far off on the horizon a single gem swims into view in the sea of black, a glowing ruby, blazing steadily against the velvet darkness. Somewhere, a gong strikes once, a low throbbing beat of golden sound. Silence falls over the restless throng of black mites. Again it rings, dull and muffled as from far below the surface of the ground. In answer comes a blinking blaze of golden flame, veined with crimson and shot with silver, and on its heels a shattering blast of sound that starts little trickles of boulders on the face of the cliffs. And after it comes a fine intermittent piping that is lost in the silence of the desert. Above, three dots of red flare into incandescent white and vanish. Below, three towering domes of silver are gone from the concrete center of the little valley, where the splotch of black is thinning, spreading out into darkness, and the drone of gnats has risen once more.

So a wandering deity, roving carelessly through space in the neighborhood of an especially insignificant little sun, might have witnessed the going of Man's three hopes out into the uncharted, untried sea of space, leaving their little planet Earth to seek charity and brotherhood from an alien race who must have solved the problem that was wasting away the life of the planet. As is the way of such minor deities, his interest might have been aroused by this puny onslaught of a race of mites, and he might hesitate in order to tamper mischievously with the wheel of Fate, balancing Success against Death in an eternal instant of indecision, then tossing down his choice and going his way, just a little bored, to create a sun or crush a solar system.

Ten long years before, a nameless aviator, crossing one of the less dangerous deserts of western North America, woke to the face of his imminent destruction with a rude start as a scorching mass of incandescent metal hurtled past him into the blank white sands, throwing aloft a geyser of powdered rock and sand, and bringing him fluttering to earth in flames. When, nearly a week later, rescuers found him gnawing his last sandwich and shying pebbles at the still hot meteorite, a few noticed that immediately around it the sand was red, and crumbled queerly into dust, while the moisture in their bodies seemed to be sucked out by the abnormally dry air. The meteor was small, and buried deeply, and nobody gave it a second thought until it forced the knowledge of its presence upon the entire world.

That year, prolonged drought made the crops in a rather isolated section of Arizona fail, but nobody cared, with the exception of a few half-breeds and an Indian or two, who depended upon them for a livelihood, and a queer old cuss with long whiskers who made millions from a mine a hundred miles or so to the north, and who raved for months because his prize roses shriveled in the sun.

Two years later, the crimson sand reached the nearest of the regular tourist stations, where another "queer cuss" with a yellow walrus mustache and a couple of degrees was hunting for a meteorite which nobody had ever heard of. Then the world woke up, and wondered why something wasn't done about it all.

It took "Swede" Hansen just two weeks from the time when he left his canteen of water unstoppered for ten minutes in the shade of a red rock to the time when he found his meteorite—and the source of the Plague. In another fortnight the place where the thing had fallen resembled a cross between an airdrome and a university. By the end of the third year, the entire understanding population of the planet knew what had happened, and what in all probability would happen in all too short a length of time.

To be brief, the meteorite, the same which had brought down the aviator, had also brought to Earth from some place far outside the limits of the solar system that dread scourge which man knows as the Red Plague. It had one new element in it, radioactive, placed by the chemists beyond Uranium, which must needs have been formed under conditions strange enough to warrant its properties. This element was the catalyst, the carrier, so to speak, of the Plague. There were also certain unknown compounds of the most inert of the known elements, which, in the presence of the new *Galactium*, constituted the Red Plague itself.

As Hansen very soon discovered, once given the clue of the empty canteen, the Red Plague meant the eventual and rapid withdrawal of water from the list of Man's resources and necessities. These new compounds, apparently as indestructible as their parent elements, attacked all silica and aluminum rocks. Activated by infinitesimal amounts of *Galactium*, which was readily soluble in them, they attacked rock and soil of almost any sort, reducing it to a crumbling crimson sand, which in turn pulverized to a fine red dust of nearly molecular dimensions and consequently of enormous surface. This either sand or dust, had practically infinite powers of adsorption for water.

The Plague Spreads

With this huge available surface in even the smallest mass of dust, and with the additional properties which amounted to the unprecedented and inexplicable phenomenon of chemical magnetism for water, any moisture that came anywhere near this red menace was immediately and complete adsorbed onto the surface of the dust. Valid physical and chemical tests proved that the water was adsorbed rather than being absorbed into any pores or used as water of crystallization. The stuff spread like wildfire, the fine gold dust going its deadly way on every gust of hot dry wind, and in no time the leprous red scabs festered everywhere in the northern half of the western hemisphere—indeed, it *must not* be so used, for to Man and to all the living creatures of Earth water is Life.

Scientists of every race and sort, led by the tireless Hansen, worked endlessly over the dust, searching for anti-catalysts, searching for solvents, searching for anything that might save America's water, or regain that which had already been lost. For no man could remove from the dust that water which it had taken to itself. Electrolysis, indeed, broke the water into its component hydrogen and oxygen, but in the vicinity of the radioactive catalyst they instantly recombined to form water, giving a beautiful and expensive explosion but nothing more. So electrolysis, and with it the entire field of electricity, was foolishly abandoned. And so the vain work went on.

Five years passed, years of toil and isolation and knowledge that death was not far off for America. In the face of the peril to the world, Europe and the rest of the nations of the planet kept a strict embargo upon immigration. Commerce was strictly one-sided: water poured from all the world into America—at a price. Everywhere were the blackened vegetation, the shriveled bodies, the empty river beds, and the dry red scabs of the Red Plague. And still Hansen labored tirelessly, with all the millions of old Ephraim Cutter, the mine-owner whose roses had withered and died, at his disposal.

Then, with the coming of the fifth year, panic broke over the world. For, whether from winds, from birds, or from other, smaller meteorites, or even, as many hinted, deliberately spread by inhuman fiends, the Red Plague burst over the planet from pole to pole, and Death stared Man in the face. Science had found that the Plague did not of itself sink far beneath the surface of the Earth, and, consequently, every day found more frantically digging men and women, striving to bury themselves blindly in the supposed safety of the Earth's heart. Soon this seemed the only refuge, and government by government, the world sought the isolation of great Man-made caverns deep in the earth. And then a young astronomer announced that it was the dust of the Plague that colored Mars!

Every eye was turned to the cloudless, blue-black skies, star-flecked even in the daytime, where Mars swam low. Madness came, frenzied curses, for many believed that it was from Mars that the meteorite bearing the Plague had come. But Science led through to sanity, showed that such a thought was ridiculous and impossible, asked why Mars should visit destruction upon a planet which might save it from a like fate. And Science showed hope, for Science knew that even as our own polar caps of ice were fast waning, and snows no longer came nor vegetation made green the river valleys, so the polar caps of Mars were *growing*, year by year, creeping in toward the red wastes of the equator, outlining the mysterious "canals" with deeper and broader green as time passed. *Mars was conquering the Red Plague!*

As the dust of the Plague spread over the Earth and outlawed traffic upon its surface for fear of carrying the dread red dust to some untouched spot, Man had taken entirely to the aid. From the broad roof-fields of every towering city, from little farms and great factories, from ocean liner and man-made floating island rose numberless ships of the air, carrying Man about his business. In a short five years the few great continental air-lines had spread over all the world. Not long since, Man had feared the air, feared to leave the surface of his planet and entrust his life and safety to Science. Now, Man feared the ground! Atomic energy became available in part, albeit at great expense, and now every man paid his government for the energy which kept him safe above the plague-infested surface of the Earth.

With the news of the young astronomer borne by the news service to every corner of the world, Man revived again the dreams of those days long before the Plague when scientist and layman alike struggled with the thought of leaving this little Earth and speeding, in great shining rockets, out into empty space, to other planets, other suns, other universes. And with the world at his back, old Ephraim Cutter turned his failing millions from the fruitless battling of the Plague to Man's last hope—a great, threefold leap into space, in an effort to enlist the peoples of Mars in the service of a helpless Earth. Three great rockets of strong, light *durium,* built by the master engineers of the world, driven by the energy of the broken atom, manned each by a crew of six experts, would drive up into the night from the still-green oval of Cutter's Hole, up and up until at last the red deserts of Mars should be beneath, and the solution to Man's problem should lie before the three ships of space, to be won or lost forever.

Rising at first slowly, then ever faster, until the broadening bowl of the Earth changed to a floating ball of bloody green, the three rockets sped up-ward and outward, glowing from cherry red to incandescent white with the friction of the atmosphere, then cooling in the absolute zero of space with a suddenness that set the sorely strained metal hull into a bedlam of creaking as it cooled. Only superb workmanship in the making of the great ships kept them from bursting under the enormous tension. In each, five men sweated and strained under the terrific heat and acceleration—men who had been trained for five long years to withstand these very burdens. Before the master control-board, sunk in the heart of the ship where no harm might come to it, sat the commander of each rocket, eyes strained to the televisor and the many dials of the board, beside him food capsules and the sleep drug, that he might work for three Earth-days without relief—in the first of the three, "Swede" Hansen. Five hundred miles of space separated the three great rockets, surrounded by the luminous golden haze of their exhaust gases, but in the televisor each com-mander stood side by side with his fellow, bristling Swede, burly spectacled Negro, and clean-cut athlete from Annapolis, guiding, by word and touch and gesture, their silvery ships of space. They were forgetful of the telescopes on mountain peak or desert plateau that search the skies for three tiny fleeting shapes with the glory of the sun reflected from their shining metal sides.

On the Way!

At the little barred windows of heavily-wired quartz, the men of the crew gazed wistfully at the green and blue globe, etched with familiar outlines and splotched with scabrous red, that grew ever smaller behind. Now and again the voice of their commander would ring from the speaker in the wall, his gestures on the great screen direct them, and they would sink panting to the floor or flounder helpless in their hammocks while the great after jets poured forth golden vapor and the starry heavens reeled and spun before the enormous acceleration that drove them ever nearer to their top speed of one hundred thousand miles per hour. For an instant, far behind in the black of space, two silver specks drove on and on along the unmarked trail that Man followed for the first time. Then the rolling thunder of a jet would shake the ship and the swinging heavens sweep them from sight. A strange and thrilling experience for these erstwhile masters of the air, now become navigators of empty endlessness.

Ahead, the Moon loomed dead and bare, its pocked and pitted face swelling into a wilderness of crater and jagged crag and bottomless crevices, blanketed in the dense white volcanic dust that once spewed from the thousands of great volcanos of a living world! Then, with the passing of the day on the chronometers, its pear-shaped bulk swung past barely a million miles below, and three little specks of silver light hurtled on into emptiness, half a million miles with each five hours.

"Swede" Hansen slept less than any man in that leap through space. On every ship were five men beside the master, each fully capable of handling the ship for a day or a week, gauging with trained accuracy the change for any slightest deflection of the course, holding to the thin silver line on the space chart, representing a leeway of many thousand miles (the line ran straight from green curse to red against the polished black) watching the pressure, the fuel, the air, the radiation rate and temperature, doing all the thousand and one things, great and small, that navigation by dead reckoning in open space must entail. On all but the flagship of the little fleet, each man took his turn of three days, so that with the last watch, at the end of the third week, each commander should take his post to maneuver his ship through the atmosphere of Mars to a safe landing. But in the leading ship the bristling yellow moustache would appear in the televisor, the blue eyes twinkle, and the jolly voice boom in the speaker.

"Hallo! How you takin' it, over there? Tell your lazy captain that the girls should be sunburned to suit his taste in color, on Mars!" Or else—

"Hallo! You there, on number three! Where's your commander—writin' love letters or playin' football? Tell him he's a thousand off the median, or else I am."

And they would come to the control room of their ships, the great bulky Negro with his perpetual grin and horn-rimmed spectacles, and the college man with a dream in his smiling eyes, and josh back at him, or send little meaningful messages from man to man of the crews.

"Hey, Swede!" the athlete would shout. "I dare you to come over and wrestle me, you big soft lump! Who called you a scientist, you blamed old walrus? If you don't chew off that fringe of bristles, right pronto, I'll send a little meteor over to clip 'em for you!"

"Never mind my whiskers, young fellow. An' don't sass your commander-in-chief, or he'll have you marooned on an asteroid to cool off. Say, kid, tell Frenchy there, your radio man, that Bill got a whale of a picture of Eros the other day when we passed it. He says he can make out water on it, but it takes pretty good eyes to make out the mountain ranges, beat that if you can."

Or the Negro, Johnson. He talked rather slowly, but moved like lightning at the controls, and always spoke in a serious tone that belied his flashing grin and the way in which he ignored his spectacles.

"Oh, Cap'n Hansen, we're havin' a little mite of trouble over here, with the vision apparatus, and our radio man has the willies from stayin' awake too long watchin' the stars. I sort of thought you might know something about it. It's been a-flickerin' off an' on, sort of like a loose connection somewhere, but we don't seem to be able to find it. I'd appreciate it a lot if you would sort of think it over some time soon, an' let me know what your idea is."

"*Say*, Johnny, where d'you keep the brains when you're off the controls? Didn't you tell me not more than a week ago that you'd moved the blamed thing up near the generator? You've got a hole in your screenin' some place, an' the generator's just naturally raisin' Old Scratch with your field."

"Thanks, Cap'n, thanks a lot. You know that I'm not just dumb, but there's a heap of sunburn to weigh me down, like you have with that shoe-brush of yours. I'll see you later when we fix the vision up a bit better."

A pleasant trio, good friends, great men and great scientists, companions to their mixed crews. And then, two weeks out, a frantic call came from the control room of the steadily decelerating ship that sent "Swede" to the board on the run with every man on edge and at his post. There was no time for more than a nod and a brief "Hallo!" to his comrades, each in his place with a grim set expression on his face. Out of space, directly in the course of the onrushing ships, a huge, widespread swarm of meteors plunged directly toward the three tiny silver specks. They could not stop, or diverge widely, could not survive the sudden acceleration of the change. At the terrible speed with which they were approaching head on the scattered cluster of iron and stone giants, any collision must be fatal, and the only chance must be to plunge through the thinnest part of the swarm, deflecting where possible, and trusting to God for the rest.

On, on, into the maelstrom of hurtling star-fragments, the smallest of which could deal destruction to any of the ships, and hence to an entire planet, the first rocket sped. "Swede," every sense on edge, every muscle tense, hovered over the controls. Here, half a mile meant life or death. A rushing bulk in the screen, the whirl of a dial, the rattling thunder of a jet, a sickening lurch, and safety—repeated in terms of seconds, with miles of crowded space in every swerve!

Again and again, time after time, then a glancing blow from a mass of rock and iron the size of a basketball, that ripped the great armored plates off the side of the ship for half its length, destroying a vane entirely and driving a deep dent in the inner sheathing—then dart and dodge and through in safety! And within twenty seconds Johnson is in it, gripping his dials grimly, cold sweat on his shining face, strong white teeth clenched through a mangled lip! Swerve, leap, swerve again, and then a blur of flame in the screen, a tearing of metal, and blackness? On the other screen a clean-shaven man grits his teeth and turns aside his straining eyes, then freezes to his work, his duty to Man. On, on, through flaying masses the size of giant buildings, fragments of lost planets, swerving, darting, slowing, a master's hand at the keyboard and dials, thin lips set in a narrow line under the strain of the acceleration! Ten seconds, twenty, twenty-five, and the way is clear. He shudders, grins into the televisor at "Swede," then freezes in horror! His voice chokes in the speaker. "So long, you— damned—old—walrus—you!" In a flash he is gone, shattered by the great thing that hurtled in the wake of the storm, or frozen instantly in the absolute cold of space. Perhaps neither was more than a hundred miles off "Swede's" course, the course of safety, a mere three second's distance, but in all likelihood ten miles would have been as fatal. It was four days before "Swede" Hansen took over the controls, to guide the slowing ship safely to its landing.

On Mars!

Down through the thin air of Mars, gliding in a long, flat spiral over the endless wastes of red sand through which jutted the crumbling remains of ancient peaks, the battered space-ship sank toward the surface of the planet, rising, become flatter, then suddenly concave. The canals were plain in the clear air, broad lanes of matted moss running mile on mile across the decayed red wastes, blending at the edges into the desert of crimson dust that swirls in great clouds over the barren wilderness. Here and there they converged, came together in great circular areas many miles across, where the crumbling rock that jutted up through the rank moss had strange, half familiar forms. Cities had been here, once. In some the moss was withering, the lanes of green velvet thinning before the onslaught of the Red Plague. Near the equator, especially, was this true, where the shattered ship must land. To the north and south, where broad ice caps glistened white, it might be otherwise. Time must tell, would tell.

"Swede" Hansen, worn, haggard, the memory of his comrades deep in his eyes, struggled through the crumpled metal port of the mighty ship that had plowed deep in the sand, its vanes twisted and scored, the edge of the gaping slash in its hull fused by the friction of the air. After him came three men. Two had been in that part of the ship which was struck, and died of the sudden shock and compression which had dented the insulating armor and burst in an inner bulkhead. A few hundred feet away the moss began, an unhealthy metallic green. Above, opposite the blazing sun, swung Phobos and Deimos, the two moons of Mars—Phobos a scant six thousand miles above the planet, and Deimos, jerked from its former distant orbit by the most massive comet in the records of astronomy, which now rotated very near its limit of disruption, and was daily drawing closer to its mother planet. Neither showed any important markings, clouds of pumice and ash from long extinct volcanoes having buried all mountainous features of their surfaces, even as has been done on a less thorough scale on the Moon. Sunlight, reflected from the red surface of their parent planet, bathed them in an orange light.

Wearily the four men dragged forth the heavy cases which contained parts of the comfortable and roomy aero with which they were to explore this new planet. There would be more room, now, for food and instruments, with two men less, they thought bitterly. Then they withdrew into the ship, leaving an electrical alarm with the cases, for a much needed rest. Now that there was no longer danger of the storeroom collapsing on the aero, and leaving them stranded, the world and Man could wait for one more day.

When the sun set once more over the red Martian wastes, a new, lithe form lay beside the crumpled rocket, speed in every line of its marvelously designed frame. The engineers of Earth had striven long and hard to provide this most perfect of Man's aeros for the expedition. Of tough, shining metal and clear crystal, stream-lined with the utmost perfection, capable of circling the Earth in a day or less, no man of the remaining crew but was proud of the trim craft. And he who had designed her, young Jimmy Van Deusen, late of Boston, strutted grinning beside her, stroking the broad stubby wings and tail surfaces, testing the resilient landing gear, looking to the lubrication of the twin propellers and trio of helicopters, and at last, at a word from his chief, leaping to the pilot's cockpit for a test flight. The atomic motors purred sleepily, the helicopters began their crescendo whine, then with a flash of silver under the setting sun he was off, and up within fifty yards, the wind whistling over the clean cut body of the aero and setting up tiny whirlpools in the red dust. Up and up, until the vanished sun once more shone gloriously on the silver bird of Man, up until only a shining speck was visible, then down, mile on mile in a screaming dive that flattened out a bare thousand feet above the sands, and changed to a mad frenzy of loop and spin and roll, climbing, diving, whirling. Then, with propellers and helicopters reversed, dropping almost vertically to rest beside the great half buried hulk of the rocket. He tumbled out joyously.

"She's great Swede!" he shouted. "With this atmosphere, and gravity like this— Wow! We're going to go places and do things with this little lady, all right, and don't you doubt it! Oh what a ship!"

"Good. We must not waste time. In the morning, early, we should go. Can we?"

"Sure! We could go right now, if we were packed. Let's stow everything away now, and beat the sun up."

So, with the rising sun, the little ship with its cargo of four eager men roared up in a golden mist of disintegrated atoms and flashed through the brightening skies to the southward, toward the greatest ice cap of Mars. As mile after mile sped by beneath, affording brief glimpses of ruined, crumbling cities and rotting red peaks, they saw with hope and joy that the green lanes of giant moss became ranker and broader, seeming to press out from the line of their flight into the red desert on either side.

Then, far on the horizon, appeared a flashing, dazzling glory of light, the mighty Antarctic ice sheet of Mars. Here was the great area over which a triumphant Mars had conquered the Red Plague, had redeemed her precious water, was doing so day after day. Here would be the Martians, skilled, intelligent beings, wiser than Man, who must be persuaded to share their secret with a sister planet before it was too late. An hour, now, and they would be there!

And with the passing of that endless hour, the green path had broadened into a mighty emerald carpet, leading straight to the base of the towering walls of ice that crowded down from the south. Rimming about the rampart of ice, separating it from the green of the converging lanes, lay water, a lake of cool, pure water, lying open and unharmed under the rays of the sun!

Then Jimmy noticed *them*, queer oblong ships that floated motionless above the edge of the narrow lake. Three were in sight, perhaps fifty miles apart and two hundred feet above the line where water and moss merged. More than the thin air and lesser gravity, these men of Earth had found it hard to accustom their senses and motions to the judging of distance on this planet of greater curvature, but comparison with more familiar objects later gave the necessary clue to their size and distance. The strange machines were about forty feet in length and twenty-five in width at the middle. They seemed to be made of pure gold. In a fifteen foot ring at each end was set a polished mirror of green stone, while above the tubular central body, which separated the rings, was a bulbous tower some ten feet in height. Everywhere were little windows of the green crystal, indicating that creatures of some sort manned the machine, though it was little more than ten feet in thickness. No other sign of life or intelligence was visible.

"Hey," said Jimmy hoarsely, "they must be pretty small, to man that. What is it, anyway, Harry? Got any ideas?"

"Certainly," replied the tall Englishman. "It seems to me to be plain enough that it is the thing that we are after, the apparatus that makes the moss grow and the Plague fail. But where are the Martians? They can't live in those."

"Hover for a while, Jimmy," put in Hansen. "If they're there, they ought to see us and make their presence known. We can afford to wait, and it won't do to make them our enemies. We will have to handle them with kid gloves."

The Examination

For nearly two hours they hovered, or circled the queer machine, trying to peer through the windows, but without result. Then "Scotty" MacRae, the third man of the crew, who had been roughly mapping the place, grabbed Harry by the arm, and pointed below. The others, seeing the gesture, looked through the ports at the surface of the planet, a hundred feet or so below.

The thick carpet of moss was buckling upward in three widely separated spots, showing the red earth beneath, which was being pushed slowly upward and outward by some slow steady pressure from below. Then a polished dome of pink metal appeared, followed by two others, and rose with a slow rotation some thirty feet into the air, revealing a ring of hooded openings leading onto a narrow ledge that ran around the entire dome. From a large opening in the flattened peak, little red figures were swiftly rising toward the aero and the queer machine, on which they began to play bright yellow rays of some sort—human figures, five feet in height.

They approached the aero fearlessly, appearing now as suits of red and white metal with crystal head-pieces above which protruded luminous green horns. As the little figures sped upward or came to rest, these correspondingly came together or diverged, showing that by interaction between them and force field of some sort these individual flyers were propelled. Where hands would have been, on Earth, two pivoted ray-tubes were fastened.

One of the little flyers rose barely ten feet in front of the hovering aero. Others joined it. The heads of the Martians were visible through the crystal, ugly little creatures, but evidently enormously advanced. The head and face were bare and shiny, with large ears pressed flat against the skull, adapted for hearing in the rare atmosphere. The chin was small, pointed, and protruding, the jaw small, the mouth thin and expressionless. Great nostrils in a nearly vertical nose made it possible to inhale great lungsful of thin air with comparative ease. The black eyes, round and goggling, and sunk deep in their sockets, regarded the men with an indifferent stare.

Suddenly the nearest Martian flashed his yellow ray full in the faces of the group.

"Who are you?" came the thought. "What do you want?"

Hansen replied verbally, pointing to his lips to indicate that he could talk.

"Do not speak. Think. I have the ray on you. Our languages are not the same."

Each mentally pictured the history of their expedition, its cause, the fate of their companions. Hansen asked to see someone in authority.

"You are from the Third Planet. We have noted the coming of the Plague. We expected you. You will be examined. If you prove worthy, you race will be aided. If not, it is wisest that you perish. Leave your machine for examination. It will be returned, if you need it. Land, and follow me."

At a sign from Hansen, Jimmy brought the aero to the ground beside the nearest dome, and the four men left it to follow the Martians. He led them into one of the openings on the ledge, which closed, leaving them in the dark. Suddenly the floor sank, bearing them down into the blackness, then stopping short many feet below the surface. They followed their little guide into a vast, dim cavern, crowded with the little red forms of flying Martians, entered a long low vehicle that shot like a bullet through the narrow streets, all the while emitting a high pitched wail. They came finally to a halt before a great windowless building of grey metal, surrounded by a wide plaza. Inside, they were shoved into a small bare room and left alone. The door, when they turned, was invisible.

Then, through a crystal oval in the ceiling, the yellow ray flooded every corner of the room. Standing there, helpless, they felt the probing questions of their examiners, pelting them with queries of all sorts, dragging every thought from their bewildered brains. They knew the futility of any failure to reply, and hence settled down to search their memories for every scrap of information that they might contain which would better outline Man's knowledge of the Universe. Now and then, when memories conflicted, the questioning took on a sharper, impatient note until the point in question was fully cleared. Once or twice, as they spoke of the atomic release that provided Man with energy, the questions were eager with the knowledge of a new, unsuspected truth. It was this power of Man to partially free the energy of the atom which proved his worth and his right to the air and brotherhood of the peoples of Mars, a race which, for all its greater age and triumphs in other fields, had failed utterly in this. At last the ray flashed out, and they sank on the hard cold floor in exhausted sleep.

Their former guide woke them, led them to an escalator, then left them. The moving metal belt rose steeply into the upper portion of the building, ran on through the dark and out into light, dim, but brighter than the outer caverns. The Martians, adapted by centuries of life to dimness, could not stand light such as they might easily have produced artificially, and when in their golden electrifying machines must needs use the green crystal to shield them from the sun.

Now, for the first time, they saw a Martian without his flying and protecting suit. They had slight, dwarfed forms, barely four feet tall, with huge chests and tiny legs. Their arms were short and thin, with large delicate hands and long, very slender fingers that seemed well on the way to the formation of tentacles. When they spoke, surprisingly enough, their voices were deep and graceful, showing that their dwarfed size was due to no disease or physical defect, but to direct evolution under the cramped conditions of under ground life.

Now the thought-carrying ray was focused on them once more, and from the ten greatest scientists of all Mars they learned indelibly what the Martian government had decided to tell them.

Several thousand years before, when the Martians had not yet attained Man's station in life, a meteor bearing the Plague fell in the heart of the most densely populated portion of Mars, and spread red destruction over all the planet. Even as Man was doing now, they had buried their cities deep into the safety of the planet's heart, and there in the semi-darkness had developed the existing race, mental giants but physical dwarfs.

Always they had striven to combat the Red Plague, which had covered all the surface of Mars and was slowly eating its way toward their retreat. There, in their great natural and man-made caverns, they had discovered the motive force of the flying suits, and of all their flying apparatus. They had developed a crystalline substance so energized in a manner analogous to magnetism, that when like poles were brought together, they reversed the gravitational field over an area depending on their strength. When they lay in the same line, it was neutralized, and the flyer hung motionless, or drifted as the mechanism of the solar system willed. At any median angle, with reversed polarity, gravitation was amplified. The use of variations of this principle for nearly all extended motion led to the ultimate development of their atrophied legs and feet, and the formation of slender, flexible fingers for manipulation of the keyboard controls common to all their devices.

Then, accidentally, they found that a very strong electronic field would effect the rapid disintegration of the catalyst, our *Galactium*, to familiar elements, leaving the other compounds harmless except for any natural adsorptive powers of a dust so finely divided. Of course, it would again become the former menace, but here it was discovered that certain mosses flourished in the newly reclaimed soil, and that they so altered the compounds as to make the catalyst impotent. Again, with the mosses removed, contact with the pure compounds would cause something like a change into the harmful forms, but this could be avoided, and moss-tracks were laid from most of the buried cities to the poles, where some water yet lingered, and reclamation began. Most important of all, the reclaimed soil was extremely fertile, and could be used in the synthesis of the energized crystal. The long, thin machines of gold were energy converters, turning the radiation of the sun into electrical energy, and laying down the electric field that destroyed the catalyst. Already, the area of permanently reclaimed land had spread remarkably, and other plants were growing where the moss had cleared the way. These, with the frequency of the thought ray, were the secrets that Mars gave to her sister, Earth, and in turn the Martians learned the application of their devices to the liberation of atomic energy, somewhat more efficient than solar radiation as a source of power.

"That is all," concluded the spokesman of the Martian men of Science. "You will be given the moss. A space ship of your own type has been prepared for you.

You may use the gravitors to repel meteors. You, of the Third Planet, Tellus or Earth, are better for physical strife than are we. Our minds are capable of greater comprehension. Let us henceforth share our knowledge, that together we may succeed where one race should soon fail. We will not leave Mars, for we are physically unfitted for the strain. It will take thousands of years to change us, for we are an old race. Meanwhile, come and go in peace and welcome. Tell us of the Universe, which we may not see for ourselves. Be our bodies and our senses, and we will aid your new minds. Farewell!"

The manipulation of the new ship was easily learned, though quickness on the unfamiliar keyboard control came hard to men accustomed by long practice to switches, levers, and dials. Soon Mars was shrinking behind the spherical space ship with its great projecting rods of crystal at top and bottom. Then space once more opened before them, and closed once more behind as the white phantom of the Moon flashed past, and Earth at last spun below.

Everyone knows the result. The Martian moss flourished, and, crossed with plants of our own, proved more effective than ever. The unsuspected value of the red earth has been quickly taken advantage of in many fields, and the crimson wastes are taking on a new appearance. Within the year, a second expedition will set forth into space, carrying the new plants to Mars, solving the shrouded mysteries of Venus, reaching out beyond the asteroids to the major planets, whose larger satellites may harbor life. The thought ray breaks down the barriers of race between all thinking beings, and it seem certain that at last the dreams of the ancient writers are to be realized in a union of the planets in knowledge and peace.

P. SCHUYLER MILLER

The RED Brain

by Donald Wandrei

This is one of the most famous stories ever published in Weird Tales magazine, best remembered for its oft-quoted last line. (Don't read it first!)—FJA
Weird Tales, October 1927

One by one the pale stars in the sky overhead had twinkled fainter and gone out. One by one those lights flaming whitely with their clear, cold flame had dimmed and darkened. One by one they had vanished forever, and in their places had come patches of ink that blotted out immense areas of a sky once luminous with hordes of brightly shining stars.

Years had passed; centuries had fled backward; the accumulating thousands had turned into millions, and they, too, had faded into the oblivion of eternity. The earth had disappeared. The sun had cooled and hardened, and had dissolved into the dust of its grave. The solar system and innumerable other systems had broken up and vanished, and their fragments had swelled the clouds of dust which were engulfing the entire universe. In the billions of years which had passed, sweeping everything on toward the gathering doom, the huge bodies, once countless, that had dotted the sky and hurtled through unmeasurable immensities of space had lessened in number and disintegrated until the black pall of the sky was broken only at rare intervals by dim spots of light—light ever growing paler and darker.

No one knew when the dust had begun to gather, but far back in the forgotten dawn of time the dead worlds, in their ceaseless wanderings, had become smaller and had slowly broken up. What happened to them, no one knew or cared, for there was then none to know or care. The worlds had vanished, unremembered and unmourned.

Those were the nuclei of the dust. Those were the progenitors of the universal dissolution which now approached its completion. Those were the stars which had first burned out, died, and wasted away in myriads of atoms. Those were the mushroom growths which had first passed into nothingness in a puff of dust.

Slowly the faint wisps had gathered into clouds, the clouds into seas, and the seas into monstrous oceans of gently heaving dust, dust that drifted from dead and

413

dying worlds, from interstellar collisions of plunging stars, from rushing meteors and streaming comets which madly flamed from the void and hurtled into the abyss.

The dust had spread and spread. The dim luminosity of the heavens had become fainter as great blots of black appeared far in the outer depths of space. In all the millions and billions and trillions of years that had fled into the past, the cosmic dust had been gathering, and the starry horde had been dwindling. There was a time when the universe consisted of hundreds of millions of stars, planets, and suns; but they were as ephemeral as life or dreams, and like life or dreams they faded and vanished, one by one.

The smaller worlds were obliterated first, then the larger, and so in ever-ascending steps to the unchecked giants which roared their fury and blazed their whiteness through the conquering dust and the realms of night. Never did the Cosmic Dust cease its hellish and relentless war on the universe; it choked the little aerolites; it swallowed the helpless satellites; it swirled around the leaping comets that rocketed from one black end of the universe to the other, flaming their trailing splendor, tearing paths of wild adventure through horizonless infinitudes the dust already ruled; it clawed at the planets and sucked their very being; it washed, hateful and brooding, about the monarchs and plucked at their lands and deserts.

Thicker, thicker, always thicker grew the Cosmic Dust, until the giants no longer could watch each other's gyres far across the void. Instead, they thundered through the waste, lonely, despairing, and lost. In solitary grandeur they burned their brilliant beauty. In solitary majesty they waited for their doom. In solitary defeat, kings to the last, they succumbed to the dust. And in solitary death they disappeared.

Of all the stars in all the countless host that once had spotted the heavens, there remained only Antares. Antares, immensest of the stars, alone was left, the last body in the universe, inhabited by the last race ever to have consciousness, ever to live. That race, in hopeless compassion, had watched the darkening skies and had counted with miserly care the stars which resisted. Every one that twinkled out wrenched their hearts; every one that ceased to struggle and was swallowed by the tides of dust added a new strain to the national anthem, that indescribable melody, that infinitely somber paean of doom which tolled a solemn harmony in every heart of the dying race. The dwellers had built a great crystal dome around their world in order to keep out the dust and to keep in the atmosphere, and under this dome the watchers kept their silent sentinel. The shadows had swept in faster and faster from the farther realms of darkness, engulfing more rapidly the last of the stars. The astronomers' task had become easier, but the saddest on Antares: that of watching the universe die, of watching Death and Oblivion spread a pall of blackness over all that was, all that would be.

The last star, Mira, second only to Antares, had shone frostily pale, twinkled more darkly—and vanished. There was nothing in all Space except an illimitable expanse of dust that stretched on and on in every direction; only this, and Antares.

No longer did the astronomers watch the heavens to glimpse again that dying star before it succumbed. No longer did they scan the upper reaches—everywhere swirled the dust, enshrouding Space with a choking blackness. Once there had been sown through the abyss a multitude of morbidly beautiful stars, whitely shining, wan— now there was none. Once there had been light in the sky—now there was none. Once there had been a dim phosphorescence in the vault—now it was a heavy-hanging pall of ebony, a rayless realm of gloom, a smothering thing of blackness eternal and infinite.

"We meet again in this Hall of the Mist, not in the hope that a remedy has been found, but that we find how best it is fitting that we die. We meet, not in the vain hope that we may control the dust, but in the hope that we may triumph even as we are obliterated. We cannot win the struggle, save in meeting our death heroically."

The speaker paused. All around him towered a hall of Space rampant. Far above spread a vague roof whose flowing sides melted into the lost and dreamy distances, a roof supported by unseen walls and by the mighty pillars which rolled upward at long intervals from the smoothly marbled floor. A faint haze seemed always to be hanging in the air because of the measureless lengths of that architectural colossus. Like a boundless plain the expanse of the floor swept forever onward with a dull-gleaming whiteness. Dim in the distance, the speaker reclined on a metal dais raised above the sea of beings in front of him. But he was not, in reality, a speaker, nor was he a being such as those which had inhabited the world called Earth.

Evolution, because of the unusual conditions on Antares, had proceeded along lines utterly different from those followed on the various bodies which had dotted the heavens when the deep was sprinkled with stars in the years now gone. Antares was the hugest sun that had leaped from the primeval chaos. When it cooled, it cooled far more slowly than the others, and when life once again began it was assured of an existence not of thousands, not of millions, but of billions of years.

That life, when it began, had passed from the simple forms to the age of land juggernauts, and so by steps on and on up the scale. The civilizations of other worlds had reached their apex and the worlds themselves become cold and lifeless at the time when the mighty civilization of Antares was beginning.

The star, because of discords arising from its enormous population, had then passed through a period of warfare until such terrific and fearful scourges of destruction were produced that in the Two Days War seven billion of the eight and one-half billion inhabitants were slaughtered. Those two days of carnage, followed by pestilential diseases which carried off three-fourths of the remaining inhabitants, ended war for eons.

From then on, the golden age began. The minds of the people of Antares became bigger and bigger, their bodies proportionately smaller, until the cycle eventually was completed. Every being in front of the speaker was a monstrous heap of black viscidity, each mass an enormous brain, a sexless thing that lived for Thought. Long ago it had been discovered that life could be created artificially in tissue formed in the laboratories of the chemists. Sex was thus destroyed, and the inhabitants no longer spent their time in taking care of families. Nearly all the countless hours that were saved were put into scientific advance, with the result that the star leaped forward in an age of progress never paralleled.

The beings, rapidly becoming Brains, found that by the extermination of the parasites and bacteria on Antares, by changing their own organic structure, and by *willing* to live, they approached immortality. They discovered the secrets of Time and Space; they knew the extent of the universe, and how Space in its farther reaches became self-annihilating. They knew that life was self-created and controlled its own period of duration. They knew that when a life, tired of existence, killed itself, it was dead forever; it could not live again, for death was the final chemical change of life.

These were the shapes that spread in the vast sea before the speaker. They were shapes because they could assume any form they wished. Their all-powerful minds had complete control of that which was themselves. When the Brains were desirous of traveling, they relaxed from their usual semi-rigidity and flowed from place to place like a stream of ink rushing down a hill; when they were tired, they flattened into disks; when expounding their thoughts, they became towering pillars of rigid ooze; and when lost in abstraction, or in a pleasurable contemplation of the unbounded worlds created in their minds, within which they often wandered, they resembled huge, dormant balls.

From the speaker himself had come no sound although he had imparted his thoughts to his sentient assembly. The thoughts of the Brains, when their minds permitted, emanated to those about them instantly, like electric waves. Antares was a world of eternal, unbroken silence.

The Great Brain's thoughts continued to flow out. "Long ago, the approaching doom became known to us all. We could do nothing then; probably we can do nothing now. It does not matter greatly, of course, for existence is a useless thing which benefits no one. But nevertheless, at that meeting in an unremembered year, we asked those who were willing to try to think of some possible way of saving our own star, at least, if not the others. There was no reward offered, for there was no reward adequate. All that the Brain would receive would be glory as one of the greatest which has ever been produced. The rest of us, too, would receive only the effects of that glory in the knowledge that we had conquered Fate, hitherto, and still, considered inexorable; we would derive pleasure only from the fact that we, self-creating and all but supreme, had made ourselves supreme by conquering the worst and most powerful menace which has ever attacked life, time, and the universe: the Cosmic Dust.

"Our most intelligent Brains have been thinking on this one subject for untold millions of years. They have excluded from their thoughts everything except the question: How can the dust be checked? They have produced innumerable plans which have been tested thoroughly. All have failed. We have hurled into the void uncontrollable bolts of lightning, interplanetary sheets of flame, in the hope that we might fuse masses of the dust into new, incandescent worlds. We have anchored huge magnets throughout Space, hoping to attract the dust, which is faintly magnetic, and thus to solidify it or clear much of it from the waste. We have caused fearful disturbances by exploding our most powerful compounds in the realms about us, hoping to set the dust so violently in motion that the chaos would become tempestuous with the storms of creation. With our rays of annihilation, we have blasted billion-mile paths through the ceaselessly surging dust. We have destroyed the life on Betelgeuse and rooted there titanic developers of vacua, sprawling, whirring machines to suck the dust from Space and heap it up on that star. We have liberated enormous quantities of gas, lit them, and sent the hot and furious fires madly flashing through the affrighted dust. In our desperation, we have even asked for the aid of the Ether-Eaters. Yes, we have in finality exercised our Will-Power to sweep back the rolling billows! In vain! What has been accomplished? The dust has retreated for a moment, has paused—and has welled onward. It has returned silently triumphant, and it has again hung its pall of blackness over a fear-haunted and a nightmare-ridden Space."

Swelling in soundless sorrow through the Hall of the Mist rose the racing thoughts of the Great Brain. "Our chemists with a bitter doggedness never before displayed have devoted their time to the production of Super-Brains, in the hope of making one which could defeat the Cosmic Dust. They have changed the chemicals used in our genesis; they have experimented with molds and forms; they have tried every resource. With what result? There have come forth raging monstrosities, mad abominations, satanic horrors and ravenous foul things howling wildly the nameless and indescribable phantoms that thronged their minds. We have killed them in order to save ourselves. And the Dust has pushed onward! We have appealed to every living Brain to help us. We appealed, in the forgotten, dream-veiled centuries, for aid in any form. From time to time we have been offered plans, plans which for a while have made terrific and sweeping inroads on the Dust, but plans which have always failed.

"The triumph of the Cosmic Dust has almost come. There is so little time left us that our efforts now must inevitably be futile. But today, in the hope that some Brain, either of the old ones or of the gigantic new ones, has discovered a possibility not yet tried, we have called this conference, the first in more than twelve thousand years."

The tense, alert silence of the hall relaxed and became soft when the thoughts of the Great Brain had stopped flowing. The electric waves which had filled the vast Hall of the Mist sank, and for a long time a strange tranquility brooded there. But the mass was never still; the sea in front of the dais rippled and billowed from time to time as waves of thought passed through it. Yet no Brain offered to speak, and the seething expanse, as the minutes crept by, again became quiet.

In a thin column on the dais, rising high into the air, swayed the Great Brain; again and again it swept its glance around the hall, peering among the rolling, heaving shapes in the hope of finding somewhere in those thousands one which could offer a suggestion. But the minutes passed, and time lengthened, with no response; and the sadness of the fixed and changeless end crept across the last race. And the Brains, wrapped in their meditation, saw the Dust pushing at the glass shell of Antares with triumphant mockery.

The Great Brain had expected no reply, since for centuries it had been considered futile to combat the Dust; and so, when its expectation, though not its wish, was fulfilled, it relaxed and dropped, the signal that the meeting was over.

But the motion had scarcely been completed, when from deep within the center of the sea there came a violent heave; in a moment, a section collected itself and rushed together; like a waterspout it swished upward and went streaming toward the roof until it swayed thin and tenuous as a column of smoke, the top of the Brain peering down from the dimness of the upper hall.

"I have found an infallible plan! The Red Brain has conquered the Cosmic Dust!"

A terrific tenseness leaped upon the Brains, numbed by the cry that wavered in silence down the Hall of the Mist into the empty and dreamless tomb of the farther marble. The Great Brain, hardly relaxed, rose again. And with a curious whirling motion the assembled horde suddenly revolved. Immediately, the Red Brain hung upward from the middle of a sea which had become an amphitheater in arrangement, all Brains looking toward the center. A suppressed expectancy and hope electrified the air.

The Red Brain was one of the later creations of the chemists, and had come forth during the experiments to produce more perfect Brains. Previously, they had all been black; but, perhaps because of impurities in the chemicals, this one had evolved in an extremely dark, dull-red color. It was regarded with wonder by its companions, and more so when they found that many of its thoughts could not be grasped by them. What it allowed the others to know of what passed within it was to a large extent incomprehensible. No one knew how to judge the Red Brain, but much had been expected from it.

Thus, when the Red Brain sent forth its announcement, the others formed a huge circle around, their minds passive and open for the explanation. Thus they lay, silent, while awaiting the discovery. And thus they reclined, completely unprepared for what followed.

For, as the Red Brain hung in the air, it began a slow but restless swaying; and as it swayed, its thoughts poured out in a rhythmic chant. High above them it towered, a smooth, slender column, whose lofty end was moving ever faster and faster while nervous shudders rippled up and down its length. And the alien chant became stronger, stronger, until it changed into a wild and dithyrambic paean to the beauty of the past, to the glory of the present, to the splendor of the future. And the lay became a moaning praise, an exaltation; a strain of furious joy ran through it, a repetition of, "The Red Brain has conquered the Dust. Others have failed, but he has not. Play the national anthem in honor of the Red Brain, for he has triumphed. Place him at your head, for he has conquered the Dust. Exalt him who has proved himself the greatest of all. Worship him who is greater than Antares, greater than the Cosmic Dust, greater than the Universe."

Abruptly it stopped. The puzzled Brains looked up. The Red Brain had ceased its nodding motion for a moment, and had closed its thoughts to them. But along its entire length it began a gyratory spinning, until it whirled at an incredible speed. Something antagonistic suddenly emanated from it. And before the Brains could grasp the situation, before they could protect themselves by closing their minds, the will—impulses of the Red Brain, laden with hatred and death, were throbbing about them and entering their open minds. Like a whirlwind spun the Red Brain, hurling forth its hate. Like half-inflated balloons, the other Brains had lain around it; like cooling glass bubbles, they tautened for a moment; and like pricked balloons as their thoughts and thus their lives were annihilated, since Thought was Life, they flattened, instantaneously dissolving into pools of evanescent slime. By tens and by hundreds they sank, destroyed by the sweeping unchecked thoughts of the Red Brain which filled the hall; by groups, by sections, by paths around the entire circle fell the doomed Brains in that single moment of carelessness, while pools of thick ink collected, flowed together, crept onward, and became rivers of pitch rushing down the marble floor with a soft, silken swish.

The hope of the universe had lain with the Red Brain.

And the Red Brain was mad.

The last human creature had been dead for over three years, and the last bird or beast or insect for perhaps an additional six months, when, at approximately eleven o'clock in the morning on June eighth, in the year—according to occidental reckoning—two thousand and ninety-seven, Thvall the Seeker brought his fourteen-million ton neutronium-hulled space-ship into Earth's atmosphere . . .

The RED
God Laughed

by Thorp McClusky

Short, but not so sweet—you never know who's watching . . .
Weird Tales, April 1939

T he city was dead. Nu Yok, the greatest monument mankind ever reared upon the face of Earth, was dead. No creature of flesh and blood moved along her thousands of miles of multiple-tiered streets, glanced appreciatively and pridefully outward and downward through dizzying azure depths from the gleaming pinnacles of her four-thousand-foot towers, strolled or lounged in her unkempt and silent parks. No silvery aircraft or fish-shaped strato-ships hurtled purposely above her Himalayan skyline, no birds or insects sang or buzzed in her wondrous hanging gardens. Grass and weeds grew in crevices in her disintegrating pedestrian walks, and fat angleworms crawled unafraid through their lush and fecund tangle.

Dry and chalk-white skeletons littered the streets—the skeletons of men and women and children and birds and domestic beasts. They strewed the dust-carpeted corridors of great buildings; they were even to be found—had any sentient creature been there to search for them—in the huge and hermetically sealed gas shelters beneath the city. The gas had lingered longer than the men who had designed and built those tremendous caverns had believed possible; thirst and oxygen starvation had snuffed out lives the gas had not been able to touch.

It was not only that way in Nu Yok and in the Americas; it was the same all over Earth. Even the yellow men, big and little, who had first perfected the gas and immediately deluged the Americas with it in that last decade of the Twenty-first Century, had also perished. For the gas had been easy to analyze, and easier to manufacture. Dying, the Americas had struck back at the yellow men with their own weapon, and gasping doom had encircled the globe. All races of mankind, all air-breathing creatures, save only the deep-sea fishes and the worms that chanced to be far underground—and, perhaps, a few toads and frogs, encapsulated and dormant in dry lake or river beds—had perished.

The last human creature had been dead for over three years, and the last bird or beast or insect for perhaps an additional six months, when, at approximately

421

eleven o'clock in the morning on June eighth, in the year—according to occidental reckoning—two thousand and ninety-seven, Thvall the Seeker brought his four-teen-million ton neutronium-hulled space-ship into Earth's atmosphere and, having already observed Nu Yok's towers and minarets from half-way around the globe, set her down as lightly as a drifting feather in a cradle of granite rocks near the southern boundary of that rectangular stretch of greenery men knew as Central Park. And, as he set his ship down gently, careful to avoid crushing the green vegetation, in Thvall the Seeker's curious soul there was a great gladness. For Thvall knew that his quest was ended.

It had been a long and a lonely search, spanning reaches of space that light will not cross in twenty thousand years. It had begun beyond the hub of our stellar galaxy, and the years of Thvall's journeying were to the life of a man as the age of the Pyramids is to a single day.

Spawn of the innermost planet of a blue-white dwarf sun deep hidden in the globular cluster in Messier II, Thvall resembled in no way save one any of the diver-sified forms of life which have evolved upon Earth down the millenniums since the red heat died from her surface rocks and permitted her seas to form. Because of that single resemblance Thvall had begun his search; only because of it had he fi-nally arrived upon Earth.

Water! Thvall, like a man, required water. The mechanical processes of his existence, and of the existence of his kind, depended upon an unfailing supply of water. And upon Thvall's home world the water was almost gone . . .

Thvall well knew, when he began his quest, the odds against his succeeding. To every hundred thousand suns there was but one, and perhaps not even one, with planets. To every thousand planets perhaps, *perhaps* there was one sufficiently sup-plied with water—*and* suitable for colonization by his kind. There were a hundred million chances to one of Thvall's finding, anywhere in the galaxy, that which he sought. And the other galaxies, even the big, near one in Andromeda, were too far away . . .

And now the quest was ended.

Thvall's selection of Sol as a star worthy of investigation had not been haphaz-ard. While still beyond the white star Alpha in the constellation of the Centaur he had noted that this modest yellow-white sun was slightly unstable, slightly variable, a star that fluctuated, though to only a minor degree, through a regularly recurrent cycle.

That periodicity might mean almost anything; it might mean that the star was on the verge of blowing up, it might be caused by the resultant of the gravitational attraction of attendant planets, or it might be merely the subsiding spasms of some ancient solar malaise. From Alpha Centauri, Thvall set his course for Sol.

He was fifteen billions of miles beyond the orbit of that planet men have named Pluto when the steadily increasing intensity of Sol's illumination, actuating certain mechanisms, awakened him from the state of completely suspended animation in which he voyaged from star to star. He awoke instantly, feeling neither refreshed nor enervated, and lacking any recollection whatsoever of the passage of time. His first, and almost automatic activity, was to reduce the velocity of his spacecraft from a hyper-Einsteinian, interstellar speed to a pace more suitable to interplanetary cruising.

During those first brief, waking moments his ship traveled Solward a billion miles.

Immediately he had slowed the rush of his ship toward the yellow sun, he applied himself to his instruments, and saw at once that the slightly nervous star was plagued with a swarm of planets. The outermost planets were too cold to support life; their atmospheres were raging seas of ammonia and methane. The planet nearest the luminary was without atmosphere; the next was heavily blanketed with an atmosphere, which was, however, full of carbon dioxide; the third planet—the one with the pear shaped moon—had an atmosphere dripping with water vapor.

Thvall, looking upon Earth, knew that his quest was ended.

His ship safely landed on Sol's third planet, Thvall began a series of routine tasks. He analyzed the luminary's radiation and the planet's atmosphere with highly encouraging results; his kind could adapt themselves to life on Earth. Next he attempted communication with the green growing life, but, although he quickly learned that Earth's vegetation possessed a dim, vague consciousness, it was obvious that its intelligence was too meager, too instinctive for the development of original thought. Obviously Earth's vegetation could not have constructed the aimless sprawling city in the midst of which Thvall's space-ship lay. It was probably therefore that the city's creators were temporarily absent. Perhaps they were nocturnal creatures, who lived during the day in underground recesses and came to the surface of the planet only at night. Perhaps they were migratory. There were any number of plausible explanations of their absence.

His preliminary scrutiny of the immediate environment satisfactorily concluded—and no motile form of Earth-life having yet appeared to inspect his ship, attempt communication with him or perhaps dispute his peaceful invasion of the planet—Thvall determined to inspect one of the buildings which towered skyward only a quarter of a mile away, to the southward. Prudently burdening himself with a variety of apparatus and weapons, which he distributed among several of his smaller tentacles, he emerged through the airlock in his ship's hull and crawled rapidly and with a light tingling of anticipation toward the nearest of the buildings.

He had proceeded only a short distance when he came upon a bleached mass of human bones, half hidden in the rank grass. Examining them, he realized at once that they had lived, but—as his own amorphous race lacked rigid skeletal structure of any sort, and any conception of motile life being hampered by rigidity was alien to him—he had difficulty in imagining what the creature had been like in life. He concluded that it had been nowhere near as motile as himself—perhaps little more motile that the vegetation.

He also noted, however, and with considerable approval, a number of fat, gray earthworms, and he paused and attempted to communicate with them, quickly discovering, however, that, though they knew fear and hunger, they were incapable of abstract thought.

Continuing onward, he ascended a long ramp which debouched upon a broad street. On the opposite side of the street the buildings began. The street was littered with a large number of small, egg-shaped wheeled mechanisms. Examining one of these through its windows of fused silica and metallic oxides, Thvall saw that it contained two skeletons.

It was obvious to him now that these dead were of the species which had built the city. Why were they dead? And had all of their kind throughout the city perished? Or were some left alive?

Uneasily Thvall, who realized only too well that the unknown doom which had snuffed out this bony form of Earth-life might also be inimical to himself, paused and made additional tests. Reassurance of a sort returned to him as he determined that Earth's atmosphere was remarkably stable and that there were no electrical or atomic mechanisms operating within the field of his apparatus. Nevertheless, he determined to proceed with extreme wariness.

Crossing the broad street, Thvall approached the base of the building and examined as much of the interior as he could see through the dusty though still partially transparent windows. The structure was internally subdivided into many small cubicles profusely equipped with furnishings which were, for the most part, incomprehensible to Thvall; he would have to see those objects in use before he could understand their purpose.

His bulk was too great to permit him to enter through any of the windows, but there were large doors which, after a brief examination, he easily opened. Entering the building, he found himself in a chamber of considerable size, which, like the smaller cells, was luxuriously furnished. The walls of this room were profusely paneled with mirrors, which created the illusion of a chamber twice as large as actuality; why this illusion should be necessary or even desirable was utterly beyond Thvall's comprehension. Reflecting surfaces in utter dissociation with any recognizable form of apparatus whatsoever were a complete enigma to him.

The floor of this chamber was littered with no fewer than twenty skeletons. Some were still partly clothed in garments of vegetable, mineral and animal fiber; some wore loose-fitting circlets of metallic alloys around their tinier appendages; many of the circlets held geometrically carved bits of crystalized carbon in claw-like sockets. Lifting and examining a small, glass-dialed mechanism which lay beside one of the skeletons, Thvall discovered that it was operated by an internal spring which had, however, lost its tension; he rewound the spring by turning a ratcheted pin provided for the purpose, and discovered that the mechanism produced a regular pulsation, which three small indicators beneath a transparent portion of the mechanism's shell revolved at proportionate though greatly dissimilar velocities. Correctly assuming that the mechanism was a device for measuring the passage of time, Thvall replaced the watch beside the skeleton of its owner and glided toward the deeper recesses of the chamber.

Here he discovered a number of doors arranged in an orderly row, and, investigating one which was not fully closed and which slid open easily, he found that it opened upon a chimney-like well. Within the well were a number of taut steel cables, which supported a square metal cage at a level slightly beneath the door. Thvall had opened the cage. Thvall saw at once it was designed to be raised and lowered from level to level of the building. Far above, a tiny pinpoint of brilliant light told Thvall that the well extended to the top of the building; he instantly determined to ascend the shaft and view the city from that vantage point.

He squirmed up the elevator shaft like a gargantuan knot of writhing serpents, and, reaching the elevator motors, squeezed upward past them and into a small, many-windowed chamber. Here an iron door provided egress to the roof of the building. Thvall opened the door and squirmed through.

On the roof of the building, in the clean, sharp sunlight, Thvall put down his instruments and weapons and sedately capered. This world was so fair, so bountiful—and, as yet, so undeveloped! There was no doubt now that its ruling race was exceedingly primitive, but they possessed intelligence of a sort, too; if they proved peaceable and friendly Thvall's people could teach them so much—so much!—in return for a bit of the planet's desert land and a single lake of water. Probably the first boon Thvall's kind would confer upon this world's people would be conquest of the plague which had slain this city's inhabitants. Yes, that would certainly be done first . . .

The roof on which Thvall stood was flat, and surrounded by a low parapet. It was encumbered by only two objects, the small structure which housed the elevator motors and a huge torpedo-shaped, steel cylinder which lay near a corner of the parapet. Some of the parapet bricks were broken, and there was a long, dull scar on the roof. Obviously the cylinder had been dropped from a low altitude, had struck the parapet a glancing blow, and had then slithered across the roof.

What was the thing, and why had it been dropped on this roof?

Thvall slowly circled the object, scrutinizing it intently. He saw that, except for a short stubby rod protruding from its pear-shaped nose, it was utterly without external moving parts of any kind. But the rod looked like a control of some sort. Thvall first rotated the rod; then, when nothing happened, he tugged on it, and finally pressed on it. That brought results. The rod moved inward easily, and instantly four small valves opened in the cylinder's circumference and a thick gray gas poured forth and mingled with the atmosphere.

For an instant Thvall hunched there motionless, watching the gas ooze viscidly from the metal cylinder and vanish in the clean, still air. Then, in a lightning-flash of utter comprehension, he understood the whole cryptic pattern—the silent city, the dead everywhere, the significance of the gas-bomb that was now pouring its lethal fumes into the surrounding atmosphere. Instantly he darted for the open door and the elevator shaft . . .

He never reached that gaping well. He detected no odor; there was no warning pain, but abruptly the flat roof was heaving and billowing like a swirling sea.

Vertigo danced in his alien brain, an intense blackness deepened before his single, thousand-faceted eye, and strength and life went swiftly together from his boneless tentacles.

Thus Thvall the Seeker died, and the knowledge that on Earth—the third planet of a minor sun deep sunk in the thinning haze of stars twenty thousand light-years beyond the galaxy's axis—were the environmental conditions and the water his people required so desperately, died with him. And on Earth the frogs and fishes were now the highest remaining forms of sentient life.

But Mars, the Red God, laughed—for though on Earth the men who had deified him and honored him with a name no longer lived to speak that name, had just claimed his last and perhaps his most significant, sacrifice.

Discord
In SCARLET

by A. E. Van Vogt

Canadian born Alfred Elton van Vogt (not Egger as sometimes misreported) in the company of his peers Fritz Leiber, Isaac Asimov, Robert Heinlein, Sir Arthur C. Clarke, received the highest accolade of the science fiction professional community by being awarded the prestigious honor, Master of Science Fiction. His claim to fame includes nearly 100 short stories and a score or more novels, "Slan" leading all the rest. I had the privilege of collaborating with him on a New Wave spoof (neither of us appreciated the short-lived frantic fad), "Laugh, Clone, Laugh", a salute to the Lon Chaney film title, LAUGH CLOWN LAUGH and A. Merritt's "Burn Witch Burn". Although as yet unproduced, I sold his original shooting script for COMPUTERWORLD to the movies. At the preview of ALIEN, knowledge-able fans clustered around him and asked how he liked the movie. "They did a good job of adapting my story", he said of the later acknowledged "Black Destroyer". When Alzheimer's had robbed him of his comprehension of who he was and what he has contributed to the realm of imaginative literature, his wife Lydia pointed to me and asked him, "Do you know who this is, Van?" Loud and clear and unequivocally he declared, "My agent!" although by then I doubt he knew what an agent was. Along with Vincent Price and Brother Theodore he gave me his last autograph. His sense of humor was the last thing malicious Alzheimer's robbed him of. He is buried in the same cemetery as Bela Lugosi and Dr. Donald (Dracula Society) Reed and, knowing that Bing Crosby is also there, he quipped, "Bing can sing to me!" The world will continue to sing your praises for lustrums and decades to come, dear friend, dear legend.—FJA   *Story from Astounding, December 1939*

Xtl sprawled moveless on the bosom of endless night. Time dragged drearily toward infinity, and space was dark. Unutterably dark! The horrible pitch-blackness of intergalactic immensity! Across the miles and the years, vague patches of light gleamed coldly at him, whole galaxies of blazing stars shrunk by incredible distance to shining swirls of mist.

Life was out there, spawning on the myriad planets that whirled eternally around the myriad suns. And life had once crawled out of the primeval mud of ancient Glor—before cosmic explosion destroyed a mighty race and flung his—Xtl's—body out into the deeps of space, the prey of chance.

His brain pulsed on and on in the same old, old cycle of thought—thinking: one chance in decillions that his body would ever come near a galactic system. One chance in infinity itself that he fall on a planet and find a precious *guul*. And never, never a hope that his race would live again.

A billion times that thought had pounded to its dreary conclusion in his brain, until it was a part of him, until it was like a picture unrolling before his eyes—it and those remote wisps of shiningness out there in that blackness. And that picture was more real than the reality. He had no consciousness of the spaceship, until he touched the metal.

Hard, hardness—something material! The vague sense perception fumbled into his dulled brain, bringing a living pain—like a disused muscle, briefly, agonizingly brought into action.

The thought slumped. His brain slid back into its sleep of ages, seeing again the old picture of hopelessness and the shiningness in the black. The very idea of hardness became a dream that faded. Some remote corner of his mind, curiously alert, watched it fade, watched the shadows creep with reaching, enveloping folds of lightlessness, striving to re-engulf the dim consciousness that had flashed into such an anguish of ephemeral existence.

And then, once more, his groping fingers sent that dull pulse of awareness tapping its uncertain message to his sodden, hopeless brain.

His elongated body convulsed in senseless movement, four arms lashed out, four legs jackknifed with blind, unreasoning strength. There was a distinct sense of a glob and of a pushing away from the hard matter.

His dazed, staring eyes, his stultified vision galvanized into life; and he saw that, in the contorted fury of his movements, he had pushed himself away from the surface of a vast, round, dark-bodied metal monster, studded with row on row of glaring lights, like diamonds. The spaceship floated there in the velvet darkness, glowing like an immense jewel, quiescent but alive, enormously, vitally alive, bringing nostalgic and vivid suggestion of a thousand far-flung planets, and of an indomitable, boisterous life that had reached for the stars and grasped them. Bringing—hope!

The torpid tenor of his thoughts exploded into chaos. His mind, grooved through the uncounted ages to ultimate despair, soared up, up, insanely. Life surged from the bottom point of static to the swirling, irresistible height of dynamism, that jarred every atom of his scarlet, cylindrical body and his round, vicious head. His legs and arms glistened like tongues of living fire, as they twisted and writhed in the blaze of light from those dazzling portholes. His mouth, a gash in the center of his hideous head, slavered a white frost that floated away in little frozen globules.

His brain couldn't hold the flame of that terrific hope. His mind kept dissolving, blurring. Through that blur, he saw a thick vein of light from a circular bulge in the metallic surface of the ship. The bulge became a huge door that rotated open and tilted to one side. A flood of brilliance spilled out the great opening, followed by a dozen two-legged beings in transparent metal armor, dragging great floating machines.

Swiftly, the machines were concentrated around a dark projection on the ship's surface. Intolerable light flared up as what was obviously repair work proceeded at an alarming pace.

He was no longer falling away from the ship. The faint pressure of gravitational pull was drawing him down again—so slowly. Frantically, he adjusted his atomic structure to the fullest measure of attraction. But even his poorly responding brain could see that he would never make it.

The work was finished. The incandescent glare of atomic welders died to spluttering darkness. Machines were unclamped, floated toward the opening of the ship, down into it and out of sight. The two-legged beings scrambled after them. The vast, curved plain of metal was suddenly as deserted and lifeless as space itself.

Terror struck into Xtl. He'd have to fight, have to get there somehow. He couldn't let them get away now, when the whole universe was in a grasp—twenty-five short yards away. His letching arms reached out stupidly, as if he would hold the ship by sheer fury of need. His brain ached with a slow, rhythmical hurt. His mind spun toward a black, bottomless pit—then poised just before the final plunge.

The great door was slowing in its swift rotation. A solitary being squeezed through the ring of light and ran to the dark projection, just repaired. He picked up an instrument that gleamed weirdly, a tool of some kind forgotten, and started back toward the partly open lock.

He stopped. In the glow from the portholes, Xtl could see the other's face through the transparent armor. The face stared up at him, eyes wide, mouth open. Then the mouth moved rapidly, opening and shutting, apparently a form of communication with the others.

A moment later the door was rotating again, opening wide. A group of the beings came out, two of them mounted on the top of a large, metal-barred cage, steering it under power. He was to be captured.

Oddly, his brain felt no sense of lift, no soaring hope, none of that mind-inflaming ecstasy. It was as if a drug was dragging him down, down, into a black night of fatigue. Appalled, he fought off the enveloping stupor. He must hold to his senses. His race, that had attained the very threshold of ultimate knowledge, must live again.

The voice, a strained, unrecognizable voice, came to Commander Morton through the communicators in his transparent spacesuit: "How in the name of all the hells can anything live in intergalactic space?"

It seemed to the commander that the question made the little group of men crowd closer together. The proximity of the others made them feel easier. Then they suddenly grew aware of the impalpable yet *alive* weight of the inconceivable night that coiled about them, pressing down to the very blazing portholes.

For the first time in years, the immensity of that night squeezed icily into Morton's consciousness. Long familiarity had bred indifference into his very bones— but now, the incredible vastness of that blackness reaching a billion trillion years beyond the farthest frontiers of man stabbed into his mind, and brought an almost dismaying awareness. His deep voice, clattering into the communicators, split that scared silence like some harsh noise, startled him:

"Gunlie Lester, here's something for your astronomical-mathematical brain. Will you please give us the ratio of chance that blew out a driver of the *Beagle* at the exact point in space where that thing was floating? Take a few hours to work it out."

The astronomer replied immediately: "I don't have to think about it. The chance is unstatable in human arithmetic. It can't happen, mathematically speaking. Here we are, a shipload of human beings, stopping for repairs half-way between two galaxies—the first time we've ever made a trip outside of our own galaxy. Here we are, I say, a tiny point intersecting without prearrangement exactly the path of another, tinier point. Impossible, unless space is saturated with such—creatures!"

"I hope not," another man shuddered. "We ought to turn a mobile unit on anything that looks like that, on general principles."

The shudder seemed to run along the communicators. Commander Morton shook his great, lean body as if consciously trying to throw off the chill of it. His eyes on the maneuvering cage above, he said:

"A regular blood-red devil spewed out of some fantastic nightmare; ugly as sin—and probably as harmless as our beautiful pussy last year was deadly. Smith, what do you think?"

The cadaverous-faced biologist said in his cold, logical voice: "This thing has arms and legs, a purely planetary evolution. If it is intelligent it will begin to react to environment the moment it is inside the cage. It may be a venerable old sage, meditating in the silence of distractionless space. Or it may be a young murderer, condemned to eternal exile, consumed with desire to sneak back home and resume the life he lived."

"I wish Korita had come out with us," said Pennons, the chief engineer, in his quiet, practical voice. "Korita's historical analysis of pussy last year gave us an advance idea of what we had to face and—"

"Korita speaking, Mr. Pennons," came the meticulously clear voice of the Japanese archaeologist on the communicators. "Like many of the others, I have been listening to what is happening as a welcome break in this, the longest journey the spaceship *Beagle* has ever undertaken. But I am afraid analysis of the creature would be dangerous at this faceless stage. In the case of pussy, we had the barren, foodless planet on which he lived, and the architectural realities of his crumbled city.

"Here we have a creature living in space a million years from the nearest planet, apparently without food, and without means of spatial locomotion. I suggest you make certain that you get him into the cage, and then study him—every action, every reaction. Take pictures of his internal organs working in the vacuum of space. Find out every possible thing about him, so that we shall know what we have aboard as soon as possible. Now, when we are fully staffed again and heading for a new galaxy for the first time in the history of man, we cannot afford to have anything go wrong, or anybody killed before we reach there. Thank you."

"And that," said Morton, "is sense. You've got your fluorite camera, Smith?"

"Attached to my suit," Smith acknowledged.

Morton, who knew the capabilities of the mournful-looking biologist, turned his attention back to the cage fifty feet away. He said in his deep, resonant voice: "Open the door as wide as possible and drop over him. Don't let his hands grab the bars."

"Just a minute!" a guttural voice broke in. Morton turned questioningly to the big, plump German physicist. Von Grossen continued: "Let us not rush this capture, Commander Morton. It is true that I was not aboard last year when you had your encounter with the creature you persist in calling pussy. But when you returned to the base planet before embarking on the present voyage, the story you told to the world was not reassuring, not to me, anyway."

His hard, gray-dark face stared grimly at the others: "It is true that I can see no real objection to capturing this creature in a cage. But it happens that I am replacing a man who was killed by this—pussy. Therefore I speak for him when I say: Such a thing must never happen again."

Morton frowned, his face lined with doubt. "You put me in a spot, von Grossen. As human beings, we must take every possible precaution. As scientists, however, all is grist for our mill; everything must be investigated. There can be no thought of shunning danger. If this voyage is to be ruled by fear, we might as well head for home now."

"Fear is not what I had in mind," said the physicist quietly. "But I believe in counting ten before acting."

Morton asked, "Any other objections?"

He felt oddly annoyed that there were none.

Xtl waited. His thoughts kept breaking up into little pieces of light and lightless—a chain of dazzle and dark—that somehow connected up with all the things he had ever known or thought. Visions of a long-dead planet trickled into his consciousness bringing a vague conceit—and a contempt of these creatures who thought to capture him.

Why, he could remember a time when his race had had spaceships a hundred times the size of this machine that swam below him. That was before they had dispensed completely with space travel, and just lived a quiet homey life building beauty from natural forces.

He watched as the cage was driven toward him unerringly. There was nothing he could do, even had he wanted to. The gaping mouth of the large, metal-barred construction closed over him and snapped shut the moment he was inside.

Xtl clawed at the nearest bar, caught hold with grim strength. He clung there an instant, sick and dizzy with awful reaction. Safe! His mind expanded with all the violence of an exploding force. Free electrons discharged in dizzying swarms from the chaos of the spinning atom systems inside his brain and body, frantically seeking union with the other systems. He was safe—safe after quadrillions of years of sick despair, and on a material body with unlimited power to take him where he would go. Safe when there was still time to carry out his sacred purpose. Or was he safe?

The cage was dropping toward the surface of the ship. His eyes became gleaming pools of caution, as they studied the men below. It was only too evident that he was to be examined. With a tremendous effort, stung by fear, he tried to push the clinging dullness from his brain, fought for alertness. An examination of him now would reveal his purpose, expose the precious objects concealed within his breast; and that must not be.

His steely-bright eyes flicked in anxious dismay over the dozen figures in transparent armor. Then his mind calmed. They were inferior creatures, obviously! Puny foes before his own remarkable power. Their very need of spacesuits proved their inability to adapt themselves to environment, proved they existed on a low plane of evolution. Yet he must not underestimate them. Here were keen brains, capable of creating and using mighty machines.

Each of the beings had weapons in holster at the side of his space armor—weapons with sparkling, translucent handles. He had noticed the same weapons in the holsters of the men at the top of the cage. That, then, would be his method if any of these creatures flashed a camera on him.

As the cage dropped into the belt of undiffused blackness between two portholes, Smith stepped forward with his camera—and Xtl jerked himself with effortless ease up the bars to the ceiling of the cage. The gash of his mouth in the center of his round, smooth head was split in a silent snarl of fury at the unutterable bad luck that was forcing this move upon him. His vision snapped full on; and now he could see blurrily though the hard metal ceiling.

One arm, with its eight wirelike fingers, lashed out with indescribable swiftness at the ceiling, *through* it, and then he had a gun from the holster of one of the men.

He did not attempt to readjust its atomic structure as he had adjusted his arm.

It was important that they should not guess that it was he who fired the gun. Straining in his awkward position, he aimed the weapon straight at Smith and the little group of men behind him—released the flaming power.

There was a flare of incandescent violence that blotted the men from view. A swirl of dazzling light coruscated virulently across the surface of the ship. And there was another light, too. A blue sparkle that told of automatic defense screens driving out from the armored suits of the men.

In one continuous movement, Xtl released the gun, withdrew his hand; and, by the act, pushed himself to the floor. His immediate fear was gone. No sensitive camera film could have lived through the blaze of penetrating energy. And what was overwhelmingly more important—the gun was no good against himself. Nothing but a simple affair which employed the method of transmutation of one element to another, the process releasing one or two electrons from each atom system. It would require a dozen such guns to do damage to his body.

The group of men stood quite still; and Morton knew they were fighting, as he was, the blindness that lingered from the spray of violent light. Slowly, his eyes became adjusted; and then he could see again the curved metal on which he stood, and beyond that the brief, barren crest of the ship and the limitless miles of lightless, heatless space—dark, fathomless, unthinkable gulfs. There too, a blur among the blurs of shadows, stood the cage.

"I'm sorry, commander," one of the men on the cage apologized. "The ato-gun must have fallen out of my belt, and discharged."

"Impossible!" Smith's voice came to Morton, low and tense. "In this gravitation, it would take several minutes to fall from the holster, and it wouldn't discharge in any event from such a slight jar of landing."

"Maybe I knocked against it, sir, without noticing."

"Maybe!" Smith seemed to yield grudgingly to the explanation. "But I could almost swear that, just before the flare of light dazzled me, the creature moved. I admit it was too black to see more than the vaguest blur, but—"

"Smith," Morton said sharply, "what are you trying to prove?"

He saw the long-faced biologist hunch his narrow shoulders, as if pulling himself together. The biologist mumbled: "When you put it like that, I don't know. The truth is, I suppose, that I've never gotten over the way I insisted on keeping pussy alive, with such tragic results. I suspect everything now, and—"

Morton stared in surprise. It was hard to realize that it was really Smith speaking—the scientist who, it had seemed sometimes in the past, was ready to sacrifice his own life and everybody else's if it meant adding a new, important fact to the science of biology. Morton found his voice at last:

"You were perfectly right in what you did! Until we realized the truth, you expressed the majority mind of this ship's company. The development of the situation in the case of pussy changed our opinion as well as your own, but it did not change our method of working by evidence alone. I say that we should continue to make such logic the basis of our work."

"Right. And beg your pardon, chief!" Smith was brisk-voiced again. "Crane, turn the cage light on, and let's see what we've got here."

To Morton, the silence that followed seemed like a sudden, oppressive weight, as the blaze of light showered down on Xtl crouching at the bottom of the cage. The almost metallic sheen of the cylindrical body, the eyes like coals of fire, the wirelike fingers and toes, the scarlet hideousness of it startled even these men who were accustomed to alien forms of life. He broke the spell of horror, half-breathlessly:

"He's probably very handsome—to himself!"

"If life is evolution," said Smith in a stiff voice, "and nothing evolves except for use, how can a creature living in space have highly developed legs and arms? Its insides should be interesting. But now—my camera's useless! That flare of energy would have the effect of tinting the electrified lens, and of course the film's ruined. Shall I get another?"

"N-n-no-o!" Morton's clean-cut, handsome face grew dark with a frown. "We've wasted a lot of time here; and after all, we can re-create vacuum of space conditions inside the ship's laboratory, and be traveling at top acceleration while we're doing it."

"Just a minute!" von Grossen, the plump but hard-boiled physicist, spoke. "Let's get this straight. The *Beagle* is going to another galaxy on an exploration voyage—the first trip of this kind. Our business is to study life in this new system, but we're not taking any specimens, only pictures and notes—studies of the creatures in their various environments. If we're all so nervous about this thing, why are we taking it aboard?"

"Because"—Smith beat Morton to the reply—"we're not tied down to pictures and notes. There will, however, be millions of forms of life on every planet, and we shall be forced to the barest kind of record in most cases. This monster is different. In our fears we have almost forgotten that the existence of a creature capable of living in space is the most extraordinary thing we've ever run across. Even pussy, who could live without air, needed warmth of a kind, and would have found the absolute cold of space intolerable. If, as we suspect, this creature's natural habitat is not space, then we must find out why and how he came to be where he is. Speaking as a biologist—"

"I see," interrupted Morton dryly, "that Smith is himself again." He directed a command at the men on the cage. "Take that monster inside, and put a wall of force around the cage. That should satisfy even the most cautious."

Xtl felt a faint throb of motors on the cage. He saw the bars move, then grew conscious of a sharp, pleasant tingling sensation, brief physical activity within his body that stopped the workings of his mind for a bare second. Before he could think, there was the cage floor rising above him—and he was lying on the hard surface of the spaceship's outer shell.

With a snarl of black dismay that almost cut his face in two, he realized the truth. He had forgotten to readjust the atoms in his body after firing the gun. And now he had fallen through!

"Good Heaven!" Morton bellowed.

A scarlet streak of elongated body, a nightmare of shadow in that braid of shadow and light, Xtl darted across the impenetrable heavy metal to the air lock. He jerked himself down into its dazzling depths. His adjusted body dissolved through the two other locks. And then he was at one end of a long, gleaming corridor—safe for the moment!

They would be searching for him: and—he knew with a cold, hardening resolve—these creatures would never trust alive a being who could slip through solid metal. Their reason would tell them he was a superbeing, unutterably dangerous to them.

One advantage only he had—they did not know the deadliness of his purpose.

Ten minutes later, Morton's gray eyes flicked questioningly over the stern faces of the men gathered in the great reception room. His huge and powerful body felt oddly rigid, as if his muscles could not quite relax. His voice was mellower, deeper, richer than normal:

"I am going to offer my resignation on the grounds that, for the second time under my leadership, an abnormal beast has gotten aboard this craft. I must assume that there is a basic lack in my mental make-up; for results, and not excuses, do count in this universe of ours; even apparently bad luck is rigorously bound up with character. I, therefore, suggest that Korita or von Grossen be named commander in my place. Korita because of the care he advocated, and von Grossen on the strength of his objection to taking any living specimens aboard—both are more fitted to hold the command than I am."

"The honorable commander has forgotten one thing," Korita said softly. "The creature was *not* carried into the ship. I admit it was our collective intentions to bring him aboard, but it was he himself who entered. I suggest that, even if we had decided not to bring him into the interior, we could not have prevented his entry in view of his ability to slip through metal. It is absolutely absurd for Commander Morton to feel responsible."

Von Grossen heaved himself out of his chair. Now that he was out of his spacesuit, the physicist looked not so much plump as big and iron-hard. "And that goes for me all the way. I have not been long on this ship, but I have found Commander Morton to be a most able intellect and leader of men. So let us not waste time in useless self-reproach.

"In capturing this being we must first of all straighten our minds about him. He has arms and legs, this creature, yet floats in space, and remains alive. He allows himself to be caught in a cage, but knows all the time that the cage cannot hold him. Then he drops through the bottom of the cage, which is very silly if he doesn't want us to know that he can do it. Which means that he is a very foolish creature indeed, and we don't have to worry very much about him. There is a reason why intelligent living things make mistakes—a fundamental reason that should make it easy for us to analyze him right back to where he came from, and why he is here. Smith, analyze his biological make-up."

Smith stood up, lank and grim. "We've already discussed the obvious planetary origin of his hands and feet. The ability to live in space, however, is an abnormal development, having no connection with natural evolution, but is the product of brain power and science, pure and simple. I suggest that here is a member of a race that has solved the final secrets of biology; and, if I knew how we should even begin to start looking for a creature that can slip through walls, my advice would be: Hunt him down and kill him within an hour."

"Er!" Kellie, the sociologist, said. He was a bald-headed man with preternaturally intelligent eyes that gleamed owlishly from behind his pince-nez. "Er, any being who could fit himself to vacuum of space condition would be lord of the universe. His kind would dwell on every planet, clutter up every galactic system. Swarms of him would be floating in space, if space floating is what they go in for. Yet, we know for a fact that his race does not rule *our* galactic area. A paradox, which is worthy of investigation."

"I don't quite understand what you mean, Kellie!" Morton frowned.

"Simply, er, that a race which has solved the final secrets of biology must be millions, even billions of years in advance of man; and, as a pure sympodial— capable of adaptation to any environment—would, according to the law of vital dynamics, expand to the farthest frontier of the universe, just as man is slowly pushing himself to the remotest planets."

"It is a contradiction," Morton agreed, "and would seem to prove that the creature is not a superior being. Korita, what is this thing's history?"

The Japanese scientist shrugged: "I'm afraid I can only be of the slightest assistance on present evidence. You know the prevailing theory: That life proceeds upwards by a series of cycles. Each cycle begins with the peasant, who is rooted to his bit of soil. The peasant comes to market; and slowly the market place transforms to a town, with ever less 'inward' connection to the earth. Then we have cities and nations, finally the soulless world cities and a devastating struggle for power— a series of frightful wars which sweep men back to the peasant stage. The question becomes: Is this creature in the peasant part of this particular cycle, or in the big city 'megalopolitan' era?"

Morton's voice slashed across the silence: "In view of our limited knowledge of this creature, what basic traits should we look for, supposing him to be in the big city stage?"

"He would be a cold, invincible intellect, formidable to the ultimate degree, undefeatable to the ultimate degree, undefeatable—except through circumstances. I refer to the kind of circumstances that made it impossible for us to prevent this beast entering our ship. Because of his great innate intelligence, he would make no errors of any kind."

"But he has already made an error!" von Grossen said in a silken voice. "He very foolishly fell through the bottom of the cage. It is the kind of blunder a peasant would make—"

"Suppose," Morton asked, "he were in the peasant stage?"

"Then," Korita replied, "his basic impulses would be much simpler. There would be first of all the desire to reproduce, to have a son, to know that his blood was being carried on. Assuming great fundamental intelligence, this impulse might, in the superior being, take the form of a fanatic drive toward race survival—"

He stopped, as half a dozen men came through the doorway.

Morton said: "Finished, Pennons?"

The chief engineer nodded. Then in a warning voice: "It is absolutely essential that every man on the ship get into his rubberite suite, and wear rubberite gloves."

Morton explained grimly. "We've energized the walls around the bedrooms. There may be some delay in catching this creature, and we're taking no chances of being murdered in our beds. We—" Sharply: "What it is, Pennons?"

Pennons was staring at a small instrument in his hand: he said in a queer voice: "Are we all here, Morton?"

"Yes, except for four men guarding the engine room."

"Then . . . then something's caught in the wall of force. Quick—we must surround it."

To Xtl, returning from a brief exploration of the monster ship's interior, the shock was devastating, the surprise unutterable and complete.

One moment he was thinking complacently of the metal sections in the hold of the ship, where he would secrete his *guuls*; the next moment he was caught in the full sparkling fury of an energy screen.

His body writhed with an agony that blackened his brain. Thick clouds of free electrons rose up within him in that hell of pain, and flashed from system to system seeking union, only to be violently repelled by the tortured, madly spinning atom systems. For those long seconds, the wonderfully balanced instability of his structure nearly collapsed into an abyss of disintegration.

But the incredible genius that had created his marvelous body had forethought even this eventuality. Like lightning, his body endured readjustment after automatic readjustment, each new-built structure carrying the intolerable load for a fraction of a fraction of a second. And then, he had jerked back from the wall, and was safe.

In a flare of thought, his mind investigated the immediate possibilities. Obviously, the men had rigged up this defense wall of force. It meant they would have an alarm system—and they would swoop down every corridor in an organized attempt to corner him.

Xtl's eyes were glowing pools of white fire as he realized the opportunity. He must catch one of these men, while they were scattered, investigate his *guul* properties, and use him for his first *guul*.

No time to waste. He darted into the nearest wall, a tall, gaudy, ungraceful streak, and, without pausing, sped through room after room, roughly parallel to a main corridor. His sensitive feet caught the vibrations of the approaching men; and through the wall his full vision followed the blurred figures rushing past. One, two, three, four—five—on this corridor. The fifth man was some distance behind the others.

Like a wraith, Xtl glided into the wall just ahead of the last man—and pounced forth in an irresistible charge. A rearing, frightful shape of glaring eyes and ghastly mouth, blood-red, metal-hard body, and four arms of fire that clutched with bitter strength at the human body.

The man tried to fight. His big form twisted, jerked; his lashing fists felt vaguely painful as they pounded desperately against the hard, sheeny crust of Xtl's body. And then, by sheer weight and ferocity, he was overwhelmed; the force of his fall jarring Xtl's sensitive frame.

The man was lying on his back, and Xtl watched curiously as the mouth opened and shut spasmodically. A tingling sensation sped along Xtl's feet and his mouth opened in a snarl. Incapable though he was of hearing sounds, he realized that he was picking up the vibrations of a call for help.

He pounced forward, one great hand smashing at the man's mouth. Teeth broke, and crushed back into the throat. The body sagged. But the man was still alive, and conscious, as Xtl plunged two hands into the feebly writhing body.

The man ceased suddenly even that shadow of a struggle, his widened eyes staring at the arms that vanished under his shirt, stirred around in his chest, stared in petrified terror at the monstrous blood-red cylindrical body that loomed over him, with its round bright eyes glaring at him as if they would see right through him.

It was a blurred picture the frantic Xtl saw. The inside of the man's body seemed solid flesh. He had to find an open space, or one that could be pressed open, so long as the pressing did not kill the man. He must have living flesh.

Hurry, hurry— His feet registered the vibrations of approaching footsteps— from one direction only, but coming swiftly, swiftly.

And then, just like that, it was all over. His searching fingers, briefly hardened to a state of semisolidity, touched the heart. The man heaved convulsively, shuddered, and slumped into death.

The next instant, Xtl discovered the stomach. For a moment, black dismay flooded him. Here was what he was searching for, and he had killed it, rendered it useless! He stared in cold fury at the stilled body, uncertain, alarmed.

Then suddenly his actions became deliberate, weighted with contempt. Never for an instant had he suspected these intelligent beings would die so easily. It changed, simplified everything. There was no need to be anything more than casually careful in dealing with them.

Two men with drawn ato-guns whipped around the nearest corner, and slid to a halt at the sight of the apparition that snarled at them across the dead body. Then, as they came out of their brief paralysis, Xtl stepped into the nearest wall, a blur of scarlet in that brightly lit corridor, gone in an instant. He felt the fury of the energy rays that tore futilely at the metal behind him.

His plan was quite clear now. He would capture half a dozen men, and make *guuls* of them. Then kill all the others, proceed on to the galactic system toward which the ship was heading, and take control of the first inhabited planet. After that, domination of the entire universe would be a matter of a short time only.

Commander Morton stood very stiffly there in the gleaming corridor, every muscle in his huge body like a taut wire. Only a dozen men were gathered round the dead body, but the audio-scopes were on; nearly two hundred tense men throughout the ship were watching that scene. Morton's voice was only a whisper, but it cut across the silence like a whiplash.

"Well, doctor?"

Dr. Eggert rose up from his kneeling position beside the body, frowning.

"Heart failure."

"Heart failure!"

"All right, all right!" The doctor put up his hands as if to defend himself against physical attack. "I know his teeth look as if they've been smashed back into his brain, and I know Darjeeling's heart was perfect, but heart failure is what it looks like to me."

"I can believe it," a man said sourly. "When I came around that corner, and saw that thing, I nearly had heart failure myself."

"We're wasting time!" von Grossen's voice stabbed from behind Morton. "We can beat this fellow, but not by talking about him, and feeling sick every time he makes a move. If I'm next on the list of victims, I want to know that the best damned bunch of scientists in the system are not crying over my fate, but putting their best brains to the job of avenging my death."

"You're right," Smith said. "The trouble with us is, we've been permitting ourselves to feel inferior. He's only been on the ship about an hour but I can see now that some of us are going to get killed. Well, I accept my chances! But let's get organized for combat!"

Morton snapped: "Pennons, here's a problem. We've got about two square miles of wall and floor space in our twenty levels. How long will it take to energize every inch of it?"

The chief engineer stared at him, aghast; then answered swiftly: "I could sweep the ship and probably wreck it completely within an hour. I won't go into details. But uncontrolled energization is absolutely out. It would kill every living thing aboard—"

"Not everything!" von Grossen rejected. "Not the creature. Remember, that damn thing ran into a wall of force. Your instrument, Pennons, registered activity for several seconds. Several seconds! Let me show you what that means. The principle underlying his ability to slip through walls is simple enough. The atoms of his body slide through the empty spaces between the atoms of the walls. There is a basic electronic tension that holds a body together, which would have to be overcome, but apparently his race has solved the difficulty. A wall of force would increase those electronic tensions to a point where the atoms themselves would be emitting free electrons; and, theoretically, that should have a deadly effect on any interfering body. I'll wager he didn't like those few seconds he was in the wall—but the point is, he stood them."

Morton's strong face was hard: "You could feed more energy to those walls, couldn't you, Pennons?"

"N-no!" said Pennons reluctantly. "The walls couldn't stand it. They'd melt."

The walls couldn't stand it!" a man gasped. "Man, man, do you know what you're making this creature out to be?"

Morton saw the consternation that leaped along that line of stern faces. Korita's thin, clear voice cut across that pregnant silence:

"Let us not forget, my honorable friends, that he did blunder into the wall of force, and recoiled in dismay, though apparently without damage to his person. I use the word 'blunder' with discretion. His action proves once again that he does make mistakes which, in turn, shows him to be something less than a superbeing—"

"Suppose," Morton barked, "he's a peasant of his cycle. What would be his chief intellectual characteristic?"

Korita replied almost crisply for one who usually spoke so slowly: "The inability to understand the full power of organization. He will think probably that all he has to fight in order to get control of this ship would be the men who are in it. His most instinctive reasoning would tend to discount the fact that we are part of a vast galactic civilization or organization, and that the spirit of civilization is fighting in us. The mind of the true peasant is very individualistic, almost anarchic. His desire to reproduce is a form of egoism, to have his own blood particularly carried on. There can be no such thing as a peasant co-operative or organization. But this creature may want to have numbers of beings similar to himself beside him to help him with his fight. But, though there would be a loose union, they would fight as individuals, and not as a group."

"A loose union of those fire-eaters ought to be enough!" a crew member commented acidly. "I . . . a-a-a-a—"

His voice sagged. His lower jaw dropped two inches. His eyes, under Morton's gaze, took on a horribly goggled stare. The commander whipped around with an oath.

Xtl stood here, forbidding specter from a scarlet hell, his eyes pools of blazing alertness. He knew with a vast contempt that he could plunge into the nearest wall before any gun could leap out at him in ravening fury. But he felt himself protected by another fact. These were intelligent beings. They would be more anxious to discover why he had deliberately come out of the wall than to kill him immediately. They might even consider it a friendly move; and, when they discovered differently, it would be too late.

His purpose, which was twofold, was simplicity itself. He had come for his first *guul.* By snatching that *guul* from their very midst, he would demoralize them thoroughly.

Morton felt a curious wave of unreality sweep over him, as he stood just behind von Grossen there in that glittering hallway, facing the tall, thick, cylindrical reality of Xtl. Instinctively, his fingers groped downward toward the sparkling, translucent handle of the ato-gun that protruded from his holster. He stopped himself, and said in a steady voice:

"Don't touch your guns. He can move like a flash; and he wouldn't be here if he thought we could draw on him. I'll take his opinion any day on that point. Besides, we can't risk failure. This may be our only chance!"

He continued in a swift, slightly higher, more urgent tone: "Every man listening in on the audio scopes get above and below and around this corridor. Bring up the heaviest portables, even some of the semiportables and burn the walls down. Cut a clear path all around this area, and have your beams sweep that space at narrow focus. Move!"

"Good boy, Morton!" Pennons' face appeared for an instant on the plate of the audioscope. "We'll be there—if you can stall that hellhound three minutes."

Korita's sibilant voice hissed out of the audioscope: "Morton, take this chance, but do not count on success. Notice that he has appeared once again before we have had time for a discussion. He is rushing us, whether intentionally or accidentally matters not, because the result is that we're on the run, scurrying this way and that, futilely. I am convinced the vast resources of this ship can defeat any creature—any single creature—that has ever existed, or that ever will exist, but only if we have time to use them—"

His voice blurred briefly in Morton's ears. Von Grossen had taken a notebook from his pocket, and was sketching rapidly. He tore the sheet loose, and stepped forward, handed it to the creature, who examined it curiously.

Von Grossen stepped back, and began to sketch again on the second page with swift deftness. This sheet he handed also the creature, who took one glance at it, and stepped back with a snarl that split his face. His eyes widened to blazing pools; one arm half reached forward toward von Grossen, then paused uncertainly.

"What the devil have you done?" Morton demanded, his voice sounding unnaturally shrill even to himself.

Von Grossen took several steps backward, until he stood level with Morton. To the commander's amazement, he was grinning:

"I've just shown him," the German physicist said softly, "how we can defeat him—neutronium alloy, of course, and he—"

Too late, Morton stepped forward, instinctively trying to interpose his huge form in front of von Grossen. A blur of red swept by him. Something—a hand moving so fast that it was invisible—struck him a stunning blow, and knocked him spinning against the nearest wall. For an instant, his body threatened to collapse from sheer, dazed weakness. The world went black, then white, then black.

With appalling effort, he fought the weakness aside. The immense reservoir of strength in his magnificent body surged irresistibly forward; his knees stopped wavering, but his vision was still a crazy thing. As through a distorted glass, he saw that the thing was holding von Grossen in two fire-colored arms. The two-hundred-and-ten-pound physicist gave one convulsive heave of dismay; and then seemed to accept the overpowering strength of those thin, hard muscles.

With a bellow, Morton clawed for his gun. And it was then that the maddest thing of all happened. The creature took a running dive, and vanished into the wall, still holding von Grossen. For an instant, it seemed to Morton like a crazy trick of vision. But there was only the smooth gleamingness of the wall, and eleven staring, perspiring men, seven of them with drawn weapons, which they fingered helplessly.

"We're lost!" a man whispered. "If he can adjust our atomic structure, and take us through the walls, we can't fight him."

Morton chilled his heart to the dismay he read in that rough semicircle of faces. He said coldly:

"Your report, Pennons?"

There was a brief delay, then the engineer's lean leathery face, drawn with strain and effort, stared into the plate: "Nothing!" he replied succinctly. "Clay, one of my assistants, thinks he saw a flash of scarlet disappearing through a floor, going down. That's a clue of course. It means our search will be narrowed to the lower half of the ship. As for the rest, we were just lining up our units when it happened. You gave us only two minutes. We needed three!"

Morton nodded, his thoughtful mood interrupted by the abrupt realization that his fingers were shaking. With a muttered imprecation, he clenched them, and said icily:

"Korita has given us our cue—organization. The implications of that word must be fully thought out, and co-ordinated to the knowledge we have of the creature. Von Grossen, of course, has given us our defense—neutronium alloy."

"I don't follow the argument," interjected Zeller, the metallurgist.

It was Smith who explained: "The commander means that only two parts of the ship are composed of that incredibly dense metal, the outer shell and the engine room. If you had been with us when we first captured this creature, you would have noticed that, when the damned thing fell through the floor of the cage, it was stopped short by the hard metal of the ship's crust. The conclusion is obviously that it cannot slip through such metal; and the fact that it ran for the air lock is proof. The wonder is that we didn't think of it before."

Morton barked: "Therefore, to the heart of the ship—the engine room. And we won't go out of there till we've got a plan. Any other way, he'll run us ragged."

"What about von Grossen?" a man ventured.

Morton snapped harshly: "Don't make us think of von Grossen. Do you want us all to go crazy?"

In that vast room of vast machines, the men were dwarfs in *gigantica*. It was a world apart; and Morton, for the first times in years, felt the alien, abnormal tremendousness of it. His nerves jumped at each special burst of unholy blue light that sparkled and coruscated upon the great, glistening sweep of the ceiling. Blue light that was alive, pure energy that no eliminators had ever been able to eliminate; no condensers absorb.

And there was something else that sawed on his nerves now. A sound—imprisoned in the very air! A thin beam of terrifying power, a vague rumble, the faintest, quivering reverberation of an inconceivable flow of energy.

Morton glanced at his watch, and stood up with an explosive sigh of relief. He swept up a small sheaf of notes from a metal desk. The silence of unsmiling men became the deeper, tenser silence of men who fixed him with their eyes. The commander began:

"This is the first breathing spell we've had since that creature came aboard less than—incredible as it may seem—less than two hours ago. I've been glancing through these notes you've given me, and I've divided them into two sections: those that can be discussed while we're putting into effect the purely mechanical plans for cornering the thing—these latter must be discussed now. There are two. First, Zeller!"

The metallurgist stepped forward, a brisk, middle-aged, young-looking man. He started: "The creature made no attempt to keep the drawings which von Grossen showed it—proof, incidentally, that von Grossen was not seized because of the drawings. They fell on the floor; and I picked them up. I've been showing them around, so most of you know that the first drawing is a likeness of the creature stepping through a metal wall; and beside the wall is an enlarged atom system of the type of which the wall is composed—two hundred electrons arranged about the nucleus, forming a series of triangles.

"The second picture was around, unfinished but unmistakable single atom of neutronium alloy, with only eight hundred of the forty thousand electrons showing, but the design of each eighty electrons with their sixteen sides clearly indicated. That kind of language is intergalactic; and the creature understood the point instantly. He didn't like it, as we all saw by his actions; but apparently he had no intention of being thwarted; and perhaps saw the difficulty we might have in using such knowledge against him. Because, just as we cannot energize the walls of the whole ship—Pennons has said it would take days—so we have no materials to plate the ship throughout with neutronium alloy. The stuff is too rare.

"However, we have enough for me to build a suit of space armor, with which one of us could search for von Grossen, whom the thing is obviously hiding behind some wall. For the search, naturally, we'd use a fluorite camera. My assistant is already working out the suit, but we'd like suggestions—"

There were none; and, after a moment, Zeller disappeared into the machine shops adjoining the engine room. Morton's grim face relaxed slightly.

"For myself, I feel better knowing that, once the suit is built—in about an hour—the creature will have to keep moving von Grossen in order to prevent us from discovering the body. It's good to know that there's a chance of getting back one of the boldest minds about the ship."

"How do you know he's alive?" a man asked.

"Because the creature could have taken Darjeeling's dead body, but didn't. He wants us alive—Smith's notes have given us a possible clue to his purpose, but let that go now. Pennons, outline the plan you have—this is our main plan, gentlemen; and we stand or fall by it."

The chief engineer came forward; and it worried Morton to note that he was frowning blackly. His usually dynamic body lacked briskness and suggested uncertainty. The implications of the lack of confidence were mind-shaking. The mechanical wizard, the man who knew more about energy and its practical application than any other living human being—this man unsure of himself—

His voice added to Morton's dismay. It held a harsh, nasal tone that the commander had never heard from him in all the years he had known the man.

"My news isn't pleasant. To energize this ship under a controlled system would require about a hundred hours. There are approximately two square miles of floors and walls, mostly walls. And of course, as I said before, uncontrolled energization would be suicide.

"My plan is to energize the seventh level and the ninth. Only the floors and not the walls. Our hope is this: so far the creature has made no organized attempt to kill us. Korita says that this is because he is a peasant, and does not fully realize the issues at stake. As a peasant he is more concerned with reproduction, though what form that is taking, and why he has captured von Grossen is a matter for our biologist. We know, as apparently he does not, that it's a case of destroy him, or he'll destroy us. Sooner or later, even a peasant will realize that killing us comes first, before anything else, and from that moment we're lost. Our chance is that he'll delay too long—a vague chance, but we must accept it because it is based on the only analysis of the creature that we have—Korita's! If he doesn't interfere with our work, then we'll trap him on the eighth level, between the two energized floors."

Somebody interjected with a swift question: "Why not energize the seventh and eighth levels, so that he'll be in hell the moment he starts down?"

"Because"—Pennons' eyes glittered with a hard, unpleasant light—"when he starts down, he'll have one of us with him. We want that man to have a chance for life. The whole plan is packed with danger. It will take about an hour and a half to prepare the floors for energizing."

His voice became a harsh, grating sound: "And during that ninety minutes we'll be absolutely helpless against him, except for our heavy service guns. It is not beyond the bounds of possibility that he will carry us off at the rate of one every three minutes."

"Thirty out of a hundred and eighty!" Morton cut in with chill incisiveness. "One out of every six in this room. Do we take the chance? Those in favor raise their hands."

He noted with intense satisfaction that not one man's hand was raised.

The reappearance of the men brought Xtl up to the seventh level with a rush. A vague anxiety pushed into his consciousness, but there was no real sense of doubt, not even a shadow of the mental sluggishness that had affected him at first. For long minutes, he was an abnormal shape that flitted like some evil monster from a forgotten hell through the wilderness of walls and corridors.

Twice he was seen; and ugly guns flashed at him—guns as different from the simple action ato-guns as life from death. He analyzed them from their effects, the way they smashed down the walls, and made hard metal run like water. Heavy duty electronic guns these, discharging completely disintegrated atoms, a stream of pure electrons that sought union with stable matter in a coruscating fury of senseless desire.

He could face guns like that, but only for the barest second would the spinning atom system within his body carry that intolerable load. Even the biologists, who had perfected the Xtl race, had found their limitations in the hot, ravening energy of smashed atoms.

The important thing was: "What were the men doing with such determination? Obviously, when they shut themselves up in the impregnable engine room, they had conceived a plan—" With glittering, unwinking eyes, Xtl watched that plan take form.

In every corridor, men slaved over atomic furnaces, squat things of dead-black metal. From a hole in the top of each furnace, a white glare spewed up, blazing forth in uncontrollable ferocity at the ceilings; intolerable flares of living fire, dazzling almost beyond the endurance to Xtl protected by a solid metal wall as well as by his superlatively conditioned body.

He could see that the men were half dazed by the devastating whiteness that beat against their vision. They wore their space armor with the ordinary transparent glassite electrically darkened. But no light metal armor could ward off the full effect of the deadly rays that sprayed, violent and untamed, in every direction.

Out of the furnaces rolled long dully glowing strips of some material, which were instantly snatched into the maw of machine tools, skillfully hacked into exactly measured sections, and slapped onto the floors. Not an inch of floor, Xtl noticed, escaped being enclosed in some way or another by these strips. And the moment the strips were laid, massive refrigerators hugged close to them, and froze the heat out of them.

His mind refused at first to accept the result of his observations. His brain persisted in searching for deeper purposes, for a cunning of vast and not easily discernible scope. Somewhere there must be a scheme that would explain the appalling effort the men were making. Slowly, he realized the truth.

There was nothing more. These beings were actually intending to attempt the building of walls of force throughout the entire ship under a strict system of controls—anything less, of course, was out of the question. They could not be so foolish as to think that a partial energization could have the faintest hope of success. If such hope smoldered, it was doomed to be snuffed out.

And total energization was equally impossible. Could they not realize that he would not permit such a thing; and that is would be a simple matter to follow them about, and tear loose their energization connections?

In cold contempt, Xtl dismissed the machinations of the men from his mind. They were only playing into his hands, making it easier for him to get the *guuls* he still needed.

He selected his next victim as carefully as he had selected von Grossen. He had discovered in the dead man—Darjeeling—that the stomach was the place he wanted; and the men with the largest stomachs were automatically on his list.

The action was simplicity itself. A cold, merciless survey of the situation from the safety of a wall, a deadly swift rush and—before a single beam could blaze out in sullen rage—he was gone with the writhing, struggling body.

It was simple to adjust his atomic structure the instant he was through a ceiling, and so break his fall on the floor beneath; then dissolve through the floor onto the level below in the same fashion. Into the vast hold of the ship, he half fell, half lowered himself.

The hold was familiar territory now to the sure-footed tread of his long-toed feet. He had explored the place briefly but thoroughly after he first boarded the ship. And the handling of von Grossen had given him the exact experience he needed for this man.

Unerringly, he headed across the dimly lit interior toward the far wall. Great packing cases piled up to the ceiling. Without pause, he leaped onto them; and, by dexterous adjustment of his structure, found himself after a moment in a great pipe, big enough for him to stand upright—part of the miles of air-conditioning pipes in the vast ship.

It was dark by ordinary light, but to his full vision a vague twilight glow suffused the place. He saw the body of von Grossen, and deposited his new victim beside the physicist. Carefully now, he inserted one of his slender hands into his own breast; and removed one precious egg—deposited it into the stomach of the human being.

The man had ceased struggling, but Xtl waited for what he knew must happen. Slowly, the body began to stiffen, the muscles growing rigid. The man stirred; then, in evident panic, began to fight as he realized the paralysis that was stealing over him. But remorselessly Xtl held him down.

Abruptly, the chemical action was completed. The man lay motionless, every muscle stiff as a rock, a horrible thing of taut flesh.

There were no doubts now in Xtl's mind. Within a few hours, the eggs would be hatching inside each man's stomach; and in a few hours more the tiny replicas of himself would have eaten themselves to full size.

Grimly complacent, he darted up out of the hold. He needed more hatching places for his eggs, more *guuls*.

On the ninth level now, the men slaved. Waves of heat rolled along the corridor, a veritable inferno wind; even the refrigeration unit in each spacesuit was hard put to handle that furious, that deadly blast of superheated air. Men sweated in their suits, sick from the heat, dazed by the glare, laboring almost by instinct.

At last, Morton shut off his own furnace. "Thank Heaven, that's finished!" he exclaimed; then urgently: "Pennons, are you ready to put your plan into effect?"

"Ready, aye, ready!" came the engineer's dry rasp of a voice on the communicators. He finished even more harshly: "Four men gone and one to go. We've been lucky—but there is one to go!"

"Do you hear that, you spacehounds!" Morton barked. "One to go. One of us will be bait—and don't hold your guns in your hands. He must have the chance at that bait. Kellie, elaborate on those notes you gave me before. It will clear up something very important, and keep our minds off that damned thing."

"Er!" The cracked voice of the sociologist jarred the communicators. "Er, here is my reasoning. When we discovered the thing it was floating a million light-years from the nearest system, apparently without means of spatial locomotion. Picture that appalling distance, and then ask yourself how long it would require for an object to float by it by pure chance. Gunlie Lester gave me my figures, so I wish he would tell you what he told me."

"Gunlie Lester speaking!" The voice of the astronomer sounded surprisingly brisk. "Most of you know the prevailing theory of the beginnings of the present universe: that it was formed by the disintegration of a *previous* universe several million million years ago, and that a few million million years hence our universe will complete its cycle in a torrent of explosions, and be replaced by another, which will develop from the maelstrom. As for Kellie's question, it is not at all impossible; in fact, it would require several million million years for a creature floating by pure chance to reach a point a million light-years from a planet. Is that what you wanted, Kellie?"

"Er, yes. Most of you will recall my mentioning before that it was a paradox that a pure sympodial development, such as this creature, did not populate the entire universe. The answer is that, logically, if his race *should* have controlled the universe, then they *did* control it. We human beings have discovered that logic is the sole stable factor in the all; and we cannot shrink even from the most far-reaching conclusions that the mind may arrive at. This race did control the universe, but it was the previous universe they ruled, not our present one. Now, naturally, the creature intends that his race shall also dominate this universe."

"In short," Morton snapped, "we are faced with the survivor of the supreme race of a universe. There is no reason to assume that they did not arrive at our present level of progress any later than we did; and we've still got several million million years to go before our universe crashes into flaming death. Therefore, they are not only billions of years ahead of us, but millions of millions of years." His voice took on a strained note: "Frankly, it scares me. We're not doing enough. Our plans are too sketchy. We must have more information before we can hope to win against such a super-human monster. I'm very much afraid that—"

The shrill scream of a man protruded horribly into his words, and there came a gurgling "—got me . . . quick . . . ripping me out of my suit—"

The voice collapsed; and somebody shouted in frank dismay: "Good Heaven! That was Dack, my assistant!"

The world of the ship became, for Morton, a long, shining corridor that persisted in blurring before his eyes. And it was suddenly as if he were looking, not out at it, but down into its depths—fearsome depths that made his brain reel.

Ages seemed to pass. But Morton, schooled not to abnormal calm, knew that only fractions of seconds were dragging by. Just as his nerves threatened to break, he heard a voice, Pennons' voice, cool, steady, yet almost unrecognizable:

"One!" said Pennons; and it sounded absolute mumbo-jumbo in that moment when out there another man was going through a hell of fear and torment.

"Two!" said Pennons, cold as ice.

Morton found himself staring curiously at his feet. Sparkling, brilliant, beautiful blue fire throbbed there. Little tendrils of that gorgeous flame reared up hungrily a few inches from his suit, as if baffled by some invisible force protecting the suit.

There was a distinct click in Morton's mind. Instantly, his brain jumped to full gear. In a flash of thought, he realized that Pennons had energized floors seven and nine. And that it was blue ferocity of the energization that was struggling to break through the full driven screens of his space armor.

Through his communicators came the engineer's hiss of indrawn breath: "If I'm right," Pennons almost whispered, all the strength gone from his voice, "we've now got that—devil—cornered on the eighth floor."

"Then," barked Morton efficiently, "we'll carry on according to plan. Group one, follow me to the seventh floor."

The men behind Morton stopped short as he halted abruptly at the second corner. Sickly, he went forward, and stood staring at the human body that sagged against the floor, pasted to the metal by almost unbearably brilliant fingers of blue fire. His voice, when he spoke, was only a whisper, but it cut across the strain of silence like a whiplash:

"Pull him loose!"

Two men stepped gingerly forward, and touched the body. The blue fire leaped ravenously at them, straining with futile ferocity to break through the full-driven defense screens of their suits. The men jerked, and the unholy bonds snapped. They carried the body up the nearest stairs to the unenergized eighth level. The other men followed silently, and watched as the body was laid on the floor.

The lifeless thing continued to kick for several minutes, discharging torrents of energy, then gradually took on the quietness of natural death.

"I'm waiting for reports!" Morton said stiffly into his communicator.

Pennon's voice came. "The men are spread out over the eighth floor according to plan, taking continuous pictures with fluorite cameras. If he's anywhere on the floor, we'll get a picture of his swift-moving body; and then it will be a matter of energizing the floor piecemeal. It'll take about thirty minutes yet—"

And finally the report came: "Nothing!" Pennons' voice held an incredulous note tinged with dismay. "Morton, he's not here. It can only mean that he passed through the energized floor as easily as through ordinary metal. We know he must have gone through it because Dack's dead body was on *this* side."

Somebody said hopelessly: "And now what are we going to do?"

Morton didn't answer. It struck him abruptly, with a shock that tore away his breath, that he had no answer.

The silence in that shining corridor was a form of death. It pressed against Morton, a queer, murky, lightless thing. Death was written too in the faces that blurred around him, the cold, logical death expectancy of men who could see no way out.

Morton broke the silence: "I am willing to accept von Grossen's analysis of how the thing passes through metal. But he intimated the creature recoiled from the energized wall. Can anyone explain then—how?"

"Zeller speaking!" The brisk voice of the metallurgist came through the communicators. "I've finished the neutronium-alloy suit and I've started my search at the bottom of the ship—I heard your question, Morton. To my mind, we missed one point the first time the creature struck the wall of force: The point is that he *was* in it. And what basic difference is there between being partially inside the wall, and actually passing through? He would pass through in less than a second. The first time, he touched the wall for several seconds, which probably means that, in his surprise, he recoiled and lost his balance. That must have made his position very unpleasant. The second time, however, he simply released poor Dack and passed on through with a minimum of discomfort."

"Hm-m-m!" Morton pondered. "That means he's still vulnerable to walls of force, provided we could keep him inside one for a long enough time. And that would mean complete energization of the ship which, in turn, would depend on his allowing us to make the connections without interference. I think he would interfere. He let us get away with energizing the two floors because he knew it didn't mean anything—and it gave him a good opportunity to kidnap some more men. Fortunately, he didn't grab off as many as we expected, through Heaven help those four."

Smith said grimly, his first words in a long time: "My firm opinion is that anything that would require more than two hours to complete will be fatal. We are dealing with a creature who has everything to gain by killing us, and obtaining control of the ship. Zeller, how long would it take to build neutronium-alloy suits for every man on this ship?"

"About two hundred hours," the metallurgist replied coolly, "mainly because I used up nearly all the available alloy for this one suit. We'd have to break down the walls of the ship, and build the alloy from an electronic base. We're not in the habit of carrying a lot of metal on this ship, as you know, because there's usually a planet a few minutes from anywhere. Now, we've still got a two weeks' trip either way."

"Then that's out!" frowned Smith blackly. He looked stunned. "And since the complete energization is out—we've got nothing else."

The usually lazy voice of Gourlay, the communications chief, snapped: "I don't see why those ways are out. We're still alive; and I suggest we get to work, and do as much as we can as soon as we can—everybody working first at making suits for the men who go out to prepare the walls for energizing. At least, that will protect them from being kidnapped."

"What makes you think," Smith asked coldly, "that the creature is not capable of smashing down neutronium alloy? As a superior being, his knowledge of physics should make it a simple matter for him to construct a beam that could destroy anything we have. Heaven knows there's plenty of tools lying in the various laboratories."

The two men glared at each other with the flashing, angry eyes of men whose nerves have been strained to the utmost limit. Before Morton could speak, Korita's sibilant voice cut across the tense silence: "I am inclined to agree with Smith. We are dealing with a being who must now know that he cannot allow us time for anything important. I agree with the commander when he says that the creature will interfere if we attempt to prepare the ship for complete controlled energization. The honorable gentlemen must not forget, however, that we are dealing with a creature whom we have decided is in the peasant stage of his particular cycle.

"Let me enlarge on that. Life is an ebb and flow. There is a full tide of glorious accomplishment, and low tide of recuperation. For generations, centuries, the blood flows in the peasant, turgid, impure, gathering strength from the soil; and then it begins to grow, to expand, reaching finally for the remotest stars. At this point, amazingly enough, the blood grows weary; and, in this late megalopolitan era, men no longer desire to prolong their race. Highly cultivated people regard having children as a question of pros and cons, and their general outlook on life is tinged with a noble skepticism.

"Nature, on the other hand, knows nothing of pro and con. You cannot reason with a peasant—and he cannot reason except as a peasant. His land and his son, or—to put a higher term to it—his property and his blood are sacred. If a bourgeoisie court orders him off his land, he fights blindly, ignorantly, for his own. It matters not to him that he may have accepted money for a mortgage. He only knows they're trying to take his property, to draw his roots from the soil where his blood has been nourished.

"Honorable sirs, here is my point: This creature cannot begin to imagine anyone else not feeling about his patch of home—his own property the way he does.

"But we . . . we can make such a sacrifice without suffering a spiritual collapse."

Every muscle in Morton's body grew taut, as he realized the implications. His exclamation was almost a whisper: "Korita, you've got it! It means sacrificing von Grossen and the others. It means sacrifice that makes my brain reel, but property is not sacred to us. And as for von Grossen and the other three"—his voice grew stern and hard, his eyes wide with a chill horror—"I didn't tell you about the notes that Smith gave me. I didn't tell you because he suggested a possible parallel with a certain species of wasp back home on earth. The thought is so horrible that I think instantaneous death will come as a release to these bold men."

"The wasp!" A man gasped. "You're right, Morton. The sooner they're dead the better!"

"Then," Morton cried, "to the engine room. We—"

A swift, excited voice clamored into his communicators; it was a long second before he recognized it as belonging to Zeller, the metallurgist:

"Morton—quick! Down to the hold! I've found them—in the air-conditioning pipe. The creature's here, and I'm holding him off as best I can. He's trying to sneak upon me through the walls. Hurry!"

Morton snapped orders with machine-gun precision, as the men swarmed toward the elevators: "Smith, take a dozen men and get Kent down from the bedrooms to the engine room. I'd almost forgotten about him and his broken leg! Pennons, take a hundred men to the engine room and make the preparations to carry out Korita's plan. The rest take the four heavy freight elevators and follow me!"

He finished in a ringing voice: "We won't kill him in the hold of course, unless he's gone stark mad. But the crisis has come! Things are breaking our way at last. And we've got him! We've got him!"

Xtl retreated reluctantly, sullenly, as the men carried off his four *guuls*. The first shrinking fear of defeat closed over his mind like the night that brooded beyond the enclosing walls of the ship. His impulse was to dash into their midst, a whirlwind of ferocity, and smash them. But those ugly, glittering weapons congealed that wild rage.

He retreated with a dismaying sense of disaster, conscious that he had lost the initiative. The men would discover his eggs now; and, in destroying them, would destroy his immediate chances of being reinforced by other Xtls. And, what was more, they were temporarily safe in the engine room.

His brain spun into a cold web of purpose. From this moment, he must kill, and kill only. It seemed suddenly incredible that he had thought first of reproduction, with everything else coming secondary, even his every other thought blurred by the subordination to his one flaming desire.

His proper action was preternaturally clear now. Not to get his *guuls* first, but to kill these dangerous enemies, to control the ship, then head for the nearest inhabited planet, where is would be a simple matter to find other, more stupid *guuls*.

To kill he must have an irresistible weapon, one that could smash—anything! And valuable time had already been wasted. After a moment's thought, he headed for the nearest laboratory, conscious of a burning urgency, unlike anything he had ever known.

As he worked—tall, nightmare body and hideous face bent intently over the gleaming metal of the queer-shaped mechanism—his sensitive feet grew aware of a difference in the symphony of vibrations that throbbed in discordant melody through the ship.

He paused, straightened, alert and tense; and realized what it was. The drive engines were silent. The monster ship of space had halted in its head-long flight and was lying quiescent in the black deeps.

An abrupt, indefinable sense of urgency came to Xtl—an icy alarm. His long, black, wirelike fingers became flashing things as he made delicate connections, deftly and frantically.

Suddenly, he paused again. Through his brain pulsed a distinct sensation of something wrong, dangerously, desperately, terribly wrong. The muscles of his feet grew taut with straining. Abruptly, he knew what it was.

He could no longer feel the vibrations of the men. *They had left the ship!*

Xtl whirled from his nearly finished weapon, and plunged through the nearest wall. He knew his doom with a burning certainty that found hope only in the blackness of space.

Through deserted corridors he fled, slavering slit-faced hate, scarlet monster from ancient, incredibly ancient Glor. The gleaming walls seemed to mock him. The whole world of the great ship, which had promised too much, was now only the place where sudden intolerable hell would break loose in a devastating, irresistible torrent of energy.

He saw the air lock ahead—and flashed through the first section, then the second, the third—then he was out in space. There was a sense of increasing lightness as his body flung by momentum darted from the side of the ship, out into that blackest of black nights.

For a brief instant, his body glinted and flashed a startling scarlet, reflecting the dazzling light from the row on row of brilliant portholes.

The queerest thing happened then. The porthole lights snuffed out, and were replaced by a strange, unearthly blue glow, that flashed out from every square inch of that dark, sweeping plain of metal.

The blue glow faded, died. Some of the porthole lights came on again, flickering weakly, uncertainly; and then, as mightily engines recovered from that devastating flare of blue power, the lights already shining grew stronger. Others began to flash on.

Xtl was a hundred yards from the ship when he saw the first of the torpedolike craft dart out of the surrounding night, into an opening that yawned in the side of the mighty vessel. Four other dark craft followed, whipping down in swift arcs, their shaped blurred against the background of immensity, vaguely visible in the light that glowed now, strong and steady from the lighted portholes.

The opening shut; and—just like that—the ship vanished. One instant, it was there, a vast sphere of dark metal; the next he was staring through the space where it had been at a vague swirl of light, an enormous galaxy that swam beyond a gulf of a billion years.

Time dragged drearily toward infinity. Xtl sprawled moveless and unutterably hopeless on the bosom of endless night. He couldn't help thinking of the sturdy sons he might of had, and of the universe that was lost because of his mistakes. But it was the thought of the sons, of companionship, that really brought despair.

Morton watched the skillful fingers of the surgeon, as the electrified knife cut into the fourth man's stomach. The last egg was deposited in the bottom of the tall neutronium alloy vat.

The eggs were round, grayish objects, one of them slightly cracked.

As they watched, the crack widened; an ugly, round, scarlet head with tiny, beady eyes and a tiny slit of a mouth poked out. The head twisted on its short neck, and the eyes glittered up at them with a hard ferocity.

And then, with a swiftness that almost took them by surprise, it reared up and tried to run out of the vat, slid back—and dissolved into the flame that Morton poured down upon it.

Smith, licking his dry lips, said: "Suppose he'd got away, and dissolved into the nearest wall!"

Nobody said anything. They stood with intent eyes, staring into the vat. The eggs melted reluctantly, under the merciless fire of Morton's gun, and then burned with a queer, golden light.

"Ah," said Dr. Eggert; and attention turned to him, and the body of von Grossen, over which he was bending. "His muscles are beginning to relax, and his eyes are open and alive. I imagine he knows what's going on. It was a form of paralysis induced by the egg, and fading now that the egg is no longer present. Nothing fundamentally wrong. They'll all be O.K. shortly. What about the big fellow?"

Morton replied: "Zeller swears he saw a flash of red emerge from the main lock just as we swept the ship with uncontrolled energization. It must have been, because he haven't found his body. However, Pennons is out with half the men, taking pictures with fluorite cameras; and we'll know for certain in a few hours. Here he is now. Well, Pennons?"

The engineer strode in briskly, and placed a misshapen thing of metal on one of the tables. "Nothing definite to report yet—but I found this in the main physics laboratory. What do you make of it?"

Morton frowned down at the fragile-looking object with its intricate network of wires. There were three distinct tubes that might have been muzzles running into and through three small, round balls, that shone with a queer, silvery light. The light penetrated the table, making it as transparent as glassite. And, strangest of all, the balls irradiated, not heat, but cold.

Morton put his hands near, but the cold was of a mild, water-freezing variety, apparently harmless. He touched the metal ball. It felt as chilled metal might feel.

"I think we'd better leave this for our chief physicist to examine. Von Grossen ought to be up and around soon. You say you found it in the laboratory?"

Pennons nodded; and Morton carried on his thought: "Obviously, the creature was working on it, when he suspected that something was amiss—he must have suspected the truth, for he left the ship. That seems to discount your theory, Korita. You said that, as a true peasant, he couldn't even imagine what we were going to do."

The Japanese historian smiled faintly through the fatigue that paled his face. "Honorable commander," he said politely, "a peasant can realize destructive intentions as easily as you or I. What he cannot do is bring himself to destroy his own property, or imagine others destroying theirs. We have no such limitations."

Pennons groaned: "I wish we had. Do you know that it will take us three months at least to get this ship properly repaired after thirty seconds of uncontrolled energization. For those thirty seconds, the ship created a field in space millions of times more intense than the energization output. I was afraid that—"

He stopped with a guilty look. Morton grinned: "Go ahead and finish what you were going to say. You were afraid the ship would be completely destroyed. Don't worry, Pennons, your previous statements as to the danger involved made us realize the risks we were taking; and we knew that our lifeboats could only be given partial antiacceleration; so we'd have been stranded here a million years from home."

A man said, thoughtfully: "Well, personally, I think there was nothing actually to fear. After all, he did belong to another universe, and there is a special rhythm to our present state of existence to which man is probably attuned. We have the advantage in this universe of momentum, which, I doubt, a creature from any other universe could hope to overcome. And in the world of man there is no just place for a creature that can even consider laying its eggs in the living flesh of other sensitive beings. All other intelligent life would unite against such a distinctly personal menace."

Smith shook his head: "There is no biological basis for your opinion, and therefore it falls in the category of 'things darkly spoken are darkly seen.' It dominated once, and it could dominate again. You assume far too readily that man is a paragon of justice, forgetting apparently that he lives on meat, enslaves his neighbors, murders his opponents, and obtains the most unholy sadistical joy from the agony of others. It is not impossible that we shall, in the course of our travels, meet other intelligent creatures far more worthy than man to rule the universe."

"By Heaven!" replied the other, "no creature is ever getting on board this ship

again, no matter how harmless he looks. My nerves are all shot; and I'm not so good
a man as I was when I first came aboard the *Beagle* two long years ago."

"You speak for us all!" said Morton.

*. . . Xtl glided into the wall just ahead of the last man—and pounced forth in
an irresistible charge. A rearing, frightful shape of glaring eyes and ghastly
mouth, blood-red, metal-hard body, and four arms of fire . . .*

SCARLET
Dream

by Catherine L. Moore

*Mary Shelley/"Frankenstein" . . . Stanley Weinbaum/"A Martian Odyssey"
. . . Isaac Asimov/"Foundation" . . . C. L. Moore "Shambleau". Catherine
Louise Moore's classic has been reprinted so many times that fans have almost
memorized it; not so "Scarlet Dream". Queen Catherine was the first beauteous
female author. Today she would shine in the company of the best of today's
women writers. She considered the odor of gasoline "glamorous". Her marriage to
legendary sf writer Henry Kuttner was amorous, her literary collaborations with
him fabulous. I had the pleasure of collaborating with her on "Nyusa, Nymph of
Darkness" and, uncredited, "Yvala". I loved her, but hundreds of others could say
that. The Curse of Cthulhu on Alzheimer's that took her from us.
She lives again in "Scarlet Dream".—FJA
Story from Weird Tales, 1934*

Northwest Smith bought the shawl in the Lakkmanda Markets of Mars. It was one of his chiefest joys to wander through the stalls and stands of that greatest of market-places whose wares are drawn from all the planets of the solar system, and beyond. So many songs have been sung and so many tales written of that fascinating chaos called the Lakkmanda Markets that there is little need to detail it here.

He shouldered his way through the colorful cosmopolitan throng, the speech of a thousand races beating in his ears, the mingled odors of perfume and sweat and spice and food and the thousand nameless smells of the place assailing his nostrils. Vendors cried their wares in the tongues of a score of worlds.

As he strolled through the thick of the crowd, savoring the confusion and the odors and the sights from lands beyond counting, his eye was caught by a flash of that peculiar geranium scarlet that seems to lift itself bodily from its background and smite the eye with all but physical violence. It came from a shawl thrown carelessly across a carved chest, typically Martian drylander work by the exquisite detail of that carving, so oddly at variance with the characteristics of the harsh dryland race. He recognized the Venusian origin of the brass tray on the shawl, and knew the heap of carved ivory beasts that the tray held as the work of one of the least-known races on Jupiter's largest moon, but from all his wide experience he could draw no remembrance of any such woven work as that of the shawl. Idly curious, he paused at the booth and asked of its attendant,

"How much for the scarf?"

The man—he was a canal Martian—glanced over his shoulder and said carelessly, "Oh, that. You can have it for half a *cris*—gives me a headache to look at the thing."

Smith grinned and said, "I'll give you five dollars."

"Ten."

"Six and a half, and that's my last offer."

"Oh, take the thing." The Martian smiled and lifted the tray of ivory beasts from the chest.

Smith drew out the shawl. It clung to his hands like a live thing, softer and lighter than Martian "lamb's-wool." He felt sure it was woven from the hair of some beast rather than from vegetable fiber, for the electric clinging of it sparkled with life. And the crazy pattern dazzled him with its utter strangeness. Unlike any pattern he had seen in all the years of his far wanderings, the wild, leaping scarlet threaded its nameless design in one continuous, tangled line through the twilight blue of the background. That dim blue was clouded exquisitely with violet and green-sleepy evening colors against which the startling scarlet flamed like something more sinister and alive than color. He felt that he could almost put his hand between the color and the cloth, so vividly did it start up from its background.

"Where in the universe did this come from?" he demanded of the attendant.

The man shrugged.

"Who knows? It came in with a bale of scrap cloth from New York. I was a little curious about it myself, and called the market-master there to trace it. He says it was sold for scrap by a down-and-out Venusian who claimed he'd found it in a derelict ship floating around one of the asteroids. He didn't know what nationality the ship had been—a very early model, he said, probably one of the first spaceships, made before the identification symbols were adopted. I've wondered why he sold the thing for scrap. He could have got double the price, anyhow, if he'd made any effort."

"Funny." Smith stared down at the dizzy pattern writhing through the cloth in his hands. "Well, it's warm and light enough. If it doesn't drive me crazy trying to follow the pattern, I'll sleep warm at night."

He crumpled it in one hand, the whole six-foot square of it folding easily into his palm, and stuffed the silky bundle into his pocket-and thereupon forgot it until after his return to his quarters that evening.

He had taken one of the cubicle steel rooms in the great steel lodging-houses the Martian government offers for a very nominal rent to transients. The original purpose was to house those motley hordes of spacemen that swarm every port city of the civilized planets, offering them accommodations cheap and satisfactory enough so that they will not seek the black byways of the town and there fall in with the denizens of the Martian underworld whose lawlessness is a byword among space sailors.

The great steel building that housed Smith and countless others was not entirely free from the influences of Martian byways, and if the police had actually searched the place with any degree of thoroughness a large percentage of its dwellers might have been transferred to the Emperor's prisons—Smith almost certainly among them, for his activities were rarely within the law and though he could not recall at the moment any particularly flagrant sins committed in Lakkdarol, a charge could certainly have been found against him by the most half-hearted searcher. However, the likelihood of a police raid was very remote, and Smith, as he went in under the steel portals of the great door, rubbed shoulders with smugglers and pirates and fugitives and sinners of all the sins that keep the spaceways thronged.

In his little cubicle he switched on the light and saw a dozen blurred replicas of himself, reflected dimly in the steel walls, spring into being with the sudden glow. In that curious company he moved forward to a chair and pulled out the crumpled shawl. Shaking it in the mirror-walled room produced a sudden wild writhing of scarlet patterns over walls and floor and ceiling, and for an instant the room whirled in an inexplicable kaleidoscope and he had the impression that the four-dimensional walls had opened suddenly to undreamed-of vastnesses where living scarlet in wild, unruly patterns shivered through the void.

Then in a moment the walls closed in again and the dim reflections quieted and became only the images of a tall, brown man with pale eyes, holding a curious shawl in his hands. There was a strange, sensuous pleasure in the clinging of the silky wool to his fingers, the lightness of it, the warmth. He spread it out on the table and traced the screaming scarlet pattern with his finger, trying to follow that one writhing line through the intricacies of its path, and the more he stared the more irritatingly clear it became to him that there must be a purpose in that whirl of color, that if he stared long enough, surely he must trace it out . . .

When he slept that night he spread the bright shawl across his bed, and the brilliance of it colored his dreams fantastically . . .

That threading scarlet was a labyrinthine path down which he stumbled blindly, and at every turn he looked back and saw himself in myriad replicas, always wandering lost and alone through the pattern of the path. Sometimes it shook itself under his feet, and whenever he thought he saw the end it would writhe into fresh intricacies. . . .

The sky was a great shawl threaded with scarlet lightning that shivered and squirmed as he watched, then wound itself into the familiar, dizzy pattern that became one mighty Word in a nameless writing, whose meaning he shuddered on the verge of understanding, and woke in icy terror just before the significance of it broke upon his brain. . . .

He slept again, and saw the shawl hanging in a blue dusk the color of its background, stared and stared until the square of it melted imperceptibly into the dimness and the scarlet was a pattern incised lividly upon a gate . . . a gate of strange outline in a high wall, half seen through that curious, cloudy twilight blurred with exquisite patches of green and violet, so that it seemed no mortal twilight, but some strange and lovely evening in a land where the air was suffused with colored mists, and no winds blew. He felt himself moving forward without effort, and the gate opened before him. . . .

He was mounting a long flight of steps. In one of the metamorphoses of dreams it did not surprise him that the gate had vanished, or that he had no remembrance of having climbed the long flight stretching away behind him. The lovely colored twilight still veiled the air, so that he could see but dimly the steps rising before him and melting into the mist. And now, suddenly, he was aware of a stirring in the dimness, and a girl came flying down the stairs in a headlong, stumbling terror. He could see the shadow of it on her face, and her long, bright-colored hair streamed out behind her, and from head to foot she was dabbled with blood. In her blind flight she must not have seen him, for she came plunging downward three steps at a time and blundered full into him as he stood undecided, watching. The impact all but unbalanced him, but his arms closed instinctively about her and for a moment she hung in his embrace, utterly spent, gasping against his broad leather breast and too breathless even to wonder who had stopped her. The smell of fresh blood rose to his nostrils from her dreadfully spattered garments.

Finally she lifted her head and raised a flushed, creamy-brown face to him, gulping in air through lips the color of holly berries. Her dabbled hair, so fantastically golden that it might have been almost orange, shivered about her face as she clung to him with lifted, lovely face. In that dizzy moment he saw that her eyes were sherry-brown with tints of red, and the fantastic, colored beauty of her face had a wild tinge of something utterly at odds with anything he had ever known before. It might have been the look in her eyes. . . .

"Oh!" she gasped. "It—it has her! Let me go! . . . Let me—"

Smith shook her gently.

"What has her?" he demanded. "Who? Listen to me! You're covered with blood, do you know it? Are you hurt?"

She shook her head wildly.

"No—no—let me go! I must—-not my blood—hers. . . ."

She sobbed on the last word, and suddenly collapsed in his arms, weeping with a violent intensity that shook her from head to foot. Smith gazed helplessly about over the orange head, then gathered the shaking girl in his arms and went on up the stairs through the violet gloaming.

He must have climbed for all of five minutes before the twilight thinned a little and he saw that the stairs ended at the head of a long hallway, high-arched like a cathedral aisle. A row of low doors ran down one side of the hall, and he turned aside at random into the nearest. It gave upon a gallery whose arches opened into blue space. A low bench ran along the wall under the gallery windows, and he crossed toward it, gently setting down the sobbing girl and supporting her against his shoulder. "My sister," she wept. "It has her—oh, my sister!"

"Don't cry, don't cry," Smith heard his own voice saying, surprisingly. "It's all a dream, you know. Don't cry—there never was any sister—you don't exist at all—don't cry so."

She jerked her head up at that, startled out of her sobs for a moment, and stared at him with sherry-brown eyes drowned in tears. Her lashes clung together in wet, starry points. She stared with searching eyes, taking in the leather-brownness of him, his spaceman's suit, his scarred dark face and eyes paler than steel. And then a look of infinite pity softened the strangeness of her face, and she said gently,

"Oh . . . you come from—from—you still believe that you dream!"

"I *know* I'm dreaming," persisted Smith childishly. "I'm lying asleep in Lakkdarol and dreaming of you, and all this, and when I wake—"

She shook her head sadly.

"You will never wake. You have come into a more deadly dream than you could ever guess. There is no waking from this land."

"What do you mean? Why not?" A little absurd panic was starting up in his mind at the sorrow and pity in her voice, the sureness of her words. Yet this was one of those rare dreams wherein he knew quite definitely that he dreamed. He could not be mistaken. . . .

"There are many dream countries," she said, "many nebulous, unreal half-lands where the souls of sleepers wander, places that have an actual, tenuous existence, if one knows the way . . . But here—it has happened before, you see—one may not blunder without passing a door that opens one way only. And he who has the key to open it may come through, but he can never find the way into his own waking land again. Tell me—what key opened the door to you?"

"The shawl," Smith murmured. "The shawl . . . of course. That damnable red pattern, dizzy—"

He passed a hand across his eyes, for the memory of it, writhing, alive, searingly scarlet, burned behind his eyelids.

"What was it?" she demanded, breathlessly, he thought, as if a half-hopeless eagerness forced the question from her lips. "Can you remember?"

"A red pattern," he said slowly, "a thread of bright scarlet woven into a blue shawl—nightmare pattern—painted on the gate I came by . . . but it's only a dream, of course. In a few minutes I'll wake . . ."

She clutched his knee excitedly.

"Can you remember?" she demanded. "The pattern—the red pattern? The Word?"

"Word?" he wondered stupidly. "Word—in the sky? No—no, I don't want to remember—crazy pattern, you know. Can't forget it—but no, I couldn't tell you what it was, or trace it for you. Never was anything like it—thank God. It was on that shawl . . ."

"Woven on a shawl," she murmured to herself. "Yes, of course. But how you ever came by it, in your world—when it—when *it*— oh!"

Memory of whatever tragedy had sent her flying down the stairs swept back in a flood, and her face crumpled into tears again. "My sister!"

"Tell me what happened." Smith woke from his daze at the sound of her sob. "Can't I help? Please let me try—tell me about it."

"My sister," she said faintly. "It caught her in the hall—caught her before my eyes—spattered me with her blood. Oh! . . ."

"It?" puzzled Smith. "What? Is there danger?" and his hand moved instinctively toward his gun.

She caught the gesture and smiled a little scornfully through her tears.

"It," she said. "The—the Thing. No gun can harm it, no man can fight it—It came, and that was all."

"But what is it? What does it look like? Is it near?"

"It's everywhere. One never knows—until the mist begins to thicken and the pulse of red shows through—and then it's too late. We do not fight it, or think of it overmuch—life would be unbearable. For it hungers and must be fed, and we who feed it strive to live as happily as we may before the Thing comes for us. But one can never know."

"Where did it come from? What is it?"

"No one knows—it has always been here—always will be . . . too nebulous to die or be killed—a Thing out of some alien place we couldn't understand, I suppose—somewhere so long ago, or in some such unthinkable dimension that we will never have any knowledge of its origin. But as I say, we try not to think."

"If it eats flesh," said Smith stubbornly, "it must be vulnerable—and I have my gun."

"Try if you like," she shrugged. "Others have tried—and it still comes. It dwells here, we believe, if it dwells anywhere. We are—taken—more often in these halls than elsewhere. When you are weary of life you might bring your gun and wait under this roof. You may not have long to wait."

"I'm not ready to try the experiment just yet," Smith grinned. "If the Thing lives here, why do you come?"

She shrugged again, apathetically. "If we do not, it will come after us when it hungers. And we come here for—for our food." She shot him a curious glance from under lowered lids. "You wouldn't understand. But as you say, it's a dangerous place. We'd best go now—you will come with me, won't you? I shall be lonely, now." And her eyes brimmed again.

"Of course. I'm sorry, my dear. I'll do what I can for you—until I wake." He grinned at the fantastic sound of this.

"You will not wake," she said quietly. "Better not to hope, I think. You are trapped here with the rest of us and here you must stay until you die." He rose and held out his hand.

"Let's go, then," he said. "Maybe you're right, but—well, come on."

She took his hand and jumped up. The orange hair, too fantastically colored for anything outside a dream, swung about her brilliantly. He saw now that she wore a single white garment, brief and belted, over the creamy brownness of her body. It was torn now, and hideously stained. She made a picture of strange and vivid loveliness, all white and gold and bloody, in the misted twilight of the gallery.

"Where are we going?" she asked Smith. "Out there?" And he nodded toward the blueness beyond the windows.

She drew her shoulders together in a little shudder of distaste.

"Oh, no," she said.

"What is it?"

"Listen." She took him by the arms and lifted a serious face to his. "If you must stay here—and you must, for there is only one way out save death, and that is a worse way even than dying—you must learn to ask no questions about the—the Temple. This is the Temple. Here it dwells. Here we—feed.

"There are halls we know, and we keep to them. It is wiser. You saved my life when you stopped me on those stairs—no one has ever gone down into that mist and darkness, and returned. I should have known, seeing you climb them, that you were not of us . . . for whatever lies beyond, wherever that stairway leads—it is better not to know. It is better not to look out the windows of this place. We have learned that, too. For from the outside the Temple looks strange enough, but from the inside, looking out, one is liable to see things it is better not to see. . . . What that blue space is, on which this gallery opens, I do not know—I have no wish to know. There are windows here opening on stranger things than this—but we turn our eyes away when we pass them. You will learn. . . ."

She took his hand, smiling a little.

"Come with me, now."

And in silence they left the gallery opening on space and went down the hall where the blue mist floated so beautifully with its clouds of violet and green confusing the eye, and a great stillness all about.

The hallway led straight, as nearly as he could see, for the floating clouds veiled it, toward the great portals of the Temple. In the form of a mighty triple arch it opened out of the clouded twilight up on a shining day like no day he had ever seen on any planet. The light came from no visible source, and there was a lucid quality about it, nebulous but unmistakable, as if one were looking through the depths of a crystal, or through clear water that trembled a little now and then. It was diffused through the translucent day from a sky as shining and unfamiliar as everything else in this amazing dreamland.

They stood under the great arch of the Temple, looking out over the shining land beyond. Afterward he could never quite remember what had made it so unutterably strange, so indefinably dreadful. There were trees, feathery masses of green and bronze above the bronze-green grass; the bright air shimmered, and through the leaves he caught the glimmer of water not far away. At first glance it seemed a perfectly normal scene—yet tiny details caught his eye that sent ripples of coldness down his back. The grass, for instance . . .

When they stepped down upon it and began to cross the meadow toward the trees beyond which water gleamed, he saw that the blades were short and soft as fur, and they seemed to cling to his companion's bare feet as she walked. As he looked out over the meadow he saw that long waves of it, from every direction, were rippling toward them as if the wind blew from all sides at once toward the common center that was themselves. Yet no wind blew.

"It—it's alive," he stammered, startled. "The grass!"

"Yes, of course," she said indifferently.

And then he realized that though the feathery fronds of the trees waved now and then, gracefully together, there was no wind. And they did not sway in one direction only, but by twos and threes in many ways, dipping and rising with a secret, contained life of their own.

When they reached the belt of woodland he looked up curiously and heard the whisper and rustle of leaves above him, bending down as if in curiosity as the two passed beneath. They never bent far enough to touch them, but a sinister air of watchfulness, of aliveness, brooded over the whole uncannily alive landscape, and the ripples of the grass followed them wherever they went.

The lake, like that twilight in the Temple, was a sleepy blue clouded with violet and green, not like real water, for the colored blurs did not diffuse or change as it rippled.

On the shore, a little above the water line, stood a tiny, shrine-like building of some creamy stone, its walls no more than a series of arches open to the blue, translucent day. The girl led him to the doorway and gestured within negligently.

"I live here," she said.

Smith stared. It was quite empty save for two low couches with a blue coverlet thrown across each. Very classic it looked, with its whiteness and austerity, the arches opening on a vista of woodland and grass beyond.

"Doesn't it ever get cold?" he asked. "Where do you eat? Where are your books and food and clothes?"

"I have some spare tunics under my couch," she said. "That's all. No books, no other clothing, no food. We feed at the Temple. And it is never any colder or warmer than this."

"But what do you do?"

"Do? Oh, swim in the lake, sleep and rest and wander through the woods. Time passes very quickly."

"Idyllic," murmured Smith, "but rather tiresome, I should think."

"When one knows," she said, "that the next moment may be one's last, life is savored to the full. One stretches the hours out as long as possible. No, for us it is not tiresome."

"But have you no cities? Where are the other people?"

"It is best not to collect in crowds. Somehow they seem to draw—it. We live in twos and threes—sometimes alone. We have no cities. We do nothing—what purpose in beginning anything when we know we shall not live to end it? Why even think too long of one thing? Come down to the lake."

She took his hand and led him across the clinging grass to the sandy brink of the water, and they sank in silence on the narrow beach. Smith looked out over the lake where vague colors misted the blue, trying not to think of the fantastic things that were happening to him. Indeed, it was hard to do much thinking, here, in the midst of the blueness and the silence, the very air dreamy about them . . . the cloudy water lapping the shore with tiny, soft sounds like the breathing of a sleeper. The place was heavy with the stillness and the dreamy colors, and Smith was never sure, afterward, whether in his dream he did not sleep for a while; for presently he heard a stir at his side and the girl reseated herself, clad in a fresh tunic, all the blood washed away. He could not remember her having left, but it did not trouble him.

The light had for some time been sinking and blurring, and imperceptibly a cloudy blue twilight closed about them, seeming somehow to rise from the blurring lake, for it partook of that same dreamy blueness clouded with vague colors. Smith thought that he would be content never to rise again from that cool sand, to sit here forever in the blurring twilight and the silence of his dream. How long he did sit there he never knew. The blue peace enfolded him utterly, until he was steeped in its misty evening colors and permeated through and through with the tranced quiet.

The darkness had deepened until he could no longer see any more than the nearest wavelets lapping the sand. Beyond, and all about, the dream-world melted into the violet-misted blueness of the twilight. He was not aware that he had turned his head, but presently he found himself looking down on the girl beside him. She was lying on the pale sand, her hair a fan of darkness to frame the pallor of her face. In the twilight her mouth was dark too, and from the darkness under her lashes he slowly became aware that she was watching him unwinkingly.

For a long while he sat there, gazing down, meeting the half-hooded eyes in silence. And presently, with the effortless detachment of one who moves in a dream, he bent down to meet her lifting arms. The sand was cool and sweet, and her mouth tasted faintly of blood.

II

There was no sunrise in that land. Lucid day brightened slowly over the breathing landscape, and grass and trees stirred with wakening awareness, rather horribly in the beauty of the morning. When Smith woke, he saw the girl coming up from the lake, shaking blue water from her orange hair. Blue droplets clung to the creaminess of her skin, and she was laughing and flushed from head to foot in the glowing dawn.

Smith sat up on his couch and pushed back the blue coverlet. "I'm hungry," he said. "When and what do we eat?"

The laughter vanished from her face in a breath. She gave her hair a troubled shake and said doubtfully,

"Hungry?"

"Yes, starved? Didn't you say you get your food at the Temple? Let's go up there."

She sent him a sidelong, enigmatic glance from under her lashes as she turned aside.

"Very well," she said.

"Anything wrong?" He reached out as she passed and pulled her to his knee, kissing the troubled mouth lightly. And again he tasted blood.

"Oh, no." She ruffled his hair and rose. "I'll be ready in a moment, and then we'll go."

And so again they passed the belt of woods where the trees bent down to watch, and crossed the rippling grassland. From all directions long waves of it came blowing toward them as before, and the fur-like blades clung to their feet. Smith tried not to notice. Everywhere, he was, seeing this morning, an undercurrent of nameless unpleasantness ran beneath the surface of this lovely land.

As they crossed the live grass a memory suddenly returned to him, and he said, "What did you mean, yesterday, when you said that there was a way—out—other than death?"

She did not meet his eyes as she answered, in that troubled voice, "Worse than dying, I said. A way out we do not speak of here."

"But if there's any way at all, I must know of it," he persisted. "Tell me."

She swept the orange hair like a veil between them, bending her head and saying. indistinctly, "A way out you could not take. A way too costly. And—and I do not wish you to go, now . . ."

"I must know," said Smith relentlessly.

She paused then, and stood looking up at him, her sherry-colored eyes disturbed.

"By the way you came," she said at last. "By virtue of the Word. But that gate is impassable."

"Why?"

"It is death to pronounce the Word. Literally. I do not know it now, could not speak it if I would. But in the Temple there is one room where the Word is graven in scarlet on the wall, and its power is so great that the echoes of it ring forever round and round that room. If one stands before the graven symbol and lets the force of it beat upon his brain he will hear, and know—and shriek the awful syllables aloud—and so die. It is a word from some tongue so alien to all our being that the spoken sound of it, echoing in the throat of a living man, is disrupting enough to rip the very fibers of the human body apart—to blast its atoms asunder, to destroy body and mind as utterly as if they had never been. And because the sound is so disruptive it somehow blasts open for an instant the door between your world and mine. But the danger is dreadful, for it may open the door to other worlds too, and let things through more terrible than we can dream of. Some say it was thus that the Thing gained access to our land eons ago. And if you are not standing exactly where the door opens, on the one spot in the room that is protected, as the center of a whirlwind is quiet, and if you do not pass instantly out of the sound of the Word, it will blast you asunder as it does the one who has pronounced it for you. So you see how impos—" Here she broke off with a little scream and glanced down in half-laughing annoyance, then took two or three little running steps and turned.

"The grass," she explained ruefully, pointing to her feet. The brown bareness of them was dotted with scores of tiny blood-spots. "If one stands too long in one place, barefoot, it will pierce the skin and drink—stupid of me to forget. But come."

Smith went on at her side, looking round with new eyes upon the lovely pellucid land, too beautiful and frightening for anything outside a dream. All about them the hungry grass came hurrying in long, converging waves as they advanced. Were the trees, then, flesh-eating too? Cannibal trees and vampire grass—he shuddered a little and looked ahead.

The Temple stood tall before them, a building of some nameless material as mistily blue as far-off mountains on the Earth. The mistiness did not condense or clarify as they approached, and the outlines of the place were mysteriously hard to fix in mind—he could never understand, afterward, just why. When he tried too hard to concentrate on one particular corner or tower or window it blurred before his eyes as if the focus were at fault—as if the whole strange, veiled building stood just on the borderland of another dimension.

From the immense triple arch of the doorway, as they approached—a triple arch like nothing he had ever seen before, so irritatingly hard to focus upon that he could not be sure just wherein its difference lay—a pale blue mist issued smokily. And when they stepped within they walked into that twilight dimness he was coming to know so well.

The great hall lay straight and veiled before them, but after a few steps the girl drew him aside and under another archway, into a long gallery through whose drifting haze he could see rows of men and women kneeling against the wall with bowed heads, as if in prayer. She led him down the line to the end, and he saw then that they knelt before small spigots curving up from the wall at regular intervals. She dropped to her knees before one and, motioning him to follow, bent her head and laid her lips to the up-curved spout. Dubiously he followed her example.

Instantly with the touch of his mouth on the nameless substance of the spigot something hot and, strangely, at once salty and sweet flowed into his mouth. There was an acridity about it that gave a curious tang, and the more he drank the more avid he became. Hauntingly delicious it was, and warmth flowed through him more strongly with every draft. Yet somewhere deep within him memory stirred unpleasantly . . . somewhere, somehow, he had known this hot, acrid, salty taste before, and—suddenly suspicions struck him like a bludgeon, and he perked his lips from the spout as if burnt. A tiny thread of scarlet trickled from the wall. He passed the back of one hand across his lips and brought it away red. He knew that odor, then.

The girl knelt beside him with closed eyes, rapt avidity in every line of her. When he seized her shoulder she twitched away and opened protesting eyes, but did not lift her lips from the spigot. Smith gestured violently, and with one last long draft she rose and turned a half-angry face to his, but he laid a finger on her reddened lips.

He followed her in silence past the kneeling lines again. When they reached the hall outside he swung upon her and gripped her shoulders angrily.

"What was that?" he demanded.

Her eyes slid away. She shrugged.

"What were you expecting? We feed as we must, here. You'll learn to drink without a qualm—if it does not come for you too soon."

A moment longer he stared angrily down into her evasive, strangely lovely face. Then he turned without a word and strode down the hallway through the drifting mists toward the door. He heard her bare feet pattering along behind hurriedly, but he did not look back. Not until he had come out into the glowing day and half crossed the grasslands did he relent enough to glance around. She paced at his heels with bowed head, the orange hair swinging about her face and unhappiness eloquent in every motion. The submission of her touched him suddenly, and he paused for her to catch up, smiling. down half reluctantly on the bent orange head.

She lifted a tragic face to his, and there were tears in the sherry eyes. So he had no choice but to laugh and lift her up against his leather-clad breast and kiss the drooping mouth into smiles again. But he understood, now, the faintly acrid bitterness of her kisses.

"Still," he said, when they had reached the little white shrine among the trees, "there must be some other food than—that. Does no grain grow? Isn't there any wild life in the woods? Haven't the trees fruit?"

She gave him another sidelong look from under dropped lashes, warily.

"No," she said. "Nothing but the grass grows here. No living thing dwells in this land but man—-and it. And as for the fruit of the trees—give thanks that they bloom but once in a lifetime."

"Why?"

"Better not to speak of it," she said.

The phrase, the constant evasion, was beginning to wear on Smith's nerves. He said nothing of it then, but he turned from her and went down to the beach, dropping to the sand and striving to recapture last night's languor and peace. His hunger was curiously satisfied, even from the few swallows he had taken, and gradually the drowsy content of the day before began to flow over him in deepening waves. After all, it was a lovely land . . .

That day drew dreamily to a close, and darkness rose in a mist from the misty lake, and he came to find in kisses that tasted of blood a certain tang that but pointed their sweetness. And in the morning he woke to the slowly brightening day, swam with the girl in the blue, tingling waters of the lake—-and reluctantly went up through the woods and across the ravenous grass to the Temple, driven by a hunger greater than his repugnance. He went up with a slight nausea rising within him, and yet strangely eager. . . .

Once more the Temple rose veiled and indefinite under the glowing sky, and once more he plunged into the eternal twilight of its corridors, turned aside as one who knows the way, knelt of his own accord in the line of drinkers along the wall. . . .

With the first draft that nausea rose within him almost overwhelmingly, but when the warmth of the drink had spread through him the nausea died and nothing was left but hunger and eagerness, and he drank blindly until the girl's hand on his shoulder roused him.

A sort of intoxication had wakened within him with the burning of that hot,

salt drink in his veins, and he went back across the hurrying grass in a half-daze.
Through most of the pellucid day it lasted, and the slow dark was rising from the
lake before clearness returned to him.

III

And so life resolved itself into a very simple thing. The days glowed by and the
blurred darknesses came and went. Life held little any more but the bright clarity of
the day and the dimness of the dark, morning journeys to drink at the Temple
fountain and the bitter kisses of the girl with the orange hair. Time had ceased for
him. Slow day followed slow day, and the same round of living circled over and over,
and the only change—perhaps he did not see it then—was the deepening look in the
girl's eyes when they rested upon him, her growing silences.

One evening just as the first faint dimness was clouding the air, and the lake
smoked hazily, he happened to glance off across its surface and thought he saw
through the rising mists the outline of very far mountains, and he asked curiously,

"What lies beyond the lake? Aren't those mountains over there?"

The girl turned her head quickly and her sherry-brown eyes darkened with
something like dread.

"I don't know," she said. "We believe it best not to wonder what lies—beyond."

And suddenly Smith's irritation with the old evasions woke and he said violently,

"Damn your beliefs! I'm sick of that answer to every question I ask! Don't you
ever wonder about anything? Are you all so thoroughly cowed by this dread of
something unseen that every spark of your spirit is dead?" She turned the sorrowful, sherry gaze upon him.

"We learn by experience," she said. "Those who wonder—those who investigate—die. We live in a land alive with danger, incomprehensible, intangible, terrible.
Life is bearable only if we do not look too closely—only if we accept conditions and
make the most of them. You must not ask questions if you would live.

"As for the mountains beyond, and all the unknown country that lies over the
horizons—they are as unreachable as a mirage. For in a land where no food grows,
where we must visit the Temple daily or starve, how could an explorer provision
himself for a journey? No, we are bound here by unbreakable bonds, and we must
live here until we die."

Smith shrugged. The languor of the evening was coming upon him, and the
brief flare of irritation had died as swiftly as it rose.

Yet from that outburst dated the beginning of his discontent. Somehow, despite the lovely languor of the place, despite the sweet bitterness of the Temple
fountains and the sweeter bitterness of the kisses that were his for the asking, he
could not drive from his mind the vision of those far mountains veiled in rising

haze. Unrest had wakened within him, and like some sleeper arising from a lotus-dream his mind turned more and more frequently to the desire for action, adventure, some other use for his danger-hardened body than the exigencies of sleep and food and love.

On all sides stretched the moving, restless woods, farther than the eye could reach. The grasslands rippled, and over the dim horizon the far mountains beckoned him. Even the mystery of the Temple and its endless twilight began to torment his waking moments. He dallied with the idea of exploring those hallways which the dwellers in this lotus-land avoided, of gazing from the strange windows that opened upon inexplicable blue. Surely life, even here, must hold some more fervent meaning than that he followed now. What lay beyond the wood and grasslands? What mysterious country did those mountains wall?

He began to harry his companion with questions that woke more and more often the look of dread behind her eyes, but he gained little satisfaction. She belonged to a people without history, without ambition, their lives bent wholly toward wringing from each moment its full sweetness in anticipation of the terror to come. Evasion was the keynote of their existence, perhaps with reason. Perhaps all the adventurous spirits among them had followed their curiosity into danger and death, and the only ones left were the submissive souls who led their bucolically voluptuous lives in this Elysium so shadowed with horror.

In this colored lotus-land, memories of the world he had left grew upon him more and more vividly: he remembered the hurrying crowds of the planets' capitals, the lights, the noise, the laughter. He saw space-ships cleaving the night sky with flame, flashing from world to world through the star-flecked darkness. He remembered sudden brawls in saloons and space-sailor dives when the air was alive with shouts and tumult, and heat-guns slashed their blue-hot flame and the smell of burnt flesh hung heavy. Life marched in pageant past his remembering eyes, violent, vivid, shoulder to shoulder with death. And nostalgia wrenched at him for the lovely, terribly, brawling worlds he had left behind.

Daily the unrest grew upon him. The girl made pathetic little attempts to find some sort of entertainment that would occupy his ranging mind. She led him on timid excursions into the living woods, even conquered her horror of the Temple enough to follow him on timorous tiptoe as he explored a little way down the corridors which did not arouse in her too anguished a terror. But she must have known from the first that it was hopeless.

One day as they lay on the sand watching the lake ripple bluely under a crystal sky, Smith's eyes, dwelling on the faint shadow of the mountains, half unseeingly, suddenly narrowed into a hardness as bright and pale as steel. Muscle ridged his abruptly set jaw and he sat upright with a jerk, pushing away the girl who had been leaning on his shoulder.

"I'm through," he said harshly, and rose.

"What—what is it?" The girl stumbled to her feet.

"I'm going away—anywhere. To those mountains, I think. I'm leaving now!"

"But—you wish to die, then?"

"Better the real thing than a living death like this," he said. "At least I'll have a little more excitement first."

"But, what of your food? There's nothing to keep you alive, even if you escape the greater dangers. Why, you'll dare not even lie down on the grass at night—it would eat you alive! You have no chance at all to live if you leave this grove—and me."

"If I must die, I shall," he said. "I've been thinking it over, and I've made up my mind. I could explore the Temple and so come on *it* and die. But do *something* I must, and it seems to me my best chance is in trying to reach some country where food grows before I starve. It's worth trying. I can't go on like this."

She looked at him miserably, tears brimming her sherry eyes. He opened his mouth to speak, but before he could say a word her eyes strayed beyond his shoulder and suddenly she smiled, a dreadful frozen little smile.

"You will not go," she said. "Death has come for us now."

She said it so calmly, so unafraid that he did not understand until she pointed beyond him. He turned.

The air between them and the shrine was curiously agitated. As he watched, it began to resolve itself into a nebulous blue mist that thickened and darkened . . . blurry tinges of violet and green began to blow through it vaguely, and then by imperceptible degrees a flush of rose appeared in the mist—deepened, thickened, contracted into burning scarlet that seared his eyes, pulsed alively—and he knew that it had come.

An aura of menace seemed to radiate from it, strengthening as the mist strengthened, reaching out in hunger toward his mind. He felt it as tangibly as he saw it—cloudy danger reaching out avidly for them both.

The girl was not afraid. Somehow he knew this, though he dared not turn, dared not wrench his eyes from that hypnotically pulsing scarlet . . . She whispered very softly from behind him,

"So I die with you, I am content." And the sound of her voice freed him from the snare of the crimson pulse.

He barked a wolfish laugh, abruptly—welcoming even this diversion from the eternal idyll he had been living—and the gun leaping to his hand spurted a long blue flame so instantly that the girl behind him caught her breath. The steel-blue dazzle illumined the gathering mist lividly, passed through it without obstruction and charred the ground beyond. Smith set his teeth and swung a figure-eight pattern of flame through and through the mist, lacing it with blue heat. And when that finger of fire crossed the scarlet pulse the impact jarred the whole nebulous cloud violently, so that its outlines wavered and shrank, and the pulse of crimson sizzled under the heat—shriveled—began to fade in desperate haste.

Smith swept the ray back and forth along the redness, tracing its pattern with destruction, but it faded too swiftly for him. In little more than an instant it had paled and disembodied and vanished save for a fading flush of rose, and the blue-hot blade of his flame sizzled harmlessly through the disappearing mist to sear the ground beyond. He switched off the heat, then, and stood breathing a little un-evenly as the death-cloud thinned and paled and vanished before his eyes, until no trace of it was left and the air glowed lucid and transparent once more.

The unmistakable odor of burning flesh caught at his nostrils, and he won-dered for a moment if the Thing had indeed materialized a nucleus of matter, and then he saw that the smell came from the seared grass his flame had struck. The tiny, furry blades were all writhing away from the burnt spot, straining at their roots as if a wind blew them back, and from the blackened area a thick smoke rose, reeking with the odor of burnt meat. Smith, remembering their vampire habits, turned away, half nauseated.

The girl had sunk to the sand behind him, trembling now that the danger was gone.

"Is—it dead?" she breathed, when she could master her quivering mouth.

"I don't know. No way of telling. Probably not."

"What will-will you do now?"

He slid the heat-gun back into its holster and settled the belt purposefully.

"What I started out to do."

The girl scrambled up in desperate haste.

"Wait!" she gasped, "wait!" and clutched at his arm to steady herself. And he waited until the trembling had passed. Then she went on, "Come up to the Temple once more before you go."

"All right. Not a bad idea. It may be a long time before my next—meal."

And so again they crossed the fur-soft grass that bore down upon them in long ripples from every part of the meadow.

The Temple rose dim and unreal before them, and as they entered blue twilight folded them dreamily about. Smith turned by habit toward the gallery of drinkers, but the girl laid upon his arm a hand that shook a little, and murmured,

"Come this way."

He followed in growing surprise down the hallway through the drifting mists and away from the gallery he knew so well. It seemed to him that the mist thickened as they advanced, and in the uncertain light he could never be sure that the walls did not waver as nebulously as the blurring air. He felt a curious impulse to step through their intangible barriers and out of the hall into—what?

Presently steps rose under his feet, almost imperceptibly, and after a while the pressure on his arm drew him aside. They went in under a low, heavy arch of stone and entered the strangest room he had ever seen. It appeared to be seven-sided, as nearly as he could judge through the drifting mist, and curious, converging lines were graven deep in the floor.

It seemed to him that forces outside his comprehension were beating violently against the seven walls, circling like hurricanes through the dimness until the whole room was a maelstrom of invisible tumult.

When he lifted his eyes to the wall, he knew where he was. Blazoned on the dim stone, burning through the twilight like some other-dimensional fire, the scarlet pattern writhed across the wall.

The sight of it, somehow, set up a commotion in his brain, and it was with whirling head and stumbling feet that he answered to the pressure on his arm. Dimly he realized that he stood at the very center of those strange, converging lines, feeling forces beyond reason coursing through him along paths outside any knowledge he possessed.

Then for one moment arms clasped his neck and a warm, fragrant body pressed against him, and a voice sobbed in his ear.

"If you must leave me, then go back through the Door, beloved—life without you—more dreadful even than a death like this . . ." A kiss that stung of blood clung to his lips for an instant; then the clasp loosened and he stood alone.

Through the twilight he saw her dimly outlined against the Word. And he thought as she stood there that it was as if the invisible currents beat bodily against her, so that she swayed and wavered before him, her outlines blurring and forming again as the forces from which he was so mystically protected buffeted her mercilessly.

And he saw knowledge dawning terribly upon her face, as the meaning of the Word seeped slowly into her mind. The sweet brown face twisted hideously, the blood-red lips writhed apart to shriek a Word—in a moment of clarity he actually saw her tongue twisting incredibly to form the syllables of the unspeakable thing never meant for human lips to frame. Her mouth opened into an impossible shape . . . she gasped in the blurry mist and shrieked aloud . . .

IV

Smith was walking along a twisting path so scarlet that he could not bear to look down, a path that wound and unwound and shook itself under his feet so that he stumbled at every step. He was groping through a blinding mist clouded with violet and green, and in his ears a dreadful whisper rang—the first syllable of an unutterable Word. . . . Whenever he neared the end of the path, it shook itself under him and doubled back, and weariness like a drug was sinking into his brain, and the sleepy twilight colors of the mist lulled him, and—

"He's waking up!" said an exultant voice in his ear.

Through the twilight he saw her dimly outlined against the Word. And he thought as she stood there that it was as if the invisible currents beat bodily against her, so that she swayed and wavered before him, her outlines blurring and forming again as the forces from which he was so mystically protected buffeted her mercilessly.

Smith lifted heavy eyelids upon a room without walls—a room wherein multiple figures extending into infinity moved to and fro in countless hosts. . . .

"Smith! N. W.! Wake up!" urged that familiar voice from somewhere near.

He blinked. The myriad diminishing figures resolved themselves into the reflections of two men in a steel-walled room, bending over him. The friendly, anxious face of his partner, Yarol the Venusian, leaned above the bed.

"By Pharol, N. W.," said the well-remembered, ribald voice, "you've been asleep for a week! We thought you'd never come out of it—must have been an awful brand of whiskey!"

Smith managed a feeble grin—amazing how weak he felt—and turned an inquiring gaze upon the other figure.

"I'm a doctor," said that individual meeting the questing stare. "Your friend called me in three days ago and I've been working on you ever since. It must have been all of five or six days since you fell into this coma—have you any idea what caused it?"

Smith's pale eyes roved the room. He did not find what he sought, and though his weak murmur answered the doctor's question, the man was never to know it.

"Shawl?"

"I threw the damned thing away," confessed Yarol. "Stood it for three days and then gave up. That red pattern gave me the worst headache I've had since we found that case of black wine on the asteroid. Remember?"

"Where—?"

"Gave it to a space-rat checking out for Venus. Sorry. Did you really want it? I'll buy you another."

Smith did not answer. The weakness was rushing up about him in gray waves. He closed his eyes, hearing the echoes of that first dreadful syllable whispering through his head . . . whisper from a dream . . . Yarol heard him murmur softly,

"And—I never even knew—her name . . ."

Lover in SCARLET

by Harold Lawlor

*Harking back to the heyday of the "Shudder Pulps," here is a story of
thud and blunder . . . proving that there are worse things than being alone!*
Weird Tales, January 1949

Afterward the members of the coroner's jury never blamed the shutter, for they couldn't blame something of which they'd never heard. Such a prosaic object, a shutter, to give rise to the dread of that Other. But then the jury never knew, either, of the thing in the scarlet cloak.

Yet that was how it began, with the shutter that thudded in the night's rising wind against the narrow brownstone front of the decrepit old four-story house.

Thump, thump, thump, thump . . .

The old man lying in the black walnut bed listened and roused and pushed himself up on one scrawny elbow to clutch his nephew with his free hand, a hand more like a liver-spotted claw now than ever.

"Sh! Did you hear?" whispered Uncle Ralph. "Footsteps!"

Fred Kolbey listened to the monotonous thudding of the shutter. He was about to reassure the old man of the true origin of the sound when he bethought himself of his recent interview with the doctor.

"I have good news for you, my boy!" the doctor had said, once safely out of earshot of the sick man. "Your uncle's heart is responding splendidly to treatment. There's no reason why he should not go on living for years, barring accidents. Just keep him in a reasonably cheerful frame of mind, and be careful to guard him from sudden shocks."

"Good news," Fred had thought sardonically, though he'd diplomatically dissembled his chagrin as best he could. Uncle Ralph would go on living, sitting on his money like a hen on an egg, too stingy to enjoy it or even let anyone else enjoy it.

Fred had felt the gall churn within him. Three weeks he'd wasted in this hellhole already. Years now, probably, before he could ever expect to get his hands on any of the money. Of all the dirty rotten deals!

The thudding shutter, his uncle's words, cut across his frustrated brooding now, and as quickly as that the idea was born. It just came to him from nowhere. It had happened before. Hunches. He got 'em, he played 'em, he always won. Didn't they call him Lucky Kolbey out at the track, in the back room at Shenley's?"

"Footsteps, Uncle Ralph?" Fred said now, aloud. He appeared to listen. "Yes, someone is coming up the stairs." He let his eyes widen then, let them turn to meet the still wider eyes of the old man on the bed. "But there is no one in the house except us!"

Uncle Ralph whimpered. "It's someone coming after my money. Or—or it's someone coming after *me*!"

"Nonsense!" Fred cried, with what he hoped would sound like false heartiness. "I know what you're thinking, Uncle Ralph! You're thinking it's *Death* coming for you!"

The aged man gasped, and fell back against the pillows, his open mouth like a purse from which the drawstring had been removed.

Fred patted the brown claw nearest him, watched with satisfaction the labored heaving of the thin chest under the sheet. "There, there, I'll go see who it is." He paused to add reflectively, " *What* it is."

Uncle Ralph groaned, the color of his skin like a faint wash of gray over ocher.

Fred had a thin smile for the darkened hall outside his uncle's bedroom. Keep him in a cheerful frame of mind, eh? Why hadn't he thought of this before? What could be easier than playing on the sick imagination of a man already at death's threshold? Once the ball was rolling it shouldn't take so very long.

Fred listened, and nodded approvingly. Already luck was with him, he noted, for the wind died just then and the thudding of the shutter muted until it died away at last into silence. He waited a moment before reentering the bedroom.

Again his uncle had propped himself on one elbow, the better to watch with rheumy, apprehensive eyes for what might come through the door. When he saw it was only Fred, he groaned gratefully, and asked in a racked whisper, "What—what was it?"

Fred let his forehead furrow. "I thought I saw— But, pshaw! Of course I didn't."

"What, what?" The swollen tongue came out, tried futilely to moisten dry lips.

"I must have imagined it. Calm yourself, Uncle Ralph! Don't you think I'd tell you, if I were sure I—"

"No!" The rheumy eyes narrowed cunningly. "You wouldn't tell me. You'd let me lie here, unknowing, and let it get me!"

"Uncle Ralph!" Fred sounded unbearably hurt. "Very well, then, I thought I saw something flee down the stairs when it heard me. Something in a scarlet cloak. I caught the white flash of—of bones, and there was a scarlet cowl that only partially hid a—a *skull*!"

The old man made a mewling piteous sound, and plucked feebly at the bed-clothes.

Fred laughed unconvincingly. "But of course, I must have been mistaken! You lie here quietly now, while I go down to my room and finish up some work I must do."

"Don't leave me here all alone!"

"There's nothing to hurt you, and I'll be right below this room. You have your bell there on the table, and I'll hear you if you ring, or if you call me," Fred said, and hurried out, purposely deaf to the frantic entreaties that followed him.

He must get away before the shutter started banging again. Better to leave the old man to his frightened thoughts, leave him to meet alone the renewed sound of the "footsteps".

Fred started down the stairs, praying to such gods as he acknowledged for the rising of the wind. Such was the power of the imagination, he thought in some amusement, that he even felt a little uneasy himself. True, he didn't hear footsteps that weren't there! Nuts to that! But damned if it didn't seem as if *eyes* were following his progress down the stairs. He felt this so sharply that he grew conscious of a chilly sensation in the small of his back.

Once in the quiet of his own room he forgot readily enough that queerly disturbing moment on the stairs. He listened instead, achingly, for the coming of the wind. And when it came, he mused, what should he do when next he was called to that room above? What should he say? Surely his own imagination was capable of depicting a yet more vivid horror, more graphic still, for the delectation of Uncle Ralph?

He listened. The wind was rising! The window rattled, and tree branches scratched the outer walls. And then it came.

Thump, thump, thump, thump . . .

Immediately Uncle Ralph's bell began to jangle fiercely. Fred grinned, and lolled at his ease, hands clasped behind his head. Let the old boy stew in his own juice yet awhile.

"Fred! Fred! Fred!"

Fred cocked his head. He could hear a muttering now, coming faintly down the stairs. An unintelligible jargon. Good! Uncle Ralph was gibbering to himself. It was several moments before a faint wail came again for Fred.

He rose at last and started leisurely up the stairs, but near the top he broke into a run. "Uncle Ralph, what is it? I was in the bathroom, and—"

He stopped on the threshold of the bedroom. His uncle had managed some-how to get out of the bed alone, to walk or crawl or drag himself halfway to the door before collapsing where he lay on the floor. Fred hastened to him, lifted the stertorously breathing body, slapped the putty-colored face until the faded blue eyes opened to stare blindly, already lost in a semi-coma.

"Go, Fred!" His uncle panted. The voice came so faintly Fred had to bend an ear nearly to the gray lips. "Money in box—under bed. But don't wait, go! *It* was here! The thing—in scarlet! It loves you! It told me so! It wants me to die so it—can be alone—with you!"

The thin body shuddered as if from a racing motor within. Then it was still. Fred stared down, unbelieving. It couldn't have happened so quickly! He couldn't have succeeded so well! Uncle Ralph couldn't be dead! And then he smiled, remembering, before easing the body to the floor.

Lucky Kolbey!

He went to the bed then, stooped, lifted its damask draperies to pull the carved walnut chest from beneath it. He turned the key already in the lock, and eagerly threw back the lip. Currency! Bundles of it, bales of it! More than he'd ever dreamed!

He was still bending over the opened chest, gloating, when he felt again that uncomfortable sensation in the small of his back. He turned inquiringly, more in annoyance than fright. Shocked unbelief held him still momentarily. It *wasn't* there? It *couldn't* be there? He was leaping to his feet then, his eyes swiveling frantically.

But there was nowhere to flee, no way he could escape the thing in the doorway. The thing in the hooded cloak with its death's-head under the cowl of scarlet, its jaws clicking ingratiatingly, its eyeless sockets giving off an unholy light of what passed with it for love. Advancing toward Fred, it extended the chalk-white bones that were its arms.

It was happy, Fred's dazed mind recognized sickly. It had received its wish. It was *alone* with him at last!

"Sweetheart!" it grated in a hideous travesty of a voice.

He had time only to make a dreadful sound low in his throat before he felt the bony arms enfold him, before merciful oblivion came to him, borne on the swift wings of horror . . .

*The thing in the hooded cloak with its death's-head under the cowl of scarlet,
its jaws clicking ingratiatingly, its eyeless sockets giving off
an unholy light of what passed with it for love.*

The WHITE Lady

by Dorothy Quick

I almost met the mysterious Ms. Quick in 1939. I rang her
doorbell in Manhattan and she spoke to me through a tube
but I never laid eyes on her, only ears.—FJA
Weird Tales, January 1949

"**M**ary Vetrell," he said, his dark, malevolent eyes flashing. "I want your answer." The girl looked into his crafty face. It had power, and one glance was enough to know he would stop at nothing to gain his ends. His figure was dark and sinister against the linen fold paneling. He was taller than Mary—a good six feet, which seemed even more due to the long black robes he wore. He was all dark—hair, eyes, under thick black brows which met over his nose. His skin was sallow, and craft had etched deep lines beside his narrow, cruel mouth. He was handsome in an evil way, and, without the churchly robes and tonsure, might have been a fine figure of a man. The only touch of color about him flashed from the jewels in the huge cross he wore suspended from a gold chain about his neck and the ring on his finger, which was a ruby heavily mounted in gold.

Mary Vetrell was afraid of him. Fear flowed through her like angry waters, but she held her head high and let no trace of it show.

If the man was dark Mary was light itself. She was tall and slim with all the grace of a young willow tree. Her eyes, brown with little golden flecks in them, under straight brows with heavy lashes, looked calmly at the man who threatened her. She had a mobile face, exceedingly lovely, her hair was a deep bronze—what little could be seen under her coif, which was of the type Holbein painted. She wore a rose-colored gown over an underdress of heavy green satin. The stiff skirts billowed away from her slender waist which was encircled by a gold girdle. The low cut square neck of her dress was outlined in gold thread and the glint of emeralds shone from the embroidery, of which were also touches on the sleeves.

Her hand picked at the rose-colored velvet nervously as she answered in a calm and steady voice that betrayed none of the havoc her emotions were in.

"My Lord Abbot, my answer is plain and short, though I have been long in

483

giving it, who weighed its cost." She drew herself up to her full height so her eyes were almost on a level with those in the saturnine face opposite hers, and shot the word at him as though it were an arrow from a bow. "No!"

"So—my nephew is not good enough for a Vetrell," snarled the Abbot. "Listen, girl, in Spain where we Telvas come from, the Telva name is a key that opens all doors at Court, and Clement has not only Telva blood from my sister, but D'Aigula blood from his father. In Spain those two names mean much—not only in Spain, but here—as you will find, lady, unless you send a better answer to my nephew Clement's suit."

"My Lord Abbott, I never questioned Clement's high lineage, but I can send no other answer to a man I do not love."

The man threw back his head and laughed.

"Love? Is that all? Love will come after mating—trust my nephew for that."

"I am no Spanish girl who sits cloistered until she is given to a man of her father's choice. I am Mary Vetrell, daughter of Sir Charles Vetrell of Tall Trees, and we Vetrell women have the right to choose our own husbands. It is so written in the Vetrell deed for Tall Trees and those acres you would join to the Abbey—that deed which William the Conqueror gave to the Charles de Vetrell who helped him win this island, and to his Anne, who saved the King's life and asked this boon as her reward. She loved her father's clerk, and when the King put in the deed that Vetrell women could be wedded as they would, she married her love and was truly happy. As I shall be, Lord Abbot, when I take me a husband of my own choosing." She emphasized "my" so that Telva could not doubt her intention.

"And have you made your choice, daughter?" once more the Abbot's tones were smooth.

Mary hesitated. What should she do? She *had* made her choice—of that there had been no doubt in her mind since her childhood playmate, John de Winton, had come back from the foreign wars as Sir John de Winton—an honor gained from his bravery in the field. She had loved him as a child, as a long, lanky boy before he sailed for France, and now she loved him as a man. But although she loved him, and he rode from Winton Castle each day to Tall Trees and spent much of his time beside her, he had said no word of love.

The Abbot stirred and Mary, throwing caution to the winds, told the truth— and a lie.

"I have, my father—of a truth I have made my choice, and ere the winter comes John de Winton and I will beg your services to make us one—"

"Though you come on your knees I will refuse."

"There are other priests in England."

"Ay—and other Kings than William the Conqueror. What one monarch gives another can take away. King Henry has been ever gracious to me, and Queen

Katherine is a true daughter of the Church. You would do well to let me choose your husband." His words were soft but there was sharp steel under the velvet.

"I am sorry, but my heart has already chosen. Nor do I think the King would greatly care whether I wed Clement D'Aigula or John de Winton."

She had struck back, but the Abbot merely smiled.

"Queen Katherine would. She likes to see her countrymen advanced. I swear to you I will get the King's ear, and chop your Tall Trees down if need be unless you'll be my nephew's bride."

"Lord Abbot, let us cease fencing. You are no cupid, nor, do I think, does Clement love me so greatly. He has position, as you say, so that marrying a Vetrell is a step down for him, not up. Surely he cannot need wealth, or if he did, he'd look to other maidens. Then why are you so strait with me, whom up 'till now you have been fond of?"

"I like your honest fearlessness. I always have since the day I took the fish hook from your hand. You were a child then, yet you did not whimper, though I hurt you sore. I have given you of my poor fund of knowledge—writing and Latin—at your father's wish, and, as you say, I have been fond of you—fonder than you guess." His voice faltered, then went on. "In fact my dream has ever been to dance your children at my knee. I sent for Clement to come here from Spain because I thought you'd make a good wife for him—far better than any of those women at Philip's court who tried to capture him. And, as I had foreseen, he loved you greatly—though you do not think it. He is of my own blood and, 'fore my God, I'd rather have you dead than wed to any other—"

"You still don't tell me why," Mary swayed a little as she stood.

"I'd rather have you dead than wed to any other," he had said, but he had not gone on speaking the thoughts that coursed through his brain. "I love you. I cannot wed you, who am wedded to the Church, nor would I take you otherwise, but if you are married to my own nephew you become almost my own. Your children will have Telva blood in them and be part mine on that account, so I can be content, for you'll be in my life for always. But if you wed another I should lose you. I could not suffer that."

To Mary he was a man who, up 'till now, she had thought of as her spiritual father, and for whom she had cherished a certain affection.

Today he had come to her from Sir Charles in a temper, though she now knew it must have been because her father refused to bend her will, she still resented it, and his obvious desire to wed her to Clement, who was a younger version of his uncle, and attracted to her not at all.

At last the Abbot replied to her.

"Mary Vetrell, I have told you why. My nephew is dear to me as my own self. He loves you, so he must have you—and have you he will, for I'll see to it. As Tall Trees' acres join the Abbey lands, so shall you two be united."

"Perhaps there sits the reason. I have heard the Abbey lands are no longer fertile, which have been over-tilled, so Tall Trees' fields are coveted. Well, buy them of my father, if you will—but not through me." Mary's eyes flashed; she had forgotten the lie she had told.

"I care not for the land, though it is true the Abbey needs fields to grow grain, but my nephew has promised if he wed you that he will bide in England. That means much to me." The Abbot's fingers played with his cross. "Mary, I beg you— think again."

"I have thought. My answer is the same."

"Then," now the black eyes truly flashed, "I say the King shall hear and, too, I say that you and John de Winton may not wed, for I'll not say the rites, nor any other priest that you may find. In matters of the church I stand supreme, and 'till the King decides the right of this you must rest as you are, and I shall pray, daughter, that God will soften your heart toward that poor boy Clement who spends his days in longing for you. I go now, but I shall come again. Take counsel, Mary Vetrell, with yourself and with your father. Nay," as she bowed her head, "today I have no blessing for one who disobeys her Holy Father's commands."

He turned on his heel and went out the door without a backward glance. Presently Mary heard a clatter in the courtyard and knew that the Abbot was mounting the snow white mule he always rode. Then came the noise of hoofs and the Abbot Telva, escorted by his men-at-arms, left Tall Trees.

Mary sank into a chair and covered her face with her hands. Through her slim fingers tears fell spattering unheeded on the green satin. It was no light thing in those days to defy the Church, and Mary knew it.

A firm step sounded near her and a strong, mellow voice cried in her ear. "Zounds, Mistress Mary, are we to play peek-a-boo?" Firm fingers tugged at hers playfully, but when her face was revealed the voice changed and became full of sympathy. "How, now, Mistress, has that Spanish knave upset you? If so, I'll wish I'd ridden him off that fancy mule of his."

Mary looked up into a typical English face.

"John," she whispered. "John," while the tears raced down her cheeks.

John de Winton had a clean-cut open countenance with steady blue eyes. He was gentle and kind, but there was a stubbornness about his well-shaped mouth that showed he would be hard to rouse, but ill to cross once he had been. His hair, yellow as corn, was cut square across his forehead and hung to his shoulders Dutch fashion. He had a great chest and arms, with a figure to match, and was the type of man that women love.

Now seeing Mary's tears, his brows tightened. Then suddenly he caught her in his arms, pulled her up, and began kissing away the tears.

"I cannot bear to see you weep, my love," he murmured between kisses.

It was well he held her firmly or Mary would have fallen with shock. For a few minutes she leaned against him, her heart beating rapidly, and then she raised her head. As it chanced—or perhaps it wasn't chance—when she moved it was just enough so that John's lips, instead of touching her cheek, found her mouth.

It was as if two souls met, mingled, and became one in that brief moment. When they finally drew apart he did not say, "I love you"—nor did she. It was not necessary. Enough had already been said for all eternity.

Mary's tears were gone and John's face was utterly content.

"If I had not wept," Mary laughed, "perhaps you would have gone on being silent forever."

"And so I might, who feared you did not love me."

"Oh, John, I have loved you all my life, I think, and often wondered why you did not speak, for I was sure you cared. Now I am grateful that the Abbot made me cry."

"When I saw you unhappy it was as though a force took me without my own volition, giving me the courage that I lacked. Quite suddenly I found you in my arms where you must ever rest. Mary, when will we be wed?"

"Never, if the Abbot has his way. Listen, my love." Mary drew John to the window seat and there, sitting close beside him, her hand in his, she told all the story of her interview with Abbot Telva.

John did not interrupt her. When she finished his face was grave.

"Here is a sum whose solution is difficult to find. Our case is hard. The Abbot will not wed us, nor suffer his priests to do to. To come by one who would do it without his sanction, as we are in his See, is nigh impossible. Yet, wed we will, and soon. It must be soon. I like not that Abbot, nor his dark-eyed nephew. In truth that same Clement has haunted my dreams of late, for I feared you liked him more than you liked me."

"Foolish!" Mary rewarded him for his folly with the first kiss of her own bestowing.

A hearty laugh parted them. The perfect counterpart for Santa Claus stood in the doorway. Big, bluff and burly, Sir Charles Vetrell had the same cast of features as his daughter. Different though they were, the relationship between them was unmistakable. His snow white hair aureoled his benign continence and he smiled with his entire face.

"So, daughter, I made no mistake when I told the Abbot you would choose your own mate—and you have chosen well. I, myself, could not have done better. John always has seemed like my own son, and I had no stomach for that Spanish whelp, though I'd have been civil if you had taken him." His laughter sounded like the distant rumble of thunder. "But 'tis well you spared my disposition the strain, my child. Come hither, both of you, and have my blessing."

Hand in hand they knelt before him as he gave it, and when they looked up there were tears in his eyes. He wiped them away with the back of his hand.

"I hope you will not take her too soon, my son, for Tall Trees will be empty and barren without her."

"It looks like we may not be able to wed for a long time, Sir Charles," de Winton spoke gravely.

Once more Mary told her tale.

Sir Charles grew serious. Hoisting his bulk into a chair he said, "This is a sorry matter. There has always been fighting between the Abbey and Tall Trees over the farthest fields. We Vetrells have the right of it, but I'd give up the land for Mary's happiness. But there is more than a matter of land here. The Spaniards know that Katherine is no longer loved by the King. They have heard, as I have heard, the Cardinal Woolsey, who governs the King and England, would pull her down and put a French wife in her place—keeping, of course, the golden dower that came with Katherine, for the sake of which Henry took her when his brother died. Now the Spaniards everywhere in England cement their stance by marrying into the families that count for something here, so when the struggle comes there will be strength behind the Queen. This Abbot Telva came with Katherine and has had much advancement. His Abbey of Chettleworth is one of the most important in the kingdom. He is quite right when he says you'll be hard put to it to wed without his help."

"It is not fair," Mary moaned, but John put his arm about her, and she gave up lamenting to ask, "What can we do?"

"The King is over all, and the Cardinal rules the King," Sir Charles said meditatively. "I know Woolsey. Once I did him a favor before he reached the heights of greatness. I do not think he has forgotten. I will write him a letter and John can ride to Hampton Court with it. I think he'll see justice done and be not overly anxious to favor the Spaniard."

John hit his hand against his knee and exclaimed, "Well planned, Sir Charles. I'll go to Hampton Court this very day, and if Woolsey helps not, I know one of Queen Katherine's maids, Mistress Anne Boleyn, whom I met in France. She might whisper a good word for us into the Queen's ear."

Mary drew back and looked at him very strangely. She was jealous and wondering if this same Anne Boleyn was perhaps the reason why John had delayed speaking of his love.

"It seems you are hasty to leave your new-betrothed, and over-quick to think of another lady," she said coldly, withdrawing her hand.

John caught it back again.

"I only go so I can make you wholly mine, Mary, and I do swear to you that until this instant I had forgotten Mistress Anne, though, in truth, she was very fair." His eyes twinkled.

Mary was about to speak tartly when her father interrupted.

"Peace; this is no time for petty bickerings. Mary knows right well you love her, John, and I hold that your idea of speaking to Mistress Boleyn is good, although if you do, you must ask her to whisper in the King's ear—not the Queen's! For it seems of late the King has found Anne Boleyn 'very fair.' John, you will walk a dangerous path at Court; see that you tread it carefully. Now I will go and write my letter to the Cardinal." Sir Charles heaved himself out of the chair sectionally.

"I ride this very day," John said, and then as Sir Charles neared the door, "would not you and Mary stay at Castle Winton 'til I return? The castle is well fortified in case the Abbot stirs up trouble. My mother would joy to welcome you."

Sir Charles pondered awhile, then nodded.

"A good idea, my boy. We'll keep Lady de Winton company until you return. I'll bid your woman pack your gear, Mary, so you can bide here 'til we leave. For in the fashion of lovers you and John have much to say."

Then he bustled through the door, and they heard him giving orders for awhile until his voice died away.

"Oh, John, I do not like to see you go to Court. Suppose the Cardinal is not friendly?"

"Fear nothing, Mary. We have two arrows to our bow. By one or the other I'll win you."

He held her close and Mary thrust her jealousy aside, and soon the joy of his kisses made her quite forget that he was going to see Mistress Anne Boleyn—who was "very fair."

A few hours later they were riding to Castle Winton where they were warmly welcomed by John's widowed mother.

Lady de Winton had been practically a second mother to Mary since Sir Charles' wife died giving her birth, so that when John told her he and Mary had at last come to an understanding she was overjoyed. But the other news sobered her.

"I do not like that Abbot, nor his nephew," she said. "The Abbot Telva's demands in tithes for the Abbey are exorbitant, and as for Clement, one of my farm men," she stopped, then went on, "told me he rode for Windsor but an hour ago!"

"To the King! I'd best to horse," John exclaimed.

"Ay, John, and beat the Abbot at his own game!" Sir Charles rumbled.

Lady de Winton bustled about seeing to the packing while John told his body-servant, Godfrey, to make ready and bring the horses. Presently the preparations were complete.

John said farewell, and he and Godfrey rode away.

Mary was very sad. She had only found her love to lose him, and her heart was still greatly troubled over the fairness of Mistress Anne.

Lady de Winton, seeing her downcast, touched her shoulder.

"Nay, Mary, do not grieve. He will come back, and it is well you early learn the first lesson of a woman who loves—that of waiting. So often it is all that we can do. But be of cheer, for of your waiting joy will come, whereas some wait and wait," here she looked at Sir Charles from under heavy eyelashes, "and profit not."

Sir Charles started!

"Do you, by any chance, mean, Jane, that you would have listened if I'd—"

A faint smile played around the corners of Lady de Winton's mouth which, despite her forty years, was almost girlish.

"I would have, Charles—and will."

Mary regarded them both with wonder. Lady Jane standing beside her looked calm and beautiful, and Sir Charles suddenly seemed to have shed at least ten of his fifty years.

"Then," he cried, "though I am somewhat large, I still will kneel to ask your hand, for I have loved you a long time, Jane."

"Kneel not. Oh, Charles, you and that boy of mine had such close mouths it took the Abbot to play match-maker. Well, I will come to Tall Trees and keep you from being lonely when Mary is Mistress here. That is-" her dimples showed, "if we've your blessing, child."

"Oh, that you have, and I *am* happy—happier than I ever thought to be," Mary exclaimed.

There followed a general kissing and rejoicing, in the midst of which Sir Charles slapped his thigh resoundingly.

"Now if only John had not gone I could have sent word to the King of our intention to wed, Jane."

Now Lady de Winton's face flushed red.

"I did tell John to mention it to the Cardinal. I thought perhaps with Mary soon to wed you might—"

As Sir Charles took her in his arms she buried her face in his shoulder and Mary quietly stole away to tell her woman where to bestow her things, for she felt she was no longer needed.

She was very happy to think of her father and Lady Jane de Winton being united. Now if only Cardinal Woolsey would override the Abbot everything would be wonderful—almost too wonderful to happen. She was sore afraid. But there was nothing she could do but pray and wait—wait for John to return from Hampton Court. The journey there and back would take at least four days' hard riding, and there was no telling how long he would have to attend the Cardinal before he had an audience—for Woolsey was the honey pot that drew all the flies. Mary sighed. There was truly nothing to do but wait.

The next day nothing happened, except that Sir Charles wrote a note to John telling him that he would soon be his father in three ways—step-father, father-in-law, and father in heart, which indeed he had always been. He bade John tell the

Cardinal and ask for King Henry's sanction to the nuptials. This he sent off by one of his own men from Tall Trees.

Of the Abbot they heard nothing, and two more days passed in quiet laziness. Lady de Winton showed Mary all of the Castle, and told her how she ordered things so that Mary would find it easy to take over its complicated management.

"If I only can," Mary murmured, thinking of John and whether the Cardinal would give them dispensation to wed, but Lady de Winton took it she meant that the Castle, being a bigger household than Tall Trees would be difficult to oversee, discoursed for a longer time on how it should be done, and Mary, whose heart was with John, and not in these household matters, had to pay attention.

On the afternoon of the fourth day the Abbot on his white mule came riding to the Castle Winton. The Castle's drawbridge was down. In face there was little use for such things now in England as the times were peaceful and, beginning with the reign of Henry's father, the great Manor Houses, such as Tall Trees, began to replace the fortified and sturdy feudal dwellings.

As the mule clattered into the courtyard, Mary, watching from the leaded windows of the long gallery, wished that time could move back and they could defy the Abbot and the large escort he brought with him.

Mary waited in the long gallery and Sir Charles and Lady de Winton, at her request, stood with her.

The Abbot paused in the doorway, making the sign of the cross before he entered, then he sat in the tall chair Lady de Winton offered and motioned the others to sit also. This they did, excepting Mary, who stood beside her father regarding Telva closely.

The Abbot of Chettleworth did not meet her glance; instead he addressed her father.

"Sir Charles Vetrell, I formally ask the hand of your daughter Mary for my nephew Clement D'Aigula, though I deem it strange to come to Castle Winton instead of Tall Trees to do so."

"A request you have already made at Tall Trees and which I refused then as I do now. Mary has made her choice—as she's a right to do—and will marry Sir John de Winton." Sir Charles was firm.

"And what say you, Mary Vetrell?" The Abbot's eyes focused on the girl.

"Nothing more or less than I told you before, my Lord Abbot." This time, however, Mary's tones carried even greater conviction, for she now spoke the truth since John had spoken his heart. She knew that though her life hinge on the balance she would wed no other.

"Then I have this to tell you. My nephew writes me that King Henry gives his consent to his suit and decrees that you and Clement be married in the Abbey of Chettleworth some ten days hence, and furthermore," he raised his hand to still their protests, "the King himself will grace your nuptials, and the Queen also. They go on progress and will stop here for the purpose. Clement rides with them. He bade me give his heart's love to you, Mistress Mary and say only the King could keep him from you, but as the King himself brings him to your arms, he needs must restrain his ardor. For you," here the Abbott again turned his eyes on Sir Charles, "I have a writing. The King's Grace does you much honor for he will lodge at Tall Trees as the Abbey is not large enough to house his retinue. So you must needs return home and make ready."

Sir Charles sighed. Well he knew what entertaining the King meant. The Court would arrive like a bevy of ants to strip him bare. It was an honor—yes, but an expensive one. Still he would have to stomach it as best he could.

"My poor house is ever at His Majesty's disposal, and so am I, but with my daughter it is different. The Vetrell deed—"

The Abbot threw back his head and laughed.

"Cease drooling of the Vetrell deed. Did I not say one King can do away with the foolish deeds of another day? See, I make jingles of it. That's what I think of your Vetrell deed."

"A rhyme for a rhyme, Lord Abbot." Mary was white to her very lips, but she threw back her head like a charger going into battle.

"I'll be Sir John de Winton's wife
Or bravely end this bitter life
Before I share a Spaniard's bed
By my own hand I will be dead."

"No, Mary Vetrell, that you'll not do, for if you do you lose your soul. I here and now pronounce you excommunicate unless you obey the law of the Church. If you take your life no one will give you Christian burial, as you well know."

Mary trembled. It was a dreadful thing he was saying.

He played with his cross. "But that's not yet, child. I forgive your rash words and we'll make an end of rhyming. Get you ready for your nuptials."

Now, Mary, desperate with fear, threw herself on her knees before him. "Oh, Abbot Telva, I pray you, let me wed the man I love. Be again my friend as you have always been—the saintly father I can worship, not the bitter Abbot who lashes me with words that drive me mad. I beg you have some pity on me whose only fault is that I love Sir John." She put her head on his knees and raised her hands in supplication.

He drew her up by them and stood holding her so. "I will be generous. If you will give yourself to God and be a holy nun, I'll put my nephew by and see the King will understand."

"No—no," Mary shrank away, pulling her hands from his grasp. "I could not be a nun—I—"

"Then get ready to wed Clement, for John de Winton's wife you'll never be!" There was hate in the Abbot's face, but the three people in the room only glimpsed it for a moment. Everything happened so quickly that he was gone before anyone had a chance to even answer back. No one followed him for Mary had fainted, and it took the united efforts of Sir Charles and Lady de Winton to bring her to. Finally they were successful but when she had regained consciousness she moaned and sobbed until finally Lady de Winton had her carried to bed and gave her a sleeping draught to ease her misery. It was the only comfort she could give, for as Clement had been successful John must have failed, and the outlook was black enough.

Later Sir Charles and Lady de Winton puzzled much over it for they could not understand why the Abbot was willing to give over his schemes if Mary entered a convent. They did not know his well-hidden, fanatical love for her, nor how her prayers had moved him, so that he had for the moment been willing to give up his dreams of helping Queen Katherine, his nephew and himself just to know Mary was safe and inviolate. In a convent he could see her and be in truth her spiritual father. That would be almost as good as dancing her children on his knee, or so he had thought in that brief moment. But he had been glad when she refused. When she was Clement's wife, the mother of his child, then he could be content—but only then.

Early the next morning they were all at breakfast when John's man, Godfrey came to them weary and travel-stained. He said that John was well and staying at Greenwich where the King held Court, and gave them a letter his master had charged him to deliver.

Lady de Winton bade him go and get meat and drink after his long journey, which he was delighted to do.

When they were alone Sir Charles opened the letter and read it aloud.

"To Sir Charles Vetrell, the Lady Jane de Winton and Mistress Mary Vetrell from John de Winton. Most urgent and private.

"I write these lines myself although my hand is poor, for it is not well that any other eye should see what is set down.

"I have seen Cardinal Woolsey. For love of you, Sir Charles, he has been kind, and, had I reached him before Clement D'Aigula got King Henry's ear, I would have better news to tell you. But as you most likely know by now I was too late. Still all is not lost. The Cardinal is on our side and will favor us, but at the moment dares not do so openly for he wishes no unpleasantness with those of Spanish blood. Mistress Boleyn I have seen and she is much interested and will try to soften the heart that needs to be softened. She bids me be of good cheer and sends her greetings to Mary and looks forward to meeting her. I come to Tall Trees with the Court. I have spoken much of the Vetrell ghost—that White Lady who walks in the narrow hall—how it always haunts Tall Trees when a Vetrell is wronged. The King desires to see the White Lady who, I have told him, resembles Mary—

*the White Lady who haunted Tall Trees when the third Sir Vetrell tried to go against the Vetrell deed
and forced his daughter to wed against her will; how, when he gave over and let her wed the man of her
choice, as the deed stated, the ghost vanished and was seen no more until the night the Abbot pressed his
nephew's suit, when the White Lady walked again. His Majesty is curious to see this visitation, so I
hope the White Lady is not shy of royalty.*

*"Clement D'Aigula is here. I needs must be civil to him, but I'll pick a quarrel and send him
to another world before he marries Mary. I still have hope, and send this ring to her who has my heart.*

"John de Winton."

And there was a seal marked with the boars of Winton.

"Now I think the boy is mad, or I have lost my eyes," Sir Charles announced.
"For we all know well that Tall Trees has no ghost, no White Lady—nor was there
ever question by any Vetrell of disobeying the Vetrell deed!"

"There's this to it," Lady de Winton said. "There's more to this than has been
written down."

Mary put her finger on the mystery.

"John has some scheme wherein the White Lady plays a part. I think the Cardinal thought of it, or perhaps Mistress Boleyn, for it smacks of woman's wit to me.
Still, if John wants a ghost that looks like me, I'll play the ghost for him if we can
find some garb of white."

"I have a wedding dress from ancient days in an oaken chest that would fit you,
Mary," and Lady de Winton began describing it. Mary suggested they get it and she
try walking as a ghost.

"But first, father, give me the ring John sent."

Sir Charles gave her a twist of gilded paper. She undid it and revealed a blue
enameled ring in which was set tiny stars of gold. She put it on her wedding finger
which it fit perfectly.

"This shall be my guard until that day when John gives me another ring and
calls me wife," she said, and then went off with Lady de Winton to search out the
gown for the ghost.

That very afternoon they returned to Tall Trees, for there was much to do.
Lady de Winton went with them to help make ready for the King.

A week went by in these preparations, a week in which Mary worked hard to
stifle the pain in her heart. She had not much faith in John's ghost, but she practiced
her part diligently until she could go from her room to the narrow hall by the secret
passage without a light, and Sir Charles swore in the dimly lit hall he could not see
the panel slip back that let her into the hall.

"John has a ghost in you, daughter," he smiled, "though, in truth, I cannot
fathom what good 'twill be."

Nor could Mary, and the face of Clement dark and saturnine like his uncle's,
only more handsome, loomed large before her.

Then a swift rider came to say the King and his retinue would be there in the hour, that they had stopped at the Abbey of Chettleworth for some good Spanish wine. Mary sighed and clasped the ring John had sent her and held it to her cheek a minute before she let it slide back to its hiding place between her breasts. She had worn it on a gold chain ever since it had come. She was very unhappy for she saw no way out of the trap she was in and did not believe the ghost—no matter how realistically it was played—would open the door.

When the gay pennants of the King's banners first appeared she took her place by her father and Lady de Winton. She wore her rose-colored velvet gown, and beneath the tight bodice her heart fluttered like the wings of a moth against a flame.

It was a beautiful sight—that long queue of richly dressed people riding up the broad approach with its tall trees. There was no mistaking King Henry's massive figure, and Mary's heart almost stopped beating when she saw the Abbot of Telva riding beside him.

It was not very long before the gallant company were dismounting and crowding into Tall Trees. Sir Charles had scarcely greeted his monarch, made obeisance to the Queen, when King Henry, whose narrow pig-like eyes had been darting about, asked, "Where is the bride-to-be?"

Mary's eyes sought and found John, who was standing a little behind the King, as her father led her forth.

John smiled as though he hadn't a care in the world and made a little motion of his head toward a very young, beautiful girl, richly appareled, who was standing beside him.

Even in the stress of the moment Mary knew this must be Anne Boleyn, and she did not wonder that her young, fresh beauty overshadowed that of the ageing and somewhat grim-faced Queen.

Sir Charles led her before the King and at the same time the Abbot Telva motioned to his nephew to step forward. This Clement did, but Mary turned her face away from him.

"Now, of a truth, girl, with such a face I'd not wish to take you to the altar myself," the King said gruffly.

Mary, not daring to say what was in her heart, lifted her hands in silent supplication. Before she had a chance, even if she had found the words, the Abbot came forward.

"As you know, Sire, she is a stubborn girl whose heart is set elsewhere. But I warrant once they're wed my nephew can change that countenance to one wreathed in smiles."

"No," Mary cried involuntarily, but the King, ignoring her, spoke to the Abbot.

"I doubt it—I doubt it greatly, but I have passed my word to you and come

Wednesday she shall wed your nephew; that is, unless the ghost, this White Lady of Tall Trees, says otherwise. For, know, Lord Abbot, I will not go against a ghost, and I have sworn to Sir John de Winton that if the ghost should make it plain it likes not this marriage to your nephew by walking in the narrow hall, or some such sign, then I will give the lady's hand so that the ghost be pleased."

"Sire," exclaimed the Abbot, "I have lived in Chettleworth these many years, and never before have I heard of the White Lady of Tall Trees."

At last Mary saw the scheme. She had guessed a little of it, of course, but now that it was spread before her in its entirety she understood John's unruffled manner, and the swift pang of jealousy that had seared through her when she saw him standing beside Mistress Boleyn subsided, for if the plan had originated in Anne Boleyn's brain, it was a good one and she was grateful.

The King, meanwhile, was looking at the Abbot, and Mary, for the first time, dared to let her clear eyes rest on those dark brilliant ones set in the heavy-jowled face. He laughed roughly.

"Well, this night, Lord Abbot, you will have a chance to see the ghost, for I invite you to watch with me in the narrow hall—you and some others whom I will select, and if the ghost walks and makes her wishes known, you will abide by them as I shall. Now, enough of these matters. Mistress Mary, whoever your husband be, I myself will see you wed and wish you well. Sir Charles and Lady de Winton, I cry my blessings on your union, though to do so I take prerogative from Abbot Telva. And now if your cellars can afford some good stout English ale, I think my stomach would relish a draught of it."

Many hours later Mary stood in her room adjusting the satin folds of the ancient bride's dress which Lady de Winton had produced from her oaken chest.

Down in the narrow hallway in an embrasure she knew the King, the Abbot, Clement, John and four other high placed lords were waiting.

The embrasure was far away from that place in the wall where the secret panel opened. The light was only where the King was so that, until she came within his radius, they would not see how she got into the hall and, with luck, she could depart again the same way. If the Abbot had not been one of the party she would have had no fear for the success of the scheme, for it was a time when men believed in ghosts and when superstition greatly over-rode better judgment.

The Abbot was a different matter. Only he suspected a trick. She had read that in his eyes, and she was greatly afraid that he would know and expose the fact that the ghost was flesh and blood.

She had no chance to speak to John. The exigencies of the Court had prevented her coming close to him, or, in fact, to anyone except in passing. She had been well watched, and since Henry had stepped into Tall Trees she had had no word alone with anyone. Even now the hall outside her door was guarded and, in fact all of Tall Trees was filled with men-at-arms who made up King Henry's bodyguard.

Had it not been for the secret passageway and panel there would have been no way for her to have gotten into the narrow hall. She rather wondered that Lady de Winton had not come to her, or her father, but Lady de Winton was probably in attendance on the Queen and Sir Charles, of course, would be with the King.

The clock marked near the hour that she had heard the King say, "The ghost will walk"—for while they had been at meat the King had talked much of the ghost— in fact, so much had he talked that Queen Katherine had asked to be of the party. But he had brushed her aside with, "Nay, Kate, 'tis best you only see the living, not the dead," and the Queen had given over.

Mary dusted a little flour, which she had made ready for the occasion, over her face and was pleased at the ghostly effect it gave her in the highly polished silver of her mirror. Then with a silent prayer she pressed the panel in her own wall that admitted her to the secret passageway.

Her feet went easily down the passageway, but when she reached the end of it and stood with her finger on the rose that would release the panel that would let her into the narrow hall she was terribly afraid. Her future, her lover, even her life, hung in the balance of the next few minutes, but Mary had made up her mind, as she had told the Abbot, that rather than become Clement's wife, she would die by her own hand—no matter to what perdition she was consigned. She caught her breath and then pressed the rose.

A second later she was in the hall. It was very silent. The people waiting in the embrasure were not talking, but she could hear even breathing which told here they were there. Slowly, her hands clasped demurely in front of her, she walked the length of the narrow hall. It seemed to her that a little ahead of her was a white shadow. It could not be her own, nor could she distinguish very clearly because it was on the other side of the ring of light which came from the embrasure. It wasn't until she reached the edge of it that she gasped with horror, for on the other side, just stepping into the light as she was doing, was another ghost, another figure in white, only this figure had a veil over its face.

A cold, craven feeling went down Mary's spine and she stopped short just as the other figure did. Was this a ghost, a real ghost, a denizen of another world? Before she had time to put her quavering thoughts into a concrete form a bevy of voices reached her.

"These are no ghosts!" the Abbot's voice was full of scorn.

"Attach me those two!" the King's tone rang out.

Mary could not move. Perhaps if it had not all come so quickly she could have regained the passageway. Her knees were weak as water and would not bear her toward it. Presently there were more lights brought by men-at-arms and she was standing in the front of the King alongside that other figure whose veil he was lifting.

"Well, Mistress Anne," he exclaimed, "so you have taken to dabbling in the spirit world?"

Anne Boleyn, for it was indeed she, sank to her knees.

"Oh, Sire, I did but wish to play my part to bring two hearts that truly love together, for I believe that in all the world there is nothing so wonderful as love."

Henry raised her gently and a tender expression stole over his face.

"Your sentiments do you much credit, Mistress Anne, as well as your soft heart, but I have sworn an oath, and no false ghost can let me break it. Because your motive was so sweet I do forgive this masquerade." Then he turned to Mary and said sternly, though she thought she could read regret written on his face, "Mistress Vetrell, you, too, I forgive because your deceit was prompted by a motive I can understand." For one fleeting second his gaze rested on Anne again. "But I cannot change my decree. Apparently the Lord Abbot of Telva spoke truth. There is no Vetrell ghost, so you must marry Clement and I wish you well of it."

"Thank you, Sire," cried the Abbot, and Clement echoed his uncle's words and then stepped forward to stand beside her.

"No, no," moaned Mary, and just then Anne Boleyn put her hand on the King's arm and cried, "Look, Henry, look!" forgetting in the stress of the moment that she should not address the King in so informal a manner. They all swung around and there standing in the light the circle made was a woman dressed in white!

"Oddsfish!" cried Henry. "Don't tell me the Queen herself has joined this masquerade."

"No, no—can you not see? It is a ghost, a true ghost. Look, her garments are transparent!" Anne cried again.

They all looked and wonder grew upon them for it was true. There stood a woman with a sweet, kindly face dressed in long white robes. She stood there and they all could see her and yet they could look through her too. She was nebulous, shining and translucent.

Sir Charles gasped.

"It is my wife—Mary's own mother come again!"

The Abbot began to cry and held up his cross.

"I exhort this figure, which must come from hell, to disappear!"

But the figure did not move and Henry, who was more courageous than the others, who had shrunk back gibbering into the embrasure, said, "Methinks, Abbot Telva, the figure comes from heaven, not hell, for she has no fear of you."

And it was true. Instead of disappearing, the figure walked toward the Abbot and, leaning over, whispered in his ear—at which the Abbot shrieked and ran from the hall, the black skirt of his cassock flying around his legs like a raven's wing.

Then the ghost of Mary's mother pointed to Clement who stood against the wall shivered. It pointed to Clement and then to the door, making plain in its sign language that it wished Clement to follow his uncle.

The King, who by now had recovered himself, though he continually made the sign of the cross on his broad chest, appeared to be enjoying the events that were taking place.

"Quite clearly, Don D'Aigula, the ghost will have none of you for its daughter, and as I swore to obey the spirits myself, neither will I. Get you gone, and tell your uncle that tomorrow either he or one of his priests will wed Mistress Mary to the man of her choice."

King Henry looked toward the ghost and seemed pleased when the visitation smiled upon him. Clement made haste to obey the King's commands and vanished from the narrow hall almost as quickly as his uncle had before him.

Then the ghost beckoned Mary and John de Winton out into the circle of light and, holding her hands above their heads, she blessed them. Then with a little bow toward the King she gradually dissolved into the atmosphere.

A great peace flowed over Mary. The benediction from her mother's ghost had wiped away everything but joy and the certainty that her life would be filled with content and happiness forevermore. At the very moment when all had seemed lost, and she had reached the nadir of hope, a miracle had happened. Mother love had materialized and made itself visible in all its manifold facets, and saved her and her love. Forgetting the fact that there was an audience she turned to John. Their hands clasped, their lips met, and there was a completeness, a satisfaction in their kiss that she had never known before.

"Well, well, Sir John," the King's hearty voice swept them apart and to their feet, "such kissing had best wait until tomorrow when the maid is yours. And fear not you'll not have her to wife for I myself shall see to it and tuck you in your bridal bed with these two hands. See, Mistress Mary, I have been harsh with you because I was constrained against my will, for I want no trouble with Spaniards now—though later," he looked at Anne, "it may be otherwise. None felt it worse than I who saw two ghosts when I expected one—yourself, as Sir John had told me. How got you in the hall, Anne?"

"I hid in the corner after dinner before the guards were set, Sire. I feared Mistress Vetrell had no way to come for I knew the Abbott watched and Sir John forgot to tell me of the secret passage, but, oh, my heart was sore when I thought I had spoiled your plan." The lovely girl smiled at Mary who smiled back again.

"Well, we have seen strange things tonight—strange and wonderful things," the King mused. "A ghost blessed us all, I think, except the Abbot and his sister's son, who liked not her message. Well, the Abbot shall wed you in the morning, and you must bring your bride to Court, Sir John, for she and Mistress Anne should become friends, who have been sister ghosts. Yes, bring your bride to Court and we will make a place for you about our person. Come now, this has been thirsty work. I think some ale—"

Mary's hand snuggled into John's as they walked along behind the King who had given his arm to Anne Boleyn.

"Sweet," John pressed her hand.

A presage of the joy to come shot through Mary.

"I will be married in my rose-colored velvet gown," she whispered.

The
WHITE Vampire

by Arlton Eadie

---

*Hang on to your seats and get ready for a
thrilling ride through the jungle, no "lion!"*
Weird Tales, September 1928

T he little stern-wheel launch gingerly nosed its way through the vast maze of
shifting sand-bars and headed for the cluster of mud huts that shimmered
vaguely through the heat-haze of the tropical noon. From beside her stumpy
funnel a plume of steam shot upward as her siren wailed over the flooded water of
the River Rinné, startling the chime-birds into frantic wheelings above the feathery
tree-tops, and rudely disturbing the siesta of the dark-skinned warriors of Imanzi,
causing them to draw the folds of their sleeping robes closer about their heads as
they muttered a drowsy charm against the shrieking water-devil of the white man.

Lieutenant McFee, the young officer in charge of the Hausa patrol of the
district, became dimly aware of the sound amid the chaotic visions incidental to the
tail-end of a spell of fever. But he recognized the import of the signal, and immediately arose, swallowed the regulation quinine tabloid, swung on his sun-helmet, and
sallied forth.

The skipper of the launch hailed him as he crossed the gang-plank.

"Sorry we're overdue, sir, but I got under way the first moment this old water-
pusher could make head against the current—and we didn't spare the logs coming
up, either. If you mobilize your gay soldier-lads to hump the stores ashore, I'll be
casting off right away. I want to get down to Yola before those flaming shallows
shift again. By the way," he added as he descended to the deck, "I've brought you
something that wasn't in your indent. It's a young swell with pots of money and no
end of a pull with the Administration. He's come upstream to shoot lions and have
a good time generally."

The somewhat caustic comment that rose to Lieutenant McFee's lips was
checked by the approach of the newcomer. For a few seconds the two men eyed
each other in speculative silence.

Lieutenant McFee saw a good-looking young man of about his own age,

501

clad in an immaculate and expensive tropical outfit. His smart drill suit still retained its pristine snowy splendor; his cartridge-belt, riding-boots and re-volver-holster were of glossy and squeaky newness. Around him lay spread a perfect armory of sporting-guns, backed by sufficient foil-lined ammunition cases to supply a punitive expedition. The Honorable Clifford Egerton, on his part, beheld a gaunt figure in sun-bleached khaki, with a tanned and thickly freckled countenance and close-cropped sandy hair. At first sight he might have been mistaken for a long-legged, overgrown schoolboy; but the grim set of the lean, clean-shaven jaws and the expression in the steady gray eyes quickly dis-pelled that illusion. A stickler for military smartness might have found several defects in his general turn-out. The only thing about him that was brightly polished was his revolver-butt—and that by frequent use.

"Ah, please to meet you, Lieutenant," said the Honorable Clifford Egerton as he came forward and shook hands. "Is there any shooting to be had around here?"

For an instant the corners of McFee's mouth twitched strangely. Then he nod-ded his head.

"Any amount of it," he answered gravely, and it was only subsequently that the questioner realized the exquisite humor that lay behind the seemingly simple reply.

In due course the launch disgorged her freight and headed downstream. The two men watched its receding smoke-plume above the trees until it merged into the misty blue of the distance. Then they turned and re-entered the native hut which formed the patrol officer's quarters.

"Do you know, I heard quite a lot about you at Lokoja," Egerton remarked as he threw himself into one of the long cane chairs and lit a cigarette. "They call you 'Fighting McFee' down there, and swear that the river tribes look on you as a real number-one-size tin god."

McFee shook his head in embarrassed dissent.

"Very often my sphere of influence extends no further than a bullet can reach. I only wish that your very flattering description of my reputation were true.," he added regretfully. "In that case I might succeed in ridding my district of one of the most infamous villains that has ever infested it."

"Indeed?" queried Egerton with quickened interest. "Who is he, and what particular form does his infamy take?"

"He is an Arab called Ishak-El-Naga, and he's a dealer in slaves."

Egerton twisted in his chair and stared at the speaker in surprise.

"Slaves?" he echoed. "Oh, come! I say, you don't mean to tell me there are slaves at the present day—in a British colony!"

"Protectorate," corrected McFee. "Of course, Ishak-El-Naga does not work openly. He collects his stock-in-trade from the tiny bush villages, either kidnapping the poor wretches, or trading them from their chiefs for gin or gunpowder, or—

what is worse—inciting one tribe to attack another in the hopes of bagging the survivors of the losing side. When he's got his caravan together he drives 'em like cattle and sells 'em to the desert tribes north of Lake Chad. It's a good thousand miles, and part of the way lies through a waterless desert. I came across his trail once or twice soon after I was first detailed here, and I can assure you it was not a pretty sight. In those days he used to leave the poor devils where they dropped; now he goes to the trouble of burying them in order to make his line of march less conspicuous."

"But a man seldom falls stone-dead from exhaustion," objected the frankly skeptical Egerton. "Some of them might linger for days."

McFee gave a grim, mirthless laugh. "Rest assured, they have to get their dying over quickly when Ishak-El-Naga is around!"

Clifford Egerton started to his feet, his usually ruddy face drawn and haggard.

"You mean that he butchers the stragglers?" he cried in horror.

"What else?" answered McFee. "Do you expect an Arab slaver to run a Red Cross convoy?"

"And, knowing this, you still allow the villain to be at large?"

The patrol officer raised his sandy eyebrows and shrugged.

"Knowing is very different from proving. He's as cunning as Satan, and he has spies everywhere. If I could but get evidence against him his career would be a short one. But evidence is just the one thing that I'm not likely to get."

"Why not?"

"Because he has found a way of preventing the natives from giving information against him. They are forbidden to speak by a mysterious veiled woman who appears to them at intervals. She is credited with possessing supernatural powers and they call her *Sitoka Kilui.*"

"What does that signify in English?"

"Freely translated, it means 'The White Vampire.'"

A sudden exclamation caused McFee to glance up. Egerton had turned and was staring with wide-open eyes at a figure which had emerged from the jungle trail into the glare of sunlight which flooded the compound.

"Gad!" he muttered half to himself. "A girl, by all that's wonderful—and a dashed good-looking one, too!"

The spontaneous tribute was not undeserved. Tall above average, she moved with that easy grace which no amount of training can impart, but which seems to be the natural attribute of the women of the South. Her flawless features were shaded by a white sombrero, beneath whose broad brim there clustered a mass of curls of the color of freshly minted gold. Her beauty was enhanced by a skin of exquisite, creamy fairness; her eyes were dark and still as mountain pools. Eyes of night, hair like sunbeams—her whole appearance, like the fact of her presence in that wild spot, seemed a bewildering, bewitching paradox. Small wonder that Egerton stood agape and wondering at the unexpected vision.

"Who is she?" he whispered. "And what on earth is she doing here?"

"She is Señorita Juanita Rasparteo, the daughter of a Portuguese trader here," McFee informed him.

"A Portuguese? Impossible!"

McFee laughed. "Fact, I assure you. You mustn't judge the whole race by the snuff-and-butter specimens you meet at Lagos."

Meanwhile the girl was approaching with hasty steps, glancing frequently over her shoulder as though she feared pursuit—a fear which appeared to be shared by the slim native girl who followed at her heels.

The reason of their haste was soon apparent. Barely had they reached the center of the compound when the bushes behind parted and debouched a score of half-naked Bhutumas armed with bows and spears. At their head was a tall man wearing the flowing draperies and green *kaick*, bound round his head by cords of twisted camel's hair, which denoted the high-caste Arab, a Hadj who had performed the Mecca pilgrimage. At the sight of him McFee's hand instinctively sought the weapon at his side.

"It is Ishak-El-Naga," he whispered rapidly, "and it looks as though he's out for trouble."

Followed by Egerton, he ran out of the hut and placed himself between the girls and their pursuers.

"Greeting, O Hadj Ishak-El-Naga," he said, addressing the leader in Arabic. "Do you come in peace?"

The man stared at him insolently for a moment, then slowly shrugged beneath his gold-embroidered *burnous*.

"As Allah wills, who giveth both victory and defeat," he answered in a tone of studied indifference. "I am come to claim this maiden, Inyoni, who hath been affianced to me according to the custom of her people. A full score of oxen did I pay her father—"

"He lies, O white man, he lies!" cried the native girl, throwing her lithe body in the sand at McFee's feet. "No oxen were paid, neither was I affianced. His people seized me while I was gathering *kava* in the woods and took me to the secret place of slaves. But I escaped and made my way back to my mistress," she pointed to Juanita as she spoke. "Protect me, *Bwana* McFee! Do not let him take me away, for I am a free maiden and slave to none."

"And that's the honest truth, Mr. McFee," said Juanita, speaking for the first time. Her voice was full and musical, and she bore an accent that showed that she must have spent some years at least in the United States. "Ishak offered his oxen to me if I'd give up the girl to him. But I wasn't trading any."

Lieutenant McFee turned to the scowling Arab.

"Bring hither the maiden's father that he may testify that thy words are true," he said sternly.

A line of gleaming teeth showed behind the black beard as Ishak-El-Naga burst into a scornful laugh. "Am I Allah, that I can cause the dead to walk?" he jeered.

McFee started and his gray eyes hardened to two points of steel. "You mean that her father is dead?"

"It was written that this morn should be his last," Ishak answered sullenly. "The man was old. He died. It was the will of Allah."

"By heaven! I more than half suspect that the scoundrel has murdered him to make good his claim." McFee muttered to Egerton. Aloud he said: "I must look further into the matter, O Hadj. Meanwhile this maiden Inyoni remains with her former mistress."

"Then is it fated that you defy me?" The Arab's words were accompanied by an evil scowl.

"It is," answered McFee curtly. "Thou hast my permission to depart."

The Arab raised his clenched hands above his head.

"O beardless dogs!" he shouted furiously. "Fools of a nation of fools! May the fire on thy hearth be quenched and thy house be desolated. As for this maiden," he went on, fixing a baleful glance on the shrinking girl, "her fate shall be whispered for generations to come. Beware, O thou accursed McFee, beware!"

Turning on his heel, he rapped out an order in the native dialect and, accompanied by his savage bodyguard, plunged into the winding trail and disappeared.

"And now," said McFee, gently raising the trembling Inyoni to her feet, "tell me how I may find the secret place where Ishak-El-Naga keeps his prisoners, so that they may be freed and he punished."

A look of distress came into Inyoni's dusky features.

"Gladly would I do so, *Bwana*," she said haltingly, "but I am afraid. Were I to name the place, the *Sitoka Kilui* would surely slay me."

"You see," McFee said in an undertone to Egerton, the "White Vampire again! By heaven! It almost maddens me to think that hundreds of lives should be sacrificed for the sake of one unspoken word. Inyoni," he went on, turning again to the girl, "you *shall* speak. You shall tell me of this secret place, so that I may gain evidence to crush this Ishak-El-Naga like the loathsome reptile he is. Speak, Inyoni— I command you!"

The trembling girl hesitated, her dark eyes fixed on the young officer's face. Something that she saw there must have given her courage, for she drew herself erect with an air of sudden determination.

"Yes, I will speak!" she cried. "If you will hunt the White Vampire—"

Above the drone of insect life and murmur of the distant river there sounded a shrill whistling note, and Inyoni sank into McFee's arms with the shaft of a Bhutuma arrow quivering in her rounded breast.

In an instant all was confusion. The hastily mustered Hausas sent volley after volley crashing through the tangled undergrowth whence the arrow had sped. But it was wasted ammunition, and none realized the fact better than McFee. Lucky indeed would be the bullet that found its billet amid that wilderness of canes and trailing vines. At length he ordered his men to cease fire and retraced his steps to where Inyoni lay. He tenderly lifted the limp form and bore it into the hut, and with difficulty managed to force a little brandy between her lips. After a while her eyes slowly opened.

"The vengeance of the White Vampire has fallen." The words came faintly between the last fluttering breaths. "Avenge me, *Bwana* . . . watch . . . beside the Pool of Ghosts . . . at moonrise . . . tonight! . . ."

Within the hour McFee and Egerton, armed to the teeth, set out to solve the mystery of the fearsome being whose presence lay like a light over the countryside. But before they left, the spirit of Inyoni had already solved the last great mystery of all.

The western horizon was ablaze with the vivid hues of the tropical sunset when the two white men reached the large, circular sheet of water known to the natives as the Pool of Ghosts.

They were alone. Lieutenant McFee—a keen student of savage psychology— had quickly sensed the superstitious dread with which the mere mention of their destination had been received by his men. Strong as a horse, brave as a lion, an adept at bush tactics, the Hausa as a fighting machine is perfection itself. But the moment his imagination begins to busy itself in occult speculations, then the thousand and one devils that comprise the savage Pantheon enter into his thick, woolly pate and he is apt to become no better than a frightened child. And on such an errand, McFee decided, a crowd of jumpy followers would be a source of weakness rather than of strength.

Twilight is always brief under the equator. In an instant the scarlet and gold of the heavens were obliterated as though a huge, invisible brush charged with indigo had been swept from zenith to horizon. Then the thronging stars of the tropics flashed forth like thick-sown gems, and it was night.

But Lieutenant McFee and his companion had no time to waste in admiring the beauties of nature. They took advantage of the last few seconds of daylight to make a survey of their surroundings, and on the ground about the margin, muddy from the recent floods, they discovered something to send a thrill through the stoutest heart.

"Lions' spoor!" said McFee, pointing to the deeply indented impressions. "Look—there are hundreds of trails—the place must be infested with the beasts!

By Jove, Egerton, it looks as though you are going to have the chance of bagging your first lion straight away."

"Nothing would please me better," was the delighted reply. "That's really what I came up country for, but things have been happening so quickly since my arrival that I'd almost forgotten the fact."

Something like a sigh escaped McFee's lips. "I had hoped there would be sport afoot more exciting even than lion-hunting," he said regretfully. "However, let us make ourselves comfortable in one of these trees and we'll take things as they come. Remember, when you draw at a lion, aim just behind the shoulder. A bullet planted there is more likely to drop him than one in the head."

Egerton made a wry face in the darkness. "I'm not likely to hit a haystack just at present. It's so dark that I can't so much as see my foresight."

"Wait," answered McFee. "There will be light enough presently."

Even as he spoke the sky began to blanch, and presently the rim of the full African moon pushed its way above the surrounding tree-tops and filled the little clearing about the lake with its cold, bright radiance.

"Hist!" the warning whisper from McFee recalled the other's wandering attention. "Look—on your right!"

For a moment the less experienced Egerton could detect nothing unusual. Then, among the tall grass, he saw a ripple slowly passing as though a gust of wind had stirred it. But he knew that could not be the explanation, for the night was still and breathless. Again the grass-stems rippled; then slowly parted, and into the moon-light there stepped a beast that caused an involuntary gasp of wonder and admiration to escape the lips of the watchers.

It was an immense albino lion!

From the top of its mane-crowned head to the ground it was the height of an average man; from nose to tail-tip it could not have measured an inch under twelve feet. But, large as it bulked, its unusual color made it appear still larger. In every species of animal there occasionally occur specimens who, through some obscure defect of the pigment-cells, fail to assume their normal colora-tion, and it was to this rare and interesting type that the beast belonged. Its color throughout was a pure, silky white except the eyes, which smoldered red as garnets in their deep-set sockets and the half-opened, fang-fringed mouth. As it stalked proudly forth, the moonlight gleaming on its mane and hide, it presented a weird yet magnificent sight; so much so, indeed, that Egerton, keen hunter as he was, felt a pang of compunction to think that this marvel of strength and beauty would soon be rolling in its death agony.

But the feeling quickly passed and one of elation took its place. What a trophy to take home! His first lion—and such a lion! Mindful of his friend's advice, he pressed the butt of his repeating cordite rifle into his shoulder and took careful aim.

The next moment the heavy bullet would have been sent crashing on its deadly errand, when he felt an iron grip upon his arm.

"Don't shoot!" McFee whispered the words with his mouth close to the other's ear. "That is no wild lion. It wears a golden collar—I just caught the glint of it beneath the mane."

Too much astonished to answer, Egerton lowered his weapon and stared at the strange beast, which had now advanced to the edge of the pool and was lowering its head to drink. As it did so the moonlight fell full upon a massive golden collar encircling its neck.

Having drunk its fill, it raised its head and sent a low, reverberating roar into the night; then turned about and slowly passed out of sight among the long grass. Lieutenant McFee at once slung his rifle and prepared to descend to the ground.

"I intend to follow that lion," he said in answer to Egerton's whispered query. "Perhaps it may lead us to the very heart of the mystery we set out to solve."

At first sight the spot where the beast had disappeared seemed to be an impenetrable thicket of aloe bushes and thorny canes. Closer inspection, however, revealed a narrow path intersecting it, and into this, with wary eyes and ready rifles, the two men plunged. They had barely proceeded a dozen paces, however, before the even straightness of the path aroused a growing suspicion in McFee's mind. Stooping down, he drew his hunting-knife and thrust it through the ankle-deep grass. A few inches below the surface of the ground the blade grated against something hard. Twice he repeated the experiment at different spots; then he sheathed his knife and turned to Egerton.

"I thought so," he said in a low voice. "Beneath us is an ancient roadway faced with blocks of stone. The thin layer of soil which has been deposited on it in the course of ages is not deep enough to enable the larger bushes to take root; otherwise it would have been overgrown long since."

"What, a stone roadway in the heart of the African bush? Impossible!"

"It may not always have been bush; I have a very shrewd idea that at one time the river came up as far as this—you know how the bends are apt to silt up. Anyway, an ancient roadway naturally presupposes something equally ancient at the other end, so come on. Keep your gun handy, but don't fire unless you have to."

A few minutes later McFee's surmise received ample confirmation. The path turned sharply and then terminated in a wedge-shaped opening in the side of a low, conical hill. Although both jambs and lintel were thickly incrusted with moss, there was not the slightest doubt that they were of artificial construction.

"Why, it's a regular tunnel!" exclaimed Egerton. "And look at the carvings! I know I'm not much of an archeologist, but they look to me exactly like those I saw at Luxor. Surely the ancient Egyptians could not have penetrated so far up country?"

McFee did not answer. He was staring with a puzzled frown at the hill before him. He had previously noticed that its outline seemed suspiciously symmetrical, but it was not until his companion mentioned the word "Egyptian" that his mind grasped the startling truth. "Why, the thing is nothing more nor less than a pyramid overgrown with vegetation!" he cried. "It's the very thing I've been trying to find ever since I've been stationed here."

Egerton grasped his arm. "You mean it is the secret slave-hold of El-Naga?" he breathed.

Lieutenant McFee unslung his rifle and pushed forward the safety-catch.

"More than that—it's the home of the White Vampire!" he said grimly. "Forward!"

Followed by his friend, he stepped across the threshold and plunged into the yawning blackness beyond. Twenty paces; then a faint flickering light became visible ahead. At the sight they pressed forward eagerly. Then without warning the solid ground seemed to slide from beneath their feet and they pitched headlong forward and downward.

McFee was conscious of a sickening blow on his head—a thousand lights danced before his eyes—then he remembered no more.

When McFee next opened his eyes the sight they beheld was so extraordinary that for a moment he thought it the figment of a dream.

He was standing on a long, raised platform in the center of a lofty hall, which, from the solidity of its construction and the character of the decoration on its walls, was evidently situated in the heart of the pyramid. On each hand stretched a sea of upturned savage faces. Their dusky features were indistinct amid the gloom, but the myriads of watching eyes, catching the wan light which struggled from above, stood out in startling contrast. Six yards in front of him, its blood-red eyes watching his every movement, crouched the albino lion. Behind him was a pillar of granite, and to this McFee's arms and legs were fastened by means of four hinged bronze staples of curious, and seemingly antique workmanship. In spite of the stifling heat of the crowded and ill-ventilated place, McFee felt a chilly shiver pass down his spine as he realized the full hideousness of the fate in store for him. A helpless prisoner, he was about to be subjected to the onslaught of the white lion!

For what seemed like hours he stood gazing into the smoldering eyes of the beast before him, dully wondering at its delay in giving play to the instincts of its natural blood-lust. Nor did his wonder lessen when at length he perceived the reason of its seeming inactivity. A steel chain stretched from the wall to its collar, preventing its further progress. For the present, at least, he was out of reach of its teeth and claws. The deep sigh of relief which he uttered was answered by a voice close at hand.

"Thank God, you're still alive, Mac!"

It was Egerton who spoke. Turning his head to the left, McFee saw that Egerton was secured to the pillar in the same manner as himself.

"Looks as if I've landed you in a most unholy mess, old chap," McFee said apologetically. "Apparently Ishak-El-Naga is about to provide an elaborately staged spectacle for the edification and amusement of his slaves, with us as the star turns! I wonder what is to be the first item on the program?"

"Probably the first item will also be the last," Egerton answered dryly. "Ishak came round while you were still out for the count, and made a long speech to the audience, and I think he was promising them something top-hold in the way of thrills. I couldn't understand what he was saying, of course, but his expression wasn't exactly benevolent. After he'd finished speaking his piece he flitted off, and in flitted the White Vampire."

"You've seen her?" cried McFee. "What is she like?"

"She's got eyes as black as" —he gave an unsteady laugh— "as that beautiful Portuguese girl's. As for the rest of her appearance—well, you'll soon have an opportunity of judging for yourself!"

A sudden blare of barbaric music echoed through the temple and from the door at the farther end there emerged a party of Bhutumas lustily blowing hollowed elephant tusks. These were followed by a double file of warriors bearing shields of white ox-hide and long, spade-headed spears. Then came four young native girls, their slender, oil-anointed bodies bending and swaying beneath the weight of a huge golden canopy, under which there glided an imposing and sinister figure which came slowly forward and halted before the pinioned men.

Lieutenant McFee and the White Vampire were at last face to face.

Draped in robes of spotless white, with a veil of the same color completely enveloping the head, the thing bore a shuddering resemblance to a walking corpse. Only the eyes which glittered like polished jet through the slits of the head-dress told that the being within, be it man or woman, was at least alive. Although McFee had steeled himself to meet the unexpected, the effect of that veiled presence was both repulsive and terrifying. Immeasurably greater was its effect on the minds of the ignorant savages. A whimper of abject terror rose from a thousand throats as they prostrated themselves face downward on the ground.

"*Sitoka Kilui . . . Sitoka Kilui . . .*"

During the hush which succeeded the utterance of the dread title, two of the guards came forward and cast something on the bronze braziers which glowed on either side of the incumbent lion, and immediately a haze of aromatic fumes floated up and began to eddy about the head of the animal. Whatever subtle drug may have been employed, its effect was almost magical. In an instant the beast's lethargy had vanished. The long, tufted tail began to lash from side to side; the nostrils to dilate and twitch; the eyes to glare furiously. Rising to its feet, with stretched forelegs and arched back, it stood for a second motionless; then, with a roar that seemed to shake the very earth, launched itself straight at McFee.

Brought up short by the restraining chain, it stood reared up on its hind legs, a vision of bristling mane and bared teeth, as it pawed the air in a vain endeavor to reach its victim. But the chain held fast, and the foiled brute retreated with a low growl, only to turn immediately and repeat its leap.

Time after time the beast threw itself against the straining chain, and to McFee's excited senses it appeared as if each successive leap brought it nearer and ever nearer to him. For a while he set this down to mere imagination on his part. Then he began to gage the forward leaps by comparing them to the cracks in the stone flooring. At once a dim suspicion of the truth entered his mind. He looked at the chain, and horror clutched his heart like an icy hand.

Instead of being fastened to the wall, it really passed through an opening, and was gradually paid out from the other side!

"It's no use, Egerton, old man," he groaned. "We're cooked this time. He intends to let that beast play with us just like a cat with a couple of crippled mice, before finishing us off. No wonder he succeeds in keeping his slaves in a state of terror. I suspected something pretty bad—but nothing so devilish as this!"

The chain tautened with a jingling crash as the lion leapt again. So close was it now that he could feel its hot, fetid breath on his forehead. The end was near.

A cold, implacable fury took possession of Lieutenant McFee. He had faced death too often in the routine of his duties at that lonely outpost to feel overmuch fear at the certainly of meeting it now. But to die without striking a blow, the sport of a rascally Arab slaver—oh, for a dozen files of his beloved Hausas, with old Sergeant Mamo Assam at their head! Oh, to hear the swish of steel and the sharp, short snap as the bayonets were unsheathed and fixed! What bayonet-play they would make among the Bhutumas, with their "long point—short-point—jab!" . . .

"Fix . . . bayonets!"

Lieutenant McFee started, and endeavored to shake off the torpor into which his mind had fallen. Had he spoken his thoughts aloud? Or were his senses playing him false under the terrible strain?

The crash of a disciplined volley, a rush of feet, the sound of the Hausa charging-yell, told him it was no delusion. When he opened his eyes it was to see the lion stretched lifeless on the ground, together with most of the slaver's guards, while the remainder stood huddled together, covered by the rifles of a score of Hausas.

But the White Vampire was nowhere to be seen.

Immediately upon being released McFee set a guard on the door of the pyramid, and then with an armed party instituted a thorough search of the maze of passages and cell-like rooms with which the main temple was surrounded. This, although a protracted task, was far from being a tedious one. It is impossible to feel bored when your next step may be greeted with a shot at close quarters.

That Ishak-El-Naga would make a desperate fight for life when discovered seemed almost certain; but the scene which actually followed took McFee entirely by surprise. Pushing open a heavy teak door at the end of one of the passages, he found the slave-dealer standing in the center of a room which, unlike the others he had visited, was richly furnished and lighted by hanging lamps. He made not the slightest movement until McFee had covered him with a ready revolver and ordered him to put his hands up. Then he merely lifted his shoulders a fraction of an inch and smiled.

"I expected your coming, Englishman," he said indifferently, as he pointed to two ivory-handled Colts and a long curved sword lying on the table beside him. "There are my weapons. I am your prisoner. But first I demand to know the crimes with which I am accused."

"They are many, Ishak-El-Naga," said McFee sternly; and for the next five minutes he recited a catalogue which sickened him merely to repeat.

At the conclusion the Arab gave an elaborate yawn. "What have I to do with these crimes?" he asked wearily. "By your own showing they were committed by an unknown person who goes by the name of 'The White Vampire.'"

Lieutenant McFee pointed an accusing finger at his prisoner.

"The White Vampire was—*yourself*!" he cried.

Ishak-El-Naga threw back his head and uttered a scornful laugh.

"Prove that to the judges at Lokoja!" he sneered. "Tell them thy fable of a veiled spirit who enslaved thousands by the mere terror of her name. Bah! The English require proof—not empty words! They will laugh thy accusation to scorn!" he drew himself up with an air of defiance. "Take me to Lokoja. I am ready to face my trial."

For a full minute Lieutenant McFee stared at the man in silence. For the wily Arab spoke no more than the truth. There was not a shred of actual proof against him. If he accused him, the case would assuredly fail. And yet—was this monster to escape scot-free? The vision of Inyoni's death-agony rose before the eyes of the lieutenant and his features set in an expression which caused the watchful Ishak to quail.

"Thou art mistaken, O Hadj," he said in a voice of terrible calm. "Thy judges are not at Lokoja. They are here."

"Here?" gasped the Arab. "Who are they?"

"Thy victims!" was the answer. "Thou shalt be delivered into the hands of thy slaves, that they may do with thee what they will."

Ishak recoiled a pace and his face appeared suddenly gray.

"But they will torture me!—I shall die by inches!" he almost screamed. "You—you dare not do this thing. Mercy, *Effendi!* Have mercy." He threw himself on the ground in his terror and strove to embrace McFee's dusty riding boots. "If die I must, at least let me die while I still resemble a man!"

Lieutenant McFee crossed to the table, took up one of the revolvers and threw open the breech. Eight little brass cylinders were ejected by the self-acting mechanism. Seven of these he placed in his pocket. The other one he slipped back into the firing-chamber, closed the breech, and laid the weapon on the table.

"There's one round left," he said significantly.

Ishak-El-Naga bowed his head as a sign that he understood, and his hand closed eagerly over the ivory butt.

"I bear witness that there is no God but Allah," he cried. "And Mohammed is the Prophet of God!"

Lieutenant McFee raised his hand to the brim of his topee in grave salute.

"I knew you'd take it sensibly," he said in Arabic. "Thou hast my permission to depart."

As he closed the door behind him there came from within the sound of a muffled shot. Ishak-El-Naga was dead.

A sudden fear clutched at the young man's heart. The adoration that Pete gave to Inez was not merely the affection of beast for mistress; for Pete was no longer a beast.

The
WHITE Wizard

by Sophie Wenzel Ellis

It's not in Oz but there is a Wizard, a dog, and a lot of tin hat tricks . . .
first appeared in September 1929, in Weird Tales. Scarier than the
following month's (October 1929) market crash and much shorter.

"Over there, across the river, where you see that tower shooting up high above the trees, lives a man of mystery," said Phil West, a slim, dark khaki-clad young man. "The natives call him the White Wizard."

Tom Bannon, rotund and heavy-faced and as youthful as his companion, reined in his horse and looked across the San Juan river toward a break in a typical Brazilian jungle scene.

"Who is he—a white man?" he asked.

"Yes, a Spaniard—Don Julian Mendoza." Phil West's fine, dark eyes snapped with interest. "He's a scientist from Madrid, who settled in this wild section of Brazil years ago, some say to conduct a secret experiment. I was told that the half-breeds won't come within ten miles of his house, because they fear he will seize them and turn them into monkeys."

Tom Bannon's explosive laugh made his big body shake. "You and your South American myths touch my funny-bone! I've knocked about with you among the Inca ruins and the Amazon jungle for six months, and not yet have you shown me a genuine mystery."

A sheepish grin spread over Phil's dark, good-looking face.

"I'll admit that the haunted shrine at Castillo was a fake; and that the River of Blood was colored with the juice from those weird red water flowers; but the White Wizard is really a man of mystery, Tom, or there would not be so much talk about him."

Tom glanced hurriedly at the banking clouds in the sky.

"There's a storm due soon," he said, in the deep voice that matched his huge frame. "It will give us an excuse to get acquainted with your White Wizard, for even he would not be heartless enough to turn us out to the mercies of a tropical storm."

"Then let's swim the horses across before it is too late."

Already the wind was lashing the narrow river into dirty cream waves. Hidden creatures scurried through the tangled denseness of the jungle. Birds screamed their warnings in the smothered trees overhead.

The two young men urged their horses into the turbulent water, and in a few minutes were inching their way over the woven underbrush on the other side. They found a dim path which ribboned through the dense growth. It led them up a steep hill to an amazingly large house on the crest, built in the rococo splendor of old Spain; a rambling, thick-walled structure that thrust insolent shoulders to the very edge of the black *selva* which swallowed it on every side.

A puzzled look crossed Tom's plump face. "Appears interesting, all right. Suppose he'll turn us into monkeys if we ask for shelter until the storm lets up?"

"I hope he does," grinned Phil.

They dismounted at the foot of a long flight of stairs which leaped up the hill to the tall gate. Before they had finished tying their horses, a small stone whizzed through the air and struck Phil smartly on the arm.

"Look out! Here comes another!" shouted Tom.

Phil ducked his head just as a larger stone cut the air close by him.

"Someone under the steps did that," declared Tom. "It was a Negro; I saw his black hand."

A peal of coarse laughter came from the direction of the steps—laughter that had a disturbing abandon in it. The two men eyed each other indignantly. Phil whipped out his automatic and stooped to peer through an opening left by the stones which had fallen away at the side.

"What in thunder!" he bawled, and stepped closer to the opening. "Come here, Tom!"

Tom hastened to look over his friend's shoulder, and in the half-lighted recess under the steps he saw a dark, bulky shape. His first thought was that it was a hideously deformed Negro; but he soon perceived the hair that covered the body, and the powerful arms that reached almost to the long-fingered feet. The creature was a huge anthropoid ape.

"Tom, did you hear it?" vociferated Phil. "It spoke to me when I first looked at it!"

"Spoke to you?" Tom eyed him oddly.

"I'm not kidding you; it said just as plainly as I'm speaking to you now, 'Good morning, master,'"

"Phil, you're crazy!" Tom announced amiably. "Those wild tales about Mendoza have gone to your brain."

Phil flushed. "You'll find out before long whether or not I'm crazy, or merely more discerning than you," he retorted.

Tom laughed good-naturedly at his choleric friend, and followed him up the steps. The gate wheezed open on rusty, unused hinges. A hound bayed dismally.

About five acres of the hilltop was enclosed in a high, wrought-iron fence, through which the dauntless jungle had sprawled into the shrubs and neglected lawns.

Their knocking at the great, oaken door rolled through spacious halls within.

2.

The door opened, and a tall, pale-faced man confronted them. He regarded them intently with eyes that were large and dark and strangely impressive, like the brooding eyes of an old master's painting.

"You wish shelter from the storm, *señors?*" he addressed them in excellent English, flavored with a slight accent.

Phil laughed a little nervously. "You are a good guesser, sir," he declared boyishly. "We can pay well for supper and lodging for the night."

"I charge nothing for my hospitality, *señor.*" He fingered his black, military beard. "I welcome you as guests, not as lodgers."

"But we hate to intrude," demurred Tom.

"Julian Mendoza deems it an honor to entertain you.

Phil's brown, sinewy hand went out impulsively toward the pale, aristocratic hand which was offered.

"You are most generous," he said warmly. "West is my name. My friend here is Mr. Bannon. We are both from New York, and have been knocking about South America for the past six months, studying the Inca ruins, mostly."

"I'm something of an archeologist myself," returned Mendoza. "Our tastes are similar, and we shall pass a charming evening, I am sure."

Through the tiled hall he ushered them into a large room, magnificently furnished. The walls and ceilings were richly frescoed. Ornate hanging lamps shed warm, colored light over the hand-carved furniture. Beyond the stained glass windows the lightning could be seen tearing across the sky in fiery streaks.

"It is a pleasure to me to have guests," said Mendoza. "I so seldom see anyone besides my one servant and my niece."

As he spoke, the curtains hanging before a door parted and a girl entered. For a moment she stood there, with one arm holding back the rich folds of the tapestry, and the other fingering the lace of her white dress. Her soft, light hair, worn somewhat longer than the fashionable bob, flowed in shining waves and ringlets about her exquisitely molded neck. A band of pale blue velvet marked the fine lines of her head and made her large brown eyes very dark. She was not more than five feet tall, and her form, through rounded in womanly proportions, was slight and frail. When she saw the two young men, a vivid blush spread over her soft cheeks and throat, and she turned to flee.

"Wait, Inez," called Mendoza. "I want to present my young friends to you."

She acknowledged the introduction with a graceful bow and a shy, dimpled smile. After passing a few commonplace remarks, she excused herself on the plea that she wished to see that dinner was properly served. As she left the room, Mendoza's eyes follower her with a proud look, and a paternal smile softened his thin lips.

"Ah, my little Inez!" he murmured. "She is the core of my heart."

"Does Miss Mendoza live here alone with you, Don Julian?" asked Phil.

"Since finishing school in your United States two years ago. Her mother was a New Yorker. Her father died when she was a baby. It is rather lonely here for her, as she sees no one for months at a time. We can cannot even keep servants, except my faithful old Ramon. But I can cannot part with her; she is the one comfort of my life. I am her only living relative, and she has no alternative but to live with me."

"Selfish brute!" Phil ground under his teeth.

"Would you care to freshen yourselves before dining, *señors?*" continued Mendoza.

The young men replied in the affirmative, and Mendoza rang a bell which summoned an ancient half-breed man servant.

"Show the gentlemen into the west bedroom, Ramon," said Mendoza.

The room was luxuriously furnished, with silk-draped walls and a huge, hand-carved ebony bed. In a few minutes they had rid themselves of the grime that covered them and changed to the extra khaki suits which they had with them.

That dinner was one which Tom and Phil never forgot. Warmed with wine, Mendoza's wit sparkled, and his fascinating personality wove a pleasant spell about them. He had a head and face of unusual beauty. His black hair and pointed beard, slightly touched with gray, contrasted pleasingly with his pale skin and finely marked features. His soft, aristocratic voice and elegant manner were not merely the result of culture; they were his heritage from a long ancestral line of Spanish grandees.

When they had finished dining, they retired to Mendoza's study. Soon Inez and Phil withdrew to a sofa before the huge fireplace, while Tom and Mendoza warmed over scientific discussions.

Above the noise of the rain came a timid tapping at the casement. It slid open and in the aperture appeared a huge, hairy form. It was the ape. His little, beady eyes snapped quickly from Phil's face to Tom's. Then he threw back his grotesque head and laughed uproariously. A frown crossed Mendoza's face, and he went to the window and spoke in a low voice to the animal, which turned reluctantly and disappeared from view.

"That brute seems to have almost human intelligence," remarked Tom.

"You have heard of my experiments?" asked Mendoza. A faint smile played upon his lips. "In that ape you are observing the result of the natural process of evolution, assisted, of course, by science. For instance, it possesses the power of speech. I have only forced nature's own issue. She is tardy in her creation, you must confess, and there is a lapse of countless ages between the dumb anthropoid and this!" He touched himself on the breast significantly.

Phil, his dark face eager with interest, left the fire and joined the men.

"Tell me," he asked, "how have you brought about this miracle?"

Mendoza laughed. "What miracle, *señor?* Is there anything miraculous in transplanting a wild flower into a well-ordered hothouse, carefully nourishing and grafting it, until it is transformed into a fragrant, perfect bloom? You do not think that wonderful. Yet an animal is but a wild, uncultivated thing. When nature is his only trainer, he develops as slowly and imperfectly as the wild flower. Bring man's genius to work, however, and in a few years, yes in a few months, you have accomplished more than nature has in her countless ages."

Tom winked slyly at Phil, as though he thought Mendoza was exaggerating.

"Uncle Julian," broke in Inez, "do stop that wise conversation, which no stranger believes, and play for us."

Mendoza's pale face flushed with enthusiasm as he picked up a violin of rare workmanship. He polished the beautiful wood with an affectionate touch; then he placed the instrument in position.

A wild, sobbing note, clear and cold and passionless, trembled from the strings. This was followed by a quick succession of staccato trills that froze the blood of his listeners. Then from under the bow there flowed a rush of music such as they had never before heard—the boom and roar of mighty cataracts, swishing, whirling, rushing; the shrieking of tornadoes on wild, desolate shores; the weird moans and cries of anguished souls; and through it all a sad, wailing minor strain that summoned involuntary tears to the eyes of the listeners.

At last the music melted into a melancholy reverie. Tears rolled unheeded from Mendoza's eyes and fell upon the strings of his violin. The tender strain suddenly broke off, and he finished with a grand finale of ghoulish shrieks which left his audience trembling and breathless. The violin slipped from his hands and his bearded chin sank upon his breast.

A heavy silence hung upon the room for many seconds.

Phil whispered hoarsely: "Don Julian, you could stir the world with playing like that!"

Mendoza raised his tear-stained face. "I had a great master," he said. "Longinotti."

"Longinotti?" said Phil, puzzled. "Not Fabio Longinotti, the famous Italian composer?"

"The same."

"But Fabio Longinotti died thirty-five years ago. You do not look older than forty."

"I am forty-one, to be exact." He turned to Inez, wearily. "Come, my dear; we will retire." With an air of apology, he added: "You gentlemen will please excuse me. Music has a powerful influence on me."

He drew Inez's arm affectionately through his and led her from the room. She paused for a moment in the doorway to bid the young men good-night, and Phil flushed with pleasure when she lifted her slender fingers to her lips and blew him a kiss.

When the echo of their receding footsteps had died away, Tom's plump face broke into a broad grin.

"Old fellow, you've made a hit!" he said. "I've a mind to punch your head off."

Phil ran his fingers nervously through his black, wavy hair. "Tom," he said earnestly, "I'm going to marry that girl."

Tom's face went suddenly grave. "Gosh, I believe you mean it! Better go easy, boy. Don Julian told me that he will never permit her to marry. Notice how he trotted her off to bed when he left? Didn't want her alone with any eligibles. And Don Julian Mendoza is a man that I'd hate to get down on me!"

3.

It was past midnight when they were awakened by the dismal howling of the hound. There was a blood-curdling quality to the animal's weird wail which made them exceedingly uncomfortable. After enduring it for more than ten minutes, Phil said:

"There is some cause for that animal to howl that way. Maybe there's a snake or something after him. Let's dress and investigate. My nerves can't stand this racket another minute."

"He's only moon-struck," said Tom.

"Well, dress, anyway, and let's quiet him. Better take your automatic."

They drew on their clothes and went out through a door in their room which opened on a terrace. The night was beautifully clear, with the freshness that follows a storm, and there was a full moon.

At the back of the house they discovered what once had been a garden, but now the jungle had crept into it, choked out the plants, and wound crushing, destroying tendrils around the sun-dials and sculptures. Here, isolated from all other buildings, was the tower they had first seen, from the tangle of the jungle it vaulted high into the moon-bathed sky. Three stories up there was a lighted window, uncurtained. At the window sat Mendoza. And under the window was the wailing dog, crouching, his eyes spread in terror toward the figure above.

Mendoza was working. His head was covered with a metal cap, connected by wires with something beyond the range of vision from without. His hands were busy in front of him. Even from where they were standing, the young men could see the expression of concentrated thought upon his face.

But as they watched, that pale, studious face underwent an extraordinary change; rage convulsed it, drawing back the thin lips from the teeth, stretching the eyes in a mad glare. He jerked the metal cap from his head and stood with clenched hands, trembling, his head thrown back. For a moment he stood thus, glaring down at the howling dog; then he snatched something that lay close at hand and disappeared from the window. His steps could be heard pounding down the stairs. Soon he dashed out of the tower with a whip. When the frightened dog saw his master rushing toward him, he cringed close to the ground and whined.

Mendoza, cursing in voluble Spanish, raised the lash in his white-knuckled hands and brought it down through the air, with a sickening swish, upon the animal's quivering flanks. Again and again the cruel whip cut bloody gashes in the poor beast's side, and yet the dog made no motion to move. Then Mendoza, screaming like a jungle animal, threw the whip far into the bushes and leaped upon the hound. One slender hand reached into the open mouth and drew out the lolling tongue. The other, wielding a pocket-knife, approached the tongue with unspeakable intent.

Phil leaped forward from where he stood in the shadows and cried: "Enough, Don Julian!"

Instantly Mendoza arose from his seat on the moaning dog's body. As a cat walks, he came forward until only three feet separated him and Phil. The moon made points of light in his huge black eyes—light that drew Phil's gaze and held it. For many seconds they stood thus, with eyes on each other. At last, when Mendoza laughed and looked away, Phil felt the blood tingle through his body as though he had stepped from a freezing atmosphere into the warm sunlight.

"Fool!" muttered Mendoza. "You play with the devil!" He laughed again, unpleasantly, and went toward his tower.

When his back was turned, the half-dead hound got up weakly and staggered off into the bushes.

"What is he, god or demon?" mumbled Phil.

In silence they made their way to their room. For many minutes they lay awake, without speaking.

"Tom," said Phil, "I'm sure that Don Julian has some sort of hypnotic power. Did you not notice that the hound remained motionless while he was whipping him? And I'll swear, Tom, that he had me all but petrified when I interfered."

4.

Phil was awake first the next morning. Through the open window he caught the flutter of a white dress. In a moment he was up and reaching for his clothes.

He found Inez sitting on a large rock, at the edge of the ruined garden. Sprawled at her feet was the ape, with his bright little eyes fixed upon her face. There was mute adoration in the animal's gaze—the protective adoration that is given only to a kind master.

Phil shouted a happy greeting, and the ape leaped to his feet with a surly growl.

Inez laughed joyously. "Dear old Pete! He is so afraid that someone will harm me." She patted the animal's hairy hand. "Were it not for him, I wouldn't dare leave the house, for there are snakes and other awful things about." She shuddered.

"He is your faithful watch-dog, isn't he?" said Phil.

"Oh, no! Don't class Pete with a dog. He is the dearest, most faithful, most intelligent—slave. If you only knew—" She bit her lips suddenly as though she were about to say too much.

Phil sat beside her, and Pete, with a reproachful backward glance, went slowly toward the house.

"You find it rather lonely here, don't you?" asked Phil.

"Very. I was educated at your Vassar. Now I never see young people."

A wave of tenderness came over him as he watched the childish little figure beside him. She was so unlike the sophisticated girls with whom he was accustomed to associate. He noticed the slender little hand lying listlessly in her lap; each tiny finger was like a delicate flower, and dimples showed even in her clenched fist.

For more than an hour he sat beside her, enjoying her bright retorts to his sallies. Then a large stone rolled down the steep incline and splashed into the stream. Mendoza was approaching. The Spaniard fixed his dead black eyes upon Phil's face, and the young man colored with uneasiness.

Mendoza took his niece's arm. "Did you not hear the breakfast bell?" he demanded.

"No, Uncle Julian," she replied in her soft voice. "Is it really breakfast time?"

"Time does fly when you are in conversation with a charming young man, doesn't it?" he scolded.

She drew away from him with blazing face and quivering eyes. Then she left them and darted swiftly over the loose stones to the house. Mendoza seemed to have forgotten the young man's presence, for he walked beside him with his head bent in meditation.

When they reached the breakfast room, Phil was startled to see Pete's huge, hairy form huddled in an armchair, poring over a book that rested on his knee. Phil had often seen monkeys on the vaudeville stage appear to read newspapers; but there was a weird earnestness about the way the manlike creature followed the lines with an awkward forefinger, and moved his coarse lips as though he were mumbling the words to himself, child-fashion.

Phil passed behind the ape's chair and glanced over his shoulder. The book in which the animal appeared to be so deeply engrossed was a first-grade English reader. The ape's awkward finger had stopped on one word as a child might do when the spelling or meaning puzzled him.

"Pete is having trouble with his lesson this morning," said Mendoza. "What is it, Pete? Can I help you?"

He leaned over the ape's shoulder, and Pete lifted the book, with his finger still indicating one of the words.

"That is 'gnaw,' Pete," explained Mendoza. "It means to bite with your teeth as mice do."

Pete uttered a grunt of satisfaction, and his finger passed on slowly along the lines. Phil nervously mopped his brow with his handkerchief. The unnatural situation did not seem ludicrous.

"Can that animal actually read?" he ventured to ask.

"Very well. He reads better than he can speak. You see, the vocal organs of the ape are not formed for fluent speech. But Pete does excellently; get him aroused, and he'll talk as well as a three-year-old child."

"And you have hopes of developing this ape to a still higher plane of intelligence?"

"I not only have hopes; I absolutely am convinced that Pete can be educated to a point where he will at least equal the lower state of savage man. I have been working on him for only five years. Pete is now grown—sixteen years old. Had I begun to educate him when he was much younger, his brain would have developed faster. Pete lives like a man now; he has his own little shack, which he keeps fairly clean."

Here Ramon entered with a huge tray loaded with a steaming pot of chocolate, delicately fried wild fowl, and a picturesque dish of tropical fruit. Pete closed his book and stole quietly from the room.

"After our *siesta* today," said Mendoza, "I have a rare experience in store for you gentlemen—an extraordinary adventure. I have decided to reveal to the world who I am, and what I have accomplished. For the first time, I will exhibit my most closely guarded creation, which even Inez has never seen." He leaned back in his chair and paused dramatically. "I will show you, gentlemen, my secret garden, where you may view the wonders of a dozen *Arabian Nights* tales!"

Tom and Phil exchanged surreptitious glances.

"You are too generous," protested Tom. "We'd like to see your garden, of course; but we can't take advantage of your hospitality. We'd better be on our way this morning."

"But you must give me the pleasure of at least a few days of your society, unless I bore you!" Mendoza smiled with rare charm. "Visitors are a luxury to us. Have pity on us, *señors!* I have my heart set on your remaining."

He passed his long, slender fingers through his heavy hair, and his beautiful eyes glowed with even more than their usual brilliancy.

His smooth voice went on pleadingly. "'Twill be such a great happiness for me to disclose the fruits of my labors to you."

"If you put it that way," said Tom, "I guess we've got to accept."

5.

While the others were taking their *siesta* after luncheon, Phil wandered restlessly about. How could he sleep, with his thoughts constantly on a small, sweet face brushed with soft, flying, golden hair!

His undirected footsteps led him to the tangled garden and beyond to the vine-smothered fence in the rear. Here, under a tall tree, he saw a small shack built from twisted twigs and vines. Through the hole that was the door he saw rude furniture—a bed padded with leaves, a chair made from a log, and an old table. He paused for a moment. The rough walls were almost covered with bright pieces of cloth, paper, gold and silver tinsel, leaves crisped and glowing with autumn tints, and many other brilliant odds and ends that made a sort of savage tapestry from floor to ceiling.

Phil smiled at this fantastic attempt at decoration, for he remembered that Mendoza had told him Pete had his own little shack. These colored bits, carefully pinned in place, spoke pathetically of long, lonely hours whiled away by a forlorn creature that was neither jungle beast nor man, but a curious combination of both. Phil hesitated before entering. To him Pete had suddenly acquired a certain grotesque dignity.

A notebook lying upon the table caught his seeking eyes. He crossed the room and picked it up. The pages, thumbed and soiled, were scrawled over in large, limping letters which resembled a child's early attempt at penmanship. A cold shiver passed over Phil. Could the great, awkward fingers of an ape really have formed those uncouth pot-hooks? Mendoza had told him that the ape could write, but this was beyond belief. He laughed weakly at his own wild doubts. The letters must have been made by some little child. Perhaps the notebook had been Inez's.

At last Phil turned to the page where the faltering attempts had been successful in a word that pridefully occupied the entire space:

INEZ

This convinced him that the book belonged to Inez, for a child's first written word is usually its own name. He breathed with relief after he had made this decision, for there was something appalling about an animal possessing intelligence which was so amazingly human.

But on the very next page he was again disturbed with doubt. In a smear of discolored blood that had, perhaps, come from a cut finger, there was the imprint of a great, rude thumb. Sticking to this dried blood that had clotted thickly were several coarse, brown hairs. Even this did not entirely convince Phil that the notebook belonged to the ape, for it is a mischievous habit of his kind to steal and hide the belongings of the master. But as the young man continued to turn the pages, he perceived that the writer was now trying to connect the word Inez into a combination of words; and on the very last page, in a fairly legible manner, a sentence struck Phil's eyes like a blow:

PETE LUVS INEZ

A sudden fear clutched at the young man's heart. The adoration that Pete gave to Inez was not merely the affection of beast for mistress; for Pete was no longer a beast.

"It can't be!" shuddered the young man. "It can't be true that Mendoza has raised this brute to where he has the impulses of a man!"

If Pete was cultured enough to write Inez's name, why should he not be capable of loving her as a man might who had passed beyond savagery and reached the dawn of civilization? Revolting as the thought was to Phil, he knew that there could be dangerous reality in it. He felt a sudden sympathetic regard for Pete. As he once more turned the pages of the notebook, he realized that, although the genius of Mendoza had destroyed the barrier that separates the brute from the man, it was Inez who was raising this strange creature to a realization of human hopes and desires.

Phil was so occupied with the notebook that he did not hear a soft footfall in the room. The first knowledge that he had of another's presence was a short, shrill scream of rage that came from behind his shoulder. Then a dull, heavy blow upon the head brought a red mist before his eyes. With a tired sigh, he crumpled in a heap to the floor.

6.

His return to consciousness was gradual and delightful. A gentle, perfumed wind fanned his face, and far-away music sounded in his ears. He stretched himself luxuriously upon a couch that was as soft as silk down. For several minutes he lay with closed eyes, breathing deeply of the scented wind that bathed his lungs with intoxicating balm. Something soft and warm touched his brow.

"He's coming to, Uncle," spoke a low voice.

He opened his eyes wide and stared about him, half dazed. He was in a garden of strange, dream-like beauty. Gathered about him were Tom, Inez and Mendoza.

Inez flushed suddenly and laid her little hand upon his. "There, sir! How do you feel?"

"Immensely happy!" He grinned up at her. "What happened?"

Tom leaned over him anxiously. "Pete cracked you on the head. It was lucky for you that I was right behind him, or he would have finished you in short order."

Bewildered, Phil felt his head carefully with his fingers. He had no sensation of pain or even discomfort.

"I remember. Something struck my head with terrific force. I guess I went to sleep after that. But why am I here?"

"For repairs, young man," put in Mendoza. "Had we not brought you here, you might never have awakened from your sudden sleep. Your skull was cracked."

Again Phil passed doubtful fingers over his head, which was unbound and apparently uninjured. "If my skull was cracked, it mended miraculously. I have no pain whatever."

To demonstrate, he sat up, and after a moment of hesitation, stood upon his feet and walked about. His nostrils quivered with pleasure as he drew in a great draft of the intoxicating atmosphere, and with every breath he felt that his physical being was becoming more vital, his mentality clearer.

"Who could feel pain here?" said Mendoza. "This is the Garden of Life. The blind, the crippled, the sick, those who suffer in body or mind, can become whole in this atmosphere. The blow that Pete gave you cracked your skull. Had this occurred anywhere else in the world, and had a physician sought to heal you, a cure would have been dragged over weeks of suffering. But age cannot wither, nor accident destroy, that which breathes this atmosphere. It was the atmosphere, sir, and my ten fingers, that mended your fractured skull in one hour."

Phil looked questioningly at Tom. His friend's face was grave, yet his eyes snapped with excitement.

"You were in a bad fix when Pete finished with you, old man," said Tom quietly. "There was a little puddle of blood under your head. See how you splashed your shirt."

Phil saw that his khaki shirt was stained with freshly dried blood.

"When we reached this garden, I thought you were a goner," Tom went on. "But that was about an hour ago. Anything could happen here in an hour—with Don Julian's magic all about you. I've seen the White Wizard in action, Phil."

Phil looked about him, half skeptically. Before his eyes stretched a garden of strange, perfect beauty. Thousands of blossoms of fantastic form and color swung in the scented breeze—great, flamboyant blooms on vine, bush and tree. Fountains jetted from flowery mounds, their crystalline spray catching the wild riot of color that glowed on every hand. Bridges and winding paths beckoned the feet and promised magic beyond the enticing curves. But not alone was the eye enchanted and the olfactory nerves delicately gratified; the vivifying quality in the air soothed yet intensified the senses. A feeling of joyousness settled upon Phil. Youth and life sang through his blood like heady wine.

"What is it, Don Julian?" he whispered breathlessly. "What is the strange quality in the atmosphere?"

A low laugh broke from Mendoza. "You are not in nature's world now; you are in *mine*. Do you see those butterflies flitting around the flowers by that fountain? They are ten years old. The ordinary span of a butterfly's life is but two days in the outer world; in mine it is illimitable. This is the Garden of Eden, sir, created by me. And here there is no forbidden fruit—no serpent." His thin lips parted over his perfect teeth.

Phil looked at Inez, and his head swam as he met her dark eyes. The long lashes dropped until they swept her cheeks. Forgetful of Mendoza and Tom, they wandered off, hand in hand, along the perfumed paths.

As in a dream, they strolled about, silent, overwhelmed by the beauty that surrounded them and the intoxication in their blood. Birds of brilliant plumage warbled in the blossom-laden trees, fairly reeling in the ecstatic joy of existence. Each moment the pair's enchanted eyes were delighted with some strange and beautiful bloom that exhaled voluptuous fragrance. By this time, the atmosphere had woven a spell of sorcery about them. Now and again their eyes met, lingered, and melted with the intoxication of the glance.

At last Inez spoke. "Are we dreaming, Phil? It is strange that I never discovered this garden. See, there is the house plainly visible. Beyond it is the jungle, dipping to the river."

When Phil heard her speak his given name, for the first time, he turned eagerly to her, jerking his head around suddenly. As he did so, his brow struck a hard obstruction, and he fell back, half stunned by the blow. Nearly blind with pain, he looked about him, puzzled. There was neither wall nor rock nor sculpture near, yet the blow had had no impetus behind it—the thing which had struck him was stationary. Again he took a step forward, and again stumbled back with a bruised brow.

"Oh, what is it?" cried Inez, gazing in horror at a thin stream of blood which trickled down his forehead.

Phil threw his hands before him. Two feet from his face they came in contact with a hard, rough surface. He stared at Inez, blankly. Her face had gone dead white.

"Am I insane?" he asked. "Or is there an unseen barrier in front of us? Feel before you, Inez—carefully."

She put out her small hand and touched something—something invisible in the air!

7.

Inez's lips trembled as she stifled a sob of fright.

"Take me away!" she pleaded, crowding against Phil's arm.

Suddenly, as though the light of the sun were eclipsed, an impenetrable darkness fell upon the garden; then, as suddenly as it had come, the darkness vanished, and a brilliant golden light streamed around. They stared about them, bewildered. The garden, in all its marvelous beauty, lay bathed in the golden light, but the outer world had disappeared. Gone was the house, the snarled jungle beyond the garden; gone as completely as a melted snowflake. Opaque walls of rock encompassed them and shut off the blue sky and the landscape. Mendoza came forward and stood before them with a cynical smile upon his fine lips.

"Uncle! What is it?" moaned Inez.

With a laugh, Mendoza threw back his head. A gentle wind blew the long, soft hair from his broad temples, and the strange light that filled the garden brought out all the delicate, intellectual lines of his face.

"Consider me Aladdin," he said, "and this my magic lamp."

He buried his hand in a thick clump of shrubbery. Instantly the stone walls disappeared, and the river, with its surrounding scenery, and the great bulk of the house came into view. Tom lifted his round, ashen face to Mendoza and gulped hard.

"Ah, you are curious," teased the Spaniard. "You would even fear, if you were not in my world, where fear and distress are aliens. But I will satisfy the agonies of your suspense, and you will laugh at the simplicity of it all."

He paused, as a cat plays with its prey; then continued in his sonorous voice:

"I have discovered a new light ray which renders the opaque absolutely invisible."

"But—" protested Phil.

Mendoza stayed his speech with an impatient wave of the hand. "Hear me out! This garden is built in the bowels of the hill. It is entirely cut off from the outer world by a surrounding wall of rock. The only outlet is the hidden trap-door in the tower, through which Inez and Mr. Bannon will recollect that we passed. The atmosphere and the light I have myself created; no matter how. By concentrating my nil-ray, as I call it, upon the walls, they are rendered as transparent as thin glass. In fact, any solid body can be made invisible when exposed to this ray."

Again it seemed to the fevered fancies of his beholders that the light gathered around him, and that his eyes—his dark, magnetic eyes—were the center of everything.

"The invisible man is no longer a fable," he went on. Think what it will mean to me—or to anyone who possesses my secret—to be able to move among my fellow men and not be seen. Permit me to illustrate."

He took a few steps to one side and suddenly vanished from view. After a moment of surprise, Phil laughed lightly.

"I've seen disappearing stunts pulled off in a ten-cent side-show," he chuckled.

A smart blow on the mouth checked him. Anger flared up in his eyes, and he whirled on his heel with clinched fists. There was no one near him. Close to his ear sounded Mendoza's characteristic laugh, and the echoes of that mocking laugh tinkled musically through the garden and blended with the dripping of the fountains and the stirring of the leaves. Even the birds and the insects sounded as though they were caught up the ringing cadences, for a sudden flurry and twittering came from every hand.

As unexpectedly as he had vanished, Mendoza appeared before them gradually. First a hand, disembodied; then an arm, and then his entire body materialized slowly and weirdly from the air. A smile of amusement was on his thin lips. He stood with folded arms crossed over his violin.

Without speaking, he raised the violin to his chin and drew the bow across the strings. Ripples of low, magnetic sounds soared from the instrument. Every shrub and tree in the garden stirred, and a multifarious flock of birds flew into the air. They settled about Mendoza, some on his very body, others on the brink of the fountain by which he was standing and others in the surrounding shrubbery. For a few moments there was a medley of fussing and scolding. Soon, hushed by the magic sounds of the music, they squatted quietly, with cocked, listening heads.

The low sobs of the violin, the strange beauty of the garden, the exhilarating atmosphere, and the sweet exalted expression on Inez's face charged Phil's blood with madness. Almost involuntarily, he sought the tiny hand of the girl and drew her close to him. His arm went around her unresisting body, and, oblivious of the others, he pressed her close.

A harsh, twanging crash sent them trembling apart. Mendoza stood before them, eyes ablaze. His clenched hand held the violin, with the broken strings dangling from it. His thin lips quivered with his panting breath. Shrieking a terrible Spanish oath, he raised the violin on high, as though to strike the young man with it.

The magnetism of his eyes held Phil paralyzed. He tried to move, but stood as motionless as a slab of marble. He tried to speak, but no sound issued from his livid lips. His blood oozed in icy streams through his body, and his mind refused to work. After what seemed many minutes to the young man, Mendoza lowered the violin. His distorted features regained their usual calm expression, and he held out his hand impulsively.

"It is the music, *señor*. It affects me so strangely. Forgive me!" His voice was pleading, almost humble.

Phil took the hand that he offered. "The half-breeds call you the White Wizard, Don Julian—and with good reason. You are a genius—a dozen geniuses rolled into one! You are a musician, a naturalist who understands biology as probably no one has ever done before. You are a scientist, a psychologist. Heavens, man! What else are you? Why don't you leave this God-forsaken spot and benefit humanity with your genius?"

A look of pain swept Mendoza's handsome face. For a moment he stood silent and pale, staring with unseeing eyes at the splendid flowers and trees that had bloomed into unearthly perfection under his hands. Then he laughed a harsh, bitter laugh.

"The world can do without me very well," he muttered.

He turned from them and walked slowly down one of the winding paths. Phil followed him and touched him lightly upon the back.

"And Pete—what have you done to Pete?" he demanded. "He is an animal with a man's brain and heart. I believe you have even given him a soul."

A smile slashed the White Wizard's lips.

"Pete is the crown of my endeavors," he said proudly. "Pete is what has made me master of beast as well as of man."

"Pete is the loneliest creature in the world," broke in Phil. "He is neither man nor beast. His instincts crave the jungles, but his high mentality craves companionship with men. I think, Don Julian, that Pete is a very dangerous combination."

"We are all dangerous combinations, my friend. The most highly civilized man has something of the jungle beast in his heart. Remember, not so long ago, we, too, lived in the jungle."

"But Pete is no longer in the jungle. You have taken him from his native haunts and given him the hopes and desires of a man. He has risen above the instincts of the ape. He reaches out, blindly, perhaps, for the same things that a man wants."

Mendoza's face flushed, and he threw out his arms in an impulsive gesture.

"And why should Pete not have a man's hopes and aspirations? As he develops, it is natural for him to have desires which he never experienced before. In a few years, I trust, Pete will be a useful citizen."

Disgust went over Phil. "Do you know that Pete has begun to love Miss Mendoza?"

"You discovered his diary?" Mendoza's smile was amused. "That is why he tried to kill you. Yes, I know that he worships Inez. It is what I wish. Love between the sexes—the love that is beyond mere desire—exists only where culture has drowned brute instinct. Even the races of men that have not reached the more advanced stages of culture know scarcely anything of love. Loving Inez will raise Pete to a higher plane of mentality."

Phil met his eyes, so strangely brilliant and black, lit by a light that threw its influence over him like a cloak.

"Good heavens!" he shuddered. "I believe you would do anything for the sake of science. You would even put the happiness of your niece at stake."

"Anything for the sake of knowledge," declared the other. "Knowledge is what raises man from the beast, and superman from the human. The more knowledge one has, the more he can accomplish. Why has the world progressed so marvelously during the past fifty years? It is because we have had all the knowledge of our forefathers to help us obtain new knowledge. If life were longer, if we were not cut down just when our minds have become filled with enough learning to accomplish something worthy, we should truly be supermen. Do you know what one man would be if he were a master of science, medicine, engineering, geology, painting, music, and, in fact, a hundred different realms of endeavor, one of which ordinarily would require a lifetime of close application to master?" he paused, smiled brilliantly, and then went on: "He would be a White Wizard."

8.

Inez did not appear at dinner that night; and when Phil remarked upon her absence, Mendoza explained that she had a headache. Phil was disappointed, for he had been anticipating an evening with her.

He did not join Tom and Mendoza in the study, where they were having their smoke. The cool night air tempted him, and he went out to wander in the open. He recollected with a thrill of pleasure his meeting with Inez that morning and was drawn toward the spot where he had found her. As he approached, a low sob from the direction of the stone assured him that he was not the only one who remembered that pleasant hour at the beginning of the day. In a moment he was beside her little huddled form. She was crying, softly.

Gently he took her hands from her face. "What is the matter?" he asked her.

She tried to draw away, but he held her tight. Her shining hair framed her face like a halo, and her delicate features were ethereal in the soft moonlight. After trying in vain to loosen his hold, she turned upon him and whispered brokenly:

"Phil—Mr. West, for my sake—for your own sake, go away from here tomorrow. It will mean nothing but sorrow and regret to both of us if you stay longer."

"Why should I go?" he demanded. "What is there to fear?"

"My uncle," she murmured.

The wind fluttered the silk scarf that she wore against his face, and his blood leaped madly. His arms closed about her drooping form and he crushed her close. For a moment he buried his hot face in her fragrant, silky hair. Blindly he found her lips and kissed her, long and deep, until her slight body shivered. It was many minutes before he found voice to say huskily:

"Can you get ready tomorrow to go back to New York with me?"

Like a startled wild thing, she drew away from him. "Oh, what have you done?" she moaned. "Leave me! Go! Leave this place tonight—now!"

He held her off and stared at her in amazement. "You love me—don't you?" he faltered. "Then why shouldn't you wish to be my wife? I know that I'm not worthy of you; but am I not a better companion than your grim uncle?"

Her face paled. "I do love you," she replied simply. "I love you very dearly; and I shall be unhappy when you leave me. But you must go."

"Why?"

"You do not know my uncle. He will kill you. He suspects that we love each other." She hid her face against his arm. "And I've known you but two days."

With a low laugh, he again gathered her toward him. "What a foolish little girl you are," he soothed, stroking her hair. "Don Julian will be glad to have a millionaire for a nephew-in-law. Have we known each other but two days?" He tilted her face until he could look into her averted eyes. "It just proves that we are made for each other."

A sudden chill crept over him. He no longer tried to restrain her, and she slipped from his loosened arms and darted up the hill to the house. He wanted to follow, but his feet remained fixed to the ground. A blind, nameless fear enslaved every faculty, and the manhood froze within him. He tried to move, and could not; he strained his throat to scream or speak, but he was dumb.

His struggles to free himself from the strange inertia were suddenly and almost violently successful, for he nearly fell face forward on the ground. For no special reason, his feet jerked his body toward the tower. Some instinct seemed trying to convey to him the knowledge that a dangerous and destructive power lay at the point to which his body was moving. He fought against the compelling influence until he gasped for breath.

A growing weakness and weariness seized him, and he would have sunk in exhaustion to the ground, but for the strange force which held him submissive. He reached the door which led into the tower, found it unlocked, and his hand mechanically swung it open.

Step by step his enslaved feet mounted the spiral stairs. His face smarted with fever, and his eyes stared wildly before and above him. He reached the top landing of the stairs and paused for a moment, with every shred of his will-power pitted against the malign power that was plunging him onward. But, step by step, his feet, like lumps of lead, moved forward, and his hand encircled the door knob.

The door opened and he met the eyes of Mendoza—the great, dead black eyes that seemed to bore into his very heart. Here was the magnet which had attracted him. Body and soul and mind were enthralled by that fascinating gaze. He was choking, drowned in those inky, smothering eyes.

Mendoza was seated before a table. On his head was the bright metal cap that Phil had seen him wear on the previous night.

"I summoned you to come to me," he announced.

An icy shiver trembled over Phil. Helplessly his eyes whisked about the disordered laboratory. In a corner crouched Pete, closely watching Mendoza. That sight of the man-like animal was a relief to Phil, for he felt that he was not entirely alone with the White Wizard.

"*Señor* West," said Mendoza crisply, "I have a few questions to propound. Tell me, how do we convey our thoughts to one another?"

"Er—by speaking—or writing—and sometimes by signs," hesitated Phil, speaking like a frightened schoolboy.

"Are they the only ways?"

"Yes."

"They are not. They are indeed the primitive methods. Man is still primeval in this respect. In the early ages man and beast alike had only their voices by which they could convey their feelings and desires. Then man rose a little higher than the beast; he learned to speak, and then to write, which is but a silent form of speech. He has been speaking and writing for thousands of years, and has never discovered a better way."

He paused in dramatic silence. The faint ticking of Phil's watch could be heard. Then again came the rich, mellow tones which burned into the young man's brain and caused his heart to quicken.

"It is known that a brain never loses an idea that it once conceives. The thought may sink into the sub-conscious mind and never be recalled, but it has graven its image upon the brain. Then why can we not discover some method to recover these buried treasures?"

He walked up and down the room excitedly, with flushed cheeks and clenched fists. Then he stood still and swept his hand toward a shelf filled with labeled glass jars, each one containing a human brain immersed in a preservative.

"There rests knowledge, genius of the highest type, *señor!*" he cried exultingly. "*It is mine!* I am the most learned man that ever lived. I have the key to every art and science in the world. The minds of the powerful and the wise are at my command."

He reached up for one of the glass jars and turned the label toward Phil.

"Fabio Longinotti, violinist; died 1893."

"This brain," continued Mendoza, "dead thirty-five years, gave me my knowledge of the violin."

Aghast, Phil let his horrified eyes crawl over the shelf. Here was the name of a great inventor; there a famous naturalist; there a noted French general who had died in the World War. All down the grim line he recognized names—names of men and women who had died recently; of others who had died a generation ago.

"In a few hours," came Mendoza's voice, "I can assimilate knowledge which required a whole lifetime to collect."

Pete stood up and came toward him. "Master!" fell from his coarse lips in a husky voice.

Mendoza put his hand on the ape's shoulder. "Pete also has learned from them," he said, pointing to the ghastly row on the shelf.

His sensitive fingers stroked his beard as he went on thoughtfully. "When we examine a brain, no matter if it is human or animal, we find that the cortex bears a visible record of the sensations and thoughts. Science has determined a few of the cortical centers, and various functions of consciousness have been localized fairly exactly. For example, the visual center of your brain is in the same area as the visual center of mine. If we had some means by which we could transfer the records of these various thought and sense centers, we could learn in a short time from the brain of a genius that which required years to wrest from the musty books of scholars, or from life and experience. In one week, from the brain of Longinotti, I acquired what a lifetime had put into its convolutions."

Phil stepped forward, forgetting his uneasiness. "Could anyone have gained immediate knowledge of music from the brain of Longinotti?

"Yes. Now listen." He shuddered slightly. "In those labeled jars are the brains of great thinkers—and of others. I have made their thought-records mine. Understand what this means. Each individual is limited in his thinking and accomplishments. One can be a great writer, or an artist, or a philosopher, or a successful business man; but he cannot be all these unless he lives several hundred years. The natural acquisition of knowledge is slow. But when one man has the brains of a dozen geniuses to draw from, he is a power—a superman!"

He raised his head with conscious dignity, and it seemed to Phil that his presence filled the room and crowded against him, until he breathed with difficulty.

The ape, with veneration in his small eyes, crept to Mendoza's feet and threw his great, hairy arms around them.

"Master!" he muttered.

Mendoza stooped and placed his hands upon the animal's head. "Ah, Pete, you and your master have both progressed!" His hands went to the metal cap on his head. "And now *Señor* West will learn something he did not know before."

He removed the cap and placed it upon Phil's head. Then he selected one of the glass jars on the shelf and connected it, by means of wires, with the metal cap.

"This," he explained, "is the brain of Psamaeris, who lived during the reign of Rameses III. His mummy lay entombed with the dust of three thousand years thick upon it, when I was fortunate enough to discover it; very fortunate, indeed, for only in rare instances were the brains left in a mummy by the embalmers. In ten minutes you shall learn more than archeologists can learn in years of assiduous study.

"Now, listen carefully. For self-protection, you must control what you learn from Psamaeris. If you do not *will* your thoughts into a safe thought-center of this brain, you may experience certain horrors in the Egyptian's life that you'll regret, for his brain and yours become as one when I press the button. Think now of a battle scene on the desert, with the Sphinx and the pyramids in the background. You will connect your brain with a similar thought-center in the brain of Psamaeris. Think!"

Immediately Phil's brain became abnormally active. He closed his eyes and dreamed. He was on a desert, surrounded by sad-eyed men in flowing robes, who spoke a language which was new yet familiar to him. The bearded men were shouting in battle. His dry lips opened, and he gave commands in the language of those around him. He roared at his followers, cursed and encouraged them, until a vast cry of victory thundered about. Then the sad-eyed swarthy men gathered around and praised the name of Psamaeris, their mighty leader.

After a wild dash over the hot plain, he was seated in a white marble palace in Thebes. Before him lay the *Book of the Dead*. With a reed pen he wrote in it; and, as he wrote, the mystic signs seemed to fall from his stiff fingers like burning coals, and he felt the awful presence of Osiris himself. He filled many pages with the strange hieroglyphics, praising the wisdom and power of Rameses III.

The scene faded like the awakening from a dream, and Phil found himself sitting before Mendoza, who held the metal cap.

Phil brushed his hand over his eyes, and tried to summon a weak laugh. "What did you do—hypnotize me?" he inquired.

Mendoza's eyes flashed. "I demonstrated to you once before that I do not appreciate facetiousness," he said curtly. "Your brain, through the medium of thought-radio, has reproduced the thoughts of Psamaeris. Had I permitted the connection to continue uncontrolled, you would have experienced many of Psamaeris' joys and sorrows; you would even have gone through the agonies of his death when an enemy gave him a poisoned drink. In thought, I died with

Psamaeris, as I died with the others. But come; understand. I will permit you to commune with—the White Wizard."

He fastened the contrivance again to Phil's head, and placed a similar one on his own head, both of them being connected by wires.

As he went toward the curtain to press a hidden button, a wave of repugnance swept over the young man. Through the open window he could see the sky banked with great clouds, cleft through by the cold, white rays of the moon. He shuddered nervously.

A thunderous roar began to pound against his ear drums. Through a blue mist he saw Mendoza take the chair in front of him. His brain was in a turmoil; it was bursting. From his nose and mouth flowed a great rush of blood, and he fell back senseless. When he regained consciousness, he looked into the pale face of Mendoza as the Spaniard bent over him.

"Ah," sighed Mendoza. "I should have known that none could climb to the heights of my mentality. You are yet too weak to read what is in my brain. Still I would glean what you know. I may learn something, and I never scorn a grain of knowledge. But I will protect you from myself."

He took the cap from Phil's head and replaced it with another. Then he once more went behind the curtain, pressed the button, and sat in the chair in front of Phil.

An itching, pulling sensation throbbed through Phil's head. Then came Mendoza's voice, in dreamy, broken sentences, relating many of the most intimate happenings of his life. More than once, the young man squirmed in his chair as Mendoza drew forth some cherished secret.

Suddenly Mendoza sat up straighter, and an expression of rage so distorted his face that Phil instinctively drew away. With a demoniacal shriek of passion, Mendoza tore the cap from his head and leaped to his feet. His face was bestial in its ferocity as he stood before the young man.

"Thief!" he screamed. "Like a thief you have stolen my Inez from me. Then die, thief!"

Snorting and quivering with passion, he raised his fist and dashed forward. Phil stumbled backward and threw out his arm to guard his face. Instantly he realized that he had no ordinary foe to confront. Mendoza was temporarily a maniac in his wrath and strength. He crouched as a tiger before its kill. His lips curled back beast-like from the teeth, and slaver rolled from his mouth.

Phil glanced swiftly around for something with which to defend himself, and his eyes fell upon Pete. A change had come over the ape. He was looking at Mendoza, but the look of subjugation was gone from his face, and in its place was the jungle beast's hatred for a cruel master off his guard. Phil took instant advantage of this.

"Pete!" he called softly—appealingly.

Pete sprang from his corner, brushing Phil aside with his great, hairy body, and faced his master with exposed fangs. Master and beast stood regarding each other in primitive malice.

Mendoza waved his fist threateningly. "Out of the way!" he commanded, trying to push the ape aside.

Pete did not move.

"Ungrateful brute!" shouted Mendoza. "Is this how you repay me for lifting you on a level with man?"

With a mighty blow he brought his fist down upon the ape's skull, and the animal's powerful form crashed in a heap to the floor. For a moment, Mendoza stood as one dazed. He passed his hand over his forehead and looked around. Sinking upon his knees, he lifted Pete's head. A groan rumbled from the animal, and he whispered:

"Master—my master!"

The effort brought a crimson flow of blood from his lips, and he fell back lifeless.

In an agony of remorse, Mendoza hovered over the body.

"Speak to me, Pete, you the noblest triumph of my genius. Speak!" he sobbed, shaking the body. "He is dead!" he muttered, rising to his feet.

Like a drunkard, he reeled to the window and gazed out at the speckled sky. Then he fell upon his knees, dropping his head to the low window-sill. A paroxysm of weeping shook his frame. He cried with all the passion and abandon of his race. Phil could have left the tower had he wished, but the strange events of the past hour stirred in him a desire to see what might happen next.

9.

Without noticing Phil, Mendoza turned from the window after his frenzied weeping was spent and went to his desk. From a locked drawer he took two small, exquisitely painted miniatures. His hand trembled as he fingered them. Phil could plainly see the faces from where he sat. One was Mendoza's own portrait, painted in the first flush of manhood. The beardless face and frank, happy eyes were alive with the vivid impulses of a youth full of fire and intelligence. The other portrait was that of a beautiful girl.

Mendoza looked from one picture to the other, his pallid lips drawn in a thin, pained line. He put them down suddenly, as though he could not bear looking at them. For several minutes he sat with his head bent in thought.

A sudden resolve seemed to possess him, for he reached for a diary and began writing in it. Phil felt awkward, as though he were viewing a scene too private for a witness.

All traces of the recent evil passions had left Mendoza's white face; again he was the proud aristocrat. At intervals he stopped writing and gazed with evident horror upon the blood-spattered body of the ape.

When he had finished writing, he left the diary lying open, and once more picked up the woman's portrait. He whispered soft Spanish words over it, crushed it roughly to his lips.

Still holding the miniature, he went over to the curtain in the corner of the room and threw it aside. A tiny machine of delicate workmanship was disclosed. In a network of fine wires revolved a small glass bulb, filled with a liquid that constantly quivered and sent out tiny shafts of white light.

Mendoza passed his hand with a gentle, loving touch over the bulb. Suddenly his fingers closed over it sharply, until the delicate glass cracked into fragments. The heavy, trembling liquid ran over his hand, eating into the flesh like acid. Mendoza surveyed the ruin he had wrought and laughed shortly.

"The inglorious end of the White Wizard's genius," he said.

Phil uttered a cry of protest, but Mendoza refused to acknowledge his presence. His right hand still clasped the broken fragments of glass. The shimmering liquid had eaten holes and ruts in the flesh; some of it still boiled and trembled in the livid depressions. But Mendoza gave no symptoms of pain, or even discomfort. He walked leisurely toward his desk and fumbled about one of the drawers.

A sudden, sharp report resounded in the room. Mendoza fell in a heap to the floor.

Instantly Phil was beside him. A tiny stream of blood flowed from the massive forehead, and the revolver still smoked in the mutilated right hand. He never moved after he fell.

When Phil had recovered from the horror of it, his first thought was the dead man's diary. Mendoza's last actions were all clear to him now.

Trembling with excitement and dread of the possible revelations, he went to the desk and read the last insertion in the diary:

I, Julian Mendoza, am about to end my life, realizing at this moment that it has been wasted in perfecting a discovery which would prove a curse to the human race; and before I take the step that will destroy me, I earnestly desire to make my confession to the world, and to ask forgiveness of those whom I have injured.

After years of study and labor I have perfected an instrument that makes possible the practicable use of thought-radio—that marvelous force of which science knows but little.

I have robbed the graves of great thinkers directly after they were buried, to obtain their brains. I have robbed museums, laboratories, hospitals, to obtain the preserved brains of many notables who have died in the past.

And I have made the education, talents, and life experiences recorded in these brains my own.

I have pillaged the minds not only of superior human beings, but also of criminals and animals. I have had connection with the brain of a man-eating tiger that was killed in a Burmese hut; with a headhunter of Patagonia; with a murderer who was hanged. My nature has some of the most fiendish passions of the fiercest beasts; of the vile, crawling things of the earth; and of men who have sinned grossly.

If I should go into the world with my mighty brain and my mysterious power, I could make it either a heaven or a hell. But I am a duel character that is a menace to civilization.

By the time this is read, the garden in the hill will be no more; for, with a shift of a lever, I have cut off the atmosphere which I created, and immediately everything in the garden passed into complete dissolution. Search and you will find a cave of dust.

When Phil finished reading, there was a mist in his eyes. He went to the dead body of the White Wizard and reverently arranged the limbs. A soft smile parted the pallid lips, giving the still face a singular expression of peace.

"He was not all brute," said Phil gently.

He covered the face with a clean handkerchief, and went to find Tom.

10.

Phil and Inez lolled back in their steamer chairs, watching the late afternoon sun flashing on the blue waves of the Atlantic. Inez was entrancing in a white serge suit. The fresh air had whipped a lovely wild-rose color to her creamy cheeks. Her light curls blew against a saucy red cap.

"It is like a dream, Phil, isn't it?" she said.

"Yes; she's a peach of a dream," replied her enraptured husband, gazing at her beautiful face.

"Stop joking when I try to be serious," she pouted. "I mean those last terrible days. Shall we ever know how much that we saw was really true and how much was due to hallucination, hypnotism, or maybe to some mysterious jungle delirium?"

The boyish smile faded from Phil's face, and he answered in a low voice:

"We doubted everything when we found that under the trap-door in the tower there lay only an empty, dusty cave, just what the diary said we'd find. But let me show you something that is almost beyond belief."

He fumbled in his pocket and drew out a notebook and a pencil. For a moment, he glanced over the ocean with a dreamy look in his eyes. Then he began writing fast and fluently. When he finished, he showed her the page covered with queer pictures and characters.

"Hieroglyphics," he said, in answer to her puzzled frown. "Ever since that night in Don Julian's laboratory, I have been able to write in the way of the ancient Egyptians. I interviewed the famous Professor Costello of Buenos Aires before we sailed and he showed me some photographs that he had taken of hieroglyphics, inscribed upon the walls of a tomb which had never been deciphered. I glanced at the photographs, and the memories of Psamaeris the Egyptian began to quicken in my brain. And, Inez, I translated those hieroglyphics as readily as though they were a schoolboy's exercise in Latin!"

Tom came up in time to hear the last part of his speech.

"I ought to be envious of you, Phil," he said. "You not only won the prettiest girl on two continents but all of the adventure fell to you. I believe that I'll turn into a rattle-headed dreamer, too. They seem to get more kick out life that we sober-minded realists."

"I told you so," grinned Phil, tightening his clasp upon Inez's hand.

The
RAINBOW Jade

by Gardner F. Fox

From the inception of his career in 1937, writing for comics, including
Superman, Fox gravitated toward the fantastic and the heroic, as
in this story which appeared in Weird Tales, *September 1949.*

The bell clanged again. Shevlin heard its vibrating peal clearly in the crisp mountain air, two thousand feet above the sun-baked Taklamakan Desert. Its notes stirred tinkling echoes from snow-capped peaks and the fir-sheathed slopes of Tokosun Gorge. His brown face tightened, listening.

Very faintly, the gong was answered by a distant baying, there were animals here that responded to the call of that gong. Not dogs, not wolves. But something so like them, and yet so—unlike—that Shevlin shuddered.

He kicked the big Karasher stallion to full gallop. The sun was a scarlet hump on the horizon, and he wanted to get off this flat stretch before the moon came up from the Gobi. He touched the walnut handles of his Army revolver for reassurance.

Shevlin was an adventurer. He admitted it, when any of his friends accused him. He told them, "I'm out for what I can get. I'm big and I'm strong. I like the feel of a horse under me, and the smell of mountain air. I can't afford that kind of thing unless I work at it. So I go out and get things for people. Things in out-of-the-way places. Maybe even things that don't exist. Sometimes I chase legends." His gray eyes lighted when he talked like that. His friends knew he was remembering some pieces of tissue-thin blue porcelain he had brought out of a bandit's lair for a millionaire; or perhaps the emerald that once had been in an emperor's swordhilt, an emerald now gracing a woman's finger in San Francisco.

When news of Pearl Harbor filtered across the Himalayas, Shevlin had stolen a horse and ridden a thousand miles to join Chennault. And when the surrender was completed on the deck of the *Missouri*, he threw his uniform into a trashbin and joined a nomad caravan headed for Paochi. He had met Talbot in Paochi, over a gin swizzle.

541

Talbot showed him a broken chip of yellow jade. The man's eyes, already un-naturally bright with fever, blazed as he looked down at the translucent stone.

"Nothing like it anywhere, old man. Positively priceless. Found it back inside, around the Sin-kiang section. Rainbow jade. That's what it is." At Shevlin's polite stare, Talbot chuckled. "'S what I call it, you know. Deuced rainbow left it with Confucius, after he'd finished that *hiao-king* book."

Talbot coughed, convulsing. He apologized, and added, "Go in back there for more of it myself if the flesh weren't so weak. Got a mind to, anyhow. Not that I need the stuff. More pounds'n I know what to do with, thanks to the *pater*. I say, Shevlin! You do work like this. Finding stuff an' things. Take a commission from me, old boy. What d'you say? Fifty pounds a month and a share-and-share split if you find the yellow stuff. Eh?"

He had agreed. Why not?

And in Kashgar, after six months of fruitless search, he found Chi Ling.

She was leaning against the painted post of a temple, cool in thin shirt and riding breeches and boots. She was not white, nor Kirghiz, Uzbek or Tatar. Her lips were red and full, her hair black as the *Ou-ni-yao* vases. Her body was bigger than the Chinese, her breasts were more full. She was the loveliest thing Shevlin had ever seen, but it wasn't her beauty that took his eye.

It was the yellow jade amulet in the form of a crescent hanging about her throat. It matched the piece Talbot had shown him in Paochi. It was so transparent he could see the fabric of her blouse beneath it.

"Where did you get it?" he asked her. "I'll buy it from you. Just tell me how much you want. I'll buy information, too. Where'd—"

He got that far when she slapped him. She turned her back and walked away; but not before, deep down in the black pools of her eyes, he had seen that she was afraid; deadly afraid.

Shevlin followed her for two weeks before she spoke to him. One night he saw her coming out of the bazaar. There was a big man with her, a man with a hooked nose and the sharp, bright eye of an eagle. He was wrapped in a dirty sheepskin, but he wore it with the ease and grace of an emperor.

Shevlin said, "Look, my name's Shevlin. The jade, now, I'll pay you—"

The girl whispered harshly, "You want the jade, yes? You will pay for it? With two horses?"

The girl put out a pale white hand, touched his briefly. Her flesh tingled against his. Shevlin scowled. He had never bothered with women, except for an occasional Eurasian or White Russian émigré on the coast. Now this girl, with electric fingers and a face that was exquisite under Kashgar moonlight—

"Not money," she told him. "Horses. *You* must buy them."

Shevlin chuckled, and the girl stiffened. Political refugees of one sort or another! The frontier towns abounded with them. Then he shrugged. It was none of his affair. The jade was what he hunted. He said, "I'll have horses. Two fleet mares. With food and water canteens. Now—tell me your name."

She looked at him as a man for the first time. Shevlin let her study the brown planes of his face, the wide, thin mouth, the level gray eyes with the white scar above the left where a snow leopard on Anne Machin almost clawed it out. The scars on his leg and arm that the leopard had engraved tingled faintly as her eyes met his. He grinned, "Well, what about it? Do I get to know your name?"

She shook her head and touched the amulet. "No, that was not part of our bargain. Only the amulet. It will be yours."

When he came back, thirty minutes later, she had the yellow jade in her palm, and her black hair was tucked up in a knot on her shapely head. She would ride swiftly, he thought. Somehow, he knew she was a good horsewoman.

She dropped the jade piece into his hand, swung up in the saddle. She looked down at him, laughing softly. "My name is—Chi Ling." And then she was off in a clatter of hooves on the cobblestoned street.

Shevlin ran around the corner where his Karasher roan was jingling its bit impatiently, and mounted. He followed them easily. They made good targets in the moonlight.

He trailed them from a distance, across the alkali plains between Kashgar and Tihwa, into the valley of Ili and beyond, past wind-eroded ruins and bleached skeletons of men and horses. For more than four hundred miles he followed. He lost them in the Celestial Mountains, the first night he heard the bell, and the animals baying.

He sat in the light of his little campfire and checked his guns, an Army .45 and a Winchester .30.30. The wind came out of the firs, fragrant and cold. Shevlin drew his big cloth cape around his shoulders, looked up at the stars. The baying was very close, now. At times he could have sworn he heard a sniffling, at not too great a distance.

Shevlin reached for the rifle, took it across his knees. Something was moving in the little copse at the bottom of the hill where he was camped. It was big as a lion, judging from its shadow. And yet the head was that of a dog. A queer mixture. Shevlin thought of the Dogs of Fo that guarded the Chin temples.

Clannng, clannng, clannng . . .

The bell was very near, alive and vibrant. It was somewhere up above him, hidden in one of the caves that dotted the mountains, where the Buddhists had placed their magnificent murals.

Shevlin came to his feet, swearing in amazement. The animals were in the clear now, bright in moonlight, coming for him. Dogs of Fo! Huge, tawny in color, mouths slavering, that deep bay erupting from their throats.

He fired coolly. The high powered rifle was as accurate as his skill and experience could make it. A dog—he had no other thought for it—dropped. Another fell, crawled on toward him, dying. A third leaped high in the air, crashed on a rock.

Then the others were on him. There was no room to wield a rifle, no time to draw the Colt. He went back with white fangs and a red mouth gaping for his face . . .

Clannng—clannng! Clannng—clannng—clannng!

The bell was fierce, now. Loud and pealing! Ordering, commanding; the dogs fell away, sniffed at him, tongues lolling. Their real eyes shone green and brilliant in the darkness. The bell clanged again, louder and faster. Summoning! The dogs wheeled, trotted off.

Shevlin drew a deep breath, put his back against a rock and wriggled to his feet. His left arm was gashed and bloody. His cheek was furrowed.

"A minute more, and there wouldn't have been anything to save. But thanks anyhow," he muttered to the bell. He winced as his left arm throbbed. He had a medicine kit somewhere in his pack. He staggered toward it, knelt down.

"I think I can do it much better."

She stood in a pool of silver light between two giant firs. She no longer wore the shirt and riding breeches; instead, a silken *sari* clung to her, of scarlet and green and yellow splashes that overlapped to form a weird, alien pattern. Her long black hair was bound in a startling coiffure with tiny hair horns protruding from her temple. Her sloe eyes stared at him out of the lovely creamy mask of her face.

Chi Ling moved gracefully. She strode freely, yet as easily as if she skimmed the grasstops.

She knelt, removed a yellow jade jar from the linked girdle. From the jar her long fingers cupped a fragrant balsam; applied it to the wounds with gentle strokes. It stung at first, then soothed.

Shevlin said, "Where did you get the gown? It isn't silk or linen. It looks metallic."

"The *shang-ti* gave it to me. They have many unusual things."

"*Shang-ti?* The heavenly ones. Never heard of them."

"You will. They ordered that I bring you to them. I had to plead for your life. They do not like—strangers. That is why they loosed the *kalfi* here. The animals who nearly killed you. They brought them with them when they came."

Shevlin frowned. "You speak of them as if they came from . . . where do they come from?"

Chi Ling slid her eyes sideways at him. Her red lips quirked. Mischievously she lifted a finger, pointed starward. "From up there. From the stars."

Shevlin snorted, laughed. The pain was lessening. He grinned, "If they gave you that salve, I'm half convinced already . . . if they come from the stars, where's their space ship?"

Chi Ling laughed. "Space ships! Space ships are only for humans. The others, the *shang-ti*, they do not need ships. They are different. They have been here a long time. Many centuries. Only a very few suspect. The Lama in Tibet, a scholar like Charles Fort, a student or two who knows why Cambodia became a ghost city, why Ming-oi was abandoned overnight! . . . but they cannot be proved."

Shevlin stared into the glowing embers of his dying fire. He had read Fort, that collector of incredible and impossible news notices: lights seen on the moon, dark objects crossing the sun, tiny coffins found in Scotland, shadows cast by unseen bodies in the sky, huge glowing wheels plunging into oceans and later rising from them toward the sky.

He chuckled. "And flying discs over the States, and an aviator chasing a strange thing . . . absolutely white except for a streamer of red that appeared to be revolving before his ship disintegrated over Kentucky!"

Chi Ling eyed him warily. He reassured her, "Just something I was thinking about, in regard to Fort. But you—how come you're so friendly with these *shang-ti?*"

"I've been bred to serve them. My family for generations has been with them as they move from place to place on earth, waiting. In their time here on Earth while they waited, they have dwelt in many places. Easter Island, Cambodia, Ming-oi. They have waited for such a long time. Soon now, they will be ready."

"Ready? For what?"

"They will tell you if they want you to know. Come! We must go to them. I've stayed away too long already."

Shevlin reached out, caught her wrist. "Suppose I don't play it that way? Suppose . . ."

She shook her head at him. She said, "You will. The *kalfi* are still out there. If they come again, the gong may not call them off."

Shevlin heard the sniffling, the panting. He shuddered and let her go. The girl arose calmly, brushing at her soft robe. Her black eyes smiled at him.

He had heard of the Caverns in the Celestial Mountains from a warrior who had ridden with Ma Chung-ying. The Buddhists had sprawled their murals on rock walls in the domed hills, inside caves that stretched back into darkness. The soldier told him that a few men had explored one cave and—had not come out.

Chi Ling took him up a tier of steps cut in the limestone, through a low-portalled cave into gray dimness. Her hand in his as guide, she led him through a series of interlinked caverns that broadened into a smooth ramp. The ramp twisted and spiraled gently downward.

There was no door, as such. One moment they stepped off the ramp into a dim grayness—

The next moment there was light and color and movement all around them. It was as if scales had been lifted from his eyes. Shevlin swore softly, staring.

There were giant caverns, many of them extending as far as he could see. Each was different. The one he was walking through, with Chi Ling a swaying graceful-ness ahead of him, was purple-walled, and floored with great plants and fungoid growths, giant creepers that lifted tangled vines and bronzine leaves toward the groined ceiling far above. It was a jungle of red and yellow and blue, of metallic bronzes and harsh silvers, of gold and amethyst and emerald . . .

The next cave was a liquid pool in whose depths queer transparencies flitted, where huge black bodies darted between trunks of coils and rounded coral. On a slim path of stone, Chi Ling pattered between rippling waters. Shevlin followed, eyeing crystalline anemones and the mad colors of fire sponge and golden corals . . .

Under the arch of the third cave, Shevlin cried out.

Chi Ling turned, nodding. "A museum of sorts."

There were many races and men in the transparent bio-plastic cases. A Roman in cuirass and greaves. A half-naked Egyptian. A Tartar of the Mongol tribes, en-cased on the wooden saddle of his shaggy pony, arrow notched to bowstring. A Polynesian, in white-feathered cape, stepping into a long canoe. On the far side Shevlin made out a Persian in chain-mail, scimitar dangling from his brown hand. Beyond him, a Crusader, red cross on his white surtout.

They went through that cavern, into one where statues and wooden carvings rioted against a backdrop of bright wall murals.

Chi Ling was hurrying. Shevlin caught no more than a glimpse of the follow-ing chambers . . .

"Here," whispered Chi Ling. "Here now is the cavern of the *shang-ti!*"

Her warm hand squeezed his, then she was thrusting aside an iridescent cur-tain, stepping onto a polished black floor of basalt. This hall was larger than the others. Its walls seemed carved from mahogany, smoothed and polished with oil until they glittered. Tiny glowing ovals swirled and danced in the air currents high above, shedding a pale bluish-white light that was almost daylight.

And on the tier of ebony blocks, vivid white against the black—*shang-ti!*

A solid, shimmering cube of brilliance. Eight feet in height, coruscating light against the darkness, revolving pinpoints of light within it, a hard core of glittering, blinding opalescence at its heart. Awesome, strange, and—

Cold!

Something deep inside him told him he had never known such cold. The white was the frost of a Siberian snow field, the glitter was the shimmering feet of ice that rims the Alaskan glaciers. The movement inside the cube was the fantastic swirl of cosmic snows, the imponderable, frozen sluggishness of the glacier. It moved and looped and shifted in the cube, that living cold. Moved—and was still.

Chi Ling pressed his hand with cool fingers. He went with her across the basalt floor to the ebony steps.

Chi Ling whispered: "Wait!"

She went up the steps, wide-eyed; arms open to the cube. Shevlin cried out, "Be careful! That thing must be as cold as—"

The cube whirled, rotated; lifted and danced in the air with bright coruscations. Swept down on Chi Ling. Wrapped and enveloped her in the opalescent garment of white hoar-frost. Faintly there was the eerie tinkle, as if ice prong touched ice-blade. A musical arpeggio, swirling up and up with cold perfection of tone—

The cube was gone.

Chi Ling stood with her back to Shevlin, hands buried in her hair. Swiftly the hands worked, changing tresses, altering the coiffure. Her skin whitened, glowed. Her body altered, mistily and as in a haze; blurred, grew, shrank, flattened . . .

The girl turned, stood looking down at Shevlin from the height of the ebony steps.

It was Chi Ling, and it was not Chi Ling. The red mouth was there . . . and the green eyes framed by the raven hair . . . but the face was altered subtly, the eyebrows arched, a pixiness in the hollow of the white cheeks, mockery in the set of the full lips, the slant of the eyes, and the flaring of the thin nostrils.

Shevlin choked: "How'd you—do that?"

The woman laughed. "You would not understand. Unless—are you a scientist? Like Edison? Einstein? Lawrence?"

He shook his head. The *shang-ti* woman came down the steps, moving with facile grace. She said: "Chi Ling may have told you a little of me, of our kind. She calls us the *shang-ti*. It will do. We have come from a very far distance, across fifty million light years, from a galaxy a dozen times the size of your own Milky Way."

Shevlin licked his lips. He was an adventurer. He had faced a lot of odd things in the past, all the way from Nepal to northern Siberia. He told himself; just another person, that's all she is. Nothing else than that. Keep it in mind.

"We are different from your people. You are carbon life. We are a form of life based on efficiency of energy."

Shevlin looked blank. The *shang-ti* woman laughed, crossed the room toward a row of ornate benches. Sank down on one, gesturing to Shevlin.

"I'll try and explain. Your life form is based on matter, mine on energy. You know heat as energy, but to the *shang-ti* there is no such thing as heat. We are energy incarnate. Within ourselves there is no matter at all, only energy. Many eons ago, our life-forms came into being on a very distant planet. Pressures, a fantastic out-pouring of incredible power from a blasted twin-sun, the right conditions—" Chi Ling shrugged, smiling; said simply, "All that combined to form the *shang-ti*.

"We exist at what you would call absolute zero, two hundred and seventy degrees below Centigrade zero. Your men of science have never duplicated that temperature, can never hope to do so. It is at that temperature that all matter transforms into energy. *Is* energy, and not matter. At absolute zero there is no pressure, and no molecular movement. There can be no gas, no matter, nothing at that coldness except—energy alone! Anything added to it becomes only more energy."

Shevlin blinked. He said slowly, "But if I were to use a flame-thrower on you, heat you—"

Her laughter carolled. "You can't heat me, as you put it. You forget that I am nothingness. No gas, no flesh. Nothing. And—nothing will scarcely absorb heat, will it? You can't multiply zero. Neither can you heat what does not exist. And nothing exists within me except pure energy."

"But that cube . . . the coldness . . . the whiteness . . . I saw you!"

"You saw only the frosting of the air that rimmed me. We allow that to be seen. We could always be invisible, if we chose. Permitting the air to frost also permits our intense cold to be felt."

Shevlin leaned forward. "But Chi Ling! You entered her body. I saw that. If all that cold touched her, she'd die!"

Chi Ling toyed with a rich black link of hair, smiling at Shevlin's excited face. "Of course she would, if matter that cold touched her. But only pure energy touched her, took over her body!"

"And you use her body to—"

The woman brooded at him. "I am Chi Ling—at the moment. Her thoughts, her memories are mine. The *shang-ti* can enter any human body. While we waited here on Earth, we have amused ourselves from time to time by doing just that."

Her green eyes mocked him. "Haven't you ever wondered why science seems to spurt every once in a while? For a thousand years man will go along in the same old rut. There was Egypt, Crete and Phoenicia. Along came Athens with its brilliant upsurge of the arts and philosophy. The dark ages, and then—the Renaissance! DaVinci, Michelangelo, Bacon, Shakespeare."

Her laughter was a tinkling triumph in the great ebony hall. "You never suspected. Not once! None of your so-termed wise men ever guessed. Columbus! Napoleon! The age of science then began in the last century. Electricity! Airplanes! Even—the Manhattan Project!

"It is something to do, to play chess with an entire world. To move races and nations like pawns—with a planet for a playing board!"

Shevlin thought: You can't square a circle. An animal can't eat itself. You can't have a black white, or any other of a dozen or more paradoxes. He said: "But you—"

Chi Ling shrugged glistening white shoulders. The *shang-ti* woman said, "Many millions of years ago, on our planet, a way was found. By Nature, in a subterranean vault where our first life forms were patterned. Cold life, Shevlin. So cold that we are perfect transmutants. In us, matter becomes energy simultaneously. There is no matter. Only energy."

"And energy," said Shevlin thoughtfully, "can't be destroyed."

Chi Ling stood up, twirled so that her skirts flew our around her legs. She threw back her head, let the long hair float in a spray of black fire. She whispered, "No one can destroy me, Shevlin. And as long as there is any matter anywhere to feed my energy . . . I will live! Life and living is a fine thing, Shevlin. You like life. I can read it in your face, in your eyes. You like Chi Ling too . . ."

Shevlin grinned. He stood up. The *shang-ti* woman slid away, laughing. "Shevlin, you might hate me if I told you why I am here, why others like me are here on Earth. Will you hate me, Shevlin?"

"No, I guess not. Not if there's anything in it for me. I'm sorry. That's the way I am. I try not to be honest about it. I was born in a city slum, grew up fighting and scratching for a piece of bread and a glass of water. It wasn't easy. I hated the cities. When I found there were things like mountains and long stretches of steppe and tundra, and horses to carry me over them, I took adventure as my job. And I take what's in it for me."

The woman came close to Shevlin. Her green eyes flared at him. She whispered, "Soon I will let you know why we are here. And there will be something in it for you. Soon!"

Her arms were white fires around his neck. Her red mouth sank over him. She breathed, "It is fun to be human, Shevlin. I am almost sorry we are not . . . kiss me! Kiss me!"

Shevlin was given the freedom of the underground caverns. He swam in the depths of the blue pool, lay in the cavern of the suns, his skin drinking in the bluish radiance. He drank of cool green wines and ate of tiny honey cakes that were a succulent mixture of meat and flour and vegetables. He wandered amid great gardens where riotous blooms and bulbous flowers nodded swollen petals. He ran and exercised in a cavern where near-living vines fought him, wrestled and almost crushed him, before he could win free of them and stand panting, wet with sweat.

There was only one place he could not go. It was the last cavern, and there was an opaque veil across it that hid its interior. Once Shevlin touched the thin gossamer shroud: found it stone-hard and cool to his touch.

The *shang-ti* woman shared his days, laughing and mocking and gently loving. Her asked her: "You aren't Chi Ling. Yet you're in her body. How do you do it?"

She lay on her back, a hand sheltering her eyes from the brilliance of the sunballs above. She said softly, "All your carbon life forms are comprised of atoms. Building blocks. They're held together by mesons. The binding stuff. Concrete between the blocks. At absolute zero, those mesons lose their adhesive strength . . . weaken . . . let the atoms separate . . . become other matter . . . or energy."

"Being energy, we can merge in a form of osmosis with other energy as soon as the mesons have been weakened by the utter cold. Reshape that energy into material form . . . appear as Chi Ling . . . or Newton . . . Bacon . . ."

Shevlin said dreamily, "Why me? How come I was allowed in here?"

The *shang-ti* woman rolled over, faced him. "You were after the yellow jade. We do not have enough of us to maintain an elaborate spy system on earth. We have to be very careful. While we cannot be destroyed, we could be set back in our—work— for countless years.

"We make that yellow jade. It's a byproduct of our—work. So we wanted to make sure . . . just why you were sent here, who sent you . . . if you were sent."

"You never asked."

Her laughter tinkled. "There was no reason to ask. You were observed, fol- lowed, when Chi Ling first reported your interest in the jade. She had been arrang- ing for certain needed materials in Paochi. We let you follow Chi Ling. We know that no one came after you from Paochi. And besides—

"You are hard! Different from the men we've known. I thought it might be fun to know you better before—"

Shevlin asked, "Before—what?"

She put out pink fingertips, ran them across Shevlin's lips. "We will take you back with us, Shevlin. Back to our mother planet. You will not perish. You see, we are going to smash the Earth. An experiment. As your own nation made an experi- ment at Bikini. This will be a cosmic Bikini. But a few life forms we will take back with us. You will be one of them."

"In a bio-plastic case?" he asked dryly.

"Alive," she laughed. "What good are you to Chi Ling or me—dead?"

"Chi Ling goes back, too?"

"Of course. And a few others. You humans are very interesting, Shevlin. So serious. Like children, sometimes, at play. It is fun, this being a human. I have learned to like it. Others of the *shang-ti* will like it, too."

Playthings. Toys. Animated slaves, to be inhabited and enjoyed as the spirit moves. Shevlin lay back and let the warm gloves bathe him. So that was to be his fate! Transported across an unimaginable distance, to be a living toy. He would be bred to make more humans, more toys to be inhabited and used. Like a pig or a chicken!

Her flat green eyes were watching him. She mocked him softly, "Do you hate me very much?"

Easy, he told himself. Go easy here. It's a tight spot, like the time the snow leopard cornered you on a ledge of the Anne Machin. His man-will had won against the snarling cat. He had not thought to come out of that alive. He knew the same dead, useless feeling now. You can't kill pure energy as you do a snow leopard, he thought wearily.

He said, "I don't know. I haven't figured out my angle, yet. What do I get out of it?"

"You get immortality. And Chi Ling. And a life of ease or exploration with us.

Adventure? I'll take you with me to planets you haven't dreamed of. I'll show you sunsets on oceans wider than the sun. Or winters on planets that are rocks, where storms are so frightful they topple mountains. There are green planets like your Earth, without people. I'll show you the palaces built on planets so long ago, even the bones of the people who built them are dust."

"Yes. That sounds good. That would be heavy for an adventurer. But destroying the Earth, now. Can't you —"

"The Earth must be smashed! It is an experiment."

He recognized the determination in the cold voice. Unshakable. He was only a pawn to her. An enjoyable pawn, but still only a toy. Shevlin shrugged—

And leaped!

His big hands went out and closed on Chi Ling's throat, tightened and clung! The muscles on his arms and back bulged and rippled.

Chi Ling went limp.

And the brilliant cube of coldness that was the *shang-ti* stood sentient and brilliant, a few feet away. Flickering. Opalescent.

A voice in Shevlin's brain mocked, "Let her be, Shevlin, She is only a carbon thing like you. She cannot hurt you. I am what you want to destroy—and cannot!"

Shevlin moved a hand, dragged his revolver from its holster where he had flung it to bathe beneath the sun globes.

"Shoot!" ordered the voice.

He pumped three shells into the blinding cube. It glowed around them, absorbed them. Transformed them into energy as they ate into its heart of living cold.

"I could just as easily absorb the full fury of an atomic explosion, Shevlin. What do you know that can destroy me, Shevlin? Bullets? Explosives? Rays? Atomic blasts? Those things—all matter—I can blend with. Absorb! Make mine!"

Shevlin stood by the sprawled body of Chi Ling. He said hoarsely, "I'm licked. What do I do now? Die?"

The voice said, "I told you I want you alive, Shevlin. You have a strong body. A good body for breeding."

Shevlin repressed a shudder of repulsion, staring at the eight-foot-high cube of coldness. That thing in Chi Ling? An indestructible mass of cold, of sexlessness, of brain. Ready to use him, like a toy, for entertainment.

It was dark in the last cavern. The sun globes were far away. Here there was only a dim grayness, like a London fog. Shevlin clutched Chi Ling's smooth wrist, drew her after him.

"Let me into that last room," he told her. "Let me past that curtain! I have to see what's in that room—what they're going to do!"

"I'm afraid!"

"They're going to smash the Earth. Don't you understand that? You and I, we've got to stop them. Somehow. There must be a way."

"They are indestructible! Haven't my people tried? Years ago they tried. The tale came down to me. They used many ways. The *shang-ti* only laughed at them. The *shang-ti* let them. Allowed it. As a lesson."

"Energy," whispered Shevlin. "They're pure energy . . . matter turns into energy at absolute zero. That's what she . . . it . . . said. But lift the veil. Let me see into the room . . ."

Chi Ling whimpered in the dimness. She stretched out a hand, touching the shrouding veil, moved her fingers in a queer pattern. The veil moved, drew back . . .

It was not as large as the other chambers. It was plain, austere. It held nothing but empty bio-plastic casings, arranged in rows, one after another, stretching into the darkness.

Empty casings—

They were not empty!

Shevlin said hoarsely, "They each hold something . . . something alive! Yes, that's it . . . each one has a *shang-ti* inside it! You see? Those whitish cores . . . very dim, as if the energy inside it were ebbing away . . ."

Chi Ling put a hand to her mouth. She shuddered. "Quick, Shevlin! Before it finds us here. Take one more look—"

Shevlin mused, "It wants to blow up the earth. Maybe create a tremendous unleashing of energy. Sure, sure. To feed those things, to bring 'em back to full life again. They're dying. Almost dead. Hundreds of 'em, waiting here like patients in a hospital for a blood transfusion."

The veil closed over the cavern. Chi Ling's fingers quivered in his hands as she drew him after her. They went back through the caverns like frightened children waiting for a bogeyman, hand in hand.

It was Chi Ling who felt its presence, as they stepped into the cavern of the ebony dais. She drew closer to Shevlin, whimpering, her unbound black hair a dark nimbus about her pale, wide-eyed face.

"It's here, Shevlin. *Shang-ti!* I—I can sense it . . . feel it!"

Shevlin put a big hand on his guns; shrugged and let his fingers drop. You can't kill pure energy, he thought wearily. He looked around the room. There was nothing visible.

A voice mocked him. "I told you I could move about unseen, Shevlin. I told you I was invisible, that I only allowed myself to be seen—like this!"

Ten feet in front of him the air swirled, stirred as by a cyclonic force. Waves of sheer cold beat and bellowed, whitened, frosted. Snow crystals formed. The cube was there, shimmering in its blinding brilliance.

"Chi Ling!"

The girl moved forward, slow step by slow step, as if drugged. The cube stood still, let her walk into the frost crystals; absorbed her.

Shevlin cried out in horror. He could see through the cube faintly, see the glowing globes and the mahogany carved walls beyond it.

Chi Ling was gone!

"Come, you too, Shevlin," mocked the cube.

"No. I'll be damned if I do!"

He choked out the words, fraught with rage and the first fear he had ever known. Even the snow leopard had never caused this fear. The scars on his left leg and arm tingled, as he remembered that battle, and the bloody claws of the giant white cat.

The cube was still, watching him. It said, "I am ready, Shevlin. Ready for the explosion that will smash your planet. The long years of planning, of preparing the planet for this moment—are over. I do not want you to die, Shevlin. I want to save you, show you those other worlds. You said you were an adventurer. I can show you many planets besides this. I—"

It was then that Shevlin leaped. A crazy, insane idea had sprung into his brain, suggested by the tingle of his long-healed scars. Bullets would not kill this thing. Nothing would that was matter. But Shevlin had one weapon left, a weapon as intangible as pure energy. If that failed—well, there was nothing left for anyone.

He went through the frost crystals, expecting the sheer cold to freeze him solid. Instead, he felt only a slight wrench throughout his body. It was as if a million tiny hands tugged at all his atoms, throwing them apart. He was a man in one moment, nothingness the next. Yet he was more than nothing. He was still himself, a mind united with a will.

A will!

In the shadow of a Burmese temple, Shevlin had seen a zealot transfix his skin with needles without pain. He knew that psychosomatic medicine was trying to unravel the mystery of the mind's effect on bodily diseases. A man could will himself to health, just as he could will himself to die. Shevlin had seen too many cases in native huts to doubt. There were medical case histories of cancers come and gone, banished by nothing but sheer will. The x factor of will, sometimes subconscious, was the curative agent. Army doctors had told him much, during the war.

After all, why not? What was a man but a will and an intellect linked to a lot of atoms?

Will!

He was dissolving, swept up into the white, whirling mistiness that faded into nothingness. Faintly, he could see the dancing ovals in the cavern. A mighty force buffeted at him, tried to beat him down, down into passive, unknowing submission.

Will!

That was the answer. It had to be. It was the only weapon left him. His body and his strength, that had choked the snow leopard to death in three hours of bloody nightmare, were gone; lost in the mad opalescence of the *shang-ti*. His intellect was being swallowed, eaten piece-meal, by a brain eons old, educated in star-systems unknown to him world.

Just the will!

He held on. He—or whatever spark it was that remained of himself in that wild exhilaration—repeated endlessly, *I will not yield! I will not yield!* He fought the questing touch of that other-mind, fought the grasp that would swallow him utterly.

And the *shang-ti* weakened. Not by much. Just by a tiny fraction. But it was enough. It showed what he could do.

He never knew how long it took, there in the caverns beneath the Celestial Mountains. When it was over, he was alone in the caverns, invisible, a conqueror who would never be known. He realized that. He was *shang-ti*, now. All its powers were his, all its knowledge. But brooding, lost somewhere within him, lay the sullen strength of the other. At the first sign of weakness, the *shang-ti* would be back, to conquer. In the soul of him, Shevlin laughed bitterly. He had won—

And lost!

He was forever chained here, in this cube of brilliance. There was no escape. But he put all that away from him. He whirled toward the cavern gateways; sealed them, one after another. In the last cavern, where the bio-plastic cases stood, he used his new-found powers.

He took dust from the floor and made energy from it and hurled it at the cases. They powdered in vivid white flashes, and the thunder of their going split the rocks.

Then, alone, he went up through the caverns to the fresh, clean air of earth, and stared upward at the stars.

They would be his home now, those stars. For an adventurer, it was the supreme adventure. He wondered idly what they would be like. He wished for company—

"Shevlin!"

It was faint, like a half-forgotten memory out of childhood. It was the voice of Chi Ling. She was lost, there in the whirling coldness of him: all her atoms, intellect and will. Perhaps, somewhere out in that vast bowl of the heavens, he would find a planet and bring her back to life.

It was a good thought. He held it warm to his cold brilliance as he lifted with the dazzling speed of light toward the stars.

A Résumé of Rays

by Forrest J Ackerman

This was first published in William F. Crawford's semi-pro magazine,
Unusual Stories in 1932 when I was 15.—FJA

The *purple* ray ere realized
Kills with its icy touch.
The *blue* holds paralyzed
All creatures in its clutch.

The *green* some authors write about
Abolishes tormentors,
While *yellow* (heat) rays always spout
From minds of mad inventors.

An *orange* ray is seldom seen—
One pauses here to wonder.
But "too violent" it might mean:
Rip Galaxies asunder!

The *red* ray, visible spectrum's last,
Was science fiction's first.
Originally it gave a blast
Considered quite the worst.

Now:
Cold . . . paralysis . . . destruction . . . heat
Should be produced
—Let 4 rays meet.
Add the other 2 and get
DESTRUCTION VAST

—And Yet;

Tho combination of all six
The *white* ray isn't one of might;
For but let the colors mix—
Result: your spectrumatic,
Nondramatic, ev'ryday FLASH light!

555

Mr. Sci-Fi

Forrest J Ackerman,

a regular on the Sci-Fi channel, edited and published Ray Bradbury's first story in 1938, edited the seminal *Famous Monsters of Filmland* magazine for years, has appeared in over 50 sci-fi and horror films, and has helped to inspire countless professional careers and his fans' lifelong admiration, including such notables as George Lucas and Stephen King. A writer, editor, filmmaker and collector of science fiction material for over 70 of his 84 years, he is the author of dozens of stories and editor of six previous complete anthologies.

He coined the term "sci-fi," received the first Hugo award (and has won 6 in total), contributed to the first fanzine, started an sf club in 1929, lives in the Hollywood Hills in the Ackermansion, an 18-room home "gem-packed" with 300,000 pieces, 50,000 books alone, 100,000 stills from fantastic films, has attended 57 of 59 World Science Fiction Conventions . . . The Academy of Science Fiction, Fantasy and Horror has twice honored him with Golden Saturns.

We could go on. His love of the genre and his pioneering efforts are truly irreplaceable: He opens his home/museum to the public most weekends, and he can be contacted via the information on the next page.

READERS OF THE WORLDS, WRITE!

The anthologist of this volume is anxious to hear from YOU!

How did you enjoy the overall contents?

What few stories did you like the most?

What few stories did you like the least?

Would you like to see a collection of FJA's own approximately 50 stories? (Starting in 1929!)

Would you like to see an Ackermanthology of a selection of Mr. Science Fiction's favorite sci-fi stories of the past 75 years? Favorite Fantasy?

Any requests for the anthologist?

Forrest J Ackerman may be contacted directly at:

> 2495 Glendower Avenue
> Hollywood, CA 90027-1110
> FAX: 323-664-5612

 # SENSE OF WONDER PRESS

Ackermanthology: Millennium Edition

From Dennis Palumbo's three page tale of truly diabolical revenge to Jill Taggart's one page epiphany on the nature of leadership and victory, the original *Ackermanthology* will arouse your sense of wonder, throughout. Stories by greats such as Ray Bradbury, Isaac Asimov, and H. G. Wells are nestled comfortably among great bursts of creativity and wonder from lesser known authors such as Oliver Saari, David A. Kyle, Anne Orhelein and dozens of others that you may never have heard of but whom you'll never forget. Thus, the original Ackermanthology fulfills its purposes: to expose new readers to the creativity and spontaneity of vision that made the golden age of science fiction and fantasy golden; and, to provide you with moments and memories that will enrich your life in ways that will continue to surprise and delight you from first page to last. Foreword by John Landis.

6x9, Paper, 306 pp., $14.95, ISBN 0-9187360-25-0, *Available Now*

Rainbow Fantasia, 35 Spectrumatic Tales of Wonder

A colorful collection of classic tales (many from sci-fi's pulp tradition) including stories by Eli Coulter, Nictzin Dyalhis, Robert W. Chambers and Brad Linaweaver.

6x9, Paper, 576 pp., $23.95, ISBN: 0-9187360-36-6, Available Now

CLAIMED by Francis Stevens

You'll never feel the same about the beach or the sea again! An eerie classic, chosen by FJA. Gertrude Barrows Bennett, the mysterious woman who wrote under the pen name "Francis Stevens" has been hailed as the greatest female fantasy writer between Mary Shelly and C.L. Moore!

6x9, Paper, 192 pp., $14.95, ISBN: 0-918736-37-4, Available now

Science Fiction Worlds of Forrest J Ackerman and Even More Friends

Long out-of-print, this classic anthology is back with 4E and even more friends and collaborators. Joining such well-known writers as Theodore Sturgeon and A. E. van Vogt are classic authors Catherine L. Moore, Donald A. Wollheim and others. Six new treats join the classic greats in this new edition.

6x9, Paper, ISBN 0-9187360-26-9, Winter 2001

Sci-Fi WOMANthology

Classic stories by pioneering women writers in the genre edited and with introductions by Forrest J Ackerman and Pamela Keesey. Includes an extensive checklist of the editors' favorite genre contributions by women writers.

6x9, Paper, Illustrated, ISBN 0-918736-33-1, $14.95, Winter 2001

Dr. Acula's Thrilling Tales of the Uncanny

"Brush your hair with epoxy resin before reading this creepy collection, otherwise you're liable to lose it when your hair stands on end."—Dr. Acula. With a preface by Pamela Keesey.

6x9, Paper, ISBN 0-918736-30-7 $14.95, Winter 2001

Sci-ANTS Fiction & Insects Extraordinary

Introduction by Donald Glut, author of an insect paperback and bestselling pocketbook novelization of THE EMPIRE STRIKES BACK.

6x9, Paper, Illustrated, ISBN 0-918736-31-5, $14.95, Winter 2001/Spring 2002

Ackermanuscripts: Non-Fiction Fangoria

Culled from 70+ years of fandom, writing, editing, and agenting, includes Forry's articles on past cons; writers and books, new and old; historical pieces on science fiction, fantasy, and horror. Includes an in-depth informal interview and bibliographic and filmographic sketches.

6x9, Hardcover, Illustrated, ISBN: 0-918736-29-3, Limited to 500 copies, $30.00
6x9, Paper, Illustrated, $14.95, ISBN: 0-918736-08-0, Winter 2001/Spring 2002

Famous Forry Fotos

Kodakerman Memories! Famous Forry Fotos, from birth to 2000—over 70 years of photos from Forry at the Ackermansion, and before: photos of science fiction, fantasy and horror writers, film greats and more, with Mr. Sci-Fi as your guide! Friends, family, monsters, some great "Con" memories and much more!

8½x11, Illustrated, $14.95, ISBN: 0-918736-32-3, Fall 2001

Metropolis: 75th Anniversary Edition

Lavishly "Stillustrated" with fotos from Fritz Lang's film and Forrest J Ackerman's 75 years of Metropolis memorabilia. Hardcover limited to 500 copies, signed & numbered.

8½x11, HC, Illus., Limited Ed., $45.00, ISBN: 0-918736-34-X, Fall/Winter 2001
8½x11, Paper, Illus., $16.95, ISBN: 0-918736-35-8, Fall/Winter 2001

SENSE OF WONDER PRESS BOOKS ARE DISTRIBUTED IN THE U.S. BY INGRAM DISTRIBUTORS

Sense of Wonder Press

SENSE OF WONDER

PRESS

BROWSE, ORDER, RESERVE, HANGOUT

http:\\www.senseofwonderpress.com

Find a complete listing of stories for all our "Ackermanthologies," updates on title availability and payment information. Or write to us at:

Sense of Wonder Press
113 N. Washington Street, Box 347
Rockville, Maryland 20850

email: info@senseofwonderpress.com

The body text in this book was set in 10.5 point Garamond. Book titles
and ancillary items were set in Garamond Book Condensed.
Book design by Lynne Rock, James A. Rock & Co., Publishing.

www.ingramcontent.com/pod-product-compliance
Lightning Source LLC
Chambersburg PA
CBHW030921020726
47498CB00001B/57